PT                          122512
2670
.036
J3213    Johnson
1987     Anniversaries II

# ANNIVERSARIES II:

## From the Life of Gesine Cresspahl

REGINA LIBRARY
RIVIER COLLEGE
NASHUA, N. H. 03060

# Uwe Johnson

# ANNIVERSARIES II

## From the Life of Gesine Cresspahl

TRANSLATED BY LEILA VENNEWITZ

AND BY WALTER ARNDT

A Helen and Kurt Wolff Book

Harcourt Brace Jovanovich, Publishers

San Diego    New York    London

Withdrawn

RIVIER COLLEGE

3 4670 000761023

VERIFIED

*122512*

This volume encompasses part of Volume Two and all of Volumes Three and Four of the German original, *Jahrestage* 1 and 2. For all translations into foreign languages, the author prepared a cut version, on which this text is based.

Pages 1–351 translated by Leila Vennewitz

Pages 352–644 translated by Walter Arndt

Copyright © 1971 by Suhrkamp Verlag Frankfurt am Main
Copyright © 1983, 1973 by the Estate of Uwe Johnson
English translation copyright © 1987 by Harcourt Brace Jovanovich, Inc.

All rights reserved. No part of this publication may be reproduced or transmitted in any form or by any means, electronic or mechanical, including photocopy, recording, or any information storage and retrieval system, without permission in writing from the publisher.

Requests for permission to make copies of any part of the work should be mailed to: Permissions, Harcourt Brace Jovanovich, Publishers, Orlando, Florida 32887.

Library of Congress Cataloging-in-Publication Data
Johnson, Uwe, 1934-1984
  Anniversaries II.
  "A Helen and Kurt Wolff book."
  I. Title.  II. Title: Anniversaries 2.
PT2670.036J3213  1987    833'.914    86-31890
ISBN 0-15-107562-X

Printed in the United States of America

First United States edition

A B C D E

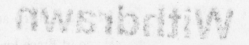

## PUBLISHER'S NOTE

Volume I of *Anniversaries*, published by Harcourt Brace Jovanovich in 1975, covered six months in the life of Gesine Cresspahl—from August 1967 to February 1968. The present volume, covering the period from February to August 1968, completes the year.

# Main Characters

*Heinrich Cresspahl*, born 1888. Master carpenter; member of the German Socialist Party (S.P.D.) under the Weimar Republic—until a serious disagreement with Party policies. Lives for ten years in the Netherlands and in Richmond, near London. On a return visit to Germany, he meets and marries—

*Lisbeth*, daughter of Albert and Louise Papenbrock. She accompanies Heinrich to England, but, becoming pregnant, insists on returning to her Mecklenburg hometown, Jerichow, where, on March 3, 1933, she gives birth to a daughter—

*Gesine Cresspahl*. She is raised and gets her schooling in Jerichow and the neighboring town Gneez. When she loses her parents (Lisbeth commits suicide in 1938, and Heinrich disappears in a Soviet concentration camp in 1945) Gesine is looked after by the displaced Abs family—Marie and her son Jakob, who works as a railway dispatcher. Eventually, after Heinrich returns as a broken invalid, Gesine emigrates to West Germany, where she conceives a child by Jakob. Before they can marry, Jakob is killed in a suspicious accident. Their daughter is—

*Marie Cresspahl*. Born in July 1957, she lives in New York, where Gesine works for a bank. Dietrich Erichson (D.E.)—also a refugee from Mecklenburg and a professor of physics and chemistry who is employed on secret missions for the U.S. Air Force—courts Gesine. Gesine intends to marry him if Marie approves.

*Albert Papenbrock*, born in 1868, owner of a granary, a brickyard, and a bakery in Jerichow, has married—

*Louise*. A religious fanatic, she transmits her mania to her daughter Lisbeth. Their other children are—

*Robert Papenbrock*. In May 1914, he leaves for South America in disgrace, not to be heard from again—until he (or an impostor) returns to Jerichow in 1935. He becomes a Nazi and during the War is responsible for a massacre of hostages in the Ukraine. He manages to survive and escapes to West Germany.

*Horst Papenbrock*, born in 1900. After his brother's disappearance, he is heir to his father's properties. Inept in business, he joins the Nazi Party and becomes involved in political assassination. He is killed in the Battle of Stalingrad, and leaves a widow.

*Hilde Papenbrock*. She marries Alexander Paepke, an attorney, anti-Nazi, and amiable loafer who squanders her dowry. Their three children are Gesine's favorite cousins: Ulrike (called "Alexandria"), Eberhardt, and Christine. Alexander dies in 1944 in the south of France. The rest of the family perishes in their flight from the advancing Russian army in March 1945.

# ANNIVERSARIES II:
## From the Life of Gesine Cresspahl

## February 25, 1968   Sunday

Many members of the Senate Foreign Relations Committee have ceased to believe government statements on the Tonkin affair, and J. W. Fulbright, chairman of the committee, claims that Secretary of Defense Robert S. McNamara has withheld important information. Calls him derelict.

Derelict: wouldn't that word apply to the English of Miss Cresspahl, who is trying to sell her labors in a country that uses this kind of language as to a drifting ship without pilot or crew? It is of not much help that the word derelict recalls Latin lessons of seventeen years ago in Gneez: *linguere* and depart, *relinguere* and relinquish, *relictus*, relic, relict, its first syllable serving only to emphasize the absoluteness, totality, and finality of its condition: derelict, the land deserted by its inhabitants, the soil renounced by the farmer, the sand washed up by the sea, the silted-up waters, the abandoned wreck, the decaying house, the ownerless objects, the unclaimed article; and at the precise moment when its meaning seems to have been contained behind barriers of knowledge, out it slips, and the next step into apparent certainty is a step into the void. For Miss Cresspahl has learned English, not American; and for a hundred years the American language has been accustomed to arrive, by way of the passive relict, derelict, and dereliction of duty, at the concept of a perpetrator in the active sense: the delinquent, culprit, liar, like those who in the eyes of police and *Times* are not merely down and out but have deliberately dropped out of society and now stand around on the Bowery, tattered and unshaven, swaying with hunger and liquor, beggars, bums, derelicts.

Mr. Fulbright has told Mr. McNamara what he thinks of him; Miss Cresspahl has listened to what the two men have to say. If she were required to give an immediate interpretation of what she has heard, she would hesitate. Perhaps her vision of McNamara on the Bowery is attributable after all to the subhead in which the New York *Times* prints the word derelict in heavy type; she would be less embarrassed at the mistake revealed than concerned over the implication that she is not completely mistress of the tool with which she is trying to earn her living.

After the war Kliefoth was appointed principal of the Gneez high school and had no time to give English lessons. His place was taken by Mrs. Weidling until Soviet counterespionage discovered that her husband was not a captain in the Tank Corps but had been employed in counterespionage and that she owed her mastery of the language to the travels on which she had accompanied Weidling. By that time Kliefoth had been removed from his posts as both principal and teacher. English through Grade 12 was subsequently taught by a junior teacher whose first name was Hans-Gerhard. He had never been to England and explained to the silent class that his professors at Greifswald University had occasionally granted him some leeway in pronunciation when he had been unable to imitate British language records. His explanation had been that he heard the words differently. It was his first teaching position, and this was his first mistake. He then drew attention to his youth and asked permission of the students, despite their right to be called by their family names, to address them by their first names; he spoke of the New Spirit of the New School. Lise Wollenberg spoke up. "But of course, Hans-Gerhard," she said. Heinz Wollenberg was still considered a pillar of society, and Lise received an apology from the young man for his outburst of rage. After his third mistake he stopped calling them all by their first names. There was no reading of Edgar Allan Poe's "The Gold Bug" in his class. With him they worked their way through "Is War Inevitable?" by Joseph Stalin. Gesine Cresspahl, the student who sat in the center block, front row, on the aisle, did not get good marks for this. There was no prospect of private lessons with Kliefoth, since he would have accepted neither favors nor money for them. H.-G. Knick contorted his lips when he switched to the foreign language, making chewing movements with his jaws; he also contorted his voice and had to listen many times a month to his students telling him that they heard the words differently, although the sounds he uttered were probably as British as it was possible for him to make them. Gesine Cresspahl graduated with honors in English, and she was accepted at the University of Halle in Saxony on the basis of a stumbling essay on the prospects for a Communist Party in a parliamentary monarchy. The Saxonians were also enthusiastic about the New Spirit of the New School, but they granted no leeway to the student to decide on its sound, and in fact Professor Ertzenberger would have liked to use her for demonstration purposes in his seminar. He was delighted to have such an example.

> *Miss Cresspahl, please pronounce a combination of k and l.*
> *Tackle. Shackle.*
> *And now in a German word.*
> *Mecklenburg.*
> *Do you hear it?*
> *No, Professor.*
> *Say: Wesel.*
> *Wesl.*
> *Your articulation is one hundred per cent Mecklenburg, Miss Cress-*
> *pahl! You can't separate the l: "M e ckl e nburg." That must go.*

At that point she started to speak English, and during the second term, while traveling on the Leipzig-Rostock express, she finally, at the second attempt, understood the passenger who was prompted by the English paperback she was holding to address her in English. In those days English passengers on the East German State Railway were, of course, the exception rather than the rule. Even at Frankfurt-on-the-Main, where she attended language school, she was not at home with the English of the children for whom she baby-sat in the American section of the city; and even at the U. S. military radio station in West Berlin she still had not reached the point of pronouncing "either" as "eether" instead of "eyether," "fast" with a short "a," and "arts" like hearts." In New York her accent is regarded as New England, and in New England as a New York hodgepodge. After nearly seven years in New York she can now refer to a dollar as a buck; but mentally she hears the English pronunciation and finds it helps her to remember that a buck is a piece of property, that it can be glimpsed, hunted, shot down. Italian or French is for her an exercise without pitfalls, subject to general observation and planning; in speaking American she no longer needs to plan her grammar, yet still from time to time she plunges into paralyzed hesitations, as if from a great height.

He called McNamara derelict.

In the place occupied in other offices by family pictures or flower vases, she has stuck a narrow strip of paper (the one considered by the Puerto Rican packer not worth classifying as "Personal Effects"), with the words THE CUSTARD APPLE IS THE FRUIT OF THE SWEETSOP. The sentence means just that and no more, but she cannot understand it, because the word CUSTARD on the billboard that she sees twice each working day at Times Square subway station has nothing to do with fruit: she knows quite well what custard is. Yet the custard apple is also known as the sweetsop or sugar apple. She cannot understand the interconnections among these words, and the faint sense of dizziness she experiences whenever she looks at this sentence is a warning not to kid herself that she could ever live on the British side of the language.

Such is the equipment with which she is to go to work tomorrow.

## February 26, 1968   Monday

"They called it the Reich Kristallnacht, the National Night of Glass?" says Marie.

"Yes."

"Like Washington's Birthday?"

"That's right."

"Go ahead, Gesine."

"Because the Jews also had their glass smashed up, or stolen."

"You've told me that the Jews were about to forfeit their lives, their businesses, their homes. A penalty of one billion marks. They were no longer allowed in the schools. Their pensions were gone. Their insurance policies were canceled. And the Government called it harsh, but legal."

"Yes, Marie."

"And was Reich Kristallnacht a phrase of the Government's?"

"No. Of the governed."

"I'm willing to believe you, but explain it again."

The week after the National Night of Glass, Cresspahl was still in Jerichow. It was a perfectly ordinary week.

On November 14, the Monday evening, the National Socialist German Workers' Party put on a social for the Party faithful at the Strand Hotel in Rande. The Strand Hotel was across the street from the jetty. The Gneez School of Music contributed some instrumental numbers, and a group of Jungmädel—the little girls who were too young for the B. D. M., the League of German Girls—sang "Red Flags Burning in the Wind." The welcoming address was given by Friedrich Jansen, in a quiet, almost tame voice. Almost every seat in the Strand Hotel ballroom was taken, and Jansen was also able to thank the local regional leader for being present. Swantenius from Gneez observed him with a veiled smile that the other man might have taken for friendly had it not reminded him of the favors done him by Swantenius at the Supreme Party Court. Jansen shouted three "Sieg Heils," and three times the ballroom responded with "Sieg Heil." A group of Jungmädel in traditional Mecklenburg costume then performed some folk dances. The National Socialist League of Women had rehearsed some songs. The final number was a play in Low German dialect, which evoked much laughter, and the prizes for marksmanship and dice scores were distributed. Dancing continued until midnight. As the people of Jerichow returned to their homes, the town was dark except for two windows in Papenbrock's house. There sat old Mr. Papenbrock, reluctant to let Cresspahl go home. Drinking had tired him out, and he roused himself infrequently with a loud sigh. Cresspahl stayed until Papenbrock was no longer aware that he was being lifted onto his office couch and stretched out on his back.

On Tuesday, the paper bag for the "pound collection" was delivered at Cresspahl's house. The bag was printed with a stylized Reich eagle perched on a swastika. Later on Mrs. Jansen turned up and apologized in the name of the B. D. M. girl who had automatically gone down her list, but the bag was already filled with semolina and waiting to be collected. The Labor Service girl could not tell Mrs. Jansen where Cresspahl was. Cresspahl was at Köpcke the builder's, and that afternoon the first trucks arrived with workmen to pull down what was left of the barn and drive off with the first truckloads of rubble.

On Wednesday, Richard Maass placed a globe in his store window. On a sheet of paper he conveyed the information that the new German frontiers were already imprinted on the globe. It was a sample, to the disappointment of the customers, but Maass took a total of twenty-one orders.

Stoffregen borrowed the sample for one of his classes. On Cresspahl's property, rubble was being taken away by truck. The child was not at the Papenbrock home, and the maid there had evidently been strictly warned not to gossip. Edith could not be made to say why Gesine was being kept at her father's instead of at her grandmother's. Meanwhile, more people than usual stopped by the parish notice board, but there was still no announcement as to whether Brüshaver would return to give the Sunday sermon. Brüshaver's oldest son had not been to school.

On Thursday, many Jerichow people had gone to Gneez. Stoffregen had reserved one and a half railway coaches for the school. New recruits were being sworn in at Gneez. On the arrival of the Air Force in Jerichow, the town had had all the delegations now appearing in

Gneez except for the National Socialist League of Hunters. The general feeling was that the Jerichow ceremony had been more uplifting. It was also said that it had been Brüshaver's fault if anything had marred the Jerichow ceremony. At Gneez the church bells rang before the swearing-in. A Protestant and a Catholic army chaplain were present and pointed out the significance of the oath of allegiance to the flag. Then "Now gather we to pray" was sung. The "Sieg Heil" had resounded more promptly on the Jerichow market square, and the response had been better at home. By evening, Cresspahl's workshop had been razed and every trace removed.

On Friday morning, two teams of Von Zelck horses arrived and began to plow up the ground on which the barn had stood. Cresspahl and Paap erected fence posts along a line where the east wall had been. If the line was prolonged in the mind's eye, it cut off a third of the garden. It looked as though Cresspahl was intending to sell or lease the strip of land. By late afternoon the charred wood was gone from the yard, and the teams of horses had plowed deeply into the yard. Then Köpcke arrived with his steamroller and turned the fresh furrows in the yard into a smooth, level surface.

On Saturday morning, the Air Force hosted a Christmas display. On show were broken toys now repaired and destined for the children of needy fellow Germans. Gneez might have its Army; Jerichow could be proud of its Air Force. Even the Air Force eagle, with its wider wings and outstretched head, cut a lot more dash than the common, or garden, variety. Even on a wreath ribbon it had an air of elegance. A wreath ribbon of this kind had been stolen from the Cresspahl grave. Mr. Stoffregen surprised three boys who were negotiating during break over the resale of the ribbon, and he forced them to return the ribbon to Cresspahl with an apology. They came back with the report that Alwin Paap had not allowed them onto the property and Cresspahl had not been around.

Anyone telephoning Jerichow 209 that afternoon could only reach Alwin Paap. He wasn't giving anything away and turned quite nasty with his abrupt replies; Cresspahl had put him up to something. There was nothing for it but to wait for Monday morning. But neither of the Labor Service girls appeared in the shops. They had both left, with their suitcases. Had Paap perhaps learned how to cook? He had arranged for his meals to be supplied by the Creutzes. He did not go to their home; the food was brought to him so that he had no need to leave the property. Papenbrock became quite sly on the telephone, wanting to know why someone was inquiring about Cresspahl. Although Köpcke had agreed that Cresspahl need not pay him before December 31, it still made him uneasy to know that the man had left town. Köpcke did not like to tell Papenbrock that he doubted his son-in-law's integrity, and said no more. No one wanted to get on the wrong side of Papenbrock.

So it could only be assumed that Cresspahl had left Jerichow on the Saturday morning. Taking the child with him.

### February 27, 1968   Tuesday

A White House spokesman says that President Johnson is convinced that Congress was informed of all the facts in the Tonkin affair before the Senators consented to the escalation of the Vietnam war. Senator Fulbright still does not believe this.

A Pentagon spokesman says that the new censorship policy announced in Saigon will have no effect on the daily and weekly casualty figures.

Louis Schein, Bronx realtor, is instructed to tell a grand jury whether he was threatened with death or beaten up by John (Buster) Ardito on account of a loan of $5,000. John Ardito is alleged to have a big say in the Mafia family of Vito Genovese, and Louis Schein refuses to say anything. He prefers punishment for contempt of court to punishment by the Mafia. He refuses even to say whether he knows Ardito.

At the end of December, two days after Christmas, Cresspahl returned to Jerichow.

"You can't do that to me!" says Marie. For the past four days she has not wanted to discuss Francine. She sees Francine at school, turns aside inquiries as if they were breaches of tact. Now something else must serve for the evenings. She seems eager, attentive; she is trying to push something away.

"He brought the child back with him."

"Where had he been, Gesine? Where had he been?"

"In Lübeck, on the market square, there was a branch of the Hamburg-America Line, the Hapag, which operated an express service from Hamburg to New York via Southampton and Cherbourg."

"You're kidding. Cresspahl in New York?"

"The adult fare began at 605 marks, and that covered a six-day stop in New York. Don't you think he would have done that?"

"Gesine, is this a water-butt story?"

"No. Only let's not talk about my mother any more. By this time she's dead."

"Did the fire—? O.K. I don't want to know about it. I promise."

"So you can't see Cresspahl in New York?"

"I don't like the idea. It would be too pat. First, quite by chance, a Robert Papenbrock, then your father. And twenty-three years later we turn up in New York. It would look so contrived."

"905 marks less for the Hapag."

"You're testing me, Gesine. The other day you said something about changing trains for Copenhagen, beside a lake, across from an island, and before that about a British consulate in Lübeck. On Schüsselbuden street, see? There must have been a Danish one there too."

"On Untertrave Street. But if he went via Rostock he could go to Grosse Mönchen Street; that's where the Danish consulate was, and there was a ferry every day, either the *Schwerin* or the *Mecklenburg*, crossing the twenty-six miles to Gedser, in Denmark."

"I don't understand. Wasn't Germany a dictatorship?"

"That wasn't what I said. Governed and administered by criminals."

"And a dictatorship lets people leave the country?"

"The majority of Germans were satisfied with Hitler and his pals. There was no reason to suspect they would pour out of the country by the million. There was an excursion ferry from Warnemünde to Gedser for which you didn't need a passport. All you had to have was an excursion voucher, which you could buy on board for twenty-five pfennigs. But as far as money was concerned, those crooks were on the lookout. The excursionists were not allowed to carry more than ten marks on them, and those had to be in coins, not bills. Then they were allowed to land in Denmark, and you can be quite sure the Danes didn't have to use force to get them back onto the Nazi boat."

"Warnemünde?"

"The mouth of the River Warnow. A harbor outside the port of Rostock, in those days. The express train from Berlin drove right onto the boat. If it was the *Schwerin*, only twelve years old, not much over 3,000 tons, 300 feet long—"

"A South Ferry! A North Ferry!"

"With smoking and nonsmoking lounges—"

"I like that, Gesine."

"And cabins with bunks and baths, verandas, promenade decks, and a magnificent restaurant, since the trip took two hours—"

"You're showing up our South Ferry. It can't have a restaurant with a twenty-minute trip. No cabins with bunks."

"Marie, that was the boat being operated in those days by the German State Railway. I'm not making it up."

"Cresspahl carried the forbidden money under his hat. That he might have done."

"He had the child carry it, sewn into her doll. That he might have done."

"He did some business for Erwin Plath in Denmark."

"I don't know about that, I don't even know whether he ever went to Denmark."

"But you can prove it. You have his passport."

"The one I stole from him in 1951 was the Republic one, not the one with the swastika. No one in Jerichow remembers now, and after the war I didn't like to ask him what had happened at the end of 1938. All I know is what I've been told in bits and pieces, and that's not one of them."

"Assume Denmark. A man alone with a child."

"Later on in my life I traveled by train a lot, from Mecklenburg to Saxony, from Bavaria to Italy, from Wales to Scotland, and I didn't have to learn how. I already knew how; maybe I learned how when I was six. In my dreams I can see hundreds of miles of railway track, with dense woods alongside the other track as far as the very spot where meadowland starts, but I don't recognize the real line, not even when I'm awake. When I came to New York with you I didn't have to discover what a boat is; I already knew all about it."

"That's not the way it is with me."

"You weren't on a six-week trip."

"So it was Denmark."

"Maybe. When we went from Copenhagen to Esbjerg—"

"Déjà vu."

"That's too fancy for me, Marie. Maybe my memory was playing me tricks when I thought I recognized the countryside on both sides of the train, the islands in the Great Belt, the bridge over the Middelfart, and finally the ferry to Harwich. But you see, your déjà vu means not only what one thinks one has seen before but also what one has experienced before; I don't have that feeling, or any premonition of what's to come. I certainly wasn't suffering two years ago from the kind of noninvolvement with life that makes one instantly dismiss the present as the remembered past—"

"I was just showing off with my déjà vu."

"—on the contrary, we visited Ingrid Bøtersen in Klampenborg and were on our way to England."

"You simply recognized it, that's all."

"Yet I couldn't register it. At the very instant of seeing, what I saw slipped into a prepared pigeonhole in my brain and became real;

the moment it was out of sight it was forgotten. That's how I felt when
I saw the Nyhavn in Copenhagen, and the Amaliegade, and the main
railway station; but not the Danish Freedom Museum in Churchill
Park, or Kastrup Airport, or Klampenborg. That other feeling, déjà
vu—"

"You don't have to keep rubbing it in."

"—I had it in a school corridor in London, at Victoria Station,
in Glasgow on the right bank of the Clyde, in the old town. Why—"

"You had been there before, Gesine. Cresspahl had been there.
He was having another look at England, at Denmark, maybe even at
Holland. To see whether there was a place for him there. He wanted
to emigrate, Gesine!"

"I wish he had."

"A man alone with a child, on a trip lasting six weeks."

"It's unclear. Many evenings alone with him in bare rooms. As
if one time I woke up, and couldn't find him, and ran through many
rooms, none of them familiar, and switched the electric light on,
wailing pitifully, and when I'd got everybody together they didn't understand me. I knew they didn't, because they all seemed so jolly. I
couldn't tell them what I wanted. That may be a dream. I also remember something about a thatched cottage with dormer windows and
four children I was handed over to; I've never to my knowledge seen
a house like that, yet the sea was not far off. Small waves, pale clean
sand in the rain. But as if I'd never been unhappy, because Cresspahl
promised to come back, and did come back. And that we were almost
never at the same place for more than a day. Anyone who tries to
imagine that can believe it."

"Then believe it, Gesine."

"But there's no way of proving it."

"I'd rather have some proof of why Cresspahl went back to Germany, to Jerichow."

"I don't know."

"Gesine, the town hadn't grown into what Richmond was. His
relatives could get along without him, so could his friends. And outside
his house, fifty yards away, there was a mound of earth covering his
dead wife."

"Maybe Cresspahl gave up."

"D'you think he might have done that?"

"Not yet."

## February 28, 1968   Wednesday

In West Germany they still have an old man as federal president who allegedly signed construction plans for concentration camps in 1944. He does not believe he did; he could not swear to it under oath. An American graphologist has recognized the signature on the plans as that of the President. A Bonn student who wrote "concentration-camp builder" after the President's name on an honor roll has been expelled from the university. The Christian Democrats, who are being helped by the Social Democrats to govern the country, reply to demands for the resignation of the suspect President: Those demanding such a step want merely to exert pressure on the coalition government and switch tracks for another coalition. This is how concentration camps rate in West German politics; that's the kind of country it is, and Mrs. Ferwalter says: I guess he had to do it; he must have had a wife.

Mrs. Ferwalter lost a portion of her life in the concentration camps of the Germans; she is aware of this, speaks of it casually, as others might of their graduation. She is stockily built, broad in the shoulders, like the country-bred servant girls who used to work so hard that they never got around to living and would fall into bed like a sack of potatoes; Mrs. Ferwalter should be able to sleep well. But she can't. Ever since the Americans found and liberated her in southeastern Europe, she has been restless, in her sleep, looking after her home, talking, unable to eliminate a look of disgust from her friendliest expression, keeps her eyes narrowed, eyes that can be big and soft and loving. Right on Broadway, in the midst of hurrying evening shoppers, she behaves as if she were surrounded by hidden dangers. Mrs. Cresspahl, the German lady, is no threat to her; she goes right up to her, smiles awkwardly, walks along with her, sometimes giving her a sidelong glance, as if at some repulsive object, in an affectionate and friendly manner. Good evening, Mrs. Ferwalter.

Mrs. Ferwalter had been with Rebecca to the Bronx, to a relative who is a hairdresser; partly because he gives her a discount, but also because he knows how to cut Rebecca's hair in layers so that it looks more European.

It is not the German but the European quality in Mrs. Cresspahl that appeals to Mrs. Ferwalter. When you mention Austria to her, she knows where that country is. It contains Mauthausen. Mrs. Cresspahl does not even look blank when České Budějovice is mentioned, she is familiar with one's lost homeland, even with the lost tip of Slovakia now occupied by the Soviet Union. Did they hand over the Jews to the Germans before they rebelled, in 1944? We mustn't ask her. Mrs. Ferwalter is not interested in that; she is interested in the other woman's boots, pale-brown leather, laced all the way up, with hooks. Is that European? They're from London, Mrs. Ferwalter. She is well satisfied. She appreciates the fact that Mrs. Cresspahl is familiar with other than American standards of propriety and understands that Rebecca's mother cannot but be offended when the child's birthday is overlooked, even with the excuse of illness. Yesterday Marie did come after all, leaving a gift in the approved European manner. And to think that it was a pen case from Switzerland! But this is not handed over to Rebecca, it is shown to visitors and later displayed behind glass in the cabinet as a sign that the Ferwalter home still maintains European standards. "From Saks Fifth Avenue!" cries Mrs. Ferwalter. "I guess you shop there all the time?" It is not worth denying it, Mrs. Ferwalter will believe it anyway. She regards Mrs. Cresspahl as "very high class" and has mentioned this to Professor Kreslil; these origins may also help her in the friendship. Now she talks about the pen case coming from Zurich, about Mrs. Cresspahl's having to do a lot of writing in her profession and hence knowing what a good pen is. It would have been better still, of course, if it had been a gift from Germany, the home of the most careful of all craftsmen.

Mrs. Ferwalter is not going to hold it against the West German President that he is suspected of having built concentration camps. In her eyes, the good Germans are excused anyway. "They didn't know about the camps." It makes her uncomfortable to think that at least the highest representative of West Germany knew about it. The dignity of the office prevents her from believing this. She is loath to be convinced. But when she goes shopping she makes sure she is not cheated out of a single cent.

Now she would like to know whether it is true that Mrs. Cresspahl, with all that European background, has taken a black child into her home.

She gives a satisfied nod on learning that it was a temporary measure; she has understood: an aberration. She keeps the nod to herself, she does not let Mrs. Cresspahl see it; she is not going to indulge in blame. She is intolerant of Negroes and believes in all seriousness that God has created them to live in dirt and poverty and sin.

Not even her religion, for which she was sent to the camps, enables her to think of Germans as anything other than goys. She has such a sharply defined contract with her God that she regards as of equal rank only those who live as orthodox Jews, whether they be poor or not poor. She is not averse to a slight preference for the not-poor in order to respect this decision of God's. She observes the feast days rigidly; quite often Rebecca and Marie are separated. On Saturdays Rebecca is, strictly speaking, forbidden to go for a walk or a visit. Friday is housecleaning day, meals are cooked in advance and kept warm so that the gas need not be lit the next day. On the Sabbath Rebecca is not allowed to take a bath. She has to accompany her father and brother to the synagogue, and if she first eats an ice cream by mistake at the snack bar, it is not so much God of whom she is afraid as her mother. Rebecca has had a long upbringing according to the stern principles of the Old Testament: am I not chastising my child? Is this not proof of my love for her? The fact that Mrs. Cresspahl was letting her child grow up freely was regarded by Mrs. Ferwalter with horrified suspicion, and it was only as time went on that she could relent a little. Mrs. Ferwalter is so firm in her principles that she disapproves of the Jewish congregations on Manhattan's Upper West Side. Services are actually held here in little stores along Broadway! After the service, the faithful stand around amid traffic and crowds of pedestrians the way other people do outside a movie! But Mrs. Ferwalter also has a bad conscience, she seldom accompanies her family to the synagogue. There is this problem about money. If she really scrimped and saved, there would be enough to pay for a Jewish holiday camp for Rebecca, who must not be deprived of any aspect of a Jewish upbringing. Mrs. Ferwalter is offended when Mrs. Cresspahl sends her child off to a summer camp outside the city; after all, Marie could have played with Rebecca, who is obliged to stay behind at the P. S. 75 school camp in order to avoid paying the fees for the Jewish one, and the uneasiness arising from that has to be hidden by a demonstration of hurt feelings. But it's all right for the playmate to be German. Whatever the Germans did to the Jews was something ordained by God.

So now that the Cresspahls no longer have a black child in their home, Rebecca is allowed to visit again and be friends with Marie. Is that what it was, Mrs. Ferwalter?

That must have been it. Mrs. Ferwalter has seen a movie that showed some European scenery, a castle in the mountains, a nobleman with many motherless children, almost constant singing, and at the end a wedding. Mrs. Ferwalter wept. She won't allow that it was corny, but she admits that for a time reality is pleasantly distorted. "Surely we deserve that." Besides, it can happen. A chief rabbi got married in Jerusalem, he was seventy, the bride was forty. Such a pious man, he had a beard down to his navel. There was romance in the world after all.

"Don't tell me you're blind in this eye too? Or have you given up, really?"

During the flight from the German camps, Mrs. Ferwalter lost her language. At home they had spoken Yiddish. At school she learned Czech, which she speaks somewhat less brokenly than the German she learned in concentration camp. In Israel she learned Hebrew, and until they arrived in America this was the language the family spoke at home. Then their son began to answer Hebrew in English, and she had to learn English. From then on she spoke Yiddish with her husband, and with their son and Rebecca an English that the children did not always understand. Then, at the New York school, Rebecca learned Hebrew, and Mrs. Ferwalter set herself the task of relearning it. For her husband and each of her children she has a different language.

"You not mind?" says Mrs. Ferwalter. For we have now arrived at the building on the side street leading down to Riverside Drive in which the family of four has been living for nine years, in three and a half rooms, all windows facing a courtyard, and evidently Mrs. Ferwalter has screwed up her courage to deal with the matter on the street and not to invite the German lady into the apartment. Home is for the family; let the outside belong to outsiders.

The thing is, Mrs. Ferwalter would like to give a word of advice. She is the older of the two, between friends this is permissible. Maybe it's nothing serious, but let's hope it won't lead to her splitting up with Professor Erichson. Right?

Not so many years ago, D. E. came one Sunday morning to the park and sat down at a distance from the Cresspahls, like a stranger who had brought along his breakfast in the form of a paper cup of coffee and a newspaper under his arm. Mrs. Ferwalter was sitting beside Mrs. Cresspahl, saw him look across, and was reminded of men whom she had come to know too well in the camps. She almost ran away, and it was some time before she could bear even to be in the same room with this tall husky gentleman from Germany without fidgeting in her chair, shifting her legs, and working her lips more than usual. Now she wishes to ally herself with him, and what has brought her to this point.

Because Mrs. Cresspahl has started something with one of the top presidents at her bank. After being so conspicuously singled out by him, with a salary increase, a grander office, more status all around, in fact. And how did Mrs. Ferwalter find out?

From Mr. Weiszand, Mrs. Cresspahl. Dmitri Weiszand. Whenever one runs into him outside Columbia University he has time for a chat, even with an unassuming Jewish lady from Czechoslovakia. In fact he had been the one to start these chats, about three months ago. Such an easy person to get along with, so kind, although the Germans had beaten him up in their camps.

Now Mrs. Ferwalter is very agitated and concerned. "I not mixing in!" she cries. "You not mind!" she says, and now it is not merely the words but the tone that implies an order.

"Who knows what's best, Mrs. Ferwalter?"

"Like I say, eh?" she says, not beaming exactly, yet complacent because she has attempted what she regards as the best. Her mouth is relaxed now, and she looks pleased, trusting, suddenly a woman who is still young.

*I like you, my German friend, see? Can you understand that?*

*No, Mrs. Ferwalter. But we're glad to hear it, and the feeling's mutual.*

---

### February 29, 1968   Thursday

is the day following the evening on which a West German publisher took part at the Hilton Hotel in New York in a discussion of the chances of a resurgence of German National Socialism today. Klaus Harpprecht introduced himself with the statement that he had been a young soldier under Hitler but was now married to a Jewish woman who had been in Auschwitz.

Please explain. After all, you're German too, Mrs. Cresspahl. Try and explain.

The day on which a report can issue from Bonn, West Germany, that the Government has banned an illustrated weekly that raised questions about the signature of the Federal President to blueprints for concentration camps. The official reason for the ban was that objection had been taken to an anthropological series and the series of photographs showing Chief of Police and Brigadier General Nguyen Ngoc Loan executing a young man in the streets of Saigon. The Government is afraid that the photographs might "brutalize" youth. But the effect on youth of time spent in concentration camps is not the subject of government statements at this time.

Please explain. After all, they are your compatriots, Mrs. Cresspahl. Try and explain.

It is the day on which the German author Hans Magnus Enzensberger publishes an Open Letter in the *New York Review of Books* entitled "On Leaving America."

Please explain, Mrs. Cresspahl. After all, you are one of those Germans. Try and explain.

In this letter Enzensberger has publicly informed the President of Wesleyan University that he is resigning as a fellow of the Center for Advanced Studies at Wesleyan University, and he begins with what he calls a few elementary considerations.

He publicly acknowledges his belief that the class which rules the United States of America (including the Government) is the "most dangerous body of men on earth." The same statement was made by Paul Goodman last October in a speech to military industrialists: "You are, at the present time, the most dangerous body of men in the world." Body of men. Who is going to quibble over a quotation? "In the world," that sounds so humdrum. No: on earth. Solemn, resonant. Biblical, no question. On earth.

Because Enzensberger was not aware of this three months ago, he is now publicly leaving the country after three months.

This West German has been told by many Americans that they are deeply troubled by the state of their nation. When Mr. Gallup mingles with the nation, he is in a position to question many people; how many Americans has this West German been able to meet in twelve weeks? To what class do they belong?

Moreover, the conclusion he has reached corresponds to yesterday's Gallup poll. He is not allowing for much knowledge on the part of those whom he is addressing.

It is just that many Americans have told him that the crises in the country, not least the undeclared war in Vietnam, are unfortunate accidents, ineptitudes, tragic errors. Enzensberger cannot agree with this interpretation. Obviously the obvious gains in obviousness when an Enzensberger says it.

The ruling class in the U. S. A., he says, has ruined so many countries; nobody can feel safe any more, neither in Europe nor in the United States itself. No one has said otherwise. But in this way he can at least tell us that he needs to feel safe.

Enzensberger admits that he has wasted our time with his truths; but although he would like to do so scientifically, he lacks the space.

The contributions of others in the field for which Enzensberger lacks the space are regarded in the American academic community as trifling, old-fashioned, boring, rhetorical; this is what he has been told, and this at least he would like to bring up to date.

He speaks of our society. It has become permissive about the old taboos of language, the ancient and indispensable four-letter words. All of society has seen fit to do this, and Enzensberger was there.

But there is also another society, polite society. This is where Enzensberger has made the acquaintance of his 98 million Americans. These have, by general agreement, banished other words. Exploitation and imperialism: in Enzensberger's polite society, these words have acquired a touch of obscenity. Among the like-minded, of course. But then, to do away with the word for a problem is far from doing away with the problem. How true.

Enzensberger now turns to the notion that bank presidents, generals, and military industrialists (see Paul Goodman) look like comic-strip demons. He would like to rectify this. They are well mannered, they are gentlemen, possibly lovers of chamber music, with a philanthropic bent; the same kind of people as there were among the Nazis. So that's what they are like. Now we know. Their moral defects derive not from their character but from their social function. After these surprising and original insights, no one, presumably, will continue to suppose that the President of the United States acts in his private capacity. What must be said must be said.

And what speaks from Enzensberger's analysis is not Communism. He has no reason to fear this time-honored indictment. Fearless fellow that he is. For Communism used in the singular has no single meaning, it has many contradictory and mutually exclusive ones. So there is not much to fear on that score, and Enzensberger is not afraid. But, just in case he is not sufficiently covered, he has at his side Greek liberals, Latin-American archbishops, Norwegian peasants, and French industrialists, Enzensberger's whole polite society. American military industrialists are the most dangerous body of men on earth, Paul Goodman says so too; but not the French ones. Furthermore, Communists do not spring to his aid, at least they do not form part of the Communist vanguard. Hence nothing can happen to Hans Magnus Enzensberger. He has stated his claim publicly; now we must be sure to back him up and not deprive him of his safety. Otherwise it would be a pile of shit (all sections of society have lifted the taboos from these indispensable words).

It follows therefore, the logical conclusion is, the consequence is: a fact. That 125 millions do not know what they and their country look like to the outside world.

No. We can't have that! How could they! And how do they look to the outside world without knowing how they look? Without having the slightest idea?

Enzensberger has realized this from the glance that follows American tourists in the streets of Mexico, soldiers on leave in the Far East, businessmen in Italy or Sweden. Sweden seems to be an alternative.

Moreover, the same glance is directed at embassies, destroyers, billboards for American products, from General Motors to IBM. An international glance the same in every country. One place where this glance is not to be seen is the territory of the United States of America.

Enzensberger has had no trouble recognizing this look. He makes no bones about it. A terrible look that makes no distinctions and no allowances. Enzensberger has felt it on himself, because he is a German.

In 1945 the Germans had to answer to the world for 55 million dead, plus the 6 million victims of the extermination camps.

In Enzensberger's eyes the citizens of the United States have assumed a comparable guilt.

Never mind about the dead. The dead can be relied upon to keep their mouths shut.

There follows the analysis of that international look. The attempt at an analysis.

The modest, tentative student who nevertheless gets to the bottom of things: that look consists of a blend of distrust and resentment, fear and envy, contempt and outright hate.

And anyone who does not believe him is welcome to meet him in Rome during the summer and find it out for himself around the fountain at the foot of the Spanish Steps.

For passersby in the streets of Mexico, the Far East, Italy (or Sweden) have already analyzed United States foreign policy. It is only people in America, and especially the *New York Review of Books* and Wesleyan University of Middletown, that are not properly informed. But now at last Enzensberger has arrived.

The look falls on President Johnson. There is hardly a capital left where he can show his face. Here an audible sigh from many of Enzensberger's listeners: if that were only true.

For of all the heads of state in the world the President of the United States is the only one whose public appearances are protected by security measures.

But because it is not true, Enzensberger rapidly proceeds to speak of the nice old lady across the aisle on the flight from Delhi to Benares. The look falls on her too. That is certainly bad news for the airline. Vast sums spent on advertising, and now passenger Enzensberger is undermining it, possibly even the flight personnel are too.

It is an unselective, blind, indiscriminate, unreasoning look. Lock, stock, and barrel.

It is a Manichaean look. This derives from the supporters of the doctrine of dualism between the Lords of the Kingdom of Light and the Kingdom of Darkness, between Spirit and Matter, out of which unseemly and deplorable union the world and Man have resulted. According to this doctrine, salvation for the world and Man is only possible if the particles of Light are separated from Matter and revert to the Kingdom of Light. This process will continue until final purification in a world conflagration. The enlightened person can further this merely by abstaining from procreation. Much can also be achieved if the Elect renounce the pleasures of meat and wine. They are also enjoined to renounce work. Property is whenever possible to be shunned. But those who lack these select insights, those who have children and eat meat and drink booze and work and for that work use their own means of production: on these falls the Manichaean look: just like that. Manichaean.

Mr. De Rosny, Vice-President of his bank, travels unsuspectingly all over the world, and in Mexico, Bangkok, Rome (or Stockholm) the eyes of the inhabitants follow him with that look, all of them old people without children, monks and vagabonds, each without possessions, vegetarians, and abstainers. Manichaeans.

Enzensberger is not happy about this look.

Although he feels obliged to tell us all this, it is to be assumed that he pities us because of it.

Enzensberger sees a connection between the blind look of the Manichaeans and the fact that he does not agree with President Johnson's views. Someone may have suspected that he does; let him be disabused. The simple fact is that whatever the President utters in regard to collective graft and collective guilt does not accord with Enzensberger's views.

True enough, he is willing to admit that the other nations also share in the pillage of the Third World. In case the public is not familiar with the process, he describes it.

What Enzensberger admires in the U. S. A.: the work of three political student groups. Hardly to be compared with Europe.

And he resents the air of moral superiority shown by many Europeans toward the U. S. A. merely because their own empires have been shattered. He knows such Europeans, and he cannot stand them. As if it were to their own personal credit. There are such Europeans, he is disgusted by them. A lot of hypocritical nonsense.

However, personal responsibility for the actions of one's own government, on this he must insist. He cannot allow us to evade this, since he cannot evade it himself. We have been looking for someone like this for a long time, someone prepared to answer for a West German President who can be suspected of signing some blueprints for concentration camps.

In looking back, Enzensberger finds all this familiar. Present-day conditions in the U. S. A. resemble those in the mid-thirties in Germany. Statesmen would arrive and shake the Führer's hand. The same thing happens in the U. S. A.

For example, that most people refused to believe that Germany had set out to dominate the world.

Just as in the U. S. A. Here many of Enzensberger's Americans have told him that they do not credit their government with the intention of dominating the whole world.

In Germany there was racial discrimination and persecution. Just as in the U. S. A.

It must be something like 300 years since German galleons sailed from the coast of Africa laden to the gunwales with black men whom they intended to take to market in Hamburg and sell off as concubines or cheap workhorses. Just as in the U. S. A.

Where you will frequently see a Negro being led through the streets, his head shaved and his neck hung with a sign: he promises never again to complain to the police about the Storm Troopers. Just like the Germany of the mid-thirties.

And finally Germany became involved in the Spanish Revolution. Just like the U. S. A.

Vietnam is the Spain of our generation! That's what such people say.

But they don't ask their friends the French industrialists for discreet donations to the warring party for whom they desire victory.

They make public speeches, in case someone might think they were secret supporters of the Americans. The friends of the lawful Spanish Government sent shiploads of medical supplies, they took along sizable checks, they armed themselves with rifles and fought in brigades against the military clique, and one man went at least to observe in order to be able to write a book about it.

Only at this point, after the Spanish Civil War, whose counterpart he sees in Vietnam, does Enzensberger find his analogy breaking down. His present masters are wielding a destructive power of which the Nazis could never have dreamed.

And if they did, and dreamed of a rocket with a range as far as New York, so much the worse for those dreams. Besides, things aren't handled as crudely as they used to be, says Enzensberger. Today verbal opposition is licensed, well regulated, and even encouraged by the powerful. So those are the ones who are encouraging him.

Enzensberger sees this freedom as precarious and deceptive. He visualizes censorship and open repression, stern and frank; but he doesn't want that either.

Dear Mr. President, he writes.

It took him three months to discover that preferential treatment would end by disarming him; that in accepting the invitation and the grant he has lost his credibility; and that the mere fact of his being in Middletown, Conn., would devalue whatever he might have to say.

He is prepared to defend himself against West German money; he feels less able to cope with the dollar.

He has been given a piece of advice: to judge an intellectual it is not enough to examine his ideas; what counts is the relation between his ideas and his acts. Now Enzensberger is acting. He is leaving a small town north of New York and going to San Francisco and from there on a trip around the world. No: around the earth.

For it is one thing to study imperialism (there it is again, that obscene word) in comfort. But to confront it where it shows a less benevolent face—indeed, my friend, that's quite a different story.

He has been to Cuba. C. I. A. at Mexico City airport were photographing every passenger leaving for Cuba!

Other countries do not allow their Secret Police to do such things: to take photographs.

Nor do they invade smaller countries and leave their traces behind them; their economic systems leave no scars on the body or mind of a small country. Definitely not.

Enzensberger has seen it for himself.

Enzensberger has decided to go to Cuba for a substantial period of time. That might be three years.

This is hardly a sacrifice, he says.

He just feels that he can learn more ("joy") from the Cuban people than he can teach the students at Wesleyan University about political attitudes.

He wishes to be of use to the Cuban people. He, personally, wishes to be of use to an entire people.

The transformation of Enzensberger into usefulness for the Cuban people, here displayed for all to see. No tricks, no double curtains, no veils!

The letter is his meager thanks for three peaceful months.

At least they were three peaceful months.

He realizes that his case, per se, is of no importance or interest to the outside world.

So he goes and gets himself published in the *New York Review of Books*.

Because his case raises questions, if nothing else.

So he does this.

Questions which do not concern him alone.

Sure.

Which he therefore wishes to answer in public.

No, not quite so self-assured, so confident. Which he wishes to try and answer.

As best he can.

As best he can. And anyway, are they the right questions?

Now let us see how he signs himself in a letter to the University President, who, by granting him privileges, wanted to disarm him, deprive him of his credibility, and devalue whatever he might have to say. How does Hans Magnus Enzensberger teach us to treat an enemy?

"Yours faithfully,
Hans Magnus Enzensberger,
January 31, 1968."

"Had this fellow countryman of yours never been in this country before?"

"He had been here many times before, and for quite long periods of time."

"Mrs. Cresspahl, why does this German treat us like kindergarten kids?"

"He is happy to have learned so quickly; he merely wants to tell us about his progress, Mr. Shuldiner."

"Ought we to go to Cuba now too? Has he nothing to do in Germany?"

"One should never read other people's letters, even if they offer to show them to us."

"But no doubt he wanted to set an example to you, as a German."

"Naomi, that's why I don't want to live in West Germany."

"Because people like that are always sounding off?"

"Yes. Good people like that."

This morning's thick haze is what's left of the fog that shrouded the river yesterday evening. From the fourteenth floor up, the buildings were invisible behind their wrappings. In the afternoon, frequent showers rattled against the windows, and in the evening.

## March 1, 1968   Friday

At six this morning there was snow in the park. In town the traffic turned it immediately into slush. By noon Lexington Avenue was almost dry, bright with sunshine.

Mr. Greene has given up. Twenty years ago he began with a tiny jewelry store on Lexington, between 81st and 82nd Streets, and he is one of the many to whom we always went, as if there were no such businesses on upper Broadway. Even in broad daylight his store was kept locked, and he would carefully inspect his customers through the iron grille in the door before pressing a button to release the automatic lock. He had penetrating eyes, almost cornflower blue; at a customer's second visit he would try to recognize him by his appearance. Marie had her first identification bracelet engraved by him. His work bench was cluttered with tools.

"Don't throw your watch away," he said, when he could have tried to sell us a new one. "It's a good watch. But where's this place Ruhla?" he said. During the last few years his store has been held up seven times and on one occasion cleaned out, and now he cannot get any insurance. His policy has been canceled, and he is closing up. His store is given an obituary in the *Times*, with a bit of personal and statistical history and some sociocritical comments from an insurance agent, such as: "Years ago the hardest thing to find was customers. Now, the hardest thing to find is underwriters." And since the police decline to comment on the situation, the *Times* notes that the police decline to comment.

Jerichow's municipal police—now, to oblige the Air Force, three men strong—was spared having to assist the Gestapo in the expulsion of Aggie Brüshaver. Aggie left of her own free will.

As a rule, the wives of clergymen were entitled to retain the home when the husband was in jail. But Brüshaver had given the state too much provocation by reciting Daniel's prayer of atonement the day before Lisbeth's funeral. Instead of denying his statement that the devil (your adversary) walketh about as a roaring lion, I Peter 5, 8, he supplied his interrogators with chapter and verse not only for that text but for the others which an attentive member of his congregation had been writing down since 1936. After serving his sentence he was committed to indefinite custody in a concentration camp. The full-length funeral accorded the Cresspahl body had riled the Ecclesiastical Council; Aggie could expect no help from that quarter, nor that Brüshaver might one day be reinstated in Jerichow. Not only had he been suspended from office: the authorities had seen fit to unfrock him. On one occasion the illegal Church committee, the Regional Brotherhood Council, had been able to get money to her. People like the Von Bobziens were not afraid to make her gifts of potatoes and game, parking outside the parsonage in broad daylight; and after she had left town Baron von Rammin publicly announced, by way of the newspaper, that he had resigned from the German Faith Movement for "National Socialist and religious reasons."

It did not escape Aggie Brüshaver that the people of Jerichow were also putting pressure on her. Her children were not molested at school, Mr. Stoffregen making one of his inscrutable decisions here; no one refused to talk to her, or greet her, on the street. But visits ceased, and Aggie noticed from their surprised and questioning looks that the townspeople were beginning to find it irksome to stick by her and Brüshaver. When she had been allowed to visit him in the Rostock jail she had also dropped in on her old clinic, where they had been glad to take her back as a nurse. Now she lived far enough away with her children, in the old quarter of Rostock near St. Jacob's Church; the expulsion order came too late to affect her, and did not pursue her there.

---

### March 2, 1968  Saturday, South Ferry Day

---

Yesterday the West German Federal President, Heinrich Lübke, appeared on his country's television. He stated that he could not remember having signed blueprints for concentration camps in the Nazi Reich. Nor that he had not signed them.

The General Secretary of the Christian Democratic Union, of which Lübke is a member, has attacked the person responsible for reviving the affair in his illustrated weekly, asserting that this editor had been an impassioned follower of Hitler.

I forgot to ask when Cresspahl started his job; by September 1939 he had already been working some months for British counterespionage.

"I don't like that," says Marie, disgruntled and annoyed. Today the weather is so cold and windy that she has inspected only the interior of her boat. Sits there reluctantly, bored, staring at the vague clouds above the harbor. She doesn't like it.

"Because he betrayed his country?"

"That too."

"But wasn't his country in the wrong?"

"Gesine, isn't this country in the wrong too? Couldn't you go on quoting examples for hours? But does that make you go and betray it?"

"We're guests here."

"We live here."

"O.K., Marie. If I ever do, I'll ask you first."

"I won't help you, that's for sure."

"And what's your other reason for not liking it?"

"Everyone in your family went along with the Nazis, and Cresspahl most of all. Now you're trying to salvage the honor of one of them at least, preferably your father."

"I have proof."

"That's just an ordinary halfpenny with George VI on the back."

"Look at the year it was minted."

"1940. You could have brought that from England recently."

"This was sent to me from Jerichow when my father died. That was in 1962, and he never went back to England after the war broke out."

"Tell me about it! Tell me! Why didn't you tell me about it before?"

"Would you have understood?"

"No. I don't understand even now. Tell me about it."

"The life insurance with the Alliance—"

"Listen, Gesine. I thought you were inventing it. I don't mind your inventions, you know that, I'll give it to you in writing. This time I'd prefer the truth. Is it true?"

"It began with money."

"You know my weak spot so well. You've got such an advantage; you know me, Gesine."

"Cresspahl had insured only his own life, for the sake of the child and Lisbeth; so now Lisbeth's death didn't bring in any money. He didn't even bother to report the loss of the workshop with all the machinery to Hamburg; then the insurance company noticed that the December installment had not been paid. In January a reminder was sent but still no money arrived. Jerichow: seen from Hamburg was way out in the country, perhaps even farmland, in any case not an area promising much in the way of correspondence. So in mid-February someone was sent there, in a car with a Hamburg license plate parked in the center of town as if the driver had merely got out to have lunch at the Lübeck Arms. Cresspahl said later: one of those tennis types, so that I picture him like Dr. Ramdohr, tall, loose-limbed, with a small head, a somewhat sleepy expression, but wide awake and not likely to be caught napping, let alone got the better of. Perhaps because Ramdohr so often had business in Hamburg. This other man attracted no attention even carrying a brief case; instead of going as far as the Gneez road he walked across the churchyard like any sightseer, emerged from the chapel gateway onto the brickyard path, and was on Cresspahl's property without being seen by many people. Now comes something I don't know."

"Use your imagination, Gesine!"

"I imagine they had met in November in Denmark (or in December in England); in that case the conversation would have begun with reminiscences. I also imagine this to have been the first approach. So the stranger would have made the proposal quite casually, like something to be taken for granted, as if it weren't a matter of life or death. And Cresspahl would have said, with equal indifference, that he would give it some thought. Or: give it some more thought. Then the man would have held out the police report on the fire and said: In a wooden building where the lumber is stored, it is easy for a lantern to fall over.

"But Cresspahl was entitled to the money!"

"Not if it was suicide."

"What do you mean, suicide! O.K. I know. Sorry."

"Cresspahl wanted to test them. He went to Lübeck and listened cautiously to what Erwin Plath's friends were saying, but they were busy with Franco's victory over the lawful Government in Spain, and when they did mention England they abused the British Government, which had collaborated in starving out the Popular Front. And that was the time when the Social Democrats were beginning to go underground. Then the visitor came again, and this time Cresspahl had no trouble believing him. For what the man brought along was a sheet of paper showing the law of February 1935 regarding foreign currency. According to this, up to ten years' hard labor was threatened for anyone failing to report his funds abroad. Cresspahl had neglected to do this for three and a half years, what's more, so a court of law could have proved: deliberately."

" 'What's it got to do with the state, where I keep my money?' "

"There speaks an American. But the state was in the control of bandits, and they were determined to get their hands on their subjects' foreign currency. Sorry: but a law like that carrying ten years' hard labor had already been passed in 1931."

"Had your father been careless?"

"He did have a healthy respect for the law. But why should he obey this one, when the only people who knew about what was left of his English bank account were Dr. Salomon and the Surrey Bank in Richmond? And by the end of 1938 it should have been used up by the monthly payments to Mrs. Elizabeth Trowbridge. But she wanted to bring up her child without the help of a person who went off and married someone else, and she kept returning the remittances until Salomon gave up sending them."

"And wrote to Germany."

"Dr. Salomon didn't reveal his clients' secrets to the mails, and certainly not to the German ones. By then there were enough refugees in London who could have warned him. And Salomon couldn't care less about what laws they had in Germany. It was the British ones he was concerned with."

"Mr. Smith betrayed Cresspahl? That I can't believe."

"And it wasn't Perceval either. T. P. had wanted to get so far away from Richmond and the memory of Mrs. Cresspahl that nothing would do but the Royal Navy. It was Gosling."

"Hence 'Gosling the Patriot.' "

"Gosling had never got over the fact that, without permission and of his own free will, the German had stopped managing Reggie Pascal's workshop for him, not exactly making a gold mine out of it but at any rate enabling Reggie's nephew to live like a lord. Gosling had finally located Mrs. Trowbridge near Bristol, and needless to say he noticed the child. He could only assume that Cresspahl was paying for the child, that it was his; he merely took a stab at denouncing him, who knows what for. He was hoping at least that the German's money would be confiscated by the British Government, and perhaps a handsome reward would come his way."

"And was sent home as a nut."

"Right. And a few weeks later had a visit from the Government he had been trying to help. The Government was represented by two grim gentlemen of whom one kept sniffing as if at an unpleasant smell in Gosling's vicinity. When they left, Albert A. Gosling, Esq., was so terrified that he determined to forget the whole affair, and particularly the money, with a solemn oath the money."

"And so the British could blackmail Cresspahl, their man in Jerichow."

"And that suited him very nicely."

"Hm, I wouldn't like to have to go to bat for that."

"It's quite simple, Marie. As long as they could believe they had a noose around his neck with that ten years' hard labor, they didn't know the true reason for his wanting to help them."

"He didn't trust them. They were blackmailers."

"And he would never have told them that he had an account to settle with the Nazis. On it were his wife, Voss in Rande (whom he had never even known), Brüshaver, the war."

"But the war hadn't started yet, Gesine."

"As long as the war hadn't been started by the Nazis, Cresspahl was uneasy, at times. It was only when they had actually invaded Poland that he felt sure of himself and, what's more, furious at the inaction of the British."

"Would the Nazis have hanged him?"

"Oh, with pleasure!"

"The fact that he had a child meant nothing."

"He didn't trust his ability to bring up a girl. He had hidden money in the country for the child, and he trusted Hilde Paepcke not only because she was Lisbeth's sister."

"You forgive him for that."

"I forgive him for that. And now he had other grounds for saying the British had gone to the dogs. Except that Alwin Paap knew scarcely anything about Cresspahl's time in England, and the wife who might have listened to him wasn't there."

"I like that."

"And there was something else that suited Cresspahl. As soon as he had accepted, the money arrived from the insurance company. A lantern falling over in a carpenter's workshop can be an accident, or just clumsiness. It was a lot of money. In those days German money was still worth something."

"So now they had bought him too."

"Blackmailed and bought and secured. Only that he had made up his mind on his own and had kept his freedom intact."

"You know, I'd keep that bit to myself."

"I do. Jakob knew about it; D. E. knows about it. Now you do."

"It's a kind of skeleton in the closet."

"Not for me. It's my father's affair; I don't care to show it to everyone."

"We've been taking the South Ferry for five years now, and we've never managed to make it in a storm! That one yesterday could easily have been on Saturday. To be on the South Ferry in a storm, that's what I'd like."

---

## March 3, 1968 Sunday

The West Germans have released from prison in Kassel, for health reasons, Robert Mulka, former assistant commandant of Auschwitz and convicted of assisting in 3,000 murders. The *Times* arrived at our apartment with two supplements of Greek advertisements. In New Haven, Church Street and the university campus were emptied by a harsh wind, 8° below zero. Now a sliver of moon is lying on its back above Riverside Drive. The sky is almost black.

Dear G. C.,

Handwritten, for your sake. That's the way you, Cresspahl's daughter, like letters. This letter would go no faster in the typewriter, maybe not at all because the standardized type face would indicate an objectivity that isn't there. Whichever way you look at it, handwriting mitigates circumstances. That's not what you mean.

I won't use the word. Not because it's too vague for me but because for you it's outlived its usefulness. By this time you've come to despise it so much that you only use it now when you want to play in the foreign language, and its etymology is involved too: in English it has a Latin ancestor, *lubēre, libēre*, intended merely to indicate the desire to give pleasure, to be kind, to do someone a favor. For instance, you'll respond to an unwelcome suggestion: I'd love to. But you do it; and you don't do the other thing. I like that.

Not that I want to avoid the word. You tease me about my liking for verbal precision; mentally I do use the word you don't want to hear and which I would have no other opportunity of uttering. I dislike it as much as you do when it is made to fit into the HaveHaveHave syndrome, whether in terms of consumer products, a person, or life. But I don't mind it when it ensures the past. In a literary work I could accept it when it applies to a dead person who can no longer benefit from it, who is no longer obliged to repay, either in money, favor, or speech itself. But I suppose that would have to be an old book. In short, and inadequately, I can use the word for the sum of the relationship between one person and another; a relationship that contains history, that is maintained, whose termination would cancel out a part of the person. Of course there is need there too, but self-interest could not survive in it; a yoked system between one person and another needs nourishment from all sides, interacting, reciprocal.

This detour around the word has taken me twenty-nine minutes. I'm writing that down too, and you are laughing.

I don't want you to marry me; I want you to live with me. You're the one who says "want"; I mean "wish."

It is a clinging to you. Not the kind Klothilde Schumann means. As a landlady in East Berlin this is what she called it when she once came into my room without knocking and Eva Mau and I fell off Klothilde's sofa together. It's that kind too. But it's more than I can bear G. C. under any circumstances. That's not a generalization, it is a summation of almost six years. (Don't counter by saying that you happen to be easy to bear.) There was only one occasion when I couldn't stand your face. That was last week, when you had a fever and allowed yourself to be treated by a pediatrician and even when you were asleep you railed against hospitals as well as against what I might have got you into. I didn't mind the obstinacy in that; more often than not it has been a cover for your good sense; what I didn't like was that you were in danger and refused to allow me to do anything about that danger. That, by the way, is the reason for this letter. Because I wasn't allowed to do anything about your obsessed, burning sleep, about your unconscious talking, I didn't come again and this is my first return to your apartment, with a bow from the waist like the ones the little boys of the Misdroy promenade were taught to make so they would learn the meaning of deference.

I'm not begging: I'm explaining my suggestion.

You think that's my life; you are politely mocking when you observe it, but you keep your distance from it. You have seen a lot; I won't deny any more that that's how it looks. That when I'm working I'm not there, or merely as a performer, not as a person. That I have long since ceased to justify my work. What the Soviets did in Mecklenburg after the war is not enough justification; what the Americans are doing in the world, now that the buying phase is over, is not enough. In this interlocking system I would be merely a cog in any job; this happens to be my job. On neither side would my usefulness extend farther than my usefulness to my employer. The other side: it didn't work. This side is at least a matter of indifference to me. You are appalled by the lack of biographical impetus. I have no biography, except maybe a tabular one. In such a situation of boredom, a person can make a lot of noise with airplanes and cars and the machinery of his job; it may deceive others, but not him. Nor you. If I am to remain alone, all I want during the next twenty years is to watch, but without taking the side of my own prognoses, merely with curiosity; not much else is left. Call it waiting.

You don't live that way; for you there are still real things: death, the rain, the sea. In my memory I know these things, but I can't go back to them. What does seem real to me is you.

Where I have an old woman with her own ways, because she is still alive, you have a past filled with characters, a present that includes the dead, and even Marie knows more precisely who she is because she is learning about her background. There is something there that I can't put into words. Never will I be able to say with such certainty of my own mother that she has at any time been more than what I have seen, heard, listened to; you calmly say: My father was not concerned with revenge, he wasn't going to soil his hands by dealing with the Nazis; an incomprehensible statement, surely, because it can never be proved. And I believe you absolutely, I believe it is a truth with which you get through life; often as the truth. Of course I know living people at the places where they do their jobs, there are some I would miss. It all seems very pleasant, even friendly, and later you look back on a few hours of companionship, with no unkindness and with mutual pleasure. And then again it wasn't that, it was nothing but some more time spent. You can't yet pass a horse without looking it in the eye, without touching it, until the horse knows who was there. You're not concerned about that; it's the others to whom that means something. I wish you would live with me.

You can speak; I can't. You say of Amanda Williams: She's flat on the ground with her soul. With anyone else I would recognize that for an uncalled-for remark, depending on how I felt, and I would either cover it up with another remark or let it stand there in all its nakedness. When you say it, I suddenly understand the sum of the relationships that go to make up a person, including the unexplained or still-unrecognized part. You also said of her that she was not heated all the way through; that should have conflicted with my system, but instead it complemented it. Not only did I laugh, I felt refreshed for days. Let's hope that by now you've heated her all the way through again. Whatever I say, even if it is a new description of something new, the moment I utter it it's a quotation. With me, something that really happened, not many years ago in Wendisch Burg, becomes dry, witty perhaps, but it turns into an anecdote. You tell Marie about someone called Schietmul, "and the other one was called Peter," and Marie sees a cat, and another cat, because with you they have remained part of life while to me they have become words. These are all things I can't explain. They are such that I have no wish to pull them to pieces; all I want is to be close to them.

You have not given up. Needless to say, I would find it incredible in myself. I must admit you are right. You've never yet tired of taking the socialists' promises at their word, you persist in challenging the imperialist democracies with their nobly conceived constitutions, to this day you can't forget that the Church included instruments of war in the blessing of the recruits in the Gneez barracks yard. If this were naïveté, I would swallow this never-ending pedagogic task with pleasure; but it is hope. You don't say so in words, for reasons other than just the Mecklenburg ones. Forget that I first tried to talk you out of the

Czechoslovakian business; by now all I want is for those people to come to their senses, if only so that for once you wouldn't have to bear the brunt. Forget the bet.

I promise that the child will not be taken away from you. She will never be mine anyway; she will always be your Marie.

If we meet again one day, maybe then we should be together.

I have written you this because once again I am being loaded onto a Scandinavian Airlines plane, and because I wanted to write it. Because the undersigned would rather not speak about it. Neither snow nor rain nor heat nor gloom of night stays these couriers from the swift completion of their appointed rounds, and if Herodotus is still regarded as one of the pillars of society the mailman should be standing outside your door with this letter about eight o'clock Sunday morning. Otherwise we will see that the inscription on the brow of your main post office is removed by chisel.

Sincerely yours,

D. E.,

a child who was not one of your classmates.

---

### March 4, 1968   Monday

If we convict four citizens for having expressed views that differ from those of the Soviet Government, says *Pravda* on behalf of the Soviet Government, this is as justified as the purges of the thirties. Now even the state has confirmed that the thousands of dead of that era enjoyed only a twelve-year restoration of their good name.

At times it seems possible. Yesterday even the New York *Times* mentioned Czech hopes for long-term West German credits. The price would be "recognition of West Germany." De Rosny could do it cheaper.

At times it does not seem possible.

Perhaps De Rosny chose the wrong employee after all and was badly advised. Not only does Mrs. Cresspahl now have to bend her head back still farther in order to make out the glass of her cubicle in the bank's tower, seldom finding the right square, but she also has to fight a shyness in herself that surprises her. In the elevator she often presses the button for the twelfth floor as if she were afraid of the higher one, and only then does she press Number 16. So the elevator sometimes stops at the old level, the doors slide all the way open, and no one steps out, unless it be an invisible person. In the upper regions the elevators are more sparsely occupied, and even if this does not make the passengers observe each other more closely, one imagines that they do. Because in the first few days Miss Cresspahl tended to gaze up at the indicator panel above the door, she found herself being greeted in fatherly fashion by a gentleman whose face she did not remember, Mr. Kennicott II, who said: "Have you settled in all right, Mrs. Cresspahl?" Beaming and embarrassed, she replied: "Yes, thank you, sir."

To lie is easier than what the Personnel Manager calls settling in. To begin with, there is the more luxurious appearance of the corridors. Here there are rugs, the fluorescent tubes are shaded not merely with glass but with plastic covers of expensive design, and their light falls not on bare walls but on prints in custom-made frames. Down below, in Foreign Sales, there had been steel doors painted green; here they are massive mahogany slabs maneuvered by great round chunks of brass. Down below it had sometimes been possible to avoid the wide tentative smile at the department's reception desk; up here the desk is manned by Mrs. Lazar, who sees that her place is taken when she leaves her post. Here no visitor gets by without inspection, unlike down below, where there is less to hide. Mrs. Lazar, a middle-aged person with the manner of a headmistress, invariably gives the new staff member an austere encouraging look, and the passing of the time of day is presented with a gracious smile, as if the inquiry after her health were tantamount to a daily birthday gift. On leaving her, Miss Cresspahl goes swiftly past the expensive desks in the spacious, elegant outer office, as if not wanting to disturb; what she really wants is to avoid any personal contact.

It is not fear of the new department; what she misses is the nature of her relationships to the others. When De Rosny presented her to his subordinates, the men welcomed her with looks of downright pleasure, and the names, which at the time she did not gather, have gradually become familiar to her from the little triangular plaques that each one has on his desk: Wilbur N. Wendell, Anthony Milo, James C. Carmody, Henri Gelliston. . . . The nameplates on the twelfth floor had not included the first names. The name Cresspahl is still absent from beside the door of her new office; certainly they won't put a nameplate here with the word Miss. Now that she is allowed to work up here she is entitled to be addressed as Mrs. Cresspahl. She would like very much to know her status in these splendid prison cells. Does Mrs. Lazar regard her as one of De Rosny's passing fancies? Is it possible that the irreproachable encounters with co-workers in the outer office do conceal doubts as to the new colleague's knowledge, or indignation at a woman being placed beside them? Even discussions about work are not feasible; Mrs. Cresspahl has her own sphere, as do the others, and is not asked about it. There are times when she is glad not to have to sit out there in the general office but behind a door. Here the doors may be closed, yet she still feels less at ease than before when her door was open, because now a knock would surprise her more.

Nobody knocks. It is left to Mrs. Cresspahl to see how she composes her memoranda; she can stretch out on the visitors' sofa if she has something to read through. The strange surroundings, the distance from the others, confine her more relentlessly with her work; all of a sudden she cannot decide to take a break. Down below, when it was possible to put off a ticklish paragraph, she could carry a mug of coffee and a cigarette over to Naomi, Jocelyn, or Amanda Williams and a chat for fifteen minutes at their desks; it had looked quite businesslike and had been a refreshing pause before the next hour's work. Rules are laxer up here; in principle she is now free to decide when she will turn up between nine and ten, whether to take an hour or an hour and a half for lunch, just as long as she is to be found in her office until five o'clock; she has not yet been able to learn such freedoms. Now she often finds herself sitting in the midst of her new work, surrounded by maps, diagrams, journals, books, and for minutes on end she has thought of nothing, has leaned far back in the swivel chair, arms dangling, mute, blind, deaf, and tired. Yet almost every four days she can hand over a file folder to Mrs. Lazar, and Mrs. Lazar invariably takes a fresh Manila envelope, addresses it to De Rosny, and staples it shut, the ordinary string closure apparently not being sufficient.

Nobody comes. Amanda was here once, to supervise the move and the furnishings, she pronounced the new office magnificent, she has not come again. They all still say hello in the elevator, ask how she is, smile as if at someone they are glad to see, yet from afar. On Friday evening Mrs. Cresspahl was in the Foreign Sales department and wanted to work out the figures for her 1967 income tax return on Amanda Williams's machine, and they were all shocked by the visit, as if by something improper. As if what they had in common had disappeared as soon as the work ceased to be on a common level. Mrs. Cresspahl's temporary replacement is a writer from Switzerland who wants to earn some money so he can spend a few extra months in New York, and because he mentioned having some difficulty with Italian Mrs. Cresspahl promised to help him. He will turn to Amanda for advice, and he will send her nothing. When the telephone does ring it is a wrong number or, once in a blue moon, De Rosny, dispensing praise and hoping she is well the way one gives sugar to a horse.

How quiet it is. When the day's work is coming to an end, what she misses most is a gentle click. That had been Amanda down below, outside the open door, packing up her coffee cup for the night and carefully placing it on her file cabinet. With that click the free remainder of the day had begun.

It is so quiet that once Mrs. Cresspahl did not go home until half an hour after closing time. She had forgotten the time. She had not liked that, and Mr. Kennicott II's appreciative smile in the elevator had not improved the oversight. Down below people had noticed each other, helped one another out a bit; up here each person is supposed to shift for himself.

Sometimes it doesn't seem possible. Good night, Mrs. Cresspahl. Take care.

## March 5, 1968   Tuesday

When people in the bank start saying that the place is about to collapse, it sounds optimistic, complacent. Today they are saying that what happened at the Chase Manhattan Bank could have happened even more easily here—a small group utilizing an accomplice in the cable department conspired to demand the sum of exactly $11,870,924.00 from a Swiss bank by means of fraudulent cable instructions. A single word saved Chase Manhattan. The gangsters had demanded the remittance in dollars rather than in Swiss francs, and this was enough to make Zurich cable back for confirmation. Could just as easily happen to us.

And yesterday when the Vice-President was concentrating so hard that he had to take his dictating machine apart, he found a nest of cockroaches inside it. Why does he have to keep a refrigerator in his suite anyway? The creatures can smell food through twenty floors. The firm must be on its last legs.

If the city were to perish, the cockroaches would survive.

We took over our apartment from two girls, one Danish and one Swiss, and at first we couldn't believe it. In the morning we would find brown wings lying on the floor, as if discarded by some minute vermin. In the dark kitchen sink there would be a collection of brown crawlers that ran away as soon as the light was switched on, concerned only with escape. They looked so single-minded. I thought it was a freak and brought my foot down on the first cockroach within range on the floor. No use, it had already vanished into a crack unsuspected by the naked eye. There could have been a disaster, for they can provoke allergies from asthma to eczema, even when they are dead, and to throw away shoes and stockings would hardly have been enough. They are too quick for such a death. The draft caused by the moving foot is carried to their powerful legs by tiny hairs, without wasting time in the brain, and before the shoe reaches the floor the creature has scuttled away. They were all over the place, in the backs of books, in the upholstery, in lighting fixtures, all with five eyes, six legs, and two highly sensitive antennae, and this time I had a good word for the supermarkets because there you don't have to ask aloud for insect sprays.

Mrs. Cresspahl was so embarrassed that she said a cockroach on the wall was a fly, when Marie asked what it was. Why shouldn't a fly be half an inch long? Marie was not yet four, and because she had found many things to be bigger in this country she accepted the explanation.

Then, in broad daylight in 1961, there was Marie sitting on the floor looking at something beside her discreetly, almost as if they were buddies.

It was a female cockroach on the point of giving birth, highly pregnant. Perhaps it was too weak to hide, or the instinct for self-preservation was no longer uppermost. Later on Marie was able to describe the sacklike container suspended from the waist over the abdomen, as plump and firm as a pillow, long and narrow, and releasing from an opening on the side little white threads in quick succession, almost like swiftly unrolling snippets of tape, and the little grublike pennants unfurled, swelled, turned faintly gray, were already recognizable as bodies, everything in clear-cut fractions of time, countless numbers every second, and while the mother was still lying on her side discharging the pupae, the first of these were already running off, complete except for their wings, and Marie asked. Because the word children could not be avoided in the explanation, she offered money as rent for the new denizens of the earth, and was horrified to see them swept up into a paper bag to be burned by the janitor that night. Mrs. Cresspahl was so embarrassed that she forbade the child ever to mention the scene, even in unintelligible German.

Then, on the benches in Riverside Park during that summer of 1961, the German woman was initiated into the lore of cockroaches. The new arrival did not rate very high, if only because her job rendered her a "temporary" mother and she could not really keep up in the detailed discussions of bowel movements (quantity and color), of wobbly knees and ingrowing toenails; also because she didn't take along any knitting. She was allowed to sit there and listen, and that was how she found out that in New York every year is the year of the roach.

The most frequently occurring type was called the German cockroach.

It was treated as a completely normal and respectable topic, and whenever a housewife denied that cockroaches shared her apartment with her she soon gave that up when subjected to the pitying or scornful looks that accused her of hypocrisy. The cockroach was discussed with respect, with hatred, with comic despair and systematic expertise, and invariably as an invincible enemy. For they devour everything, from dry furniture glue to the impregnated head of a match; and even if poison temporarily makes life difficult for them, after a few years they have developed a resistance to it and consume as dessert the very thing designed to bring about their extermination. When one of the more senior matrons talked about the happy year of 1940, when chlordane was still effective against cockroaches, her description was listened to not as folklore but as a bit of American national history. Theories were expounded, such as that of the cyclic wave, or that the creatures survive because with them reproduction ranks first in importance, not third, as, say, with rats. The last supposition was dealt with at greater length and with more enthusiasm than that of the cycle. Horror stories were told, such as the one about the elderly lady who had recently been looking at television in her darkened hotel room in Mexico and watching an American movie while fingering a brooch on her bosom. "Suddenly I realized I wasn't wearing a brooch." Even the New York *Times* had heard about her; indeed, in January the *Times* was able to devote what was almost a scientific article to the cockroach, including such facts as that its flight mechanism functions in .003 of a second, a world record. In New York the cockroach constituted, and constitutes, a respectable topic of this nature.

When the German lady, embarrassed and prepared for a hasty retreat, began to talk about her first experiences, she provided the ladies on the benches around the playground with some pleasurable excitement. Now it was possible to repeat the history of the cockroach for her benefit. This time they casually dismissed the notion that cockroaches might have reached this country on German ships. After all, weren't there some American types too, and Oriental? They wrote out a long list of sprays for the new neighbor, the list going at a good speed from hand to hand because each housewife vaunted her specialty. Then came the advice: always wear a mask over mouth and nose while spraying—although the cockroaches may absorb the chemicals without discomfort, such chemicals are dangerous to humans. Don't mop the floor too often—the Orientals like nothing better. Shake out clothing after each wearing, as well as before. Examine purchases carefully all over before placing in refrigerator. Triple all safety measures when your neighbor paints his apartment—they will move across to yours. Then came new horror stories: how one desperate housewife simmered a panful of cockroaches for three hours at 300° and how they then all got cheerfully to their feet and went their ways, except for one, which, however, was not dead, merely unconscious. In retrospect it was an enjoyable hour, full of merriment and helpful suggestions; but Mrs. Cresspahl would be reluctant to admit to a visitor from Denmark or Germany that cockroaches are a hallmark of this city, let alone hold forth about them.

There is an alarming aspect to this state of affairs. The cockroach happens to be the oldest flying insect surviving in the world today; it is 250 million years old; at one time the age probably belonged to the cockroach, and not to coal formation, and it has remained the cockroach's. They are useful to science on account of their powers of resistance and their terrifying fertility. They can go without food for months, and on realizing that no food is going to materialize they move elsewhere. They can grasp certain things, they are intelligent, they can learn. Granted that they appear to have no reason for their five months of life, since their sole aim seems to be procreation, but nevertheless they are there. They live among the poor as well as among the rich, and even Francine believes this now; they live in airplanes, on the South Ferry, in the highest buildings made of glass; they are New York's lowest common denominator; they may very well land on the moon before man. They are a cunning lot.

For a whole three months we lulled ourselves into believing that our apartment was virtually free of them and were satisfied with the line of sprinkled powder drawn by the building management's pest-control agent. Then, during the weekend, the heating broke down, and now that warm air has returned since Monday the cockroaches are trying a new tactic to cope with such eventualities, coming defiantly right out into the open and stinking with fear when attacked. Nowadays our comments on the Society for the Prevention of Cruelty to Animals represent sheer self-defense. When Marie is reminded that she once offered to pay rent for these creatures, she redoubles her efforts and wields the spray can with increased vengefulness as she follows the vermin around with unchallenged curses.

De Rosny has quietly vacated his office, without protest or punishment of any offender. There is no offender, either in the building or anywhere else. De Rosny knows when he is beaten. Here he has accepted defeat.

### March 6, 1968   Wednesday

When asked who he was, it seems that Che Guevara gave his name and said: Don't kill me. I'm more valuable to you alive than dead.

The New York *Times* still gathers many news items in Munich, but via its very own correspondent in Prague it has conveyed the information that the Party Presidium no longer wishes Jiri Hendrych to be its secretary for ideological matters—Hendrych, who was so good at lambasting dissident writers and students. Moreover, it appears that the sale of foreign books and newspapers in Czechoslovakia is shortly to be "normalized."

For the official list of those from the New York area killed in Vietnam, the *Times* no longer uses standard type, but prints today's names in the very smallest.

Cresspahl had taken his child to the Paepckes. Because they had left Mecklenburg they were known in the family as "the Berlin-Stettin ones," and for the child they also seemed a long way from Jerichow, from Cresspahl. The trip had been an innocuous overnight one by train, and although Cresspahl had explained the journey by saying they were moving house, and her clothes and toys accompanied them in a trunk, she did not believe her father would desert her. Across the center aisle, lounging comfortably against the upholstery, sat two bored Navy crewmen exchanging insults. "Watch it—I'm going to tell my ma!" said one of these two grownups, in broadest Mecklenburg. It sounded as if he couldn't speak proper German. The pair were voices and two glowing cigarettes. For the child they were her very first "sailors." The fact that she couldn't be sure what the sailors were laughing about stuck in her mind. She fell asleep in the train, and the moment she woke up next morning she firmly closed her eyes again because of the shock of finding herself among total strangers. Then she jumped up and ran through the Paepckes' house, lost her way, finally found the front door. Cresspahl had already left.

The two older Paepcke children kept a sharp lookout to see if the Cresspahl child deprived them of anything. She did not deprive them of anything. Alexandra kept her place next to her mother, tubby Eberhardt was not required to sacrifice his place beside her, Christine on Hilde's other side was in no danger anyway. Gesine sat at the other end of the table, keeping her eyes on her plate and eating her bread in a special way: first the crust all the way around, then the soft center, in slow careful bites, as if it were something precious. The Paepcke children were allowed to eat any way they wanted, and when one of them licked the butter off his slice Hilde would calmly spread some more on. After breakfast the new child was no trouble either, obediently joining the others, falling in with any suggestions for a game, not taking advantage of being the oldest. After a while she went away to find a place in the attic to cry in. In the afternoon she let the others tell her all about Stettin, the movies, the harbor excursions; obviously she had nothing to boast about with her Jerichow.

In the evening it turned out that the newcomer had won something after all. Now her place was beside Alexander Paepcke, who normally liked sitting at the far end all by himself with enough room for his newspaper and his glass of beer. This evening he was so busy questioning the child from Jerichow that he almost forgot to eat. Did Methfessel still ask people if they would like to be a lion? Had Cresspahl started giving her any pocket money? Would she like to see how you balance a walking stick on your nose? He demonstrated, and he gave her some "pin money" that was five pfennigs more than Alexandra got, strictly according to age, and the Cresspahl child did talk to him, although she was reluctant to raise her eyes. She remembered the duties of a guest that had been dinned into her by her father, and tried to be obedient. Finally Paepcke desisted. In the end he was about to stroke her hair but caught Hilde's warning glance in time. Then his own children claimed from their father the right of which they had so far been unaware. Paepcke was now quite puffy in the face, had never looked so worn out, was slower; but he only had to make an effort and for the children he was instantly magician, joke maker, and buffoon all rolled into one. He made a great effort that evening, and there was plenty of laughter in the kitchen, yet it was not long before the Cresspahl child asked whether she might go upstairs to bed.

That evening, at great expense, Paepcke put through a call to Jerichow 209. He wanted to have a serious word with Cresspahl. It was only right and natural for him not to want to deliver up his child to the rigors of Grandma Papenbrock's religion, if only because he felt that his own wife had been destroyed by it; it was a good thing old Mrs. Papenbrock had been told all this without receiving any support from the old man or Hilde. There she had squatted like a great fat offended bird, feathers ruffled. And she had wept too; by this time the family was familiar with her tears, whatever the occasion. But Paepcke didn't happen to want to live under the same roof with an unhappy child, and he had no faith in his ability to console the child since she took after Cresspahl and would be obstinate even in her grief. "Hinrich, even a dog would take pity on her," said Paepcke. At the other end of the line there was a long silence, but Paepcke did not think he could hear a sigh. Then Cresspahl said: "Alex—" in a certain way, utterly devoid of hope, and Paepcke troubled him no further. He was very dissatisfied, and that evening Hilde did not once say to him: "Do stop drinking, Alex!"

About ten o'clock his daughter came downstairs, having found the Cresspahl child's bed empty. But Alexandra, in order to spare herself a sermon on hospitality, would not say where the newcomer was, and Paepcke had to search the whole house before finding Gesine in the attic, crouching in the dark among trunks and baskets so she could cry in peace. Paepcke was so furious that he shouted at everyone, not only at the child, he even got the maid out of bed, and next morning the Widow Heinricius reported at the grocery store that Paepcke had tried to kill his wife during the night, shots had been fired, and the fire brigade had arrived.

Paepcke sat at the breakfast table and said, looking at the Cresspahl child: "What some people have to put up with!" Here he was, with an important post in the Army Ordnance Department. It just didn't seem right. And that evening, instead of going home he stayed at the Podejuch station bar until midnight. Paepcke could not bear seeing children unhappy. That's how it was; it was eventually to lead to his death. And if he had to get drunk he preferred to do so away from home.

*You must never forgive me for that, Gesine.*
*I've forgiven you, Cresspahl.*

## March 7, 1968   Thursday

As the *Times* understands it, a major general of the Czech Republic is now in this country, having found it no longer possible to support President Novotný. Just why, however, is not quite clear, since in his own country he was just about to be arrested for the misappropriation of $20,000 worth of state-owned alfalfa and clover seed (although he had been Party secretary at the Ministry of Defense, not of Agriculture). In his own country the hope has been expressed that he will not meet with a fatal accident, and here the hope is to profit from the defector's military intelligence.

"You're trying to make Cresspahl look better than he was," says Marie.

She never mentions Francine now. At school she looks past her, does not talk to her. She cannot get over the knowledge that Francine had not wanted to return to her own mother. For her this is a breach in her understanding of Francine which she has not yet been able to repair. Francine has evidently hurt her.

"Gesine!" she says.

"You don't believe me."

"I can't believe it of him. A carpenter, even though he was living right next to a military airfield—"

"He was employed at that airfield as a carpenter. Headquarters had asked the guild in Gneez to suggest someone, and most of them found it quite proper for Böttcher to put forward Cresspahl's name. The man had lost his wife, and his workshop as well. He must have work, otherwise he'd go nuts.

"At the airfield he gets no farther than the door he's supposed to fix—"

"The first was the one in the casino, where a drunken Party functionary had taken his revolver and tried to shoot holes in the shape of a swastika in Böttcher's solid woodwork. Right?"

"See? And now and again he builds a veranda onto one of the houses for the civilian staff, for his own account—"

"And at Semig's house he had to build an entirely new study, with six-foot paneling with space for Lieutenant Colonel von der Decken's wall safe. It was Cresspahl who made a door to hide it."

"See? Your father was a safe-cracker."

"He didn't have to be."

"Good enough. But your lieutenant colonel, and von der Decken at that, he would only speak to a workman like he would to a dog. 'Good boy, good boy.' You say to yourself. Maybe he saw a few airplanes from way off."

"From close up, Marie. Even from a distance he could have counted them. It already meant plenty that he could count the civilian employees, and their jobs."

"And you're trying to make out that he knew something about technical military matters too."

"No one's trying to make out anything. I'm just trying to tell you."

"O.K. Now the British know how many airplanes there are at Mariengabe near Jerichow."

"And which ones are stationed there, which are only visiting, and which bring supplies in or pick them up. As for the trucks carrying fuel or bombs, Cresspahl could see those on the streets of Jerichow. Sure, his masters, or those who thought they were, would rather have used someone like Professor Erichson, who could have drawn a plan of the airfield from memory that same evening. But they had to make do with a workman who could memorize such type numbers as He–111–P and enough of the exterior to be able to recognize a fighter plane. That was enough for the transport plane Ju–52 or for the He–59, one of those little biplanes. And as for the Ju–87, that horrible monster, it wasn't exactly the talk of the town in Jerichow—"

"A minute ago I believed you, Gesine. Now you're exaggerating again."

"The Ju–87 was a Stuka, a dive bomber. When they swooped down on their target, built-in sirens gave off an infernal howl. That was known then as psychological warfare. They were called Jerichow sirens."

"After the trumpets carried by those old priests marching around those old walls till they came tumbling down?"

"That worked only in one city, Jericho in Jordan. Joshua 6. And the story of the destruction of the city is a legend; you can ask our friend Anita the Red about that, she was working at the dig to get her Ph.D."

"Jericho sirens. That's one coincidence too many."

"I don't like it when something's that pat. So we have Jericho sirens in Jerichow, not invented."

"Not by me. And Cresspahl also knew that the Ju–87 had machine guns on its wings, and that during the Spanish Civil War the long-distance reconnaissance plane Do–17–P used to be known as the Do–17–F. That could be picked up from a conversation as a harmless workman was passing by. And it was useful if he could pinpoint where the aviation fuel was hidden in the ground. In London that was a good enough target on the map."

"Harmless workman! A man who had lived in London."

"And who merely nodded when asked whether after the glorious rebirth of the German Fatherland he had no longer wanted to stand aside. That made him reliable enough. The man looked somewhat slow. He had evidently not done too well in England. Besides, there was always his work—that counted. And weren't they queer, the tales he told about London? 'In London there were dormitories where you lay right on the floor. But under your head they string a rope, that's where you rest your head. In the morning they drop the rope, that's how they wake you,' he said. He was having fun with them."

"There are times when I have a vague notion that I'm beginning to understand."

"See? And Cresspahl was by no means limited to the airfield. In one or other of the taverns, the Foresters' Tavern or the Rifle Club, suddenly men in uniform would turn up who were not from the area, and they couldn't resist showing off with their parachutists' knives. That was just before the planned offensive against England. And so he found out that the parachutists had training schools in Stendal and Wittstock, that they were paid 50 pfennigs a day but that for every practice jump they got 27 marks, which was why they were drinking beer at the Foresters' Tavern and chasing every skirt with that stuff about one last time before they were killed. Cresspahl didn't have to do all this alone. Erwin Plath was somewhat beside himself over the fact that the national soccer eleven, with their trainer Sepp Herberger, was to play against the Hungarians: Sunday, April 7, 1940, was to be the historic date; but he also puzzled over why the motorship *Hansestadt Danzig* had tied up in Lübeck-Travemünde at the Ostpreussen pier; although she was now painted gray she was instantly recognizable from her days in service between the Baltic seaside resorts rather than in the Navy. The *Danzig* had also docked at Rande, near Jerichow. On Sunday they roared in the Berlin Olympic stadium at the heroic 2–2; in the evening the *Hansestadt Danzig* sailed from Travemünde carrying in her belly the 1st Battalion, Infantry Regiment 308 of the 198th Infantry Division, that had been recruited in the collapsed Czechoslovak Republic, in the 'Protectorate of Bohemia and Moravia,' mostly Swabians and Sudeten Germans, of whom many had hoped that the annexation of their own country would be the last warlike act of the century. The day had begun with a ground frost and had later warmed up to 45°, and the sky remained cloudless. What was starting, though, was not spring but the occupation of Denmark. This could only be guessed at by the soldiers, and by Cresspahl too, for the orders were not opened until April 9, by which time the *Danzig* was sailing through the Belt. But for London it was not too late for intelligence as to which troops had been sent to Denmark or for a memo that affairs of this kind could start in the harbors not only of Kiel and Swinemünde but also of Lübeck."

"D'you mean that in or near Swinemünde and Kiel there were people like that, people who went and betrayed their country—?"

"They were betraying the Nazis. And just as with Cresspahl, there was nothing special about them, nothing noticeable. Cresspahl wasn't a Party member, of course, but that was all the more to his credit as far as the Air Force was concerned: remember the swastika punched out with bullets in the casino? Cresspahl didn't have a Blaupunkt magic-eye radio like Alexander Paepcke's, one that could get foreign stations, which it had been forbidden to listen to ever since the war started. Cresspahl had something known as a Volksempfänger, a 'people's receiver,' a VE 301, including antenna 76 marks, 'created in memory of the People's Rising of January 30, 1933.' Besides, by that time people in Jerichow had almost stopped discussing Cresspahl. They might have said he'd become a bit odd since his wife's death. Held his head like a stubborn horse, had got into a way of nodding that looked as if he were deaf, a shade too deferential. This was often taken for stupidity, so that sometimes an order would be explained to him twice, as if he hadn't understood. Then it turned out he *had* understood, and still he nodded again. And some people in Jerichow had their own highly personal reasons for keeping their mouths shut, for during the fire at Cresspahl's workshop quite a few things had been pinched, things that could still be used; Alwin Paap couldn't be everywhere at once. There were mornings when tools were thrown over the fence marked with a C. Maybe they didn't do it only because the initial might have given them away. And it was safer to keep your distance from a person who got mixed up with bad luck—

*Go away, blackbird,*
*Buf I'm black*
*The guilt's not mine alone,*
*The guilt's my mother's*
*For not washing me*
*When I was little,*
*When I—*

—and to have blackbirds in a tree behind the house, there was nothing special about that either. There were a lot of them, a lot were braver than he was."

"That's not how I meant it, Gesine."

"A lot were braver than he was in betraying."

At seven the darkness was quite clear. The skyscraper on the far bank of the Hudson is lit up as if for a holiday. Seen from New Jersey, our Riverside Drive looks as if it were lit up for a holiday.

## March 8, 1968  Friday

The New York *Times* is delighted to find that now it too has been parodied by Harvard students. Among other items on the witty title page, the Parthenon is shown as collapsing, and at the top left there is a double-column report on the failure of an air bridge near Khesanh: because the parachutes fail to function, tanks and heavy guns fall mercilessly on men below. . . .

The time spent at the Paepckes' in Pomerania seemed long to Cresspahl's child, more than six months; yet not too long.

There were evenings like the one in late May of 1939 when the strawberries were ripe and left juice in the sugar. They were eaten with silver forks, at the table in the garden, and Hilde kept heaping new heaps onto Gesine's plate. The child was so absorbed in eating that she didn't notice until she had finished that everyone had been watching her, helpless with silent laughter, without envy. The child had long since ceased to feel observed, suspected, exposed. She could laugh with them.

At the Paepckes', a child had no duties, no burdens. When Gesine and Alexandra offered to go to the grocery store, Hilde pretended to be thinking it over and often refused if she had thought up another new game for the children. "May I turn the potatoes in the pan?" Gesine would ask. "Yes. Turn them in the pan," Hilde would snap, in an offended tone of voice that promised dire punishment. She could not keep it up for long, and would end by laughing. But she would rather a child didn't approach the range in the first place, since a child can so easily get burned.

The way Hilde carried on with Alexander, I've never seen anything like it. Alexander would come home and hang up his uniform tunic in the closet; Hilde would come up to him and put her arms around his neck. "You're not well!" she would complain, and Alexander would shake himself as if he had swallowed some bitter medicine. "What would I do without you and the noosties?" he would say. Hilde could tell as he approached which evenings he was not going to be put off, even with words. Then all Hilde would worry about was to get supper over with quickly, the big girls had to look after the little one, each felt a hand pass over hair and cheek; but then Hilde would follow her husband into the living room and was unavailable for the rest of the night.

Heard from a distance, when the child was very tired and could not see her, Hilde's voice was her mother's. From her the Cresspahl child learned the manner in which Lisbeth had stopped speaking to her child. The second syllable of her name drawn out, not commandingly or admonishingly, the way people did later, but tenderly, constantly surprised by new pleasure.

Hilde was standing beside the range, and Alexander looked her up and down reflectively. After sufficient consideration of the matter he said: "I used to think you had beautiful legs. But you haven't at all."

Hilde looked at him quizzically, but rather saddened, and Alexander decreed once and for all: You've got lively legs, that's what they are—lively!"

Neither of them minded the children hearing this. What has remained is a sense of infectious enthusiasm, of the pleasure of sharing in such a life. (The other side was jealousy; that one was kept from the children.)

Even when Alexander let himself go on the subject of the "Nazi swine," Hilde would pay close and sympathetic attention to what he said. Lisbeth had nervously and reproachfully interrupted. (Remember the child, Heinrich Cresspahl!)

Alexandra and Gesine were supposed to go to the doctor for an inoculation, and Hilde wrote a letter of excuse: "On March 21 my children will be unable to attend as we shall be celebrating the first day of spring."

My children. Gesine had no doubts about that. She knew quite well that she was Cresspahl's child and had to live with him; she knew that inside of her. Outwardly she was one of Hilde's children.

Whether it was the first day of spring or the birthday of one of the two cats, such events were celebrated with vigor. And even if the sky was dark with threatening rain, Hilde would still help Auguste the maid string up paper lanterns in the garden. She invariably filled the garden with the children she invited, except for those of Storm Troop Leader Bindeband, although he had six to offer, with names like Gerlinde and Sieglinde and Brunhilde and Kriemhild. They played Blinking, and Johnny Squeak, and Musical Chairs, and Hilde cheated remorselessly whenever a child was in danger of losing too often. As she shifted the bowl closer to the blindfolded child's groping stick, she would look conspiratorially at the others, and they all consented to this narrowing of their own chances of winning. The author is reluctant to say so, yet it was typical of Hilde: she had a good (deleted).

Then Alexandra and Gesine were invited by Mrs. Bindeband to play with her children. Her girls wore braids down to their backsides; they were dressed in garments of sackcloth, hessian aprons. The "playing" turned out to be a celebration of a heathen Easter in a villa that had once belonged to a Stettin Jew. The Persian rugs, the oil paintings, everything still seemed intact. In addition to the guilty conscience there was the feeling: My God, how poor we are. When they got home Hilde was not angry, just disappointed. From then on the children would not allow themselves to be inveigled into the Bindebands' house.

At the Army Ordnance Department in Stettin, Paepcke did find some people whom he was not obliged to classify as Nazi swine, and he would often bring three or four of them home unannounced; those were long evenings for the children too. There was no need to notice the children, they simply shared in the gaiety of the grownups. They knew they were not unwelcome. Alexandra would sit beside her father as he solemnly held forth (we're going to lose this war too; we've had enough practice, haven't we?) and press against him until he fell over in a side-splitting pantomime of a nonswimmer dropping from a great height into bottomless water.

And no matter how often it was threatened, no child ever had to "go to bed without a caress."

For their photography the Paepckes had a bellows apparatus, and this they believed in. The subject had to be exactly six feet away, and if possible the sun was to be behind the camera. Hilde kept this object in the kitchen closet, and scarcely had Christine torn down a curtain than she had her picture taken. (Am I six feet away? she asked the tiny Christine.) The children used the remains of the curtain for a dress-up party, and they had their pictures taken too.

In the Paepcke house, when a child sat drawing or cutting up material Hilde would never pass by without praising the handiwork in detail, not with flattery but with inquiries. At the Paepckes the children learned to be aware of who they were.

Hilde knew that the neighbors expected her to reflect her husband's profession and rank in her dress; she enjoyed wearing her hair tied back in a scarf, like the women who worked in the fields. She made many of her own clothes, liked to wear pants, responded to derogatory greetings with innocent friendliness, as if she had not understood.

At the Paepckes', you could lie around on the property surrounding the house as if you were in a forest beneath pines and acacias, on the smooth needle-strewn ground. You were never disturbed while doing that. When the child returned from solitude, Hilde would be holding a ribbon and tie it around the child's forehead. And she was not mistaken: the child had indeed been with the red Indians.

During the summer the Paepckes drove with their family to the Fischland. The war had not yet begun. Evening on the High Coast looked strangely different from evening on the North Coast near Jerichow. Cresspahl arrived on their last day at Althagen. He looked old, smaller than she remembered him, emaciated. He stood unannounced on the boundary path, and Gesine knew he was going to take her with him.

Because she knew the Paepckes to be behind, she was too embarrassed to run toward Cresspahl. Then she heard Alexander talking in a very loud voice about birds' nests and realized that none of them was watching her. Then she ran.

The next morning nothing could be more fitting than for her to

go to Jerichow with him. It was already wrong to leave the Paepckes
behind.

*If you had written that down, Gesine, it would be an outright
bread-and-butter letter.*
*It's meant to be.*
*Are you grieving for us too?*
*Yes.*
*We wouldn't have believed that of you during our lifetime. Not
while we were alive.*

## March 9, 1968   Saturday

Cloudy, mild, around 54°; not a day for the South Ferry after all.
Marie has dressed as if for the boat, pants and hooded parka, for bad
weather, when her clothes have to be rough and not too valuable.
Marie has chosen this day of no school to straighten things out with
her friend Francine, but she could not locate her by telephone in the
city welfare hotel. Now Marie was going to try to find her on the streets
of the Upper West Side slums. For that you don't wear a London coat;
she might easily get yelled at if she did, even have things thrown at
her.

Our slums are around the corner, a foreign district. The slums in
our area are not quarters especially built for the poverty-stricken, like
the jerry-built tenements for workers run up by building speculators in
the cities of Germany, a Bidonville in Paris, or a prefab village for
refugees. The slums of New York were not built as slums; here a slum
is a drifting jellyfish in society.

In the side streets between the avenues, slums are now to be found
in many of the brownstones. These are four-story buildings named for
their original façades of reddish-brown sandstone, and after the Civil
War they were the hallmark of bourgeois affluence. The wide steps
were designed to enhance their owners' public image, the four floors
were intended for a single family plus servants, the interiors lavishly
equipped with fine wood paneling, oak floors, marble fireplaces, carved
doors, turned newel posts. Inside, there had been receptions, glittering
parties; outside, elegant coaches once waited. They were luxury dwellings and, although by now the façades are peeling or carelessly painted
over, there is still an incongruity about the dirty front steps, the decaying
furniture and mattresses, the uncovered garbage cans, the grimy windows, and the aftermath of the garbage collectors' strike, refuse strewn

about that will lie there indefinitely if it can resist the rain and is too heavy to be blown away.

These are abandoned homes, built for White Anglo-Saxon Protestants. The Irish who arrived in swarms in the 1870s concentrated in the apartment houses along Columbus and Amsterdam Avenues, but many of them saved up for one of these fashionable brownstones and could be property owners by subletting. The Irish were the most powerful political group in the area, before the Jews from Harlem, unable to cope with the growing proximity of the Negroes, migrated there. Then came the Negroes from the ghettos of New York, after World War II the waves of Puerto Ricans; and the white immigrants, now well adjusted to the scale of values they encountered, abandoned one street after another. That's to say, not quite. A single-family house of this kind can be turned by the owner first into four apartments, one to each floor, and the increased rental revenue makes up for the loss in property value. Out of these small apartments the landlord can in turn make single rooms. By now he has increased the former rental revenue many times. Since, if they come from Harlem or Brownsville, his tenants are bound to regard such living conditions as an improvement in their lives, and the Spanish-speaking inhabitants are initially incapable of resistance, the landlord is free to continue putting off repairs, to economize on heating, and to do without a janitor. The laws are specific and provide for fines for all such instances of neglect, but people without education or sufficient knowledge of the language get nowhere with the bureaucratic apparatus, and the courts are lenient toward the slum landlord, representing as he does the concepts of acquisition and property.

Acquisition and property are what create the slum in the first place: the ugly, flimsy partitions, the missing windowpanes, the defective locks, the broken mailboxes, the slippery encrusted dirt even in the corridors, the rusty kitchens, the contamination of the cubicles by vermin and by the rats over which the people's representatives laughed themselves sick last summer. Mrs. Daphne Davis in Brownsville, Brooklyn, spoke of how her daughter played with a rat last summer. The creature was so big that the child said: Here, pussy, pussy, here. When it gets to this point the city inspectors give up, whether they come to inspect the water mains or the fire exits, and even the garbage collectors catch on fast. Here garbage is collected less often than in better-class streets, and in a casual manner that knows no sweeping up afterward. But it is not acquisition and property to whom the riot act is read.

If a family like the Carpenters III on West End Avenue wish the best for Negro families while an apartment in their own well-maintained but not fashionable building is not part of that best, at least Liz Carpenter III discusses the slums and convinces herself that these blacks simply wouldn't know how to live in a civilized community, as if this were an innate characteristic of theirs. Scarcely one of those arguments aimed at impeding a reasonably equitable distribution of social property makes any effort at cogency or even the appearance of logic. Moreover, this particular one overlooks the fact that not all Negroes live in slums and not only Negroes live in slums. The prejudice of the American nation against a long-settled tenth of their community is incomprehensible; the issues defended with the aid of this prejudice are concrete enough. These are: jobs as a means of income, education as a means to a better income, and the right to rights as a safeguard of income. The name of the game is rat race, and the fact that some rivals are handicapped can only improve one's own chances.

No group has had to fight so long for its rights as the Negroes. Runaway and freed slaves who arrived last century in the more casual, less arrogant North, were nevertheless segregated there in special areas, exploited by "white" landlords and businessmen, denied equal rights to education and job training, always the first to be let go, always the last to be hired, and they had to look on while group after group of immigrants found their feet and were recognized by other citizens: the Germans, the Italians, the Jews, and in the fifties the Puerto Ricans. Eight years have passed, yet John F. Kennedy's classic figures still apply: "The Negro baby . . . has about one-half as much chance of completing high school as a white baby born in the same place on the same day, one-third as much chance of completing college, one-third as much chance of becoming a professional man, twice as much chance of becoming unemployed, about one-seventh as much chance of earning $10,000 a year, a life expectancy which is seven times shorter, and the prospects of earning only half as much." Kennedy made this statement in a TV address in 1963. Hence whatever may be the roots of this traumatic exclusion by the whites, the Negroes as a group must accept the highest losses in the struggle for work, and they consistently form the largest group of those who have given up hope of work, who were never in a position to have this hope, who let themselves sink down into the slums.

The slum is a jail to which society consigns those whom it has itself mutilated. These are dwellings in which bedbugs and cockroaches cannot be held at bay by even the most patient effort, in which the function of the refrigerator is not to keep food cold but to act as a safe that the vermin cannot crack. When whole families, without the money for vacations or attempted flight, have to live in a single room, the children become witnesses to inevitable quarrels, they arrive at school tired out and upset, their homework incomplete; their achievements are bound to lag behind the demands of the curriculum, they leave school as early as possible, they "drop out" and start working in inferior occupations that will die out as technology develops, and they are trained for poverty. If two thirds of the Negroes on the Upper West Side are single men, this is because a family that has been deserted by the breadwinner is entitled to welfare support; science has helpfully invented the "factor of single-room occupancy." Negroes in the slums feel neglected by the police; their streets are patrolled less frequently, break-ins evoke boredom more than anything else, when there is a fight the black is more likely to be arrested than the white; yet all the Negroes want is more police, more reliable protection (while the whites can afford to demand a citizens' board to supervise the forces of law and order). (The Communist Party of America has been canceled.)

Resistance is futile. If slum dwellers attempt to strike against their landlord by withholding rent, the landlord has the courts on his side. If he fails to evict them, he lets the building die. Above all he can depend on cold. Then the city moves the inhabitants into armories; they cease to be his responsibility. Still, it is worth paying a small tax on the property to prevent the city from taking over a building that is staggering under mortgages and Brother Wind; there is always the hope that his particular site will be taken over for a community project. Should stubborn tenants stay on, they are taken care of by hoodlums, drug addicts, and metal thieves. Of these not all are kind enough to turn off the water main before they dismantle the pipes. When the ceiling is dripping and all the doors have been knocked down, the last tenants move out, and the property is finally in perfect order.

Where there is no longer any question of order, garbage is thrown out the window, and if it lands in a back yard it might be a message, a missive from the air. As a group, the whites do not hear; the occasional white passerby may hear something when a bottle smashes at his feet on the sidewalk. The whites often remind me of figures in shrouds, specters, corpses on their way to the cemetery. Since the whites as a group refuse help, why not hold a knife to the heart of the lone white and help yourself from his wallet, his till, his apartment? Since for the slum prisoner the way out into a worth-while life is blocked, why should he hesitate to evade life in the illusions and sicknesses of drugs? Since society has erected a fence around this life, why maintain the norms of society, why treat the social worker other than as the bringer of an installment payment, why not send the kids out to beg, why still live under a roof? Since connections with society have been broken off, why not rip out the cables of public telephones; why leave an address when you go away, whether you end up under a bridge, in the Bowery, in jail, or in the Vietnam war?

His Honor the Mayor, John Vliet Lindsay, is fairly sure of his ground here. He often mentions the slum ghettos in his speeches, and one of them, Brownsville, in Brooklyn, he calls Bombsville.

The word slum also exists as a verb. Mrs. Cresspahl and her daughter went slumming this afternoon, and in our slum areas the children were out on the street. Among these were some who had to use the street to relieve themselves, and others who might have a bathroom but no water to bathe in. Some whose clothes had been washed and mended over and over again and who would not risk wearing them to school and appearing before the teachers in them. Some who were searching a long-since disemboweled car for some overlooked salable object. Sometimes they ran like crazy and played baseball with a broomstick. Others were too shy to play games and stood around like men out of work, bored, hostile. All of them had learned to recognize a drug addict, a homosexual, an alcoholic on the street and to look on him as a normal inhabitant of the neighborhood; but a dog barked at the lurching figure with the bottle, and kept on barking. We saw this. This is where we live.

Francine was not at any of the places where she usually whiled away the day. But the man at the wicket of the Mediterranean Swimming Pool, a strangely soft person in his white T-shirt, one of those with the mild voice, the defensive tone, had a message for us.

"May I have another look at your card? Is that how you pronounce it: Crisspaw?"

"Most people do."

"Might a Negro girl have been asking for you?"

"Yes. Called Francine?"

"Mhm."

"Did she leave a message?"

"What kind of message could she have left, Mrs. Crisspaw? She wanted to know whether you were in the pool. And that's just where you were. Then she left again."

"I don't understand, Mr. Welch."

"That goes for me too. Only the police ask questions like that and then go off so a person really doesn't know what it's all about. This afternoon she turned up again. Of course, anyone can make a mistake in the number."

"Oh, of course, Mr. Welch."

"And by mistake I told her you and the young lady were in the pool here. This time she even wanted to come in."

"Is she still there?"

"Think again, Mrs. Crisspaw. The wilderness of the street has swallowed her up."

"Mr. Welch, if she comes again we want to pay the day rate for her. Whether we're here at the club or not."

"But she's a black girl."

"We know her. She's a friend of ours."

"Does that mean you'll guarantee for this child?"

"That's what it means. Here's a dollar."

"A dollar's a dollar, Mrs. Crisspaw; but I hope you know what you're doing."

Since the new Czech Government abolished censorship two weeks ago, the New York *Times* is encountering unfamiliar difficulties in Prague: Is it the Government speaking, or is it merely the voice of a TV commentator, that warns against premature purges in the ranks of the Stalinist old guard? If Alexander Dubček wishes to implement his economic reforms, will he succeed without cleaning up the bureaucracy? "He is said to be against blood revenge." Such uncertainties, when a Communist ceases to use the country's television as his private property!

### March 10, 1968   Sunday

It was a visit with friends.

In the American sense of the word, Jim and Linda are our friends. They let us share when they rent a house by the sea in New Jersey, they want us all to have meals together, they drop in for a drink, they inquire solicitously after our health and let us in on the private doings of their children, parents, aunts, so that we are left with a pretty complete memory of them even if we haven't seen them for five months. Maybe the visit was too centered on politeness. The O'Driscolls have moved away from the Upper West Side and have finally entrenched themselves in a Greenwich Village basement, so now the Cresspahls must come and see the new apartment. Jim has put on even more weight, and often the only way he can move in his armchair is by heaving his bulk around, but he has painted the walls himself and fixed up the plaster and woodwork in the rooms, a great barrel of a man who has recently acquired a mournfully drooping red mustache. He still enjoys watching Linda, secretly congratulating himself not only on finding her five years ago in Greece but also on bringing her back to New York. Linda has learned his kind of English, New York with strong Irish overtones, and has also acquired such notions as running a kindergarten co-op when the city ones fall short, Linda with her peasant braids, her black glances of jealousy, her look of astonishment at the sight of one of her own children, as if Patrick and Patricia were miracles that had befallen her. At the O'Driscolls', the children behave as if every day they had to win their parents afresh; they seem to be forever coming in from the little back yard, hugging Jim around the neck, clambering onto Linda's lap, to make sure they are not forgotten. Toys were lying all over the place because Jim works at an office where his job is to apply his knowledge of psychology to thinking up new markets for the toy industry; the visitors felt welcome, comfortable, among old friends.

On arrival Mrs. Cresspahl was welcomed with the eager question as to what was the good word, the good news, the answer to which is supposed to be that Ireland is free or that President Johnson has stopped an elderly widow lady on the street and insisted she hand over her last lamb, nor is there any way of avoiding a big hug or, from Linda, a few carefully planted kisses on the temple, and Marie was greeted like a children's nanny who has been anxiously awaited for days and turns out to be not an old battle-ax but a well-educated young lady to whom one can hand over the responsibility for Pat and Pat with a sigh of relief. In the kitchen. Lunch is prepared as a joint effort at the counter. Rolls with smoked salmon and ham and cheese. Surrounded by bowls of salad, sherry, and Irish whisky.

Talk. About the trend in the U. S. toward a police state. Jim is convinced that the Government has provided for the coming rebellions of the blacks by setting up detention camps into which people will be herded without trial on the sole basis of skin color. Whether the O'Driscolls should go back to Ireland; Jim's father, after all, had been the first to emigrate. Rambling argument about Linda's Greece, which they cannot go back to. About a choice between Nixon, standing for a vague war program, and Rockefeller, unable to produce any peace program. About Hans Magnus Enzensberger. About Jim's father. About mail from the family in Nauplion. From the yard the subdued noise of the children.

Maybe it's been too long since we saw the O'Driscolls. During a pause Jim's brooding remark: What Himmler did to the Jews is what in effect we've done to the Indians.

Now it was no longer "Jee-zine" but the German woman who was expected to explain Himmler.

The awkwardness persisted, no matter how much Jim regaled them with gossip from the office, with his physical condition. Ten days ago he had come out of a bar on Third Avenue and fallen over a car. No question of being drunk, after only five gin and tonics. More likely a fainting fit. Heart—? When Jim talks about himself, he seems to be mystified by many things about himself. Even the action of raising his glass to his lips seems to amaze him.

The awkwardness was enough to discourage the idea of a walk. Instead they would go to a film club. The communal nature of the event, the system of donations rather than regular admission, were discussed in such detail that Mrs. Cresspahl missed the name of the movie. I missed the name of the movie.

It was *Under Cover of Darkness*, and one other.

I left after the first. It was in Brooklyn.

Between the brownstones the air was thick with fog. Behind a screened window children speculated on the solitary pedestrian. The bottom of Second Street seemed to drop off into the harbor. Foghorns. On Seventh Avenue the Irish bars were full, delicatessen stores were looking after Sunday customers, kids were teasing the sales clerk by chinning themselves on the glass counter. Gray-haired alcoholics stood helplessly at street corners.

We missed the beginning of the movie. The French narration was embarrassingly polished. The photos of starvation, of humiliation, of corpses caught in the electrified fence, the children's home, the gas chamber, the utilization of remains by industry. The photographs taken after the war strongly tinged with red from the brick walls. Again the dreaded picture of the Allies' broad shining bulldozer blades pushing and shoveling the corpses into their grave in the ditch. The acres of dead bodies. The stacks of burning corpses.

Picking up her child from the O'Driscolls' apartment. "Didn't you like the movie?" The hall had been rented from a church. When the light was on you could see the inscription on a crossbeam: The Place Where We Meet To Seek The Highest Is Holy Ground. In the dark, sweat lay so heavy, as if the skin would soon be unable to breathe.

They have been good friends for many years. They see me, and they think of the crimes of the Germans.

Without meaning to hurt. They take it for granted, it is only natural. That's the way it is.

## March 11, 1968   Monday

It looks as if they really do mean to houseclean the Czechoslovak Republic. There have been secret ballots at Party meetings. Antonín Novotný is urged to go before the people and ask for an expression of confidence. In the trade-union journal, the Rector of Charles University in Prague, the neurologist and psychologist Dr. Starý, declares that many people in Czechoslovakia are suffering from split personality, caused by fear and by a system in which people are manipulated as though they were cogs in a machine. On the anniversary of the death of Foreign Minister Masaryk, who twenty years ago jumped or was pushed from a window in his office, 3,000 students were allowed to assemble at his graveside. The President of the Supreme Court is planning to correct judicial errors. It is publicly stated that innocent people are being held in jails.

Had Cresspahl left his child with the Paepckes she would have been dead long ago. If he had sent her to Aggie Brüshaver she would have been dead even longer ago. Because of its proximity to the airfield, he regarded Jerichow as a dangerous place. His taking the child back there was directly attributable to Hilde Paepcke's letters. By means of lengthy and detailed descriptions she had tried to make him see that in Podejuch, Gesine was missing nothing; this had made him realize how much of the child he was missing. Perhaps he did not mind the possibility of her being killed as long as he was there too.

There had been no regular cooking at Cresspahl's for a long time. Cresspahl saw to breakfast, and to the bread for the cold supper, and when Gesine came home from school at noon she took Swenson's bus to the airfield. There she sat with Cresspahl in the canteen for civilian employees, and there she did her homework. She was only eight, and Cresspahl took her along when he went to the Strand Hotel in Rande in the evening for a beer. Sometimes Kliefoth would join them, and every two weeks a stranger, whom at first the child had not recognized. Now Cresspahl was bringing up his child himself.

He taught her:

What I see, and what I hear, and what I know is mine alone.

Even when I know that a name is wrong, that an address is wrong, I must stick with the wrong information.

What my father does and knows belongs only to him. Only he may talk about it, not me.

It is not wrong to lie; as long as the truth is protected. It is amusing that all other children are taught differently; it is not dangerous.

We have a different truth, each has his own; the only person I may share mine with is Cresspahl.

## March 12, 1968   Tuesday

About eleven in the morning and at one thirty in the afternoon, snow pattered against the office windows. It burst apart on the street, trickled away on the warmed sidewalk. At five o'clock, when people were let out of their glass cages onto the street, fat drops of rain were falling. The upper floors of the buildings had vanished; tomorrow morning they would be waiting there intact. Grand Central and the trains leaving Times Square were strangely overcrowded, and some of the station police had grown too hoarse to shout. The trees in Riverside Park were now throttled in white stuff.

When the German troops occupied Prague in March 1939, snow-flakes hung in the air.

Mayor Tamms's official proclamations in 1942: the use of hot-water heaters, refrigerators, gas heating and cooking ovens is prohibited due to overburdening and icing conditions in the transportation system. Blackout will apply from 8 P.M. to 7 A.M. Attention is again drawn to the following: anyone traveling for pleasure will be fined or, in serious cases, sent to a concentration camp!

Jerichow's worry was the Poles. On the Schwenzin estate one of them had thrown his pay book at the inspector's face, yelled at him, struck him with his pitchfork; in Granzlin, one of them had thrown a pot of hot coffee at the farmer's wife. It was not sufficiently reassuring to know that they had been safely condemned to death; something must have given them the courage to put up a fight.

Cresspahl's daughter had few worries. On Air Force Day in Jerichow North, Cresspahl had appropriated a paperweight made of enemy airplane parts before it was auctioned off together with other loot, which meant that for the last three weeks Gesine Cresspahl had had more friends than usual at school and had to keep taking the object out of her satchel and show it around.

She had a minor worry. She could not get out of her head the lines that her teacher Mr. Stoffregen had made them learn by heart:

*Adolf Hitler is our Führer.*
*Adolf Hitler loves us kids.*
*All the kids love Adolf Hitler.*
*All kids pray for Adolf Hitler.*

It was not the learning by heart that bothered her but the fact that it kept coming back when she didn't have to recite it. When you thought about it, it seemed all of a piece. How do you cope when you don't believe a thing yet you can't pull that thing to pieces?

Cresspahl had a worry of another kind. The George VI halfpenny had not done the trick, even though it was minted in 1940.

"That's what I wanted to tell you ten days ago! That halfpenny may have been in the pocket of some British flier who got shot down, maybe he'd forgotten he had it, or it was a lucky charm! And it was the Germans who set it as bait for him! Maybe he was working for them all the time, and not for those English bastards," Marie says, not with much conviction but hopefully. She had been saving up this protestation since the previous Saturday, for the moment of maximum effect. She doesn't like someone betraying his country.

"But then he didn't find that out after ten days."

"O.K. So he found it out right away."

"And at first he seemed satisfied with that kind of proof. He didn't insist on a second; he referred to it just once."

"He was scared."

"It didn't turn out to be that hopeless. But of course he was hoping to save his skin, maybe even for the child's sake—"

"In a situation like that, a child just doesn't count."

"—and at the end of March he got a message. That was at a rendezvous to which he was supposed to take the letter allegedly written by Werner Mölders, the Inspector of Fighter Pilots, to the Provost of Stettin before crashing in November 1941 near Breslau. The letter made the Nazis so mad that they threatened to send to a concentration camp anyone found distributing copies, and the British wanted the letter for their leaflet propaganda, whether it was forged or not. Cresspahl had not been able to find the letter; from time to time a silent toast was drunk to Mölders at Jerichow North airfield."

"Don't they say that the Germans knew nothing about the concentration camps?"

"Maybe those who didn't read the *Lübecker Generalanzeiger*. Cresspahl had listened to Gesine's stories about Alexander Paepcke's magic-eye radio, and on March 25 he started out on a trip, a pleasure trip actually, although it might have meant concentration camp."

"A man with a child."

"It didn't look too serious, and it might even have appeared justified. Incidentally, it wasn't a pleasure trip only; his job was to have a look around the Rechlin area and find out what all that nighttime banging was about. Sounded like rockets. It wasn't too far from Wendisch Burg, so this was a chance for Gertrud Niebuhr to get her annual visit from Gesine. While Cresspahl was sitting in front of Alexander's magic eye in Podejuch, Kliefoth was on leave in Jerichow from the Russian front, listening to the B. B. C. and being much surprised at the story that was broadcast following the four Beethoven notes. He knew a different version."

"Alexander was risking his neck."

"Alexander was working for the Army Ordnance Department in Stettin, don't you see? Who would want to tangle with him? Sure the kids were sent out of the room, sure he stayed right by the set so he could instantly switch to another station; but if Heinrich happened to want to know what it was like to listen to London, he'd be glad to do him the favor."

"Fire away, Gesine. You win—I'm believing you again. I'm a sucker as usual. Fire away."

" ' "The memorable hero Robin Hood—" ' "

"As if I hadn't known."

" ' "—having been unjustly accused by two policemen in Richmond Park . . . was condemned to be an outdoor and went and lived with a maid," who was called Lizzie *Pope* near a *brook* where there was no forest. . . .' "

"Lisbeth *Papen* and *brock*. They might have spared him that."

"And then again, no. They proved that they knew about him."

"And what had the policemen in Richmond Park wanted of him?"

"Only he knew that. In the summer of 1931, before his wedding with Lisbeth, he had gone for a walk one night in Richmond Park at a time when the police were on the lookout for a purse snatcher. 'Would you mind giving us a hand, sir?' Half an hour at the police station in the church square. Remember the blue lamp?"

"Yes. And in Jerichow there was no forest."

"Near Jerichow there was the Gräfin Forest, to the west, far enough away. And now he was condemned to live outdoors, beyond the doors of England."

"They figured that all out like buddies."

"It certainly had sentimental value."

"Heck! I believe you, Gesine."

"And are you satisfied? Or do you need to hear the story of a British pilot who is shot down and makes his way at night to Cresspahl's house and for a while lives in the attic, behind a solid wall of stacked-up firewood, till Gesine can take him by the hand and lead him to an address in Gneez, once again a man with a child—?"

"That'll do. I'm satisfied, Gesine."

"And when on the night of March 28 the Royal Air Force attacked Lübeck with 230 bombers and, more by accident than design, blew up a hangar at Jerichow North, Cresspahl was far away in southeast Mecklenburg by a lock in the forest."

"You're overdoing it again. Again it all fits. You and your exaggerations, Gesine!"

"It was a coincidence, Marie. It wasn't worth while sending someone like Cresspahl away from a place where the R. A. F. was about to unload their shit. He wasn't that important. He was a bit of thread in a net, not even a knot. He was replaceable. The net could easily be mended."

"Gesine: at least let him hang for a sheep."

"If it *was* treason, you want it full-blown?"

"Not minimized."

"Treason is a bore, Marie."

"Now that I *don't* have to believe."

"Gestapo! Gestapo!" shout the students in Warsaw at the militia cracking down on them with truncheons.

---

### March 15, 1968   Friday
---

The Deputy Defense Minister of Czechoslovakia, Colonel-General Janko, has shot himself: according to one story, in the staff car that was taking him to face an inquiry into his involvement with the military plot in favor of Antonín Novotný; according to another, in his apartment when he discovered that the cabinet had discussed his involvement.

In Bentre, the city in the Mekong Delta that was destroyed by the Americans during the Vietcong offensive "in order to save it," the South Vietnamese Government has so far not provided one brick, or one sack of cement, for its reconstruction. 2,500 families are homeless; 456 civilians have been killed, and an additional 200 applications for death certificates are still being checked.

Cresspahl returned from Wendisch Burg to Jerichow on Sunday evening, in good time for his appointment at the Strand Hotel in Rande; he waited there for an hour and a half, twice as long as agreed and permitted. This made him believe that his contact had not been living in Berlin after all but had been sitting all the time in Lübeck by his radio until the British air raid got him. His memory of the man was so vague that he could not even imagine him dead. His absent-minded behavior, his brisk educated voice, his roving gaze, had made it hard for Cresspahl to believe that the man was absorbing and retaining all those figures and names. At times the presence of the Party badge on his lapel seemed conclusive, at others not reassuring. In Rande there seemed to be people who knew him, who called him Fritz. Fritz sounded too boyish, too casual, for the staid fifty-year-old, and to Cresspahl's ear too familiar, but Fritz and Heinrich it had had to be. By the time others had approached the table, the man was always well into some dissertation on birds or game; perhaps he had been a teacher. Cresspahl would have liked to ask him just why he was working for the British; as a defense against any such discussion the man had assumed an armor of formality, of arrogance even.

The following day, March 30, 1942, the Polish prisoners of war from the Jerichow area were all taken to the airfield to clear away the rubble of the hangar. The brick walls had collapsed, as had the roof; but the steel framework was still standing, although at one end on crippled, jagged struts, like a dog holding up an injured paw. The parachute mine had shattered windowpanes over a wide area, and Cresspahl helped Freese to reglaze them. Freese did not have enough material for all the windows, and he grumbled at having to put in tar paper. The topic of what had happened to Lübeck during the night from Saturday to Sunday between eleven forty-five and three thirty was hardly discussed by the workmen; Lübeck was only a few miles away, and the accidental unloading might just as easily have happened over Jerichow. At the canteen Gesine, in answer to Freese's questions, talked about school. Stoffregen had told the children that the choice by the British of a night of brilliant full moon for the attack had been a piece of arrant knavery. "The things they teach kids these days—!" said Freese, with an awkward shake of the head and a challenging look at Cresspahl. But Cresspahl kept his head bent over his plate, as the child had also been doing.

That evening Mayor Tamms called on Cresspahl. Jansen had resigned his office "on account of overwork." He had sold the brickyard to a Lübeck manufacturer just so he could pay his debts, and the local Party office was now housed in Oskar Tannebaum's store. Ed Tamms had cleared up Jansen's legacy at the town hall in three weeks and then proceeded to make himself welcome on his own merits. From now on there were no more favors at town hall, permits were issued according to need, and under Tamms it was no longer possible to convert building repairs into a new building. Now that Ete Helms knew he was backed by Mayor Tamms, it was no longer as easy to intimidate him with a Party badge, and if someone failed to pay a fine Tamms was quite prepared to follow it up with a summons. That must have hurt; that was in the old tradition. The big swastika flag continued to flutter above the town hall, Tamms would fling out his arm by way of greeting; Tamms was regarded as a "convinced National Socialist," but he seldom talked about it. In his late thirties; had studied political economy without graduating; married, had three children. In conversation quiet, not slow, not evasive. It bothered some people that he did not beat about the bush like a true Mecklenburger, although it was clear that he saved not only his own time but theirs. He was from Mecklenburg, from Olden Mochum, so called because of the large number of Jews who had at one time been living in Alt Strelitz. Jokes of that kind did not go over well with Tamms; he would look coldly at the visitor, who was obliged to hurry if he wished to state his business. Tamms was quite capable of holding the door open for a visitor.

That day Tamms had made a survey of unused living quarters in Jerichow, politely and relentlessly, with no nonsense about "national solidarity," impervious to complaints. Resistance was half-hearted after he had spared neither the Papenbrocks nor Avenarius Kollmorgen, although they were the first with whom he came to terms. At first Louise Papenbrock had not been inclined to prepare ten rooms for total strangers; Tamms had said: "The Führer expects it of us—"; on Jansen's lips that would have sounded like a threat. Tamms was stating a fact, and since Louise privately took him for a gentleman she further consented to set up her laundry room as a communal kitchen, for the sake of good publicity for Papenbrock philanthropy, and Tamms thanked her in just the way she wanted; surprised, a little touched, yet as if taking something for granted.

Tamms came around the back of Cresspahl's house and found him in the kitchen, not alone with the child but sitting with two of the French prisoners of war, who preferred to eat their cold supper there rather than squatting on their bunks. It was a punishable offense to eat at the same table with P. O. W.s; Tamms did not refer to the infraction and, although he did not shake hands with the Frenchmen, he bade them good evening in their own language. Every room in the house was fully occupied, and Tamms accepted this information, although Cresspahl offered to show him over the house. By this time there were P. O. W.s even in Lisbeth's bedroom. During the war there was a lot of shifting around in Cresspahl's house. Tamms had had a full day and accepted a chair at Cresspahl's after the Frenchmen had said good night and left. Monsieur le Maire did not curse the British. He spoke of Germans (not: *Volksgenossen*) looting ruins in Lübeck and selling food at inflated prices. He spoke of the death sentences in a tone of grudging acceptance. Tamms said: "That's war for you."

On March 31, a Tuesday, the *Lübecker Generalanzeiger* once again got through to Jerichow, with three photos of the destruction of the city; one headline said, "Hasty U. S. attempts to secure positions," and the other, "Outcry against British desecraters of culture."

On April 2 the newspaper ceased to exist: the Charles Coleman publishing company had now been amalgamated with the National Socialist publishing company of Wullenwever, stolen by the Nazis from the Social Democrats. *Lübecker Zeitung* was the new name and, on the basis of confidence in final victory, it was to appear seven days a week.

Train tickets to Lübeck were obtainable only upon presentation of a certificate issued jointly by police, municipal, and Party officials, and anyone failing to buy a return ticket was likely to be arrested in Lübeck. Cresspahl had to depend on the news in the paper. The business quarter below St. Mary's Church had been almost completely destroyed. The church towers still stood, burned out. St. Peter's was in ruins. Two thirds of the Old Town had been destroyed in the conflagrations. Tuesday morning the bombed-out Lübeckers arrived in Jerichow. Louise Papenbrock could not understand why she could not get these people to work, or even to talk. It was up to her to see that the children were clean and meals were prepared, and she reveled in being so busy and running about the house; she did it all in a pious, aggrieved manner, and it was not easy to be grateful to her.

On April 5 Wallschläger preached in the packed church on the subject of the desecration of Palm Sunday by the ruthless, heathen British nation, a people in league with the Antichrist.

On April 5 the *Lübecker Zeitung* carried the first announcement of a mass grave. Cresspahl noted from the private death announcements how the survivors explained the attack to themselves and the readers:
Still beyond our grasp is the sudden death of . . .
As a result of the British attack that defied international law . . .
An immutable fate snatched from our midst . . .
During the disastrous night of March 28/29, Fate so decreed
   that . . .
As a result of the heinous British attack . . .
During the sneak enemy attack I, too, lost . . .
As a result of enemy action . . .
Due to a tragic destiny . . .
At the airfield Cresspahl gathered:
That the flak had not shot down a single plane. Added to the rage felt by the Jerichow North crews at having to look on helplessly at wave

after wave of fresh bombers, there was their annoyance over the fact that the *Lübecker Zeitung* reported twelve downed British planes and a captured R. A. F. crew, and described the bunglers of Lübeck as heroes.

From Rostock came a letter from Aggie Brüshaver in which she spoke of the envy of high-school students at Lübeck, and not Rostock, being once again at the head of the list.

On April 6 the *Lübecker Zeitung* reported an official figure of 280 dead. On April 11, 295 air-raid victims were reported.

*You were to blame for that, Cresspahl.*

*I was also to blame for Coventry.*

*And you could bear it?*

*They attacked Coventry on November 14, 1940, the Germans, 450 bombers. There was a cathedral in that city too. Between November 19 and 22, 1940, they were over Birmingham three times, they killed 800 people with their bombs.*

*Are you balancing accounts?*

*No, Gesine. Except that it was the Germans who started it. They invented a word from it, "to coventrize." What they do is against international law when others do it.*

*You didn't like the Germans any more.*

*Not those Germans.*

*Nor the people of Lübeck.*

*Gesine, remember Rostock, remember Wismar. From then on Lübeck could sleep in peace every night. The Red Cross moved its parcel clearing house to Lübeck, and there were no more air raids there.*

*They showed their gratitude, Cresspahl.*

*Once again they presented one of their citizenship awards, this time to the President of the Red Cross. The thing they were celebrating may not have exactly gladdened the hearts of the other towns.*

*And that Churchill visited the mass grave in Birmingham, and Hitler didn't visit the one in Lübeck.*

*That was Churchill's bounden duty, Gesine.*

*And suppose Tamms had made you put up refugees from Lübeck after all?*

*Gesine, our house was under the same sky as Lübeck.*

*And suppose the refugees had lost children in the fire, or a wife had lost her husband?*

*I'd already lost a wife, Gesine.*

*See? You are balancing accounts.*

*No, Gesine. I'd moved on by then. To where there were no more comparisons, no accounting. In those days no one understood me, and today you don't either.*

*Yes I do, Cresspahl.*

*Never mind, Gesine. Lies are a thing of the past now. You don't need to lie any more, Gesine.*

---

### March 17, 1968   Sunday

President Johnson has decided against the bankers. While he is not sending the 206,000 soldiers to Vietnam that his man Westmoreland had ordered, he is sending 35,000 or 50,000.

For the first time since the coup in Czechoslovakia, veterans of the Spanish Civil War or those who fought on the side of the Allies in World War II have been allowed to gather in Prague. For twenty years the important thing about them was not what they did against the Fascists but that in this way they came to know people in foreign countries.

When Alexander Paepcke traveled, he made preparations. He looked up at the fastest trains and the best connections, and from the moment they left the house his family was permitted to go by no other watch than his. When he traveled to the Fischland in that wet June of 1942, the train to Stralsund did not go by Alexander's watch and arrived too late for the Ribnitz train, which had already left. Alexander felt injured at having to wait two hours in Stralsund. Although he now served the war in the civilian administration of the occupied French territories, he did not recognize the war in the guise of a delayed train, it being a train in Germany that had done this to him.

So the Cresspahl child had a long wait on the station platform at Ribnitz, standing under an advertisement for Schachenmair wool, reluctant to believe that Alexander would leave her in the lurch. She waited until it was almost too late before setting out for the harbor. On the Fischland steamer they were just pulling in the gangplank. There sat the steamer like a fat black duck in a hurry. The child sat down facing the stern. Her father had sent her away, although in Mecklenburg the schools were still open. The spire of Ribnitz church sank behind the boat, then the Körkwitz one, then the Neuhaus dunes. She might never find her way back to Jerichow.

For half the afternoon she stood on the quay in Althagen Bay, a nine-year-old child in a washed-out dress that was too long for her, her cockscomb of hair awry. She had no return ticket. She had spent almost all her pocket money on the boat trip. She had no way of proving that her home was in Jerichow. She was afraid that after three years' absence she would not be able to find the Paepcke summer home. She stood on the right side of the bay, which even in those days tended to be overgrown with reeds. The ship's screw had torn plants loose in the water.

Then Paepcke arrived with the steamer that brought the workmen home from Ribnitz. By now he was, in a determined way, satisfied. Stralsund had been useful after all, for he had been able to visit a toy shop where he had bought some gifts. He was returning to Mecklenburg, wasn't he? Here he was no corner-pisser from Stettin. Paepcke was arrayed in white trousers and a white hat. He took it for granted that little Gesine had been consoled by his apologies in the form of a gift, but the pocket knife from Alexander was identical, except for a little scratch, with the one she already had.

Paepcke asked about Jerichow, about Methfessel, about Gesine's French, about Aggie Brüshaver. Hadn't there been some children there with delightful-sounding names: Martin, Matthias, and Marlene Dietrich? Gesine said: But they're dead.

Alexander did not understand. How could such little kids suddenly be dead!

They had been living in Rostock, on the street beside St. James's Church. On April 25, when the R. A. F. visited Rostock, Aggie had been on night duty at the clinic, and her children were alone at home when they were burned to death.

Paepcke, rather embarrassed, extracted a promise from Gesine that she would not tell his children about this. She did not understand: they hadn't even known Marlene.

The village street was shady. The light that did come through courtyard entrances was white. The houses were sheltered from the wind by high windbreaks. When the two village boys stopped with their barrow in front of a gap in the dense bushes, Gesine recognized the house. It was a long brick cottage with a thatched roof, the west wall white and then painted over in yellow. There was one dormer window (not two) in the roof. The way in from the windbreak went so far down, onto the floor that was lower than the threshold, that it felt like sliding into the house.

The garden was completely overgrown. Carefully laid out, with one terrace for flowers and a lower one for vegetables, it was now a tangle of grass, weeds, and struggling flowers, surrounded by rambling bushes. Facing the Bodden, the shallow inlet, there was a gate leading to a grassy patch, again hedged in on all sides, and the "giant stride" was still intact: when three children hung onto its ropes and took off

REGINA LIBRARY
RIVIER COLLEGE
NASHUA, N. H. 03060

at a run, they were soon flying high above the bushes in a circle. Now the vacation was getting off to a good start, for they all landed safely, not one of them banged into the iron pole.

The rooms had names. Upstairs, in the Bodden Room, slept Hilde and Alexander. The Duke's Room was Great-Uncle's domain and was kept locked. The children were put up in the Studio. On waking up they could hear a steady thudding sound. It came from the coast batteries, practice-firing out to sea from the High Cliff. Alexander's voice would ring through the house. He was cursing the military for always turning up like a bad penny.

Great-Uncle Alexander had bought the house way back around 1902, from a painter who had built a studio onto the cottage. Of course, there had to be a tiled kitchen in the basement, also a dumbwaiter and a pump for the kitchen. But what the Paepckes really liked best was to fetch their water by rope and bucket from the well in the yard. Never again have I seen such clear water.

From the East Room you could look way down onto the morning-white Bodden, the Bodden meadows that stood under water for weeks. The water came to your ankles. It felt good to walk about in it because of the squelching sensation under your soles, and faintly alarming because it behaved like the bogs described in books. Often there were fishing boats lying motionless on the faint horizon, their brown sails furled after the labors of the night.

Westward, toward the sea, the land rose sharply. To this day, when on some steep path, I expect the Baltic, seen suddenly from above by the child of that time.

A west wind, as nearly always, blew in our faces.

Paepcke was determined that this should be a vacation. No newspapers. Shut up, radio! He would swim way out; and on his return, breathing comfortably, Hilde would repeat his name in a reproachful tone, as if she had just started to call out to him. Alexander taught the children to swim, one way being to persuade them that they already could. He mentioned a "sandbank" a couple of yards from the shore, and when he had coaxed the children that far they would continue swimming after him.

The beach was sparsely occupied with beach chairs. It was very quiet, not many of the Althagen cottagers rented out rooms, and anyway the place was considered a village, while neighboring Ahrenshoop, in Pomeranian Prussia, was known as a "resort." Althagen had only one hotel, named after the Baltic it faced: it spelled itself with a circumflex accent, and Paepcke tried to explain this to Gesine. Unfortunately she knew all about it from "her" Frenchmen in Jerichow, and he had immediately to think up something for the other children so their feelings would not be hurt.

Meanwhile another youngster had arrived, Klaus Niebuhr from Friedenau, in Berlin. The boy thought pretty well of himself for making the trip here ("out into the lowlands") all alone, but Eberhardt Junior, too long in the company of the three girls, had acquired a new way of looking at the world. Instead of supporting the male side, he pointed out that Gesine had also made the trip on her own. Klaus the man was hurt, and to be outdone by a girl at that, and now at last there was a chance to give away a pocketknife.

Alexander Paepcke could have gone with his pals to the hotel for a drink, but they did not care for the beer there. The Kurhaus at Ahrenshoop? The company was too high-class. Paepcke thought of himself as company, of himself as high-class. Sometimes he went with Reineke Voss to the Seezeichen, the Sea Marker, but their favorite spot for a drink was Mrs. Saatmann's Konditorei. In winter a hangout for the locals, in summer it was also an outdoor café. Malchen Saatmann was a trim woman, sturdy and buxom; I could not describe her face, yet I would recognize her. Malchen was not one for chatting, not even to the kids, but even kids felt they were getting their money's worth.

On rainy days Alexander played Parcheesi with "his" children. But he called it pakesi, the way Cresspahl had pronounced it from his London days, after the Hindi word *pachisi*, meaning twenty-five; and because it was a foreign game it was played with its own rules: for example, two pieces of the same color may stand on the same square and even form a barrier; a piece on a starting square of any color is "free" ("Home Rule"!); and three sixes are too much of a good thing and mean a return to base. Paepcke's Alexandra was the least able to bear her men being sent back; her blush would color her whole skin deeply, and this embarrassed her still more. A player preoccupied with losing did not care to notice when things turned out well for him in the end. Paepcke found it hard to maintain his good nature, and he would end up glaring mutely at his lost game.

The house was no longer as seigneurial as Alexander's great-uncle had planned, with antique furniture and bare walls. Alexander had lugged along discarded pieces from his former homes, half broken, with torn covers, the very thing for kids. There were flowers in all the rooms. A child could be by himself in every room. There, on a wobbly sofa with gently rearing armrests, I would read my way into the Orient, walk down marble steps to the water where great fish came to rest, and was Harun al-Rashid.

In the evening, on our way back from the sea, we ran into children of our own age who were driving the cows home. Night on the Fischland was too harsh for milk cows. Alexandra gazed spellbound at Inge Niemann and the cow ambling along so peaceably in front of her stick, and Paepcke asked Inge to surrender cow and stick to his child. Paepcke was absent-minded that day and walked on. But all the cows walked on too, and Alexandra's stood stock-still. It even took the liberty of munching a little grass from the verge. Alexandra looked at me, but I did not like to advise her to beat the animal. In her desperation Alexandra gave the beast a friendly shove, and the cow looked back in surprise, straight into our eyes. From this predicament we were rescued by Alexander, who had indeed been thinking about the children as he walked along.

And never to bed without a caress.

*Be wise then, children, while you may*
*For swiftly time is flying.*
*The thoughtless man, who laughs to-day,*
*To-morrow will be dying.*

Cresspahl, who had been sure he would not be able to come, arrived at the end of July. Alexander looked forward to a whole week of evenings and said: You're a good sort, Hinrich!

One day Paepcke was obliged after all to go to the post office in Ahrenshoop, took a few of his children with him, and walked along the Bodden dike, past the Dornenhaus and the mill (no longer in existence) as far as the old earthworks. On the Ahrenshoop road he saw Cresspahl walking along with a man who could not possibly have come from anywhere but the Kurhaus, a high-class personage indeed. A man with Berlin, civil servant, Party badge, written all over him. Paepcke caught sight of the Party badge as he overtook the two men, and he could hear Cresspahl talking urgently to his companion. "Fritz," he called him. Cresspahl turned up at the post office on Paepcke's heels. "He mistook me for a Kurhaus guest," he said without waiting to be challenged, and Paepcke decided to believe him. But it was not like Cresspahl to allow a stranger to address him as a Kurhaus guest and, moreover, to walk along the road with him, deep in conversation, his hands clasped comfortably behind him.

*Alexander didn't deserve that, Cresspahl.*
*And if I'd told him, would he have deserved that, Gesine?*

*You didn't trust hm.*
*I didn't want him to have to trust me.*

During the night the Allies bombed Hamburg. Hamburg was not
visible from the Fischland.

That summer Alexander plucked up his courage to ask Cresspahl
something, his debts now amounting to a few thousand marks more
than he could handle. Cresspahl was not considered stingy but he had
a reputation for thrift, and Alexander, to his incredulous amazement,
was relieved of all his obligations in one fell swoop. Cresspahl did not
even ask for details. They skimmed over the subject of repayment.
Cresspahl relied upon Gesine's receiving a share in Paepcke's Althagen
house when Alexander inherited it from his great-uncle. It was not
binding, but Alexander kept his word and in Kiev he added it to his
will. Hilde never knew about it. Thus Cresspahl tucked money away
for his child in many places in Mecklenburg; in case they caught him.
Executed him.

It was a very quiet summer. There were no planes in the air as
there were in Jerichow. The early-morning booming of the coast batteries was forgotten during the day, and so was the nighttime foghorn,
which was not visible either.

Cresspahl was also called upon to settle the Paepckes' argument:
whether the beacon that could be seen from the High Cliff was the
Warnemünde one or the Poel one.

Alexander Paepcke had some rather vague tales to tell about the
civilian administration of occupied France. He was not looking forward
to leaving by the Berlin-Paris furlough train, and the inflated fellow
sighed when he appeared carrying a small leather suitcase that had
escaped the children's notice. The suitcase contained a kepi for Paepcke
Junior. For Christine there was a doll in Breton costume, and she slept
with this doll for the rest of her short life. For Alexandra there was a
doll's gilded tea set. Klaus Niebuhr got a ruler with a French inscription,
and the suitcase, a grownup's toy, was for Gesine. And what was there
for the soldier's wife? The children were thunderstruck at there being
presents all over again when Alexander was about to leave, and in his
pleasure over their excitement Alexander said casually, of the doll's tea
set specifically: I took it from a hotel. The gold looked very convincing,
and his daughter asked, horrified: But is that all right? Paepcke's reply
was a broad complacent: Suuure; then he caught Cresspahl's eye and
added, embarrassed and quite the major of the Reserve: I'll have you
know I paid for it!

Once Hilde asked unthinkingly about the night Lübeck was bombed.

Cresspahl could be evasive because he had been in Wendisch Burg.

But he did tell her what people in Jerichow had been saying: that it had looked like a peaceful fire in the bright night, and a good thing it had made such a noise, although it had been fifteen miles away.

And once again the choice was up to Gesine. She could stay on in Althagen if she liked. The Mecklenburg school vacation ended on September 1, and until then she could go with the Paepckes to Pomerania. Cresspahl took care not to look at her, shading his eyes with his hand as he searched the evening sea for something. She looked up at him, could scarcely make out his face, and said without hesitation: I want to go back with you to Jerichow. Take me with you.

*A good thing the fire in Lübeck made such a noise?*
*The bombs, Gesine. That way a person could imagine less. The noise took that away.*

---

### March 19, 1968   Tuesday

---

The Communists in Czechoslovakia simply cannot make up their minds to get rid of their Antonín Novotný by force. In the Party paper they refer to him merely as Mister instead of Comrade, they do not allow him to appear on television, but his resignation is something they expect him to attend to himself.

Robert F. Kennedy began his campaign for presidential office yesterday by calling President Johnson's Vietnam policy "bankrupt." Then he went on to say in his speech to university students in Kansas: "I will work for you and we will have a new America."

Don't forget that spring officially begins tomorrow morning at 8:22!

In June 1942 Dr. Avenarius Kollmorgen, long-time Jerichow attorney, became tired of life and relinquished it.

Only then did Jerichow find out how he had spent his last few years. Since 1935 his practice had been clamped down. After that he had still been seen on walks around the town, but he had chosen routes where he was sure of not meeting anyone he knew. Anyone hoping to be asked just once more whether one was "getting along all right" encountered a painfully confused man who stepped impatiently from foot to foot, waiting for the conversation to end, nor did he so much as raise himself on his toes and with solemn shining gaze dispense learned opinions. At first he would take his exercise before lunch; by 1941 he was already going after lunch, until finally he left it until just before dark, and then he gave it up altogether. But at night the light from his windows had fallen longer and longer onto the market square:

that and the shadows of slow movements inside seemed to indicate activity. During those nights Avenarius had been preparing for his death. Instead of all his books standing upright on the shelves, most of them now lay neatly stacked, ready for packing. In each he had entered the date on which he had read it for the last time; he had got through all but two rows. His desk was found to contain lists, inventories of the entire contents of his house, with a column for the future owners, already completed. Geesche Helms's sister, who had worked for him for over twelve years, received the complete set of Kollmorgen china, as well as some pieces of furniture. The proceeds from what was not given away were to go to the University of Erlangen, together with his library. The library was catalogued. Any documents of a personal nature had been removed by Dr. Kollmorgen; his aim was to leave behind nothing of himself other than the Avenarius mystery. In the open desk drawer Ilse found, as she had been told she would, the sheet of instructions to be followed in the event of his death, from the calls to be made on Dr. Berling and Swenson to directions for the funeral. He took leave of certain people with old-fashioned printed death notices, but he did not need them, everything having been previously arranged and paid for. The words "No religious ceremony whatever" appeared in the neat flourishes of his handwriting. In that, and in his prudent arrangements, Dr. Kollmorgen's voice was audible once more, now no longer comfortably pedagogic but grumbling, disappointed, not without contempt. It would seem that after all he had not been so pleased at the town's having honored his desire to be left alone.

There were not many people who entered his living room one morning for a last look at him. In life he had been short, children had had to be told not to laugh; in the coffin he looked imposing, commanding respect. He was dressed as for a formal occasion in a bygone age, his arms were at his sides as if he were standing upright, an observer, an appraiser. Around the eyes he looked softer, almost as if asleep. He was close to eighty. Swenson looked in several times, but the mourners continued to stand around Kollmorgen, not impatient, solemnly whispering as if they had to make up for all those visits they had failed to make. Then, by the open grave, an attorney from Hamburg intoned something in Latin which the Jerichow mourners did not understand, and none among them wished to add anything. It had been Avenarius's way to live and die alone.

Ilse interpreted the legacy of the china as a hint from Kollmorgen that she should now finally take a husband, and in the fall of 1942 she married a fisherman in Rande who had waited five years for her. Ilse Grossjohann was her new name, a highly respected housewife, envied for her dowry. Now when she came to Jerichow to do her shopping she no longer had the face of a girl in helpless wonderment.

For Gesine Cresspahl a little sealed package was delivered "with compliments for March 3, 1954."

Because Avenarius was under the ground, Cresspahl had to take a letter to Kliefoth in November 1942. It was in French, postmarked Leipzig, in Dora Semig's handwriting. "Chers amis," Cresspahl vaguely understood that much. And it was urgent.

He did not like going to see Kliefoth. He was from Malchow, a burr-picker; Kliefoth was an educated man, he had lived in England but at universities there. True, they had World War I in common, but by 1918 Kliefoth had long been a lieutenant. Until the very last moment he had continued to subscribe to French and English newspapers, every eight weeks from a different *département* or a new county, but when war with France broke out he volunteered at once, after they had refused to take him against the Poles because of the blots on his Berlin registration card. After that he was on continuous active service until, after he had reached the age limit, they finally sent him home, and as long as he made his reconnaissance flights over the Soviet Union his wife continued to hang out the swastika flag for him. Cresspahl did not find it easy to penetrate that man in a hurry.

The evening was a very long one, lasting almost until midnight. Kliefoth came to his front door in full uniform, asked the carpenter in with casual but unmistakable politeness, saw the other hesitate, took the plunge, and showed his colors.

Kliefoth kept on repeating the same words: The Army. The Army, as if that were all that counted.

They had soon found a sector of the Russian front which they might have been on at the same time in 1916.

Cresspahl was not ready yet.

Kliefoth talked about having flown with the II Army Corps to Jersey, "at the King of England's expense." He had been the only one to like the English breakfast, "Bring on that porridge!," and the Italian waiters were as delighted as the French ones had been flattered at his fondness for their national dishes. Bring on that porridge!

This was of no help to Cresspahl. From Böttcher's son Klaus, the world traveler, he had heard that during the advance into France Kliefoth had driven past the marching column leaning back in the car like a lord, a leather-covered silver brandy flask to his lips.

Now Kliefoth made another effort. How in 1940 he had sworn to the Aryan origin of a schoolgirl with a Jewish name.

---

*Something like Katzengold.*
*Don't tell me her name whatever you do!*
*No?*
*Right, Mr. Kliefoth. That's about the size of it.*
*And though it was perjury it wasn't a sin and I'd do the same*
*again.*
*I suppose she's still alive*
*She's living in Hamburg! It's about time you learned to trust me*
*too, you old burr-picker you!*

Kliefoth then proceeded to translate Dora's letter. Arthur was still alive too. After the occupation of Czechoslovakia they had tried Switzerland, but they had been allowed to spend only two days there, on straw, in a camp. They had run out of money. They had spent it all near Paris. By the time the Germans arrived in France they had actually managed to escape to the unoccupied zone. During those seven days on foot and in overcrowded trains, Arthur had "come to life." Not that he could be persuaded to go to Marseilles and try to get overseas; but he had managed to find an apartment near Cannes, obtain some forged papers, and land a job, all within barely a week. Arthur, she wrote, hardly felt his sixty years, yet he was working now as a butcher. Not such a bad thing really, his having studied veterinary medicine. Chopping up the beasts he was trained to cure. The illegal nature of both job and accommodation made it impossible for her to give an address. "Please tell our parents this too, who won't reply. Our most affectionate remembrances to Lisbeth and your little girl. You and Arthur should have said 'Du' to each other after all, before we left; Arthur is sorry he didn't bring it up, since he was the older. And thank you for everything. Lisbeth, don't let things weigh so heavily on your conscience. D. S."

Kliefoth deplored the lack of an address. He knew people in German counterespionage who even after the Italian occupation of the Riviera would have been willing and able to help the Semigs, and Cresspahl believed him.

Kliefoth advised Cresspahl not to take the letter home. Kliefoth again praised Dora's French; by comparison, his own was "schoolboy stuff." The letter was placed in *Chambers's Encyclopaedia*, beside page 467, Vetch and Veterinary Medicine.

Kliefoth was right. Next morning the raiders from the Gestapo turned up at Cresspahl's, and he could tell them with a clear conscience that he had thrown the indecipherable letter into the fire. Whereupon they had tried to nail him for not reporting Dora's letter.

---

*And why didn't you ask your French P. O. W.s to help you?*

*How come you say you didn't recognize the handwriting?*

*If the correspondence was being carried on by your wife, we'll have a word with her. And make it snappy!*

---

### March 20, 1968   Wednesday

Someone writes to Miss Cresspahl, the employee, from West Berlin, Germany, saying that, although she does sometimes embellish reports on Vietnam with unkind adjectives, "surely that's the least one can expect."

So there are people in Germany who are concerned about the correctness of my behavior. It is for their sakes that I am supposed to put an end to the Vietnam war.

That, I would think, would be more than the least.

I could write a letter to the New York *Times*; I could go to jail for life for an unsuccessful attempt on the life of President Johnson; I could publicly set fire to myself and burn myself to death. There is no way in which I could hold up the machinery of war, not by one cent, not by one soldier; nothing.

Nevertheless, there are people in Germany who reproach me.

---

### March 21, 1968   Thursday

A West German actor, who was once an East German actor, has returned to East Germany because he knows that the rulers there do not support the suppression of Negroes in the U. S. or the American war in Vietnam. He did not know that before. If your conscience is burdened by the crimes of a certain country, you simply move to another.

There are also critics of the war holding the rank of former Marine commander. General David M. Shoup estimates that merely to defend the population centers of South Vietnam up to 800,000 American soldiers are required. The U. S. could only achieve victory by invading the North. The war was not worth the cost.

The school in Jerichow had sufficiently indoctrinated Cresspahl's child that in November 1942 she was letting her "people's radio" whisper beside her as she sat over her homework, turning up the volume after every victory fanfare heralding a "special announcement." She was waiting for the Soviets to lose Stalingrad. In one way she wanted to know that the battle had been decided, yet she was on the side of the German troops. Cresspahl had his reasons for giving her the biography of Reich Air Marshal Göring, and books like *Stukas* and *Mölders and His Men*; while in school the child was to show a harmless enthusiasm for the German forces, especially for the Air Force; Cresspahl got his camouflage. The child got her hurts. (Cresspahl consoled himself with the hope of an end to the war in spring 1943.)

In those days the Jerichow school had eight grades. After Grade 4 the children were separated into those who had to do no more than meet legal school requirements and those whose parents were able to send them on to high school in Gneez. Gesine was unaware that, starting in 1943, she was to go to Gneez, and she had settled into the Hermann Göring School as into a home, her Jerichow home.

The principal was Franz Gefeller, a Sudeten German who had taken part in the Henlein *Putsch* and was a regional Party speaker in the district of Gneez. He had discovered that, when he drew back his lips, he resembled Reich Propaganda Minister Goebbels in almost every feature. He made a point of assuming this expression when punishing children. In his normal state he could be taken for a conceited, diminutive little man. When he shouted, his voice tended to become very high; when he stretched out his arm for the Nazi salute it suddenly seemed too short.

*You are a* German *child,*
*So remember all life through*
*What cruel acts the foe*
*At Versailles did to you.*

The first year, when she learned how to write the Gothic script, Gesine's teacher was Prrr Hallier, and she had no reason not to equate his teaching methods with school in general. Lessons did not begin until his class had been drilled to sit down and stand up in a body. The pupil who was a split second late was the first to be questioned. Hallier was one of those "whom they hadn't taken." Beneath the picture of Hitler he had put up a shelf with a vase, and it was regarded as a privilege to provide fresh flowers for the idol. He suffered from the fact that making friends in a small town is slow work, and he would often announce that he was coming to call. Gesine had regarded him as "her" teacher, and she felt betrayed at not being allowed to be present at his first conversation with Cresspahl. He was called Prrr because he used to interrupt a pupil as if he were reining in a horse. He handed out the reports on the sandy playground in front of the school after the children had lined up and sung. He betrayed the Cresspahl child again by not giving her an A for Conduct, never once had he told her she was not behaving properly. Had been watching her for a whole year, never warned her, pushed her into the trap. Then "they" took him after all, and in June 1940 he was killed.

Cresspahl was also upset by the B for Conduct. It impressed on him the fact that by diligence in this subject children were to be made to toe the line and learn obedience for future life.

Then came "Old Miss" Lafrantz, proud of her family name, bitter about the one the children dubbed her with: since at forty she could still call her hair red, she considered herself to be of marriageable age. Freckled, scrawny, like a storybook governess. For Gesine she was now no longer merely the school but a person in her own right, and they clashed. "Old Miss" was hurt by the Cresspahl child's making herself conspicuous; the child was hurt because she was not allowed to make herself conspicuous. Fidgeting, standing up without being called upon, contradicting, were nothing but attempts to attract the teacher's attention. As examples in her math class, Miss Lafrantz used Brownshirt columns in rows of three and groups of six. She introduced the Latin script to replace the Gothic on the grounds that Germans should write in the same way as the world empire they were about to conquer. ("So the nations will be able to understand our Führer's orders.") She was a good-natured person, sometimes complaining as if she were driven by something. Gesine Cresspahl did not realize that she could ever call the children a burden. Conduct: B.

In Grade 3 the Cresspahl child had her first experience of confusion. She noticed a boy by the name of Gabriel Manfras, because he seldom spoke a word. Even his face remained closed and silent, Slavic in the cheekbones, slanting about the eyes. But when the teacher called upon him, he would speak. The Cresspahl child wanted this boy to notice her, and she swung between two desks, arms braced, until her shoe slipped off her foot. She retrieved it from below the blackboard, asked the other children to watch, and repeated the feat. This time the shoe flew through the windowpane, with an inexplicable swerve to the left. It was during break, and immediately there was total silence. In those days children were intimidated to the point of downright fear by the hierarchy that began with the teacher and culminated in Adolf Hitler; moreover, many of them came from farming families. Manfras was among the most scared; Old Miss had never had to witness a crime of this nature. She did not even dare mete out punishment. The Cresspahl girl was sent to the Principal.

She found it unjust that she should be punished for an accident. A deliberate flouting of the rules—now that she would have answered for. She left the school building, wearing only one shoe, picked up the other from the snow, and ran to the only public telephone booth on the market square to call Cresspahl. For Mr. Gefeller to remove his tinted glasses and look at her with his intense black eyes was an undeserved punishment. According to Miss Lafrantz, the charge was damage to public property and waste of war-essential material such as glass and fuel. Cresspahl summoned Gesine to the airfield, rectified the damage that evening with glass from the supplies in his own basement, and did not take her along to the interview with Miss Lafrantz. Conduct (pained): B.

The next teacher was Ottje Stoffregen. By now he had come to accept what Jerichow had made of his first name, had learned to put up with the Nazi suppression of the local Mecklenburg historical journals, and considered himself wise. When he did rouse himself to resistance, it was to practice the old Gothic script, "so you can read your grandparents' letters." There were not many letter-writing grandparents in and around Jerichow.

Ottje Stoffregen used to beat his pupils. Latecomers had to walk slowly past him, and Ottje would poke painfully, at least three times, with his cane on the soft part between neck and shoulder. The first time this happened, the Cresspahl child at once said it did not hurt, so as to lessen her disgrace in front of the others, and Ottje repeated the ceremony. Ottje never forgot that this was the child of Lisbeth, to whom he used to propose, with poems and letters, until he became the laughingstock of all Jerichow; his behavior toward the child alternated between severity and indulgence. Alcohol had made him susceptible to wistfulness, and sometimes he would look at the child as if he had tears in his eyes. He also developed a violent temper and was capable of hurling the Cresspahl exercise book all the way from his desk to the back of the room, clear across four rows of desks. The child had written the heading "Better Betimes." Stoffregen never forgot that by rights he should have been made principal, rather than Gefeller, that "phony German," but he obeyed the Principal's orders, even if the latter arranged for a two-hour class at eleven and, after a break, a further sewing class for the girls at two. On those occasions the Cresspahl child would be absent from school, bringing such excuses from Cresspahl as "My child had to eat," and asking whether Stoffregen might be planning to change the lunch hour at the Air Force mess? Cresspahl had only a vague notion of Stoffregen's courting of Lisbeth, because it would have upset him; Stoffregen looked upon Cresspahl's note as the depths of sarcasm. Stoffregen lashed out at Cresspahl's child in a manner that he privately called caustic and spoke with such righteous indignation of Cresspahl's demands for "an extra slice of cake" that the child had a fleeting vision of a large piece of gooey chocolate cake. It was impossible to listen to Stoffregen then. One might look as if one were enjoying the delicious flavor. Conduct (outraged, maudlin): B.

The discipline introduced by Mr. Gefeller was uniform and predictable. In the spring of 1943 a farmer accused a boy of having frightened some horses. Mr. Gefeller took the trouble to interrupt Stoffregen's class. He called the boy up to the front, a backward pupil who was taller than the others and scared of school. The boy tried to defend himself against the charge. Most likely the farmer's horses had bolted because the boy had run toward the team; however, he was accused of having tickled the horses' ears with stinging nettles. Because of his denial the boy was made to let down his trousers and stand in front of the whole class in his long hand-me-down underwear. Gefeller then grasped the boy with one hand and struck at him with the cane he held in the other, all the time shouting about crimes against the national economy and about being sent to prison, and since the boy was strong from working in the fields he was able to twist and turn and pull Gefeller with his cane in a circle after him, moaning and whining as if the blows were hurting. Gesine Cresspahl knew quite well that she was about to do something risky, but she could not stop herself, and during the next break in the schoolyard she spat at the ground in front of the Principal's feet. That was how much she trusted in Cresspahl's protection. Conduct: D.

After she had learned all these things, Cresspahl sent her to school in Gneez. She did not mind the solitary train trip twice a day provided she did not have to go to school in Jerichow.

If Gefeller and Stoffregen had had their way, the D in Conduct would have warranted sending her to a special school, preferably straight to the reformatory in Hamburg. But Dr. Kliefoth, holder of the highest distinctions, author of a dissertation on the French word *aller* and a prince in the realm of the Gneez School Council, swore to the good behavior of this child.

### March 23, 1968 Saturday

Each additional soldier sent by President Johnson to Vietnam costs the nation between $20,000 and $40,000. (The family of a soldier killed in Vietnam receives $300 toward funeral expenses; enough to cover an Army funeral.)

Antonín Novotný, since his Party will not touch him, has resigned. (His son has resigned too, although only from a sinecure.) The Party presidium of the Communists estimates the victims of justice between 1952 and 1964 at 30,000.

Today Mrs. Cresspahl has been to the place where the men of America are at home.

It was one of those called by D. E. "his," this time one on Third Avenue, Irish by its very name, and a sign had just been hung in the window specifically inviting ladies to visit the establishment. It was suspended by a fine chain, the elegant antique lettering picked out in black and gold, and this means that around seven in the evening business with male customers tails off and must be made to pick up again by admitting prostitutes; unescorted women are also welcome. That was why, as soon as D. E. sat down, he said: "You know my wife, Wes."

"Pleased to meet your wife I'm sure Professor congratulations," said Wes all in one breath, casually, without so much as a glance at her. He is the boss of the two bartenders behind a forty-foot bar, the master of the house; but he does his full share of the work, waiting on ten or more customers seated in front of him and each one expecting his very own personal conversation with Wes. Among his diplomatic skills are those of correctly filling and refilling the glasses of the non-utterers and not missing any of the good nights cast his way, of solemnly welcoming new arrivals, and finally keeping vacated stools free for friends who have been feeling at a loss in another preserve until Wes beckons them over and seats them in his. In addition to all this he is a private bank, cashing his customers' checks, giving personal loans, holding bets in safekeeping, all without interest. Wes is a clearing house of information, he knows the whereabouts of someone missing in Galway or Lisbon, and imparts or withholds the information with unerring discretion, never faltering as he says into the ever-jangling telephone: "I'm sorry, madam, your husband's not here," having previously held out the receiver toward the harried spouse, waiting for the latter's desperate head shake. By the time Wes has twice paced his preserve between his customers and the seventy bottles, he was woven a close network of handshakes, glances, and conversations; today he looked openly several times at the lady next to D. E. before making up his mind to assume that the Professor had not been pulling his leg.

Wes is tall and hefty, about fifty, with almost no expression around his firm mouth, his gray eyes. All his glances are silent appraisals, and possibly the secret of his enormous turnover is that a man may well be prepared to forfeit the respect of his wife but not that of Wes. Wes shows his face very little, keeping his eyes on his work with bottles, glasses, strainers, sink, and when he has to blend two ingredients by shaking them, he stands sideways so as to be seen in profile, a solemn figure performing a strict ritual. His hair curls closely over his head, like Cresspahl's, only reddish blond instead of gray, and these things, the abstracted pose of the head, the concentrated listening, have deprived me of yet another degree of sharpness in my remembered image of my father.

Wes filled up D. E.'s glass and informed him categorically, to ensure that the necessary had been done: "I like your wife, Ericksen." Looked askance at the lady to see whether she was offended, accepted with grave satisfaction D. E.'s reply: "So do I, Wes."

And now D. E. got his very own personal conversation with Wes for this evening. In the course of it Wes prepared drinks for others, took a customer's money, placed change in front of him, wiped the bar clean, stacked glasses skillfully beside the cash register, but it was D. E.'s turn, and the other customers pretended not to be listening.

"I like your wife, Ericksen."
"So do I, Wes."
"That deal with Aer Lingus is on again."
"I might be able to use a ticket in August. For a giant, as usual?"
"For a giant, no extra charge. But I don't want you to think I don't like your wife."
"I guess you know what you're doing, thinking, and feeling."
"It's a free country."
"Once you've paid your dues. See you later, alligator."
"After a while, crocodile."

D. E. didn't talk much. He greeted friends with a measured lift of his glass, looked around, patiently listened to the confidential confessions of the tipsy man next to him, making sure with an occasional glance at me that I realized he was having a good time, and inviting me to have a good time too.

Here in this home from home, men and women are not judged by the color of their skin. If a person doesn't bother his neighbors, wants to relax rather than get drunk, has enough money to pay for his drinks, and can even claim some knowledge of the horses, that's all that's asked of him. That makes him an ordinary person, and welcome. Here a man was a man; a white rowdy gets thrown out; a quiet black devotee of firewater is respectfully addressed with the bourgeois title sir.

A man sitting next to me took me for someone on the make. "You a stewardess or something?" he asked. "I mean, because of that wheel with wings on your cigarette pack. Guess that's what gave me the idea," he said, then caught Wes's disgusted shake of the head, felt bitterly censured and warned, picked up his money, and went off with his tail between his legs.

The men are considerate with each other here, showing real concern, even affection. One of them has a problem with his glasses. Can't see too well. Wes goes over to him and hands him a napkin. Mimes a wiping gesture. He would never interfere in his customer's private affairs. Gratefully the man wipes his glasses. Returns the napkin with a sigh of relief. What would I do without you, Wes.

Another customer had just been served his Canadian stuff. A bottle of soda water stands beside his glass. He could pour it himself. "Mix it?" says Wes. "Want me to do it for you?" The man is sufficiently burdened without having to make this extra effort.

A fat little manikin with a dainty double chin replies to the inquiry after his health: "I feel I'm going nuts." Wes replies, carefully tipping the brimming jigger over the ice: "That's just how you look." This satisfies the sad little fatso. At least one person who understands him. He goes on: "I'm about ready for the funny farm, that place in Nutsville where they straighten out the kinks." Now he really does look like a deeply hurt child on the verge of tears. One moment Wes is leaning toward him with an expression of concern, the next he barks at him callously: "Be sure and let me have your address, just in case I want to visit you, O.K.?" For Wes is busy, at this point he has to extricate a miniature onion out of a narrow jar with the point of a short knife ("Why don't you use your fingers?" says the customer, who couldn't care less), and now he suddenly has to pick up a piece of ice and throw it accurately into the cash register of the western preserve twenty feet away, to give George a surprise and the customers some entertainment, he's busy. Someone has knocked over a bottle of soda water, by mistake. Wes picks up the half-empty bottle, holds it aloft over the bar, and splashes the contents out onto the counter. "Is that the way you like it?" The sad manikin already feels much better. "I guess I'll buy a return ticket after all," he says.

Quiet, relaxed talk. Not a word about the war. Beyond the windows, the warm busy street night. As if there were peace.

*Sometimes I come here to enjoy myself, Gesine. You ought to try it sometime.*

*I am, can't you see? I am.*

## March 24, 1968   Sunday

Twice the East German Communists have rejected an invitation from Prague, as if they felt that this would render democratization in the Czechoslovak Republic less likely to play into the hands of West German capitalism. Alexander Dubček, instead of behaving like a thwarted child, took a train to Dresden and tried to explain matters to the comrades there. Meanwhile the latter have gone so far as to confiscate newspapers from the socialist brother country.

In the fall of 1942

the Von Bobziens near Jerichow had no further difficulty keeping walkers out of the Gräfin Forest. Two men had hanged themselves on trees there, and had money in their pockets.

Goebbels called the Winter Aid Program a "unique ledger of German socialism," but the *Lübecker Zeitung* contained an inordinate quantity of Wanted to Buy ads and swap offers. Böhnhase the tobacconist was taken away from Jerichow for bartering smokers' supplies in exchange for produce. Seven years in jail.

Almost every villa behind the Rande dike was requisitioned, and a third of them were rebuilt. "War-essential housing for the Air Force." The officers were now trying to burn driftwood in their fireplaces, all the pieces they had worked so hard to collect that summer on the beach. The wood stank, refused to burn, went out in clouds of dense smoke. The officers, who prided themselves on their rustic efficiency, had forgotten to let the rain leach out the salt in the wood.

The Governor of Mecklenburg issued a public warning against rumormongering in connection with the bombing of "a" Mecklenburg town. Now the merry-go-round of tales of looting and corpse-robbing whirled even faster.

Leslie Danzmann was now living in one of the villas by the Rande dike, as "housekeeper." She had the place virtually to herself, since the owner was required to remain within reach of a number of telephones at the Air Force Research Department in Berlin, which meant that his trips to Mecklenburg's Baltic coast were limited to occasional weekends. On such occasions Cresspahl was a guest at the villa, not of Leslie Danzmann's. He used to take the child along, and Leslie would mend her clothes while Cresspahl spent the evenings in the study with her Fritz, drinking. All she saw was the leftover bottles later that night.

The serialized novel in the *Lübecker Zeitung* was entitled "G. P. U.":

G loom
P anic
U pheaval

and the double-headed eagle on the paper's masthead now appeared, more stylized than ever, to the left of the cumbersome new lettering and, within the old shield but replacing the former coat of arms, it bore a swastika.

Leslie Danzmann's Fritz may have been in an impregnable position in Berlin; in Mecklenburg he could not help her. She was put to work at the Labor Office in Gneez, not sent to a munitions factory, because of her high-school education. It took her almost an hour to travel from the Baltic to Gneez, in the company of the women munitions workers from the country. When they got home in the evening they still had children, house, and barn to look after; Leslie could take off her shoes and put her feet up. Yet never in her life had she craved sleep so much as during this period. She was not accustomed to working.

The weekly newsreel was offering a new service. If a person recognized a fallen son in the pictures from the front, he could order a copy of the picture, which might have been the last. It was sufficient to describe the scene in detail, or merely the preceding or following one. The service applied only to the dead. Horst Papenbrock, who fell near Stalingrad, had not appeared in the newsreel.

His brother Robert had been sent to the Soviet Union as a "special leader." From there he had been sent back to the Papenbrocks a twenty-two-year-old girl, blonde, tall. His parents were to keep her for him in Jerichow. Louise treated her as a maid. ("On August 12, the birthday of our Führer's mother, the German Mother's Cross of Honor will be awarded." Thus Edith had been forced into marriage. Edith had left the house.) The Russian girl was called Slata. She knew enough German to do the shopping in Jerichow. She did not behave like a prisoner of war, and no one knew what the Papenbrock family were cooking up again this time. As a result, people were polite, even friendly, to her. The annoying thing was that she accepted this as of right.

Cresspahl was asked about his future relative. The Russian girl reminded him of Hilde Paepcke, among other things because she wore a head scarf, although a white one, and he tried to praise her. But more often he would talk about the term special leader, since *sonder*, for special, might mean one thing or the other, but if one went by the Dutch equivalent, *zonder*, that simply meant: "without" or "no."

On Monday, November 2, 1942, the clocks were to be put back one hour.

Kliefoth found himself waylaid while walking to the station. In the opinion of Swantenius, Regional Leader, it was not right that a certain someone was not in the Party and that he, Swantenius, would be held solely responsible for this. The scanty, vague news from Stalingrad depressed him, and he spoke of the Eastern Front reproachfully.

*You mean, you were on the Eastern Front?*
*It was just that I no longer have a full set of teeth to produce. Otherwise I'd be doing my bit in Italy now.*
*Hm, I see. Too bad when a fellow like you won't join the Party.*
*No time.*
*All we've got in the Party is odds and sods.*

At that time Kliefoth wrote on questionnaires, under the heading "War Decorations": Iron Cross 1st and 2nd Class, World War I; Iron Cross 1st and 2nd Class, WW II, "etc.," because there was not enough room. "The stuff a fellow accumulates in two wars."

Leslie Danzmann's job at the Gneez Labor Office was to act as counselor to the foreign women doing forced labor, and she was scared of the "black divvel." The black devil in question was a Yugoslav who owed her nickname to her wild black eyes and the threats and ferocity with which she blasted the people of Mecklenburg. The men were more scared of her than the women were. Dunya the Yugoslav failed to see why she had to live in a foreign country and, to add insult to injury, work there as well. She would stay in one place for four, even six, weeks, but she would not tolerate abuse, or a cut in her rations, and whenever a request was put to her in the form of an order she would throw down whatever she happened to have in her hand. Then it was up to Leslie to find her another place, and in her good nature she would tremble at the woman's airy threats that her friends would beat Leslie up. Dunya's contempt for the Germans was so abysmal that she did not even take the trouble to learn their language.

Sometimes Leslie Danzmann could persuade the head of the Labor Office to issue blank travel permits. She used to wonder why Cresspahl wanted to spend so many weekends traveling by train; but Leslie Danzmann was always glad to do someone a good turn.

Death announcements from the front did not always state that a boy had "given his life while loyally fulfilling his duty to Führer and Reich," sometimes it was stated that he had to forfeit it, or at least that he had "met a hero's death in supreme fulfillment of a soldier's duty," as if it were something a person seeks.

Lisbeth Cresspahl had now been dead four years.

The Air Force had built Cresspahl a new workshop on the airfield, poor in comparison to the one he had lost, but it was good enough for the construction of "dispatch boxes" of knot-free pinewood and ammunition cases of beechwood; minimum thickness of sides: one inch. Since Cresspahl's requisitions bore the stamp of the airfield command, the Hamburg-Altona Regional Guild Center allotted him an occasional permit for iron. Permits for iron entitled one to stands for machinery. Many Gneez carpenters were now obliged to make do with wooden stands. When he could do so inconspicuously, Cresspahl would pass an iron permit along to Böttcher. By now he had also acquired a zinc machine for lining the boxes and cases, as well as a rotary polisher.

The head of the local Gestapo branch, who shall be nameless, claimed to have returned home one night to find his wife had been killed by an ax, whereupon he pursued panic-stricken investigations, against himself in Herbert Vick's opinion. Herbert Vick, Criminal Police Commissioner (not from the Gestapo), traveled around the district of Gneez questioning people, including those of Jerichow, in his menacing way ("National Socialism must remain pure!"). Who, during the night of the crime, about 2 A.M., had seen a girl standing in a doorway sobbing? Who had seen through a gap in the curtains (a charge of infringement of blackout regulations was already being laid)—who had seen two men and a woman seated in conversation at a table in the window of the Café Heidebrecht? Who has any information about the motorcycle found next morning, totally destroyed, outside the local police station? Who had picked up a member of the Air Force when a patrol approached and driven him away in an automobile without switching on the headlights? At this point Herbert Vick's National Socialism achieved purity. The head of the Gneez Gestapo branch shot himself through the head, two and a half years before his colleagues did the same.

Principle No. 1 of the Mecklenburg constitution had been: Things will stay as they are.

---

**March 26, 1968   Tuesday**

---

De Rosny, an ideal man for our times.

The East Germans and the Soviet Russians are offering the new Czechoslovak Republic a substantial credit, to prevent the West

Germans from granting one, and they are doing it in the form of an ultimatum.

De Rosny on the telephone, his vocal cords comfortably relaxed: "I call that *good* news! Whose applecart is being upset, Mrs. Cresspahl? We'll just carry on!"

He's not the one who has to do the carrying on.

All he has to do is prescribe the image of an enterprise: from his higher vantage point.

His first defense is: In exchange for their hard currency the West Germans would insist on the Czechoslovak Republic taking up diplomatic relations. But De Rosny is De Rosny, and all relations with him are diplomatic ones.

His main battle position is: The Czechoslovak economy does not need the soft currency of the Council for Mutual Economic Aid; the currency it needs is from the dollar empire. And in that empire he is one of the princes. Nothing is going to happen contrary to his will in a hurry.

Sleeps well. On awaking is instantly present, with no desire for those protective miles of dreams. Sleep is for him the interval between battles; dreams are flaws that he causes to be repaired. He drops into the day as into cold water, accepting. Enjoys the massage. Spreads affability around himself so that the staff may give it back to him. Enjoys his solitary first meal of the day, the plans that have so wondrously grown, branched forth, blossomed, in sleep.

Impatient with anticipation. By helicopter he could get from Connecticut to downtown New York! But unwilling to make a statistical risk of a life like his. A gamble such as his life is.

He knows other kinds. Alone in the car with his man Arthur, he enjoys hearing about Arthur's life, and the big black man, dignified with the acquired gestures of service and slow aging, tells his boss about his wife's illnesses, the progress and setbacks of his kids in school, the anniversaries and quarrels of his relatives. De Rosny sits in a spectator's box, sees children playing far below.

Arthur has been saving for over ten years, hoping for other rewards from De Rosny than wages and his Social Security. He asked him for a hot tip on the stock market.

De Rosny enjoys telling this story. His chauffeur approaches De Rosny, assuming him to be benevolently disposed, and asks him about easy money. That isn't the kind of money De Rosny is after. (He doesn't talk about money, he talks to it.)

When the tale fails to evoke the usual laugh, he adds: To be fair, he had given Arthur a raise instead of a hot tip. The last sentence is so obviously tardy and contrived: perhaps the truth would have arrived faster.

Why shouldn't De Rosny supply the Soviets on behalf of the Czechoslovak Republic? He has his secrets too, discusses them with a few enemies, like smart schoolboy pranks.

Arthur's work may be Parcheesi, that of De Rosny's subordinates chess; De Rosny's may have some aspects of poker, but his stakes are beyond comparison.

And he goes and loses thousands at one sitting; is incapable of annoyance. He sees his repetitions as experiences; defeats happen to him to make room for triumphs. But both give him the feeling of being alive.

He never gives a thought to manners; they have been instilled into him by family tradition, private schools, universities. Even the machine that looks after his daily life supplies him imperceptibly with symbolic and tangible funds, clothing to meet required conventions, homes in capitals, by the sea. Because he does it, whatever he does is right; unchallenged he sits in the restaurants of the world, alert despite the genial demeanor, bored behind the epicure's mask; waiting. As soon as a pastime invades his privacy, he breaks it off.

Among equals less equal. De Rosny of the De Rosnys. First among his second chief executives, to leave his hands free. Who keeps track of his victories, dollars coming second. Not vulnerable. Dangerous. Magnanimous.

Terrible, that business with his wife.

Unassailable. Sympathy declined. Unapproachable even via that route.

When he does spend a night in town, it is to work.

Picks his secretaries for their qualities of unobtrusiveness. So he won't be distracted.

Secure in the belief that something is happening where he has given orders.

Leaves his exterior to the doubts of others, whether his handicap refers to golf or bluffing; uses his own doubts not for self-enlightenment but to fall asleep enjoyably.

Sleeps well. Knows how to wait.

## March 27, 1968   Wednesday

At the time of Stalingrad's fall back into Soviet hands, Wilhelm Böttcher had his son home on leave, that same Klaus who since 1934 had been trying to escape from his father's workshop, first to the Hilter Youth, then to the Reich Labor Service until, in April 1939, the Army relented and "took" him. In February 1943 he came home, aged twenty-two, slept for three days, and spent the evening of the fourth day at the City of Hamburg Hotel in Gneez with Weidling, one of the teachers to whom he owed his defeat at the Gneez high school, now on equal terms with him. For although Weidling came from somewhere or other as a Tank Corps captain, he was not free to enlarge on his counter-espionage assignments; his pupil wore on his tunic the Iron Cross 1st Class, the Wound Badge, the Attack Badge, and all the rest of the hardward so necessary to his masculine pride. Only five years ago Klaus Böttcher had been too skinny, too weak-lipped, too much of a little runt, for a soldierly bearing; now it seemed tailored to him. Later that evening they were joined by Kliefoth, another of the young Klaus's former enemies, but all he could report to Cresspahl was that Klaus Böttcher, the ingenious yarn-spinner, had kept his counsel and used the other two men as drinking companions and to find out the name of a doctor who would certify an extension of his leave.

Whenever the young Klaus had run into Cresspahl he had stopped him and reeled off stories in a sly, smug manner. These stories concerned his experiences far away from Gneez, from hearth and home. Cresspahl regarded his colleague's son as one of those people who, not content to dig potatoes in the middle of the field, prefer to have two rows at the edge so that they have something to look at while they work and can thus, at least through visual distraction, escape from work. Now he no longer believed that the boy was trying to pick up careless remarks; rather, that he felt at ease in flexible and fluctuating situations, particularly since these also provided the opportunity to hatch amusing little plots, and that that was what he talked about. Now Cresspahl listened to him as to a ne'er-do-well whose deeds harm no one and in fact serve as light entertainment.

In 1938, while doing his Labor Service, Klaus had narrowly escaped having to submit to the rigorous discipline imposed on everyone else. But, as it turned out, he never learned so much as how to hold a spade, for when he found that no one wanted to be a tradesman he reported for carpentry work and from then on lived as a free man. The quartermaster needed replacements for thirty stools that his predecessor had either burned up or sold, and he must have regarded Böttcher, the Labor Service recruit from Gneez, as a worker of miracles. Undeterred by the absence of wood, he stole a load of railway ties from the Schwerin-Ludwigslust line, chopped them up in a little carpenter's workshop twenty miles away, and made the thirty stools for the quartermaster plus another twenty for himself so as to have greater freedom of movement in his private business transactions. This was how he became head of the carpentry department, obtained orders by others who had meanwhile caught on to his strategy, and was given leave to go to Neustadt-Glewe whenever he wanted. "That wasn't how things were in your day, was it?" Klaus Böttcher had said, in that provocative way of his that was aimed at prompting Cresspahl to˙acknowledgment rather than annoyance.

How someone like Klaus Böttcher lived in Bromberg, in Poland, in 1940: He avoided German girls, their fathers had Party jobs. On the whole he found German civilians distasteful, "failures" living in confiscated Jewish villas, armament racketeers, profiteers, currency speculators. No, Klaus went out at night with a Polish girl, turning up at his barracks every morning at six, in charge of training and instruction. It was possible with Benzedrine. ("Benzedrine"? asked Cresspahl.) Leave regulations had been relaxed, the regiment having come from Schneidemühl on the German border and the men's names being enough to label them as relatives of the local inhabitants. However, the men were only allowed out in pairs, and Poles were forbidden the streets after 10 P.M. So Klaus got hold of a military coat and cap for his girl, and in this way they strolled through the town at night. Army personnel were not allowed to remove their side arms even in restaurants; but Klaus gave his girl a small lady's pistol so she could defend herself against any Germans who became obnoxious. He spent Christmas with his girlfriend's chums and showed them how Germans celebrated it: *Gemütlichkeit* is essential, but no boozing under the Christmas tree. Klaus was then ordered to appear before the commandant. In battle dress. On the desk lay Klaus's letters and photos, all taken from the Polish girl. The Lieutenant had known him during their training period together, from evenings at the Café Residenz in Schwerin, called him by his first name, bawled him out for therapeutic purposes when Klaus tried to ask about the girl. "Are you going to denounce me for racial desecration now?" Klaus had ended by asking Cresspahl, in his sly, droll, half-despairing manner. "If only I knew whether she's still alive!" Klaus had said, suddenly no longer man of the world, proud of his exploits, but doubting his plans for his life.

However, the day before his leave was up Klaus did start talking about his life again. Ill-at-ease, they were sitting in Böttcher's parlor. Each person there must have known the dark misdeeds he shared with Böttcher but not why he was there with the others. At first they had to discuss such matters as lifting the ban on hairdressers' giving permanents. That's how it was, but would it last?

Cresspahl and Kliefoth were the only ones invited from Jerichow.

The awkwardness arose not only from the presence of a Party member from the Gneez Tax Office, but also from Klaus's unsure, hesitating behavior. Shoulders hunched, he sat on the sofa between his parents, a far cry from the smart, brisk non-commissioned officer, now more like a boy whose leave ought surely to have been extended. Klaus brushed the hair back from his forehead, shook it down again, trying to keep his distance with gruff no-no's and unfriendly glances, until Mrs. Böttcher went over to the buffet, opened the liquor compartment, and placed the bottle of kümmel in front of her cherished son, her own child, leaving it there for him to help himself. "If I can't sleep, then I want to know why," she says.

*I can't tell you a thing. They'll shoot me.*
*Klaas, lad, we're your parents, that's Kliefoth, that's Cresspahl—*
*I'm sorry, I can't.*
*Come on now, Böttcher! Pretend you're in school!*
*O.K., O.K. There was a whole bunch of us drivers, around fifty it must've been, and our job was to escort 180 Belgian cart horses, on foot, from Bialystok to Smolensk, to the horse depot. Twelve miles a day. At night we used to drive the horses into stables, or into private homes. The houses were too small for the beasts, the drivers refused to go in there with them. The horses would get scared and start kicking out all over the place. And me in charge. A shit game.*
*Klaas.*
*The SS?*
*Well, that's how it is, Mr. Kliefoth. I wouldn't say the SS is hated, when it comes to a battle they'll fight to the last man, you have to say that for them. But the fact is they're Nazis, and they might as well be the first to die. That doesn't bother us; there were times when, as the enemy was approaching, I'd park a few trucks clear across the road, set fire to them, and then, holding a sign I'd stolen from the M. P.s over my camouflage coat, lead the SS Death's-Head Division straight to the Russians.*
*You took off, Klaas.*
*I wouldn't be sitting here otherwise, would I?*
*You did quite right.*
*Well, I dunno—.*
*Fire away, my lad.*
*I was wounded, you know.*
*Oh, my boy, so you were. Klaas.*
*Oh, quit that. That time in the military hospital at Schaulen, I was looking out the window. There was a fence around something or*

other, sheds and what was left of the town. They were keeping civilian prisoners there. In rags, sort of.

What did the SS do to them?

Nothing, Ma. Not when I was looking.

And later on?

Now, Dad, who wants to watch something like that!

Hm, I see.

Now you see what I'm getting at.

Tell us about it.

Well, when we got to Smolensk we were confined to barracks right away. Me being an N. C. O., I didn't think that applied to me. So off I went with a pal for a stroll outside the town—

Klaus!

But we never did find what we were looking for! In some woods on the edge of town we found a pile of corpses. Five feet high. Like this, up to your shoulder. Civilians. Stacked up like for burning.

Partisans. Saboteurs.

Kids, Mr. Kliefoth?

Oh, no, Klaus!

Kids, and women, like they'd just come from work. From shopping.

Got a picture, Klaus?

We were just taking some pictures when the M. P.s turned up and hauled us along to the SS. They were going to shoot us on the spot.

How ever can you take such risks, Klaus!

The risk was already there when we arrived. Well, as I say. Report on the double. Marching orders. We had to swear.

Swear what, lad?

That we'd never seen it! That there was no such thing, Ma.

It can't be true.

Can't it?

How can they let you go on leave if it's true? You might tell the whole story!

The leave's the reward, don't you see? For swearing.

D'you believe that, Mr. Kliefoth?

The SS does do such things.

Not the Army?

The Army!

Klaus doesn't have to do such things?

No.

I can't believe that.

Wouldn't have helped me anyway.

Kids?

*Kids too.*
*But they're Germans, the SS!*
*Sure they are.*
*You mean, regular civilian kids?*
*Jeez, Ma! It wasn't all that dark. One of them, she looked, you
know, like she could've been Cresspahl's kid.*
*Cresspahl, d'you believe that?*
*Yes.*

## March 28, 1968   Thursday

starting right after lunch, is Professor Kreslil's day, that schoolteacher
from Budweis, Bohemia, who left his pupils almost twenty years ago
and is now trying to lead some kind of life on Manhattan's Upper East
Side by translating from and into Czech as well as giving a few private
lessons in his own language.

At first he tried to maintain a classroom atmosphere, sitting there
so carefully prepared for the lesson, all kinds of teaching aids arrayed
behind his desk, as if he were still responsible for not one but all those
thirty pupils of so many years ago. It seemed as if, with the display of
professional trappings, he was trying to insure himself against the slightest doubt that he was earning his fee down to the last cent. For the
old man needs the money. To him the United States had not been
the land of reassuring success stories; indeed, its sole function had
probably been that of its adequate distance from Czechoslovakia. Where
he lives, the East Side is no longer the segregated precinct of the affluent:
instead it is an undefended multitude of decaying four-story buildings
on the edge of the German and Hungarian section. And finally, the
translating of scientific and technical processes does not come easily
to him, seeing that he had taught languages as long as the Germans,
and later the Czech Communists, had allowed him to do so. The
presentation of the check at the end of each lesson was an embarrassing
event for him, implying as it did the instant transformation of his efforts
into mere money; yet he was relieved not to find himself cheated out
of his remuneration, and he would thank Mrs. Cresspahl in his Old
World, deferential way. "I am very much obliged to you," he was still
saying at the end of November.

He it was who turned their Thursday afternoons into a social
occasion, as if between friends. As Mrs. Cresspahl enters the room he
cannot refrain from rising, advancing toward her, bowing, and kissing
her hand by way of greeting: she, for her part, does not insist on the
lesson starting immediately in return for her good dollars, with the

result that the occasion gradually deteriorated into trial and later genuine conversations, after the second month in Czech, now no longer
the sole purpose of the visits. Moreover, Professor Kreslil prefers, in
the case of a lady, to extend carefully phrased compliments rather than
to praise her as a pupil, however pitifully she may have mangled the
thickly consonanted syllables in her throat. It was Kreslil who, in his
courtesy, wanted to save the lady, his client, the trip to the upper
nineties, who would suggest walks, accept invitations to Riverside Drive,
and even turn up at the bank, a venerable gentleman, his shabby
garments hanging loosely about his thin figure, his carefully composed
features kept severely in place from sheer bewilderment at the sight of
a sixteenth floor in a bank, until he could walk through Mrs. Cresspahl's
door with a stately bow and a formal expression, one which recently,
however, has taken to combining recognition with a sense of fun.

The reason for this is not the increase in his fee, although for
each lesson this amounts to the taxi fare in both directions and he can
save almost all of it by taking the bus or the subway; the offer of
playfulness and complicity in his expression is based on mutual understanding. The first time they stood in the doorway to Lexington
Avenue he said: How often he had walked past the Petschek Bank in
Prague without ever dreaming that financial barons rested their eyes
on paintings, that their feet needed to be cooled or warmed on hand-
woven rugs, or that their self-image required the presence of antique
furnishings. He spoke without heat, without indignation, more in
amusement and surprise, as at stupidities. Mrs. Cresspahl tried to deny
her guilt or participation in the magnificence of her false surroundings;
Professor Kreslil could not turn his full and serious attention even on
this, and he met her eye with a sprightly look, as if wanting only to
recognize her, not where she is.

*You are a Slav, Mrs. Cresspahl, one of the Obotrites, we are closely
related.*
  *Maybe that explains it, Professor.*
  *You say you come from the German Baltic? But the land comes
to an end up there!*
  *And how about Bohemia-on-the-sea?*
  *You're certainly not German.*
  *I most definitely am, Professor.*
  *No, no. Smím se Vás na něco ptáti?*
  *Prosím.*
  *If you would say Anatol, I could say Gesine.*
  *But you're the senior one, Professor.*

*Perhaps it would be my privilege; I have become wary of privileges.*
*Whenever you feel like it, pane Kreslil.*

Now under his supervision they no longer read a solemn text from
the previous century; instead they read *Študáci a kantoři*, by Jaroslav
Žák, *Students vs. Teachers: Strategy, Tricks, and Self-Defense*, a handbook published in 1937, a pseudo-scientific pretense at instructing high-
school students in the art of battle in a hostile environment, and it
never ceased to delight the schoolteacher's heart in Kreslil that we in
Mecklenburg behaved in much the same way as these students of the
Czech Socialist Republic, from diverting a teacher's attention onto his
favorite topic to the best way of dealing with sneaks, and when it is
a matter of finding student equivalents for school authority Professor Kreslil can forget himself and try his hand at a German expression
after all. The reply to a question on the battle situation at the "Mecklenburg" high school led to information on Cresspahl's job as
mayor after the war, until gradually segments of our pasts began to
intertwine.

While I had been learning the Gothic script, Anatol Kreslil, high-
school teacher, was hiding with his wife at the home of relatives in a
village near Vyšší Brod, not far from the former Austrian frontier.
Gesine the schoolgirl was spending her vacation by the sea; that summer
the Kreslils were betrayed to the German occupation forces by neighbors
of his father-in-law, and they subsequently lived in hiding, in the
suburbs of Prague, in the homes of four families who occur in Kreslil's
tales not as "Czechs" but as Elžběta and Bohumír, Viktorie and Jakub,
Jiřina and Mikuláš, Růžena and Emil. Cresspahl's child was lying in
her own room in her own bed, dozing as she listened to her father
telling the story of Robin Hood's earthly sojourn; the Kreslils in their
hiding place were listening to a Jewish neighbor who was visiting Růžena and hoping to spend the last of her money on a pair of lace-up
boots for her five-year-old child, for the deportation journey to the
extermination camp. Because, knowing what their destination was,
Růžena gave the woman the boots, the Kreslils did not like to continue under her roof, they preferred to starve among others, until
Mrs. Kreslil starved to death, only a few days before the arrival of
the Allies; and the Cresspahl child was tidily eating the crust of her
bread first in order to save the precious middle part of the slice to
the end.

*It's all in the past, Mrs. Cresspahl.*
*No, it isn't.*

*You hear me tell you about it. As something that was.*
*Yes, something that was.*

That is how Thursday afternoons have been recently.

## March 29, 1968  Friday

As far as he is concerned, Antonín Novotný does not acknowledge that the Party is always right, repeat always, in fact invariably. Let others be losers, he refuses to be one and pushes aside the microphone of a radio newsman to whom he could surely have told this.

The new President of the Socialist Czech and Slovak Republic is reputed to be a friend of the Soviets. Holder of the St. George Cross of Tsarist Russia, a Hero of the Soviet Union, holder of the Order of Lenin, former minister of defense, then deputy premier in charge of physical culture and sport, until the Stalinist purges relegated him to the bottom of the heap. Then came Nikita Sergeevich Khrushchev asking after his good friend. Novotný hurriedly summoned General Ludvík Svoboda from his job in a collective village, and Khrushchev embraced him and seated him at his side.

The appointment of Ludvík Svoboda is regarded as an attempt to soothe the Soviets, and the Soviets are defending themselves furiously against the assumption that they are trying to throttle democratization in the Czechoslovak Republic. All that is happening there is an "activation of Communist Party organizations and the state administrative apparatus," and this seems to meet with their approval.

In Memphis, Martin Luther King, Jr., led a march of 3,000, but there were young people among them who ran away from the demonstration, smashed store windows, and looted. The police resorted to clubs and tear gas. A sixteen-year-old boy is dead.

In the summer of 1943, the Niebuhrs from Berlin-Friedenau decided for a change to spend their vacation, not at the Wendisch Burg lock, but at the Baltic, near Cresspahl. They asked Cresspahl to find them a place to stay. Jerichow airfield was, in his view, too close for comfort, and he found them accommodation in Rerik rather than in Rande. Moreover, Cresspahl preferred to be on his own, unobserved. In Rerik there was only the flak artillery training school; besides, he had been able to find the Niebuhrs an Air Force officer's house for two weeks, instead of just one hotel room for two adults and two children, one of whom, Günter Niebuhr, was only a few months old.

Gesine was sent to Rerik for the second week. This involved taking a train from Jerichow to Gneez, then another to Wismar, then via the

Rostok line to Neubukow. From there a bus did the eight miles or so to Rerik in half an hour. She was not happy to leave Jerichow, merely obedient. Cresspahl had stressed that she would be the oldest child, and she foresaw nothing but work. She was puzzled, too, by his telling her not to ask older people for "Rerik" but for "Old Gaarz," as the little place had been called before the Nazis elevated it to the status of a town in 1938, intending with the new name to revive memories of a vanished trading center of which only a few ruins remained. At Neubukow station, just as she was boarding the bus, the child asked whether it was going to Old Gaarz for sure, and the driver nodded vigorously, reassuringly, approvingly. Now there was a properly brought-up kid for you. He saw to it that she got a front seat.

Outside Rerik post office stood Klaus Niebuhr, once again far from pleased that this Gesine should be allowed to travel around without parents; yet he was too much of a week-old connoisseur of Rerik to refrain from being her guide through a town in the center of which there were thatched cottages, not at all like Berlin-Friedenau. The church, with its massive tower, standing on high ground, was visible from almost everywhere, yet Klaus compared it unfavorably with his Church of the Good Shepherd at home. But he did not hurry, taking her to see the ancient barrows as well as the walk along the High Cliff. The countryside was quite bare under the white sky, treeless. From that height one could look down onto the Salz Haff, the lagoon, onto the roaring surf. But over to the west lay Poel Island, the steep coast of Rande, Jerichow.

Just as in Jerichow, there were constant air-raid alarms, and Gesine could not understand these Niebuhrs, who felt they were safe simply because the Wustrow Peninsula was not Berlin. The first time the sirens wailed, she got up from the table, ready to run down to the cellar and, even though Klaus was forbidden by his parents to make fun of her, she was aware of their smiles. Besides, the Niebuhrs seemed different this time. Peter behaved less naturally to her, treating her with a neutral politeness, asking for her approval of every plan, and while he would rebuke Klaus he would not rebuke her, as if she had the rights of a grownup. An uncommonly tall man whose whole body was still skinny. There was so little flesh beneath his cheekbones that his lips looked pursed, as if they had tasted something sour. His eyes behind dark glass. He played games with the children, but not for fun the way Alexander Paepcke had, and soon left them to themselves to follow his wife wherever he found her. I didn't know then that he was no longer considered indispensable at the Ministry and that after the vacation he was due to go to the Eastern Front. He had invited Cresspahl's child believing this to be his duty; would have preferred to be alone with his family. It was the last time; even Cresspahl said after the war that Peter intended to desert to the Soviets the first chance he got.

It seemed that during that summer Martha Niebuhr showed a side of herself that no one had ever seen. If you came upon her in the kitchen, you would find her crying. She was impatient with Klaus, always after him. The surprised way that Klaus looked up at her showed that he sometimes did not recognize her, but by now he had learned to keep out of her way. If he did fall down in her sight, instead of worrying about the pain or the wound he would brace himself for his mother's scolding. Yet in photos from other years she looks gay, tender, her lips half open in happy anticipation, a dark girl with big eyes, leaning her head against Peter's arm at every opportunity. Gesine counted the days to Jerichow.

They were not many. There may have been a trip by rowboat across the lagoon, to the woods of Tessmannsdorf. Walks, perhaps to the Bastorf lighthouse, to Diedrichshag Hill. Then came that Sunday.

The air-raid warning on Sunday afternoon had already lasted three hours. All the grownups had come up out of the air-raid shelter into the fresh air, as well as the older children, headed by Klaus. Gesine stayed down below beside Günter the baby, embarrassed at excluding herself, obstinate in following Cresspahl's instructions. The baby was asleep, half naked, breathing heavily in the heat. From time to time Gesine would blow across his face. It was a puckered, laboring little face. She was alone with the baby in the spacious, comfortable cellar. The building was the property of the Air Force, and the shelter had been built according to standard specifications. A supporting wall had been constructed under the center of the ceiling; bunk beds had been attached to the walls. From somewhere outside came the murmur of the radio announcer's voice, describing the map co-ordinates in which the Allied planes were approaching. In front of the steps leading to the outside was an iron door framed in rubber, ajar, and beyond that a kind of antechamber, again with an airtight door, standing wide open. This arrangement had been explained to Gesine as a gas lock. So she would be able to give Cresspahl a better idea of this gas lock, she stood up and went over to the steps. Outside in the garden the grownups were standing around, among them an officer looking through some binoculars. The planes were hanging tidily in the sky, like a net, shining in the sun. Suddenly the officer's voice rang out in surprise and in- dignation. "They're dropping them!" Gesine heard. She was back again standing in the middle of the cellar. She watched Klaus Niebuhr fall into the open gas lock and then, in slow motion, onto the cellar floor. As soon as the first bombs hit the ground, mortar dust hung like flour in the air. In one of the cellar walls there was a hole. The lights had gone out. Gesine heard the baby screaming, groped her way over to him, ran back to the hole in the wall, and held the howling infant up to the air. She was very deep under the ground. But the children were being looked for in the gas lock, which had now almost disappeared under the rubble. The blasts had been so loud that it was a full minute before she realized that people had been calling her name several times. Since she was carrying the baby she had to nudge Klaus, who was still lying on the floor, with her foot, to wake him up. She was the oldest child. He crawled outside across the slanting pile of rubble, dragging her after him. Now she had only one arm free for the baby. The baby's head was lolling back pitifully. She knew it ought not to look like that. She was scared, because now the baby's cries were reduced to whimpering.

In the garden she could not see all the grownups, because many of them were lying on the lawn. The house that belonged to General Pirrmann of the Air Force seemed intact, but all around it craters had been torn into the ground. Grownups were lying around on the street too.

The children were not consulted when the buses from the flak training school arrived. They were bundled into them, driven to Kühlungsborn, and put up in hotels. There was another air-raid alarm that night. The shelter did not conform to standard specifications. She saw the water pipes all over the walls, woke Klaus Niebuhr with a whisper, and crept with him and the baby over to some stairs where the night was visible beyond. Now she knew she was afraid. Next morning Cresspahl appeared in Arendsee (now called Kühlungsborn—Arendsee had been known as Aaronssee in the days when Jews were still allowed to swim there).

The telegram to Cresspahl had said: "Children alive," as if one of us might have lost our legs.

So it was that Gertrud and Martin Niebuhr acquired two children whom for the next ten years they could call their own.

So it was that the child Gesine lost a little blue straw hat.

So it was that Peter remained with his wife Martha, sharing a coffin in the Wustrow earth.

By this time the child Gesine had become familiar with funerals. She knew all about the three handfuls of earth on the coffin.

## March 30, 1968   Saturday, South Ferry Day

"What were you like as a child, Gesine?"

As they waited at the ferry dock on the Manhattan side, the little round panes of glass in the doors seemed like holes in a prison as the faces of arriving passengers hove in sight beyond them. How childhood fears live on.

"What do you mean, a child not fit for school!" she said indignantly, somewhat annoyed too. Now she would be less free to boast that she didn't inherit a fortune but can provide for us both simply by selling what she has learned.

"Because I was one of the new girls in Grade 5 at the Gustaf Adolf School in Gneez and, what was more, came from Jerichow, out there in the sticks, it was my job to stand outside in the corridor and, as the enemy approached, to dash into the classroom shouting 'Look out!,' so that as the teacher entered the room the entire class would be standing up, right arm outstretched, ready to shout Heil and Hitler. The routine was new to me and should have been enough to keep me on my toes if I had only known what it was all about. So instead I stood daydreaming beside the open door, and the teacher, her hand clamped on my shoulder, propelled me into the classroom where the kids were still throwing blackboard sponges around or chalking a big question mark on the seat of the teacher's chair. I got beaten up."

"Did it have any effect?"

"So you don't mind them pulling your mother's pinafore over her head and beating her up? You're supposed to respect me, don't you know that?"

"I've had a licking at school too, with no warning from you. And then I'm supposed to love you! And respect you."

"It did have the effect of scaring me but not of making me reliable. Then another girl got the job. They'd written me off as too dumb."

"For that, yes! But you were great at lessons, straight A's."

"Maybe the career of Adolf Hitler. They hammered that into our heads till we could reel it off mechanically. But when it came to using my brain, doing fractions—"

"Gesine, our very existence depends on your knowledge of math, let alone doing fractions!"

"Marie, on the classroom wall facing us in Jerichow there had been a motto about German boys having to be as hard as Krupp steel, as tough as leather, and something else. Even that I hadn't understood, because I knew all about leather, it wasn't tough, we used to say of something that 'it tore as easily as sheepskin,' and all I could do was be glad I wasn't a boy. In Gneez they had had these words painted in big brown letters on the classroom wall:

> You are the Germany of the future
> And so we want you to be
> The way this Germany of the future
> Shall and must one day be.      A. H.

nicely centered."

"So?"

"It's like this. When you have that in front of you for hours on end, you think about it and don't listen to all that about fractions. And getting your face slapped had no effect. I got mine slapped one time because once too often I had left my math exercise book at home. I still resent that, and I'll never forgive Julie Westphal for it. It never occurred to her to explain to me why you mustn't leave your books at home. I felt only fear for her, not respect. That wasn't because she had come to Gneez from Jerichow because of a shortage of teachers rather than on merit. Cresspahl never slapped me, not even when I forgot something. So I spent the hours in class poking my little finger into the cap of my fountain pen and enjoying the smell of dried ink. In those days we often had to go to the school hall, stretch out our right arms, and sing both national anthems; I didn't mind, that just used up more schooltime. When we had to write an essay, instead of describing the cat on the basis of what our biology teacher had taught us about *Felix communis* I wrote what I knew about the Cresspahl cats: what they looked like, how many whiskers they had, and their various moods, where they deposited mice, and 'the house cat has 32 teeth.' An E."

"I don't think I like that, Gesine!"

"*I* like it."

"Tell me, Gesine, were you punctual at least?"

"Some of the teachers would smile as soon as I arrived, partly because of the laboriously contrived excuse I felt courtesy demanded. It wasn't easy, I couldn't even have the train from Jerichow arrive late, since Lise Wollenberg had come by the same train and was on time. Only once was I ever punctual in Gneez, ahead of time in fact. Cresspahl had forgotten to put the clock back to winter time, and I took the train to Gneez with a lot of sleeping men who got out at Gneez Bridge, still half asleep, for the Arado factory. They seeemed to me like a hidden army, and I knew for the rest of my life that they go to work unseen, unknown, and yet governments claim to know them. There I stood on the rough cobblestones outside the school, a whole hour too early, yet I got a scolding just the same, this time from the janitor. I was on time at the City of Hamburg Hotel, where Elise Bock served me the daily special (without ration tickets). I was on time for the train back to Jerichow. I was often late reaching the air-raid shelter under the City of Hamburg Hotel. Ever since the attack on Hamburg in July 1943, Gneez had been pretty quick at giving the alarm, because of the rocket factory of course, and I ran in record time through the streets for fear of being shoved down into a strange shelter, and I was always scared by the Hitler Youth Cubs, who would yell after me and order me to stop. The Cubs were a menace."

"Gesine, why did you care whether you were killed by a bomb or not?"

"Out of obedience to Cresspahl. Or I thought he would miss me if he had to live without me. Forget it, I don't know. Why try to trap me with a question like that?"

"Because, say what you like, you lived like a dog when you were a child, Gesine. Having your lunch among strangers, no help with your homework, getting up at six, all when you were ten years old!"

"That was the life Cresspahl had arranged for me. Had to arrange for me. That's why I didn't mind. And again I had to make a choice. Alexandra Paepcke would have liked to go with me to the Empress August Viktoria School in Stettin, not by herself, because after the big attacks on Stettin the school had been evacuated to the island of Rügen and turned into a boarding school. I would have liked to please Alexandra; Alexandra was my favorite of all the kids. Cresspahl read Hilde's letter aloud to me, looked at me, had me in his grasp. So I became a commuting pupil from Jerichow. The food at Elise Bock's wasn't as good as at the Air Force canteen, but I did rather like being a hotel guest. Cresspahl would ask me about my homework, not casually either, but I could tell he was a bit uneasy about checking over my Latin assignments. So I used to say they were all done. It was then that he began to speak English to me. The idea was to help me. And every morning he would sit at the table, breakfast all ready, and wait for me, every school day he would walk me to the station for the 7:08 train; he use to make me my sandwiches, and he would even give me some money to buy a snack in Gneez, a roll stuffed with chopped herring—"

"Gesine, you lived like a dog."

"I was fine."

"Gesine, why are there no pictures of you as a child?"

"Marie, your grandfather was a tradesman! If his wife had lived, maybe she would have taken up photography like Hilde Paepcke. Even at the Papenbrocks a 'studio photographer,' Horst Stellmann, used to be summoned to the house, and only on special occasions at that. And Cresspahl needed no pictures to help him remember. He was secure in his memory. I was the first one to take pictures; I was the first in the family to be afraid of forgetting."

"Those Paepcke photos. Where are they?"

"They were destroyed when the Paepckes died."

"Don't tell me about it."

"I won't."

"Gesine, what did you look like as a child?"

"I thought I was fat. I stuck out my lips. That makes you feel fatter. My worries were scraped knees, torn pockets; I had learned to cope with those by myself. I looked at people in a way that was not unfriendly, but frowning, so they wouldn't stroke my hair and call me poor. I wasn't a poor child. I had a secret of my very own; that was my father."

"And a D in Latin."

"An A."

"Oh, I see, Gesine. In that case."

## March 31, 1968    Sunday

On the far shore of the Hudson the light was so clear that the buildings stood out sharply, closer, too close. Normally the polluted air gives the impression of a hazy region on that side, with trees, as if the river might have prevented New York from continuing over there.

## April 1, 1968    Monday

For his renunciation the New York *Times* gives the President three banner headlines covering all eight columns, as if he had died. It has noticed tears in his eyes. And if the paper is to express any opinion, it has many to offer: that he was evidently even more deeply determined not to be rejected at either the convention or the ballot box; that he was not to be taken too seriously and, after a treaty with North Vietnam, might be glad to return as the President of Peace; that he may already be too late. What does the *Times* call the war? "This dreadful, cruel and ugly war—the war that nobody wants."

The situation in the Czechoslovak Republic is now such that in the very heart of Prague 3,000 citizens are permitted to assemble who were imprisoned, tortured, and ostracized for not being Communists when the Communists seized power. They are allowed not only to mourn their dead but also to ask for belated justice for the living and the dead, and this with the full approval of Government and Party.

Radio Moscow has reported President Johnson's bombing halt but not his renunciation of office. Over there, truth is dispensed like medicine, as it suits them.

In today's mail there is a letter postmarked with the single word Jerichow, with oversize stamps representing two oak trees as well as some people with books; addressed in an unfamiliar hand.

Don't accept it, Gesine. Return to sender.

"Jerichow, 17th March, '68, My dear Gesine—"

March 1968, for all contrary winds.

Gesine, you don't know who this is writing to you. But you know me. You wouldn't recognize me. I'm old now, a regular pudding, my hair's quite white, I'm getting wrinkled around the eyes. All that tennis didn't help much. Can you picture me now?

I don't live any more where you think. Don't have a house either, just a room on the market square in Jerichow. Yet I might've gone to Berlin and lived as snug as a bug in a rug, or I might've died in a cellar in Schöneberg. Now d'you know?

And just imagine, I speak with as much of a Scottish accent as Mary Hahn in Rostock: "On the spur of a moment"? Like Lisbeth's English was?

I'm writing you posthaste, you see, because you never write to me and it's better you shouldn't. At the post office they have a kind of screening list, if you know what that is. It's not that I'm scared. If they crack down on Gerda Wollenberg for going to Italy on a travel permit for West Germany, all I can say is she should've known better. Why should I be scared of sheep when there's a dog in my pocket? It's just that I don't want to be asked how come I'm writing to you, I believe I'm not supposed to.

Gesine child, what have you gone and done? Did you write a letter to the Rande Community? What was in it? Were you cheeky? You weren't cheeky as a child. You didn't want to take off your dress when I had to mend it, and when I pricked you you looked at me wide-eyed, and said nothing. I can still see the look in those eyes. Those clothes of yours, they were nothing but rags. You were an easy child, tall for your nine years, your cockscomb of hair always a bit crooked. It was just that you behaved toward grownups as if their being older didn't mean a thing. Except with Cresspahl and of course Cresspahl's daughter is what you have become.

I knew Cresspahl too. People say I went to bed with him. He didn't want to. There. Now you know who I am.

If you did write a letter to the Mayor's office in Rande the comrades there must have gulped. It seems you asked for figures, and apparently not the founding year but something to do with Jansen and Swantenius's Thousand-Year Reich. Methfessel won't say. I knew Methfessel when he was a child; that child, now 35, refuses to answer an old woman, just walks away from her! Methfessel and the Party mean the same as the guild and the Party, and he was the first who had to take an official interest. Schettlicht is a schoolteacher in Rande, from Meissen, I'm not going to ask him. Kraczinski is the local headquarters in Gneez, I'm not going there. The same goes for all the others, and whatever the information you asked for was, they didn't like it. At their Party meeting they had it on the agenda.

It's true! But that was a mistake for now they can't shift the blame onto one single person, instead the whole lot of them wrote you and signed the letter jointly. Methfessel reluctantly. He went to school with you, after all. The letter was dictated by Schettlicht, I s'pose he wanted to show his bucolic comrades how such matters are handled in *his* circles, face to face with the class enemy.

What was it about Gesine? Methfessel goes around looking as if they had officially declared you a child of imperialism, a warmonger, and all those tricks you New Yorkers are up to! Methfessel says: After a letter like that I wouldn't want to show my face again in Jerichow.

Yet they want you there: they think you should come Gesine! The whole 4,000 miles, and across the frontier into East Germany! Just for a couple of days. And I know why. I can't believe it.

What they thought was: maybe it can be smoothed over. Amicably, you understand. They went to see Kliefoth. The screening list at the post office, you know. They wanted to know whether you two correspond.

You should know, says Kliefoth.

Then tell us what she writes about, they say.

You should know, says Kliefoth. They say he's to tell them anyway.

Kliefoth: Do you have a search warrant?

There's not much they can do to him, you know. At 82. And he's got friends among professors in England. Birmingham I believe.

Would he co-operate in a delicate matter?

Kliefoth: I'm an old man, the only letters I write these days are personal ones—you can imagine what he said.

Kliefoth speaks of you as if you were close friends, on equal terms, and as if that pleased him very much. Did you know that?

They came to see me too. The rumor about Cresspahl in my bed, you know. Forgive me, and it really isn't true. Wanted to know whether you and I corresponded.

Maybe they think someone at the post office slips up sometimes with the screening list.

They couldn't believe we don't correspond and they don't want to believe it. For now they have no one who can write and tell you to forget that letter and they'll make you another one, as good as new!

I didn't even have your address. Kliefoth wants first to ask your permission for me to know where you live in New York. Emmy Creutz, they were at her place too, imagining all kinds of dire things. It's a small town, of course.

Gesine, you won't believe this. The brickyard path, the Ziegeleiweg, is to be renamed. It's to be called Cresspahl-Weg, and your old house is to get a bronze plaque, and the kindergarten that was set up in there is to be called the Heinrich Cresspahl Kindergarten.

I don't imagine your papers carry much about what's going on over here. What is going on is that the Soviet Union has dug up its Richard Sorge. But such people aren't called spies, they're known as scouts. And Cresspahl is supposed to have been one of these scouts. Not for the Soviets, that would really take the cake; but for the British, in other words, against the Nazis. Gesine, is such a thing possible? Child, I can't even bear the thought of it! Gesine, write me at once and say it isn't true!

Just so I know. (Don't write to me, write to Kliefoth. Then I can ask him whether he's had a letter with a No, followed by a full stop, that he didn't understand.) That's about all you can do.

It was in the paper, in our *Volkszeitung,* used to be the *Gneezer Tageblatt,* but now they print it in Schwerin, and Gneez just has a distribution office.

The paper had this piece about someone called Ludwig Krahnstöwer on his 70th birthday. A hero of the anti-Fascist resistance or something. Claims to have been a radio operator in Hamburg from 1943 to 1945 with the station code name of Jürss, or J. Ü. R. S. S., but for the Soviets and the British simultaneously, and that he got a lot of his Mecklenburg reports from one man, and he says: Cresspahl. He admits he never met him personally. He says: Cresspahl.

I'd sooner believe Jerichow's going to get a streetcar line to Wismar! So that's our latest rumor.

In that case after the war Cresspahl could have lived like a king! Because the Soviets would also have used his reports! Gesine, to keep something like that under one's hat, I don't believe the man's been born who could do such a thing, it just can't be true.

Just imagine, you might be unveiling a new street name and a memorial plaque here!

Maybe an honorary citizen of Jerichow, how would you like that!
You won't do any such thing, I know that.

There's one thing more I'd like to say: I'm an old woman, I have my pride too, but never mind that. I was very fond of you, even when you were no longer a little girl. After all, you were Lisbeth's little girl. I'd have liked to bring you up, Cresspahl wouldn't part with you. You didn't notice an old woman passing by, someone who had once sewn on your buttons and pinned up your hair. You greeted me nicely enough and walked on. There were times too when the town made fun of me. And you had Mrs. Abs, she became your mother, I suppose. I just wanted you to know that I'd have liked to be that too. Not because of Cresspahl, because of you.

Now you know who's writing to you. I won't be seeing you again. It may be because of my former life that at least I don't want to be forgotten. Not by you. Never had a child, you see.

A friend and well-wisher!

## April 2, 1968   Tuesday

Justice in Mecklenburg during the Nazi war:

Fedor Wagner, Polish farm hand in Gross Labenz, said that Germany was guilty of the war against his country. Arrested September 3, 1939. Removed from Bützow-Dreibergen Penitentiary to Auschwitz. Never seen again.

Wilhelm Zirpel, of Michelsdorf, near Belzig, bargeman, had listened to Radio Moscow and made antiwar statements in Malchin. Arrested December 11, 1939, five years' hard labor at Bützow-Dreibergen; after January 26, 1945, at Sachsenhausen concentration camp.

Johann Lehmberg, of Rostock, engineer, expressed antirearmament opinions. In penitentiary from 1939; on January 22, 1940, removed to Neuengamme concentration camp, later murdered there.

Louis Steinbrecker, of Rostock, greengrocer, conscripted as worker at Walther Bachmann aircraft factory in Ribnitz, arrested December 27, 1939, for "malicious statements," sentenced February 1940 to two years' hard labor, removed from Bützow-Dreibergen to Buchenwald concentration camp, where he died July 31, 1942, "of pneumonia."

Eduard Pichnitzek, of Neddemin, laborer, talked to Polish

P. O. W.s in their own language and drank beer with them. On April 22, 1940, sentenced to three years in jail. As a result of confinement at Bützow-Dreibergen contracted tuberculosis, which brought about his death on January 25, 1943.

Karl Saul, age 43, of Schwerin, plumber, repeated news broadcasts from foreign radio stations. On June 4, 1940, sentenced to three years' hard labor, his wife to two years' hard labor.

Martha Siewert, age 27, of Teerofen near Karow: for listening to the B. B. C. and denouncing the war, sentenced on June 17, 1940, to two years' hard labor.

Hermann Kröger, of Schwerin, mason, spoke on August 12, 1940, to two Frenchmen and gave them some cigarettes. He said workers of the world must unite. He was sent to jail for eighteen months.

Harald Ringeloth, age 20, from the Reich Labor Service Camp, Grevesmühlen: for making subversive statements was sentenced on August 14, 1940, to two years' hard labor.

August Spacek, of Elmenhorst near Rostock, dairy worker, allowed four Polish workers to listen to foreign radio stations in his apartment: for this was sentenced on October 2, 1940, to four years' hard labor.

Friedrich-Karl Jennewein, of Güstrow, laborer, was sentenced on November 29, 1940, to two years' hard labor for subversive activities, transferred July 3, 1942, to Mauthausen concentration camp, and died at Güstrow in 1946 from the consequences of confinement.

Otto Trost, grocer in Schwerin, listened to the B. B. C. and discussed the news reports with his customers. For this he was sentenced on August 8, 1941, to two and a half years' hard labor, and on October 20, 1943, died at Bützow-Dreibergen Penitentiary.

A tailor (small, deformed) and his wife carried a pail of water over to some parched, half-starved P. O. W.s so they could have a drink. The next day the couple were picked up by the SS and never seen again.

On October 9, 1941, Erdmann Fünning, age 60, boatbuilder, was arrested at the Kröger Wharf in Warnemünde. For spreading B. B. C. news reports among his fellow workers, he was sentenced on January 21, 1942, to ten years' hard labor.

Paul Koob, munitions-factory worker in Malchow (I. G. Farben), described Adolf Hitler as a swindler and the Winter Aid Program as a war loan. On June 9, 1942, he was given two years in prison.

A Rostock baker named Köhn sold some thousand loaves of bread (between fall 1942 and early 1943) to Polish forced-laborers without demanding ration coupons. That cost him two and a half years' hard labor and a fine of 1,000 marks.

Johann Schulz, of Warin, age 68, employed at the rail-car factory in Wismar, was arrested for the second time in December 1942. On March 8, 1943, he was sentenced to five years' imprisonment for spreading facts detrimental to the war. He lived to see the liberation of the Bützow-Dreibergen Penitentiary in May 1945, and on May 12, 1945, while on his way home, died in Zernin from injuries to his health suffered during his imprisonment.

On November 10, 1943, four members of the Lübeck clergy were executed: Catholic Chaplains Johannes Prassek, Hermann Lange, and Eduard Müller, for listening to and spreading foreign radio news reports, and Protestant Pastor Friedrich Stellbrink, allegedly on account of the sermon he preached on Palm Sunday 1942, following the air raid on Lübeck.

Walter Block, shaft foreman and Communist Party functionary in Malchin, was rearrested in May 1939 for illegal Party activities, spent six years in the concentration camps of Sachsenhausen and Neuengamme, and on May 3, 1945, drowned in Lübeck Bay with 8,000 prisoners whom the Nazis had intended in April to remove by ship.

Wilam Simic, a Serb, employed as a cook at the North German Dornier Works in Wismar. For giving food to Soviet P. O. W.s at the factory, he was sentenced on February 25, 1943, to six years' hard labor.

Walter Jahn, of Güstrow, master mason, conscripted as a worker at Priemerburg, in July 1943 predicted a German defeat, and on October 11, 1943, was given a jail sentence of three years.

Theodor Korsell, State Councilor and Doctor of Law, age 52, stated on a Rostock streetcar, after the fall of Mussolini, that the Führer should resign too, it being obvious that Germany could now no longer win the war. "And we don't all want to be burned to death, do we?" He was executed on August 25, 1943.

Friedrich Schwarz, of Waren, age 54, laborer, expressed his satisfaction, in the presence of fellow workers, at the downfall of Mussolini. On November 16, 1943, it was reported in the *Niederdeutscher Beobachter* that he had been executed.

Wilhelm Schröder, of Schwerin, cabinetmaker, said after the air raid on Hamburg on July 25, 1943: "What? You still believe in victory? I don't, and I never have." On May 11, 1944, he was given a two-year jail sentence.

Karl-August Grabs, of Grabow, age 64, cattle dealer, said at the end of 1943 in the presence of others that for Germany the war was lost. For this he appeared before the First Senate of the People's Tribunal on February 26, 1944, and was sentenced to death.

On March 21, 1944, at 11 A.M., the Polish forced-laborer Czeslaw Nowalkowski, age 23, was hanged in the village fields of Stove, near Wismar.

Otto Voth, age 41, farmer in Zeppelin, district of Güstrow, was arrested by the Gestapo on March 29, 1944, for stating that Germany's defeat was now inevitable. On January 25, 1945, he was sentenced to five years in the penitentiary, his term to be served at Bützow-Dreibergen.

Karl Willführ, of Eldena, bargeman, conscripted as worker at the explosives factory (Dynamit A. G.) in Dömitz, protested against the ill-treatment of Soviet P. O. W.s. In September 1943 he was arrested by the Gestapo, in 1944 sentenced to three years' hard labor, and on January 25, 1945, murdered at Gollnow Penitentiary in Pomerania.

Ella Kähne, of Beckentin near Grabow, in 1944 gave a Soviet P. O. W. some rubber solution to mend his boots. One year's imprisonment.

On November 30, 1944, Josef Molka, laborer, born in Poland, in Germany since 1929, was arrested, together with his three sons, for giving food to the P. O. W.s on the Mörslow estate near Schwerin and telling them about the situation at the front. It also counted heavily against him that he had urged his sons not to go to war for the sake of getting shot. On January 15, 1945, he was sentenced to death, and on February 6, 1945, was executed at Bützow-Dreibergen.

At Ziebühl, near Bützow, August Schlee, farm worker, declared that his village should surrender without a struggle to the Soviets. On May 2, 1945, he was shot by an SS commando.

Marianne Grunthal, of Zehdenick, age 49, schoolteacher, on hearing of Hitler's death exclaimed: "Thank God, now this terrible war is over at last!" On May 2, 1945, she was hanged from a lamppost in the station square at Schwerin. The square still bears her name.

The execution cellar at the Bützow-Dreibergen Penitentiary is now preserved as a museum.

It was a whitewashed cellar. Beyond one vault of the ceiling a steel beam had been mounted in front of the rear wall. From this beam hang three hooks. Beneath the hooks stand three low stools. Strung along the ceiling are two cords, and two curtains can be pulled along these cords so as to form three separate death cubicles. On each side of the entrance arch hangs a piece of dark cloth. These could be drawn in such a way that the victims walked into a narrow, dark tunnel, unaware that anyone was hanging from a hook beside them.

I can visualize Cresspahl in this place.

## April 4, 1968  Thursday

The clouds hanging this morning over the Hudson resemble the cloudy sky of the summer of twenty-four years ago over Ribnitz and the inlet of the Saal Bodden, when the Paepckes set out on their last vacation. This time, however, they all met the train bringing the Cresspahl child, Alexander in an unfamiliar uniform yet instantly recognizable in his pleasure, his businesslike manner, his mock officiousness. Now anticipated delights were replaced by the real thing. Alexander said: "Many children, many blessings, said the verger pocketing his christening fee."

It may have been too late for the Althagen boat, with probably no transportation available for six people plus bag and baggage. Alexander led his retinue diagonally across the station square to an ambulance that looked alarmingly official. Addressing the children as if they were patients, he stuffed them peremptorily onto, under, and alongside the stretcher, enjoying their horror, surprise, and delight at the new adventure. A vehicle of the municipal hospital drove north along the Fischland road on very urgent business. Alexander was proud of the favor done him by an old Leonia friend, and prouder still that such a thought had occurred to him. He sang loud and happily with the children the whole way, and not one of them had any suspicion.

The evening seemed very long to the children, but Alexander would not let them leave the house. They did not feel observed; he did not let them out of his sight. Gesine had to tell them about Jerichow, and in fifteen minutes he taught her how to do fractions, something the school had been unable to get into her head. Alexandra was sent to the clothes closet and told to come back dressed as the Queen of Sheba. Alexander had returned that morning from Soviet Russia and had seen his family again for the first time at the Stettin station. He asked Paepcke Junior all about school and taught him some new cribbing tricks, "for when you're at your wit's end, my boy." For Christine's benefit he demonstrated how she had drunk out of a mug at the age of two. When it was full, she used to hold it tight with both hands; as soon as it was empty she simply let it fall to the floor. Christine was now seven and delighted to see that as a small child she had genteelly crooked her little finger as she held the mug, before discarding it as useless, just like Alexander; she laughed even harder than the others, not a bit hurt. Alexander was incapable of hurting a child's feelings. That evening they talked a lot about the past, and about Lisbeth. Lisbeth's child realized that her dead mother was known among them as a thoroughly likable person, beautiful even at the age of eight, the friend of humans and animals throughout her life, her mocking manner designed to hide tenderness. Lisbeth's sister did not say much, prompting Alexander with half-sentences and sometimes pressing both forefingers to the inner corners of her eyes, as if pushing back pain. To the children she merely seemed tired, and no one suspected a tragedy. Christine and Eberhardt fell trustingly asleep on Hilde's lap and, with their heads against Alexander's chest, were carried out, put to bed, gently kissed, and looked at as they slept.

Next morning the High Cliff coastal batteries were firing out to sea, and after the first dull rumble Gesine waited for Alexander's voice to penetrate the ceiling and denounce the Greater German Army for its unseemly behavior. But Alexander was no longer there.

The morning was almost white, with fringed cloud-boats in the sky. The reflection of the light from the Bodden was an exquisite pain in the eyes. The paths between the cottages were warmed and protected by the tall brushwood. Artists sat about in the meadows, as they did every year, each one doing her best to commit the Dornenhaus to canvas, although the old cottage was barely visible beneath its sagging hip roof, hidden as it was behind rambling thorn bushes so high that they hung down over the roof, bent to an angle of forty-five degrees by the wind, thick and impenetrable. Alongside the Mecklenburg-Pomerania border road ran the familiar blackthorn hedges, the cliffs fell away as steeply as ever just where Pomerania began, and the children recalled Alexander's tales of how the sea had broken through at this very point. Bare on the Althagen side, the border road on the Ahrenshoop side was densely built up with houses painted in wonderful colors, the famous blue, with gardens protected from the wind, nurtured by the sun from the south, way down below the steep slope up to the road, with bright-hued hollyhocks growing right up to the roofs. The children thought of Alexander's solemn explanation that these houses had a back door to the north, dating from the days when Mecklenburg and Pomerania had been on bad terms and the inhabitants were not allowed to use the border road. It was the Fischland, yet not the real one. Without Alexander the vacation did not seem possible.

By the time evening came, Hilde could see that the children were at odds with her and the world. Alexander had not been on leave, he had been ordered to southern France and had left the train, against orders, to help her take the family to Althagen and see the children once more. It was more than he could ask of himself, to say good-by openly to the children. Hilde tried to make out that it was her fault he had had to go back to his post early that morning. Then she sternly ordered them to write letters to Alexander and in that way salvaged the prospect of the next day.

Hilde sent the children out into the fields with the harvesters. They rode on the bumpy wagons, ran alongside the mowers, tried their hands at binding sheaves, sat and ate with the harvesters on the narrow strips of earth between the two bodies of water, came home parched, dumb with fatigue, and thought they had been working. In the Fischland the haystacks were built not in the shape of roofs, as they were around Jerichow, but round, making excellent wigwams in their games. In the damp woods, the Mückenwald, the part that had once been cut off from the Darss by the inroads of the Baltic, the children looked for blueberries, and they were given them for supper with milk and believed they were living off the fruit of their labors. Hilde was quite capable of running all the way to the Mückenwald after a child who had forgotten to take along her sun hat.

The Althagen house was surrounded by a solid gravel dike whose purpose was to distribute rain water from the roof evenly over the soil. It was considered an honor to be entrusted with weeding the dike. The regular evening walk down to the beach for a swim was a kind of wages. On the Niehagen side a path ran through a very high field to the High Cliff between willows and poplars protected from the wind, an ordinary cart track that always seemed to stop abruptly at the edge of the abyss down to the sea. Letters were written to Alexander about the watchdog at the Nagel farm that refused to allow the public to walk through to the dike and the Bodden path, about people they had run into in the village street, about visits to Alexander's friends. So it was that a vacation could be invented once the art had been learned from Alexander.

Today I know that the vacation was not like that.

Not far from Althagen, on the other side of the Bodden, was the Barth concentration camp. The camp held prisoners from Soviet Russia, from Holland, Czechoslovakia, Belgium, and Hungary, people who were forced to work at an evacuated Heinkel aircraft plant. Dr. Stejskal, a Czech, has kept a list of the women and the men who were buried in the Barth cemetery and mass graves. There are 292 names. The bodies of 271 prisoners were sent from Barth to the Rostock crematorium. Causes of death were given as "tuberculosis," "pneumonia," "suicide." People were "shot while trying to escape," and if a woman persistently refused to help build airplanes that were destined for use against her own country, she was taken back to the Ravensbrück concentration camp and murdered with gas. We did not know this. Hilde Paepcke took us to Barth, over the swing bridge, so we could have a

look at the town. We saw nothing. The railway line by which Cresspahl's child had come to the Fischland passed Rövershagen. At Rövershagen there was a concentration camp whose inmates were forced
to work at the Heinkel plant. Today I know this.

The gifts left behind by Alexander for the children consisted of
white raincoats from Soviet Russia made of some rubberlike material.
They felt brand-new and still smelled of the factory, but in the pockets
there were sunflower seeds. When Alexander told them about the
reoccupied Baltic countries, it had seemed very strange that the Baltic
was there too, in such dense heavy forests. The Baltic was there like
a shining snake in the forest.

After the war I found out the following: Alexander's job was in
the "Todt" organization and consisted of putting civilians to work who
had been handed over to him by the SS from among the Russian
population. In one instance he had protested slightly against accepting
a group of fifty Jews because it included children. He got off without
a court-martial. The Army had taken him back and sent him off to
take a noncommissioned officer's training course. More could not be
done. By this time it was no longer possible to argue with the war. All
the Paepcke family connections were of no avail, neither through Leonia
(the Mecklenburg student fraternity), nor through former Reichswehr
officers, nor through the Army Ordnance Department in Stettin. It
was almost incredible that the family should have been unable to get
him moved to a safe place.

At Althagen they played a game in which Alexandra Paepcke sat
on one side of the turnstile in the border hedge, Gesine on the other,
and as they went around and around they would sing: Now I'm in
Pomerania! Now I'm in Mecklenburg!

The turnstile, the vacation, are part of the memory of that summer. It was not like that.

---

### April 5, 1968   Friday

*I'm sorry they shot him.*

*You're not sorry, Mrs. Cresspahl, madam.*

*We've been living in this building, you and I, for six years, Bill.*

*Martin Luther King was a black man, like me. You belong to the
whites.*

Yesterday evening the Reverend Martin Luther King, Jr., was
fatally shot in Memphis. It was about 6 P.M., seven o'clock New York
time. He had spent the whole day in his room at the Lorraine Motel.

He had chosen it because it belonged to Negroes. He had gone to Memphis to help the sanitation workers who had been on strike since Lincoln's Birthday, since February 12. A week ago he led a strikers' march that ended in violence; the last rally had taken place on Wednesday. Just before six he came out of his room onto the balcony and chatted with friends who were standing around in the courtyard parking lot below.

"You mustn't believe that of our country, Mrs. Cresspahl. It's not like that."

"It's just like that, and worse."

"A Nobel prizewinner gets shot in this country, he only has to be a Negro and demand civil rights for Negroes."

"Both stock exchanges expressed grief at the news on opening today, the national and the New York one. And at eleven there's going to be one minute's silence."

"Do you know a Negro with a seat on the stock exchange?"

"Tonight the rebellion's going to hit New York."

Dr. King was leaning over the balcony railing. He was rested, genial, looking forward to the evening. He was dressed to go for dinner with a pastor in Memphis. His driver warned him of the evening's chill and advised him to wear a coat. Dr. King promised to do so. A friend introduced to him the musician who was to play later that evening at the rally. Dr. King had asked for the Negro spiritual "Precious Lord, Take My Hand." He greeted the man and repeated his wish. Then the shot was fired.

"He predicted it."

"When he flew to Memphis, all the baggage had to be searched and the plane kept under guard, because of him."

"Last night you could still see him live on TV. They showed his speech of Wednesday night. That his people will reach the Promised Land, although not necessarily at the same time as he does."

"They ought to abolish television."

Dr. King collapsed to the floor of the balcony. He was visible from below because the railing consisted merely of iron rods painted green. Blood gushed from the right side of his jaw and neck. The explosion had torn his tie to shreds. He had just bent over; if he had been standing

up he would not have been hit in the face. Someone ran over to him
as he lay there and tried to stem the blood with a towel. Another person
tried to cover him with a blanket. Then came someone with a larger
towel. It was ten or fifteen minutes before a Fire Department ambulance
arrived. His head covered by the bloodstained towels, he was carried
away on a stretcher. He had been in the open for just three minutes.

"The Negro leaders smiled at his efforts to achieve equal rights
without violence."
"Many people hoped he was right."
"Now they have to believe in their own violence."
"Tonight there'll be white blood on our streets."
"Here we sit like in a cage."
"By tonight the Negroes will be able to blockade all the trains."
"No white's going to be able to leave town."

The sound of the shot seemed to some people to come from a
passing car. To others it sounded like a firecracker. One man nearby
had been watching television, to him it had sounded like a bomb.
When the fifteen or so people in the motel courtyard turned toward
the direction of the shot, all Negroes and friends of Dr. King's, the
police came running up from all sides, mainly from the direction of
the shot. The police were carrying rifles and shotguns and wearing riot
helmets. Moments before the shot, a squad car containing four policemen had driven past. The police first cordoned off an area of about
five blocks around the Lorraine Motel. Then 4,000 National Guards-
men were called out, and a general curfew was declared. Dr. King
died at 7:05 (8:05) P.M. during the operation on his neck, "a gaping
wound."

"It can be overdone, you know."
"Flags at half-mast! After all, he wasn't Kennedy."
"The blacks ought to be smoked out, block by block!"
"Maybe they did it themselves."
"Since last night my hairdresser has had to wear dark glasses after
a Negro struck him under the eye with a knuckle-duster. In spite of
his being French."
"What did he say?"
"He just took off his dark glasses and looked at me."
"Do you really believe no one was killed in Harlem last night?
They just want to reassure us."

"A single headline in the *Times*, and half of what was under it was other news."

"Like I say, it can be overdone."

The police believe the assassin to have been a white man in his thirties who had been hiding fifty to a hundred yards away in a flophouse. Dr. King's driver saw a man "with something white on his face" creep away from a thicket across the street. The police assume that the killer's getaway car was a late-model Mustang. A .30-06-caliber rifle was found about a block away.

"That must have been a trail laid deliberately."

"D'you suppose he was alone?"

"D'you believe Oswald was alone?"

"D'you suppose it'll be like with Kennedy?"

"They may find the killer, but not the ones who hired him."

After Dr. King had been pronounced dead, his friends gathered in his motel room for consultation. They had to step over the drying pool of his blood outside the door. Someone had thrown a crumpled cigarette package into the blood.

"If the bank is going to close early anyway, why don't they close at noon?"

"By this time the Negroes have mined all the tunnels and bridges."

"The Negro soldiers in Vietnam send weapons to themselves back home. You've no idea how many machine guns the post office delivers every day in New York!"

"And hand grenades too. And plastic bombs."

"On Madison Avenue they stabbed a white woman and her child to death because she was wearing a mink coat."

"And then we even send them to Vietnam to learn close combat!"

"First the Indians. Now the blacks."

*I'm sorry they shot him, Bill.*

*You're always so polite, Mrs. Cresspahl, I know that.*

*I'm sorry.*

*And yet, if the black people from Harlem came here tonight, I wouldn't lift a finger to help you, madam. Do you even know the meaning of fear?*

*Yes.*

*You know nothing. You're not black.*

## April 6, 1968   Saturday

"Mrs. Martin Luther King
St. Joseph's Hospital
Memphis, Tennessee

Dear Mrs. King:
For the personal loss you have suffered
that has been caused you
that the Whites have inflicted upon you, I would like to
express m—"

"Mrs. Coretta King
Lorraine Motel
Memphis, Tennessee

My dear Mrs. King:
In view of the loss that you and your children have suffered,
that has been inflicted upon you and your children by the Whites, the
national significance of which cannot be mitigated by the official sympathy of the Federal Government, you will find it strange that in your
city, as in New York, people are walking along Broadway, enjoying
their free Saturday, even taking pleasure in the sunshine. You know
about yesterday's memorial march through New York, the longshoremen's work stoppage in the harbor, Mayor Lindsay's visits to the ghettos.
Certainly some stores here are closed, including Jewish ones that on
this occasion are attaching to the Sabbath a different meaning from
that of their own religion, on handwritten cardboard signs, out of
affection and respect for your husband's memory. But there are plenty
of people about doing their Easter shopping, the sports events that have
been canceled for today and tomorrow will be scheduled later, possibly
even for Tuesday night, and I would like to assure you that not everyone
agree—"

"Mrs. Martin Luther King
Southern Christian Leadership Conference
Atlanta, Georgia

My dear Mrs. King,
After first intending to apologize for the telegram my daughter sent you

last night, I now merely want to say that she is not yet eleven years now I feel I would like to share in the impulsive, spontaneous tone of that telegram, in a wa—"

*Why can't I do it! Tell me!*
*It's something real, Gesine.*
*It isn't an ordinary death, you see.*
*A death like your own. Predictable, likely. But also just as unlikely.*
*Because he wasn't Kennedy?*
*Because he was a Negro. Whether he preached nonviolence or violence. He had simply become too visible.*
*All the more reason I should be able to write—*
*No Gesine. What sort of country are you living in, of your own free will? In a country where Negroes get killed. What do you think you can write?*
*Yes. Nothing. Nothing.*

### April 7, 1968   Sunday

News pictures of the riots in Washington show dirty smoke billowing through the streets, spreading far out over the city. It obscures the White House, says the caption. Another picture shows low lines of buildings from above, close together, some of them burned to empty shells, their façades collapsed. There is enough left of others for the fire to consume. These are American buildings, recognizable as such by the flat roofs, the parallel lines of windows. This is what a war in American cities would look like.

In Mecklenburg, at the Gneez high school, they were still saying in January 1945: First you'll be given orders, after that you'll be told! in a paramilitary tone, as if all the teachers were amateur noncoms. Sometimes they phrased it more elegantly, saying: Leave the thinking to the horses, their heads are bigger than yours! whenever a child said: I thought—.

The Cresspahl child did not say what she thought, she sat there with a pleasant expression, noting how the teaching staff handled a child who had thought something. The Cresspahl child had a secret. She knew the war would soon be over. She reported to Cresspahl what they had been told in school about London dying under the V-2 rockets, and her father had been unable to suppress a surprised and then a hearty laugh which made him look as though he were choking. But the secret meant that within a few weeks school would be finished.

Any child could see what was happening. In Jerichow there were still families where the parents believed in national solidarity and bought no food on the black market, and in those families the children went hungry. The farmers and tradesmen had reverted to barter. Cresspahl and his pipe did not suffer, his French prisoners of war saw to that; but on her way to school Lise Wollenberg would walk the whole length of the train in search of a recklessly discarded cigarette butt for her father, cigarette rations having once again been cut to ten cigarettes per six coupons, and these had to last four weeks. Children could see what was happening just by looking at the railway station at Gneez. Express trains had been discontinued; ordinary trains could be used only by people working out of town or by schoolchildren. The Allies had finally managed to destroy the German railway network. Gneez station was very quiet these days. Occasionally a ghost train for official use only would stop, met by a scattering of people on the platform. There was a ban on all mail to Wendisch Burg except postcards, and the Jerichow mailwoman's bag contained more letters with out-of-town addresses that she had to "return to sender" than there were letters *from* out of town. The Cresspahl child had been stopped on the road to Rande for riding her bicycle to the Baltic just for the fun of it: the use of bicycles for distances of over two miles was banned by a regulation that applied even to the Hitler Youth. The Cresspahl child had passed on to her father her teacher's inquiry as to when she was finally going to join the Jungmädel, seeing that she was now eleven, and Cresspahl had written a note saying she must be excused since she was an out-of-town pupil, but privately he had said: No sir! We don't have to worry about that any more, Gesine.

But among Jerichow grownups conversation often turned to the flocks of waxwings that had suddenly descended upon the area from the north, graceful creatures with feathers of reddish gray, soft white, and reddish yellow, in size and build resembling crested larks. The old folks had respected these birds for their ability to predict the weather, their sojourns and travels being so variable; generally speaking, their arrival was supposed to herald a severe winter. For some people this severe winter signified Germany's defeat, while others said that a Germany still able to maintain the railway from Jerichow to Wismar (or Lübeck) could never lose the war.

Then the airfield grew very quiet. Takeoffs were no longer worth counting, landings scarcely more so. The Mariengabe Air Force base, Jerichow's pride and joy, began to die.

*Hamburg, Lübeck, Bre—men,*
*Don't need to feel ashamed—and*
*Jerichow is much too small*
*To be worth shitting there at all.*

And Otto Quade was given a box on the ears. For a while the words of that song had not applied. Jerichow had had the Air Force.

The Mariengabe Air Force base had been a typically Jerichow affair, right from the start. When it had still formed part of Berlin Air Force Region III it had been planned merely as an auxiliary base, a small knot in a far-flung network, a landing strip of 500 by 1,000 yards running west, later a farther one perpendicular to it. The fact that it had taken three and a half years to complete was due not merely to the inadequacy of the local construction industry but also to the abandonment of plans for long-range bombers, whereby those fellows in Berlin had overlooked the importance of Jerichow, a blow to local pride. True, the number of troops stationed at the airfield had then gradually increased beyond the 300 posted there back in October 1938, just for the sake of appearances; but then the airfield had been assigned instead to Hanover Air Force Region XI, where all they cared about was Hanover, under Air Force Command 2 (North) in Brunswick, where all they cared about was Brunswick, and Air Force General Helmuth Felmy had not taken the trouble to pay a visit to Mariengabe, although he would have had his public welcome in Jerichow, with band music on the market square and a torchlight procession at night.

Jerichow North's first commandant, Lieutenant Colonel von der Decken, left Jerichow before the town had had time to get used to him properly. The home he had established in what had once been Dr. Semig's villa was a quiet one. The people living along the Bäk caught a glimpse of him every morning and evening when the car with his adjutant at the wheel drew up at the front door, as if an airfield commandant were an employee doing an ordinary job. A few times he accepted invitations to the local estates, where he had some relatives; the town had no part in these. Mrs. von der Decken did her shopping by having what she needed either delivered or picked up, and she behaved toward a tradesman as if she were scarcely aware of his presence. When Cresspahl built a wall safe for her husband she had a plate of stew placed in the kitchen for him. Her Hanoverian airs, the visits to the theater in Schwerin, her expression of pained boredom, all this had been considered appropriate enough for Jerichow: it was just that previous ruling powers had been more in evidence, had revealed more about their lives. What people did remember were the two von der Decken girls, twins of fourteen, blonde, very Berlin, sharp of feature like their mother. Instead of attending school in Jerichow they were driven in a staff car to the Gneez high school. They were known as the dolls. In what had formerly been the veterinarian's stable, horses were kept for the two girls, and at harvest time they went riding in the Gräfin Forest and along the coast, often accompanied by a young officer, and Jerichow was once again offered an example of how to provide for one's children's amusement, even more thoroughly than in the Papenbrock style.

Then the commandant had left for the Eastern Front with his fighter squadron, and the family moved to Lower Saxony; a group and a half of the squadron returned, their numbers were brought up to strength, and they flew to the Soviet front and did not come back. As a result of transfers and postings, Jerichow now had its fifth commandant; they had become steadily younger, now they were all majors who never even brought along their families but lived at the base instead of in town. The last Air Force Day, when the airfield was thrown open to the public, had taken place in 1940; after that both fuel and funds were lacking, and Mariengabe had become Jerichow's secret, tightly fenced in, secured by guards, patrols, sentries, a sound, often incidental, that awoke the town only when there was a northwest wind.

Things had gone on like that until 1944. The unit that took over the airfield in 1940 had been training pilots until it was transferred to France, leaving behind a battalion for basic instruction to which was then added a company for air-reconnaissance training. The acquiring of domiciliary rights as promised by von der Decken was striven for, now somewhat less ambitiously, by the staff officers at the base, older men from the Reserve. The *Gneezer Tageblatt* published a dramatic report of the night of March 28, 1942, so that people living around the airfield should realize it was still functioning: how the crews, equipped with gas masks, steel helmets, and rifles, run into the bunkers and trenches, how the medical orderlies, the aircraft mechanics, and the fuel attendants take up their positions in order that landing fighter planes may be swiftly dealt with, "and, its engine roaring, the slender bird rises up into the night to face the British terrorists."

This had not sufficed for the invention of new games for Jerichow's younger generation. On one occasion the senior classes of the Hermann Göring School had been packed off to the Archduke Hotel in Gneez to hear a holder of the Iron Cross with Oak Leaves tell them about his experiences; an increase in applications from draftees to join the Air Force had resulted, as desired. Since 1943 fighter crews had been stationed at the airfield, turning night into day with march music from the duty barracks, their Messerschmitts leaping across the Baltic, to Berlin, and they had been shot to pieces not only by the British but by the German flak too. Airfield troops were still rushing to take cover or into position whenever there was an alert, but their own fighter planes never came back to Jerichow North, and the Allies sailed in broad daylight high above the Baltic coast and into Germany, invulnerable, arrogant.

Just as in Rostock there were schoolboys who were jealous of Lübeck's prime position in terms of air raids, so there were boys in Jerichow who were annoyed that the British and Americans did not consider their airfield worth even a light attack. All they got were the foil strips dropped by the Allies to confuse the German radar-tracking system. In Wismar and Rostock there was a regular trade in flak splinters. In Jerichow they had only just got around to supplying antiaircraft machine guns; in other places cannons had been set up.

*Hamburg, Lübeck, Bre—men,*
*Don't need to feel ashamed—and*

Now that Mariengabe was no longer a base for fighter planes, Cresspahl was receiving fewer and fewer inquiries about it. The rearming and retraining of enemy-aircraft trackers to handle landing equipment for instrument flying and night pursuit had been the last items that his employers had been keen to have confirmed; after that they were not even disappointed that he was unable to locate the new bomb-sighting mechanism which they assumed was being tested in Jerichow. From time to time he would pass on information as to which flight engineer had recently been put in charge of civilian airfield personnel, or which person was now looking after the day-to-day administration of the base; from early in 1944 his job consisted of trips with official permission from Leslie Danzmann or sanctioned by an Air Force rubber stamp from Jerichow North. Anyone traveling in the direction of the Rechlin Air Force testing site has to be visiting relatives there or hunting up spare parts or lumber; near Ribnitz there was not only the Walther Bachmann aircraft factory, there was also a child to be brought home from vacation. Wherever possible he included in his reports details of the Mecklenburg concentration camps, so that, although the Heinkel works would be hit, the bombs would spare the foreign forced-laborers near Krakow, at Rentzow near Rechlin, at Neustadt-Glewe,

Rövershagen, and Reiherhorst near Wöbbelin, and particularly at Comthurey near Alt Strelitz. He had seen the inmates of this latter camp, not far from the station, as they were being herded to work on the estate of a senior SS officer, Oswald Pohl, beaten half to death, human beings shuffling along like starving animals.

*All the Germans knew about it, Gesine.*
*Are you still not keeping score, Cresspahl?*
*No, Gesine. I'm keeping track in my own mind.*

So Cresspahl had managed to save his skin. The airfield command had repeatedly carried out security tests, but Cresspahl's doors at the airfield were kept closed as required by regulations. Once an officer from the Air Force Regional Command had appeared on the scene, an elderly major, and for two days Cresspahl was conscious of being watched. It turned out that the Major had simply heard the story of Lisbeth, from the von der Deckens. Counterespionage had infiltrated men at the airfield who gave out that they had been transferred; they asked around, invited confidences by making derogatory remarks about the SS, and they had invariably been obliged to give him up as a harmless old gaffer who had gone a bit soft in the head, his wits affected by a tragedy with his wife.

*Maybe I had, Gesine.*
*Yes. No more than I had.*

Once again people in Jerichow were saying that Cresspahl sure knew how to look after himself. After the very young and the old had been mobilized into the Volkssturm, a kind of home guard, Cresspahl wore the uniform of an Air Force sergeant major with a regular pay book in his pocket. On the airfield the war would quietly come to an end, and once again he was one of those who has to come through it without shooting or being shot.

Jerichow North had no more fuel and carried out basic training only, a new bunch every three months. The airfield was silent now.

At the end of January a collection was taken up in Jerichow for Army and Volkssturm, articles such as underwear and clothing "of all kinds," rucksacks, spades, sunglasses, yet this time the Hitler Youth boys returned to Party headquarters with almost empty handcarts. The donations included boots and shoes that were not worth repairing. Some had given a ragged horse blanket so Friedrich Jansen would not come looking for it. Käthe Klupsch had donated her father's uniform belt from World War I, for Käthe Klupsch was superstitious and believed that *one* person's good will might serve where others had given up. Cresspahl had stopped giving.

By the end of January the front was near Breslau. In Jerichow an air-landing alarm was announced: one long siren wail lasting five minutes, or the ringing of church bells.

*You certainly knew how to wait, Cresspahl.*

*I'd given up waiting by then, Gesine. There was nothing left, you see, only you. For a person like me there was no more to expect.*

### April 8, 1968   Monday

Yesterday the family of Martin Luther King was photographed beside the open coffin: Yolanda, Bernice, Martin Luther III, Dexter, and their mother. Their father's head is lying strangely low. The youngest daughter, Bernice, whose chin hardly reaches the edge of the coffin, tries to look across it. The other children know they have to look at the body. But they are not used to the vertical angle.

The Attorney General has declared the murder to be a Federal crime. The reason for this exception is that Federal agents were assigned to help in the investigation under a Federal law making it a crime to violate a person's civil rights, in this instance to deprive Dr. King of his life.

In our area, west of Broadway at 96th Street, a clothing store next to Charlie's "Good Eats" has today been broken into and looted for the second time. The boarded-up window bears plaintive handwritten signs. Some passersby stop to read them and sign the proffered petitions. They are watched by Negroes standing around in waiting attitudes.

On one sign the store owner has written the question: When is this going to stop? Someone else has written, in red, the words: When we kill you, you'll see. You're soft.

### April 9, 1968   Tuesday

Martin Luther King was buried today.

On the grass in Central Park, families and couples sat around on blankets having picnics in the sunshine.

Schools, banks, stock exchanges closed.

The 4,000 seats facing the orchestra shell in Central Park were packed, many more people stood behind the police barricades. As usual,

Leopold Stokowski's hair fell over his forehead while he conducted. There was a girls' choir in red gowns and the American Symphony Orchestra. As we arrived they were playing excerpts from the *German Requiem*, then came the *St. Matthew Passion*, and finally the "Ode to Joy."

The zoo, the merry-go-round, and the pony ride in Central Park were packed with children intent on making the most of the extra school holiday. The park was at its fullest springtime green, clustered with yellow and pink blossom, and colorful with cyclists, girls with dogs, people out for a stroll. From the transistor radios came news of the progress of the funeral.

At Columbus Circle a hot-dog vendor had run out of sauerkraut, and he kept on apologizing: this was the busiest day he'd had this year. The seats in the subway were almost empty. Perhaps Negro employees had not turned up to work in full force because of the televised proceedings from Atlanta.

Young people, mostly students, stood outside City Hall keeping silent vigil, bareheaded. They had been standing there since ten o'clock and stayed until the clock struck noon.

Now the signs in the closed stores no longer all bore the handwritten words: We mourn Martin Luther King. Meanwhile some indicated, in printed, embossed, neatly inscribed lettering, that the store was not only showing respect to the dead man but doing so in a respectable manner.

People stopping behind us occasionally spoke of Negro threats to stores unwilling to close voluntarily.

One often heard the words: Just like with Kennedy. All the church bells ringing—

Females may have lunch at Wes's bar as long as they do not expect to be served at the bar itself. From our nook we could look comfortably across at Wes. Once he went with outstretched arms toward a girl who was waiting behind the male customers until he noticed her. Welcoming, beaming, he held out his arms, come to my heart, until the girl said: Two bottles of that and that. "Oh well," said Wes, disappointed, his hopes shattered. As he passed her order to her over the men's shoulders, he challenged his male customers to secret grins.

The following drifted across to us from the conversation at the bar:

"How come there are no tow trucks around here today? Things haven't been this normal for a long while."

"They're all in Harlem today. Otherwise things'd get out of hand there."

"*Some*thing good at least."

"Well, Wes, what's the good news?"

"That's right, sir! The country's on fire!"

He hasn't noticed us, and Marie doesn't ask why we have come to this place.

In the afternoon the department stores along Fifth and Lexington opened up again. During the morning the streets had had a holiday air about them, quiet and almost empty; now cars were thrusting their way through, horns blowing, and pedestrians were bumping into each other with their grocery bags.

Shortly before five we found ourselves on Third Avenue outside the window of a television store. The company was advertising its wares by showing all the sets in operation. For a long time the colored picture showed nothing but the coffin in Atlanta, shining in the sun, resting on a mule cart that was stuck fast in the crowd. From time to time the camera would try swinging to the brightly colored U. S. and U. N. flags, over the heads of the mourners, to return optimistically to the cart, yet still the coffin had not moved on. But the sun had gone, and the coffin no longer shone.

Tonight the theaters are to have one minute's silence before their performances begin. Then the shows will start.

"Speak to me, Gesine. Speak to me, will you!"

"Yes."

"If you don't buy us a TV set right now, I'll see that someone gives us one, either D. E., or Mr. Robinson, I don't care who!"

"No. We can rent one."

"At the very least!"

"But what for? King's funeral is over."

"For the next one, Gesine. For the next person they assassinate. For the next one!"

---

### April 10, 1968   Wednesday

---

The murder of Martin Luther King has led to violence in 110 cities. The whole city of Washington has closed down; banks, restaurants, businesses, stores, have not opened. The Chicago jails contain twice as many people as they are built to hold. On the other side of the river, in Newark, fires are still burning. Dr. King has been buried, and the New York *Times* is worried about the future of the American soul: "Nothing of irreplaceable material value has been lost, but . . ."

Opening of the baseball season.

The Communist Party in Czechoslovakia has now filled the Government entirely with people who were not accomplices of the Stalinists. General Pavel, Minister of the Interior, is familiar with his country's prisons from many years spent inside them. Moreover, the Party requires of itself that the State Security organs have the sole function of protecting the country against hostile acts from abroad and may not be used to solve questions of internal policy. It sounds like a textbook.

In March 1945 a forgotten crocus bloomed in Lisbeth's garden. Swarms of bees flew around in the sunshine, cleaning themselves. The tree behind Cresspahl's house was black with starlings. From the marsh the first plovers could be heard.

In March, on a country road in western Pomerania, a truck belonging to the Army Ordnance Department of Stettin was fired upon by low-flying Soviet planes and half burned out. Except for the driver, all the occupants were killed. Cresspahl did not receive the telegram until Hilde Paepcke, with Alexandra and Eberhardt and Christine, had already been buried in a grave which we could not find when we looked for it after the war.

## April 11, 1968   Thursday

It is starting all over again. The questions resemble those raised after the murder of John Kennedy.

Why, shortly after the shooting of King, did the Memphis police order a search for a white Mustang, with the additional statement that the car was equipped with an antenna as if for a citizens-band radio receiver and transmitter?

Who, on April 5 at 6:35 P.M., thirty-four minutes after the assassination, radioed from "police car 160" that he was following a white Mustang driving east in the northern part of the city?

Is there someone in the Memphis police who wanted to divert the Memphis police in order to open up a western escape route for King's killer toward Arkansas or a southern one toward Mississippi?

Why did the police report at 6:36 P.M. that a blue Pontiac had now joined the chase for the supposed getaway car, and at 6:47 that someone in the white Mustang was shooting at the blue Pontiac?

Why were there subsequently no more broadcasts about the three cars? Because headquarters had by this time diverted enough police cars to the wrong direction?

Why did the driver of police car 160, Lieutenant R. W. Bradshaw, say yesterday that he had neither seen nor chased a white Mustang, and today that any further comment would have to come from his superiors?

Would the business of the false radio report ever have got out if a radio-equipment dealer had not been monitoring police radio calls?

How could he have heard it, since his monitor could not have received the report from the spot where police car 160 actually was?

Yet how could the call have come from a private car with a citizens-band radio, since it is impossible with such a radio to transmit to police headquarters as if the message were coming from a police car, unless some fiendishly clever experts had been at work?

Why did the police know of a second man in the killing yet persist for days in claiming, jointly with the Federal Bureau of Investigation, that the assassin had worked alone?

Why has the F. B. I. waited five days before taking up the trail that indicates a murder conspiracy?

If a government commission ever presents an official report on the assassination of Dr. King, it will explain all this away.

In 1965 a new version of the history of Wendisch Burg, to com-memorate the 800th anniversary of its founding, was published by the committee in charge of centenary celebrations from the regional head-quarters of the Socialist Unity Party. According to this version, the preserving of the town from artillery fire and bombardment is attributed to two people, Alfred Wannemaker and Hugo Buschmann, both mem-bers of the then illegal Communist Party and today occupying high positions at the Rostock regional headquarters and an East Berlin min-istry respectively. This book says that during the night of April 29, 1945, these two men, together with a Polish forced-laborer, made their way stealthily through the forest to the south of the town until they came upon the first Soviet troops and were taken to a commanding officer. At that point there is mention of time-consuming, justified suspicion, but A. Wannemaker apparently had with him a city map of Wendisch Burg, and for the benefit of the Soviet comrades he entered on this map the German troop positions, complete with numerical strengths, quantities of vehicles and fuel supplies. The negotiations were interrupted by a skirmish with some scattered German units, and H. Buschmann was obliged to take cover on an office floor in the village school while he telephoned to the Mayor of Wendisch Burg and arranged terms of surrender. The Pole as interpreter, the class-struggle solidarity of the nations, and the Red Army, all marched into Wendisch Burg along Old Street, between its undamaged timbered gables.

Cresspahl would begin his story with a memory: You know what he's like, as if his listeners were able, as he was, to summon an instant visual memory of Martin Niebuhr, of a stooping figure with long arms, wearing blue mechanic's overalls, who applies his strength without haste, is slow in speech as in decisions, even a bit somnolent, who suddenly "wakes up" and acts not only prudently but also swiftly, if need be cunningly and deceitfully, and, as it turned out, correctly.

What had awakened him had been the notion of an SS Storm Troop leader to blow up the lock on the River Havel at Wendisch Burg and use all the water dammed above the lock to sweep away the Soviet units to the south. To begin with (spoken scarcely with indignation but quite at ease, in terms of his own legal position): To begin with, this was Martin Niebuhr's lock. His sole superiors were the Department of Waterways and possibly Berlin, but in Berlin the front ran along by the Halle Gate and Alexander Square. The SS plan violated instructions, it was downright totally illegal, and Niebuhr the civil servant was not of a mind to support an action in defiance of official regulations by means of tolerance and connivance. He had worked on the damming of the water since he was a boy, whether stacking fagots or learning the job of lock-keeper, and it went against his ingrained nature to flood the Strelitz countryside, his own work, with the River Havel. Incidentally, the explosion would also scatter the maintenance buildings and his house all over the map, and he was well aware that the Department of Waterways would never give him anything but this Wendisch Burg lock, and not even that if it should ever be rebuilt. It was Cresspahl who explained Martin Niebuhr's thoughts and motives to us; Neibuhr's own comment was brief and final: Can't be done.

He supposed that with this official reply the matter would end there; fortunately for him, he was confronted not by the SS but by two engineers, sent by the SS and not all that happy about their assignment, the SS having comfortably dug itself in outside the south gate of Wendisch Burg and the two sappers being off on their own in an area already completely cleared of German troops and, moreover, half a mile or so closer to the enemy. One of them is reported to be an architect in Hamburg today, so that possibly he had some knowledge of engineering and the destruction of an entire lock went against the grain for him too. For the other, the SS was not far enough away; he was afraid of a court-martial and being shot, so he went busily to work unpacking the dynamite from the motorcycle sidecar and was evidently determined to make a huge hole in the ground next morning at nine o'clock sharp. (This was on the eve of April 29.)

Gertrud Niebuhr had overheard the time set for the blasting, but first they all proceeded to have supper. Seated at the table with them were two children, a boy of ten with his two-year-old brother. Since Gertrud Niebuhr was in her own home rather than someone else's, she spoke her mind freely about this plan to flood the homes and fields of her neighbors in the villages to the south, and as she reeled off all the names, Martin Niebuhr had time to think over his problem undisturbed. He sacrificed two unopened bottles of schnapps that he had earmarked as down payment on a cow; he left nothing undone. Then he came out with his opinion that the blowing up of the lock, if it had any military function at all, was directed more against the civilian population. He could draw a map for his guests of the Mecklenburg heights

*Call them hills if you like. Even if they're Meecklenburg hills. They're still hills!*

beyond which the Red Army could advance unmolested toward the north, even if the Bolter lock on the River Müritz were blown up too, without having to hasten unduly to occupy a large damp patch south of Wendisch Burg! And a patch it'll be, no more! Many times when I stood on the lock after the war I would look at him to see whether he was capable of shouting, but I found him quietly good-tempered, patient, more of a grandfather than an uncle to his brother's two children. Yet at the time, the Niebuhrs had a young tank soldier hidden in their attic, a deserter, and Karsch says he could hear Martin's voice loud and clear through the ceiling. The older boy, Klaus Niebuhr, secretly carried Karsch's share of the meal up to him, and Karsch realized that there must also be a telephone at the spot the Russians had now reached. No use denying it, Karsch.

At this point Cresspahl would imitate his brother-in-law Niebuhr as if he had actually seen him on the phone. Would place his hand against his ear as if holding the receiver, register astonishment at the absence of a dial tone, hold the receiver out at arm's length like some repulsive object, put it down again. His normal telephone was connected to the post office, but the SS had put that switchboard out of action. Niebuhr had wanted to summon the courage to use a line that could be monitored by the Secret Police; he was more reluctant to use his second phone, linked to the Waterways Department's own system, for a purpose that surely must be called private. But he was in a hurry; he could not rely on the two soldiers remaining much longer in the company of his wife and the brandy without becoming suspicious. The first lock south of Wendisch Burg came on the line with a solemn: What a business! Man, what a business!

"Yeah," said Martin Niebuhr. Also, he was hampered by the cover story he had wanted to use on the open line. "They're right here," said Ewert Ewert. I visited him near Strelitz in 1952, and that's how he told it too. Niebuhr never did have to initiate his high treason on his own, it was a Russian officer who took the receiver from Ewert and demanded information on the situation at Wendisch Burg. Since the officer's German was almost without accent, Niebuhr had to ask him to say something in Russian. "I can't understand you: say something in High German," the Russian said in Russian. Niebuhr still believed it to be an SS trap and felt obliged to ask once again for Ewert. "It's the Russians all right!" Ewert confirmed, and now, after the time-consuming and justified suspicion, the Soviets obtained their picture of the enemy.

The SS had marched into Wendisch Burg on Hitler's birthday and immediately imposed a gift for the occasion on the town. The inhabitants had been forced to dig tank traps in a semicircle around the south gate. The road appeared intact but actually had been mined. The gate looked inviting, open, a tourist attraction, just as the guidebook said; but inside it rails had been laid along which a wall of solid rocks could be shunted. Here, to the left and right of the city wall, the SS had set up machine guns. Inside the town there was only one unit, guarding the high school where the inmates of the shut-down concentration camps were being held after it had become impossible to move them any farther. The guards were to shoot the inmates the moment a German victory in Wendisch Burg was in doubt. Martin Niebuhr confirmed to the man at the other end of the line, in great embarrassment, that these doomed people included Soviet citizens. The SS had forgotten about the harbor; the town lay open to the whole lake. To the north were army units, but they had wanted to move on before the SS assumed command over them. "Thank you for your struggle on behalf of peace," said the voice to Niebuhr, in its strange, deliberate German, making him shake his head as he returned to the front room and his guests. He told them he had been on the phone and that Ewert had said the Russians would be there in half an hour.

They entered Wendisch Burg from the north, while it was still barely dark; on the lake side of the town they met up with the units that had crossed the lake just before midnight, and the only shooting was around the school, but that did not last long. Not until they had liberated the inmates did they turn their attention seriously to the SS at the south gate, and the remnants of the SS drove off hurriedly past the lock and took the first turning to the west. The engineers at Niebuhr's then took off their uniforms, sold him the dynamite and the motorcycle, and made their way on foot through the forest in the direction of the River Müritz, to a village where Martin Niebuhr had friends.

Next day the Red Army formally marched into Wendisch Burg, flags flying, between the undamaged timbered gables of Wendisch Burg. Phones were certainly busy that night.

Cresspahl would round off his story with a motto carved into a beam of a house on Wendisch Burg's Old Street, three doors down from the post office, and it may be there to this day: ONLY / A FOOL TRIES TO / PLEASE THEM ALL.

*I don't want people to talk about me, Gesine. If only Cresspahl had kept his mouth shut.*
*Isn't it the truth, Uncle Niebuhr?*
*The truth. The truth. Bullshit.*

---

### April 12, 1968   Good Friday

But the bank is open.

And De Rosny's friends in the Treasury Department seem to be less dependable than he would like. The Government refuses to initiate any negotiations regarding the return of the Czechoslovak 20 million dollars in gold and insists on awaiting an offer from Prague. One reason given: So as not to compromise Mr. Dubček in his reforms.

"How quick your people are to learn," Mr. Shuldiner said last night on the telephone. A leading figure in the Socialist League of German Students, Rudi Dutschke—although his purpose is "change through force of argument" rather than the violent overthrow of society—was wounded yesterday afternoon in West Berlin by a stranger firing three shots. Mr. Shuldiner was anxious to do Mrs. Cresspahl a kindness, to make sure that the German lady would not be late in hearing the German news. The Germans are quick to learn. That's how it looks from outside. The New York *Times* adds, almost in amazement: Mr. Dutschke had no police protection. They still have that to learn, anyway.

President Johnson has called up 24,500 Reservists for active duty in Vietnam. A few days ago he was still talking about 13,500.

At Easter twenty-nine years ago, Cresspahl sent away a Jewish refugee from Berlin. The man had escaped from a concentration camp, was wearing ordinary clothes again, his white summer coat and green felt hat looked like a disguise, and his manner was so lightly assumed that it seemed about to fall from him any minute, leaving him with nothing but remembered and present fear. Gronberg; his first name has been forgotten. A tobacconist from Schöneberg, in Berlin. He was hoping to find a fisherman to take him to Denmark. Cresspahl kept him in the house as long as he could account for him as a man asking the way, he may also have invited him to stay for a meal; but he did not accompany him to Rande to help persuade a fisherman. After his long journey, the man still had nearly an hour's walk to the coast, and Cresspahl sent him on his way alone. After the war he explained to me that he had not been free, for the sake of this one man, to jeopardize his affairs with the British (against the Germans). I often thought I could understand this. I would so much like to understand Cresspahl in this too.

Tonight the Jews begin their commemoration of the Exodus from Egypt more than 2,000 years ago, and in the Ferwalter home only the china reserved for this annual occasion will be brought out, with the pastries and the wine, symbols of the mortar and stone of the Egyptian pyramids, and Rebecca will put the four questions marking the opening of the celebration, the Ferwalters will drink wine four times: to the deliverance of the Jews from serfdom, from slavery, from dependence on Egypt, and finally to their elevation as the chosen people, the elite, and once again Marie will not be allowed in her friend's home tonight. All Marie feels is curiosity.

The Ferwalters' Passover china comes from Germany. We appealed to Karsch for assistance, and in fact he did manage to get it cheaper, sending it in several packages each of which was below the New York Customs limit. It is a valuable set, with a cobalt-blue border, very high class, but we have never set eyes on it. Except during Passover it lies undisturbed, wrapped in linen and plastic, in the Ferwalter linen closet. It is Rosenthal: the name leads Mrs. Ferwalter to believe that the manufacturer is Jewish.

Louise Papenbrock had a Rosenthal dinner service, a pattern of green fish twisting through reeds, and the Papenbrocks called this set "the Rosenthal dishes" even when the Semigs occasionally came to dinner.

Today our bakery on Broadway has turned Jewish. All bread is unleavened because in the haste of the Exodus the dough had to be taken along in that state, and the usual pastries have been replaced by little cakes made of nuts, raisins, apples, and cinnamon, called by Mrs. Ferwalter macaroons. For Mrs. Ferwalter has followed us into the store, placed herself beside us with pleasure, and embraces us over and over again with her affectionate, somewhat repelled gaze.

What could Dora Semig have meant by declaring herself to be "Jewess that I am"? Had she adopted the Jewish faith while living among the Czechs or the French? Was it possible that Semig abroad had tried to live like the Jews?

Mrs. Ferwalter does not know how salt can be kosher, how at the supermarket these days you can no longer find goods printed simply with the word kosher: some also bear the rabbi's official stamp, "kosher for Passover." Is it because no flour is used in Passover baking? How can salt be kosher? She does not know. She shrugs her fleshy shoulders, swinging her kindly, repelled face from side to side as much as to say, What's the difference? The customer ahead of us put a large package of matzos down beside the cashier, saying to her companion: I'm sick of matzos!

Mrs. Ferwalter drew attention to this unorthodox person by smiling broadly, as if she had suddenly pricked up her ears, as one might raise a forefinger in the classroom to show how something should not be done. Then she paid for her own matzos, a small, frugal package.

On the way down 95th Street it occurred to her that she did know why after all: "They're just out to make money!" she exclaimed. "Everything is business!" she repeated, very satisfied with her role of the older, more experienced woman who is privileged to instruct young Mrs. Cresspahl and her child in the ways of the world. In saying good-by at the corner of West End Avenue, she pressed Marie warmly to her massive hips, like her own child. Then, having bestowed on us some of her festal joy, she went her way, somewhat laboriously on those stout legs that had been ruined by the German SS.

In the subway stations there are ads showing an old Indian with a weather-beaten face, braided black hair beneath a black hat, eyes sparkling with pleasure at being able at that very moment to take a bite of a Jewish product:

> *You don't have to be Jewish*
> *To love Levy's Real Jewish Rye.*

Some people like to draw swastikas on these ads. Not quite accurately, mind you, but this evening I saw one more than this morning.

*April 13, 1968  Saturday, South Ferry Day,*

but from the St. George pier we went by bus across Staten Island and then onto the Verrazano Bridge, high above the open neck of the harbor, raised high up into the blue-white, warm-embracing sky, and through south Brooklyn to Coney Island, where people on the board-walk wearing colored shirts and dresses are stealing a march on summer, as far as the Stillwell Avenue subway station, at the entrance to which, says Marie, there are the best hot dogs in New York, the only ones that are not poisoned, and for an hour we rode back underground, under the East River and right through Manhattan as far as our 96th Street at Broadway, and in the evening were as tired as if we had just come back from vacation. En route Marie wanted to make her mother lose the war.

"So—how did the Russians treat you?" she asked, looking more than a little suspicious, prepared to discount at least half of my un-sensational stories about the Russians because I did not, as she did, regard the Soviets as beyond the pale, or merely as "the others." She has learned her anti-Communism as part of the air she breathes.

"But it was the British who occupied Jerichow, Marie."

"The British, sure. Because Cresspahl had dealings with the Brit-ish, it had to be they who came to him. In your stories everything has to jibe, to fit, no tag ends, not even the tiniest loophole!" she said. It was her last throw. There was still time for me to admit that, although the entry of the British into Jerichow may have made Cresspahl's deal-ings with them more likely, it did not make them true. For the last time she was trying to clear her grandfather of treason.

"It was the British, and Cresspahl didn't care one way or the other, Marie. He was finished with them, don't you see? The job was done. In January 1945 he received instructions from Hamburg to go under-ground and stay there, and to be sure to take no more risks."

"That was decent of them, I must say."

"Decent, yes, and they knew how to hold their tongues too. They never bothered him again, till Ludwig Krahnstöwer's tongue ran away with him, and all because it was his seventieth birthday."

"It can't have been all the same to Cresspahl whether or not he was to have his child grow up with the Russians, Gesine!"

"He made no attempt to cross over with me into Holstein. He had a cousin there, on a farm, he could have put us up. The Marien-gabe command—"

"I wish you'd say: Jerichow North. It's as if you wanted to drag my name into it."

"The command would have gladly issued him a travel order to East Holstein, no questions asked and all properly stamped. But he was quite satisfied with a formal discharge from the German Air Force, along with the rest of the civilian airfield personnel, antedated to mid-April. Kutschenreuther, commandant at Mariengabe, even offered discharge papers to the military personnel, but so few wanted to leave that even on the morning of May 2 the regular routine was still being carried out at the base, complete with flag-raising, drill, and technical instruction."

"How come Jerichow was safer than some other place?"

"It was halfway. On April 29 the British entered Bremen and the Soviets occupied Wendisch Burg. From Jerichow you could wait and see who got to Wismar first. If you went to the west too soon, you merely ran slap into the war. Even so, an old woman on School Street was now getting a lot of business as a fortuneteller. And the town pharmacy was broken into one night because Dr. Berling refused to prescribe lethal pills, not even if it turned out to be the Russians who came. But by then there wasn't a sleeping tablet to be found, the Party brass had grabbed the lot for its own purposes because the Party officials had all had to surrender their firearms to the fighting troops."

"And at the airfield Cresspahl was still making 'dispatch boxes' for a German victory."

"He borrowed a team of horses, removed his machines, and carted them into a brick shed next to the house. I seem to remember that he simply unloaded them, covered them up, locked the door, and that was that. Sat in the sun, his pipe at a comfortable angle between his teeth, and warmed his hands. Waiting."

"He didn't want to abandon his property."

"In the eyes of the law it was my property, Marie."

"You know me, Gesine. You know I'm a sucker for fathers."

"He even forbade me to take the train to school in Gneez. The first time I came home and told him that all we had to do was recite poems, 'Archibald Douglas' and stuff like that, but so the school wouldn't lose face he sent them a certificate from Berling and one from himself, 'my daughter is needed at home.' Those were happy days."

"What a lazy kid you were, Gesine."

"Yes. And I used to sit with 'our' Frenchmen on the milk bench and teach them the forbidden song. In the Army it was a punishable offense to sing it, in Jerichow North you stopped in the middle when you saw your superior coming, but Cresspahl stood there quite content listening to the clumsy attempts of Maurice and Albert. Deutsch eine swere Sprack."

"Sing it for me."

*"Everything will pass,*
*Nothing's going to stay,*
*Hitler's turn in March,*
*The Nazis' turn in May—"*

"It's true, you can't sing. Sorry."

"Here comes the 6th Airborne Division of the British."

"Great. All those white parachutes in a sky like this one, descending on Jerichow North airfield."

"The 6th Airborne Division came through Gneez on May 2 and went off quickly in the direction of Wismar. All they sent to Jerichow were a few men in trucks."

"Not even tanks?"

"In Lübeck the 11th Tank Division was entering the city. Why go to Jerichow?"

"You *never* make the war exciting, Gesine!"

"For your benefit?"

"Well. Yes."

"They let Kutschenreuther surrender the airfield to them and ordered him to carry on with the administration. They fired Tamms as mayor and ordered him to carry on in a provisional capacity. Then they proceeded to look for a new mayor."

"And Cresspahl showed them the halfpenny with the year 1940 on it."

"It wasn't like it is in the movies. They first thought of Kliefoth, but Kliefoth felt it necessary to present himself in full uniform, hung with all his decorations and badges of honor. So Papenbrock was next in line. Some officers had billeted themselves at his house, and Papenbrock slipped back into the old days, tried to wangle something, give away something, get back something. They had a look at the old gaffer's son-in-law, and since here was a man who could talk their language they made him mayor, with Tamms as deputy."

"Gesine."

"Well, if you insist. The first week in June the security officers of the Second Army followed in the wake of the fighting troops and checked out the mayors. They had Cresspahl on their list. And it was for those people that Cresspahl fetched a piece of wood that had once been a level, unscrewed the brass in the middle, and showed them the coin."

"I can't picture that without an embrace. Or without fine words."

"Marie, they were officers. Career officers. Cresspahl had got along fine with Kutschenreuther by being on time and acting dumb, but after all Kutschenreuther was a Reserve officer, a shoe manufacturer from Osnabrück, hard-working and circumspect, no doubt, a little man who gave orders as if he didn't really think they would be obeyed. The men who went to see Cresspahl were a different breed altogether, the kind who can think of themselves only as being apart from the rest of society, single-minded about their work as if it were something sacred, more introverted in a way. And they carried their swagger sticks tucked between elbow and lower ribs, just the way I had seen it in photographs."

"Gesine, what did they say?"

"Thank you for taking the trouble to see us. We apologize for taking up your time."

"And Cresspahl?"

"That it was to remain a secret. They took that as a faux pas, as if he were doubting their professional honor. Nodded to him and drove out of the yard. They had walked past the refugees in the house without seeing them."

"Was Jakob already there?"

"Yes."

"Not now, Gesine."

"Whenever you like."

"And there's really nothing thrilling to tell me about the British? Shots in the night? Attempts to blow up Jerichow town hall? Something exciting?"

### April 15, 1968   Monday

5:20 P.M.

Two Negroes are standing astride the open space between two cars on the West Side subway, singing in howling plaintive voices faintly reminiscent of a religious service. The Negroes inside the car are solemn, hiding their expressions in fatigue, suffering from the damp air that has crept into the tunnel. (Thin clouds of rain had been hanging around Grand Central.) By glancing at the singing Negroes a white man is trying to persuade other people to grin, in vain. Not one of the passengers in the rushing, swaying car could care less about the danger to the two misplaced Negroes. If the subway police take them off the train before the other passengers reach their own stations, there is bound to be a delay. We don't want that, we want to get home, we're on our way from work, clickety clack! The men are singing, they want to put some life into somebody.

## April 16, 1968   Tuesday

The New York *Times* is lenient in its comments on the restless students in West Germany, intent on being fair, an old lady who believes she understands young people. Her true concern, however, is that the East German Communists might exploit the unrest for their own purposes, and in no time at all its opinion has turned into a message to the Soviet Union: would they kindly refrain from encouraging Mr. Ulbricht?

The Soviet Union had long since installed its Ulbricht group in Friedrichsfelde, near Berlin, even before the capitulation of the German forces; but Jerichow felt safe with the British.

The British in Jerichow wished to show that they demanded respect for their mayor, and each morning they sent him a jeep with a driver to take him to work and from one end of the insignificant little town to the other. They placed a Union Jack on his town hall and planted a sentry outside his office. They gave him their assistance and transformed his official proclamations into reality:

The following sentences were imposed by the military court: for stealing 30 kilos of potatoes, one year in jail, 15 kilos, 6 months; for using a motorcycle without a permit from the military government, 9 months; for breaking curfew, 3 months;

but for spitting at Cresspahl a person got 9 months in jail for insulting a representative of the British Crown and had to serve his sentence in the cellar beneath Cresspahl's office. And Cresspahl was the only German in Jerichow who was allowed to use electricity for more than a radio. The counterespionage officers who had come to check out Cresspahl had been forced to decide to take Edward Tamms off to a prisoner-of-war camp, despite Cresspahl's pleas; now the untrained Mayor often sat up until all hours in the town hall and, with the help of Leslie Danzmann at the typewriter, put together his proclamations, word by word, by electric light.

Thus Jerichow gradually came to look quite respectable. When Karsch managed to sneak through to Jerichow from the Soviet-occupied territories, the town seemed to him nothing short of opulent. True, the store windows were empty, and the tradesmen had hung signs on their doors to say that continued knocking was useless, and even Karsch's little bottle of kerosene from Wendisch Burg yielded him a positive fortune in cigarettes; but in Jerichow there were no line-ups at the town hall, no refugee was forced to spend the night in an open field, and any army straggler was picked up at the very entrance to the town and taken to the camp at Jerichow North, investigated, fed (officers from the rank of major upward were still fed according to Air Force Commissariat Regulations, Para. I, the administration still being in Kutschenreuther's hands), and sent off after a few days in a westerly direction, even if he wanted to remain in Jerichow. There under the white summer sky the town lay small and reassured, as in peacetime. On June 15 Montgomery lifted some of the orders he had issued in March; now British soldiers were allowed to talk to German children and play with them. Every evening at nine the town obediently became silent and dark; by this time even the children had become familiar with hunger. The untidiest house was Cresspahl's.

He had given over half the house to accommodate refugees from Pomerania and later from East Prussia; he had no time to keep that part tidy. In the house two children were ill with typhoid; he relied on Mrs. Abs to keep them alive and perhaps cure them with the soups she made from boiled husks. It was the face of Jakob's mother that I saw above me that summer, gaunt, dry, narrow-eyed; despairing when we were too weak to eat.

"And Jakob?" says Marie.

"Jakob wasn't staying in the house. He had taken the Abs horses and was working at a village by the sea for a share of the harvest. He didn't often come to Jerichow."

"Start from the beginning, Gesine."

"When the refugees' carts had been unloaded, Jakob took all the horses to ride out into the marshland. Cresspahl had told him where to find safe water holes for the horses. He was five years older than me. One of the grownups. He had a grownup's face, reserved, severe, stubborn. There was a bandage around his neck, underneath was a wound he had got in an air attack. I wanted him to like me and pretended to know all about horses. After they'd been in the water the horses got quite frisky, and Jakob asked if I could canter. Again I said yes. He had given me a bay, a lively young creature, and I didn't have to make him canter. He began to leap forward when he saw his companions leap forward. And to the animal's great surprise I flew headfirst over his head and landed at his feet. The horse had stopped with such force that from down there it looked as if he were going to tip forward. Looked at me reproachfully. After that I tried to avoid Jakob. Not that he wasn't concerned as he picked me up and sat me back on the horse after trying to reassure me, but he was so silent as he gazed straight ahead that I felt he might be laughing inside."

"And then?"

"Then I kept out of his sight. The typhoid had made my hair fall out and left me with rheumatism in my shoulder and knee so that I hung all askew in my bones. I didn't want him to see me like that."

"And when he did see you?"

"He said: 'It'll come back, just wait a while.' And I knew he was promising me new hair."

"Then you didn't even know each other!"

"No."

"And it wasn't the first day of the rest of your life?"

"Would you know?"

"Yes, Gesine. I'm not from Mecklenburg. I would know."

## April 17, 1968   Wednesday

In the final week of June 1945 Cresspahl announced that the Western Allies had now agreed with Stalin on the date by which they would withdraw from their occupied territories of Mecklenburg, Saxony, and Thuringia and would move instead into the western sectors of Berlin. Sunday, July 1, 1945, was the date set for the Soviets to arrive in Jerichow. The British had long since done away with the travel ban in their area; from Mecklenburg roads were open to Holstein, Lübeck, and Hamburg as well as to Lauenburg and Lower Saxony. Shall we go with the British, shall we stay?

You couldn't go by Brüshaver. Brüshaver hadn't found his wife in Rostock; he had already once believed her to be dead, the first time the R. A. F. coventrized Rostock, for concentration camps never received the printed red cards which air-raid survivors could mark with an X to show they were still alive. Brüshaver believed that if he was going to meet up with his wife anywhere, it would be in Jerichow; after walking for three days he arrived in the town, emaciated and covered with dust, found the parsonage evacuated by Wallschläger, and his wife mopping the floors. After that Brüshaver thought no more about fleeing from the Russians and turned all his attention to his sermon.

The old Papenbrocks' decision seemed obvious. Old Mr. Papenbrock's business had also made money out of supplying the Air Force, they would take that away from him. And the bakery. And his house full of refugees, he would never get them out. It was extraordinary that the old man refused to budge. It was true, of course, that he had missed the exodus of the local aristocratic families, and now he couldn't get hold of a single horse and cart for his belongings; could it be that Albert was too embarrassed to leave his home on foot? Was it possible that in his all-embracing wisdom Albert had neglected to stash land and money away in the British Zone? Papenbrock no longer walked erect when he went out, his shoulders were bowed, and he had let his hair straggle, unkempt, below the bald pate that now looked sick rather than handsome. If Papenbrock stayed it was his first blunder.

Many people thought that a certain person would turn up: Dr. Arthur Semig, veterinarian.

People were saying that it was an outrage, a breach of trust, for the British to deliver Jerichow up to the Russians! The Mecklenburg soul felt it had acquired a right to be taken care of as long as the British were there.

On the morning of July 1, the first Soviet patrols arrived in Jerichow, in two heavy American trucks. They drove straight through the town and out the other side. At the airfield they found only a few remaining British troops. Any aircraft that had still been intact had been fueled up by the British and flown off to their own zone; what was there were the empty buildings and the runway that Kutschenreuther was supposed to have blown up. The British had taken along every last one of their prisoners. Among them had been a lieutenant general who had told Papenbrock that without the Soviets' technical arms assistance and the Lipezk pilot-training center of the twenties, the Greater German Air Force could never have become what it finally did become. Apparently the officer relied on this to help him with the Russians. But in the end he had himself moved to the west with the others after all.

Now there was a breathing space until next morning.

Pahl the tailor had lost all his relatives in the fires of Hamburg. He was reluctant to move to an area where he would be among strangers and dependent on the kind of assistance that he had refused to homeless refugees. He went off with his family to the marshland, where they all drowned themselves in the bog. Others tried to do the same in the Baltic.

Dr. Berling swallowed some of the tablets he had refused to prescribe for his patients. In Dr. Berling's care the P. O. W.s and forced-laborers had been treated almost as human beings, certified sick when necessary; in Gneez there had been doctors who held a pencil instead of a stethoscope to the chests of sick men and women and said: A-1— get going! Dr. Berling had no reason to fear Soviet retaliation, and he committed suicide, that hulking, morose, black divvel.

Nothing was heard of Robert Papenbrock except that the Soviets would kill him if they could lay hands on him. Horst's wife was said to have been taken prisoner near Danzig while driving an army truck. The Böttchers had heard that their son was in a camp in southern Russia; they had received eight anonymous letters when his name was read out over the Moscow radio. Methfessel the butcher, who a few weeks earlier had succumbed to melancholia in a concentration camp, had been taken by the Nazis to a clinic where, in accordance with the Führer's orders, he was given a lethal injection as being a worthless life. Friedrich Jansen had slipped away to somewhere near Lauenburg, where his Mecklenburg activites were not known; during an identity check the authorities discovered the pistol he carried on him for emergencies, and the British sentenced him to death for possessing a weapon and shot him in Lübeck without knowing who he was.

From Alexander Paepcke there had been a letter brought to Jerichow by a straggler, written in Kiev and dated early June. In it Alexander promised his niece Gesine Cresspahl a share in the Althagen house if he should inherit it. In September 1944 he had reopened the letter and urged Cresspahl to persuade Hilde to move with the children from the east bank of the Oder to the west bank, if possible back to Mecklenburg. Alexander asked Cresspahl to take in his family if he should be killed at the front. Around the bloodstains on the letter a Frenchman had written that the owner had died on September 29, 1944, but not where he was buried.

Maurice and Albert went with the British to Lübeck. (There had been a third one too, whose name has been forgotten. A country boy from around Clermont-Ferrand, who had kept himself apart from the two urban types, as well as the Germans.) They did not say good-by to the Cresspahl child, and she was disappointed to find different people in the room. The two men had taught her how to say good morning and good afternoon in their language. They had sung songs together. The child had felt there was no enmity there, not with her.

During the night of July 1, a lot of digging went on in the yards and gardens of Jerichow. Papenbrock brought the family silver to Cresspahl, who had to reopen the part of the cellar that he had already walled up.

"Did Cresspahl stay because of Lisbeth's grave?"

"He didn't want to set out on the road with two kids who had typhoid."

"Wasn't he scared of the Russians?"

"Why should he be, Marie?"

"Gesine, he left you with the Russians!"

"It was good training, I wouldn't have wanted to miss it. And after eight years I was free to leave."

The walnut trees outside Cresspahl's house were still there. That kind of wood is used for making gunstocks.

Hanna Ohlerich still did not know why she had been sent away from home. Her parents had hanged themselves in Wendisch Burg as soon as she was out of the house. Karsch could not bring himself to tell her when he saw her ill and feverish.

On the morning of July 2 the Soviet occupation forces entered Jerichow along the Gneez road, the men in low, rattling horse carts, the officers in American jeeps. The town command, the Kommandatura, was set up in the brickyard villa across from Cresspahl's house. There they hoisted the fourth flag of the century. That one stayed.

That evening the green board fence around the Kommandatura was almost complete.

That evening Cresspahl was driven there from the town hall. The commandant wanted to see how his mayor lived. He saw the refugees' cramped quarters in Cresspahl's house and that the Mayor slept in the same room that was his office. He offered to have the house cleared immediately of all outsiders, and he acquiesced reluctantly to Cresspahl's quiet head shake, No. Whenever possible Cresspahl avoided talking to the Russian; there was so much about him to observe.

The Soviet Major was an old man, burly, thickset, sad. He sighed a great deal. Whether he was sitting down or starting to speak, he automatically emitted a heavy rasping sigh. He asked Cresspahl to clear the table. Then he called for three bottles of vodka to be placed on it, dismissed the orderly, seated himself with a sigh, and began the task of getting acquainted with this German. "Iff you plees, Mayor," he said, pointing to the other chair.

Outside it was still light. Because the night was so long in coming, Cresspahl's child came creeping up to the door to have a look at the foreigner, and he called to her patiently to come in, made her stand in front of him.

"You, Fascist," he said, teasingly.

The child had wished him good night, making the little curtsy she had learned from the Papenbrocks, and it confused her to find that for this man that was not enough. Her shoulder hurt as if it were being pounded. She was embarrassed by the kerchief around her head. The fever had made her giddy again, half deaf. Cresspahl watched her as if she had to pass a test and he was not allowed to help. It was an effort to keep her eyes open. The man looked at her as if he were having fun with her. She wanted to go back to bed and lie down, so she obliged him. This gave him a comfortable sense of pleasure, and he repeated the game.

"You, Fascist," he said, in a voice of threat and delight.

"Me, Fascist," said the child.

## April 18, 1968   Thursday

The New York *Times* takes a generous view of John Vliet Lindsay and only casually mentions that he has rejected the proposal for broadcast commercials in the city's subway as an "invasion of privacy" of subway users. Privacy is the fanatically maintained silence of the imprisoned passengers, alone with themselves, driven back into themselves.

Once again it is possible for the Party newspaper in the Czechoslovak Republic to report that district organizations representing 31 per cent of the Party's membership were in favor of an extraordinary Party congress, for the purpose of electing a new central committee, one without the last-surviving Stalinists. According to the statutes, only 30 per cent are required. Then comes the editor of the newspaper *Rudé Právo* after a session of the Presidium and orders the article removed from the second edition as if it were not true. On radio and television, however, it is allowed to stand as the truth.

Last year there were 746 murders in the city of New York, most of them during weekends, fewest on Wednesdays. The most frequent reasons were lovers' quarrels and insulting remarks. It pays to be polite!

If De Rosny so desires, Thursday afternoon is canceled, Professor Kreslil is out one check, and Miss Cresspahl is invited to a baseball game at Shea Stadium. The employee's child is also summoned. De Rosny is about to prove that he has been seen in the company of a lady.

The invitation is a business one, for on Long Island, on the approach to Grand Central Parkway, De Rosny tells his driver that during the game he is to pick up a deity by the name of Rutherford from the Regency Hotel and bring him to the stadium for a conference. Arthur swallows the anticipation he had been indulging in and replies good-humoredly: "Whatever you say, Chief." De Rosny cannot bear a mood of bitterness around him, it might damage his own mood, so he says: "I'll make it up to you by letting you have the box sometime in June, all to yourself, how's that, Arthur?" Arthur knows he must now give a sigh of relief and say, as if dismissing the whole thing: "That'll be just fine."

De Rosny passes the time by playing a game with Marie that

consists of inventing a conversation between a teaching-computer and a student. Apparently he has decided against buying Xerox and is now making friends with computers. As the car drives up to the huge triple-tiered bowl of the stadium, from which one eighth has been chopped out, De Rosny ends their game in the role of the computer, speaking in the slow, stilted voice of a machine: "You did re-al good."

And Marie, in the role of the courted young lady, not only in the role of the student, says: "You mean *well*, don't you?" and they are united in their pride at having jointly committed and corrected an error. He has Marie walk immediately behind him, ahead of Gesine.

The ushers give him the royal treatment and for his benefit pull the rags out of their hip pockets to dust off the yellow seats in the box with extra thoroughness. The boxes are labeled with the names of the season ticket holders. Here is the name of De Rosny's only superior, the President of the bank himself, and with casual, carefree gestures De Rosny makes his guests comfortable. Twice they have to change their seats so they will be sure to realize that their whims are being sufficiently catered to and that they are helping to bolster his enjoyment.

The flag is still at half-mast.

In the great seat rings, painted light green at the top, pale blue in the middle, and orange at the bottom, the spectators are in a state of happy excitement, catcalling and tootling. 50,000 people are bent on having a good time.

At last the text of the national anthem is projected onto the advertising screen. Yells of delight when it is over. This anthem ends with a question mark.

De Rosny indulges in explanations: "A ball like that has a speed of ninety-five miles an hour. If you get hit you can't sue, Marie! Read your ticket!"

Most of the players move as if they had wet their pants. Sometimes one of them hurls himself at a catcher like a runaway tank. When a player is injured the music instantly switches to soothing sounds.

"A gentleman's game! Without violence!" cries De Rosny enthusiastically. Maybe it looked different from where he was sitting.

Every two minutes airplanes rise from La Guardia, their engines roaring. In the quiet intervals the vendors shout stridently: "Peanuts here!" "Beer here!"

In addition to enjoying the game, De Rosny has the pleasure of being able to explain it to Marie. She knows the rules of baseball, she listens to him with great docile eyes, following his pointing finger. He describes a home run, when the hitter can run around all the bases without stopping. De Rosny describes a circle with one finger, he has also held forth several times on comparisons with the ballet.

What? Don't we know why they've hung a green screen behind the flag? So the catcher won't be dazzled when looking at the pitcher.

Then De Rosny turns himself from the man of the world into a little boy staring intently ahead as he talks about Willie Mays, whom he has been watching for as long as he can remember, and always with a quickening pulse. At nineteen this Willie Mays still went back to Harlem after the game. That self-same large-as-life Willie who, wrapped in an aura of sanctity, is swinging his bat down there on the diamond! Used to play baseball with the kids, with a broomstick. Stickball.

Where the boss lives, people don't know that to radical Negroes Willie Mays is a traitor. He has refused to support a boycott of the Olympic Games by black athletes.

De Rosny has never spoken to Willie in his life, never even seen him close up, yet he speaks of him as of a friend whose sufferings are his own, and he always looks up to him, for De Rosny cannot do in baseball the things for which Willie Mays is famous. According to him, Willie has grown quieter, but also sadder. A word that doesn't exist in the world encompassed by De Rosny's orders, but for the black hero with the baseball bat it does.

After hinting at Willie's marital troubles, De Rosny comes to a decision. It is unprofitable, it will not bring in any money, it is a display of emotion, yet it is to be. In a firm tone of defiance De Rosny promises the distant, bat-wielding, madly running friend: "Someday when he's all through—he'll get a job in our San Francisco branch!"

Tirelessly the airlines belabor the suffering spectators with their symbols, especially TWA and Braniff with its Easter-egg colors. Beside the 727s the lower-flying propeller planes seem antiquated.

In the outfield Willie makes a basket catch, hands to stomach, that's his trademark, explains De Rosny solemnly for Marie's benefit, and she takes note of it with a studious nod. Doesn't she see that De Rosny's soul mate has just made a much higher catch? Is what De Rosny wants the only reality?

Balk! There goes someone trying to throw beyond the boundary line, and he fails. "Only happens once in a blue moon! Today you're getting the works, d'you know that?"

The hitter moves on to the next base, the man on third is home free. Mrs. Cresspahl is not the only one who wishes she were somewhere else. In front of them sit two girls who take it in turns to hold up alternate homemade signs, listlessly.

Something historic is happening. The coach yanks the pitcher, he doesn't trust him with the bases loaded. The new pitcher is solemnly driven onto the field in an open car, they remove the coat from around his shoulders as if he were a gladiator.

At the start of the seventh inning, people rise for their team, De Rosny for the San Francisco Giants, so does Mrs. Cresspahl for San Francisco, and is amazed at herself. At a baseball game with the boss. Around them people remain seated.

"Willie'll get them all home!"

Toward the end of the seventh inning the New York fans rise. There are some 30,000 of them, it is not lonely around them, and De Rosny has to raise his chin somewhat.

Then Arthur arrives with Rutherford, the deity, a white-haired, erect old man with no eye for the diamond, a golfer. The spectators in this stadium do not read the financial section of the New York *Times* and are unaware that a lord in the realm of the dollar, indeed a prince, has come among them. The two men withdraw to an empty box at the rear, paying no further attention to the brilliant grassy expanse. Both put on their glasses and read from little scraps of paper for about twenty minutes. Then De Rosny raises his hand, and Arthur is ordered to drive the illustrious guest to the Los Angeles plane. However, the conversation was satisfactory, for now De Rosny has no wish to wait for the end of the game and is content to listen to it over a cab radio. The business transaction was very profitable, for once again Arthur is promised that he will be able to take his whole family to the bank's private box "sometime during the summer."

"Wasn't it a wonderful afternoon, Mrs. Cresspahl," says De Rosny challengingly.

"It certainly was," says his employee Miss Cresspahl.

*Don't you like the country, Gesine? Afternoons like that in a strange country?*
*That's what you're hoping to hear, I'm sure.*
*If you don't like the country, go and look for another.*

---

## April 19, 1968   Friday

---

"The New York Mets gave Willie Mays another chance with the bases loaded," says the New York *Times*, "and that was a mistake." That's for sure. 5–3. That was a mistake.

Much obliged, Auntie Times.

No nostalgia.

There are awakenings with terror along the nerves, reluctant to recognize the dense gray light beyond the windowpanes, searching for other windows; and even the April colors no longer seem right, the morning blue of the Palisades, the cloud-dimmed river, the hard trunks of the plane trees in the pallid green of the park. Then the hundredfold-familiar sight engulfs expectation.

There are mornings when the seething glitter of the sun on the East River disappears in the shadow of the Venetian blinds, and Long Island becomes a different island. The dirty gray haze transforms the crush of buildings in Queens into a gently vibrating landscape, wooded meadows and views of a church spire as I once saw it from the sea while the boat was tacking, a spire like a bishop's miter obscured by folds of the earth and suddenly only a stone's throw beyond the High Cliff.

That does not call me back. I have lived in Jerichow, Mecklenburg, Saxony, Frankfurt, Düsseldorf, Berlin. There it is the places that have remained, not the dead, Cresspahl Jakob, Marie Abs. Those whom I was.

Nine more hours, one more day facing the humming clacking machine, a sloping wedge of light from outside that wraps the voices of the others and the mechanical sounds and my own voice in a gray twilight that by noon will have many layers.

Then Marie will be standing on Broadway at 108th Street, beside the car she has chosen for the journey "to America." She has insisted on one thing: it must not be a Mustang.

Then we will greet each other like strangers, and she will scan my face for traces of my work, follow me with her eyes, discreetly, secretly gay, concerned. As if she could not let her charge out of her sight.

That's how she describes it: I'm keeping a watch on you!

"I'm guarding you": the words Cresspahl sometimes used when asked what he was doing. I remained a child for a long time; Jakob used to say so too.

## April 20, 1968   Saturday

The water is black.

Above the lake the low sky is shut, morning darkness of the pines encloses it, rising from the muddy bottom an inkiness suffuses the water. The swimmers' hands circle forward as if against a heavy tincture, and coming out into the air they look surprisingly clean. On all sides the shores are near, in the half-light an observer would have thought he saw two ducks in the middle of the lake, one dark-feathered, one light. But it is too early for humans. Silence makes the lake seem somber. Fish, birds of water and land, do not care to inhabit the dredged hollow, the sickly trees, the chemically treated countryside that has been adapted for people who pay. When you let yourself sink two feet below the unmoving surface, you have lost the light and find instead a greenish blackness.

"How many lakes does this makes for you, Gesine?" asks the child, asks Marie, asks the alien fish popping up from a long underwater swim. "How many lakes have you made in your life?"

Two voices over the water, in the close-hung silence, one an almost eleven-year-old soprano, rough at the edges, the other a contralto of thirty-five, smoothly rounded, not carrying far. The child won't allow the Baltic.

It was in the Baltic that the child I was first swam, the Fischland behind me and in Lübeck Bay, on the maritime border of Mecklenburg, once a province of the German Reich, now a coastal region of the German socialist state. Swam with children now dead, with sailors of the conquered German Navy who spoke of the mighty Baltic as the flooded meadow among the oceans. But in the geography books of America it is called the Baltic Sea, and Marie won't count that as a lake. This is an American child.

How many lakes has her mother swum in, taken in, made; what is the record?

The local people, starved for children who are unobtrusive, considerate, well-mannered, call her a European child. Politely Marie had stood in the early-morning haze at the edge of the lake; patiently, into the bone-cold water, she followed the mother who has been her partner through thick and thin all her life and whom she cannot yet do without. And, as taught by the nuns in schools, she shows good manners, carrying on a conversation as they swim. Much as she would prefer to spend her time underwater, she keeps her head above it, trying to register interest in her determined, water-smoothed face.

How many lakes in thirty-five years?

Swimming in the Gneez municipal lake, Physical Education at Fritz Reuter High School after the war, and the child Gesine Cresspahl was to be trained for competition swimming at the public beach on the Gneez side. Gneez municipal lake, again in a group, on the south side, the kids' swimming hole, Grades 10, 11, and 12. Swimming at home in the military swimming pool that had been overlooked by both the German Air Force and the Red Army, with Lise Wollenberg, Inge

Heitmann, and the boy from the Jerichow pharmacy. Never in Dassow Lake, only about seven miles from my father's back door and out of reach, the lake shore being the line of demarcation, the state boundary; the water: British Occupation Zone, the Federal Republic of Germany, "the West." With Pius Pagenkopf in Cramon Lake, an hour's bike ride from the town where I went to school, between Drieberg and Cramon, in 1951. Alone, between Jerichow in the northwest and Wendisch Burg in the southeast of Mecklenburg; in Schwerin Lake as far as Lieps Island, in Goldberg Lake, in Plau Lake, in the River Müritz. With Klaus Niebuhr, Günter Niebuhr, Ingrid Babendererde, Eva Mau, in all seven lakes around Wendisch Burg, right up to 1952. In Leipzig, in Halle: lifesaving courses in indoor pools as late as May 1953. The last time in Gneez municipal lake: at the end of May 1953, and Jakob lifted up my pierced foot as if it were a foal's, and the gesture sent a shiver through my body with no pain at all.

Never with Jakob. Jakob was still working in Cresspahl's house, in the villages, when we used to hurry out from Jerichow in the evening to do six laps in the "Mili," the military pool, stubbornly called the "Mili" (the Mariengabe military airfield would now never be known as anything but Jerichow North). Jakob left town to take up a job with the railway, a picture was taken of him at the Pfaffenteich Ferry, in Schwerin (with Sabine Beedejahn, Protestant, age twenty-four, married). Jakob used to go fishing with friends in the lakes, bringing back bucketfuls of live crab from the Mecklenburg lakes, and I did not know those lakes, and he went without me, with fishermen, with girls, with fellows from work, and I hardly knew Jakob.

After leaving the East German authorities behind me: with Anita almost every day for ten days in Wannsee in West Berlin, where the frontier was farthest away. In West Germany: public swimming pools in Frankfurt, Düsseldorf, Krefeld, Düren. In Geneva. In the U. S.: Lake Winnipesaukee, Lake Chippewa, Lake Travis, Lake Hopatcong. Once again with Anita, in France, in the Vosges Mountains.

"Eighteen allowed, four disallowed, one doubtful, and a gold star for Lake Travis in Texas!" says Marie.

But the boat dock is now only a quarter of a mile away, and with that she lays her head sideways in the water, so sure is she of her challenge to a race being understood, and after a long shallow plunge she moves off in a swift crawl, with sharp precise strokes and scarcely a sound. She wants to get back to the borrowed house, that costly affair made all of glass and mahogany beams, where there is a phone and news on TV and possibly, from the village store, the New York *Times*, and soon, tomorrow afternoon, they will be on their way home, to

Manhattan in New York, Riverside Drive and Broadway, corner of 96th Street.

Patton Lake this one is called, named in glorious memory of a general of this country. Until 1944 heavy tanks were practicing here for the final onslaught on Germany, until the thick old tree trunks were stumps and the ground so churned up by caterpillar treads that the area had to be made into an artificial lake, homeless trees and substantial returns from a summer colony. From here came the Sherman tanks that also quartered market squares in Mecklenburg.

"And you swam all the way here from Mecklenburg!"

Marie, an easy winner, is already standing on the dock, hand on heart, saluting the flag hoisted in stadiums in honor of the victor, then greeting the loser as she comes swimming up at her feet. She utters the English words with pleasure, because it is permitted to feign mockery, and with delight, because here at last is a chance to substitute the language of her own country for that awkward German.

Vacation in the country. Somewhere north of New York, but no more than three hours' drive from the city and at the other end of a telephone line with which the bank can haul back its employee Gesine Cresspahl whenever it likes from her two-day break.

"And so I swam all the way here from Mecklenburg."
"And so you made the nineteenth lake in your life!" says Marie.

An afternoon of much heavy black Patton water.

### April 21, 1968   Sunday

Vacation in the country; this time something of a chore for Marie.

"You need your New York *Times*," she said as soon as we were out of the water, thus pre-empting for herself the right to the mile's walk to the general store, to some time by herself in the woods. With this house in the country we had acquired not only a houseful of Finnish furniture but also a mechanized home, amply equipped; at noon Marie went off again, to get two lemons which the meal could have done without. It would still be a long while before they started for home, yet already she was fixing up the car for the trip, and anyway she still had plenty to do outdoors working on a map of the surrounding countryside, a gift for their hosts. She announced her comings and goings as if making suggestions, she did her fair share of the housework as if voluntarily, she always managed to get away; she wanted to be alone, now and again.

We have been living in each other's pockets for nearly eleven years, and she has had to work at coping with this mutual dependence. In 1957, for the twenty-four-year-old Gesine Cresspahl the child Marie had been a part of herself; Marie had to accept this fact for many years. She did see Jakob's mother, but Mrs. Abs wished to live alone and not to be near us when she died; if there is any memory of a grandmother, Marie never mentions it. Marie had to cope with the supervisors at the child day-care centers in Düsseldorf; but it was up to the only person entitled to care for her whether to hand her over to those strong-minded ladies or to rescue her from them. Cresspahl made one last trip to the Rhine, "to the West," he pushed the child around in her buggy in the Hofgarten, but he wore his black overcoat from 1932 and kept lapsing into Low German dialect with Marie, and she may have been scared of such a grandfather. And Cresspahl went back to Jerichow.

Marie spent her first years among strangers waiting for that one familiar person to return from those incomprehensible absences to her place of work. In the morning she would try to ask whether she must share the day with that unconquerable work or whether the day would be theirs to enjoy together until they fell asleep, and she could not really make herself understood. She was given her birthday breakfast with a second candle and remained silent. Gesine had plans for her child, plans as misguided as they were obstinate. First of all, there was to be no getting around speaking proper German. Marie would not have minded giving this other person that pleasure; for the time being she took to watching her, to showing her something or taking something away from her. As for conversation, she had no wish to embark on that even with caution. For in addition to having to get her tongue around the awkward combinations of German vowels and consonants, she was also required to produce the words in sequences in which there was rarely any choice. And if she was not mistaken, this other person turned her into someone who deliberately refused information on dry sensations in the throat either for fun or from tact or stubbornness: three mimed offers, three possible forms of consent with her own face as the sole means of expression. This, though, was the period that saw the beginning of a secret between them: Marie talked with this other person as she did with no one else, with neither her teachers nor her classmates, who in their own way were learning the profession of being a child; even the wordless understanding between her and the other person was not intelligible to outsiders. And there was no one around to make things easier for her and with whom it would have been worth taking refuge: there was only this one partner, who was both available and tiresome.

There being no father in her life, for a long time the word did not exist for her, and for a long time it was no more than an idea. Moreover, at two and a half she did not understand questions about a mother. She did not have one; she led a life with a person who was called Ine, Sine, Ge-sine, as a protection tolerable, as a companion a bit too smart.

This person did not insist on obedience, her wishes did not become instant law; one could get one's way about when to go to bed, also about where to go on outings, and after one had asked for no lighted candles on a tree, that person could be relied upon to hide a flame bursting from a match. And the other person desired resistance so urgently that the child had to concoct and even remember things that would have been more soothing as feelings or forgettable sights. However, one was no match for that part of the other person called work (friend? foe?). Work required a plane trip to West Berlin, work required living in strange houses among people with an even stranger language; here obedience was not enough, and curiosity helped, since there was no choice without or against the other person. Then the child was reconciled to sojourns abroad by a return in days that could be counted, and went along trustingly to France and onto a ship to America. After a week at sea the other person proved to have been too smart. The journey had been a removal, work—the accomplice or the hostile power—prevented a return to Europe, and the habit of morning separation had turned without warning into a bargain, to be carried out in a primary school on the Hudson in a totally new language. After living two years in New York, Marie could still describe the room she had left behind on the Rhine. For a long time now she had been using German as if it were a first foreign language; yet she would point to rights that had been left behind, to an awareness of injustice, and she had accepted New York as a gift, defending the newly acquired city as a right.

"Life with my mother wasn't easy": this is the kind of sentence Marie may think, though disguised in English, to be kept in reserve for a future in which a listener has yet to be chosen. Her mother had brought along from her Europe ideas the child was supposed to use here. Everyone was equipped, or to be provided, with equal rights. How was Marie supposed to act on that? She could show her mother that she offered her seat on the bus to a black woman as casually as to a pink one, she can go down to Jason in our basement and console him for the long long hours until sundown; but to take the only black girl in class, Francine, under a European wing, what would that lead to with her light-skinned friends? It was necessary to omit some of this in telling her mother about school, and worst of all was her mother's unshakable confidence in a truth that existed only because of a lie and because of precisely that kind of action, performed for Francine's benefit, which Marie would have liked to avoid.

Her mother taught that there was a difference between just and unjust wars. How is a child supposed to switch from the year 1811 (revolt of the Shawnees under Tecumseh) to the American war in Vietnam, since the very first attempt resulted in threatened friendships and almost a rebuke? At home, without committing oneself, it was possible to criticize today's war, perhaps in the hope that her mother would assume her behavior in school to be equally intransigent. But the hope was a vague one, the lie was inherent in answers and in questions and in silence, and it was the lie that her mother was determined to regard as unthinkable. Couldn't she understand that her code, while it had been accepted, was only possible in the other language and not translatable into either thought or action? She herself was not honest, she claimed to favor the socialist cause yet worked in a capitalist country, in a bank! And a child cannot very well suggest a move to a socialist country merely for the sake of consistency, for then the child would lose her whole city of New York along with all her friends and the subway and South Ferry and Mayor Lindsay, so she has to put up with dishonesty, which is not supposed to be. But then, when her mother follows her convictions, unchallenged by her child, and leaves New York in aid of the socialist cause, possibly this summer, the younger Cresspahl will be in the soup, and she has helped to stir it. This is what Marie will one day say about her mother, Gesine Cresspahl (Mrs.): Life with her was not an easy alliance.

A two-day vacation in the country. Variable cloudiness, occasional gleams of sunlight in the torpid water.

Marie has many things to attend to around the school on upper Riverside Drive, around Broadway on Manhattan's Upper West Side; at Patton Lake it was quiet. In town she has to spend only a few hours with her mother; at Patton Lake she had sometimes squatted on the boat dock looking as rootless, as out of place, as if waiting in a desert, and she would have welcomed an army helicopter's landing as a rescue from this continual togetherness, and the consciousness of it.

"No," she said, "not by the Army. By Boston radio." Then she was loyal to her own politeness and referred to self-inflicted boredom.

Every time Marie left the house for a walk she would change her clothes. The other summer homes were scarcely occupied this early in the year. She might meet the young woman from the filling station, or a couple of dogs, and at the store she would be associating with the local farm people. But she changed her slacks and sweater for a proper dress, suitable for going to church, and she pinned her hair back into a neat ponytail and cleaned her shoes for the walk around the lake. The locals must not be able to say that a child from New York does not know how to behave in the country.

And after the first stranger had wished her good morning, she exchanged the time of day with all the subsequent ones, for New York's sake.

She would come back and puzzle over people in New York who meet Mrs. Cresspahl for the first time at a party and after half an hour's conversation promise her keys to a summer home at Patton Lake. (She brought it up casually; nevertheless, it was intended as praise for Mrs. Cresspahl. Her mother must be handled gently; tomorrow morning work begins again.)

Then she had to put up with half an hour in the company of Sergeant Ted Sokorsky, the local policeman, custodian of their hosts' keys. Mr. Sokorsky lowered himself amiably to the boat dock, shyly accepted a beer, and in tactful terms began to discuss the weather. He spoke very softly, and Marie took this for a token of his respect for Mrs. Cresspahl, a lady visitor from New York. He was quite young, and Marie would have very much liked to ask him to drive her around the lake on his clumsy motorbike, but she preferred to offer him an example of the ladylike reserve in which certain mothers train their children. Mr. Sokorsky was not sparing in the use of "madam" for Mrs. Cresspahl, and after locking up the house he managed a bow from the neck; Marie will never see him again, and for years when the conversation turns to the police she will refer to one of them, named Ted Sokorsky, not brawny, more of a lightweight, and the reverence with which he treated my mother, I'd like to demonstrate it to you.

But now the vacation in the country is over, for some time now we have been driving on the freeway over the Palisades, with Manhattan on the other side, and Marie already thinks she can see the spot among the finely sculpted apartment towers where the moist mauve reflection of the evening sun strikes five windows, the ones behind which she will switch on the lights, all at the same time.

"If that's all right with you, of course, Gesine. By your gracious permission."

## April 22, 1968 Monday

In the morning a thick haze hung over the Hudson, astonishingly light, and like a breakfast guest it occasionally lifted an eyelid over a blindly blinking white eye.

But a person who still does not understand New York's weather lands up in a gentle shower of rain on the rise from 96th Street to Broadway, she was already running down from the newsstand into the subway, like many others she trotted along Lexington Avenue holding the folded New York *Times* like a roof over her head.

From under the edge she squinted up to the traffic light on 45th, saw on the inside of the roof the report of the war over the weekend: 31 Vietcong dead in fighting northwest of Saigon on Saturday, yesterday morning a further 15 north of Saigon . . . stepped forward with the crowd, hemmed in by the elbows of strangers. Not until noon did she gather from the dried-out newspaper that the New York *Times* chooses to see the fighting for the foreign capital not as American defense but as an offensive.

The paper's forecast for today: sunny and mild. Not these sharp showers.

Sunny weather prolonged by steady heat: Marie was not happy about it as the sole memory of that first summer of Jerichow's New Era, yet it is almost ninety-one seasons ago and more than 3,500 miles away. Laziness in telling the story is what she called it. Squatting in front of the vacation fireplace, building a fire until by careful probing she found the piece of kindling that would light that other fire. "I understand the Russians didn't play fair as victors," she said.

*Tell her, Gesine.*
*I was just a child then. Twelve years old. What can I know about it?*
*What you've heard from us. What you've seen.*
*She will make wrong use of it.*
*She is a child, Gesine.*
*It's easy for the dead to talk. Were you frank with me?*
*Improve on what we did.*
*And so she will know where she is going with me, and to whom.*
*And for our sake, Gesine. Tell her.*

Jerichow, all of western Mecklenburg, was still occupied by British troops, blocked off by armed lines, yet the Soviets had long since arrived, invisible yet present in conversation as in suppressed fears: as rumor. They were no longer the indistinct subhumans with which we had been indoctrinated by German Reich propaganda since 1941; they were not even the photographs of East Prussian villages where German units had been allowed to counterattack and snap pictures of abused female corpses, of male bodies crucified to barn doors; the Reich Government had invented too many stories and tried to substantiate them with faked pictures.

In my father's house there was a sick child, Hanna Ohlerich from Wendisch Burg, whose parents, while skeptical of most Reich propaganda, had believed this, and had hanged themselves: in advance, before seeing the foreigners from the East with their own eyes, hearing them with their own ears, said the survivors, even people in Jerichow, secure under British administration. Then, early in May, the rumors came no longer from the collapsed Reich Government but from friends and relatives in other parts of Mecklenburg under Soviet occupation, and they amounted almost to reports. In Waren an anti-Nazi, known to the last as the Red pharmacist, had celebrated all one night with his liberators from the Soviet Union until they raped all the women in the house anyway and the family committed suicide with the poisonous medicines that had not been saved for this purpose at all; the report was substantiated by a name, a market square, a business on the ground floor of a gabled building. In Malchin, Güstrow, Rostock, the subjects of the rumors had tried to wash potatoes in toilet bowls by pulling the chain and had proceeded to threaten the unsuspecting Germans with firearms for committing flush sabotage. From Wismar came the report that one night three Soviet soldiers had hauled a grandfather clock through the British lines to a clockmaker for him to convert into thirteen wrist watches, these having become scarce in the Soviet area of Mecklenburg due to the foreigners' habit of not winding wall clocks and throwing them into the bushes or the water as broken. A number of country seats were burned down because the spectral looters did not believe in electric light even when it was still available and would light paper spills to aid them in their searches. For a microscope from the pathology department of a university they accepted two bottles of liqueur, they shot at pigeons with rifle ammunition, and they were said to be incapable of singing their melancholy songs. All this, plus their infatuation with children, was incredible and well known in Jerichow when the British withdrew, and once again local people and refugees in the town drowned, hanged, and poisoned themselves, but not all out of fear of the new occupation: Pahl had not known where to go to now, and for Dr. Berling all his studies had been of no avail against melancholy. The rest—on July 3 an estimated 3,500 persons—stayed on in Jerichow.

The people in Jerichow, whether residents or refugees, stayed on for the sake of a roof over their heads, whether their own or borrowed. In any case, from July 2 on, the British allowed no one with household goods to cross the Trave Canal, their new boundary; now a person would have had to swim across without baggage. Wulff stayed on not only for the sake of his combined inn-keeping and grocery business; he had also been a member of a banned party (the Social Democrats) as well as unfit for military service, and without precisely expecting any reward he was probably counting on a fair deal in terms of business. ("Curious, that's what he was," said Marie.) As for Papenbrock, by this time it was fairly obvious what was keeping him. My father stayed because the British had made him mayor and he wished to hand over the affairs of his office in good order. And the locals put their faith in the outward appearance of Jerichow.

For what could the foreigners see in this little town so far from the highways, in the midst of a corner of land beside the Baltic, without even a harbor to call its own? From whichever direction they came, all they could see from a distance was a low cluster of insignificant buildings. The spire that looked like a bishop's miter, no matter how high it reached or how densely enclosed it might be by the foliage of 600-year-old trees, was a symbol of past riches, not present wealth. They may have seen the country seats of Mecklenburg, magnificent urbanesque mansions surrounded by parks; no doubt they had marched along streets flanked by the commercial buildings of the inland towns, tokens of imperial times; but in Jerichow they found few buildings more than two stories high. Those that were stuccoed showed great holes in their brickwork, the result of wartime economy, and the beams of the timbered buildings had already had to wait too long for paint or even creosote. And the vehicles of those entitled to claim victory, what did they drive on as they entered town? Not on asphalt, but on a bumpy pavement of large rounded cobblestones, without even a smoothly paved double path for cyclists (which corresponded to the rumor about the victors' lack of skill on bicycles). There remained the brickyard villa, and in that they set up their headquarters. From the town residence of the Von Lassewitzes, now Papenbrock's, they had backed off immediately on finding all the rooms full of refugees (which implied some truth in their alleged fear of epidemics). Lindemann's Lübeck Arms had been used by the British for their club: now the Soviets could put up their own name over it. To the uninformed, the market square may have seemed a little too spacious; certain owners of three-story buildings might well have to face confiscation. Apart from that, to the Soviets the municipality of Jerichow must have seemed a uniformly poverty-stricken area where there was nothing worth looting because there was nothing displayed.

By the Sunday following the entry of the first Soviet troops, by the evening of July 8, only one rumor had become fact. At Otto Quade's Plumbing & Heating, a Red soldier had entered the store and pointed beyond the low partition to a prewar display of a drain. "Draan," the Red Army had said to Bergie Quade. Bergie, who, following all the current advice, was dowdily dressed, grubby of face, and wore a napkin smeared with chicken manure under her skirt, had retorted with typical Quadian presence of mind that she had no intention of "drowning" herself. Not she. But if he would like to know the names of all the local people who had drowned themselves, in the marshes or in the Baltic—? The Red Army had not waited to hear the list and had marched off with a shake of the head that Bergie felt looked like a reproach, she couldn't help it. This was the only unaccompanied soldier seen in Jerichow during that first week. The commandant had had himself and his troops boarded up in the brickyard villa and com-municated with the Germans by way of decrees which he ordered Cresspahl to post outside the town hall. As for the military airfield at Jerichow North, that unfortunate evidence of the town's participation in the war of the others, no Soviet airplane had yet landed there and, although with its barbed-wire enclosure the area would have made a suitable prison camp, the new people did not use it even for that.

Well then, what was the atmosphere like in Jerichow that first week of July 1945?

All those rumors, pretty exaggerated, I'd say (B. Quade).

And if they're not exaggerated, the Russians aren't going to risk anything among people who've had experience of the British occupation (Dr. Kliefoth).

But Ilse Grossjohann did get raped (Frieda Klütz).

They're not interfering with the town administration, they're not using the airfield—that won't last (Mr. and Mrs. Maass).

So I guess the British will be coming back, Papenbrock (Creutz Senior).

The things Cresspahl is doing, and he's not even embarrassed (Käthe Klupsch).

Maybe we'lll be given back to Sweden. It was only 200 years ago, after all (Mrs. Brüshaver).

Papenbrock belongs to the elite, you see. Businesswise, I mean (Else Pienagel).

They must be scared of us. Curfew, indeed! Scared, that's what they are! (Frieda Klütz).

Maybe they're moving around at night (Frieda Klütz).

In wartime such things are called latrine gossip (Alfred Bienmüller; Peter Wulff).

You just wait (Gesine Cresspahl).

---

### April 23, 1968   Tuesday

---

For a moment she was still alone. Yesterday's evening sky, painted over with broad brush strokes, had crept into the last images before waking; the dream hung on in dawning consciousness like a protection. As if for the first time in a long while she had got up again. Was nobody; a field of recollection, recollection in which grew alien grasses, a thundery sky over the Baltic, the smell of grass after rain. A few glances toward the Hudson, and with the light in her eyes the sense of time would move faster, and in it would be herself, Gesine, Mrs. Cresspahl, employee, a four-digit number after the telephone exchange 753, not here, midtown. Not yet.

There were postponements. For a while I was still I Gesine, still I Marie, still we the child and I and the voices from the dream. Gradually the felty sensation of sleep disintegrated into dry powder. Although a bit dazed, she could register pleasure. Marie had tied up her hair in a bunch so tall and tight that for a while it stood upright. The roles separated us. An eleven-year-old pouring tea for the older person. Gesine searching for herself as Mrs. Cresspahl, reflected in the child's appraising glance: my mother, age thirty-five, she does not see the single gray hair among all those dark ones. Disguised for an office, equipped for a day outside the home, now less recognizable. A child hostile to school talking as if looking forward to the paragraphs she has to write, to make it easier for the other person to go out into the world as a workingwoman. Once more Marie's concerned, sleep-softened, un-American face in the closing door. Alone.

With time to drift along, although on appointed routes, proceeding punctually from square to square; yet alone. That was she promising the newsvendor a good morning, she will never bother him beyond that; connected because they are acquainted. She was almost disappointed to find herself once again underground among strangers on the express side of the platform, and relieved to see yesterday's young lovers run down the worn steps at the last moment, inexperienced, unsure of each other, separated in the train as it hurtled off. Still, she extricated the New York *Times* from under her arm; good weather over North Vietnam; 151 bombing missions. That was she letting the crowds beneath Times Square push her so close to the toes of a Transit policeman's shoes that he dodged aside, all but saluting her. On the shuttle train to Grand Central she walked through the swaying doorways between the cars, not for the sake of the three seconds saved but so she could move along inside a moving vehicle. She scanned the underground display windows, satisfied that she needed nothing she saw there. Passing the ticket counters with renewed thoughts of a possible escape, that was she. Still, on Lexington Avenue she relaxed in the comradeship, the diversity, of the passing crowds, in the brick buildings that had such a provincial air among the high rises, the pizza maker, seen every day afresh, holding the broad disk out to her like a salutation. The low-fronted hideaway for men, the wooden table with the breakfast beer right by the window, again she saw it, again she did not yet want to understand it. Between the façades with their many windows she sought the sky over the city and sure enough the edges of the buildings swayed in the passing clouds. Only a few more steps, and the walk through the city that surprised her every day was over. The person being swirled through the marble bank lobby, sucked out of one throng into a thinner one and into the last elevator lane, that was not she, that was Mrs. Cresspahl, employed here for the past four years, formerly a foreign-language secretary, fourth and eleventh floors, now transferred to the sixteenth floor, far from indispensable, temporarily and for a limited time incorporated into the workings of the company. "How are you!" she is repeatedly asked during the ride up in the sealed capsule, and she will reply: "How are you!," a smile thinning out her lips, the corners of her eyes unmoving. That is someone else.

That's our German girl, that's our Danish girl. She's not married, she's available; she's married, she's a widow. Engaged; seen by Wes on Third Avenue with some guy from Kansas. No, Nebraska. She has a foster child, no, two, no, it is her own. Jee-zine. She is witty; she might say: You wouldn't find my village on the map, I must pencil it on first, yet she says: I was born in Jerichow, that's in Mecklenburg. Yay-ree-show. Looks taller than five feet four. There's something between her and the Vice-President's son; after three years she was moved into the fat cats' tower. Is allowed to eat in the bosses' dining room but at noon takes the elevator down to Sam's off the lobby; she's wrong to do that. Right, and goes back to her old departments, and doesn't burn her bridges. Helps her friends check their letters of credit; must have something to do with her Communist past. A whim of the Vice-President's; De Rosny's like that. Special mission. No memos issue from her desk; her number is not on the company telephone list. Yesterday she took a French scion to lunch; she's De Rosny's left hand, that's all. She has an outside office, with windows facing out; a safe has been hauled up to her office by the bank. Miss Cresspahl. No, Mrs. So she *is* available. Pesonnel's not saying. Who's that? A girl from the sixteenth floor; where there's supposed to be men only. Won't be long before she's transferred to the Milwaukee branch. 10,000 a year. 11,000, more likely. Cresspahl, name sounds Jewish. Celtic. In other words: No one knows who she is. That might be just what the fat cats on the sixteenth floor want. Sum total: Unknown. Nobody, camouflaged. Not recognizable.

The sun beating through unprotected windows takes her back once more. The spacious office with its functional and domestic furnishings is full of hot, mid-level, eastern sunshine that heats the haze over the low settlements of Long Island City to the color of an ocean seventeen years ago. There she had once been, holding a sextant against the sun. That had once been she.

Later, beyond the Venetian blinds tipped perpendicularly against the sun, the day sinks toward evening, toward the slow return trip to Riverside Drive, to our home, to where we live. "Is that what your Mecklenburg looks like?" asks Marie. She has got up specially from her homework, places herself behind her mother's chair, even brings her cheek close so as to have at least a parallel line of vision.

It was nothing. Ragged mist drifting over the river. A gap in the ever-astonishing foliage seems to open up a cloud-hung inland lake, and beyond it memory once more places with delight the bluish pine forests on the Palisades of the far shore, the landscape of the past again and again made transparent and unreal by the frame of trees.

"There now," says Marie, reassured and reassuring, as if to a shying horse. What would happen to her if her New York with river and shore were something else, or even comparable to something else. To her it is incomparable. Time stretches ahead for her here.

## April 24, 1968  Wednesday

In the Czechoslovak Republic three high-ranking members of the judiciary have been dismissed, and these were not ushers or porters but three deputy general prosecutors, and one of them was also chief military prosecutor. The spokesmen of the new government do not explain the dismissals. As if those guardians of the law in former times had become guilty of crimes.

The Soviets had been occupying Jerichow barely a week, and on the second Monday in the first July after the war the local inhabitants were convinced that one man was responsible: Cresspahl, my father. "To blame for the Russians," so went the judgment upon him, and applied not only to complaints about the foreigners. It really did one good to utter the phrase, as if without Cresspahl the foreigners would never have come in the first place.

The British had made Cresspahl mayor of Jerichow. Although they may have regarded him as one of the other Germans, that is, a traitor, they still trusted him, almost as a friend. The British intelligence agent had thought nothing of it, had saluted him as they left! And a military salute at that! Even some Americans had turned up from their Schwerin area and had spent nights in Cresspahl's office, and if they did question him for his reliability in Western terms, this had certainly not been done without drinking and fine words. Then the Soviets had moved in and left Cresspahl as mayor. That was their ploy, aimed at concealing their secret quarrel with their Anglo-Saxon allies. However, they did not exactly take Cresspahl over, nor was anything said about confirming him in office. They "put him to work." Under the swastika this phrase had stood for something exceptional, for "emergency action," for stopgaps, for exertion beyond the common need, whether it was "helping out with the harvest" or the deployment of dispersed troops, or the putting to work of officials who had not been elected and whom it had not been necessary to consult in advance. Now Cresspahl had in turn betrayed the British and had posted a notice on the town hall to the effect that, by order of the Soviet commandant, he was now a stooge of the Russians, a tool in their hands, in other words: he had been put to work.

In May and June it had been the Western Allies, as represented by the 6th Airborne Division under B. L. Montgomery; by this time Jerichow had become quite accustomed to that now vanished authority. Hardly had they gone before Cresspahl was in the service of the local commandant, K. A. Pontiy, the Russian.

Cresspahl had helped the Russians to take over one eighth of the municipal area of Jerichow. For their fence surrounding the brickyard villa had not long sufficed as their boundary. On the fourth day following their occupation of the town it became clear why they had only threaded a few strands of barbed wire through the laburnum bushes on the west side. That morning eight able-bodied men were ordered to report at Cresspahl's office in the town hall: not by decree but summoned by name; in fact Mina Köpcke had had to appear on behalf of her husband's construction company. And what were they to do? Clean up the Lübeck Arms, wrecked by the British, so Jerichow would get back its hotel? No, they were to build a fence. A fence running due west from the local command headquarters, the Kommandantura, beyond the back gardens of the Bäk, then straight north as far as Field Street, east as far as the back yards of the houses on Town Street, and back to the already occupied lot! Mina Köpcke had been doing the accounts and supervising repairs for her husband ever since he had been missing with an antiaircraft gun in Lithuania; now she was keen to show him what she could do with a building contract carried out by herself, and Mrs. Köpcke was put in charge. Once again Cresspahl displayed his toadying to the Russians by handing over all his lumber supplies, and after that Mina was free to tear down fence boards in Jerichow wherever it suited her but not Köpcke's enemies. For this she had a requisition with a Soviet stamp, and what she could add was: Cresspahl was to blame (for the confiscation; for the construction ordered by the Russians). Unlike him, she believed she was behaving patriotically by not setting the fence posts as deep in their stone foundations as she would have done had she been building a fence for herself; and when she ordered the paint to be diluted thinner than for a German customer she thought she would be able to blame the harsh sea wind. But what did Cresspahl do? Hadn't he once been a fellow businessman and the protector of Jerichow's interests? He had one of the original fence boards sent to her as a sample; and when her paint job still turned out pale green, the can of synthetic resin was weighed in her presence on the town scales, and she had to sign a receipt. Then she turned up at the town hall with her bill, and did Cresspahl file her vouchers without demur, the way you would expect among victims of a foreign power? Late that evening Cresspahl was observed, in company with his crony K. A. Pontiy, pacing out Mina's fence, for all the world as if they were friends out for a stroll, one of them wielding a surveyor's rod and the other being amused by the great swerves of the compasses. Once again the Köpcke company was summoned to the town hall, and Cresspahl demonstrated with square meter and cubic meter that she had fiddled. He said nothing about defrauding, or even about errors: he merely asked her to submit another bill. Sat hunched at his mayor's desk, his elbows drawn in too close, and despite all his fatigue should have looked her in the eye more often than just that once, that surprised upward glance from under his brows. Mina Köpcke stuck by her figures, signed her aggressive bill, and accepted a draft on the local savings bank for deferred payment. For the time being she received no money, and she blamed this on Cresspahl, as being the Russian way of doing business, as his fault, in fact.

And he was even benefiting from his betrayal of Jerichow to the Russians! While Mrs. Köpcke and her seven men were fencing in the Bäk, a notice saying EXPROPRIATED was being nailed to one house after another on that street, and since the fence was being built from both south ends the Bäk was turning into a sack with an opening that was getting smaller every day. The Bäk had been a residential street of solid brick houses not more than forty years old, with attics often generously extended, one of them Dr. Semig's almost baronial villa, and all had ample gardens separating them from the narrow Town Street lots, and now the householders in this prosperous area had to get out and move into the overcrowded town, forced into billets on orders signed by Cresspahl. They could take only what they could carry; each room was to be left in a condition permitting immediate occupation by the foreigners. And Cresspahl refused to see them in his office and listen to their complaints about the single room they had now been allotted at Quade's or over the pharmacy and which they might even be sharing with refugees! But he would listen to the refugees billeted in Bäk homes, waiting so much more patiently for him after this third or fourth relocation within six months, and to these refugees he could allocate the rooms that the Jerichow people had intended to keep for themselves or their relations simply because he was as familiar with every house in town as the locals were with his. Then the north end of the fence was extended right across the Bäk, and that was the last of this street to be seen by the people of Jerichow to this very day. The people living in houses along the Town Street side of the enclosure complained about the shadow now cast by the tall fence on their shrubs and flower beds, which did not take kindly to so much shade. Who was to blame?

But Cresspahl's entire house and property lay outside the fence, on the other side of the brickyard path. And he had looked after his friends: the Creutz nursery garden was inside the fenced area and, although its produce had to be handed over to the Kommandantura, Amalie was allowed to go on using the path that led past the parsonage to Town Street, and the ground leased by the Creutzes next to the church was included within the fenced area as if it were going to be theirs for all time. Pastor Brüshaver, too, another of Cresspahl's neighbors, was permitted to live on unmolested in his house, situated as it was at a strategically weak point so that its inclusion within the green army fence would have been necessary to create a complete stronghold. And Cresspahl had secured himself against looters and unwanted visitors: the only approach to his property was via the brickyard path, but here a sign had recently appeared, the first in all its history, an arrow-shaped board inscribed КОММАНДАНТУРА. Who was likely to go in that direction unless he had to? Cresspahl had not even provided a German translation. It certainly looked like a strong suggestion that they learn Russian, and they wouldn't put that past Cresspahl.

And he had forced Bergie Quade to set foot in the Kommandantura. The Red Army soldier whom she had so quick-wittedly enlightened as to "draan" turned up again at her shop, this time with a boy, a refugee from Pomerania whom Cresspahl had taken into his home. About seventeen, but broad in the shoulder, and he looked Bergie in the eye as if he had long been a man, and taciturn at that; this one was not to be shoved off, talked into retreat. The Red Army soldier looked at Mrs. Quade as he spoke, and she felt almost attractive under his recollecting gaze. The boy did not smile, he merely translated. It sounded reliably North German, even when he had to ask the Red Army a question. Bergie Quade could not resist the urge to wash her hands again. Meanwhile she had decided to be co-operative, so she invited the visitors into the kitchen. She hid her satisfaction as she walked down Town Street between the two men, as if being led away, like an honest German housewife under arrest, and she even managed the requisite expression of grim determination. She followed the two men across the Creutz property, stopping for a minute to talk to Amalie, who was supervising the fence builders as they transplanted some gooseberry bushes, and then actually entered upon the confines of the occupying power.

In the next few hours the Red Army learned swearwords from Mrs. Quade that for some time were to circulate inappropriately in the linguistic resources of the Soviets of Jerichow, and Jakob Abs earned praise from her for the delicate precision with which he implemented her instructions, as if he were an expert plumber. The last German owners of the brickyard villa had preferred to leave sawn-through drain-pipes behind for the Soviets rather than intact ones; on kitchen and bathroom faucets Bergie found suspicious evidence of hammer blows, and she was secretly astonished that people who were after all aristocrats could have treated a house in such fashion. Then Bergie Quade could choose between a bill to the municipality or a half-liter of unlabeled vodka, accepted her husband's solace and even had a free drink from it with Draan the Red Army soldier, seeing that he had lent a hand with the job.

When Jakob escorted her through the front door of the brickyard villa onto the civilian brickyard path, she was tempted to look in on Cresspahl to make sure he didn't need any help with the refugees and the child. But Jakob shook his head, and Bergie walked along past the cemetery wall toward Town Street as if on some ordinary errand, firmly grasping her tool bag and with the bottle under the apron that had previously concealed the manure-smeared napkin, and pondering deeply on whom she should tell about this expedition. The way she saw it, her obstructionist tactics had cost Cresspahl time as well as effort. So at least he was not to blame for that. But it so happened that Mrs. Quade's reticence was enough for her neighbors to blame Cresspahl once again.

But meanwhile Cresspahl had had to post Order No. 2 issued by the military commandant of the town of Jerichow, and the citizens were required to hand in their radios, batteries, typewriters, telephones, microphones, cameras, "etc." within three days at Papenbrock's granary. "Etc." was explained by Cresspahl overnight as meaning weapons, explosives, rifles, guns of all kinds; and one day later K. A. Pontiy's Order No. 4 also required all gold, silver, and platinum coins and bars, as well as all foreign currency, to be handed in at the Farmers' Credit Bureau, including even documents relating to foreign assets, and once again Cresspahl was regarded as an accomplice of the Soviets. For in the morning he was seen walking toward the town hall with his telephone tucked under his arm, and once with two army carbines which somebody had thrown onto his property during the night, but the collection of people's radios or "etc." in Papenbrock's granary did not amount to very much. Then Cresspahl provided his fellow citizens with further proof that he had not lived among them for twelve years for nothing by putting up a notice outside the town hall referring to the list on hand at the post office of former owners of radios and telephones. Some of these did turn up, but their idea was to fling the equipment at the feet of Cresspahl the toady and they had a long wait outside the granary because the Mayor announced his imminent arrival every two hours and failed to show up. Finally the Kommandantura threatened to hold any householder responsible under whose roof any confiscable articles were found, so now the local people forced the refugees to hand over what *they* still had, and what they had not buried they burned, including the genuine Russian rubles the prisoners of war had saved to do business with once the British occupying forces had returned (or the Swedish ones had arrived). However, they could still hold Cresspahl responsible for their losses: there were receipts to prove that he was to blame.

The shameful extent to which Cresspahl was in the pay of the Soviets was demonstrated to Jerichow by his behavior toward the Papenbrocks. These were his own parents-in-law to whom in their old age he continued to send fresh batches of homeless refugees to camp in the old man's office. He had not lifted a finger to prevent the Red Army from removing the Von Lassewitz furniture from the Papenbrocks' house and spraying it with Lysol right out in the market square before carting it off to the Kommandantura. Papenbrock's yard and granary were confiscated, with all the grain they held, these becoming the supply depot of the Red Army, and Cresspahl was free to carry on after despoiling his own relatives of their property. And if he should live to be ninety, how was he ever to wipe out such guilt?

As for the Soviets, they did not respect him: the British had had him driven around in a jeep from morning till night; the Soviets let him walk, from the brickyard path to the town hall, from the hospital to the gasworks, from one end of Jerichow to the other—unaccompanied, defenseless, alone!

### April 25, 1968 Thursday

The new Prime Minister of Czechoslovakia has praised his Czechs and Slovaks for their good work since 1948, as befits the start of a new program; then Mr. Cernik proceeded to paint a picture of the result of that good work: the per-capita national income is thirty to forty per cent below that of "advanced capitalist countries," delivery of manufactured goods to customers often lags two to three times behind delivery times in the West, transportation, housing, and the retail trade are also in poor shape, and he actually refers to the deficit of $400 million in foreign trade with capitalist countries as being relatively small but "very unpleasant and inconvenient" because it involves short-term loans. Since December Mrs. Cresspahl has been calculating and reporting all this for the bank records; she has been useful to the firm and need not start worrying about dismissal on being summoned to the management floor in the midst of her work and can look down without too much anxiety onto two segments of Third and of Lexington where people down there in the depths appear not merely foreshortened but distorted.

Twelve years ago the bank had not been here, and it would have been inclined to handle a little matter such as $400 million with some trepidation. As for a female being assistant to a vice-president, this was unthinkable.

It was a family bank, not only in terms of ownership but also in its business transactions, and in its name it still reveals its beginnings, when in small Midwestern towns it had given loans against wheat on the stalk, bribed the sheriff, and accepted a man's word as willingly as a promissory note. The name, with its rustic overtones, reminiscent of forebears and filial piety, has remained.

There is a photograph in existence, in the brownish detail of around 1880, showing a village branch of the bank in North Carolina: outside the winow with its garland of gilt letters stands the justice of the peace chatting with blacksmith and storekeeper, all in frock coats, and leaning in the doorway is the bank manager, dressed as if for church, with eyes guileless and blurred under his hat brim, the whole group bisected by a wooden rail to which in those days genuine cowboys used to tie up their horses. The picture refuses to remain fixed in the second for which the photographer of ninety years ago told them to stop breathing, the scene is about to move on, to the rattling stagecoach as it pulls to a halt in a cloud of dust, the relief driver up front shot through the eye, the horses high-stepping and frisky, townspeople pouring out of the neighboring buildings, ladies looking down from the upper windows of the hotel, the strongbox, roughly pried open, hanging by its last strap, and a shot rings out, and fresh horses are brought up for the chase after the robbers—will they be bandits or Indians?—and finally, with a roaring echo, the fade-out and the sign at the entrance to the bank: CLOSED FOR FUNERAL.

Quite a number of people in the building claim that the photo has been retouched and that all it shows is the set for a Western movie. Others claim to have seen this very film and swear they recall the scene. But a person saying the opposite—that the location of the filming derived from this picture—is suspected of harboring foreign notions, of flippancy even, and Mrs. Cresspahl does not say it again.

Around the turn of the century the bank made it to Chicago, in the heart of the Loop it had a mansion to call its own, narrow but noble of chest, and from 1945 on it was almost prosperous. But the family that owned it thought so too, it wanted to hold onto its gains yet multiply them, it wanted to eat its cake and have it too—the bears' attitude to life. Hence the family council believed the rumor of 1947 about the imminent decease of New York City, and it kept a decent distance from the notorious area where human beings are devoured like money. In 1951 they came too late. They were looking for a fitting location, and they found an old building 500 yards from the Wall Street subway station, and although they decked it in marble and inscribed it in gilt, this merely debased it further. And not only did they fail to improve their appearance: they came too late for the Bretton Woods Conference, they hardly distinguished themselves by boldness on the stock exchange, and they might have guessed the name Chad to stand for a detergent. The head office remained on Lake Michigan, directing furious and defiant glances at the sick child on the Atlantic Coast yet continuing to keep its crippled offspring in funds. When Gesine Cress-pahl arrived in New York in 1961 the bank's name was all but unknown to her, she might innocently have confused it with a brokerage firm or a finance company, although she was quite at home with such empires as the Morgan Guarantee Trust. But now there she is high up in the new building, standing at a window, barely discernible from the sidewalk, waiting till De Rosny is free, waiting for the Deputy Chairman of the Board, the Deputy General Manager, the Deputy Omnipotence: in fact, for De Rosny.

There had been a time when De Rosny laughed at the notion of associating his good name with that of this financial institution.

In the mid-fifties a report came from the Golden Gate more often than by chance: De Rosny was looking for something in the East. Reason: his wife could no longer stand the California climate.

It was a reason typical of De Rosny, and if his partners smiled for a moment, taking it for one of his familiar leg-pulls, what were those of a lesser breed to suppose, whose names he no doubt regarded as belonging to some harmless characters from the great American fairy tale? The offers made to De Rosny were few, and those few did not emanate from that place near Wall Street. De Rosny did not need them. If he wanted to go east he had only to place a few phone calls, and ten days later all his household goods would have been hauled across the continent and installed on Long Island Sound in a family mansion the very twin of the one he had left behind in San Francisco. De Rosny had not worked his way up into money, nor had he married money; his parents had provided him, and only him, with it, and he had been breathing through that pungent, nourishing, protective husk of money ever since knowing his own first name, and not merely since starting, out of boredom, to learn the banking business in Singapore. So that was the word: De Rosny was not available. There on the white hills where he sat behind his telephones, he was paid whatever he liked over and above the salaries of others, merely because he was related to Money, was descended from it, had become Money. De Rosny would never concern himself with such an unimportant dilemma, even if it were possible to solve it on the East Coast.

De Rosny was said to be unpredictable. He was prepared to risk a quarrel with Howard Hughes, publicly critical of Howie's business (not private) investments in Hollywood; De Rosny's vacations were spent not there but with the aristocracy in Britain. As for business, he did enough with aircraft companies and had no need of Howie's inventions, especially since these days planes didn't stay up that long. Others spoke of him as not being serious enough. They did not mean what he did with money. No, he didn't know how to live. The dinners, those satisfying rewards for a day of board-room battles, bored him, and he showed it. De Rosny never drank hard liquor, he could have pleaded religious conviction rather than say he wasn't interested. Familiarities, no sir! Does anyone know De Rosny's first name? He once sent his suit to the cleaners after someone gave him a friendly slap on the back! He allowed very few people into his house; those he did were certainly not his friends, and they took away almost nothing worth telling. In his home De Rosny served imported white wines from a place in France where there was some hill or other. Feeble stuff, hardly loosened the tongue at all. While others had to be grateful for being photographed with Eleanor Roosevelt in a restaurant, De Rosny had long been spending evenings by the fireside with Franklin Delano, without anyone's taking his picture, and F. D. R. had even gone so far as to misrepresent these business chats as exchanges of prep-school reminiscences. In the midst of the war against the Huns. No, too many things came De Rosny's way too easily, it wasn't fair. So he knows where God lives, but he doesn't even thank Him. And this smart scoundrel, this all-too-flexible fifty-year-old, his whole physique trained by something other than tennis—this was the man one was supposed to approach about some trivial matter in New York, just because he wanted to come east? (Because the sunny Pacific climate did not agree with his wife.)

De Rosny stopped off in Chicago and stayed not at the city's super-luxury hotel but at the Windermere, and the Windermere's conference room saw some unfamiliar guests, and five companies far away in the South became two, and two became one, and all of a sudden New Orleans appeared on the market with a product that sold with childish ease, and a child could have thought of it, and was that what Matthew 18 meant? (Ask those Gideon fellows.) And for six months the Windermere was swamped with reservations. But De Rosny did allow himself to be approached about some minor Eastern problem, and annoyingly enough he knew all about it and began by pointing out the considerable expense involved. In Chicago they interpreted this as his remuneration; they interpreted him wrongly. De Rosny permitted himself to be seen in New York, ostensibly back from inspecting his mansion in Connecticut, and at the Waldorf Towers his visitors included some from Wall Street who had had to invite themselves. De Rosny needed no notebook, no secretary, for his conditions, he obviously intended this trifling matter to yield him a degree of amusement commensurate with the time he was devoting to it.

His conditions were said to be: That the Board of Directors would never attempt to appoint him president.

The remuneration he deemed appropriate for a Vice-President De Rosny and the annual rate of increase are the kinds of figures that will never come to the knowledge of an employee such as Mrs. Cresspahl.

Then came that terrible business with his wife. Now he must be glad to have moved to the Atlantic, even if it had meant paying for it out of his own pocket. However, careful provision for these expenses had been made in Chicago, and once again he had come off better than he deserved.

Except for his wife. It was four years before her story became known, and then as such a vague rumor that it was just not worth the telling.

De Rosny moved into the aborted shack on Wall Street and for a long time after was seen no more. Obviously De Rosny was having fun. He even left the problem child's rustic name unchanged, although the public-relations department had greeted him with a snappy new pseudonym. De Rosny insisted on the old-fashioned lettering being reinstated, and where there had been a comma there was to be an & in the fashion of yesteryear. Maybe he did realize that he had to prove himself, so with his friends he established a branch in California. (De Rosny lends De Rosny the following sum on the following terms and conditions. . . .) The financial world found those of De Rosny's methods that came to their knowledge disappointing, positively old hat; De Rosny held his conferences not in the presence of the press but in the building. In the building word got out as to the meaning of all that big talk in Chicago about expense. It was an enormous sum. Outrageous, in fact. This time there was no De Rosny to help them out financially. He had even made his San Francisco people deaf in that ear. In Chicago they had to choose. As a resigning Vice-President De Rosny would be very expensive; his sole condition had a nasty catch to it. It was a challenge. They could bear the idea of De Rosny picking up his hat. What they could not bear was the sequel: De Rosny putting on his hat, turning in the open door, and taking leave of a bunch of cowards. De Rosny remained in his deputy chair, in northern California the Air Force bought a fair-sized rocky plateau. In New York talk persisted that De Rosny had not measured up.

Although by that time the Elevated no longer raced along on its stilts above Third Avenue, nevertheless between 40th and 60th Streets that great artery of Third Avenue was still lined mostly with low, four-story buildings, each like the next in its brick angularity, built for high-class renting and lower-class living. While science was visualizing the death of New York City, the "L" left behind more business for Third Avenue; from Grand Central Station the commuters went to Park and Madison, and there a clientele developed for new stores at street level, bars, invisible mending, hairdressers, even little hideaways, and on the upper floors many of the buildings had been blinded by grime or window shades, with only a few monuments to prosperity standing awkwardly among them.

It was upon one such block between Third and Lexington that a horde of brokers descended, bidding and counterbidding, and there was no one they could have named as their principal, except possibly a superbroker. Whenever an owner hesitated, the wrecking balls went into action next door, and the whole area became a wasteland. The owner of a corner property was still suing while above his head the steel skeleton of the new building was going up, like an absurdly enlarged product of a child's imagination, and since at night the scaffolding was illuminated to the very top, the New York *Times* commented on it and reinforced its opinion with a picture. The construction site could be observed through generous ovals in the fences, even Gesine Cresspahl walked innocently by and stopped and marveled to see bricks actually being stuck between steel girders, oddly enough from the top down, where they hung naked in the air, exposed as a concession to tradition. The man at the corner went tirelessly from one court to another, complaining to the construction company and the world that General Lexington (or was it Washington?) had once slept in his building, which was why he was the only owner in the block to have left the original timber intact and painted it green and white, and De Rosny relented. It was not specifically De Rosny, but he may have leased that part of the building from the construction company, and apparently it was at his discretion to preserve the historic little corner building by means of a cement superstructure, and once again a venerable and ambitious Chicago and Wall Street bank managed to get itself forty-three lines and a picture in the New York *Times*. Two enormous towers went up, one at each end of the block and faced with strips of blue glass, even the connecting structure between them was fifteen stories high, and the manner in which the builders had dug into the earth was not exactly tentative. The name of the construction company appeared in large (albeit removable) letters above the entrances, and for the time being the bank's street-level windows had the appearance of a branch office, temporarily rented. De Rosny held a lease for the entire leviathan, his subtenants being attorneys as well as United Nations delegations which, only three blocks away, had been waiting all that time for office space. Finally it reached the point where the bank was paying itself rent, and now it was time for an entry in the land registry and an insertion in the New York *Times*. The bank is still a long way from wanting to occupy the entire building itself, but it is free to evict tenants for all the additional space it may require, and its old-fashioned rustic name with the & marks this milestone of uncompromising architecture as being its property. Yet even this name is not chiseled in marble, it too is removable. For De Rosny's pride basks in the fact that the building has been constructed in such a way that it can be torn down in thirty days and the empty lot sold to the next sucker at a nice profit.

De Rosny, incidentally, had been at work all the time. Thus the meaning of Chad was being circulated through the bank, to some people the word was becoming painfully familiar, and De Rosny is also spreading knowledge about other parts of the globe. The head office has moved here from Chicago, the head of the family now lives at the top of one of the towers with roof garden and swimming pool, he is wearing the emperor's new clothes and De Rosny is doing the work. All day long people emerge from the subway under Lexington Avenue, from Grand Central they are swept northward, and De Rosny is not above accepting their current and savings deposits. He has made the building more than a few feet taller than the Union Dime Savings on 42nd, and he must have enjoyed seeing the Chemical following him quite a bit later and also building on Third. And the type of advertising that shows young ladies with their lips voluptuously parted,

> *when a girl thinks of a bank,*
> *she gets a Chemical reaction,*

is quite foreign to him; he can just bring himself to accept the advertising department's five-stroke logo composed of the bank's initials, the employees in the lobby are allowed to wear it over their hearts but De Rosny's chauffeur may not, his uniform is more in the English style. In the machinery of the building everything is dovetailed, from the space allotted to each employee to the underground parking, but the pattern is not discernible, De Rosny keeps it in his head. He is considered strict, merciless even, as a boss; throughout the building he is known as D. R., with an undertone of respectful amusement. The voice of the President, the head of the family, is to be heard over the intercom in the cafeteria and receives rather less attention than the rain beating against the double windows; De Rosny's hard-nosed utterances are greeted with laughter, and a staff rumor amounts almost to a sincere wish that he would finally get around to switching the damned P. A. system to television. This, they feel, will allow them to get at the truth, as if a De Rosny would let the cat out of the bag before the deal has been completed. For the time being only three people in the entire bank know what De Rosny has in mind with Czechoslovakia, and one of these estimates the business at somewhere around $400 million, based on those bloodthirsty short-term loans he's been reading about in the paper.

De Rosny seems perplexed with Mrs. Cresspahl. He hurries through his door to meet her, hastily closes the door behind her, starts striding up and down on the wide expanse of carpet. A man in thought. A man struck by amazement. He might be a teacher, one of those thin-lipped and absent-minded ones who look over the heads of their students and after ten years give no inkling of all that accumulated familiarity and comradeship, and move on to the next stage in the syllabus.

De Rosny cannot understand the Communists, in particular the Czech and Slovak ones. How can they go publicly revealing details of their national budget to the man in the street! And even telling him how they intend to spend it!

To Mrs. Cresspahl it all seems according to Hoyle.

To De Rosny it seems to contradict the rules. Not only is this a case of Communists behaving like Communists: they are ruining the market for the loan he intends to slip them *in petto*, sub rosa.

This in turn would be according to De Rosny's rules. Observations of this kind are now permitted to Mrs. Cresspahl in this room: innocent, knees together, gaze fixed on the space between De Rosny's eyes, the student. De Rosny is enjoying laying a trap. Wouldn't his efficient Gesine Cresspahl like to make a quick dash over to Prague, disguised as a tourist, and tell the new leaders something about De Rosny's private life?

Mrs. Cresspahl does not like being De Rosny's efficient tool, she would first have to discuss such a trip with her child, tomorrow she has appointments with the dentist and the hairdresser. She would rather not, and she has to say: Of course. I'll be glad to. Tonight?

No. The Communists would not take a woman seriously. Not as an authorized spokesman for a bank in New York.

Mrs. Cresspahl disagrees. Equal status of women in socialist countries.

With an unexpected twitch of his eyelid De Rosny reminds her of the statistics prepared by her on this very subject. Now he has her at his mercy and starts off with an assessment of her Tuesday's report.

He says: But with me, in the pay of us murderous man-eating capitalists, that's where you'll see equal status. A real bombshell! Just wait another four months!

"Very good. I don't mind waiting, sir," says Mrs. Cresspahl.

This is our life now. This is what we live on.

---

### April 26, 1968  Friday

---

Yesterday, in Times Square, New York commemorated the anniversary of the rebellion in the Warsaw ghetto twenty-five years ago, and we missed it. More than 40,000 men, women, and children died after forty days of fighting against German troops, and yesterday 3,000 living souls stood on sidewalks and traffic islands separating Broadway and Seventh Avenue, and we were not there. Fifty-five Jewish groups joined forces in memory of this and also of the six million people killed elsewhere by the Germans, and we didn't know about it. Speeches were made, telegrams read out, and a tenor from the Metropolitan Opera Company, wearing a skullcap, chanted the memorial service of *Yizkor* for the dead, and we didn't go. There is nothing we can do about it; since yesterday the demonstration area is to be known as Warsaw Ghetto Square, and we'll have to remember that.

Cresspahl was converting the orders of his town commandant into regulations and rules of behavior for Jerichow, he would like to have known what he was doing and scarcely ever understood K. A. Pontiy.

It was not a matter of language. Since early July Schwerin had had a Soviet Military Administration for the Mecklenburg and West Pomerania Region, a bureau that issued its orders in German, signed by Colonel General Fedyuninski, countersigned by Major General Skossyrev, and one after another these orders were handed to Cresspahl at the brickyard villa ready for posting outside the town hall. And K. A. Pontiy's German, although not good enough for teaching the language, sufficed to make him understood, at least in terms of what he required of the people of Jerichow. And Cresspahl did not understand him. His child received curt replies

> *That's the way he wants it.*
> *But he can't do that.*
> *He can.*
> *Then why do you do it?*
> *He's the winner.*

*Is that what winning means, Cresspahl?*
*Times have changed, Gesine. Well—*

and soon stopped asking. (The child had plenty of other things to do.)

When Cresspahl tried to understand him in military terms, he did occasionally hit on something. If Cresspahl had had to erect fortified quarters inside a small town without their being readily visible, he would no doubt have set about it much as the Soviet commandant had done. Beyond the fence stood the buildings on the west side of Town Street, innocent enough, they could not betray him. Entry to the street known as the Bäk had been closed off with painted boards, no barbed wire, let alone a gate: it might well be called a blind spot in the town. Anyone wanting to approach the Soviet fort from the west would have had to trample down ripe grain. The only access was from the southeast, a sandy side road that looked more like a lane petering out between cemetery wall and drying sheds than an approach to a Kommandatura with armed sentries, triumphal arches, and barbed wire. Since Cresspahl had been made a noncommissioned officer in 1917 not solely for the purpose of attending a lecture course, he regarded Pontiy's layout for a hideaway as strictly consistent with the book of rules.

Meanwhile, feeling himself to be on trial yet out on bail, he had been able to observe his commandant over the past two weeks, both at midnight and in the early morning, and no matter what he saw he could make neither head nor tail of it. K. A. Pontiy, with his pale, shell-colored eyes, no eyebrows, and blunt, naturally bald head, his ponderous movements (due either to age or to an old shoulder wound), must have been roughly Cresspahl's age, not much younger. That steady, unconscious sighing might be attributable to illness or to grief, but it did not mean he was susceptible. Perhaps he did not like standing with the German because the latter could then still look down onto his bald pate, and after a while Cresspahl was ordered to sit, officially. As Cressphal came into the room K. A. Pontiy would stretch back in his chair behind his piles of papers, while beside him, hand sometimes on holster, his lieutenant stood at attention, adjutant and attorney combined. Now and again it would cross Cresspahl's mind that there was something Pontiy was afraid of losing, his uniform perhaps, or his dignity. When angered Pontiy would get up and cram on his cap. He was suspicious of the German, and this suited Cresspahl. However, the threat that hung over him was not dismissal but a bit of autobiography. He was quite familiar with agricultural problems, Pontiy informed him, his voice low, sharp, dangerous, his eyelids twitching. Nobody could pull the wool over the eyes of a technical man like himself, Pontiy warned sneeringly but then switching to a tone of almost friendly persuasion. He had attended the Frunse Academy, and he stood for the honor of the Red Army, K. A. Pontiy would have his mayor know in what looked like blind rage, on the point of pronouncing arrest and death sentence, but then he could appraise Cresspahl with a look almost of amusement and dismiss him like a naughty child who will benefit from a good scare. Cresspahl could not make him out, not even on the surface.

From a military academy, and sixty years old: why did K. A. Pontiy hold the rank of major, a narrow row of medals and no more? Why did his army allot him an insignificant little town like Jerichow?

He claimed to be of peasant stock yet was surprised that the sharp ends of the fence posts had been charred before being set into the ground, and he was unaware that he could have demanded tar oil and creosote. (Perhaps he had needed a fence in Jerichow but none in Russia?)

A technical man yet wanted to calculate the dimensions of his fence in square meters with military compasses and was amused by the clever (and just as innacurate) instrument as if he had never in his life seen a surveyor's rod.

He wished to defend the honor of the Red Army, among other things as head

of the military post

of the government bank

of the Soviet occupation forces

of the town of Jerichow,

representing his nation as against the German nation, and demanding not from that nation but from individuals their gold and silver, their English and Dutch shares, the entire platinum stock of Jerichow (whether the owners of such articles had profited by the war or not, whether they had run after the Nazis or kept their distance from them), and instead of presenting these valuables to his country had kept them for himself, bartered them for liquor, distributed them among guests and subordinates. When Cresspahl was queried about Order No. 4 he could say things like: The "harvest" is coming along, and he himself had handed over not much more than his obsolete statements from the Surrey Bank in Richmond. He found the Red Army soldier they called Draan lighting a fire with these in the brickyard villa fireplace, and so one or two pounds sterling were lost after all to the Red Army and their government bank. Cresspahl did not report this, he had no wish to expose the fellow with the unaccountable name to punishment, this business of honor was beyond him.

When the Red Army started circulating Dr. Kliefoth's coin collection in Jerichow as regular currency, Cresspahl held out two Lübeck talers (Schwerin 1672) on his outstretched palm for the commandant to see, and K. A. Pontiy pounced on the coins like a chicken, looked at the more recent tooth marks, and slipped the museum pieces into his breast pocket. Head of the military post, that he certainly was. Cresspahl was given to understand that this was how the German Army had behaved in K. A. Pontiy's own country, and what could he do but nod? But now he had insulted the Red Army by comparing it with the Fascists, and was to be shot, forthwith, for convenience's sake against the cemetery wall! Cresspahl got off by casually inquiring about street names. He had gone to the Kommandantura to complain that that silly child Gesine had been so careless as to wear a brooch that had been torn off her by a nighttime looting patrol. It was the German Imperial five-mark piece that Lisbeth Cresspahl had had made into a brooch in October 1938 by Ahlreep the jeweler, in defiance of the Nazis' gold-snatching, and around two in the morning Cresspahl acquainted his Major Pontiy with the difference between a coin and an ornament. K. A. Pontiy nodded solemnly, from either weariness or satisfaction, had one go at shouting, and seemed relieved when the German did not back down. He admitted he was right. Two days later an embarrassed Red Army soldier turned up in Cresspahl's kitchen, beckoned the child Gesine outside, and handed her the brooch, knotted up in a silk handkerchief. *Izvini pozhaluysta* means: "Please excuse," and *Nye plakat'* means: "Don't cry." Cresspahl looked in at Ahlreep's to thank them for not reporting the concealed valuable, and days later K. A. Pontiy was still reminding him with a happy, crafty smile that he had vindicated the honor of the Red Army.

There were occasions of less formality. Cresspahl had wanted to know whether the Kommandantura intended the fence as a temporary or a permanent fixture, and K. A. Pontiy refused to tell him whether he would be giving the area back very soon to the British or later to the people of Jerichow. (This meant that Mrs. Köpcke had to pack more stones in around the base of the posts.) The Russian had replied, with an almost Mecklenburgian delight at the trap he had seen and hurdled: For everr, Mister Mayorr!

If only we could ask Cresspahl! From a child's-eye view, the association of these two often had the air of a vehement friendship, staggering between unconditional loyalty, murderous quarreling, and ardent yet sulky reconciliation.

Would Cresspahl's memory have reached that interpretation to-day?

After walking through town between the two foreign 98K carbines, Cresspahl was very late getting home that night. K. A. Pontiy had sent guards to escort him from the town hall, and at the villa it all turned into a party. Cresspahl, after being greeted for the very first time with a handshake, was wined and dined until midnight, and when they parted outside on the steps K. A. Pontiy's hand missed Cresspahl's shoulder several times before succeeding in slapping him heartily on the back.

Cresspahl handed over both his telephone and his radio simply because he and his household would have had to expect a more severe punishment than those others who had merely read the order. However, this turned out to be a mistake, for, although his commandant referred to the many Russian telephones and microscopes that Germany had to make good, he had nevertheless credited Cresspahl with more brains. Socialism was now a promise, he said, and life without telephones or radios would be impossible. For some people no, but Cresspahl must be able to hear Pontiy, whether over the phone or on the radio. This time he shook hands as Cresspahl left, because the latter had confirmed the reference to socialism with a nod, and from his personal supplies K. A. Pontiy sent him an eight-tube superhet which the refugees in Dr. Berling's home had turned in from either gratitude or superstition. Now the huge blue-black object stood on Cresspahl's desk, silent, side by side with the memory of Lisbeth's first attempt at suicide, not to mention Dr. Berling's defiant death. Pontiy came to check up on whether his mayor had consigned to the attic this proof of confidence in the elect.

Pontiy paid calls. Not to the town hall, but to Cresspahl's bed. Whether it was midnight or two hours after, he ordered him to be wakened, gave him two minutes to dress, and, sighing, sat down with him to talk about nights like this beside the lake when everything looked so low yet with a sky like the one over Leningrad, if not higher. But just as Pontiy was host at the brickyard villa, so Cresspahl was expected to be host in his own house and, as of late, even to offer vodka. (The Mayor was not required to make personal use of the black market, for which activity he had to issue penalty threats in his official notices: the job was done for him by Jakob. Jakob, believe it or not, had supplies of brand-label liquor hidden somewhere in the house in a cache that was never discovered, and Cresspahl did not like to ask the boy. Only, Jakob ought to have told him their equivalent value and not offset it against a right of his mother and himself to live in the house.) And one morning Hanna and I were awakened not by the birds but by two men, seen as dark figures lurching through the half-light, and one of them was saying in a queer, surprised voice: *Dyeti, Dyevushki*. The other confirmed: Children, girls: the voice unfamiliar, awkward, like a mechanical dictionary, and it was my father after spending the night drinking as if with a friend.

He did not understand him. K. A. Pontiy, a major in the Red Army, an expert on atheism, turned up one Sunday in church accompanied by four soldiers. He waved graciously up to the organ, which had fallen silent, impatient until it started up again, and wandered benevolently up and down between the pews full of singing worshipers, performing the sweeping movements of a conductor until Pastor Brü-shaver began his sermon. One almost expected him to sit down facing the congregation. After eight minutes this uniformed visitation came to an end. The delegation then proceeded to inspect the front part of the cemetery, and K. A. Pontiy commented on the arch of shade afforded by the trees against the July heat. He also deplored the neglected state of some of the graves. On Monday the commandant issued Order No. 11, prohibiting all further burials in the cemetery as well as the placing of bodies in the chapel beside the brickyard path. Even before this first skirmish with the Church of Mecklenburg was being discussed at the lower end of Town Street, Aggie Brüshaver had to escort an urbane, almost gallant visitor to her husband as he sat at his desk: K. A. Pontiy, military commandant. Brüshaver was expecting a ban on Church services, and Pontiy asked him to explain the liturgy to him. He said he was looking forward to the next event of this kind. He noted with regret that the Nazis had had time to melt down the zinc and copper of the new bells for making cannon. A question about the funerals made him flare up for a moment, as if his friendliness were being ill repaid. By the time Pontiy left, Pastor Brüshaver had gained the impression that St. Peter's Church had been promised bells in the very near future, who knows where from. In Jerichow it was being said that the only clergymen whom the Soviets treated like that were those who had been in concentration camp. But the Catholic parish house, although lacking such credentials, also received a visit from K. A. Pontiy (who asked Böhm if he wouldn't mind letting Brü-shaver have one of his bells, the smaller one at least). If that was atheism, then it was one with devout singing and bell chimes almost at the gates of the villa occupied by the unbelieving Kommandantura.

## April 27, 1968   Saturday, South Ferry Day,

but the free day had been planned otherwise.

It also happens to be the day when the Veterans of Foreign Wars wish to demonstrate their loyalty to the country with parades, in dark dress uniforms, white gaiters, white bandoliers girdling hips and chest, cops with buttons pinned to them, rifles shouldered, and flags of union and state in slings braced against the belly. Marching with them will be the Catholic-school bands and youngsters from drill groups sponsored by veterans' organizations, and a contingent of longshoremen; Fourth Avenue in the Norwegian quarter of Brooklyn and Fifth Avenue in Manhattan will be hung with national flags, the Archbishop will lead the marchers and, together with the Mayor, review the parade. But today's march, the twentieth since 1948, is dedicated to the memory of the deceased Cardinal Spellman, who was very fond of war, and for the past two years Loyalty Day is to be taken not only as a token of support for American troops in Vietnam but also as a threatening fist raised against the war resisters. We might have gone to watch that.

We had an alternative. On its Food  Fashions  Family  Furnishings page the New York *Times* shows us a picture of Mr. and Mrs. Scanlon with their children Rebecca (2) and Caitlin (5): they have bought a house in Brooklyn, built in 1894, and instead of tearing it down they are preserving it and are thrilled with the bathroom and its original bathtub on claw-and-ball feet, the marble sink, stained-glass windows, pull-chain toilet, all genuine, right here in New York City. We might like John Scanlon's Irish mustache, we might like the Italian Mrs. Scanlon even more, and the *Times* gives us their exact address: 196 Berkley Place. By subway to Grand Army Plaza. But Marie didn't want to go there either.

She opted for the peace parade in Central Park, and for this occasion she dressed as carefully as a grownup. The police will be there, so one must be able to run well in what one is wearing. Marie insisted on her mother's taking off her dress and putting on slacks, plus an old blue cotton shirt (capable of withstanding a policeman's grip, one that would not hurt the feelings of the black peace marchers from Harlem). Thus, clothed defensively, in deliberately unpolished flat shoes, Marie was finally ready, took stock of herself, and learned from the mirror that she should undo her braids and keep her hair in place with a simple black headband (Shawnee Rebellion under Tecumseh, 1811). This is how we set off up 95th Street, a white squaw and a coltish, sinewy, fair-haired Indian maiden.

At the corner of Amsterdam Avenue we have to stop and scan the façades of the apartments, the pavement, the corner store. Here there used to live four children, allies if not friends, who allowed their parents to move them from New York to one of the suburbs, where the sapphire-green lawns are not genuine and the imitation village street of plastic and aluminum is not genuine either. Marie cannot understand such a move; maybe the kids at least have come back to New York's Upper West Side. Not today.

The streets were dry after the early-morning rain. The pallid sun threw out some warmth in front, enough for a holiday.

Often as we zigzagged between the blocks we passed houses like the one the Scanlons wanted to salvage, once haughty bourgeois dumps designed for living on three floors. From many of them the steps and windows had already been torn out, while some of their brownstone comrades had already been entirely gutted. The demolition sites were screened by the doors from the interior of the dead house, many of them cracked and split, weathered to various colors, inadequate fences around a grave.

Marie was not depressed by the wounds inflicted on her city by speculators, and she observed the passersby with care and Indian in-scrutability. But when she was hailed as Great Chief or with the war cry of the original inhabitants, she did not close up her face as she usually did with strangers. Without exactly opening her mouth, she did smile back. These were citizens of New York, she and they were walking in the same direction. Kindred spirits, friends of peace, friends of the Indians.

Right on time, at 11 A.M., we were at Central Park West, corner of 101st Street, just like the *Times* said, and the parade was not yet in sight.

The sky had meanwhile clouded over, permitting fitful gleams of sunshine, and the close air threatened rain.

The people lining the sidewalks were packed not much closer than a normal crowd of pedestrians, but these of course were waiting. Helpers of the parade committee were darting among them, trying to sell "original" buttons as mementos of the morning of April 27, 1968. Marie was disappointed at such commercialism. She was not surprised, she must have expected it; but the celebration was starting off on a jarring note.

She accepted the free handbill, propaganda for Senator Eugene McCarthy, with pictures of war atrocities. The Communist Party was also giving away special leaflets, but the *Daily Worker* offered her a language such as the New Germany had once offered me, and neither of us quite understood it. Many of these were soon fluttering to the ground. Marie kept hers tucked under her arm ("which I undertook solely to keep New York City clean"), for Mayor Lindsay's sake.

Then she saw children holding balloons over their heads, green, blue, and yellow, with the word PEACE, but the dignity of her almost eleven years would allow her no more than a few kindly, patronizing glances in their direction. Then came grownups with black balloons bearing the Ban the Bomb symbol. Marie got down from the park railing and reached into her pants pocket. Although no more balloon-sellers came by, she held onto her dime.

She was watching the police, the eyes of an Indian narrowed beneath the black headband. The officers of law and order were standing in small groups at the intersections, along the curb, chatting together. The conversations appeared to be personal ones. Now and again they would soil their hands lugging the barricades into place to block off the side streets and contain the parade. There were still a few cars moving along the street, only the buses had already been diverted. Marie wanted to know how many demonstrations her mother had taken part in to date. She was more prepared to believe the number of over fifty than that we had not been allowed just to stand on the sidelines and look on.

"You mean you were *made* to march?" she asked. "But that's what we intend to do too!"

On the third floor of a building across the street a young man, naked to the waist, climbed out onto the window sill he had rented. On each of his grimy bay windows he stuck a stenciled sign objecting to the military occupation of the Negro section. The black residential areas of the city are not under military occupation. Then the agitator displayed himself with a telephone receiver at his ear, talking defiantly and belligerently with his distant friends. Then he ensconced himself on the sill for the duration. Marie kept looking up at the unathletic figure as if the sight bothered her. She refrained from comment, his behavior was not unusual for New York, she could not forbid anything he was doing; she looked for a new place for us somewhere else.

But the street was now densely lined with people, and when spectators stepped forward into the gaps there was a feeling of jostling. Into the low murmur of voices fell the sharp chatter of the helicopters belonging to the police and private radio stations; no machine fell into Central Park.

Ten minutes to twelve, and the parade started off with a group of motorcyclists. The drivers were dressed in brown suits with yellow stripes. The Magnificent Riders from Newark. (Their machines did not

roar (as the *Times* will perforce write), they whispered. Because of the
slow rate of speed the riders had to keep braking with their toecaps.
They were followed by the V. I. P.s, who were surrounded by a hands-
locked square of fifty burly bodyguards. Marie recognized Pete Seeger
and waved to him ("Where Have All the Flowers Gone?"; "If I Had a
Hammer"; "Turn, Turn, Turn"). Pete Seeger's presence in the demonstration almost redeemed it for her, but she was too shy to run across
and join in behind Pete Seeger's bodyguards. She let many more groups
go by, mentally checking her knowledge of New York against the names
of the various sections of the city being held aloft. Everyone was cheerful, as if on a picnic. Agitators gaily shouted: WHAT DO WE WANT? and
the choruses replied in syncopated high spirits: PEACE NOW! Or: WHAT?
PEACE: WHEN? NOW! Just when she wanted to step off the curb and join
the kindred spirits, along came the show.

The show consisted of a row of girls in Vietnamese costume, black-
smocked under conical straw hats. Petite American girls dressed up as
Vietnamese women. They wanted to show us who, in place of them,
America was killing in Vietnam. This was not their place. As if they
were being killed here and now, on Central Park West, corner of 101st
Street. And as if they weren't really all that serious about it.

Marie could have joined them, we would have met up again; what
spoiled it for her?

Then we also saw the senior police officers who were accompanying the not very wide marching column, one carrying a walkie-
talkie, another some file folders. Next to Marie on the sidewalk stood
a ten-year-old Negro girl with a steno pad, wearing a PRESS badge on
her blouse and earnestly leafing through the notes she had made. Marie
turned in such a way that the child could have asked her a question,
but the other child did not want to see her. Remarkably few homemade
or handwritten placards in the parade. People in crash helmets; in
shabby fatigue jackets but with shoes polished to army regulations. The
few women elected to wear sunglasses; one of these, in a hound's-tooth
costume, could have been me (in a photo). By now we were moving
along the sidewalk, looking for a subway entrance to get away, neither
admitting it to the other.

We also saw a tall youth from a mediocre college team, with a
flushed face. He was holding the elbow of a diminutive Chinese girl,
doing his best to encourage her; she was desperately, speechlessly unhappy. (From a distance we had one more glimpse of the show-off
hamming it up on his window sill, achieving the desired effect of being
hailed and applauded by many of the groups as he raised his clasped
hands over his head.) At 96th Street we found ourselves side by side

with the unhappy couple, now she was wearing his jacket, but she still could not forgive him for what he could not suspect, at least not until evening.

But it was not all over at 96th Street, we ought to have gone as far as 72nd and into the park as far as the Sheep Meadow, where the rally with the speakers was scheduled for that afternoon. Mrs. Martin Luther King was expected, Pete Seeger was there, Mayor John Vliet Lindsay would be coming. Sitting on the grass, community singing to pass the time, chatting with one's neighbor, about the weather, about the city.

"John Lindsay?" Marie said, incredulously. "But he was at the Loyalty parade!"

She refused to see that the Mayor can appear in public with enemies as well as supporters of foreign wars, an equal friend to both, desiring the votes of all for the term following December 31 of next year. For the first time ever she pleaded rather than announced: "It's Saturday, after all! Let's make it a South Ferry Day!"

So we took the IND as far as the I. R. T. and at Battery Park boarded the *John F. Kennedy*, which took us right across the harbor to Staten Island. During the trip Marie braided her hair, her head more averted than usual, and her fingers moved slowly, as if she were entwining her thoughts with the strands. With a piece of glass that had been lying handily around on the deck, she cut the headband with the embroidered Indian symbols and could now fasten the ends of her braids. From Staten Island we went by bus across the Verrazano Bridge to Brooklyn and from there underground back to Riverside Drive. It is six thirty now, and over the Palisades hangs a yellow strip that stands out sharply against the hazy blue of the upper sky. The sun has a yellow hole. Minutes later the yellow cell melts away among the darker colors.

Marie knows a lot about her Mayor John Vliet Lindsay: not only his birthday but also the names of his children and where they go to school; she keeps pictures of him from the New York *Times*, she has adopted his phrase "the fun of getting things done"; she has thought of him as one of her friends. She makes some remark as she tears his pages out of her scrapbook, but that's not for the record, Comrade Author. O.K., you can say she bawled maybe, while she was alone in her room, but then no more.

---

**April 28, 1968   Sunday, Change from Winter to Summer Time**

---

The Sheep Meadow in Central Park, 522, 725 square feet divided by the minimum space for a seated person of 9 square feet, provides room for 58,080 people (with 5 square feet left over). That's how meticulous the New York *Times* is. When Mrs. Martin Luther King entered, the meadow had been only half filled, the paper said: she read out ten commandments for Vietnam, and Dr. King had been carrying them on him when he was murdered, and the tenth was: Thou shall not kill. Prolonged applause.

Yesterday there had been another demonstration, in Washington Square, not announced in advance because "the streets belong to the people." Those who resisted the police were wrestled to the ground by plain-clothes men, kicked, kneed, beaten with leather blackjacks, and those who tried to take pictures of the demonstrators being loaded into waiting vans were also taken into custody. This doesn't help Marie, she wishes she hadn't missed it.

The day before yesterday a doctor committed suicide in the Czechoslovak Republic; under Stalin he had been a doctor in the Ruzyně prison in Prague and Josef Pavel, the new minister of the interior, stated that he had been tortured by this doctor. And there is even to be an official investigation of the case. What the Communist brother parties negotiate among themselves the Czechoslovaks now wish to do publicly, and they have not yet banned a Club for Independent Political Thought either, not even the part of the socialists that aims to introduce unrestricted democratic life. What next?

Cresspahl was now in his third month as mayor of Jerichow, and he was still learning his job.

A mirror image was not much use to him. As mayor, to demand of local citizens what had been demanded of him as a citizen would not do. He remembered when his taxes had been due and carefully posted the dates well in advance: business tax by August 10, property tax by August 15, income and corporation taxes by September 10, and so on at quarterly intervals. But Leslie Danzmann helped him discover that most of the May and June taxes for 1945 had not been paid. A number of Jerichow people had already stopped paying while the Nazis were still in power; under British occupation they waited to see what would happen; and under the Soviets they had no wish to hand over any taxes, either current or overdue. K. A. Pontiy had no other suggestion than ruthless enforcement backed by one of his orders and the pretext that all taxes other than municipal were still "Reich taxes" although the Reich had been demolished (just as there was still a German Reich Railway although no Germans were allowed to travel on it). Cresspahl had nobody to collect back taxes; however, for the tax record of each delinquent taxpayer Leslie Danzmann had to compute a penalty of 5 per cent of the outstanding amount, retroactive to the German Reich months of March and February. The Mayor's office could put up a notice to this effect, in flagrant cases it could also send out notices; this put the treasury into debt with schoolboys for messengers' wages, but "Hitler's taxes for Stalin" did not materialize. Since the treasury had no money, it could only be in the pockets of the townspeople, and anyway in an age of barter it had no value; but the citizenry persisted in maintaining a defiant self-image that would render them subjects of the Soviets and not members of the community of Jerichow.

Men like Peter Wulff gave power of attorney to the town to deduct taxes from their bank accounts. But the bank accounts were frozen, and no one was allowed to touch them, neither Cresspahl nor the owners nor even K. A. Pontiy.

K. A. Pontiy ordered that the people of Jerichow be required to pay a penalty of an additional 5 per cent of the unpaid balance. This enabled Leslie Danzmann to calculate in tenths, and she found the job easier. It got no farther than the paper it was written on, and K. A. Pontiy ordered "executive action" against assets of delinquent taxpayers if they refused to hand over cash. Cresspahl asked to have the term explained to him.

What the commandant meant was the confiscation of marketable objects: machinery, motors, tools. Things like that.

Cresspahl suspected that, with the loss of means of production, labor would cease and consequently its taxable products. K. A. Pontiy bowed, sighing, before the omnipotence of dialectical materialism and ordered such tools to be left in the hands of the owners but not in their possession.

The Mayor could not make him understand, he could only warn him, that this really would mean the cessation of all work. Pontiy was agreeable to ordering people to work. At times Cresspahl could not suppress his laughter, it looked like a cough shaking his shoulders, and Pontiy sighed. What a strange country, this Mecklenburg.

All right—*kharasho*. Order: confiscation of private homes. Wholly or in part.

But this would remove any obligation to pay property taxes.

K. A. Pontiy stretched to his full height in his chair, as if wanting to have the problem shot. It had once been Papenbrock's office chair, and behind Pontiy's bald head two inlaid lions were intertwined. He looked sternly around at his second lieutenant, indicating that he should remove his hand from his holster. Then he gave Cresspahl the order to assess the amount of unpaid taxes and confiscate real estate accordingly. As a punishment and an example. Satys-fied, Mister Mayorr?

Cresspahl drank the schnapps that was meant to signify mutual consent (Pontiy had already placed his Mauser on the table as a sign that his mayor should drink), but he could not return to the town hall with any sense of satisfaction. Many, almost all, of the Jerichow houses had belonged to the local aristocracy, there were few of these who had not moved to the West, and they paid no property taxes to the town of Jerichow. However, the property of those who had left Jerichow after May 8, 1945, had been appropriated by the town—temporarily, but permanently if the owner should fail to return within one year. So while it was true that the town was now the owner of quite a number of houses, the taxes on these would have had to be paid by the town to itself, and it did not have the money.

(The Mayor's office might have raised the rent on the town's own property. But rent increases were strictly forbidden. And the people of Jerichow were holding back the money for leases and rent for the benefit of the owners who had fled—legally, as they felt here too—and the town got nothing.)

Cresspahl introduced monthly instead of quarterly payments of wage and business taxes. ("The Kommandantura hereby declares a state of emergency.")

However, Jerichow had been the workshop for the surrounding countryside, and the tradesmen were not getting enough work from the town. The local estates and village communities, now subdivided into independent Kommandanturas, paid in kind insofar as they were able (or permitted) to place orders in Jerichow. The town farmers recompensed their farm hands not in money but in food and drink and shelter plus the promise of wheat in winter. Was Cresspahl to order taxes to be paid in kind?

Mrs. Köpcke, of Köpcke Construction Co., offset the town's debt to Mrs. Köpcke against Mrs. Köpcke's personal debt to the town for any taxes levied against her by town or Reich up to—for the time being—March 3, 1946. She claimed to have entered each of these amounts as paid. Cresspahl signed. Received: one fence plus taxes (not in cash).

There was a further nocturnal dispute with K. A. Pontiy. Pontiy took the side of the German Reich and declared all obligations to the Reich valid beyond that day on which the German Reich had capitulated to him and to the Western Allies. The freezing of bank and other accounts had no effect in terms of civil rights. The days of civil rights were over!

Well then, Cresspahl said, the Red Army was a force majeure that had rendered all monetary institutions insolvent.

Pontiy would not go for that and sent away his mayor with the order to see that the dog taxes were paid. Cute, affectionate creatures, dogs were. Eh? A fine for failing to report. Per dog! Let's say: 150 reichmarks.

Cresspahl eliminated the corporation taxes. Such corporations no longer existed in Jerichow.

Then he seized the cash resources of the Farmers' Credit Bureau and paid the staff of the hospital, gasworks, and garbage collection, wages that had been owing them for the past three weeks ("since the Russians"). But he had the amount deducted proportionately from the remaining assets of the estate owners, whose accounts had not even been frozen—again because of their absence.

"A mayor like that always has one foot in jail."

"Yes, Gesine. Mm. But your father wasn't a crook. Like John Vliet Lindsay," said Marie. That was yesterday. She did not want to be consoled, and Cresspahl's trend toward Socialism was lost on her.

## April 29, 1968  Monday

Those for whom work is waiting in midtown still have to leave Riverside Drive at eight thirty, but the sun is rising differently. The change to summer time has moved it way over to the left again so that its downward dazzle is as it was six weeks ago. But the bottom of 96th Street was deep in shadow, and the lost hour gave one a genuine feeling of early morning in the shade.

When the Cresspahl child awoke, the July sun had already moved around the house, and the shade had cooled off the room. But it was too early for sounds of people moving about the house, and as for the Kommandantura across the street, that was still fast asleep. In the silence, in the shade, Gesine climbed out of the window and crept about yard and house looking for signs of Jakob.

It wasn't easy to find him; all of a sudden there he would be where a moment ago there was nothing.

It was an act of desperation to look for him, and a girl of twelve does have her pride. Jakob was not in Jerichow. He had hired himself out, with his horses, in a village way off to the west, it would take hours to walk there. Two open windows next to the front door were a good sign, Jakob's mother kept them closed at night in spite of the Soviet notice posted on the house to protect it. Gesine Cresspahl walks by, with the merest glance at them; she is on her way to the pump. Nor is there anything special about her going out into the yard, every inch a girl out for a stroll, she can casually turn around and check whether the chimney is smoking, an even better sign. For nobody starts the fire for breakfast as early as Jakob. But this wakes up Cresspahl, who plods to the kitchen in stocking feet (so as not to wake a sleeping child) and helps Jakob drink his coffee. There is no reason why the daughter of the house should not enter and sit down at the table, she is entitled to some breakfast. But it would look odd, it is too early, the children get their first meal of the day from Jakob's mother, and both Cresspahl and Jakob changed their tone the one time she did join them. As if she were not grown-up. The year of Jakob's birth, 1928, and the year of hers—subtract one from the other and the result is always the same stupid figure. Five whole years. You could sit in the shade beside the rotting beehives and figure out the years, and all of a sudden there was Jakob standing by the pump unwinding the scarf from around his neck. How could he walk so softly on bare feet! (On the path from the back door lay sharp gravel, strewn there years ago by Cresspahl to discourage his child from walking barefoot.) The wound on Jakob's neck had healed, but it still looked red and raw, and Gesine Cresspahl felt embarrassed. She hoped she was out of sight, but there he was calling her. And there you stood working the pump like a kid and had to splash water over the head and neck of a seventeen-year-old grownup, your face showing how exploited and ill-used you felt. But since Jakob did not say thank you, and just nodded, the child could not even refuse to be thanked! Then he is gone, and there wasn't even a chance to ask him about the red fox, and everything's gone wrong, it would have been better not to have seen him at all.

One weekend, late in the day, it was almost evening, Gesine Cresspahl was sitting high up in one of the walnut trees in front of the house. Don't worry, she has things to do up there. You can take a knife and cut something into the bark. Or, when she was crouching right up at the very top, almost above the branches, she could count the roof tiles. Or the ones with too much moss on them. Or look for a broken one. She most certainly wasn't up there in the tree because she could see across to the west without being seen by someone. You can't believe your eyes when a faint stroke appears on the horizon, quivering in the setting sun, and the next instant the path across the field is quite empty. He might come out of the forest too, at that bare spot called the Rehberge. But for that you have to climb right into the treetop, where it thins out dangerously, and the swaying tree would betray a child, she's too smart for that. By now she had made up her mind that the figure at the corner of the Russian fence was a stranger, not Jakob, then she heard his voice. She was so startled that her foot slipped, making a scraping sound. That might easily have been a bird. Only she couldn't see Jakob. The Abs windows were open, but his voice didn't sound as if he were indoors. Low, but as if he were in the yard. The place was empty. "Devyatnadtzat'," nineteen, said the voice, and down below she saw Draan the Red Army soldier, squatting by the trunk of the tree. The man shook his head and began a long story with "posledniy dyen'," the day before. "Nyeyasno," that's not clear, said Jakob in a friendly tone, and now she could see him too. He was squatting there like Draan, both gazing at the upper floor of the villa beyond the green fence, apparently concerned not with bargaining but with friendship between the German and Soviet peoples. But she could see a handful of blue-and-white bills, the money the Allies used, nobody in Jerichow would accept it as payment, Jakob tucked it into his shirt sleeve. (Into his shirt sleeve.) After what seemed an eternity Mr. Draan got to his feet and tramped off to the gate in the green fence, which was where he belonged, and Jakob stayed squatting under the tree. He did not look up, oh no, he was just resting there until Cresspahl's daughter grew quite stiff from sitting motionless on one and a half branches.

That night she was also up in the tree, and sure enough someone came out of the house, tinkling softly. It looked like a very fat person, for he walked very gingerly and his trouser legs were monstrously stuffed. This unknown person stopped by Gesine's tree and thumped it so hard that the upper branches actually shook a little. And said in Jakob's voice, dreamily, savoring the thought: I wonder when these walnuts will be ripe?

Blushing is something you can feel happening, some people learn that when they're kids, even on a very dark night.

And he preferred Hanna Ohlerich, that was obvious. Probably because she was a few months older. True, he did bring Gesine an egg too, but hers he placed in front of her while Hanna's he put into her hand. Hanna could say so casually that Jakob was in the yard, she had known as much for the last half hour, she might even have spoken to him, yet she wasn't the one who had been waiting for him! It was next to a girl like Hanna that you had to lie at night, and no matter how wide the bed was, the distance was never big enough. *She* slept, *she* wasn't thinking about . . . people in the night that tinkle like glass. Hanna sat beside him on the milk bench and asked him questions! And seemed to think nothing of it. True, he did call her Child, whereas he called the Cresspahl one by her first name. Because Hanna's parents were dead. Hanna told him about the time she had worked as a mechanic at sea, yet it had only been the Baltic, the flooded meadow, and she had been allowed to touch the engine of the cutter only to clean it! So another child has to sit there too, to make sure the boasting doesn't get out of hand. Squatting there at a distance, not because she wanted to join in the conversation. So Jakob came from Pomerania, did he? Gesine had known that for ages, the name of the village too, and that it had been on the River Dievenow. But some kids go on to ask about the island of Usedom. So it had been of no use to Jakob that the Poles hadn't bothered to take it? None. So Jakob has decided to stay on in Mecklenburg? Some people hold their breath until he says: We don't know yet; and how else is a girl to hide her disappointment, that sinking feeling, except by asking whether Jakob knows Podejuch? Podejuch in Pomerania. Jakob had never heard of Podejuch. So if a girl doesn't know what to say next, she had to drop out of the conversation, her whole body feels it has lost a battle, it feels all shrunken.

And the way the grownups monopolized Jakob, so that a child never got to talk to him! Supposing there were such children. Jakob was the newspaper for the house. If Jakob said the Germans were allowed to use electricity in Lübeck, even if only to listen to their radios, there was no point in doubting him. Maybe he crossed the boundary line. Jakob said: Stettin was in ruins, and the Poles would allow only 40,000 Germans to remain; so: Stettin was in ruins and there were only 40,000 Germans living there. It was useless for a child to then slyly ask about Haken Terrace, for he actually knew it. Sitting there looking rather sleepy, good-natured, eyes a bit lackluster, too much dark hair, inconspicuous. That must be how he got around so much. Or did he pick all this up from the papers? But there weren't any.

Not long after that, Jakob was sitting at the dinner table at Cresspahl's, which was where he belonged after all, yet he almost never came to Jerichow. Jakob said something about nuts. Wondering when those walnuts would be ripe.

How long before a child can leave the kitchen, without overturning the table or banging the door off its hinges!

High up in the black-market tree, not in the other one, Gesine Cresspahl found a piece of paper tied to a branch. It wasn't a piece of paper. It was a newspaper! The news sheet of the British Military Government published in Lübeck by the 21st Army Group. A real live newspaper, there was even a price printed on it.

Gesine Cresspahl would have liked to believe that for her sake Jakob had swum the Trave Canal or Dassow Lake to reach Lübeck. It was too much to believe; most likely he'd had business there.

But now Cresspahl's daughter shared a secret with him, she alone.

And when later that evening Cresspahl wanted to read the news from Lübeck, she denied to his face ever having heard of a newspaper published in a Western occupation zone.

And again Jakob had betrayed her to the grownups, for Cresspahl said: It was a secret, and could she keep her mouth shut yet again, and the thing was in the right-hand walnut tree, on the top of the fifth branch pointing east.

"Is that what it's like, being in love, Gesine?"

"That's what it was like for me."

"Is it hereditary?"

"Are you embarrassed for me, Marie?"

"No. Not at all. Only maybe I'd go about it differently."

"By all means."

"Shall I tell you when the time comes?"

"You won't."

"Because you were like that as a child, I must—"

"No. Not because of that. You're free, independent, not subject to direction and all that."

"Did the British newspaper feel damp?"

"It hadn't been in the water, if that's what you mean."

"Good. And what was in it anyway?"

"Nothing much. Things I've forgotten. And that at the end of July 1945 a plane crashed into the Empire State Building."

"A plane? Gesine!"

"A B-35 bomber, it rammed the seventy-ninth floor of what was then the tallest building in the world. The Empire State Building, 350 Fifth Avenue, between 33rd and 34th Streets. A familiar sight to every true New Yorker."

"You're trying to connect Jakob with New York, even if it has to be via a newspaper."

"If I want him in New York, I'll take you."

"Thanks for the information."

"You mean about the B-35 bomber?"

"No, that my father knew that the state of New York is known as the 'Empire State.' And that we have a building here that has 102 floors."

"101, according to his count."

"Yes. And I'd like to apologize too."

"Don't."

"I must. Ever since Saturday I've been unbearable."

"No, you haven't."

"I have. I've been sulking, I've not been answering you properly, just because of that Lindsay, that elected official, I've been unbearable."

"Forget it."

"And if I forget again what my father was like, let me know."

## May 2, 1968   Thursday

Today Auntie Times for once has something to report about her own family. She has visibly elevated two of her most faithful nephews in her undimmed eyes, and one of them finds that during his tenure the paper has already become "lighter in appearance and more inviting to read." Does he imagine we hadn't noticed? However, he reinforces our aunt's lofty principles as being unalterable: "To be the accurate, objective newspaper of record. To serve adult needs by being complete in our coverage. To explain, explain and explain again—not in the sense of a primer but in order to fill in the gaps for readers." We will remember that, we won't forget.

Nor will we forget the girl in the moving strip above and to the right of the ticket counter at Grand Central Station who, to the greater glory of some manufacturer, ceaselessly, perpetually, keeps combing and combing her hair.

The child that I was had lost her hair from an attack of typhoid that first summer after the war. She kept aloof from other people; there had been friendly types who had tried to encourage her by pulling off her beret to show that her appearance was not distasteful. Jakob acted as if he did not see Maurice's old beret on Gesine's head; when you were with him you could forget it and were only reminded of it by the sweat. He tried to help, but not with force, not even with words. He sent a stranger to the property, shorn like a Red Army soldier and, since he was wearing civilian trousers, rolled to the knee, and an oversize shirt, he could have been a Red Army deserter on the run who had turned up all unsuspecting at the very gates to a Kommandatura. The stranger did not seem nervous, he sat down on the milk bench behind the house and waited. It was early morning, and although it was harvest time there was no one around to see him but Cresspahl's daughter. She went outside, then back into the house to report the beggar, but he called after her. His voice was just like Jakob's but she did not recognize him until she cam back with the mirror. He studied his reflection, grasping the frame of the mirror on his knees. She stood beside him. In the mirror she saw almost no hair at all, a long, shiny skull above a naked face, slightly familiar around the eyes. He sat staring somewhat morosely into the mirror, as if critical of the handiwork of the hair stylist who had made him look like that. He did not need to utter a word, she understood the wager, child that I was, and took off her beret. The mirror showed that she was ahead of him with hair, although the sight was still a shock to her. Then it grew again, my hair.

## May 3, 1968    Friday

Now the Communists in Prague have the $400 million from Moscow almost in their pockets, and they can admit that the delay in wheat shipments from the Soviet Union has not been all that bad. On the contrary, they had recently been more abundant than the original agreement had called for; the New York *Times* thinks this is a bit fishy. The U. S. Government tries a different tack and speaks openly of its "interest in and sympathy for recent developments in Czechoslovakia, which seem to represent the wishes and needs of the Czechoslovak people"; indeed, in the face of dwindling gold reserves and in an election year it would be prepared to discuss supplying gold to a Communist country; unmoved, Mr. Dubček sends special greetings from the May Day Parade to the Soviet Union, "whence our freedom came and from which we can expect fraternal aid." He will not allow a quarrel to be stirred up. He tries to smooth matters down on the other side: maybe the Czechoslovak Republic will use the Soviet dollars to acquire manufacturing licenses in the United States. Of course, as far as the U. S. Government's position is concerned, it was "irresponsible and unacceptable." Time to get down off the fence.

The town of Jerichow lay surrounded by wheat fields, close to the fish of the Baltic; yet it did not have enough to eat. The townspeople of former times would have been able to help each other out, craftsmen bargaining with farmers; now that the refugees were occupying rooms, attics, and stables, there was not enough bread. The military commandant wanted to be not only a good paterfamilias but a proud one, and he ordered the unclaimed harvest brought in.

The Mayor had a different approach and ordered that all those who
(1) owned a scythe
(2) could wield a scythe
report to the town hall, Room 4, now designated a labor office. By July 12 the office had been notified of the existence of eight scythes in all of Jerichow, most of these having been reported by spiteful neighbors rather than by their owners. Ten times as many people as scythes turned up for mowing, almost all of them women and refugees at that, and

all of them claimed they could mow, they had even brought along their small children to tie the sheaves, to steal the grain. It was a motley, ragged crowd, some were prepared to tackle the stubble barefoot, and all were emaciated by hunger. A bottle of water and the prospect of a handful of grain, that was to be their lunch. Cresspahl remembered the heavy swing wrenched from the shoulders by the scythe; in the presence of such people he must not sigh.

He escorted this band of walking refugees out of town to a field that had once formed part of one of the landed estates. He led off by mowing one length along the side, then took off his jacket and looked back. The women were far behind him, and still farther back the children were running about carrying sheaves that were collapsing in their arms. So now he lost a morning showing them over and over again how to plant one's legs firmly on the ground and shift one's weight so as not to be thrown to the ground by the swing of the scythe. And the children, many of them from towns, could not understand how a handful of stalks can be twisted under the elbow to form a cord that you knotted underneath. One of them, his own Gesine, was so eager that she seemed to have two left hands. As midday approached he had little more from his team than the promise to keep trying. "Cresspahl's bunch of cripples" is what they were called in Jerichow, but on the second day the sheaves stood too thickly to be counted at a glance, despite the resemblance to a rough sea offered by the stubble. And the dumbbells who had responded to Cresspahl's summons were paid half in cash and half in grain from last year's harvest, weighed out daily in Papenbrock's granary. For a time there were women in Jerichow, wives of respected citizens, who would have gladly put in a belated appearance with forgotten scythes, or merely to tie up the sheaves.

Then some of the women were attacked by comrades of K. A. Pontiy, and did not return. One was found too late, lying with a smashed jaw in a hawthorn hedge, and she died on the way to the hospital, carried in a horse blanket, a heavy load for four women. K. A. Pontiy disclaimed responsibility for men under the command of other Kommandanturas, he was already involved in a dispute with the commandant of Knesebeck. There a Red soldier had returned to quarters with scythe wounds all down one arm and across his back, with a story of a Fascist ambush, but it had merely been children trying to defend their mother. Pontiy started a search in Jerichow for Hitlerite Werewolves, and Cresspahl was repeatedly on the point of being shot. Reconciliation followed, and Pontiy solemnly declared his willingness to provide the volunteers with an escort from among his men. Now the women refused to go to work under such protection. K. A. Pontiy ordered the harvest brought in forthwith.

There were still men on the local farms who had harvesting machines, but Cresspahl had great difficulty in persuading the men to take these to the fields owned by the local aristocracy, this time for legal reasons. The crops had been sown by the Plessens, they had always been looked after by the estates: wouldn't they be stealing if they harvested them now? As elsewhere in Mecklenburg, people in Jerichow regarded it as a sin to let wheat rot on the stalk; but this was outweighed by their dread of the anger of the landowners who had fled. Cresspahl was finally able to persuade them to start salvaging the wheat, in trust, so to speak. Now they cleared the fields lying beyond the leased areas, and at night they also guarded the crops that were not theirs with cudgels and dogs (for which they did not pay the new tax). Those who persisted in refusing had their equipment confiscated by Cresspahl as soon as they were through with their own harvest. And he found it easier to take possession after stopping ration coupons to any Jerichow family that did not have at least one member working. (When the Mayor wangled a card for Gesine on the grounds that she was working and then gave it to Mrs. Abs for her son Jakob, this was regarded as fraud.) Being made to take their equipment to the fields was looked on as compulsion, and the work that went on there lacked the appetite that is aroused by ownership, with the result that tools and machinery tended to break down more readily. It was of little use for Cresspahl to talk about a benefit to the town: they saw it only as a benefit to the Russians. The fact that Red Army soldiers were to be seen racing their horses along the paths did not help matters either. And even worse was that a detachment turned up in one field just outside Jerichow and proceeded to exchange the horses hitched to a cart for two worn-out nags, just as if it were wartime, with revolvers at the ready. If twenty people had leaned against the spokes they could have pushed the cart, but that day no more work was done. That evening Gesine arrived, leading the two sick Russian horses, which no one had wanted to take along, and waited for Cresspahl outside the door of the Kommandantura. Inside, Cresspahl was busy negotiating the return of a tractor that had been "borrowed" by the Red Army, the commandant having required it to take him to Gneez, where he had absent-mindedly left it behind. K. A. Pontiy was not entirely comfortable, there was also the matter of several cans of diesel oil, and he casually mentioned the Ukraine. In the Ukraine, it seemed, the people got together to carry in the grain for threshing, they didn't need any vehicle for that; and apparently the women and children pulled the plow, and anyway the milk yield from cows did not begin to decrease appreciably until after four months, see also agricultural results obtained in Switzerland. After listening to these items of cultural information, Cresspahl repeated his question. "What tractor?" said K. A. Pontiy, confused for the moment and at a loss for some while.

He regarded the return of the horses by Gesine as a sign of honesty, a restitution of army property, and waved to her to go around the corner of the building into the Bäk. But the child wanted them replaced, by new ones—*noviye*, she said, scared though she was of mispronouncing the word, and Pontiy explained to her in a kindly, affable manner that as horses these were not *noviye*, no comparison with the Ukrainian breed! Cresspahl grabbed the reins from the child's hands and left the trampled front garden of the brickyard villa without another word. Later, when it was dark, K. A. Pontiy went to see him and threatened to have his mayor shot if he did not ensure that the town had enough to eat.

What made the commandant uneasy was the prospect of a comparison with the way things had been run under the British occupation, and one day he asked Cresspahl point-blank about this. My father decided to let Pontiy stew for a bit, and he described the rule of the British over Jerichow as having been bearable if not beneficent. Their administration had been good because they knew exactly when they were going to leave. They had lived on the available supplies, there had been plenty for eight weeks. When they left, the railway had no more coal and could neither take milk to Gneez nor bring potatoes to Jerichow. The Jerichow gasworks had had to be shut down, not without damage to the furnaces; the employees wandered around in the fields, depressed and unskilled. The bakeries were still without fuel. The British had made generous distributions from the warehouses, of sugar and salt and oil, and the villages and estates had trustingly done their best to deliver their quotas of beef cattle and milk. The British had let Cresspahl use town funds to pay all outstanding wages and accounts. Under their rule, even the school had been open, two days after they arrived. They were concerned to leave behind a good memory of Western methods so that the Soviets would have trouble doing likewise with their own. They were maintaining their favorable image from a distance and supplied electrical power to Jerichow from their Herrenwyk power station, and Pontiy was not pleased to hear this. Cresspahl was half expecting an order to build an independent electricity supply for Jerichow, but for the time being his job was to feed the local inhabitants as well as the British had done, and in four weeks better.

The Mayor's office in Jerichow made a contract with the fisher-

men's guild in Rande, represented by Ilse Grossjohann, for a daily
supply of at least two cases of fish. (This was the old guild that had
been dissolved by the Nazis and re-established by permission of the
British.) Mrs. Grossjohann's counterdemands changed frequently:
sometimes the fishermen needed sailcloth, sometimes they needed nails
and sometimes lubricating oil, and Cresspahl could not find all these
things in Jerichow to confiscate. He told his commandant nothing
about these deals, and the latter did not mention it either, but after a
week had gone by Pontiy's jeep turned up one morning in Rande with
Red Army soldiers demanding the "fish for Jerrichoff." Not only had
Mrs. Grossjohann learned something about law during her years of
employment with Kollmorgen: by now she had been a prosperous
fisherman's wife for three years, and she insisted on the contract being
carried out, even if this meant invoking force majeure. Before Cresspahl
could set off to lodge the complaint, two bales of plaice and blackcock
had been delivered to his home, his share in Pontiy's socialism. He
sent the fish to the hospital and arranged with the fishermen's guild to
change the landing places, but even so Pontiy got in ahead of him
often enough.

From the Soviet administrator of the Beckhorst estate (formerly
the Kleineschulte farm) Cresspahl was offered both beef cattle and milk.
The people on the estate needed string, crude oil, leather for machinery
belts. Cresspahl could picture the cows, tough old crocks, but he was
willing to take them sight unseen. It was a complicated business. First
the town had to loan Alfred Bienmüller to the Beckhorst estate so that
he could repair the motor and combine which lacked crude oil and
leather. However, Alfred Bienmüller's outfit had meanwhile become
the official repair shop for the Jerichow Kommandantura, and K. A.
Pontiy's trucks had priority, especially the one he wished to exchange
for a roadster—to the advantage and disadvantage of the Knesebeck
commandant—for purposes of reconciliation. Bienmüller applied for
a permit to go to Beckhorst, for family reasons, and Pontiy had no
choice but to sign it and have it stamped. Milk was scarce in the town
because the local cows, like those that had been seized from trekking
refugees, had been herded together on seven estates; their milk went
to the Red Army, not to the district offices and not to the rural towns
and villages, and even among its friends the Jerichow Kommandatura
had a reputation for self-sufficiency. The milk from Beckhorst did not
find its way to Pontiy. One night Bienmüller walked along the coast
and next day repaired the machines on the estate; the following night
he planned to escort the truckload of milk cans back to Jerichow. At
the edge of the forest he was challenged by the Mayor of the village,

who was having a row with the Soviet administrator and needed the milk for his refugee children because the farmers were now pressing butter into barrels. Cresspahl did not invoke force majeure, he renegotiated this part of the deal into an exchange of salt for butter and supplied the string from Papenbrock's stores. The cows got as far as the Rande highway, and from there the Red Army herded them into their little hideaway in the Bäk. At least, that was where Klein the butcher had to slaughter them, not in his yard where they could have been seen; his display window remained empty. By the end of July it had been a long time since people had been getting their three and a half ounces of meat per head. Cresspahl could not even get the daily half-pint of milk per child that he considered essential (as did Pontiy. But Pontiy got as much as he wanted from the dairy, with the invariable remark that he had children in his fortress too). Cresspahl would have preferred it if the foreign commandant had made off with food intended for Germans out of hatred, to punish them, if you like; he could not accept the game that Pontiy made of it, complete with soulful *nichevo* and lordly *shistkoyedno*.

Cresspahl ordered each poultry-keeper to hand over one egg per day, such eggs to be exchangeable only for coupons from children's ration cards. What he got was complaints of chickens being stolen, particularly from those houses with back yards bordering on the Soviets' green fence. There was no need for him to go chasing after the birds. You could hear them in the Bäk, a street that had once been far above such things as poultry-keeping. Now, because the heads of hens and cocks were sometimes left behind by the thieves in the miraculously undamaged coops, poultry began to be slaughtered secretly in Jerichow. Cresspahl could prohibit this. And at Pontiy's banquets he could stuff his pockets with hard-boiled eggs.

It was not that he was afraid of his people "going a bit hungry"; there was no starvation yet, that would come with winter. But he was powerless against talk, against the vague insidious rumblings—more resigned than malicious: nothing made sense, everything was going to wrack and ruin, everything was for the Russians. This could turn into panic, enough to tip the delicate balance of maintaining food supplies in the town.

The Mayor decreed:

The town of Jerichow has sufficient stocks of

last year's potatoes to cover its requirements and was given permission to prohibit the harvesting of new potatoes before August 15, 1945. This was interpreted to mean that he was obviously foreseeing a shortage of potatoes and was actually trying to warn the town; that in his heart of hearts he was a Mecklenburger after all, and on the side of the Mecklenburgers. During subsequent nights, the townspeople stole their own potatoes, hid them in their cellars, and produced them as a new currency in their haggling with the refugees. The Jerichow Kommandantura stopped a group of workers on their way to the fields and forced them to dig up an acre of new potatoes, yet it wasn't even the end of July. Mind you, the Mayor couldn't forbid his Soviet masters anything; he didn't want to blame them for liking the fresh new taste, but he didn't like them making nonsense of his efforts to feed the town.

And once again he started up business on his own, something that with the arrival of the victors had been forbidden,

since the end of World War II the U. S. A. has been holding $20 million of Czechoslovak gold bullion as security for confiscated American property. The people in Prague are offering 2 million for restitution and settlement. The United States is demanding $110 million. Whose turn is it now?

and used an electric motor at Alfred Bienmüller's and a set of rubber tires in Knesebeck to bring off a business deal, plus a considerable quantity of window glass and lubricating oil, and in Rande found that the harvest truck he wanted to make road-worthy again had disappeared but in its place maybe a pile of freshly dug new potatoes and a couple of hundredweight of wheat in brand-new sacks. Civilians were forbidden to accept articles of daily use or items of food from Soviet soldiers. But for the window glass he had given his word, and those who had dug potatoes for the Soviets had been allowed to take home from the Bäk two cauldrons of hearty stew such as he had not been able to obtain for the hospital.

One thing, however, he had managed to accomplish, to the considerable dismay of the commandant. The next time K. A. Pontiy behaved like the Queen of Hearts on the rampage, threatening him with execution, Cresspahl was able to nod pleasantly and as if in agreement yet without abandoning his cause. It resembled the scene where the Cheshire Cat's head was to be cut off because the cat only wanted to look at the King and declined to kiss his hand. But all the cat revealed of itself was its head, and a grin. The executioner refuses to cut off a head unless there is a body to cut it off from. The King says that anything that has a head can be beheaded and enough of all this nonsense. But the Queen wants everybody executed all round, if something isn't done about it in less than no time,

*in less than no time, Gesine!*
*is he going to shoot you, Cresspahl?*

and the cat's head stays up in the sky and the executioner comes back and the cat has vanished, head, smile, and all.

---

## May 5, 1968   Sunday

---

The military commandant of the town of Jerichow, K. A. Pontiy—he might shoot at birds with a rifle, he might stroke a cat or give it a kick, he might take Cresspahl's daughter to task for not sweeping the path to his villa quite clean enough, but he did not entirely forfeit her respect. She was, quite simply, grateful to him. He had removed the corpses from her sight.

The British had made dead people public in Jerichow. They were the inmates of the Nazi concentration camps of Neuengamme, twelve miles southeast of Hamburg, and its Mecklenburg subsidiary camps of Boizenburg and the Reiherhorst at Wöbbelin. At Neuengamme the German Reich had left it too late. When the German Reich had to evacuate the camps of Majdanek, Treblinka, Bełżec, and Sobibór in occupied Poland, it put gangs of prisoners to work to open up the mass graves, dig up the bodies, and grind the bones. The bone meal was strewn over the fields, the gas chambers and ovens were blown up, and after flattening the camps to a state of virgin smoothness the inmates were killed for their efforts. In Austria the Germans were obliged to abandon the camp at Mauthausen, and at Neuengamme they also left it too late. The Danish Government negotiated the return of their nationals until, in April 1945, it could arrange for their transportation by the much-discussed "Convoy of Ninety-two Buses" to Frøslev and Møgelkaer. At Neuengamme more than 6,000 prisoners remained behind under German command: to prevent the British from finding them, these people were evacuated. To begin with, on the journey to Lübeck via Hamburg 500 died in the freight cars, unable to endure still further starvation and deprived of medical care. Four carloads of sick were not even transferred to the ships; the prisoners, screaming in their fever, were shot to death, and if someone failed to hear this in Lübeck's outer harbor, he may have picked up the sounds of revelry made by the German SS in the grain silo right next to it as they celebrated final victory with the best brandy and delicacies from stolen Red Cross parcels. The prisoners, of whose existence the people of Lübeck were unaware, waited almost ten days at the dock, in freight cars of the German Reich Railway, in the open, or crammed into the *Thielbek* and the *Athen*; alongside the harbor the dead continued to be buried in shallow graves. In 1944 the *Thielbek* had been bombed and she was still far from seaworthy again; two tugs were needed to tow her down the Trave and out into the bay. The *Athen* could move under her own steam and was transporting batch after batch of prisoners from Lübeck's industrial harbor to the *Cap Arcona* in Neustadt's bay. The three ships packed with concentration-camp inmates were clearly visible from land and a familiar sight not only to the fishermen. The *Thielbek*, 2,815 gross tons, 350 feet long, drawing 21 feet, had carried freight for Knöhr & Burchardt in Hamburg. The *Athen*, somewhat smaller, was also equipped to carry freight, not human beings. The *Cap Arcona* had been built for passengers, a luxury liner of the Hamburg–South America Line, 27,560 gross tons, 687 feet long, drawing 29 feet. Before the war she was on the Rio de Janeiro run, thirty-five days, first class only, for 1,275 reichmarks. "Avoid part of the winter—relax in southern sunshine and mild sea air!" The *Cap Arcona* was built to carry 1,325 passengers and a crew of 380; now she had 4,600 prisoners in her hold, the sick at the very bottom, without medicine or dressings, the Russian prisoners in the banana hold, without light or air and for the first three days without food; the dead were stacked up on deck. The vessel stank of the dead, of disease and the excrement of the living; a sink of putrefaction, and stationary at that. For the *Cap Arcona* was not seaworthy either, since she had no fuel. There was almost no food for the prisoners, they were not even given water to drink, but roll call every morning was compulsory. It took longer to die here than in the gas chamber, but the day was in sight when they would all be dead.

Then came liberation. Liberation came on May 3 over the clear sunny bay in the form of a squadron of British bombers. At about two thirty they crossed over Neustadt harbor and went to work on the *Athen*. The Germans defended their prisoners with antiaircraft fire; after the third direct hit they hoisted a white flag. The British pilots may well have seen this, for they switched their attack to the ships lying in the outer bay. After twenty minutes the *Thielbek* turned onto her side and disappeared without trace below the surface, the water there being sixty feet deep. The *Cap Arcona*, with the captain's bedsheet at the mast, lasted an hour, then she tipped over onto her port side, slowly, then faster and faster until she lay on her side with twenty-seven of her eighty-seven-foot width above water. Meanwhile death was proceeding swiftly and variously. The prisoners could die in the fire, in the smoke (the fire hoses had been cut), from the rifles of the German crew (the crew had life jackets), squashed among hoarded food supplies, crushed in the panic-stricken throng, from the heat of the still-glowing hulk of the *Cap Arcona*, in the plunging lifeboats, by leaping into the water, or in the water from the cold or the blows and shots from the German minesweepers, or on land from exhaustion. 3,100 people were saved. Between 7,000 and 8,000 died. At about seven o'clock the British took over Neustadt, which, like Jerichow, was in the British Zone; contact was still permitted between the two towns, that's how we heard about it.

The dead drifted onto every shore of Lübeck Bay, from Bliestorf to Pelzerhaken, from Neustadt to Timmendorf Beach, into the mouth of the River Trave, from Priwall to Schwansee and Redewisch and Rande, right into the Wohlenberg creek and as far as Poel Island, the other Timmendorf. They turned up almost daily.

Too many found their way to the coast near Jerichow for the finders to bury them all secretly in the sand. The British occupation authorities had ordered that all corpses found in the water be reported, and they insisted on this. The British brought along a truck and rounded up men who had been members of the Nazi Party. They were driven along the beach, and wherever a black lump lay in the white sand the British stopped. The Germans were given no gloves, or even forks or shovels, for the job of loading the bodies onto the truck. The British drank their whisky while the Germans were loading; despite this medicine, even they had to vomit. The British provided no special cemetery for the dead from this watery camp. When the truck was full they drove the load far inland, all the way to Kalkhorst and even Gneez. When they drove into Jerichow the side flaps were let down. The military police made the Germans come out of their houses so they could see the load as it was driven at walking pace down Town Street to the cemetery. Slower than walking pace. The contents of the truck were not readily identifiable. The remains were damaged by bullet wounds, charring, bomb splinters, blows, recognizable by the faded, burst garments of clinging striped cotton. Often the human remains were incomplete. Limbs were missing, or limbs without torsos lay on the floor of the truck, one day only part of a head, much of it eaten away by fish. The British rounded up the townspeople on the market square. In the middle lay the first load of corpses. The commandant presented the Germans with their dead, made the Germans a gift of them. He allowed them to place the mortal remains from the sea into coffins. Then they were permitted to close the coffins and carry them to the cemetery. When the mass grave had been covered with earth, the British fired a salute into the air. At the cemetery gate stood a sergeant holding a box on which he stamped ration cards. Those who had not accepted the dead would not eat.

"It was their own dead, they belonged to those lousy British!" said Marie. "You guys let them get away with anything, and then some!"

"They belonged to the Germans. The Germans had kept them prisoner, loaded them onto ships; only, they would have died more slowly if they had kept them."

"The bombs came from the British. They must have seen the prisoners' uniforms, yet still they fired at them. That's the truth."

"The British wouldn't accept that truth. You could be locked up for less than that. German submarines had been lying all around the ships, above the surface, they were never hit; to whisper about that was too risky."

"You knew all about it."

"It certainly wasn't news. A few days before, one might have seen prisoners like that in striped clothing in Mecklenburg (probably not in Lübeck), but as far as talking about them went, they didn't exist. Now the British were bringing along corpses and decreeing the cause of death any way they pleased."

"Even if the Mecklenburg people lacked guts, the British certainly didn't."

"By 1956 they had published five volumes dealing with the air attacks on Germany up until the end of the war. On May 3 the war was still on, but nowhere is there any mention of the bombing of Lübeck Bay."

"Official history. Deadpan."

"It's also official history that the British arrived before the German submarines had time to sink the prisoners themselves. Official history also is the monument in the Old Cemetery at Jerichow."

"And one in the British Zone?"

"At Pelzerhaken near Neustadt. And four years later the British gave permission to the owners of the *Thielbek* to salvage her. The sea had not managed to wash out the vessel entirely, there were still some bodies left behind, piles of bare bones; it was quite possible to repair her. Let's call the old tub the *Reinbek* and have her run till 1961, until it's worth selling her. Today if you happen to see a *Magdalena* flying the Panamanian flag, that's the *Thielbek* of May 1945. The *Cap Arcona* was fit only for the scrap yard. But in 1946 the *Athen* became the Soviet *General Brusilov*, when she was put on the run from Gdynia to Buenos Aires and Rio de Janeiro for the Polish Line. All that's left of the *Cap Arcona* is the ship's bell; you've seen that."

"In the Freedom Museum at Copenhagen!"

"At Churchill Park, in Copenhagen!"

"And you still didn't mind swimming in the Baltic?"

"We ate fish from the Baltic. The Germans are still eating fish from the Baltic. There are nearly 3,000 prisoners lying at the bottom of the sea."

"And K. A. Pontiy wouldn't allow it?"

"He wouldn't allow the education of Germans by corpses being transported overland. That flotsam had to be collected in the cemeteries of the coastal villages, outside his territory. That cost—"

"—and he let Jerichow pay for it."

"Send a complaint, Marie."

"No. I would have been grateful to him too."

Jerichow had long since had its other cemetery, the one K. A. Pontiy had ordered, to the left of the Rande highway between town and Air Force base, on land confiscated from the aristocracy. It was not fenced in, but Pastor Brüshaver had stood there and performed the acts and spoken the words he had deemed necessary for a consecration. From the land side it was reached by going around the town, about a mile and a half, maybe half an hour longer by horse and cart.

Known today as the Central Municipal Cemetery. Surrounded by a low wall of rough stones and, inside that, by a ring of briars. The chapel, built in 1950 and much more solid than a garage, cannot be seen from the highway.

The old chapel, near Cresspahl's house, has been torn down and replaced by a section of white brick wall between the red bricks of 1850. And the churchyard is considered worth a visit because it has remained virtually untouched for more than twenty years.

### May 6, 1968 Monday

Yesterday, the 150th anniversary of the birth of Karl Marx, the New York *Times* took part in the ceremonies in and around the house where he was born in Trier, West Germany. Students shouted "Ho Chi Minh!" as the President of the Social Democratic Party, the owners of the building, was entering. The East Germans staged their own show. At the former, Ernst Bloch said at the symposium that many errors had been committed in the name of Marx. "Some people not only do not know anything about Marx but they tell lies about him."

Cast of characters:

MONSIEUR HENRI ROCHE-FAUBOURG, one of the heirs to a French banking firm. Age twenty-one, weight 136 lbs., complexion sallow, race Caucasian, hair black, the ends split, curling over his shirt collar. A Frenchman, graduate of an elite school in Paris. Has begun the study of law and political economy. Sent by his father for one year to

New York. A person who feels insulted when he is not immediately received by a New York colleague of his father's but instead is handed over to a subordinate of the boss for preliminary treatment. At a meal at the Brussels two weeks ago he was capable, until coffee was served, of refusing to believe in the French spoken by the lady accompanying him, clung to his role as the only person in New York who could speak and understand French, although the waiter offered proof to the contrary. He regarded his language as his exclusive property and, although unable to punish encroachment on this with the whip, he did resort, and generously, to lack of comprehension. He then kissed the hand of the lady who was paying the bill and said, with a smile on his red impatient lips: "What a charming remark you just made!" It had been a comment on the enamel-like quality of American make-up and, like all her previous remarks, had been made in French. He replied for the first time in this language. Can muster thirty-one words of American, of which thirty are English. Wears long jackets, reaching to the tips of his extended fingers, nipped in at the waist.

DE ROSNY: First name unknown.

The scene is a descending elevator in the rear bank. It is an ordinary elevator, not reserved for top executives, the time is one hour after closing, and the Vice-President is alone in the elevator with Mrs. Cresspahl. He is reproducing for her benefit a conversation he had had with ROCHE-FAUBOURG, switching alternately from himself to the young scion.

DE ROSNY: Well, what was it you had in mind with us?

ROCHE-FAUBOURG: My father has left the decision up to me.

DE ROSNY: Looks like he's a typical American father. The other day he seemed quite normal.

ROCHE-FAUBOURG: My father's health is excellent, thank you.

DE ROSNY: I guess I'm about to behave like a German father—

ROCHE-FAUBOURG: I beg your pardon—?

DE ROSNY: Because there's something I wish to tell you. You must complete your education.

ROCHE-FAUBOURG: Yes, I had been planning to study business administration.

DE ROSNY: What nonsense—business administration indeed! You'll learn that when you take over your father's business, and if you turn out to be a flop you can delegate the job to somebody else. And all the other jobs too.

ROCHE-FAUBOURG: I thought—

DE ROSNY: Your career has been laid down for you—right? In a few years' time you'll be taking over your father's business.

ROCHE-FAUBOURG: I flatter myself—

DE ROSNY: So it's your duty to enjoy the free time you have left. Before it's too late!

ROCHE-FAUBOURG: The American idea of enjoyment—

DE ROSNY: If you really want to, you can work here for a year. Hurrying through all the departments.

ROCHE-FAUBOURG: Perhaps six months.

DE ROSNY: Although for that, of course, you would need to be interested in the labor situation in the United States.

ROCHE-FAUBOURG: That would mean—

DE ROSNY: You could read a few books. What you have to do right now is live. How old are you?

ROCHE-FAUBOURG: Twenty-one.

DE ROSNY: First you have to learn *how* to live. And in June you should pick up a sports car and spend two months driving around the country. Go to a Communist Party rally. Our Mrs. Cresspahl will be able to tell you what you ought to know about New York.

ROCHE-FAUBOURG: I recently gained the impression, in the most charming way—

DE ROSNY: There you are! But don't take up too much of her time, she's working for me.

ROCHE-FAUBOURG: Do you suppose I might occasionally—

DE ROSNY: Business administration, what nonsense! That's all right for someone who's never going to take over. You are going to take over your father's, aren't you?

ROCHE-FAUBOURG: If my brother—

DE ROSNY: And when the year's up you're to come back to me for tests. G'bye.

ROCHE-FAUBOURG: Good-by.

As they walked along, the Vice-President repeated parts of the scene, to the amusement of other subordinates, who walked quickly past him, trying to make their haste look like tact. The Vice-President is in another kind of hurry, he has no train to catch, his black, air-conditioned limousine is waiting for him. But he keeps fingering his cigarette without bringing it to his lips, for he needs his lips to say: "You must get the picture, this confrontation between me and that young man. No one had ever spoken to him like that before, and it was only by the skin of his teeth that he didn't miss it. And yet people always think German fathers are dictators, tyrants I guess, and there was I, an American, telling a French boy: What you have to do is such and such. You must finish your education. . . ."

"Karl Marx won't be of much use to him now, Mr. De Rosny."

"There I go again, forgetting you had a German father. Can you ever forgive me, Mrs. Cresspahl?"

"No. Never."

"You're O.K., young lady. If only everyone who works for me were like you. If only they were all like that."

---

## May 7, 1968   Tuesday

So what has Alexander Dubček brought back from occupation head-quarters in Moscow? "Understanding" for the initiation of democracy in his country, "full respect of mutual rights," and very nearly the hard-currency loan from the leading treasury. He said he had been "happy to explain" his type of socialism to the Soviet comrades.

In the eyes of Jerichow it almost served Papenbrock right to be taken away by the Russians. Maybe not exactly right, but fair enough considering how Albert had profited from Göring's Luftwaffe. So now the former tycoon of Jerichow was going to have to pay his back taxes.

That's what it looked like. The conquerors had driven onto the market square one Sunday evening in mid-July in a two-ton truck; there was no sign of K. A. Pontiy, thus the impression was given of some official action on the part of his superiors. Three men walked into the house, all officers, not with drawn weapons, yet as if they were about to make an arrest. The fact that they spent half an hour inside must mean they were searching Albert's office for his earthly gains, and the silence with which they went to work only made the surprise visit more ominous, plus the recollection that Albert was by no means the only one whose friendship with Göring's Luftwaffe might offend the Russians. Only one person sent for Cresspahl, Bergie Quade, but her husband Otto was back in Town Street much sooner than the Mayor, whose slow-paced approach seemed to say that the very fact of their relationship meant there was nothing he could do to help.

Papenbrock was already being led out of his house, wearing a work shirt and shabby trousers, shoulders bent, eyes on the ground, arms hanging empty at his sides. People used to describe how the old man tried to step over the tailboard into the truck but slipped back, and again placed his lame foot on the board, and how again it had scraped down the side, this time landing sharply against his other shin, and how the officers had stood looking on as if he had been a sick animal not worth helping. Then Louise came running out of the house, bawling her head off and brandishing a bulging holdall, as if intending to injure herself or one of the officers. Finally one of them gave Papenbrock a gentle shove, but not as if wanting to hurt him; Albert lurched forward onto the floor of the truck, the officers got in after him and bolted the tailboard, the truck turned and drove off again to the south, perhaps to headquarters in Schwerin, possibly even to a larger prison. Although they had taken the holdall from Louise, they gave it not to her husband but to the driver and, although Albert might have a bit longer to live under surveillance, it did not look as if he were ever coming back.

Although there were few onlookers, accounts of what happened were not fragmentary. They had kept a respectful distance so as not, inadvertently, to share the trip with Albert, but each of them claimed to have felt a shiver when Louise, still a stout woman, tugged twice at the jamming front door, with both hands, apparently weakened by her tears, until she got it shut and bolted it on the inside. Thus the witnesses were spared having to express their sympathy, but in stepping back and turning around they found themselves confronted by Cresspahl, known to them as the Russian stooge and a traitor. Close to him as they were, nobody wanted to say to his face that now he had even failed to rescue his own father-in-law, and they felt trapped in his silent, challenging gaze. Cresspahl had been amused by the Russians' flight from Louise's copious tears, so he seemed almost relaxed as he stood with his head tilted toward the evening sky and looked at his watch. "It's nine o'clock," he said, as a reminder of approaching curfew, the Russian minion, instead of staggering under the misfortunes of the family, and they let him walk down Town Street alone. He had not even volunteered any information. However, nine o'clock it was. All of a sudden one could smell the hour, sweet, not nourishing, slightly greasy, the smell of lime blossom.

If one imagines Jerichow as the central point of a clock (at which on maps of Lübeck Bay the Hydrographic Institute places a compass rose), the village and bathing beach of Rande would be at approximately one o'clock. Looking from Jerichow, at about eight o'clock but far beyond the edge of the clock face, lay the Old Demwies estate, southwest of Gneez, in what had once been the principality of Ratzeburg, far enough removed from Jerichow. Those who had hidden their telephones instead of handing them over still could not get through to any other exchange, the post office still had no letters to deliver, the travel ban took care of the rest, and so for some while Albert Papenbrock was believed to have vanished without trace. It was toward the end of 1945 before a rumor started up in Jerichow that someone was managing the distant Old Demwies estate for the Russians, someone named Papenbrock. If the reports were to be believed, he did not behave like an old man of seventy-seven, he ordered the farm hands around just like an overseer of the old days, and he talked to his Soviet superiors in a manner that gave no inkling of his ever having soiled his hands with the Nazis, he certainly didn't sound bashful. And if a person's described to you only in words, do you recognize him right off? It was said he had found his way there from over by the River Müritz, maybe it wasn't the Jerichow Papenbrock. Cresspahl couldn't be asked, Papenbrock's wife pretended to know nothing about it, so maybe it wasn't he. When the Soviet counterintelligence people visited Jerichow, the interpreters almost always got the same answer in a tone of convincing indignation: You nabbed that fellow long ago! Don't you people even keep a list of the ones you put away?

Early in August Jakob made a wide detour from Lübeck to Jerichow via Old Demwies and was able to tell Gesine something about her grandfather. She would find it hard to recognize him. All week long now he wore much-mended old clothes, a ragged shirt, and patched trousers. Also a black straw hat, which he did not take off, so his bald head was not visible. The commandants of Old Demwies, known as the Twins, had not understood his name properly and called him the Pope; he did not correct them. In the village he was known as the Pastor because he could speak so mildly in the mornings when allotting the work and bellow so fiercely in the evenings when the daily target had not been reached. To Jakob the estate seemed to be run on model lines, they had their wheat in from the fields and were already starting to thresh it. The farm hands respected P. for this, under him they were looked after with extra allowances and the right to decent housing just as under their former masters who had fled; they would have liked to have him more strongly on their side. Like any employee, he avoided arguments with the Twins. At night the Russian soldiers would stroll through the farm workers' cottages, turning their flashlights on the beds as they looked for grown girls, but all they found were small children; one could complain to this overseer but all he did was send one to the commandants, the two young fellows who were never seen apart and who laughed together over the nightly disturbances. On one occasion the Red soldiers had been touched by the sight of so many sleeping children lying cheek to cheek, they had stood there a long time, shining their flashlights on them, surprised to see all those little ones lying there like so many peas, sleeping like little peas in a pod. This family was offered a room in the manor house, the Twins having interpreted this as lack of space and not as what that pastor could have told them. For the daytime, the Pope had persuaded the Twins to provide a police force for the estate consisting of Red soldiers, just so he could get the work done; at night he shut himself up indoors and did not hear the knocking, no matter how violent. The Soviets had put him into the foreman's cottage, into the complete household of the former regional Party leader, who had hanged himself together with his wife and children; the Pope had not wanted the advantage or the honor and had taken two refugee families into the cramped rooms, as if he did not want to be alone at night. Jakob had seen the old man only from a distance, he thought he seemed vague, and Jakob did not want to scare him with a visit from Jerichow. Besides, Cresspahl had given him no message to take to the old man.

Papenbrock had scarcely put up any resistance to the deal. He was sure he could explain to any Soviet court, even a military one, what he had been doing during the last twelve years. But ever since 1935 he had preferred to listen to Cresspahl rather than to his own sons. Since Lisbeth's death this habit had increased until it amounted almost to docility, when in June 1945 he realized that he was no longer capable of making his own decisions, whether it was to bury himself in Jerichow or to flee across the demarcation line to the British. Louise had wanted to keep on the house and if not the business, then at least the bakery. Papenbrock had stayed, not for this reason, not even for her sake, but merely because he lacked the self-confidence to take his wife away by force. Then Cresspahl turned up with the news that the Russians would be searching for the father of Robert Papenbrock, who had become well known in the Ukraine for his executing of hostages. So the old man let himself be sent to a place very close to the border. So K. A. Pontiy was in a position to demand certain supplies from the administration of the Old Demwies estate; he had sent them an overseer with excellent agricultural qualifications.

*This'll come back to us, said the farmer, as he fed his pig some bacon.*

## May 10, 1968   Friday

The Government of the German Democratic Republic never interferes in the affairs of foreign countries; tomorrow it is sending over its German Reich Railway a special train to Bonn, with 800 seats for West Berliners who wish to protest against an emergency law, the round trip payable at less than tariff rates. It does not interfere in the internal affairs of independent states; it publishes a report in the newspaper that American and West German troops are about to enter Czechoslovakia to take part in a war film. The embassy on Schönhaus Avenue promptly denies this, but still you could read it in the *Berliner Zeitung*. The sources, of course, are invariably "informed," and they had heard Mr. Ulbricht, the East German leader, telling his Soviet friends that the aggressive actions of the West Germans made it imperative to "strengthen the Warsaw Pact forces on Czechoslovakia's western frontier." The new troops included East German ones. But, no matter how you coax them, they never interfere.

However, for the twenty-third time the Communists in Prague express their gratitude to the Red Army for liberating them from the Germans and reiterate their promises of friendship with the Soviet Union. And a wreath is bestowed on the liberators of western Czechoslovakia: placed on the destroyed monument to American soldiers in Pilsen. Plzeň. As to the movements of Soviet troops on the frontiers of Czechoslovakia in Poland and East Germany, these are genuinely supposed to be connected solely with military maneuvers. If you ask the Foreign Office in London, the reports are "hard to believe."

K. A. Pontiy, commandant of Jerichow, had provided his townspeople with a new cemetery: now he would like a special one for his army.

Cresspahl tells his commandant he hopes none of his subordinates are going to pass away during his tenure.

"A powerful race, the Russians!" Pontiy says, in solemn agreement. Perhaps this was not enough in return for the German's compliment, and he nodded to him, with extra emphasis as if to a child.

At first Cresspahl said nothing, regarding this as a whim of the other man's. After all, Pontiy had already caused a long flag with the hammer and sickle to be hung from the post office tower, merely because an officer was monitoring the telephone exchange, yet he had not permitted the removal of the sign saying GERMAN REICH POST OFFICE.

Pontiy cleared his throat slightly. He certainly did not have a sore throat, it may have been unconscious.

It was early one evening toward the end of July. Cresspahl should have been checking up on the day's labors of his squad of cripples out there in the fields, he had a pile of paperwork waiting for him at the town hall; now he was ordered to take a rest sitting down. Pontiy's office with its southern exposure was now dry and cool. Beyond the top of the green fence Cresspahl could see his own roof and one of the walnut trees. The tree swayed a little at the top, yet there was no wind. The chimney was sharply lit up by the western sun, the smoke had a yellowish tinge as it emerged from the weathered bricks. The air was so laden with a sweetish taste, it could not all be coming from the lime trees. Had the garden of the villa ever smelled of jasmine? Had Hilde

Paepcke planted jasmine here? It was not the laburnum. Now the top of the walnut tree dipped again. As if there were a cat sitting up there.

What K. A. Pontiy wanted was not some common or garden cemetery but a field-of-honor cemetery! But he was no longer capable of scaring the German. Cresspahl shifted his shoulders a little, as if recalling his thoughts from elsewhere. "Where would you like it?" he asked, somewhat absently but still in apparent obedience.

The Red Army in the person of this commandant had had the market square in mind.

During his first years in Jerichow, Cresspahl had been constantly struck by how big the square was in this little town. And the wide-open area surrounded by the colorful gabled buildings had been full of activity, even at as late an hour as this. At harvest time the wagons started coming in from the fields early in the morning to be weighed on the town scales; while they waited drivers brought water for their horses from the town pump, stood around chatting, hired a boy to watch the horses, and went off to Peter Wulff's for a drink. Also on the square stood the one- and two-horse carriages of the ladies of the local aristocracy who were calling on the Mayor's or the Pastor's wife. When the wheat and turnips had been unloaded, the wagons would continue in a wide curve in front of Papenbrock's yard into narrow Railway Street, where the horses were coaxed, the wheels rattled louder without a load, and the wagons reappeared on the far side of the square.

In the southwest corner stood the panel truck belonging to the fishermen's guild, in defiance of Emma Senkpiel's egg shop, where Papenbrock had often taken what he called offense. After the arrival of the noon train, the porter of the Lübeck Arms would appear with his handcart, the weary summer guests following him like sheep. There had once been a time when an automobile had stood outside every second building on the square, even if it did not belong either to the building or to Jerichow. When Swenson, owner of the transportation company, was lazy, he would leave his bus standing there overnight. The east side of the square had been considered too high-class for shops, it had appeared on picture postcards, like St. Peter's Church. Not quite yet but in an hour, the carriages of the aristocracy could be expected to draw up outside the Lübeck Arms, if the gentlemen should wish to avoid being seen in Schwerin or have quarreled with the inn-keepers of Schönberg. There was plenty of room in the square, no doubt of that. When the Air Force had come marching into town, you could see it was large enough for them to drill on. Now it was empty, and the unused space had an almost hypnotic effect, a person could get some strange ideas just by looking at it.

"Kharasho," said the commandant, in cheerful agreement. It was not certain whether what pleased him was Jerichow's vanished and perhaps re-emerging business life or the available space. Cresspahl had thought the foreigner had got away from his idea, but no, he was firmly in its grip. Pontiy was looking forward to having the center of the square measured out, and he may well have regretted that the dignity of his rank prevented him from marching around there personally with a pair of compasses. In the center, then, was to be the obelisk, marble, with a red star on top and tablets on all four sides.

Cresspahl emerged reluctantly from his daydreams. Didn't the commandant think the dead ought to be by themselves, undisturbed by the gaze of foreign eyes?

On the contrary, those foreign eyes would enhance the dignity of the Red Army every time they looked at the obelisk! He had no suspicion of what Cresspahl had to tell him; for him this was still an enjoyable conversation, because it was a practical one.

Cresspahl proposed the square facing the station. They could make use of the opportunity to remove the monument to the victorious armies of the Franco-Prussian War of 1870/71, and needless to say the square would not be used for a memorial to *this* war. In terms of space, not to be compared with the market square, of course, but large enough for a dozen graves. By now Cresspahl was in command of his thoughts again, and he added that everyone in Jerichow had to go to the station some time or other and would have to go past the memorial honoring the Soviet heroes.

This was one of the rare occasions when Pontiy did not let out a few sighs. He had difficulty inhaling sufficient breath and passed his hand over his sweating bald head. It was obvious that he was deeply committed to someone. It was also possible that he had not yet received instructions as to the Red Army's official policy toward the dead of the Franco-Prussian War.

Cresspahl offered him a number of other sites, the grounds of the Rifle Club, a section inside the new main cemetery, a gentle rise alongside the Rande highway from where there was a view of the sea. Pontiy rejected them all, ever patient. Then it become evident that Cresspahl wished to hide the dead and Pontiy wished to display them. It remained a power play.

Cresspahl had reckoned that the Red Army dead from the surrounding countryside would also have to be brought in to Jerichow in order to invest the number of dead with the required dignity. Cresspahl mentioned the cemeteries used by the aristocracy and the villages.

Now he had got Pontiy's dander up, but good. Pontiy had become somewhat redder in the face, and his voice came from farther forward in his throat. He spoke of craftiness and deceit. Over and over again he had been willing to trust his mayorr, and now his mayorr was trying to palm off single graves for the *geroyam Krasnoi Armii*, and was even suggesting the roadside! That was how dead Fascists lay in the Soviet Union, beside a stick with a helmet on top, like dogs they lay there!

Cresspahl was prepared to give the Russian credit for not simply issuing orders but trying to convince him. He did not want the discussion to reach the point where Pontiy would spring to his feet, put on his cap, and start shouting, in that windless heat. He asked when the first burial was due.

In a voice toneless with contempt, Pontiy ordered him to have four workmen and a stonemason on the market square by the morning of the day after next. Five would be better, since the cobblestones would have to be removed before the burial could proceed. The workmen were not to be criminals who were being made to atone for their Nazi connections by performing menial tasks: they were to be real, genuine, honest-to-goodness workers.

Cresspahl thought of the order to bring in the harvest, and said no more. Because of the dearth of the kind of worker Pontiy was demanding he would have to ask women to help at the funeral, he would have to call this very evening on Kliefoth and go with him to see the firm of Alwin Mecklenburg, Gravestones & Ornamental Masonry, now run by his widow, and explain to those people how to go about building an obelisk; but he gave up. He had wanted to save the foreigner from being tripped up by local custom, he had tried often enough to initiate him into the area now under his command; that evening he had had enough. It was not merely fatigue.

Pontiy made him read through a copy of a well-thumbed mimeographed sheet. Orders required memorial tablets for soldiers to be made of granite, for officers of marble. The inscription to be in crimson enamel. Evidently the rear echelons had caught up with K. A. Pontiy.

The commandant was conscious of being watched, and sensed that if he reached for the vodka this evening he would not be turned down. The two men had often been able to see into one another without words. On this occasion Pontiy judged wrongly and credited the other man with hostility toward the dead of the Red Army. Neither Mayor nor townspeople were invited to participate in the ceremony.

The body that was driven along Town Street in an open coffin was that of a young man, nineteen years old. He had died on the Rammin estate, no word had got out as to how. His face had a blurred, uncertain look above the uniform collar. He seemed to have stumbled on some secret, too much for the boyish forehead, the unpracticed lips. Gesine had inadvertently caught sight of him outside the Kommandatura villa.

When one bright morning five people dig a hole in Jerichow market square, and two officers and eight soldiers look on, a square of that size can seem pretty empty.

---

*May 11, 1968  Saturday*

---

From the life of D. E., known as Professor Erichson. Questions by Marie.

He produces it reluctantly, one might almost say he is embarrassed, were he capable of such a thing. The point is that he regards his life as perfectly ordinary, stamped out by the dies of the machine that is society; a standard product, not worth discussing. But he cannot sit with us over breakfast, the morning sun coming through the windows, playing Family Life and then refuse information to a member of the family; he realizes this as he glances up painfully from under sparse eyebrows, staring into the bowl of his pipe as if into a bottomless pit. At least it is only the Cresspahl child who wants a sample; the other Cresspahl has raised the newspaper in front of her face, she is reading. She is hiding her secret delight at the trap in which our crafty fox has been caught. Mustn't laugh.

As a child D. E. had to wear his hair parted.

It is not much really, but Marie, kneeling on her chair, grabs his hair and divides the gray mass into a thick bunch and one tiny narrow strip hanging down over one ear. About like that? He nods, not very happy. Each darts a glance toward the edge of the newspaper at the other end of the table, it has not moved.

Here is a child from Mecklenburg, just beginning to emerge, and there is hardly a thing he began the way we did.

Born 1928, grew up in Wendisch Burg. Wendisch Burg, is there anyone who doesn't know where that is? Near Jerichow, people nod overhastily, searching furtively in the region of Genthin, not around Lübeck and on the Baltic. Never one of Mecklenburg's three "spokesman towns" in Parliament, it was certainly not dominated by the rural aristocracy or under the thumb of the dukes of Strelitz, but, rather, linked to the Hanseatic League from way back. Until the very end of the war express trains stopped there!

From your life, D. E. Never mind about the German Reich Railway.

To the northeast of Wendisch Burg the German Reich Railway

had torn up the land to make a switching yard for the freight trains to and from abroad. Right to the end, freight cars continued to arrive loaded with ore sent from Sweden for the war and were rerouted westward, around Berlin. The Königsberg-Stettin line sent its international arrivals there too, later its loot from Poland and the northern part of the Soviet Union, also prisoners en route to the camps near Berlin. Spanning the wide area that was crisscrossed with tracks there was a viaduct, with a narrow sidewalk for pedestrians. Here a boy used to stand, abandoning himself to the dense clouds of black smoke, to the snorting of the Doppler effect issuing from below the viaduct. A lively child, the head somewhat narrow, by nature a bit enigmatic. With a parting (fair hair). Light-colored knit jacket and shorts, brown knee socks. With a gift for squinting in family photographs.

Son of a barber, offspring of the old-established firm of Erichson, High-Class Ladies' and Gentlemen's Hairdresser, on Old Street in Wendisch Burg, next door to the Three Crows. (On Adolf Hitler Street.) The boy refused to sweep up the hair on the green linoleum floor after he had done his homework, even when it became war-essential material, that's what his younger sister was there for. Father Erichson wanted to rule over more than a family and in 1939 immediately thrust himself forward for the Army; in 1940 they took him. The boy disliked being ordered about. Would go off to his viaduct, to the Lower Lake.

His mother was from the country, vaguely related to the Babendererdes of Wendisch Burg, who were fisher folk. They wanted to prevent the child from aspiring to middle-class pretensions, they cut their own hair and the boy's so that Old Man Erichson could huff and puff over the insult to his professional reputation. First escape from home, from the snooty town house to the thatched cottages by the sea. Even as an adult, D. E. is still grateful to his relatives for teaching him not to look down his nose at them merely because he was forced to attend high school; he learned his Latin and at night joined them to go fishing. Learned how to boil tar. How to paint a rowboat with the hot acrid tar. Sadness for a pike found floating in the reeds, white belly uppermost. Freeing a finch from the fish traps left on shore to dry. A bucketful of eels tipping over. Rowing in the rain against the west wind, working. But even the fishermen arranged each other one summer's day by the shore to have their picture taken, and the male children were given the brown caps of the grownups, of the Storm Troopers, with the swastika on them, maybe because that band of robbers was supposed to break the bonds of usury. It was here that D. E. achieved his best squint under the peak of the cap that hung down to his thirteen-year-old ears. Germany was already at war with the Soviet Union.

And those famous affairs, D. E.?

Before that there was the sister, five years younger. And Heike would join them on the ice when he skated with the fishermen's children. Hand in hand with a girl of eleven, sure, but they didn't speak; now she is married to the head of the taxi guild of Wendisch Burg. That was all? That was it.

However, there was nothing wrong with D. E.'s eyes, and his father's dream was for him to be trained by the Nazis to serve that Austrian as a future general or executioner. Mrs. Erichson mislaid the prestigious invitation, and the boy was obliged to do no more than his service in the naval Hitler Youth. There he learned to row in a crew; he would rather have been alone on the water with his sailing kayak. During the summer an H-class yawl crossed the two lakes and tied up at the lock. Never knew the Niebuhrs, Marie; never exchanged a word with them. A report to the troop leader: Squad Leader Erichson seen handing food supplies to the Sedenbohms (mixed marriage, no privileges, wearers of the Star of David).

Photos cut up, torn up, burned. One may have been put away in the bottom of a cabinet in Fürstenberg. It showed a wintry day in 1943, and four young people of about sixteen standing in a field north of Oranienburg, behind them a few sparse pine trees, in the mist, in the dirty snow. Three were boys, dressed in the uniform of the air-defense Hitler Youth, blue-gray. True, they are not wearing the wide swastika armband on their arms, as required by regulations, they are keeping them in their breast pockets, for crazy superiors. Each of the three has managed to get hold of an Air Force belt buckle, now that as soldiers they feel superior to the Hitler Youth, and they wear their uniform shirts belted outside their trousers the way soldiers wear their tunics, not stuffed inside their trousers like kids. The fourth person in the picture was a girl, maybe she was the one who saved the photo.

D. E. renowned for his brilliant affairs. Only a week before, the searchlight battery had had to assemble behind a village inn to be instructed by their commanding officer, a lieutenant, holder of the Iron Cross Second Class, suspected of having had sexual intercourse with a Polish female slave laborer on the estate. He ordered the boys to present themselves forthwith for "hygiene inspection" after each act of copulation, and this was how D. E. first heard of such diseases. It never amounted to more than shy or overbold letters via the Air Force mail service in Berlin.

It certainly wasn't the steelworkers that he was guarding, that much he realized.

At school he worked hard at only two subjects, and in the

antiaircraft course he attracted attention by his knowledge of sonic velocity at varying temperatures and the running of machinery; he was taken out of the searchlight course and served during the air battle for Berlin as a flight observer at an antiaircraft telescope. Despite such improvements to his status, the Sedenbohm affair had not been forgotten; he was neither popular nor envied. "People from the ducal residence seem to have swallowed a poker" (alluding to his place of birth, Neustrelitz). Sometimes he forgot for whom he was on duty; the Liberator B–24s hung uncannily close in the view finder, narrow of wing, thick of body, oval hulls of the twin tail-units, perfect tools. His eyes turned out to be more useful than those of others. The other Air Force "helpers" staggered about when they were roused from sleep, despite the dimmed red light; he had excellent night vision and was now a "senior helper." He had already learned to use the ring-funnel directional finder, then he was moved to the most recent radio tracking device, built by Telefunken, the 41 T. The word radar was unknown to them. The radio tracking device located enemy bombers fifteen miles away and transmitted the varying target altitudes automatically via the antiaircraft tracking device to cannons and launchers, which then adjusted their range with a violent jerk as if guided by an invisible hand. The machine did the killing, there was no need to touch it. Yet some officers had tried to kill Hitler, and since then the high-power battery had been fenced in, barricaded off, a prison camp. No matter how many men and machines were shot down in bits, they came down over the field like hard hot rain: Berlin was burning. In January 1945 they exchanged his red antiaircraft gunner's tabs for black ones and sent him to the Oder; on the way there he deserted.

For the sake of the girl from Fürstenberg? I suspect so, Marie. Except that Old Man Erichson had been missing since February 1942 and his mother was alone with his sister in Wendisch Burg. He had to be there in time for when Sokolovsky got through.

The conqueror of Berlin? Who died yesterday? That's the one. General, commander of the Soviet armed forces in Germany, marshal and Hero of the Soviet Union, directed the Berlin blockade. 1897–1968. Who would not believe in an American victory in Vietnam, except with nuclear arms, which would lead to World War III.

The deserter waited in a forest ranger's home belonging to one of the estates by the Upper Lake, about four miles from Wendisch Burg. The house was full of strangers. An SS tank unit was making the area unsafe, looting the last of the food supplies, grabbing the men of fighting age. D. E. spent a good deal of time sitting in trees. Then, when the first Russians arrived driving their low-slung horse carts and keeping their eyes peeled, it was up to D. E. not to hide but to keep guard. He would sit on the edge of a desk by the window, watching the path that led past the woods to Wendisch Burg. As soon as he saw Red soldiers he had to run through the house and warn the women so they could escape through the back doors into some dense underbrush. He did not stare continuously at the path, he relied on his ears. There was a lot of luggage lying around that had once belonged to those who had hanged themselves in the woods, and in one suitcase D. E. had found a reprint of Albert Einstein's comments as they had appeared in the treatises of the Prussian Academy of Sciences of 1915; Jewish physics. This he read more slowly than anything he had ever read in his life, while at the same time listening for the sound of hoofbeats, of rattling carts. The fifth time around he had to admit to himself that although he could learn the theory of relativity by heart he could not really grasp it. His thinking came up against a solid barrier, it was actually painful. Sometimes the effort gave way suddenly to a sensation of flying, of an effortless soaring motion. Then the automatic pilot would collapse, with no clear explanation for the crash. D. E. was not yet eighteen and was forced to acknowledge that there was in fact a limit beyond which his thinking would not go. That this would be his life. A talent, if you like, although a small one. In mid-May the rumor came across the lake that the Red Army was going to reopen Wendisch Burg High School, with Sedenbohm as principal; he set out then and there. Thus he missed his sister, who had run away to join him.

"That keeping watch as you sat on the edge of the desk in the woods, was that because of the rapings?" Marie asks. She is no longer kneeling close to D. E., she is leaning away from him. The two of them can now observe one another as if in a contest, neither yielding, neither relenting. The older of them nods glumly, no doubt he would have welcomed some help from the other Cresspahl. She folds her newspaper, lays it aside, and observes him too, with some curiosity. If you want to be part of our family you must also try your hand at education, D. E.

"It was," says D. E. in a deliberate manner, "because of the rapings."

"That was your job, so to speak."

"In return for my board and lodging."

"And the forestry people had relations in Fürstenberg, and one of those girls had gone into hiding in the woods near Wendisch Burg."

"Who started this business of my affairs! It was hers too, wasn't it?"

"And who is *that* one married to now?"

"To a surgeon in Hamburg, if you want to know."

"It was a risky trip for her, if the Russians were already in Fürstenberg."

"She was pretty smart for her seventeen years. She got through all right."

"And," says Marie, as coolly as he, "did you take an oath on Hitler?"

"Three times."

"Is it correct to call him that 'that Austrian' so often, like that lady whom we both know?"

"Quite correct, that's where he came from. The lady in question also believes that many of his helpers came from Austria and Styria. No doubt she would have preferred it if the North German Federation had kept itself to itself after the Franco-Prussian War in 1870."

"It's no use trying, D. E. You won't catch her out. She won't let herself be caught."

"Which I undertook solely to keep New York City clean."

"And is she wrong?"

"It wasn't an Austrian type of madness, if I'm to believe my doctors."

"What did you do with your steel helmet?"

"Buried it."

"When others, the farmers, found it as they were plowing—"

"—the skeleton was missing."

"And your sister?"

"Died in May 1945."

"How old?"

"As old as Gesine in July '45."

"That's all you're going to tell me?"

"That's all, my dear Mary, the rest I shall hold in reserve."

"And is that really true, about Red Army cemeteries in Mecklenburg market squares?"

"Not in Wendisch Burg. In other places there was an obelisk with a red star, lit up at night."

"D. E.!"

"Connected with the street lighting and the local power plant by underground wiring."

"And what'll we do now?"

At last D. E. is allowed to assume his other role, that of planner, protector, initiator. "We might take in the rides at Palisades Park." But Marie refuses to sacrifice a whole Saturday for such childish things even if he wants to. Any ideas in the paper? In the *Times* there is a picture of the Y-shaped bridge in Saigon, taken from the air, so that the street fighting can only be guessed at; it looks something like our Triboro Bridge, on the other side of Manhattan. Neither of them wants to go there. A trip to Boston is out, the right train to Philadelphia has already left, finally a journey to the Atlantic is decided upon, to Rockaway Beach. But not the way D. E. imagines it. "By subway!" says Marie. By subway! Like that, his car will stay parked outside their building; like that, he can't drop us off on the way home; like that, she will have him for the evening, maybe even for tomorrow.

---

## May 14, 1968   Tuesday

Czechoslovakia's new Economic Council is discussing the plan to make the Czech crown convertible now instead of in five years' time. It would be the first currency in the Eastern bloc to be acceptable on the capitalist market; dispute seems inevitable. The country could then pay in its own currency and would no longer need dollar loans, and Mrs. Cresspahl would not have to be transferred away from New York.

From time to time Cresspahl considered moving away from Jerichow. It would be he, not K. A. Pontiy, who would have to go to jail for the crimes by which he carried out the commandant's orders, from crooked bookkeeping to dealing in the black market while in office, sometimes to the town's advantage, sometimes to its disadvantage. However, he could not see Pontiy forgetting himself to the point where he would dismiss the Mayor, assuming he continued to lack sufficient grounds for having him shot. He did not have much to take with him to the West, just his own child and Hanna Ohlerich, if she wanted to come along; at least he wanted to know where he was taking them to.

He found this out from someone who, back in August 1945, was standing one Sunday afternoon beside the pump as if he had dropped from the sky. He was a man about my father's age, but slightly built like a youth of eighteen, though the whiteness of his hair was not due to the dust from the road. He asked Cresspahl's daughter if he might draw a little drinking water from the pump. Such courtesies had not come her way in a long time, and she claims that she immediately took him for someone from Cresspahl's area. She shook her head and ran into the cool stone house to get him a mug of water. He went on standing there, looking at her as he drank as if his eyes would jump off the end of his nose, so tightly did he crinkle it. For some unaccountable reason he then asked her the time, and when Gesine looked up at the sky he sat down on the pump stone, sighing over the aches and pains of old age, which he did not have. He wore his wristwatch just above his ankle, he was ingenious, besides which he had managed to get through, all the way across the frontier. Now she recognized him as Erwin Plath, not so much as a guest at a funeral in 1938 as one of Cresspahl's wartime secrets. She took him into Cresspahl's office without being seen and immediately ran off to the fields; this was not someone she could take with her through Jerichow.

That was one of the few times Cresspahl exerted his privileges as master of the house and told Mrs. Abs to serve him supper in his room; he was anxious not to miss even fifteen minutes of such a visit. Then Gesine was sent for a bottle of Jakob's barter goods, and when she got up to go to her room at bedtime Erwin Plath drew her down onto a chair, explaining solemnly that he must look at her a little longer. Cresspahl looked at his child doubtingly, his eyes lost in a memory, he did not send her to bed, or Hanna. The children watched the grownups, who were enjoying the reunion like kids, eager, in utter confidence, each delighting in the other, in constant happy anticipation, and constantly telling each other how things had gone for them. Then Cresspahl put his question.

Plath began to nod, but he drew his lips back from his teeth as if he had bitten into something rotten. He was no longer living in Lübeck, he had landed up in Itzehoe. He was vague about the move, also about his new business beside the River Stör, but he had plenty to say about the British. Evidently they did not watch themselves as carefully as they did in an occupied zone where they did not want to leave a bad reputation behind for their Soviet brothers in arms. Did Cresspahl know the barracks at Itzehoe—the Gudewill, the Waldersee, the Gallwitz at Long Peter, and the Hanseatic by the cemetery? Cresspahl did. That's where the British were, there wasn't nearly enough room for them. At the end of May they had requisitioned the best residential area in Sude, ninety-five houses, most of them modern villas; they gave the occupants three hours to get out, taking only valuables, underwear, and bed linen with them. Now those houses were occupied by English families with one or two children and the Germans had been crammed into every last attic, into sheds, even into cellars. And no doubt Cresspahl knew about Itzehoe's sewer system. That there wasn't any. Yes. The Military Government had permitted one sealed room per house where the Germans could store their belongings; the belongings turned up on the black market, so that was how much the British respected seals. They had taken over the Hammonia Hotel, the covered cattle market, and both movie houses, they had appropriated all the sports grounds for themselves. Much of the requisitioned space was standing empty, but they held onto it just the same. Sude was out of bounds to Germans unless they worked there. One morning the Mayor walked into his office to find his desk gone, together with all the furniture, occupation headquarters had appropriated it. The British also went on private raids, from German homes they took furniture, pictures, radios, cameras, stamp collections, and other war-essential items, without even bothering to pretend they were acting on orders. They drove through Itzehoe in their jeeps like maniacs, not caring how many people they killed. One division was called the Desert Rats, they were quartered in the Hanseatic barracks, which they dubbed the Richmond Barracks. Desert Rats.

Hanna asked about the net factory, where her relatives were known. Plath knew them, they were still living near the gasworks, waiting for raw materials, they could not produce. Hanna, silenced, thanked him; she was looking for some place for herself other than Jerichow, now one more was lost to her.

"Richmond Barracks," said Cresspahl, puzzled, but he was referring to the behavior of the British.

Plath waved all that away, suddenly concerned with business. He had not come on account of the British. Cresspahl had been given some kind of order, hadn't he, to found political parties? The British permitted nothing of that kind. But look at the Soviets!

"Yes and no," said Cresspahl, his conscience somewhat uneasy. There had been some sort of order from K. A. Pontiy, which he had lost sight of. The commandant was demanding the formation of a local group of Social Democrats, another of the Christian Democratic Union, and a Communist one. But Cresspahl couldn't behave like the Creator and form political parties in Jerichow just like that!

Now Plath woke the sleepy children by saying good-by to them. He led them into the bedroom like sheep, so gently that they were scarcely aware of it, and to each he had something nice to say about her hair. After he had gone back to Cresspahl it was quiet for a long time, and the children fell asleep to the sound of little patterings. These were the night creatures flying through the open windows onto the globe of the kerosene lamp.

Plath protested to his old socialist friend that he could not go without a successor, assuming he did mean to leave Jerichow.

Cresspahl grunted a reply. Perhaps to convey that things might run better without him.

So it was up to Cresspahl to form a party to the commandant's liking. A Communist one. And from among those members this fellow Pontiy would accept a new mayor.

Cresspahl could not even form a Social Democratic Party.

"Oh, the Socialist Party—forget it!" said Plath, as if impatient with his own party. Then it came out that he had already been scouting around in Jerichow for former members. They had given him short shrift, one of them, Peter Wulff, citing no other authority than Cresspahl himself, who, Wulff said, also thought all this parliamentary stuff was crap.

"That bunch of crap all over again," growled Cresspahl, suddenly flaring up.

Plath had found only one man, named Kägebein, for the Christian Democratic Union Party.

It suited Cresspahl that an outsider should be taking some of the load off his shoulders. He couldn't even repay him with jokes, he said.

Now Plath became patient, and at the same time eager, and took an indirect approach. Cresspahl was reminded of his days in the Social Democratic Party, the secret agreements arrived at before a meeting, the prepared interjections and questions on procedural rules, until the result of the vote was a foregone conclusion before anyone had so much as put up his hand. The result had been little mice. And one battleship. Cresspahl merely listened.

Plath did not let himself be reminded that at the artillery barracks in Güstrow he had been Cresspahl's junior. He put it to Cresspahl that the Communists were only anxious to build up the Social Democratic Party in order to swallow it up later in an alliance. That business of "United Action," in 1931 and 1935. Erwin Plath was now here to see that the right people got in among the Communists on the ground floor. Not merely refugees who were hoping for new farms; no, local people too who could not easily be accused of opportunism. Communists of the very first hour, yet secret outposts of the Social Democrats. Alfred Bienmüller, the Jerichow blacksmith, was prepared to make the sacrifice. Why wouldn't Cresspahl?

It was for this that Erwin Plath had slipped across the "green frontier" near Ratzeburg, and Cresspahl managed to spin out the evening with Plath's reminiscences and another half-bottle of vodka, nor did he even let his disappointment show. But it was there. He had thought Plath had come for his sake, not for the sake of the cause. For one moment he had considered saying Yes, merely to please his friend. In the morning he was relieved to find that Plath had gone on during the night to a new local group. But for the children the visit had been a delight, and Hanna Ohlerich asked Cresspahl to write down then and there the address of this nice friendly man from Itzehoe.

But Cresspahl was not once asked by K. A. Pontiy to become

Party chairman for the Communists. His mayor was to form the parties for him, it seemed, but not to join any of them. That was the way it looked.

The newspaper *Rudé Právo*, the organ of the Czech and Slovak Communists, appeals to its readers with a questionnaire filling two thirds of a page:

Does the internal democratization of a Communist Party provide a sufficient guarantee of democracy?

Should the Communist Party carry out its leadership role by devotedly promoting free progressive socialist development or by ruling over society?

Can you speak of democracy as being socialist when the leading role is held only by the Communist Party?

Can you imagine that?

## May 15, 1968  Wednesday

This morning the subway was even more crowded than usual, and at 96th Street a young man kept pushing against an old one who was trying rather too desperately to force his way in. "Don't grab like that!" he said, and actually managed to push the old man back onto the platform. Behind the closed door, as the train moved off, he could be seen still shouting abuse. The old man tried to hide among those who had been left behind, white in the face, avoiding all eyes; to judge by his accent, a Jew from Eastern Europe.

The East Germans have written a letter to the Czechoslovak Republic. It says: "The victims of German Fascism from Buchenwald, Majdanek and Mauthausen as well as Lidice are a warning signal that should keep one from illusions about the possibilities of cooperation with German imperialism." Radio Prague feels itself handicapped by the millions of dead who rest behind these names, otherwise it could be described as "downright piquant" that one should be reminded in Berlin, of all places, of the victims of the concentration camps. That was the day before yesterday.

Today we hear again from Moscow that Thomas Masaryk, founder of the Czechoslovak Republic, paid 200,000 rubles in 1918 to an anti-Bolshevik terrorist to kill Lenin. In Prague they want to rename a street for Thomas Masaryk.

Mrs. Ferwalter is no longer interested in news from Czechoslovakia, in March she had already dismissed such matters with a wave of the hand, and since she used both hands to do this she seemed to be pushing aside something heavy and threatening. It may have seemed that way because of the irritated and disgusted expression that she can never banish from the corners of her mouth, although smiling all the while. Today she intercepts us as we emerge from "her" bakery, her face transformed in a joyful grimace that was hardly rigid at all. "Mrs. Cresspahl!" she cried, "Marie, my dear little Marie!," so urgently did she want to share her joyful news with us. Not that she has found one of her long-lost relatives again, nor has her husband been given a raise for his backbreaking job at the shoe factory; it is simply that she has her papers.

She has to tell us all about it, we are friends of the family; besides, we helped her. We could sit in the park and discuss our children's progress in school or the price of bread, and sometimes she would turn her great friendly bulk to face us and suddenly say, with a sly wink: "1776?" and we would confirm that that was the year when the States declared their independence. We also listened to her recite the amendments to the Constitution, who General Grant was, and the making of a president, and she would keep switching to a different topic with bits of knowledge that kept coming back to her. Often she was discouraged, an old woman whose brain was racked with nervous twitching and sleeplessness, no longer capable of learning, and she would let herself be comforted like a child. When we did not succeed, she would say good-by with a protracted handshake, her face averted, and walk off sadly and awkwardly on the legs that the Germans and Austrians had ruined; but she could also start off with concealed anticipation that broadened her lips to a smile until her whole pudgy face was puckered with the joy of American citizenship. Now, since yesterday, she has her second, third, and fourth papers.

She was reluctant to admit her pleasure outright, as if this would jeopardize it; she mentioned tax advantages. She could not hide the fact that the prospect of an American passport loomed before her like a new protective shell, one more bulwark against the past.

It was also our job to correct her German. This was not easy; maybe even she does not realize which of her words originates in her store of Yiddish, Czech, American, Hebrew, and German, and she seldom achieves whole sentences in a single language. We have weaned her away from the "German Federation" so that she can learn to believe in the Federal Republic of Germany; and we have warned her about speaking of a *Liebelei* ("flirtation") with her daughter Rebecca, we won't even allow her a *Liebschaft* ("love affair") with the child, although these are indeed more exact words for the love she bears her last-born. But we have not protested against the *Meine sehr geehrte Frau Cressepfal* with which she addresses us, if that is how she wishes to express friendship, and Marie allows herself to be called *liebe Mariechen*, however much she detests the diminutive; she will continue to make errors in certain German forms of address. Let us hope the West German Embassy makes no demands of this kind.

For when our Mrs. Ferwalter becomes a United States citizen she will be entitled to demand personal compensation from the West Germans. In the case of an Israeli national, which is what she once wanted to become, the money would find its way past her into the state treasury of Israel. That much we have gathered and are loath to discuss with her the squaring of murders with money. Moreover, the survivor has to prove that she once lived under German rule; apparently the American certificate of discharge from Mauthausen concentration camp is not enough. The corner of Ruthenia that contained her native village found itself sometimes on one side of the frontier and sometimes on the other, and were she to admit to Hungarian sovereignty she would be directed to an as yet nonexistent diplomatic representation. So she says. Hence the West German Embassy demands that she show some knowledge of the language of her persecutors. So she says. She is not actually required to go to Park Avenue and, in German, indicate on a map of Slovakia the spot where she was picked up; she has to write a letter. She came to the apartment and asked for our advice concerning herself. "Am I a housewife, a *Hausfrau*, Mrs. Cresspahl?" she asked. We know other words for her, we did not contradict. She was so intent on being honest that, instead of taking the corrected draft home with her, she copied it out at our table, perched uncomfortably, knees wide apart, on the edge of her chair, bowed laboriously over the paper, writing swiftly, in alarmed fits and starts. She considered this less of a fraud and, if it was one, we would do it again.

Not only is she happy with her citizenship papers, she has already acquired pride in this country. "Doesn't the Government send out checks all over the place?" she says, not forgetting her dignified satisfaction that the Government does not have to help *her* out with checks but only those for whom God has in very truth decreed poverty: the Jews who were not smart enough, and the Negroes whom Providence had unfortunately doomed to blackness. Are we to spoil her pleasure and contradict? Are we to desert her because she has acquired citizenship in a country that is bent on exterminating another country in Southeast Asia?

There is no escape, she has to tell us about the examination. In the middle of 95th Street, right beside the threatening wire-mesh fence of the school playground, she has to show us how she placed one foot in front of the other when she was finally called. So she tried to keep her head up, and she would deny that her chin trembled. In trepidation and dignity she entered the room, unsupported, defenseless as a lamb, trying to hold onto herself with two fingers at the sides of her dress until the nails dug through the material into her flesh. No, she did not want to receive it as a gift, she wished to pay for it in pain. When the learned gentlemen in their dark suits realized that she was nothing but an old Jewess, they wouldn't hurt her, and they didn't hurt her. She remembered only one of the questions. Who will be president if Mr. Johnson dies? "Gott ferbitt!" she cried out, and passed the test.

She celebrated the occasion by going home in a taxi rather than by subway. One can picture her as she describes the scene, stretching out her arm more like a first-class citizen than she would have done the day before, waiting by the taxi until the driver reached back and opened the door for her, wasn't she an American citizen now? In the taxi she leaned almost all the way back, hanging her wrist in the loop just as she had seen other people do, and high over the Hudson she had herself driven home, a little wistful over the extravagance, a little fearful at the thought of the pleasure coming to an end, quite determined to keep it alive through talking about it, and weren't the Cresspahls among the first to be told the story?

We're only too pleased, Mrs. Ferwalter, and we duly congratulate her.

And this Czech movie, *The Fifth Horseman Is Fear*, it's probably not too suitable for a celebration, is it? Something about fear, that's not for her any more. On the other hand, if it's something from the good old days, with music—

Better not, Mrs. Ferwalter. It's not from the good old days, and the music is sometimes used to emphasize pangs of conscience and permeates most of the rest of the movie too.

"And how are you, Mrs. Cresspahl?"

"Ještě dělám chyby." This is about the best phrase we can muster. I still make mistakes.

"No! Never!" she says hotly. On a day like this no friend of Mrs. Ferwalter is allowed to be under the weather, and for the first time we are invited to her apartment, to a cup of "real European" coffee, and also to look at the citizenship papers. And would Marie like her milk hot or cold?

So in spite of her new status she reverted to her native land. The Jews in western Czechoslovakia, she said, had been assimilated just as in Germany, for instance. But in Mrs. Ferwalter's village they lived apart, in a separate group, yet still respected. Under Thomas Masaryk what had they to fear? But the Germans could seize upon a tightly knit community, there was no place to hide. And she didn't even bother running away from the Germans, convinced they had already got everyone on their lists. The Hungarians were not to be trusted. She would not go back to the Czechs, or to the Slovaks, not even with an American passport.

That reminded her that she was now entitled to a United States passport, and because Marie happened to be sitting next to her she received a lengthy hug.

"Such joy!" said Mrs. Ferwalter, close to tears. "Such joy!"

---

### May 18, 1968   Saturday

Yesterday the Mayors of Moscow and New York were observed on a black leather couch in Mr. Lindsay's office. So how did the other Mayor deal with strikes by municipal employees in Russia, Lindsay wanted to know? "Strike?" replied Vladimir Fedorovich Promyslov. "In fifty years of Soviet power it has not happened once."

Cresspahl had problems with his police.

He needed someone, a few years younger than himself, a resident of Jerichow in pre-Nazi times, who commanded the respect if not the esteem of the local inhabitants, level-headed, incorruptible, and Peter Wulff had turned down the job. Cresspahl had sought out this friend two days after the end of the war, six and a half years after the publicly witnessed quarrel ordered by the Social Democratic Party; they told each other who had smuggled flowers onto the grave of Friedrich Laabs each March, to the unsacred memory of the Kapp *Putsch* and who had watched in hiding while the flagpole outside the Nazi Party headquarters was being sawn through during the night. Cresspahl did not mention his business with the British; Lisbeth's death could not be discussed. But as far as the German Social Democratic Party was concerned they had by now reached a tactit agreement not to forgive their Party for that meddling in personal relationships. There were plenty of other things, both men enjoyed sharing their leisure hours, and soon it was no longer for old times' sake but with the joint intention of getting their town of Jerichow back on the rails, in a new direction. It pleased Wulff that the British had made his friend mayor, and under the Soviets he continued to stand by him with kidding and advice, but he was not prepared to back him up by taking on the police job. Wulff preferred to turn up each morning at the schoolyard when work was being assigned, and to lug sacks of grain or help dig holes for K. A. Pontiy's fence rather than go down into the cellars or up into the attics of his fellow townsmen. He saw that Cresspahl was stuck with his job for the Soviets, and he did not want to risk getting himself into a similar situation. He proposed Fritz Schenk.

Pontiy and Jerichow demanded a manly figure.

Cresspahl would have preferred Mrs. Bergie Quade at his side.

The war had left few men behind among the locals of Jerichow; Fritz Schenk was one of them. From 1939 on, he had warded off conscription by tirelessly submitting certificates, petitions, and declarations; and so that the women would not look askance at him he had kept the town supplied, sometimes unasked, with detailed descriptions of his abdominal complaints. For the sake of his job as town clerk and registrar he had been a member of the Social Democratic Party since 1928, expelled (to his satisfaction) in December 1932 for conspicuous criticism of a Reich government's yielding to violence; confirmed in his job under the law covering the rehabilitation of the German civil service, loud in his praises of his beloved Führer *and* Reich Chancellor, and coy in response to invitations to join *that* party; since February 2, 1943, deaf to such blandishments, and until Germany's capitulation in May 1945 registered unfit for military service. Cresspahl was inclined to regard this as a skillful ploy, he recalled somewhat overpatriotic congratulations on registering the birth of a child in March 1933. He did not trust his antipathy toward the fellow and recommended him to Pontiy. Possibly what he disliked about Fritz Schenk was his pasty complexion, the long thin stick of a man, his smooth manners, the lips that were too full for a man of fifty and pursed in sensations of victory. And Peter Wulff recommended him mainly so that Schenk would make a fool of himself, not to mention keeping his own hands clean.

Cresspahl looked around for others. He could not take a refugee, since they were not familiar with the town's back alleys and back doors. He was dissatisfied, he had to load his desk with the extra paperwork of the Housing Office and the registry when he appointed Schenk chief of police in Jerichow. Schenk took it as an affront, and Cresspahl realized what had lain behind Wulff's suggestion. Schenk had only just ceased being town clerk, and now his alternatives were either to fill in bomb craters or to act as one of Bienmüller's minions. Schenk chose the administrative job and referred, as he had twelve years earlier, to making sacrifices for the New Era. "I hold myself responsible for the records to this very day!" he said. Cresspahl could detect Schenk's pleasure in the thought that the carpenter-turned-mayor would now finally mess things up, a cobbler who had not stuck to his last. "You're the boss!" Schenk cried, moved by his subservience, standing to attention so that he would not have to stand responsible for his orders.

When Schenk was sworn in, Pontiy asked him teasingly, playfully: "You Fasceest?" Schenk was not familiar with the commandant's private indulgences and, breathing heavily, rejected any such suspicion. He spoke of the German people's feeling that the war would mean life was over, and of the German people's relief when life was not over. Cresspahl watched Schenk's antics in embarrassment; such speechifying might be all right coming from Wulff. But Wulff's lips would never utter such stuff. Pontiy was merely disappointed that his chief of police had concocted such a speech. He called him You good example, You show others, You be Communist, put on his cap, got to his feet, and swore him in.

Cresspahl still did not know what Schenk thought he would get out of such a job. And when Schenk was asked about the Social Democratic Party he had shuddered with such palpable disgust that Pontiy decided to use him to form a German Communist Party in Jerichow. Once again Cresspahl tended to distrust himself. If Schenk had hated the Nazis to the extent he avowed, maybe that had been the truth and Jerichow had simply failed to recognize it.

As his subordinate Schenk picked Knever, Berthold Knever, former senior postal official, relegated in tireless wrangling with the postmaster to working behind the wicket and finally to delivering mail. Cresspahl had no objection. It was Knever's business if he chose not to believe that the postal service would continue to function under the Soviets, and the old fellow would no doubt be able to keep an eye on Schenk. Knever had been pernickety in the extreme, not only about the post office scales but also in his attire, patched though it might be, and the storekeepers would set their clocks by Mrs. Knever, so strict were his demands for punctual meals. If Cresspahl was right in his suspicions Knever was capable of dispelling them and keeping a sharp eye on Schenk, grimly alert, bristling, as befitted his nickname of the Voiceless Parrot. So to Knever also, as well as to a man from East Prussia, Friedrich Gantlik, Cresspahl gave a stripped German Army uniform and had each of the three men's white POLICE arm bands stamped with the town's insigne, from which the swastika had been cut out with a pocketknife.

They began their duties on July 4, 1945, and on their very first round did not take along the 98K carbines they had been ordered to carry. Pontiy may have wanted to prove to his mayor that he was serious about the Red Army's chivalry toward women, and that if ever a black sheep did turn up it would be the job of the German police to deal with him with a weapon. Cresspahl's police felt this was a fearsome prospect. He could hardly object to Gantlik's reluctance to exchange shots with Red Army soldiers; Gantlik had taken on the job with the municipality mainly to earn his right to residence papers, he was undersized but tough, a landless farmer, and the long trek from the River Memel to Jerichow may have rendered him less than cocksure.

Cresspahl sent the three men to Pontiy to have their marksmanship checked out; they returned with good reports plus a stern warning from the commandant that the careless wounding of a Red Army soldier would be considered unforgivable. Schenk regarded his mayor with a deadpan expression, his swelling lips pursed. Cresspahl spoiled his malign pleasure by appealing to his men's manhood. After that they sometimes made their rounds armed. But when the full-scale looting at Karstadt's department store was underway and half Town Street was milling with people and strewn with bales of yard goods and pots and pans, the police hopped around on the edges of the excited crowd like bewildered hens, incapable even of firing shots in the air. Schenk did fire into the air when Hanna Ohlerich ran away from him after coming down from a cherry tree that Amalie Creutz had pressed her to climb. The police took along their weapons when summoned to a quarrel among Germans; if a Soviet incident was reported, they would stroll off from the town hall to make sure they did not arrive in time, rifles shouldered instead of at the ready, and Miss Senkpiel came to complain that they had chosen *her* store in which to leave their firearms, just for fifteen minutes, and sometimes it was evening before they came to pick them up. So the bands of harvesters remained without protection, few lapses from Soviet chivalry could be proved to the commandant, and two Red Army soldiers with their followers were able to put eight people out of Kliefoth's home onto the street.

In their minor duties Jerichow's police were meticulous. Anyone digging up new potatoes in defiance of the law was reported. Anyone putting up a notice offering to swap baby clothes for a work shirt on his own gate instead of on the official notice board at the town hall was brought in to Cresspahl for punishment; he had in fact been forced to forbid the posting of such notices. When Pontiy changed his mind about attending a rally of former members of the Social Democratic Party, the police appeared on the scene and ordered the group to disperse. An inadequately swept stretch of roadway made them very cross. And dogs without license tags had a hard time of it.

What Cresspahl's police liked doing best was entering private homes. For this they had ample orders from the Kommandantura or the municipality. Here the cattle and poultry had to be counted so that the plans for their surrender could be drawn up after August 10. And if a sheep had to be put to the knife ahead of time it was necessary to check up on the skin. The children had had to surrender their textbooks for German (reading and grammar), history, geography, and biology; all material in Cyrillic script also had to be turned in, so the police came again and planted themselves in front of bookcases. The tradesmen had to report their stocks of raw materials and fuel, so the police checked, lifted floorboards, crawled around under the roof, and reached into water barrels in order for the list to be complete. The hunt was also on for Köpcke's motorcycle, because it was not registered at the town hall, until one day Mina Köpcke dismounted and showed her permit, signed not by the Soviet Military Administration in Schwerin but personally by K. A. Pontiy, so that his fence would be completed faster, and overnight the motorcycle had been turned into a panel truck.

On their tours through kitchens and parlors and stables Messrs. Schenk, Knever, and Gantlik saw enough to keep them entertained. Their eyes would light on beanpoles that only partially screened outlines of a barrel; they would say nothing for the time being and then report the find to Cresspahl. He could not object, he needed goods that were in short supply for his deals with the Soviet Beckhorst estate or the Rande fishermen's guild, so he would send in his application for permission to confiscate to the District Office in Gneez and trust to Slata's good offices at the regional Kommandantura. The Gneez regional area was extensive; besides, it was up to Slata to report emergencies to the municipal council, and probably she did not care to remind anyone of her previous life in Jerichow, so sometimes the document from the courthouse would arrive too late. Sometimes Schenk would seize the goods prematurely, "to forestall collusion," as he would say, flippant in his unassailability. It was not Schenk who was cursed for the removal of an eighteen-month supply of chemical fertilizer, it was Cresspahl who got tagged with the blame. He did not mind, just so long as Berthold Knever did not report cases of fraud. Then, in one of the homes, which until then was thought to have no cellar, coal was found: the house was sitting on a coal mine of briquettes, enough to supply Jerichow with gas for five days, and next door lived Duvenspeck, gasworks superintendent. A brigade of women had to go to the house with handcarts to return the black gold to the gasworks, and eventually half a ton was missing from the quantity Duvenspeck was prepared to admit. This was not accounted for by the two briquettes that each refugee carried away under her apron: Cresspahl's police had gone shares with the stool pigeon, and Knever the conscientious civil servant, the upholder of legality, did not report the fraud, for in his own storeroom he had erected a neat tower of briquettes, in perfect alignment, tapering off toward the top and camouflaged as a wall, Gesine had seen it when

she went to take a message, these days she could not take her eyes off
storerooms. Cresspahl did not care only about legality: from time to
time the regional Kommandatura removed supplies from Jerichow for
which Cresspahl had applied, and he could not manage with shortages.
He did not like to search the homes of his policemen on the evidence
of a child, so he went to the commandant and asked him merely to
give appropriate instructions to his forces of law and order. Pontiy would
not rest until he knew the nature of the goods. He was delighted to
hear that the gasworks contained coal for his winter. On the spot he
invented the proverb of the ox which thou shalt not muzzle when he
treadeth out the corn. "Yes, the ox," said Cresspahl. Pontiy supported
him with emphatic nods.

Meanwhile in the neighboring countryside there was a young man
going around calling himself Gerd Schumann, formerly a member of
the National Committee for a Free Germany in the Soviet Union,
sent, after a course in administration in Stargard, Pomerania, to this
out-of-the-way corner as a canvasser for the Communist Party. Cresspahl had talked to him and found him easy enough to get along with,
although a bit too educated in his speech for the area. A youth of
twenty-three, stocky and already running to fat, aggressive yet covertly
watchful, invariably dressed in a military tunic that, strangely enough,
showed no signs of wear; he even squared his shoulders in a paramilitary
way. Although nicknamed Red, his hair was somewhere between white
and gray, with a silver sheen to it. "From now on

the great flag
of the Freedom
of the Nations
and of the Peace
of the Nations
will wave
over Europe!"

he would shout, unaware of his audience's aversion to yet more flags.
He would make such proclamations in a graduated tone that rose and
fell in a kind of singsong and, again like Pastor Brüshaver in church,
the young man would quote chapter and verse: Generalissimo Stalin,
May 9, 1945. This manner of speaking had become second nature
with him, and thus he would work his way through the entire ten-
point program of the Communist Party of Germany as he faced the
weary farmers and farm hands whom the village commandant had
rounded up for him after work; and because he demanded such things
as battle against starvation, unemployment, and housing shortage, many
a coin was dropped into the collection plate, and he could distribute

all his handbills as well as many applications for membership. In terms of power he was far superior to Cresspahl. He wore a highly visible pistol in his belt, and with this and the Russian language he could defend himself against uninformed Red Army soldiers; he had a say in the allocation of housing, he had money, he could use bedsheets and red paint to make banners right across village streets, and when asked by refugees about their lost East Pomeranian territories he simply banged his fist on the table and calmly expounded the war guilt of the entire German nation in singsong phrases, reverberating pauses, and an elevated melodious tone. By the end of June his Party had almost 1,000 members in Mecklenburg/West Pomerania. By the end of July more than 3,000, by the end of August nearly 8,000. Cresspahl could see that this untrammeled moving about from place to place suited the man, as did the evening performance and the variety of lodgings, yet he invited him to stay in Jerichow. Once he had a place to live in Jerichow one could probably offer so adroit and fearless a person the job of police chief. (Cresspahl was secretly inclined to hope that this rival king would succeed him as mayor.) The young fellow refused even to hold a meeting in Jerichow. "It's your baby, Cresspahl!" he said in an unexpectedly Berlin tone of voice, with such a mocking twinkle in his eyes that Cresspahl felt the other man had seen through him.

The young man demanded power, and did not take it. Cresspahl was stuck with his worries over the police: like the cuckoo with its song.

---

### May 20, 1968   Monday

---

Charles de Gaulle has found the right word for the French general strike: "La réforme oui, le chienlit non": Reforms, yes; shit in our beds, no. The Grand Old Man.

Near Manhattan Avenue and 119th Street, in the Morningside Park area, the following procedure has been discovered: the bus driver sees a pretty girl at the bus stop, pulls in to the right, and opens the door. But instead of the girl getting onto the bus, three or four boys slip in who had been crouching down so they could not be seen by the driver. They hold a knife to the driver's throat, seize his money-changer, and disappear. The whole operation takes less than thirty seconds. The New York *Times* describes the location as Upper West Side, where we live; our neighborhood.

Moving clouds, white bursts of sunshine, one more snowball thrown by a child onto the roof, rolling off and leaving a thick trail, falling apart in the hand.

In the winter of 1945 one worry for Cresspahl's daughter had passed.

She did not want the two Abses to move on. She wanted Jakob to stay; she wanted Jakob's mother to stay. She cooked my meals for me and showed me how to manage with my hair, she helped me in what was to her a strange land. I remember the evening I stood with my hands clasped behind my back. "Gesine," she said, lightly and courteously touching my shoulder with her rough hard hand; I remember her rather soft, hurried way of speaking. I remember her face: long and bony and in the narrow dry eyes already far advanced in age. I had a mother all the time. All the time.

Mrs. Abs felt that in Jerichow she was not only in the wrong place but in the wrong house.

Here in this little town, hidden by the sea, hidden among the wheat, her husband would never find her. He had not actually promised to find her and the boy. On being released from the military prison at Anklam and dispatched to the East Prussian front, he had secretly made a detour across the River Dievenow and spent two hours during the night on the Bonin estate, to give her his verbal last will and testament. She had not believed it. She promised him to cross the Oder and even the Elbe but in such a way that he could find them. That was only five months ago. Von Bonin drove off with nine heavy covered wagons when the Wolin regional Party leader threatened punishment by death for anyone moving to the West; all that was left for the wife of the missing estate manager was an open potato cart, a superannuated horse, and instructions to look after the estate. Long before the regional Party leader ordered evacuation to the West she had already left the island.

Near Augustwalde she found herself on the Berlin autobahn being attacked by low-flying Soviet planes. Jakob was the more scared of the two, she had blood from his neck wound on her face. After they had laid the dead to one side there was a horse left over, a sorrel. She wanted to take the boy to the hospital at Podejuch but he would not agree to that now they could hitch two horses to their cart. From then on it seemed that he was in charge. Via Neubrandenburg and Malchow he kept them heading in the direction of the Gries area, and after reaching the mouth of the Elde they were forced farther and farther northward, no matter how minor the roads they took, as far as Wismar, and they had reached Jerichow because the road by the sea had been so empty and had seemed so safe from German Army and Nazi patrols.

She had stayed on because for the first time they were offered hospitality, because Jakob wanted to wait out the end of the war; then because of the British occupation of the town, because of the two sick children in Cresspahl's house; then so as to wait for the British to return. But in Jerichow her husband would never find them. He had taken her from a farm in the Gries area, the seventh child, the unpaid farm hand; an inspector for the local milk producers, a former student at Neukloster Seminary, had wanted her for his wife. She had not left her family on good terms, it would be a long time before she could go back there; if he came to look for her, surely it would be near Eldena. In Hamburg she had dutifully learned to be a cook, she was already thirty and had trained for three years there while her husband had been in Brazil looking around for a place for them both until he was forced to return to ruined Germany. She was thirty-eight when Jakob was born in an estate manager's home near Crivitz, that was where her husband would look for them, in Hamburg, near Hagenow. Since the post office had been accepting postcards again she had sent Cresspahl's address to the offices of eleven estate managers, to schoolteachers and church offices, wherever her husband might suppose her to be; she had even brought herself to write to her family. She had not received a single reply, and she did not believe Cresspahl when he said he would find her husband if ever he should come to Mecklenburg. Cresspahl wanted to comfort her; she was ready to believe that his offer of hospitality would stand indefinitely.

There was so much about the house that did not make sense to her. The house did not belong to this man Cresspahl, it was the property of his daughter, a twelve-year-old child, and if you didn't believe it you had only to ask Papenbrock. Papenbrock as father-in-law: how could a man like that, with his great palace of a town house in the market square, fit in with what was left of a carpenter shop behind the cemetery? Papenbrock had one son who was dead, for him he was permitted to erect a memorial plaque in the family burial place; the other son was not supposed to be talked about, he had murdered children in the Ukraine, set fire to villages. Yet the Papenbrocks had had a girl from the Ukraine living with them, first as a maid, then from December 1944 officially as a fiancée, and the Germans had acknowledged her on the street, for the family's sake. In Pomerania, on the Bonin estate, the forced laborers had been kept like cattle that had the power of speech. The girl Slata had not been deported "to Siberia" by the Red Army, she was now working as an assistant at the regional Kommandantura, the Angel of Gneez was the sobriquet she was said to have earned for herself, and in Jerichow people had recently been denying rumors that she had knelt at Pontiy's feet and kissed his hands.

Now the wealthy Papenbrock had been ordered to work as manager of a Soviet estate south of Gneez, and control of the house had passed from his wife to refugees and Russian soldiers, who at night turned the big parlor into a dance hall. Cresspahl was the mayor, he could have stood by his mother-in-law; she never came to him for anything, he walked past her house. For several years Cresspahl's child had not been allowed to visit her grandmother. So people said. Now and again Mrs. Abs would hear someone talk about "our Lisbeth"; Lisbeth could have told the Mayor what to do, soon Lisbeth would have been dead seven years. "Our Lisbeth" cropped up in conversations outside empty store windows, during rest periods in the fields, and for a long time Mrs. Abs thought she was a woman living in Jerichow, an invalid perhaps.

Jakob discovered that she had been Cresspahl's wife, since November 1938 to be visited only in the cemetery. She had died in a fire, they said, maybe by her own hand. The husband did not look after the grave, since early in 1945 Amalie Creutz had not been able to do much for it, the mound had almost collapsed. Mrs. Abs took Cresspahl's child along and showed her how it could be replanted and kept up; the father looked the other way when the child now set out for the cemetery with the watering can. But when Mrs. Abs made a vegetable garden behind the house he was almost overcome with astonishment, and actually thanked her. He knew what people in Jerichow had been telling her after three months, about the house, about his wife's death and the Papenbrock clan; he praised the food, talked about the weather, asked after Jakob, whenever his mayoral duties gave him time to come home. And besides, it suited the Soviets to have him as mayor since he had been given the job under the British; meanwhile he had frequent sharp clashes with the commandant that involved shouting matches and sudden adroit appeasement; he could not count on a salary, or on thanks, ahead of him lay many years of trouble with the low opinion of him that Jerichow was cultivating. He had once said something in this connection that made sense to Mrs. Abs. Someone had to do it, hadn't they? That made sense to her. Someone had to do it. But there was too much about the man that did not make sense to her.

To repay him for board and lodging she ran his house for him. He had taken in more homeless people than he was obliged to or than K. A. Pontiy had wanted him to, and now the top of the stove was crammed with pots and bowls and pans. Mrs. Abs could not stand the constant bickering, the hiding of food, she had been trained to manage a large kitchen and after a while did the cooking for everyone. The guests in Cresspahl's house, even the schoolteacher from Marienwerder, accepted the authority of the tall rawboned woman whose gaze could be so quiet, whose voice could be so level. After all, she did have the backing of the master of the house and had been there longer than most. That put an end to the furtive eating in bedrooms and attic: meals were taken communally at the big tiled table in the kitchen. There were still hidden supplies of grain and potatoes, since it had been agreed upon that each person was to contribute something toward the meals, and after a while the food supplies that had been such a bone of contention could lie side by side in the storeroom behind an unlocked door. When Jakob came home with his wages he was allowed to give the children an egg or an apple, the piece of bacon or the rabbit went into the common pot. Mrs. Abs contributed her share, sometimes great hunks of meat, by doing the washing for the commandant and his two officers. There was not always enough to satisfy everyone's hunger,

*Mrs. Abs! There's a horse lying right by the path! A dead horse, Mrs. Abs!*

*How long has it been there?*

*It fell there today.*

*Who knows about it, Gesine?*

*Only me. But we can't eat horse!*

*You'll get something else. Can you keep your mouth shut?*

*I'll be as silent as the grave.*

*Then give me the knife.*

The children would rather there had been a lock on the storeroom door. But there was less quarreling in the house, the grownups could go off with Cresspahl's squad of cripples and earn their ration cards, and the teacher knew that her baby was being looked after. From Mrs. Abs the children learned how to keep their own room clean, and Cresspahl's too, and they were at least shown how to clean windows. She would have been glad to make dresses for Gesine and Hanna out of the ones hanging in Lisbeth's bedroom; she asked Cresspahl for permission, and next morning they had gone. Jakob swapped the patterns that Cresspahl no longer wanted to see for parachute silk and uniform cloth, and for five days even a sewing machine came to the house, until it had to be turned into liquor. There was work to be done in Cresspahl's house, that was enough for Mrs. Abs. She could put ointment on the children's arms and legs where they had been scratched by wheat and rape stubble, she could treat their swelling boils with a salve and give them ever so slightly thicker slices of bread and molasses to take with them to the fields; sometimes she felt that the children were reason enough to stay.

She had won Hanna Ohlerich over immediately; Gesine remained aloof for a long time, perhaps because she had surfaced from her fever by such minute, hesitant stages and took that long to recognize her. Neither of them called her Mother, or Auntie either for that matter; and, although they almost always used her family name, her Christian name did slip out now and again. Hanna Ohlerich was herself a guest in Cresspahl's home; from time to time her unfocused, narrowed gaze would betray the fact that she had visions of living somewhere else; after all, the child really did not care with whom she had to live. With Gesine, Mrs. Abs felt she was at least half welcome. Gesine would give her a faraway look, ask her things in a roundabout way, stand silent and withdrawn when Mrs. Abs ran to meet the mailman and returned disappointed. When Mrs. Abs could hear Jakob with the children, she would open the flap of the kitchen window a little way. She noted Gesine's unexpected, urgent questions about Podejuch, how Jakob would pull her leg, how Gesine would silently go away and return crestfallen to the kitchen. And if she ever smiled at such twelve-year-old anguish, she did not do so in front of me. By the time I had learned not to show it, she had helped me.

Gesine did not like seeing Mrs. Abs dress to go into town and pack her black bag. It was a leather case you could use for traveling. A person who was free to leave the house to go to work was also free to leave the town. How was Mrs. Abs to be made to stay in Jerichow?

---

### May 21, 1968  Tuesday

First the French Communists have neither seen the general strike coming nor supported it, now they want a coalition of the entire left, a truly republican regime, and they also see it as being on the road to Socialism.

The Polish Communists, on the other hand, have finally discovered why they have not been understood by the Poles: the fault lies with the Czechoslovak Communists. The way they permit themselves to be publicly questioned as to their contemplated changes can only be harmful.

The East German Communists have let themselves be caught in Sweden with buried radio transmitters and mail pick-up boxes.

The Czechoslovak Communists still have Aleksei N. Kosygin as a visitor. In Prague they assist at the opening of a city office for Pan American Airways, eighteen years after it was closed following the coup d'état, after two years of negotiations, and the air fare as far as London may be paid for in Czechoslovak crowns. At the spa of Karlovy Vary, Karlsbad, the Soviet Premier strolls openly through the streets and is taking the healing waters.

Today we intended to quit buying at Don Mauro's.

Don Mauro runs a store on Broadway (board the last car of the West Side Express, leave 96th Street station in the opposite direction to the train and walk south), a modest little trap crammed with smoking supplies, candy, and cheap stationery. A row of telephone booths may attract a few customers, he does not sell newspapers, and there is not even a bench with which Don Mauro might entice his customers to stay a bit longer than is required to exchange money for goods. It is a shoebox of a trap, thriftily partitioned off from next door, the fan blades circling lethargically in the ceiling seem almost a luxurious embellishment. But in fact Don Mauro is a pillar of the Puerto Rican community on Manhattan's Upper West Side, an ornament of the Church council, respected by the police, chairman of the citizens' association, and if you want to win an election in this area you would do well not to begin without Don Mauro's good will.

When Don Mauro arrived from his island eighteen years ago, he could scarcely afford an apartment and had a hard time finding a job, only he started out differently from the blacks. The blacks still say, even today: See? That's the way they treat us. He began right off with: They're not going to treat *us* like that. From the word go, Don Mauro had more equal rights, was more of a U. S. citizen, than other people; he was aided in this by his family's lighter skin and the "right kind of hair." Here in this very store was where Don Mauro started out, soon he was teaching his oldest son how to handle the police and single-entry bookkeeping; now he is already training nephews for the stores that he is going to find, stock, and lease to them. *They* may still have to pay protection money to the guardians of law and order; in Don Mauro's store the latter must pay for their purchases, a proffered box of cigars is already an honor. (Maximum one cigar to a uniform.)

Don Mauro stands at the far end of the counter chewing on the same cold cigar butt from morning till night, maybe the whole week long. From time to time the butt in the corner of Don Mauro's mouth shifts and alters his pensive expression as if he had just spat out something, but in fact a thought has just occurred to him. He supervises the nephew standing at the cash register, he runs the expiring lease of the laundry next door through the calculating machine in his head, he chews delicately around on the kernel of a clause, until it opens under his knowing bite. Not only does Don Mauro look contented; his ceaseless planning and discovering are expressed so agreeably in his face that the existence of pleasures behind them may be assumed. Every two years he goes back to check up on the Estado Libre Asociado de Puerto Rico, to visit his mother, attend mass in his native village, and assess his young relatives in terms of their suitability for New York, and willingly, albeit somewhat morosely, he will tell them about this corner of Manhattan. There are places there that look like home, with store signs, neon advertising, bodegas. The buildings may be taller, but down below them there are holes with music of the island floating and throbbing up out of them. There are churches with services in Spanish, movies that now offer only programs in the island's own language; homesickness won't be that bad, and it won't get any worse. There, as here, the family will stick together, and one family will stick to another; and on Sundays you can see the girls in the park, respectable, nicely dressed, still Spanish-looking. If the skin is light, a lack of English won't be too serious. So every year a new youth stands beside Don Mauro's cash register, acquiring the English of the Yanquis, moves on to become a store manager, eventually perhaps a proprietor. Those who understand this may sometimes be put in sole charge of the store while Don Mauro climbs a narrow staircase in the side of the building, the discreet approach to an office on the second floor where he talks into the phone: what, nobody knows; there he keeps his money in the safe, there he has his secret bottle of cough syrup. The staircase leads only to this office, who's going to know about it, apart from the janitor? You hardly meet a soul on the stairs. The door in the alley is half hidden by the garbage pails and sacks from the hotel, just a slit that opens and shuts quicker than a wink. This office and the dime-store padlock on the door provide much food for thought; then the customers seem dreamlike, only a moment ago there was no one here.

Is it a customer? It is a Yanqui, a man about fifty, wearing a white shirt but in need of a shave, with marks on his neck like abrasions, he says something about dimes. Is he asking for change?

The suppliant fancies himself lucky, looks anxiously and paternally at the youth behind the counter, a boy of sixteen with a narrow hard head, a dreamy expression, friendly in a way beneath the furrowed brow, the still childlike waves of gray-blond hair. The man tries to repay the favor with politeness; for the sake of his own feelings, too, he has to do something, so he says, rather rashly: "I'm not really a bum, you know—" and for support he turns to the lady beside him, and she smiles, not pityingly but meaning to encourage him.

Enter Don Mauro, who sees the apprentice's fingers in the till, No Sale. The group stands transfixed, he has covered the distance to them from the door very swiftly, but each of them has seen him stride in, an old man, stiff in the shoulders, his dignity enhanced by the rage contorting his face. The boy receives a whiplash delivered in tonelessly whispered Spanish, a wound that won't heal before Saturday. The beggar is driven out of the store like a diseased steer, each of his submissive gestures intercepted by Don Mauro with a thrust of the chest and hisses of abuse as the latter nimbly maneuvers the victim until he manages to escape onto the sidewalk, the beggar, the failure, the parasite—you bum! you dirty bum!

Scarcely out of breath Don Mauro steps up to the lady customer, now just a plain-dealing businessman who has come up the hard way. The youth jerks back as if pushed by two hands. Sullenly, ominously, impatiently, Don Mauro growls: Yes, madam?

He knows this customer, he knows what she buys. But she apologizes. She has made a mistake. She needs nothing in this store.

"Are you going to give up smoking, Gesine?"
"Not exactly."
"Do you want to change the business structure of the entire city of New York?"
"Not exactly, Marie."
"Are you proposing to walk ten more blocks each time, to the next Don Mauro, Don Fanto, Don Alfonso?"
"No."
"You give to beggars, and you said it was your own business."
"I remember, Marie."
"You've taught me that it's wrong."
"No."
"Yes. You've betrayed yourself, Gesine."

## May 22, 1968   Wednesday

In its erudition the New York *Times* not only gives us its interpretation of Charles de Gaulle's remark about the soiled bed of his nation. An all-round education is what it has in mind for us, and today it offers a key to the language of the American armed forces. Light losses are those that do not affect a unit's capability to carry out its mission. Moderate losses mean that a unit's capability has been impaired, and heavy losses mean that the unit can no longer perform its designated function. Solution: If an installation in Vietnam reports light losses, it is quite possible that out of 3,000 men 100 have been killed. In this language these men do not count.

Last Tuesday East German border troops tried to annex 500 acres of West German territory near Wolfsburg, basing their claim on a map of 1873 showing the border between Brunswick and Prussia that was fixed as the demarcation line by the Allies in 1945. The West Germans admitted that there had been deviations from this line in their favor but insisted on the decision and will of the Soviets of that time. "The Russians can err too," said the East German Colonel. As the border inhabitants recall it, his friends did not err in 1945, the line had been drawn in return for gold watches or bottles of schnapps; then, with their British partners, they would repair to a tavern and draw the demarcation line on a beer coaster or a cigarette pack. Today this is a shooting matter.

By October 1945 the people of Jerichow had long ceased to believe in the arrival of occupation troops from Sweden, they had resigned themselves half-heartedly to the continued presence of the Soviets, and my father was now once more being greeted on the street, he had only to indicate he wanted to be.

The Mayor was being given credit for making things so unpleasant for the refugees that most of them had left town. A man who relieved the townspeople of the nuisance of hospitality could not be all bad.

It was under Cresspahl's regime that the schools were reopened. From October 1 the youngsters, who had been running wild, were finally kept busy again; besides, each was given a rye bun in school.

Perhaps it was Cresspahl who had succeeded at the end of September in having a real live locomotive turn up at Jerichow station, with three passenger cars in tow. Now every morning a train left for Gneez, and every evening it came back again. Heinz Wollenberg was happy that his daughter Lise could attend her high school again, and he had advised her to be polite to Gesine Cresspahl. Cresspahl was merely doing his duty. "Hi there!" said Lise on the station platform, the first time since June; such carefree nonchalance seemed a bit suspicious to Gesine, but she answered: "Hi there."

Cresspahl was paid 120 marks a month plus 20 marks housing allowance for working from early morning until far into the night. He could not supplement his income with carpentry, having neither time nor opportunity to get hold of materials from the black market, he was hitched to a wagon that carried K. A. Pontiy and the Red Army. He derived no benefits from his office; he was welcome to whatever harm he suffered.

Although he may have given orders for bicycle registration so as to provide his friend Pontiy with a survey, it did help somewhat to reduce theft.

No, Cresspahl was still needed. It was his achievement that Jerichow was getting fish from the Baltic, even if only for the hospital; and on ration coupon 10 there had been an unexpected allocation of salt. He would continue to pester the District Office of Gneez until it allocated some coal for running the gasworks. And those out-and-out squandermaniacs the British had cut Jerichow off from their Herrenwyk power plant, the town was in darkness; Cresspahl had got hold of an auxiliary plant for the hospital in exchange for Mrs. Köpcke's truck and the last few spare tires remaining in Swenson's hideaway, the two victimized firms had been compensated at peacetime prices and told to pipe down. For was it they who would succeed in getting Jerichow linked up with an eastern power circuit, or Cresspahl?

When in mid-October all male and female persons between the ages of sixteen and fifty were ordered to report for examination for venereal diseases, "as authorized by the Town Commandant," people in Jerichow spoke of a victory by Cresspahl over Pontiy. Women of over fifty turned up, bringing along girls of under sixteen. Pontiy had not realized the consequences, but the Mayor of Jerichow had. It looked as if Cresspahl was beginning to take the lead.

The Jerichow treasury had recently begun collecting taxes again. The new City Bank, formerly the Co-Op Savings Bank, no longer kept open from 10 A.M. to 10 P.M. merely at the commandant's orders: now the tradesmen were depositing their take daily; word had got around that the money was not disappearing but could be used for expenditures, with signatures and checks just as in the old days. It was, of course, an impoverished economy, a hungry life, a barren town, but Cresspahl had helped to get it moving.

On October 22 Cresspahl was visited by two Soviet officers who were not known in Jerichow. It was evening, already dark, the movements of the figures around the jeep in front of the town hall were indistinct. Leslie Danzmann was able to add that Cresspahl had gone along without a struggle. Not even the kerosene lamp had been knocked over. Then Cresspahl's secretary was arrested too. Pontiy instructed Fritz Schenk to proclaim his Order No. 24:

In the interest
of stabilizing
the autonomy of the administration
and increasing
the productivity
of the town's economy
and introducing
a stricter order into the affairs
of the Town of Jerichow
I hereby release Mr. Heinrich Cresspahl as of the 21st day of October 1945 from his office of mayor.

## May 25, 1968   Saturday, South Ferry Day

In the IRT subway the management, may it suffocate from the heat, has removed one of each pair of ventilators! When the cars crawl toward the curving platforms below the ferry station, screeching in the tight squeeze, the passengers in the front cars have first to walk between dark tunnel walls, and inside the station ramps have to be moved up to the train doors. Only then are the doors opened, and today the stuffy atmosphere fed the anxiety that they would not open at all.

"So that means I had two grandfathers with crminal records," said Marie as soon as we were on the boat. She was trying to adopt a devil-may-care attitude toward these revelations as to her origins, ancestors like that had once again made her uneasy. No matter what she heard at home, it had cut no ice against what she was taught in school, where an arrest is as good as proof of guilt. That was something she was not supposed to learn: white middle-class thinking. That's the way she thinks.

"Jakob's father never faced a court, Marie."

"He was in a military prison, in Anklam, you admit that. Did he at least refuse to do military service?"

"Perhaps you wouldn't have approved of what he did. And I don't know what he did."

"He might have been your father-in-law. He's my grandfather, Gesine."

"All I know about him is that he was born in 1889, the seminary in Neukloster, Brazil in the twenties, his jobs as estate manager in Mecklenburg and Pomerania, being called up by the Army in 1943, prison, the things I picked up during those fifteen years with Jakob and his mother. Before Jakob died I was in no hurry to ask questions. Before Jakob's mother died, I didn't like to press her. Neither of them ever volunteered anything about Wilhelm Abs, and I only know his first name from the will. If I were asked when his birthday was, I could only say July, and I'd have to look up the exact date."

"And where he's buried?"

"Until her own death his wife refused to believe in his. If you like, he'll be seventy-nine in five or six weeks."

"In the Soviet Union. We wouldn't recognize him."

"Surely you wouldn't mind a stranger, Marie."

"Tonight I'd like to write down his birth date. Not to celebrate, just so one of us knows it."

"And no criminal record."

"Make Cresspahl innocent, Gesine. If you could just lie a little."

"The officers who arrested him began by treating him as if he were innocent. He wasn't pushed into the jeep, they patiently held the door open for him till he found a seat in the dark. They didn't handcuff him, they gave him a blanket. There was some mention of the chilly evening, the approach of winter, the threat of frost to the potatoes. When Cresspahl asked them to take him to his house for five minutes, they didn't refuse him rudely: they seemed amused, as at someone new to a strange world. They gave him some mahorka tobacco for his pipe, as if he were a guest. At Wehrlich station they locked him up in a henhouse."

"That was something he could never forgive. He couldn't even talk about it!"

"They apologized. They didn't want to go any further that night, one of them had a friend at the Wehrlich Kommandantura; at the ranger's station there were no prison cells. Besides, he wasn't supposed to be seen by the German personnel. What else would you have done with a prisoner like that?"

"Just go on lying, Gesine. And they brought him his supper on a tray."

"They may have forgotten that in their delight at seeing their friend again, in the party that followed. Cresspahl could hear their voices until far into the night, the singing, the toasts, why should they give a thought to a henhouse?"

"Now the escape."

"The lock was meant to protect the former chicken occupants not only from foxes but also from two-legged thieves, with no light it was hard to pick. They had pushed their jeep in front of the door, it was too heavy for him to tip over. There was no window, the walls were solid brick, the hatch was for chickens. Nor did he want to admit right off to guilt by escaping. Actually Soviet patrols searched our rooms more than once during the following week, they were waiting for him in Jerichow. The henhouse wasn't too bad for sleeping in; they had left him the blanket. Only that at first he collided with the low perches, and that the stench of old manure was revived by the damp night air. A sour smell penetrating the clothing, the legacy of three generations of chickens; even so, in the morning the Soviets found their prisoner asleep. They now drove on in a stinking jeep, trapped with the smell by the rain, and they cracked all the jokes about hens and cocks they could think of. Cresspahl was given a hunk of bread, a mouthful of vodka, some coarse mahorka tobacco, as if they were all going off together on a vacation, only that he alone did not know their destination. The destination was the cellar below the Gneez courthouse; his companions took their leave with encouraging though cautious shoulder slappings. After that Cresspahl felt that in the Red Army an arrest wasn't considered a disgrace, at most a bit of bad luck that could happen to anyone. They wished him luck. That was the beginning of the first stage."

"You walked to school over his head."

"The girls' school in Gneez had been turned into a hospital for the Red Army, the younger classes were put into the Sacred Heart School—"

"—in a parochial school. Like me!"

"—a municipal school, named after a convent and a chapel commemorating the ritual persecution of the Jews in 1330, long since burned down. From the ruins of that venerable courtyard to the station I only had to cross two streets diagonally, that brought me to where my father was and I never knew it. All I saw was the war memorial to the Franco-Prussian War, black and shining like a newly polished locomotive, and the two red tongues of flag rising out of the courthouse roof. That's where the German police took the black marketeers, people caught with weapons, members of the German Army who had been arrested during the July registration, youngsters suspected of underground activities; never did it occur to me that Cresspahl might be locked up underneath that building. It was common knowledge, no one had to tell me: anyone picked up by the Soviets would be sent 'to Siberia.' "

"Now comes the bit about torture, the water cell, the starvation diet."

"To Cresspahl it seemed as if they had picked him up just to put him away and had then forgotten him. Twice a day the guards brought food to his cell, sometimes in the evening too, bread from their field bakery, fish soup made from water and cods' heads, remains of the soldiers' meals. At school we learned to write and speak Russian, but Charlotte Pagels may have been using a book from German Army stocks and told us that kasha was cabbage soup,

shchi i kasha
pishcha nasha

yet actually it was a gruel of buckwheat or semolina with jam or a few shreds of meat, the arrival of which would have helped my father to mark off the days in prison, had he been allowed a calendar. When the cell door was unlocked he had to stand at attention, his head touching the wall, so he wouldn't be able to look out into the corridor. When he did this according to regulations they would hand him the bowl. They didn't like to hear him speak. They called him *otyets* and *durak*, father and dope, neither meant as an insult, and little by little he learned. The inscriptions and drawings on the encrusted wall had evidently been counted, the existing quantity was not to be increased, so Cresspahl earned one foodless day for starting a calendar. He found monthly charts from the spring of 1945 scratched into the wall, final comments before transportation to the camp at Bützow-Dreibergen, the notes of the British national anthem with a blasphemous text, little swastikas with invocations for luck in battle, all that could stay. It may at one time have been Dr. Semig's cell, but he found nothing from his hand. To teach him a thing or two about secret possessions, they would from time to time rip open his straw mattress and scatter the contents all over the cell, and they would praise him like a child when by evening he had put together a new mattress. In December they noticed he was shivering, they stuck a thermometer in his mouth. He wasn't allowed to see what it showed, with the next meal he was given a blanket. More unbearable than the cold was the lack of light, it came for only a few hours through a conical shaft that opened below a grille at the rear of the building. In the next cell there were two or three voices; he remained alone.

The departure was quite a ceremony. The young fellows in their trim uniforms had accompanied him often enough to the washroom, nudging his arm gently, for to them he seemed blind; this time they helped him remove his beard and gave him some warm water. He was given parts of uniforms, Air Force below, Army above, for the first time in seventeen weeks he no longer stank of chicken manure. Sitting all alone on the bench of a covered truck he was driven south, the blurred spring green along Schwerin Lake taught him to see again. He was handed over to the Soviet Military Tribunal in the capital, now he was to speak."

"The unauthorized withdrawals from the bank accounts of the aristocracy."

"Those he had restored as soon as enough taxes had been collected (with the result that the Jerichow treasury remained bare to the very bottom). Maybe he hadn't been able to bring himself to pay interest on such loans, and remissness of that kind was part of Stage One."

"Being wakened up in the middle of the night to recite figures."

"In Schwerin the Soviets worked around the clock, so the court calendar decided when it was his turn. Of course for days they didn't need him for anything, he almost learned how to live again in the heated cell, with ample light from above; without warning they would come for him in the night. The court ran like a machine, demanding from defendant and plaintiff alike trot, walk, and instant gallop; Cresspahl couldn't blame those conducting his case individually. One of them seemed to be a military man, the other an auditor, they took turns. They had prepared themselves for his case, the files from Jerichow town hall lay on their desks, and at first Cresspahl was required simply to give an account of each procedure. If one of his reports pleased them, he was allowed to repeat it. They observed him uneasily, expecting him to defend himself rather than pronounce one judgment after another against himself."

"With a clear conscience, Gesine. He had taken nothing for himself."

"It was a matter of another advantage, not his. Although K. A. Pontiy had officially abolished civil rights in Jerichow, he had not announced the new kinds of guilt. The gentlemen of the Schwerin Military Tribunal read out to Cresspahl Law No. 4 of the Allied Control Council; according to their interpretation, for the time being those laws were valid that had been in force on January 30, 1933. But he had had no way of knowing this."

"What he had done was sufficient defense."

"You and your truth, what a little American you are! It can be used one way or another."

"But the facts!"

"Cresspahl had no desire to go beyond his own truth. Some strange things came out. He had had two bags of roasted coffee beans confiscated from Böhnhase, with the permission of the Gneez public prosecutor's office, but then the hoarded merchandise was described to him in Schwerin as having originated in a crime, and now it wasn't even coffee any more and in defiance of nature had turned into crude oil for the hospital power unit. In other words, Cresspahl was supposed to answer for the hidden hands through which the coffee had previously passed, for a past that was unknown to him. He couldn't see it that way, so he didn't sign. The two interrogators were amused by his awkwardness. They went along with his quirk of not wanting to name any other names than were on the paper, they weren't short of names, they helped him out. Gradually he was led to believe that not only Leslie Danzmann but also Gantlik was in jail, and Slata, and Amalie Creutz, and Peter Wulff, Böhnhase, and the Mayor of Beckhorst village. For a long time the conversations remained friendly, he was not required to remain standing, his chair was moved from the side of the

room up to the desk, and when it came to remembering tricky details
he would stand beside the interrogator like a partner, bent over the
files, searching, turning the pages. Since he was used to a pipe he was
allowed to choose one from the storeroom and found an English one,
scarcely damaged, with a curved mouthpiece like the one Uncle Joe
used to smoke; at the start of each session it was taken out of a drawer
and at the end it was locked away again, like a doctor's instrument. Sometimes he was even given some shag tobacco instead of
mahorka."

"I must know about Uncle Joe."

"Must know, there speaks an American. Iosif Vissarionovich was
always shown to the public in this country smoking that kind of a pipe,
in the days when he was still supposed to be an ally. The picture
showed him with a roguish eye, like a jolly uncle."

"The defendant with a resemblance to the supreme boss of the
tribunal."

"That didn't bother his interrogators. They came from a different
country, they may never have seen that picture."

"Did they also call Cresspahl Little Father?"

"They called him Mister, like the bourgeois he was. They wanted
him to feel competent, like an adult who could make mistakes while
in full possession of his faculties. These mistakes had been established,
now it was up to him to admit to the crimes. To help him, they showed
him bits and pieces of their thinking: Slata had been taken to another
tribunal, in the Soviet Union. Her name had served merely to prove
Cresspahl's connection with the perpetrator of a crime against humanity. Amalie Creutz was not under arrest at all. Why should she be,
according to Cresspahl's own evidence he had had no hesitation in
believing she was pregnant, his application for an abortion had been
found at the Schwerin Department of Health and had been countersigned by him as proof
    of the aim
    of the defamation
    of the honor
    of the Red Army,
Mrs. Creutz was no longer needed as a witness. And certainly the
interrogators were prepared to summon Fritz Schenk for a confrontation, they positively warmed to the idea, only Schenk was no longer
in Jerichow, and the German comrades reported him as being indispensable; so it was clear, wasn't it, that even a Soviet interrogation
judge had his limitations. A gross exaggeration, this talk about omnipotence."

"Whose side are you on, Gesine! You belong to Cresspahl's, and you don't speak for him."

"Why should I be on his side? What I know has more than two sides."

"Would Cresspahl agree to that?"

"They covered the ground with him right back to the year 1935. He had done carpentry work for the Jerichow North airfield, until 1938 and again till 1945. He admitted it. This meant that, since 1935, with no evidence of coercion, he had helped German militarism onto its feet and into the air. Although Cresspahl realized that one implied the other, also that outwardly they wanted to regard him as having helped clear the way for the Nazis, he refused to accept the bridge they had built for him that led to the economic sabotage in Jerichow pursued by him as a past and present Fascist; he would not sign. They tried again, this time offering something in return. When he asked about his child in Jerichow they sternly refused information, shaking their heads at his denseness; after two weeks, however, they revealed that the student Gesine Cresspahl had been transferred to the Bridge School in Gneez with a B in Russian. He thanked them for bending the rules, he did not depart from his own. They chided him, somewhat pained; they had failed in their goal of at least placing him somewhere between subjective and objective truth. By this time they had all the facts they wanted; they no longer needed him. He was sent to a camp where formerly the Nazis had kept their prisoners, he was to help clean it up."

"Was that his sentence?"

"It was a holding camp. The gentlemen of the Schwerin Soviet Military Tribunal hadn't threatened him with any definite penalty; only once, since they didn't seem to be getting anywhere, they had asked him whether he would actually prefer to remain in jail for thirty years rather than fifteen, or at most twenty."

"He was smart enough, you got mail from him."

"The camp was well guarded, with dog patrols between the double row of barbed wire, with searchlights at night. He was there with others, but they were transferred in quick succession for sentencing and removal from the country; they couldn't take messages. Even at his work he couldn't smuggle out any news; the bedsteads, the window frames, the barrack sections, all these remained inside the fence. Anyway he could only guess at the nearest town or village. He might be anywhere in southwest Mecklenburg. Others knew for sure and referred to Neustadt-Glewe; that didn't fit in with the route, as far as he had been able to recognize it while he was being taken there at night."

"What date are we at now?"

"August 1946."

"Then I'll be your guide through Staten Island, New York, as of May 1968."

The Czechoslovak Communists have had to pay a price. In order to avoid having 11,000 special troops stationed on their soil and the creation of a military Cominform within the Warsaw pact, they are to permit maneuvers in their country in June. The East Germans dismiss as a West German provocation the report of the stationing of friendly troops in Czechoslovakia; and on the planned liberalization of Socialism they have this to say: "The wheel of history cannot be turned back." History as a winch that winds up the past, irrevocably, for all eternity. Onward!

---

## May 26, 1968   Sunday

All that Marie showed me yesterday of Staten Island, the city and district of Richmond; *you know now, Gesine, I don't have to tell you again.*

After the two-story brick wilderness on the north coast of the island, there were finally trees again at Silverlake Park, scenery, protectively aligned in trellises and windbreaks. Gentle road humps, tolerantly following the ups and downs of the land. Some country houses from the past, naïvely decked out with columned porches, ancient Greece in wood. Verandas under shady trees, windows dark against the heat, behind them quiet, creaking rooms. Buildings with colored brick facing neatly pierced by white window frames. Tall branches, eroded by the breath of the Atlantic, lush, whispering clouds of foliage. Assemblies of seagulls on shingle roofs in the lee of the wind. Exposed cables on rough-hewn poles that were often askew, from the days of modest technology. Grass between the paving stones, rank weeds and bushes around the steps. Sloping gardens, cool, with overgrown hedges. Neighborhoods. What would it be like to wait here at the window, in the vaporous, overcast air of early summer, later warm in bare, damp November. *Here you'll have a life in the country, Mecklenburg, California; stay here, Gesine. Here, as soon as I can, I'll buy you a house.*

The trains of the S. I. R. R. across the island do not achieve the sound produced by their name. They pretend to be the Staten Island express line, related to the Baltimore & Ohio Railroad; in fact they are a rattling, chattering suburban line. Wobbly coaches from post–World War I days that stop every mile at narrow platforms under minimal roofs. Impatient clanging at level crossings, hollow hooting approaching stations; how bravely the little train moves along, as if it were going all the way to the Gulf of Mexico. On one of the pinched little bridge houses a glimpse is caught of a date, pompously set into a concrete step: 1933. Straggly bushes close to the electrified rails. *Start here, Gesine; stay here.*

Verrazano Bridge extends wide traffic decks across the railway underpass toward New Jersey. Beyond Oude Dorp, Arrochar, small planes suspended in the air, lodgers at the airfield off Richmond Road, along the streams flowing into Arthur Kill. *Here you could get away and we could visit you, by land, by water, by air.*

The ferry building at the southern tip of the island has grown even hollower, it is shedding its planks, the rows of piles in the fetid water are standing awry. The water has worn its way right up to Tottenville station, chewing at the garbage, nourishing the rust and the ooze. The station at Tottenville was built to serve the ferry to Perth Amboy, that end was silent, firmly encased in wire mesh as if no boat had crossed over to New Jersey for a long time although there had been one since colonial days. The far shore lay waiting motionless, cranes, warehouses, a church, roofs glinting among the trees, nothing stirred in the midday heat. Across Arthur Kill, to the north, a bridge on stilts, frozen like a rheumatic cat in mid-stride. Building rubble, oil drums, scrap iron along the beach, splintery posts in the water, farther out cruisers and fishing boats against the light. Wherever one looked, vegetation reclaiming the sick land, covering the scars and wounds of the ground; *the externals of vacations, Gesine.*

In Tottenville death passed by. In the white, sun-stretched light two couples wearing dark clothes walked toward a building that looked like a high-class dairy or private school. The skin of the two women was all warm beneath the transparent material. A man in a business suit, ill-at-ease, brought up the rear, as if embarrassed by the anticipation of seeing the recumbent person or by the prospect of himself being carried in through the rear door of the funeral parlor within a few years. (As if he were visiting his future home, himself inside it, without having given any thought yet to the move.) *When you're dead, Gesine, I won't let the embalming place get you.*

In Tottenville crippled houses huddling together, decaying, draped with pieces of plastic. A little shed of a synagogue with a skin of asbestos shingles. Italian plaster figures on dried-up bits of lawn. A living cat, white with wide black eyes, wants to be seen, knows something. Kids on the porches, an old woman with a book sits watching them. Swings, wading pools, in the back yards. Smell of hot wood, acacia blossom.

A love affair of D. E.'s in 1949 in Berlin-Wannsee, whole evenings spent leaning beside a girl against a garden gate, the scent of acacia in the air; during the day the little white blossoms hid among the leaves; in 1949, the wish she expressed to a man with black-market connections was not for chocolate or a gramophone but for a swim cap. *Or you could live among poor people, Gesine.*

Suddenly a broad field of tall grass, overgrown with wild shrubs. A freighter as close to the shore as if she had run aground. Against the horizon, framed by foliage, a white gable, a sloping roof projecting from an almost square wooden box of a house. Behind the dark windows, on the long veranda facing the Atlantic, not a sign of movement. An overgrown path for the mailman. *Or this, if you like.*

On the gravel roads, dotted with puddles, a few lonely cars were moving, as if scared by field and thicket, far from the eight-lane highways and the high rises. Swamp areas, no longer passable on account of broken glass and rusty cans. A decaying colony of summer cottages. Children staring at the strangers walking by, giggling at the citified appearance of the strange child. Close by the water a couple sat helplessly in their car, ready to drive off. Look, real reeds. These are plantains, good for cuts. We used to make soup out of goosefoot. This the rabbits used to like. A red maple. Chicory. Ribwort. Shepherd's-purse, we used to eat that. Chopped nettles were good served as spinach. Good weather for a suntan. *Don't forget why I showed you all this, Gesine.*

### May 28, 1968   Tuesday

In the morning the train waited beyond 50th Street station in the dark. The distance to the lighted platform was hard to estimate. Memory kept reporting a light place beside the track, fifty yards on, eighty yards on, seen the day before yesterday, an opening to the light, a staircase to the surface. This ever-returning search for an exit marked time, pushed aside all thought. In the motionless silent crowd, fear of each extra minute grew until, incredibly, the train started to move. On the steps below Times Square, policemen were standing around casually, hands comfortably clasped over the night stick behind their backs. They looked at the scared passengers, as much as to say: Are they all after you? Did they let you out this time? You're running as if you're going to get free candy.

After Cresspahl had disappeared, Jakob took over his household, reluctantly.

His mother had tried to do it alone. The refugees in the rear half of the house kept to the rules she had introduced, in the kitchen as well as in taking turns to clean hallway and stairs; they may have believed in some last-minute instructions of Cresspahl's, and Mrs. Abs felt this was dishonest since she had been given no such authority. Had it not been for Gesine and Hanna Ohlerich, she might well have packed her things and sought refuge where Jakob was working, two hours from Jerichow, where she was not known as the housekeeper of a mayor whom the Russians had taken away. Not that she was afraid of being arrested herself, it was simply that she expected nothing good from the authorities; to the day she died she would not be persuaded otherwise. She had such difficulty dealing with the messengers from Warnemünde or Lübeck who turned up at night outside the house with business that only Cresspahl could make head or tail of. There were the children. For Gesine she had to create a morning and an evening as they had been before her father's disappearance. Ohlerich's daughter had to be persuaded that Cresspahl's house was not now among the unsafe ones. Every morning she took Gesine to the Gneez train, Hanna to the school in Jerichow, in the evening she had to keep them both busy in the kitchen with mending and homework and, because she did not trust herself as a storyteller, she leaned heavily on the deeds of the King of the Wends.

One such evening, as they were sitting by the kerosene lamp that stood on Cresspahl's desk, the first house search took them by surprise, two unfamiliar Soviets with Mayor Schenk and Gantlik as witnesses, a well-directed whirlwind that was soon outside again, leaving not so much as an overturned chair. Nevertheless, she was so frightened that she spent the night on a chair beside the girls' bed. She left Cresspahl's room in disorder until Jakob had been brought. Jakob would not grant her wish. Arrests like this did not happen only in his mother's vicinity, he knew of day laborers as well as the Lübeck Arms. In all of Mecklenburg they would find the climate no different, the frontier to the new Western Poland had been closed since November 19. His mother let him finish all the reasonable arguments, and he came to realize that he owed her an unreasonable one. He stabled his horses with his partners at the border, he remained in Jerichow. For him it was the wrong kind of arrangement. He still had a credit of grain for wages, this was now being fed to the bay horse and the decrepit gelding. For his work in repairing the gasworks he was paid only in money, working on the land he could have earned potatoes. It was not even that he owed this fellow Cresspahl anything, he wanted to do him a favor.

*Because we could no longer get to Lower Saxony with the horses, Gesine.*

*That's why you stayed?*

*What were people to think?*

*That the two of you were leaving and deserting me, I know, you wanted those bastards to take away your bread bit by bit.*

*And we were aiming to grab hold of your house, young Miss Cresspahl.*

*You've always been good at teasing me.*

*A youngster sister like that was just what I needed. Pure selfishness.*

*I was the selfish one, Jakob.*


How does a young fellow from the country who lands in a strange town go about heading a household that has not even been entrusted to him? The boy started by charging rent, retroactive to July 1, the arrival of the New Order. He had measured the house in his head, the people in Cresspahl's house hadn't even received a warning when he placed a receipt book on the kitchen table. It was no more than Mrs. Quade or the Maass family were charging, but still it was annoying because it was an innovation. The teacher from Marienwerder threatened to lodge a complaint because he could not produce a rental agreement. At the mention of this the others suddenly tumbled to something, and they began to pay, it was only money, wasn't it. So the Cresspahl child did receive an income, and it was enough to cover the cost of boarding a friend. They were free to take the matter up with the town hall; there the name Abs was not unknown, for in applying for his ration cards he had insisted on being registered as a manual laborer. The weekly 2,450 grams instead of the regular 1,700 had led to a battle, until in the end they had to be granted to the gasworks laborer; in the commotion a residence permit for him had been entered, inadvertently, and it was irrevocable. Moreover, it was hard to dispute the fact that the children were entitled to 0.43 reichsmarks for every 1,600 grams of bread. And that was not all; young Abs had also taken along forms for the latest listing of occupants, and it was up to him to fill them out. "You are required to enter all persons forming part of the household as of December 1, 1945, regardless of whether they were present or temporarily absent on that date." The name Cresspahl, Heinrich, born 1888, was firmly entered as head of the household. The Abs family signed as his deputy, not as caretakers. "Do not include members of the occupation forces." Perhaps young Abs would get into trouble because he did include a Mr. Krijgerstam as a member of the household since this smart survivor from the Baltic provinces sometimes wore the uniform of the Red Fleet. But then, he was also to be found in his dressing gown in Jakob's room, a sallow-faced man in his forties, smelling of fruit; solemnly, and with the manners of a superior waiter, he would offer ladies' underwear for sale, some even of silk, a private Soviet citizen. Young Abs ate off the same platter with the Russians, addressing them by their first name and patronym. He had not withdrawn his investments in the black market when Pontiy's detachment was transferred, even Mr. Draan still came to the house. Jakob had a room to himself, simply because from time to time he held German-Soviet conferences there, and without a scruple he had moved his mother into Cresspahl's room, perhaps as a guard outside the girls' bedroom; but he had seen to it that the Housing Office forgot to inspect the house of which he was the head. Although he might not escape punishment later on, for the time being no one objected to his contributions to the evening meal. With small jugs of milk for her son he had brought the confused teacher from West Prussia to the point where she was saying he had "a heart of gold" (Jakob had been prescribed the milk by a doctor). He had quickly put a stop to the girls' habit of giggling at such utterances; not only did they learn to feel sorry for the unfortunate woman but they also wanted to please him and secretly kept their eyes on him when he relaxed at mealtime. His face had become blank, his eyes often held a faraway look, yet he did not miss much of the general chatter around the table. Sometimes his lips moved on their own, then he would dryly swallow a smile. Gesine felt herself trapped in his gaze; she was often reminded of his bay horse when it was drinking and the way it would fasten its eyes on the person holding the pail. What the others saw in Jakob was that he had been stirring cement or shoveling coal for ten hours at the gasworks, and for the time being they accepted him as the man of the house.

Jakob was not satisfied with himself as head of the household.

It was no more than his duty to cut Amalie Creutz down from her wire noose; his mother had had to fetch him because old Mr. Creutz had been afraid to enter his dead daughter-in-law's room after fifty years of living beside a cemetery and supervising burials. Jakob laid the dead woman on her bed, his mother washed her and changed her clothes because Creutz refused to leave the laburnum bushes along the Soviet fence and stayed away from the house until next morning. That was all the Abses intended to do, they owed nothing more to this stranger. That evening Cresspahl's daughter came home from the station and behaved with calm courage. She asked about the coffin, the appointment with Brüshaver, the transportation arrangements for the body. She also knew that there was a letter for Cresspahl, and Mrs.

Abs admitted to having found it in the dead woman's jacket; it was placed among Cresspahl's things under the floorboards. The child would have tackled this family friendship alone, without a qualm, oddly at ease; but the Abses decided to help. Jakob, armed with some Schlegel-brand liquor, took the train to Gneez to see Kern the carpenter and returned with a coffin, Mrs. Abs wrote a letter of excuse to Gesine's school, and together they drove off with Amalie Creutz on Swenson's (Kliefoth's) rubber-tired cart to the New Cemetery. Jakob stood like a mourner at Creutz's side, only because the old man needed a firm grip on his arm, and Pastor Brüshaver shook hands with Jakob too, then with his mother, then with Gesine. In the eyes of Jerichow they stood there representing the house of Cresspahl, but also representing the Red Army, and, although Cresspahl might not have objected, in the end it would do his cause no good.

Looking after a house for Cresspahl meant not only banging a lock back into shape and replacing it in the door, meant more than taking the children's minds off their hunger or putting up shutters. Jakob could only guess as to whether Cresspahl wished his daughter to be kept so permanently away from her grandmother. He would see this Mrs. Papenbrock behind the counter, she could appear so wistfully bitter when she asked after Gesine. He had seen her in church at Amalie Creutz's funeral, he had noticed the brimming eyes that were directed less at the coffin than at the front pew, on the left at the back of her granddaughter's neck. (After five months Jakob could not know everything about Jerichow; old Mrs. Papenbrock's gift for tears did not strike him until much later.) She did not send for the child, she did not come for her herself; yet Jakob saw her waiting, a fat, melancholy bird with ruffled feathers. Did Cresspahl also mean a time like Christmas? His child nodded. Did Gesine mean that? She looked at him with clear eyes, did not stop to think, and asked: "Must I?" She would now do whatever he said, he had taken Cresspahl's place. Jakob shook his head, and again after Gesine had left; from now on he was somewhat shorter with Mrs. Papenbrock. He could not be sure if that was what Cresspahl wanted.

How is Christmas celebrated in Jerichow? By going to church? With everyone in the house? With the two children alone? Jakob was worried about this. He was sure only of the presents, a toboggan for Gesine, a bicycle lamp for Hanna Ohlerich. Then old Creutz brought his Advent wreath as he did every year, the children asked for a baked apple for their Christmas dinner and prepared everything themselves. When they came to fetch him the table was all ready, and he felt he had got off lightly.

What is the head of the household to do when it gets out after all that December 25 is his birthday and everybody in the house shakes hands with him and thanks him?

Jakob was not satisfied with himself as head of the family.

## May 29, 1968   Wednesday

Cost-of-living index, base period 1957/59 = 100.

### UNITED STATES

|  | April 1968 | Percentage change from March 1968 |
|---|---|---|
| All items | 119.9 | +.3 |
| Food (incl. restaurant meals) | 118.3 | +.3 |
| Housing (incl. hotel rates &c.) | 117.5 | +.3 |
| Apparel and upkeep | 118.4 | +.7 |
| Transportation | 119.0 | 0 |
| Health and recreation | 128.8 | +.4 |
| Medical care | 143.5 | +.4 |
| Personal care | 119.0 | +.5 |
| Reading & recreation | 124.9 | +.6 |
| Other goods & services | 122.5 | +.1 |

### NEW YORK

| All items | 122.5 | +.3 |
|---|---|---|
| Food (as above) | 118.8 | +.3 |
| Housing (as above) | 121.1 | +.2 |
| Apparel (as above) | 122.8 | +.5 |
| Transportation | 119.1 | −.1 |
| Health & recreation | 133.3 | +.5 |
| Medical care | 145.2 | +.5 |
| Personal care | 115.6 | +.8 |
| Reading & recreation | 136.6 | +.7 |
| Other goods & services | 127.7 | +.2 |

What cost $10 ten years ago is now $2.25 more expensive. Some workers lost 13 cents a week in purchasing power. The dollar is now worth only 83.4 cents. Will we be able to make out here?

If Jerichow had been given to the West:

Town Street would be a canal at ground level, blacktopped, its sides consisting of plate glass and chrome. Even in the poorest houses the window frames would have been removed and replaced by display windows or by double-glazed sealed affairs made to open both upward and sideways. Two driving schools, a travel agency, a branch of the Dresdner Bank. Electric lawn mowers, plastic household appliances, pocket radios, TV sets. Methfessel Jr. would have had his butcher shop tiled from floor to ceiling. In the entrance to the yard, the helper's sports car, complete with roll bar.

One would, of course, still be able to buy wicks and glass cylinders for kerosene lamps, centrifuge filters, carriage whips, axle grease, and the kind of chain the cow steps on to prevent it from running away when the farmers turn up in their Gran Turismos to do the milking.

And there would still be bargaining over the counter, that would have remained.

Jerichow would belong to the zonal border district of Lübeck, deputies in the Kiel Assembly. Grumbling about Kiel. The surviving nobility would stand for the Christian Democratic Union.

Newly counted among "prominent families": garage proprietors, liquor merchants, Bundeswehr officers, public-works officials. Not Bienmüller; he wouldn't allow his son to join the Federal Navy, although he wouldn't mind listening in to ship-to-shore telephone conversations via Kiel radio. (And to those via Radio Rügen as well.) Vacations in Denmark, television from Hamburg, light music and a TV channel from Lower Saxony, Hanover broadcasting station. The officers of the Federal Border Defense would patronize the Lübeck Arms (which would be known as the Lübeck Arms); lower ranks would go to Wulff's tavern. And here nobody would set fire to jeeps.

Jerichow would have five picture postcards to offer rather than two. The new ones: the red-brick addition to the town hall (Hamburg style). The rebuilt Swan's Nest (formerly Foresters' Tavern). The monument reminding one of "Divided Germany" (or of the prisoners of war) on the station square.

A small town in Schleswig-Holstein. Perhaps the farms would now be measured in tons, in acres. From Jerichow to Travemünde via Rande there would be a coast highway with room for three cars abreast.

By 1952 Papenbrock would have become rich again from administering the new hegemony, the estates of the aristocracy. Before his death he would have disposed of the Von Lassewitz town house. The town would renovate it, even bringing stucco workers from Hanover for the garlands under the windows. The building would be half museum, half a cave for civil servants. The good-natured German Socialist Party of Gneez.

Meanwhile the town council would have laid sewer pipes under almost every street. The brickyard would have turned into a factory for plastic household goods to keep a labor force in Jerichow. Fluorescent streetlights even along the Bäk. The market square would be lit up at night by a neon mushroom on a long pole. The hospital would have become the gatehouse for a clinic with an operating theater. In the station restaurant the ceiling would have been lowered, the furniture that was used for fuel would have been replaced by Gelsenkirchen Baroque, there would be a refrigerated display counter for cakes and wall-to-wall carpeting.

The old inn on the way to the Gräfin Forest would be mentioned for a while in travel guides. Set fire to in the mid-fifties, rebuilt as a three-story, L-shaped building, hotel and restaurant. The swans would not recognize the Foresters' Tavern, they would not read the new name. A rapid turnover in lessees, first surprised then horrified at the lack of guests. Hadn't the publicity spoken of a "gem" of Nordic urban architecture, invoked the beauty of the countryside?

Once again Jerichow would have succumbed to the district capital. The highway to Gneez would carry five buses a day, to the greater glory of Swenson's family enterprise. The signs on the buses would read, not JERICHOW but: GNEEZ–RANDE (VIA JERICHOW). Gneez would attract and draw housewives, workers, civil servants, moviegoers, students. In Gneez, not only the movies would be as fresh as those in Ratzeburg or Lübeck. In Gneez, night school would offer language courses, illustrated lectures, readings from novels. The people of Jerichow would be annoyed over the new building for the Gneez finance department. Jerichow's best-known attractions: an elderly Air Force swimming pool and a location slightly closer to the border.

Rande would have grown, and Jerichow would hardly have benefited. The beach area of Rande would have been built up to a depth of over half a mile with weekend cottages, condominiums, villas. Band concerts in the pavilion across from the Archduke Hotel. The latter might have been renamed the Baltic. Even in Rande there would be goods and entertainment unavailable in Jerichow. Rande would have a spa treatment center, a heated salt-water swimming pool, a more modern movie house than the one at the Jerichow Rifle Club, and many of the stores would remain open also in winter. The Rande streets would have been resurfaced twice or three times. On the signposts approaching and leaving Gneez the name Rande would appear more often than the name Jerichow. Ilse Grossjohann would not have remained mayor for very long. But she would have two cutters moored at the new landing stage, and where the excursion steamers from Denmark docked she would have built a cozy little trap, well planted with shrubs and bushes, the Naiad Garden Restaurant.

Jerichow North airfield would be Mariengabe airfield, licensed only for private aircraft, rivaling Lübeck-Blankensee. After all, the landing strips were more than 6,000 feet long, with the sound workmanship of 1936 to boot. Mariengabe the annual mecca of international air rallies. Noncommercial, private, close to the border and as peaceful as can be.

Near Rande a radar monitoring station would have been erected, on the cliffs not far from the border, screened from view. (The Federal Republic, to this day not yet sovereign, was permitted to take over the establishment in 1960 from the British as a military partner.) As late as 1968 the three old naval barracks on the east side of the little sports ground. They would still look temporary. The rotating radar screen can be rapidly dismantled from its support and loaded onto the three trucks parked in such a way that they seem to be waiting to drive off. A flagpole outside the entrance, a lost Alsatian dog beside the sentry box. Here the sound of the Baltic would be spoiled by the droning of the engines. At three corners signs below the barbed wire: Military Security Zone, No Trespassing. Be Prepared for Weapons to Be Fired. Barracks Commandant, Federal Minister for Defense. Liable to Prosecution under §100, Section 2, 109g. Jerichow wouldn't have that.

Sometimes, and more often than not, the people of Jerichow would behave like country bumpkins. Closing off Town Street for an entire three days, merely to change a cable. Let the tourist make a detour, they've nothing better in mind than a trip to the beach! The excavator digging the trenches is the latest model, and with it the driver can cut the edges as foursquare as Heine Klaproth used to do during his Labor Service. The young fellow can even make derogatory asides about the stupidity of the gaping visitors. Heine Klaproth might be his father. Though the ingenious, orange-painted monster would have been rented from a Lübeck firm.

Graves would still be dug by hand in Jerichow. For Amalie, it would have been too late. At Christmas, families visit the cemetery. The silver firs they take along may have been stolen, although not from someone unknown to the deceased (that might give offense). Then they go home and feed the cows a second time, as a Christmas treat. But all have to be there. Evening service at church. Brüshaver would be under the ground, not in the pulpit. One of the graves would be old Papenbrock's. Cresspahl would be tired of life. Someone else could carry on.

The visitor asking at the pharmacy where she could find a dry cleaner would not only be directed to the building "across from the Shell station," she would also get a verbal report on the length and quality of the process. That would have remained.

Legal advice: Dr. Werner Jansen. Real estate: N. Krijgerstam of the firm of R. Papenbrock. Taxi and bus service: Heinz Swenson. Information on regional names and local history: O. Stoffregen. They, perhaps, would have remained.

Friends in Wismar would have to be over sixty-five to be able to visit people in Jerichow. Change at Bad Kleinen into the interzonal train to Hamburg via Schönberg and Lübeck. Would seem like strangers to one another.

If Jerichow had been given to the West.

---

### May 30, 1968   Thursday, Memorial Day

---

On May 30 one hundred years ago, General John A. Logan issued an order. He was then Commander-in-Chief of the Grand Army of the Republic, and he could well decree that this day be set aside to decorate the graves "of comrades who died in the defense of the country in the late rebellion." It has gone further than that, the commemoration is now to include the dead of all foreign wars, and in particular the unknown servicemen.

In our neighborhood they look for him around the corner, at Riverside Park and 88th Street, the site of the Soldiers and Sailors Monument. In front of the useless, noble little temple, modeled after the Choragic Monument of Lysicrates in Athens, they came marching along this morning with drums, trumpets, and glockenspiels, men and children in uniform, so that even where we live the air is full of the sound of fife and drum roll.

We were on our way to Grand Central Station when the rest of the column swung into 95th Street, there was no escape. It consisted of sections of a women's regiment, fiercely determined ladies who were not the least bit reminiscent of clerical work or nursing in the Korean War, so erect did they hold the flag, so stiffly did they swing their arms and throw out their legs. The two run-down buildings on the south side of the street were draped with flags. As many as three heads could be counted in each window. On our side stood the alcoholics, bemused, helpless, patriotic. One of them was holding a toy flag, without knowing it. The parade was flanked by boys and girls running back and forth with machine pistols and handguns made of plastic, they looked almost exactly like the real thing, and at least the noise was convincing.

Schools, post offices, stock exchange, and banks are closed for the sacred occasion. The holiday is to last until Sunday.

Holiday in the country, on Long Island Sound.

Holiday with Amanda Williams, Naomi Prince, Clarissa Prince. Mr. Williams is staying behind in New York, Mr. Prince has divorced his wife, Clarissa Prince is five years old. Marie Cresspahl will have to earn her holiday.

The house belongs to Naomi's father, an accountant, he has worked for it all his life. His loneliness is present in the living room, displayed in the study: yearbooks of the New York Stock Exchange, and the *Collected Best Plays on Broadway 1931*. In 1931 he got married, in 1942 he went to war against Japan, in 1943 Naomi's mother moved to an unknown place in New Mexico. Collections: pipes, shells; each of them abandoned shortly before achieving distinction. Rooms dimmed by foliage.

Today and two more days: shared meals, walks until the general cleanup on Sunday morning. On the screened terrace, a boat deck on stilts, it will be nice to watch the rain, if it rains. Saturday night we shall watch the presidential candidates debating on television, McCarthy the workhorse versus Kennedy the high-strung foal. Maybe we will forget them. At night before going to sleep there is talk, semisincere. That afternoon two young men arrive, friends of Naomi's, maybe of our Mrs. Williams, both called Henry. They drink very moderately, discuss work prospects in New York; every fourth sentence is addressed to the outsider, Mrs. Cresspahl. Certainly this part of the world is to my liking. In the evening they return and pick up Amanda to go to a barbecue in a distant garden; Mr. Williams's call from New York comes minutes before she leaves. Who will go to the phone and lie to him? We all speak differently from the way we do at the bank, workday familiarity is broken up into caution, awkwardness, reticence. All of a sudden Amanda has become nervous, hardly entering the conversation, yet she is the one with the glibbest tongue. Naomi and Amanda know something about Mr. Prince that they still have to discuss, but only with each other. It is as if Amanda were afraid of the children; yet a house with so many wooden rooms must contain more children. A cleaning woman come to start cleaning was sent away, Naomi offers no explanation. You like the rain? My father isn't exactly strict, but he doesn't expect people to behave otherwise. Did you have to train a father too? I'm sorry to say I tried it too, Naomi. You see, don't you? The moment before night reaches the ground, the instant before anxiety, the children return. They have only been as far as the beach.

The beach is the shore of a bay, curving away from the Sound. Hard sand. In the bluish light, pretentious villas beside the water. Beyond the bathing beach, motorboats lying at anchor, a tiny sail moving northwest. Reeds, marshy meadows. Fifty acres of mixed forest, narrow access roads. On the other side of the spit, a marina. Not many boats in the water. Sophisticated revolving cranes, several floats. The water almost black, still. One's fingers phosphorescent in the darkness. On surfacing one's face feels pulled, as if it had slid back into an earlier shape. On the center ramp a carpet has been spread under the open sky, next to it a shower; here by the water one can live. At last someone came walking toward us, he knows no neighbors who would go swimming at this hour. He stops beside the visitors, greets them cordially, starts to chat about temperature and humidity. And he wishes us a good night's sleep, a restful holiday. As if we had come home.

## June 3, 1968   Monday

Yesterday the Mayor of Saigon went to inspect the main battle line in his city, in the company of other friends of Vice-President Ky, mostly police officers, plus some relatives. They entered a school, now turned into a military command post. Almost at once the building was ripped apart, as if by a rocket from an American helicopter gunship. Now the Army claims that it was not using any helicopters in that vicinity. The United States mission, less circumspectly, has apologized to the South Vietnamese Government with "deepest regrets and condolences," also to the families of the victims. The Honorable President Nguyen Van Thieu, on friendly terms with yet other Americans, suddenly has seven sinecures available for some of his minions, and if he should ever publish his memoirs in the Occident he could teach us a thing or two on the subject of the home front.

The new Communists in Prague would and would not like to bring the old ones before the courts for the murders committed on Stalin's behalf. Suspensions from office, yes; commissions of inquiry, fine; but "settling accounts within the Party in public," no. Alexander Dubček is reluctant to inherit his predecessors' reputation for vindictiveness, and his comrades obey his urgings not to expose Soviet involvement in the crimes of the fifties, in fact to spare these friends. What business is it of people outside the Party, however much they may demand public probity? As yet they are not being governed against their will, but this particular desire is denied them. They had merely been bystanders, on the inside if you like, but not inside the Party.

Hanna Ohlerich had wanted to wait until Easter 1946. By that time Cresspahl should have been released and back in his workshop and she an apprentice to his trade. She took this for granted, after that she had to force herself. She began to write letters, not even secretly, she wanted Mrs. Abs to see. But she would not allow Jakob's mother to read them.

She had immediately gone over to her side, but only to a person somewhat like a mother from whom she expected comfort, help. (One could more or less guess what kind of household the Ohlerich parents had maintained. Whatever came their way had been dealt with by Mr. Ohlerich, whatever outward steps had to be taken were decided by him. Hanna's mother had been allowed to run the kitchen, the cellar, the home, but under his supervision. He had had the last word, with no further explanation than his will, right up to the rope he gave her and the one he took for himself. Stern but affectionate, easy for a child to admire. Just as he had exercised authority within the home, so he had provided protection outside the home.) For this she pinned her faith on Cresspahl, not on a woman.

She also relied on Jakob and on many evenings followed him out into the yard, so that he would postpone his business deals and go off with her to the marsh, two idle strollers in the damp May twilight, sauntering along like a long-established couple (then the Cresspahl child did not like to be seen as deserted, deprived of suitable, well-merited companionship, and she would withdraw into the walnut tree, firmly intent on not looking toward the west, where the other two were merging into the misty vapor that hid the setting sun). Jakob was allowed to read the notes, they were intended more for him than for her relations in Warnemünde. To him they seemed imploring, as if Hanna needed to be rescued from a den of thieves that was becoming more fraught with danger each day that Cresspahl failed to return home. "Get me out of here," he read. Jakob acted like a big brother, explaining nothing to Hanna except the difference between her actual situation and her description of it, and talking her out of her distrust of her Warnemünde relatives and into a distrust of Erwin Plath, until she finally pretended that all she had wanted was encouragement. He was not satisfied with himself as head of the household.

He urged Gesine to behave considerately toward her friend, she knew of no inconsiderate behavior toward Hanna. What did they not share? They lay in one bed, one did not like to fall asleep without the other, they did their homework together at Cresspahl's desk, wordlessly united they waited in the long line-up for the soggy Papenbrock bread, visitors to the town took them for sisters. When Gesine asked Jakob for money beyond the weekly allowance, she held out her hand a second time for Hanna's share, and together they went to the market square to buy a packet of grass seed each at Wollenberg's, just to buy something because Wollenberg wanted to sell something, and each would water the other's test plot. Didn't she treat her friend as a guest? On her birthday accepted from Jakob Lisbeth's box camera bought back by him from Vassarion, giving Hanna a half share in it? She even paid the forty-pfennig fee for Hanna's ration card, as was only right, without minding. They shared their hunger, their pimples, and once even a CARE parcel. Jakob knew all this, what was he thinking about? Didn't they see, hear, think alike?

For the harvest he loaned us out to the Schlegels. She did not resist. We had had enough of waking up every morning with sagging stomachs, of having to walk around all day almost doubled up with hunger, of having to leave the table bravely every evening while the teacher from Marienwerder was still sitting there feeding her little son. Besides, Jakob had promised to visit us over the weekends.

At the Schlegel farm we were greeted as "Jakob's girls," we were put to work that very afternoon but only to eat thickened milk with sugar, and certainly we were allowed to accompany Inge at her chores about the farm but not to do any of them. She would have let us pick strawberries, but only as many as we could eat.

From outside, the house looked like an ordinary timbered building under a thatched roof, a classic textbook example of a Lower Saxony farmhouse; inside, nothing was to be hidden from us. We were allowed to climb into the hollow space beneath the living room and inspect the distilling apparatus; we saw the tobacco field planted with concealing sunflowers (more than 200 plants); moreover, we could not help noticing the collection of rifles in the settle around the stove, so massive-looking to outsiders. That was how much weight Jakob's introduction carried. But as to where he slept here, that we never found out. It was no longer a farmhouse. Where otherwise the wings of a farmhouse contain open stalls for horses and cows and sheep and pigs, these had been partitioned off from the hallway by walls between the roof supports, while inside a carpenter had laid wooden floors over the beaten earth; also, the stall hatches had been enlarged into proper casement windows, so that on each side of the hallway there were three nearly square rooms, and six doors gave onto the big dining table that reached almost from the entrance to the kitchen. From the northeast came a sea breeze, everything smelled of warm, clean wood, the walls as well as the doors and windows were intact, as if the war had not passed this way. Nor was Inge Schlegel in the least afraid of being all alone on the farm with a polite Doberman and two half-grown girls.

The work of the farm took place on the other side, in a brick building whose factorylike appearance vanished with a second glance at the thatched, moss-free roof. Inside it the ten-year-old Schütte-Lanz threshing machine looked two years old, so well oiled and polished was it; a smithy neat enough for an exhibition; the storeroom racks amply stocked with containers, drums, cases; the stables smelled occupied and active, the pigs ran around freely in their wallow so that once again the girls could not shake the illusion of peace, for not everything could be explained by the semicircle of forest shutting off the farm from the sea and the east.

In the evening, with the return of the reaping machines and the farm wagons, they did notice that the war had passed this way and stayed. The rooms along the passage, once occupied by laborers and sometimes by summer visitors, were now filled with refugees. But they were not like the refugees in Jerichow. These people had come to the Schlegel farm with open eyes, they did not promptly lie down and wait for pity, they wanted to earn their keep by working. Although it benefited a stranger's property, and not their own which they had lost in the east, most of them had been here for more than a year, and few of them wanted to move on. Johnny Schlegel had given his farm a constitution, the newcomers participated in the profits according to the number of horses they had brought with them and the amount of labor they contributed, just as he had started out before the war, following textbooks on land resettlement until the Nazi Germans prohibited it. Yet in 1946, apart from the estates of the fugitive local aristocracy, there was only this one large farm, not even Kleineschulte had left anything like this behind, and the Jerichow girls remained mystified.

As time went on they put two and two together; that first evening Johnny began by handling them differently. They hardly raised their eyes from their plates, no longer because they were still hungry but, rather, in dread of their employer for the coming weeks, worrying about where in the world Jakob had sent them. They noted that no prayers were said at this table. From their fleeting glances they gained an impression of an old gentleman (he was fifty-eight) who had worked in the open air all his life, with only one arm, ludicrously tall (in the evening he was six feet two), with a tapering head, bald (for many years a little plot of curly blond hair continued to grow on his turret-shaped skull), an intellectual because sometimes he raised fabulously tiny, oval-lensed spectacles to his eyes. While the rest of the company, confident of their equal status, chatted back and forth across the table, especially with their children, Dr. Schlegel was silent, his expression grimly calculating, and the Jerichow girls were afraid of him. And they saw no chair for Jakob here.

Then they heard Johnny's bass voice, with no preparatory throat-clearing, and were startled out of their skins. For he was talking about them, spoke their names. Sheer obedience made them almost stand up. They learned that they were the children of "my friend Cresspahl" and of Gustav Ohlerich, "a man from Wendisch Burg," "good Mecklenburg children placed in the care of our Jakob," "now they belong to our farm." That was all, it transformed the kind glances of their table companions into something like encouragement, now they felt welcome. Inge Schlegel was still wearing Alwin Paap's ring, she might easily have been able to give special news of Cresspahl, particularly as to where he no longer was; and there was no doubt that Johnny could have told more about how Hanna's parents had died.

In spite of their relief, they still felt there was a threat to their wages of hundredweights of wheat, and they asked about their jobs. "We'll see about that," said Johnny casually, and the girls shyly asked what they would see about. Johnny had imagined them as a sort of emergency stand-by, when extra hands were needed at the kitchen stove, or to pick apples, or to churn butter (he said nothing about tending geese). Didn't we protest jointly, proud, no doubt, of our ages of thirteen and fourteen, almost with one voice? That we hadn't come here for a vacation but to do some serious work with the harvest! Weren't we instinctively of one mind?

Full involvement in the harvest? We wanted no mercy? We were sent to the wheat fields. Johnny Schlegel's commune was covered with endless rows of wheat sheaves, forty to sixty feet above the sea, at first the gently undulating ground seemed to us a nice change. The summer before, at Jerichow, we had been allowed to distribute the wheat shocks over the whole field; here technology sent us to the edges, out of the dips, and we were always on the run, pursued by the miraculously returning machines, moving the bundles that were not much smaller than ourselves. The days passed in a flash; where we had been working yesterday, the plows were already moving along, turning over the stubble, deep for the seed and fertilizer drills, shallow for the sugar beets, for a day in July is worth as much as a week in August: as Johnny taught us during his frequent visits to see whether Jakob's girls were ready to give up. We could never have faced Jakob; what he had brought us from here had been earnings, not presents. Sometimes Hanna was older than I and said about our thirst: It's worse at sea.

The bad days were those on which the binders had to run without yarn, for the straw rope did not easily reach around the sheaves that the machine could tie, and it was harder to foresee the end of one's work. Gradually we came to realize that Schlegel might not, after all, have saved his 400 acres from expropriation by cuts in the land registry; more likely the Soviet officers from the Beckhorst estate had helped, the ones who often came over for a visit at dusk, casually and fearlessly greeted as guests. Maybe; but why was Johnny's missing arm the cause of such tireless laughter, even for Johnny? We were equipped with pieces of truck tire which we fastened to our feet with gas-mask tapes as sandals, but even so the ankle-high stubble found its way in, and in the evening Hanna would put ointment on my feet and bandage them, as I did hers. We dreamed in gray and white and yellow, of the massed clouds in the sky, of the wheat ears, the stubble, the firm sandy tracks. At breakfast there was also a B. B. C. program in which over and over again the Austrian had to scream out that business about the last-remaining battalion on earth.

We learned how to stack the wheat on the wagons. It took far too long for the skin to harden. Whiskers of wheat in our faces invariably alarmed us. Grain is what the earth bears, and in every country corn is the name given to what is most important: to maize in America, to rye in Germany, to wheat in France and Mecklenburg. *Triticum vulgare*, said Johnny. When the wagons drove home, Hanna sat high up on the wheat, I preferred to walk beside Jakob's chestnut and wanted him to recognize me. I meant it to look like affection when I took hold of the harness as if to lead the horse, but actually it was more like clinging for support.

When the thresher started up with its flapping belt it looked clever, yet more primitive than the simple trick that nature might still have up her sleeve for exploiting the corn. The wheat. The other children had spent the harvest days in the orchard, or cleaning out the stables, helping in the kitchen. Hanna and I were trained to operate the Schütte-Lanz machine. She was allowed to go onto the threshing floor first, to cut the sheaves and pass the wheat to Mrs. Von Alvensleben, fanned out in a veil over her arm. The names of the people on the farm were: Inge, Johnny, Johnny's old woman, Mr. Sünderhauf, Mrs. Von Alvensleben, the Lieutenant, Mrs. Lakenmacher, Mrs. Schurig, Mrs. Bliemeister, Mrs. Winse, Anne-Dorthy, Jesus, Axel Ohr, hen and chicks, the Englishman, Epi, and then the children under thirteen:

there was, by the way, an old roll of film in a drawer here, but it was for a box camera that had been left behind in Jerichow, so all the faces except four have been forgotten. Out in the fields, Anne-Dorthy had stuck close to us; at the farm she acted like Johnny's goddaughter. We suspected her, but only in a vague kind of way, of having something to do with our new clogs. Newly carved, with an arched sole, lined with cotton under the leather, fastened with real tacks and wire, there they were one morning hanging from our ladder, and they fitted, once our feet had healed.

Behind the thresher was where Cresspahl's daughter reigned, leaning on the handle of a pitchfork, and every few minutes she would scoop the long straw onto a box wagon; but if there was yarn for the baler the other children had to take a hand, those who were stationed at the chaff, the sack outlets, the short straw. Little by little the whirling hum separated the brain from the inside of the skull. Every hour Hanna and Gesine would change places so that we worked continuously as a team. Anne-Dorthy was nineteen, we had never seen anyone so pretty, we would never get to look like that; the clogs couldn't have come from her.

Johnny crawled with us under the machine, explaining, there in the dark, the route taken by the precleaned grain through the bucket elevator; that's how delighted he was. Right on schedule, on August 20, he had reached his goal, eighty hundredweight had already been delivered to the Beckhorst Soviet estate, all of it against bilingual receipts, duly stamped, and now those gentlemen were nicely in debt to him with yarn, crude oil, and good reputation. When were Hanna and I not together? Our places at table were fixed, in the fields a bottle of ersatz coffee would be sent out just for us two, at times we were addressed as a single person, and we slept side by side in the hay in the apple loft over the living room. Of course we didn't tell each other everything. I was now certain that Cresspahl had slept like this beside pears and apples stored on slats at Schmoog's farm when Granny had died; I felt the subject of dying was still taboo with Hanna. True, by now she was aware of her resemblance to Alexandra and wanted to know about her. Where I thought Alexandra Paepcke would be now, if. Whether Alexandra could have coped with the wheat harvest, if. During other nights we would think up exceptions for some of the other grownups, bashfully, cautiously. For Mrs. Von Alvensleben, without hesitation. For Johnny, with reservations. Hanna could fall asleep with a great sigh, as if she were sinking into bottomless depths. Not a word about Anne-Dorthy.

Yes, Jakob kept his promise and came for a visit. We soon noticed when he was approaching the farm. Anne-Dorthy's chair at the supper table would remain empty, and when it came to our bedtime she would emerge from the forest into the hall, her hair more carefully arranged than normally, and wearing her one and only gray knit dress. Within a few minutes Jakob would be standing in the doorway, relaxed, cheerful, as if he had not been walking for two hours. Maybe it was the wind off the sea that had tousled his hair. Then, before disappearing into the living room for his business with Johnny, he would speak to us. Chat with us. Concern himself with the children. Like a guardian. That was all he had promised. We never followed Anne-Dorthy, yet we would see her on the path leading through the pine trees to the sea. Sometimes on her return her hair would be wet, Jakob's too. Now we knew why we had never found a bed specially for Jakob. During the nights of Jakob's visits we would lie silently in the moonlight shining from the sea, pretending to be asleep; neither was wakened by the tears of the other, we were too tired to talk in our sleep.

We also lay like that during the rain that destroyed the rest of the harvest over the whole area. That was on August 27, 1946, a rain, they said, such as there had not been within living memory. The clouds emptied themselves with a violence that Johnny could describe to us as tropical

like the torrents of rain which, a little while ago, at 2:45 P.M., filled the space between the buildings on Third Avenue with such darkness. In the flashes of light the hurtling drops seemed sharpened. The darkness returning with thunderclaps made the bottom of the canyon look wintry, the smooth pavement reflected the full light of the store windows just as at night. The thick panes rattled under the impact of a normal New York rainstorm

and only such work was assigned as could be done under a roof. A thick sack folded into a hood became wringing wet in the fifteen yards to the farm building. Not even the livestock could calmly accept the phenomenon that was darkening the stable doors for so long. There were places in the yard that looked like deep lakes. Johnny informed us of the normal annual average for August in the area, 2.64 inches. By evening he claimed to have estimated the rain at 7.5 inches, just for this one day. The enforced inactivity, the creeping dampness, had soon emptied the hallway, even we couldn't stay with Johnny, and we lay down on our canvas strips in the apple loft. The thatched roof rustled and smelled more and more of crushing weight. Although it was as dark now as at night, we could not close our eyes. Worse than during the dreary monotonous motions in the wheat, a single thought went around and around itself, returning unchanged: to be a countess like Anne-Dorthy, that was not in our stars. But one day we would be nineteen too, with faces as lively as hers, with a bosom that could be seen, firm of flesh, conscious also of our legs; only not at the right time, too late. It was so quiet in the cavern under the torrential rain, perhaps Hanna thought I was asleep. The empty darkness woke to her angry voice. She cried, not loud since she was lying flat: "I'm not a child any more!" It sounded determined, without remorse, and I hated her for not suffering enough from a misery that I had believed to be as overwhelming for her as for me. Once again she was older than I.

*If the young fellows talk to you, don't answer them, don't look at them, and don't turn your head. If they still won't stop, then give them short shrift: Yes. No. Maybe. Don't know. Like that.*

*If a young fellow has peeled an apple or a pear and offers it to you, be sure to leave it there and not eat it.*

*If the young fellows sit down by you and want to start something and try to hold your hand, pull your hand back and put it under your apron, and if they still won't stop, turn your back on them, don't say a word.*

*Then if the young fellows come at night with musicians or think up some other nonsense as they sometimes do and come to your bedroom door, say to them: D'you think I'm here because of you? Not likely, who d'you think you are?*

*The boys from next door are always the worst.*

Cresspahl's front door, hitherto sealed with a Protection Order, stood open until late evening. The Russians in the Kommandantura were strangers to us. So this was the third lot since K. A. Pontiy.

"It's the Twins," said Jakob. We were sitting with his mother, talking over our experiences. We had had a long journey. She kept us close beside her, one arm around each of us, and exclaimed, in the pleading tone that she otherwise used to express disappointment at naughty children: "What a sight you are, girls!" She was so quiet and hollow-eyed; without movement she would have looked dead. Everything in the house spoke of Sunday evening. We boasted about all the food we had had and refused supper. Hanna inquired politely as to who was sticking up for Gesine's grandfather, now that the Demwies Twins were in command of Jerichow. Jakob, the psychologist, the appointed guardian, the expert on young girls, let slip the remark: "Papenbrock has been . . . transferred. They've transferred him."

"Arrested him," supplemented Hanna. Gesine felt more of a shock, but she merely blinked. The house attracted danger. It was not safe here.

She was given no time to collect her thoughts. On September 8 the N. K. V. D. went to work on Sunday. In Jerichow the following were taken away from their breakfast: Mrs. Ahlreep the jeweler's wife, Leslie Danzmann, Peter Wulff, Brüshaver, Kliefoth. Tireless rumor knew for sure that a carrier pigeon had been sighted over Jerichow. Hanna had meanwhile lived long enough in Jerichow and was more inclined to see a connection between all these names and Cresspahl than to think that the Red Army was angry over some unsurrendered pigeons or a banned club. That evening those arrested were released, to avoid causing a stir at their places of work. Rumor had already put them in the Neubrandenburg concentration camp, as company for Papenbrock; they had been held in the town hall cellar. All were enjoined to strict silence. Because Jakob started with Leslie Danzmann he wasted an hour, she lied from fear. Wulff, Kliefoth, and Brüshaver all assured him that during the interrogation possibly two questions may have applied to Cresspahl. The first probed Cresspahl's military service on the Eastern Front in 1917. The other attempted to bracket him with a privy councillor named Hähn in Malchow. Kliefoth had heard the name only in connection with some arms deal in the early twenties.

Hanna thanked Jakob on his return from Warnemünde, but merely as for a duty performed. (In our new style we no longer favored this person with more than cursory attention.) Her fishermen relatives had got into trouble with the People's Police during the communal elections, they were said to have already sent for Hanna. In order for her departure to the British Zone not to attract attention, Hanna was to go aboard the vessel as it lay off Rande.

Jakob was not to take her there. While Hanna was saying her good-bys, Gesine stood outside the door, not wishing to see how she would behave with Jakob. In Rande Hanna did not want to board Ilse Grossjohann's cutter alone. About midnight we were at the spot known as de Huuk, 11° 7′, eastern longitude, 59° 2′ 4″ northern latitude. Later Gesine realized that she had been embraced as if she had been a boy.

For days afterward she could revive in her arms the sensation of pushing Hanna onto the other boat. She also found it easy to conceive that Hanna had been meant to stay with her.

When Gesine returned at dawn to the empty bed, she found Hanna's clogs next to hers, all four standing neatly in a row.

## June 4, 1968   Tuesday

The size of the armed forces of our country now exceeds 3.5 million, approaching the highest level since the peak of the Korean War in 1953; today, voters in the California primary polls will give Robert F. Kennedy some indication of his qualifications for the presidency; the address of the armed robbery marked for today is 71 West 35th Street; with the permission of the new Communists, the people of Czechoslovakia may now officially know that the great and good Antonín Novotný was dishonest in his political procedures not only in 1952 but also in 1954, 1955, 1957, and 1963;

the East German Communists have released an art historian of Columbia University, although, for purposes of his doctoral dissertation on Berlin architecture, some "restricted" buildings may have got in front of his camera, and without the American side having to give anything in return. "You could say it was done with mirrors."

This was something the certified translator, Gesine Cresspahl, resident in New York for seven years, had to look up, to keep abreast of the vernacular: a conjuring trick. Nine months in jail, and yet returned without trial to the outside world. Sleight of hand. Magic.

Cresspahl had not yet been twenty months in jail; he wanted to be tried. No matter where to, he was now anxious to go beyond just the next day.

Until that wet March of 1946 he had been busy, it had felt like movement. The camp on the western border of Soviet Mecklenburg had been intended as a holding camp, yet an inmate ran no risk in volunteering for work. The commandant gave no reward to someone who went over a barracks building from floor to roof until it was as sound and weatherproof as a house; thus the German internees had little to envy Cresspahl for. But he had his craft between himself and anticipation of the future, over which the others drove themselves crazy with rumors, quarrels, and bragging. In wanting to keep such buildings in good shape, he did not expect thanks. If he carved himself a spoon from birchwood, why not another one for the fellow in the next bunk? He would rather have taught some skill to the two left hands of such an intellectual. He would go as far as accepting two pinches of tobacco if a thank-you was not considered enough, but he would not be persuaded to go into manufacture or trade. Besides, since he divulged almost nothing beyond his name and "somewhere near Jerichow," he could believe himself to be ignored, at best tolerated, in his bunkhouse.

Then, without warning, he was fetched by a sentry and taken to the guardroom, not returning to the bunkhouse until almost midnight to find that quite a few had waited up for him. This was something he could talk about. In front of the commandant had been a wooden suitcase, the kind of which Cresspahl had made several. It had just been confiscated in the carpenter shop and still lacked the customer's initials. When challenged, he confessed to being the creator of this piece of evidence. Questioned about a false bottom, he misunderstood even the second translation, finally admitting the possibility.

Here was the order. It earned Cresspahl more sympathy than mistrust from his fellow inmates, as being forced labor. He spent almost four weeks over the birthday gift for the commandant's granddaughter, a little chest eight inches high and consisting of three partitioned drawers, a roll top, a wooden lock, and, yes sir, a secret compartment. This ticklish commission had led his thoughts for once in a different direction, toward his own children: how he would build them an even more cunning miniature chest of drawers, and using proper tools at that. He shared the fee, two packets of shag, with anyone who asked, there was nothing for him to learn as far as tobacco was concerned; he should have kept it for himself. Meanwhile the others revealed themselves to be good neighbors; they became more seriously concerned when the lower ranks now started ordering suitcases, for what else could this mean but the imminent departure of the Russians, perhaps next week? Cresspahl, however, had to produce such containers for yet more Germans, for a trip back to Roebel or Lauenburg, and thus was protected from the outlandish fantasies of the masses. He had been told: You wait. That is how he managed.

He did not spend the winter in the bunkhouse, which, in spite of the nearby River Elde, he had hoped would provide some warmth, at least during the morning hours; from December 1946 he was kept below a solid building he imagined to be the Schwerin arsenal. The cellars were wet, but not from Parson's Pond in Schwerin. The task set him was a second curriculum vitae. He did not produce very much, for when the running water in the cell froze overnight how were his fingers to relearn the use of a pencil? Moreover, the light from the courtyard, gray and checkered by a grating floor, once again turned him a little blind.

The first version of the second curriculum vitae turned out to be not much more than a tabulation, so that he was often beaten; he counted himself lucky that the blows did not break open his skin. By now he had spent too long on a starvation diet of soup for him to expect his body to recover from open wounds. He realized that his invisible masters were insisting on completeness rather than promptness; this was enough to strip him of his childhood years. Born 1888 the son of Heinrich Cresspahl, estate cartwright, and his wife Berta née Niemann, daughter of a day laborer, at Easter 1900 I was apprenticed to master carpenter Redebrecht in Malchow, Mecklenburg. All these people were dead; but there might still be some Von Haases around, who were remembered not only by the five-year-old gooseherd Cresspahl but also by the thirty-one-year-old member of the Strikers' Council in Waren that had dug up weapons on the Von Haase estate which were destined for the Kapp *Putsch*. That family's treatment of sick farm hands was familiar to him even before his mother died. He was quite happy to see people of that kind chased out of Mecklenburg to the other side of the Elbe; but it went against the grain for him to denounce them by name. This tore such gaps in the chronological order of his account that he was struck with a rifle butt in the kidneys when a particular year was marked in the interrogation room as unsatisfactory, in the neck if he was failed.

The young fellows in the service of the M. G. B. were aware of the approximate extent of the treatment prescribed but not of the day-to-day reasons for it; so it appeared that they were merely urging their charges on in the underground corridors. Passion was hardly ever to be felt. No hatred was required to keep an inmate awake, the truck motors took care of that with their outdoor concerts during the interrogations, and for four nights a circular saw. During the daytime the written work had to be continued. Cresspahl finagled a week of solitude for himself by side-stepping to his grandparents and the years after 1875; he only slightly exaggerated the genealogical part of the question. He could accept his confinement in solitary as a form of repayment. The choice was up to him. His new bosses, the expert from the Kontrasiedka and the auditor of the Soviet Military Tribunal, had left with him the analysis of his class position and his personal role in the wrong turns taken by history, all typed up and ready; he chose not to sign his name to it. It was not stubbornness that made him resist, since he was bound to be still wanting to return to his girls. Truth alone cannot have been his concern, for soon he was describing himself as someone who had been in this world for fifty-eight years without dealing, speaking, or co-operating with any other person. Perhaps he wanted to clear himself with the New Justice as long as he could keep the others out of it. Sometimes the inspectors of his learning process prompted him a bit: for instance, for an essay covering the year 1922, with the name Hähn, Privy Councillor and weapons agent. Whenever the pupil failed in a subject, he could envisage with almost perfect accuracy the kind of beating due the following dawn, yet he would escape from his present life into carefree daydreams about a different life, one that might have taken place with equal reality: from 1904, not immediately without Gesine Redebrecht, continuing for a while with her, after 1930 with Mrs. Trowbridge in Bristol, avoiding Richmond all the time, with a thirteen-year-old Henry, or killed by a bomb with both of them, after 1920 with Mina Goudelier, but not for long in the Kostverlorenvaart behind the Great Market in Amsterdam, preferably on the River Fella, in Chiusaforte, where he could have not only learned intarsia but worked in it, no, not where the Germans would turn up as occupiers, rather in . . . Australia, supposing Goudelier's daughter to have gone that far with him, across other seas than Papenbrock's Lisbeth, who would then have been allowed to survive that November in 1938, or with all four together in a memory of other High Streets, lake shores, Broadways, dawns, picnics in the grass. He was not hurt that the lazily passing visions included him only marginally, or left him out entirely. Only, when the Red Army did grant him a tablet it consisted of nothing but aspirin. They need not have been dreams.

Nor did his conscience bother him at being confined with board and lodging and with an occupation he knew very little about, while all around the prison people were helping each other with work to get back to normal life (that was how he imagined it). Responsibility for him had been passed on to the M. G. B., let them answer for his useless presence. With such ample encouragement he had by January 1947 written his way up to his military service in Güstrow (and his stupid daughter never asked), by the end of February up to his footling dispute over his honor with the German Socialist Party (and his stupid daughter meant to wait with her questions), so that by this time there were 260 pages written in his hand, but only two typed sheets with his signature, the first version. He persisted in regarding himself as the partner of his judges, known by number and name, with the right to trial and judgment, moving along a more or less agreed path, not only in time. By the end of February they terminated the agreement. He was ordered to report for transport "with all his belongings."

"Belongings" were something he had not owned since his last move, and he joined the group in the barracks yard like someone merely ready for an evening's stroll. The transfer took place on foot, in columns of unkempt men who had been under arrest for only a few days and who carried out the orders of their guards with Prussian regard for ceremony. Out of curiosity they took the doddering old man under their wing, holding him by the arm as he staggered along. Before long they gave him up, once they found he could only answer questions about his "case" with "I d-dunno," his words were slurred, his sentences broken off, and there seemed to be something the matter with his throat. "I'm fifty-eight," the fellow said, perhaps because they had called him Grandpa, more as if to himself, and they all chipped in to give this odd ragged character a cigarette. It was his first tobacco in eleven weeks, it made him feel like those Australian dreams so that later he could not be sure whether the march had actually started from Schwerin. His eyes, too, were not in good shape. At Rabensteinfeld he became aware of the direction of their journey, and when at crossroads the others cursed at the unwavering easterly direction he was able to believe that the whole thing had been set up for his benefit. For the route through Crivitz should have reminded him of something, a promise maybe, he could not put his finger on it. At Mestlin something should have struck him, it kept bothering him for the next six miles, then he recognized it as the turnoff to Sternberg and Wismar and Jerichow, now passed beyond recall. After Karow he was tormented by being unable to make out the railway line that surely should have been to the left of the road, as if he were going the wrong way. Reluctantly he trusted the sight of Old Schwerin, there was something missing at the station, Krebs Lake confused him, finally he saw the compass rose on the old windmill outside the town and no longer needed to resist: they were letting him have one more look at Malchow. Only that everything was way above him. As in a dream, knowing that he was a boy again, he once more entered the summer of 1904, the music from the lakeside promenade wafting over the water on Friday evening, he entered the fair on the children's playground that lasted the whole of the next day; the band of the Parchim Dragoons was playing, wearing its colorful fairy-tale uniforms, and three horsemen were riding out through the town gate; in the midst of the leisurely throng of the dead stood a youth with the master's daughter between Linden Avenue and the great canvas tents, seen by all, discovered by none, oh that you're my darling, but you got no money, no clogs, no shoes, in 1920 the workers seized the town of Waren, and Baron Stephen le Fort of Boek fired on the town hall with a cannon, that was when the delegates of the Strikers' Council could get no further with the people of Malchow, those fellows are shooting, and only a forester on a count's estate, who refused to supply his employers with wagons for collecting wood and tried to beat them up, lost his home and was driven off the estate. Never use a peeled stick to beat man or beast, whatever you beat with it is sure to perish. Yet it was Old Malchow on the island, the Gierathschen surrounded by gardens and jetties and gables, Mill Hill, the tiny bit of mainland that had not tolerated the churches, a storm 150 years ago had helped, the people of the underworld needed a place for their Midsummer

Eve. A hole had been blasted in the causeway to the other shore and sloppily filled in, it looked insecure, one might just manage to swim as far as Weavers' Hill, the old Wendish fortifications past which the six-year-old boy had herded his geese, the people of the underworld were invisible when they went to the Laschendorf farm at noon, but a shepherd heard them calling A hat! A hat! and got a hat for himself and put it on and saw them standing in front of him, a lot of little monks wearing three-cornered hats and then they jumped at him and scratched his eyes out and took away his magic hat. They say the dwarves of Weavers' Hill made lovely music.

Here is Fünfeichen, the sanatorium! Brown and foursquare it lies there with its bunkhouses and its guardhouse in the midst of a desolate expanse amply equipped with muddy boardwalks, barbed-wire passages, and squat watchtowers; beyond its tar-paper roofs the hills of Lindental and Tollense Lake rise toward the sky, green with fir trees, massive, and gently fissured; prominent signs along the fence inform the nature lover, in Russian, German, and English lettering: Prohibited Zone. Keep Out! Firearms Used Without Warning!

The Red Army is still in charge of the installation. Wearing military decorations on his Russian blouse that hangs way down over his baggy breeches, his head erect under the dun-colored cap, his automatic rifle at the ready, the Red Army soldier herds the prisoners along the camp road; hardened by knowledge and in amused amazement, he has a curt and taciturn way of keeping the patients under his spell—all these individuals who, too feeble to set their own laws and keep to them, are handed over to him, body and mind, to find support in his severity.

It was early summer before Cresspahl came to; he was furiously bent on concealing this. In all seriousness he regarded himself as rotting, tainted, no longer fit for this world and on the shelf.

For one thing, he had no memory of how he could have come from Kloster Malchow to Fünfeichen. He knew the Red Army from the first autumn after the war, they would have shot him at Weavers' Hill if that was where he had gone off the rails. That the other men in the column, strangers, should have dragged him along to Waren and Penzlin and all the way to Tollense Lake—he could hardly believe it. With no inkling at all he had waked up in a lower bunk at Fünfeichen Camp, as if from nowhere, too weak to eat, too tired to open his eyes, weary of life. For another, all around him in the crowded bunkhouse he heard men constantly mentioning the Neubrandenburg Camp. But this was Fünfeichen, two and a half miles from the Stargard Gate; as late as 1944 he had been ordered by the British to have a look not only at the Trollenhagen air base but also at the conditions under which the Germans were keeping their prisoners of war at Fünfeichen. If he was to believe his eyes, he was in the old south camp of Fünfeichen, in Bunkhouse 9 or 10 S, next to the barbed wire of the vegetable garden, facing Burg Stargard, and to the north was the fenced-in complex of workshops and storerooms, just as on his old drawing. Could he be that much mistaken? Why did everyone else think it was Neubrandenburg, only he thought it was Fünfeichen?

And finally, why could he still not get rid of his hankering after a trial, to make an end of it? For him this *was* the end.

He looked around the camp for the inmates who had come with him from Rabensteinfeld. Scarcely a face was familiar, it is hard work searching among 12,000. The prisoners were driven out of their bunkhouses only when the Operations Detachment of the camp command arrived with the German Kapos (inmates appointed by the Soviets to run the camp) to search the bunks. He found nobody from this last piece of his past, all of them having been on their way to somewhere else; he had been dumped here, finally disposed of. As they searched, the Kapos not only tossed the rags about, they also tipped over the bunks; for hours the inmates quarreled over confiscated or scattered possessions. Cresspahl could look on. When the soup was doled out he had to wait until someone pushed his own container toward him, contemptuously, as if he were a sick dog, and by that time the soup kettle was often empty, but still he had to pay for the loan by washing it out. He would soon have had his own bowl, except that permission to work also had to be paid for. Whatever he was wearing was beyond barter. He volunteered immediately when the German Kapos needed replacements for latrine duty; he had to march ten yards in goose step in front of the well-nourished representatives of the Soviets while proclaiming in crisp military tones: "I am an old Nazi swine and I want to carry shit!" But still he did not get the job. He tried to see it as a blessing that spared him the stench; he soon had to realize that the other inmates moved away from him, even without much room to move, because he stank. He had lain too long, unconscious or asleep, in his own filth, whatever it may have been; now he was defenseless against fleas and lice. Hot water had its price, he could have paid it by informing on his bunk neighbors; but he had no information, and the Kapos handed him over to the Soviets for leaving the bunkhouse at night, having themselves picked him up from there at night. He expected solitude from the lockup, but there he was penned up even closer with others than in the bunkhouse, only in the dark and with no food. Just because a scarecrow wore better rags than he, one of the

Kapos reported him (for neglect) to the Soviets, from whom he had instantly to step back five paces; in the clothing storeroom, the Kapos had no witnesses and could continue to bully him with beatings until he recited what they wanted: "A shitty Nazi cripple, / I lean upon my stave, / My pants are full of shit, / I shit into my grave." For the German administrative personnel disapproved, although the only clothing to be issued was that of dead inmates. However, he managed to keep his old shirt and rinsed out the caked pus from the one they gave him; after the third washing he was able to exchange it for the bottom half of a fish can, a bit rusty but without holes. When the Kapos attacked an inmate, the others would uneasily move aside, but it looked like collaboration, as if pandering to the bullies. No matter what there was to learn, Cresspahl probably picked the wrong thing.

So many people from Mecklenburg (although hardly one among the Kapos), and it was so easy to set them at loggerheads with each other. Was that a lesson? The Kapos paid in bread, in half-cigarettes, very rarely with a job in the barbershop; that was enough to break up any solidarity. Cresspahl saw one man (he refused to name him) who was tormented by his neighbors, to pass the time or because his frightened, moist-eyed expression was an invitation. With wild tales from the Eastern Front they drew him into their confidence, appealed to his comradeship, offered proof of friendship with gifts of soup, promises of a pipeful of tobacco; at last he confided in them, after being promised secrecy, and told them about his background and that he had been seconded to perform as a violinist at Reich Governor Hildebrandt's state occasions and banquets; soon the Kapos made him re-enact his decorative postures and gait, like training an animal. He cried then, whether from exhaustion or because his pride was broken; but his fellow inmates prevented him from running off into the electrified outer fence, they watched over him gloomily, less ashamed or conscience-stricken than because the Operations Detachment was familiar with such deaths and took out their inexpediency on those involved. The latter showed relief when the Soviets led away their violinist like a rabid animal; would they have been justified had it meant their release from camp?

Release was not mentioned in a single one of the rumors. Cresspahl sat in on one of the forbidden cultural groups, the subject of discussion being the Hague Land Warfare Convention and the illegal incarceration of civilians in a prisoner-of-war camp; he stayed close to the speaker until the latter was arrested so as to avoid any suspicion of having denounced him; he refrained from commenting that, in terms of international law, Fünfeichen had been a "special camp" of the Soviets since 1945. A seventeen-year-old deserter, also here "by mistake," had attacked his elders for the shooting of hostages in the Soviet Union, somewhat vehemently; for that they had beaten him up at night and strangled him by mistake. A medical orderly who had studied medicine for three years lectured on the soggy camp bread's actual calorie content and that which the camp administration calculated, and he arrived at the unexpected conclusion that the Soviets must have adopted SS concentration-camp calorie charts; for the medical student no hour had been too early or too late to clean out an inmate's boil or to give him advice, everyone had listened to him, one word would have saved him from the insulator; even Cresspahl held his tongue. What kind of virtues were those he had renounced? Or were they new ones?

In March people were still being brought in to the camp, men who failed to grasp its remoteness from civilian life and gaily rattled off the electioneering slogans of a Socialist Unity Party with which it had been possible to offset the curtailed paper allocation to the bourgeois parties; in a trice they were locked up, they would never return. The process was known as leaving, a sort of substitute for dying. Cresspahl chased his thoughts incessantly around the news that the Soviets could not get along without elections and that paper was used for such purposes. One new arrival described it as a war crime that the Soviets had fired on the town of Neubrandenburg until it burned down, leaving the area within the walls completely cleaned out except for Great Woolweavers' Street, then he "left." Cresspahl said nothing about the town's refusal to capitulate and mentally tried to make a drawing of the destroyed town hall, a charming little building with a turret perched on the middle of the roof, designed as if it had been lifted many years ago from a box of Christmas toys and set down in the market square of Neubrandenburg for the magistrate and townspeople to play with. Admittedly, he had become feeble-minded from exhaustion, from sitting around all day in the stench and chatter of the bunkhouse; maybe he was confused, because his thoughts so often wandered past the others. Could he have overlooked the possibility that he had merely lost courage, that he was no longer prompted by courage? How did he behave when a newcomer was brought into the bunkhouse, a man who only yesterday had been sitting at his own supper table in Penzlin and now found himself being shoved from bunk to bunk, finally ending up on the drafty floorboards? Why did Cresspahl let him discover, all by himself, that he was interned, that he would never ever be able to send news to his family, that the foul brew represented the very best breakfast soup and that the route via the hospital led not to comfort but to a filthy and miserable end? He knew what help was needed; he himself had not been given it. Was this callousness? What were his intentions?

For old friends he would occasionally do something. In August 1947 Heinz Mootsaak appeared in the doorway of the bunkhouse, in trousers and shirt sleeves as if picked up straight from the fields. He looked completely dazed: after the silence between the barbed-wire fences and the huts he probably had not expected such a noisy crowd at such close quarters; he was still the shy peasant, politely entering a roomful of strangers. For this man Cresspahl stood up, on this man he turned his back so as not to betray mutual recognition and to make it possible for them to meet later on as if by accident, without arousing suspicion among the rest. But he miscalculated, he assumed too much. For Heinz Mootsaak had no idea who that decrepit bag of bones in the bits and pieces of tattered uniform was supposed to be; by the following morning he had already "left" for the lockup.

In October, it was getting cold. Cresspahl was drawn into an escape plot by two inmates who may have taken offense at his new concept of sociability. They could not very well recruit him as a full partner, they affected camaraderie. The Cresspahl of the past would not have hesitated, there would have been no mistaking his expression, and merely for the record he would have added: Nonsense. Don't be such idiots. The man of 1947 hesitated, for the sake of good relations, and answered obligingly: "The nobility won't stand for it." He got himself off the hook by asking for time to think about it, now he was trapped. Meanwhile it had got around the room that that morose old curmudgeon had finally nibbled the bait, or that a new threesome was cooking up something.

There was really nothing to think over in the plan. It would take months to pry three floorboards loose and fasten them in such a way that an innocent step would not allow them to snap up yet so that they could still be removed at night in a few minutes. Their plan was to go under bunkhouses 10 and 11 S to the southern edge of the camp, then follow the barbed wire past the center watchtower, again under the entire length of 18 S as far as the inner barbed wire, under that to the auxiliary power unit, switching off the charge, and finally to force their way out over the last fence, roughly in the direction of the Soviet staff barracks, behind which ran a road. One of them claimed to be an electrician. It was neither pity nor concern that prompted Cresspahl's efforts to dissuade them; he merely did not wish to owe them anything. He mentioned the Soviets' swivel-mounted searchlights, the 500 yards of crawling and tunneling in a single night, the empty open spaces all around. Out of politeness he did at least applaud the escape route for immediately leading away from the long eastern edge of the camp. He warned them of armed patrols in the Rowa Forest, of the soggy meadows of Nonnenhof, of the Red Army's extensive prohibited zones north of Neustrelitz. One of them pretended to be hurt, perhaps the author of the plan. Both men thanked him loud enough to be heard three bunks away; after all that whispering it was good and noticeable.

After a second twenty-four hours had passed, Cresspahl believed himself out of danger; it took that long for him to be summoned before the Soviet administration. At the staff barracks a signed and sworn statement lay on the desk: Instigation to escape on the part of Internee C., ruthless designs on Soviet people's property, insulting comparison of the Red Army with the feudal aristocracy caste. Attached were sketches of the south camp and the continued escape route via Nonnenhof and the Lieps Canal, reconstructed on the basis of the accused's suggestions. Once again Cresspahl had a chance to prefer the Soviets to the German Kapos. The Soviet Operations Detachment entered camp road and bunkhouses unarmed, and they ordered no worse punishment than standing at attention for up to three hours; when one of them did hit out it was obviously good nature giving way to a desperation no longer able to put up with the behavior of a prisoner, regardless of his offense. But the German camp police intensified their interrogation with sausage and bread placed within reach of the internee, coffee poured into cups before his eyes; true, it was ersatz coffee, but it was hot, and there was milk with it. The Soviets kept their interrogation rooms as offices. They actually did not beat him. Because of his allusion to the aristocracy he was made to stand for an hour and a half by the stove, spine hollowed, hands held stiffly along imaginary trouser seams. When even then he could give no other explanation for this libelous phrase than the domination of the nobility in the Mecklenburg-Schwerin Parliament of 1896 and the remoteness of the Malchow railway station, the Russians presented him with a statement to sign. In it he was permitted to deny every accusation except for that single conversation that had been observed by too many people, and he signed. By this time, getting on for 4 A.M., the officers were in a jovial mood, although not without contempt for this wreck of a human being. They thanked him for his devotion to the truth, regretted having disturbed his rest, and expressed the hope that he would soon go back to sleep. Then they handed him over to the German Kapos.

The Kapos kept him in a detention cell of the north camp until the following noon, there were groups of four, taking turns, they used whips. Can a person refuse to speak solely because he has decided he does not wish to speak? How is he to know that, on losing consciousness, he did not speak? Did his offense warrant their injuring him right off so severely that he could ignore everything except the pain? Can a person refuse to utter a word to others merely because he does not understand them?

After the Soviets had had ample time to observe what Germans are capable of doing to one another, they ordered an end to the interrogation. The Kapos of the last shift resented having personally to drag the copiously bleeding bundle along the camp road. The Soviets would not let the regular internees lend a hand, but they did let them watch. They needed the Kapos as powerful hunting dogs, they did not want popularity to soften them. Since the Russian guards supervised the transport to the very end, Cresspahl was laid almost gently on a bunk in the barbers' quarters in the north camp.

His wounds took until the following summer to heal, he could walk by the beginning of December. That was when he went back to square one: food dish, hot water, rags for his feet. Among the north camp inmates he very quickly became known as deranged, for when questioned on his silence toward the Kapos he actually did have an explanation, and it sounded convincingly confused.

"I didn't like them," he said.

At Christmas they gave him another chance and offered him a job in the burial detachment,

    a chance

    to demonstrate

    a change of heart and

    an atonement as well as

    the forgiveness

    of the community,

plus supplementary rations and a change of clothing. Since it was work, involving exercise, the prospect was tempting. Why should he not be able to do what others could? The corpses looked bloated, they no longer weighed much. More often than not there were only a few to be picked up each week, always two bearers to a stretcher. The main thing was to be able to survive the day the corpses had to be removed from the cellar where they were collected and dragged onto the truck; on the drive to the Fuchsberg cemetery he would be able to take a breather. He felt no horror at the thought of undressing the cadavers before burying them, if anything he doubted whether he would be able to dig the graves, at first. He did not want to do it for the sake of the dead, nor for a few extra potatoes in his soup, nor in order to survive; he wanted to be occupied. At that time, career officers had appointed themselves as an illegal German camp committee, they talked him out of accepting, with mild threats. They could not rely on his remembering the correct figures, and for a while they held firmly onto him in the back row during roll call, until the Kapos gave up. The job went to an inmate who was considered worthier of the extra rations and the drive outside the camp merely because it was closer to Berlin. For the men of the burial detachments were suspected of keeping count and were often replaced or shunted off to other camps, with the result that the lists of the dead could be made up only from approximate fragments; for Fünfeichen the figure was 8,500, not entirely supported by names. Thus Cresspahl lost a chance to escape before he even knew, the Kapos could not rid the camp of him and still had to remove the two conspirators from the old bunkhouse; Cresspahl was compensated with a month's priority in getting a shave and owed thanks to nobody. Was this something he had to learn?

It had been a long time since he had given any thought to an escape, although in the past he had observed one. The march to Fünfeichen had taken them right through the town of Goldberg. Suddenly, as the column rounded a corner, one of the prisoners stepped out onto the sidewalk, grabbed a much-startled housewife by the elbow and, with loud cries of recognition, compelled her to walk on with him. "My God, Elli!" he shouted in his exuberance. Possibly the scene appeared convincing enough to the Soviet guards; as they left the town they replaced the fugitive by picking up a civilian who happened to be digging in his garden. For a while Cresspahl had hung onto this example of Red Army punctiliousness with which to regale Gesine; then the tale had been told at Fünfeichen a few times too often, and the gardening enthusiast had had to be shot two miles beyond Goldberg because of his unreasonable panic, or he was still being kept in N 22 without a clue, sometimes the woman was called Herta, sometimes the fugitive had shouted: Hey there, Aunt Frieda! Eventually Cresspahl began to wonder whether he had actually seen the whole affair.

Flight, revolt, liberation, these things no longer meant anything to him. According to Fünfeichen rumors, the piece of land near Ratzeburg received in exchange by the British from the Soviets had grown to the whole strip west of a line from Dassow via Schönberg to Schaal Lake, and if it was not American parachutists who were expected the following day at the gates of Fünfeichen, it was at least the Swedish Red Cross. Cresspahl recognized in the others the feverish, intoxicating effects of latrine gossip, he feared them for himself for he was often in that state when his thoughts moved at an unconscionable distance from the talk around him. He had never read the warning sign on the camp fence from the front; he had no doubt that Western military commis-

sions were begin kept away, even as far off as Burg Stargard and Neubrandenburg by multilingual warnings. He could not understand what
the other inmates expected of their former enemies. The occupants of
the camp were turned over with such regularity that informers were
not immediately detected, no matter how thickly larded with them the
bunkhouses were; if there was more than one participant, a conspiracy
was as good as blown. On his own he could not even plan an escape.
Once he reached the other shore of Tollense Lake he might have made
it in nine days to the legendary new border of Mecklenburg; however,
at the place where he would have had to pick up the girls the Soviets
would be waiting for him, and once his escape became known they
would keep their hands on the girls. Thus in Fünfeichen he was less
separated from them. And anyway an escape from Fünfeichen was
inconceivable.

Fünfeichen had become the world. Life outside did not enter.

There were breaks in the monotony. There were the transfers to
the concentration camps of Mühlberg, Buchenwald, Sachsenhausen,
Bautzen, familiar from the reports of new arrivals. Like Fünfeichen,
they were eternities, they stood still. And a person could also choose
death, voluntary by starvation, voluntary at the fence.

Fünfeichen offered a number of ontologies.

But Cresspahl would have preferred trial and sentence.

## June 5, 1968   Wednesday

"Where were you, Marie! Where have you been!"

"It's now a quarter to six, and I'm home. That's your rule."

"Where have you been all day?"

"And you, Mrs. Cresspahl, you didn't get home one minute earlier
than usual either."

"Should I have? Is that a reproach?"

"You're an employee, you're not allowed to leave your work.
Maybe in wet weather, or if the subway's on strike. But not for personal
reasons."

"Marie, how did you hear about it?"

"In the park."

"That's not on your way home from school."

"O.K."

"We'd agreed—"

"I know, West End Avenue. As if the police formed a cordon
there! I've been accosted there a million times. I can take care of myself

just as well in Riverside Park, in broad daylight. I'm not a child any more, Gesine!"

"You don't understand."

"I don't understand you."

"By the time I got to Broadway the New York *Times* was sold out."

"I went through the park because on Wednesdays the first period is on the sports ground. That's in Riverside Park, corner of 107th Street and—"

"All right."

"I left the building as if I'd become invisible. Eagle Eye Robinson was busy on the stairs, with his back to me. The elevator door was open, Esmeralda's posh handbag was lying on the stool, unguarded, she was nowhere around. Not a single neighbor, not a soul waiting for the bus. So there was no one to warn me. Sitting on a bench by the Firemen's Memorial Fountain was a young man, all by himself. Nineteen. Not a student, more likely a shift worker off duty. Baseball sweater, long pants, thick white wool socks, not a tourist. Crew cut. Sprawling comfortably across the bench, arms stretched along the back, not a care in the worldd. Beside him his radio, a portable, agitated voices. That's where I heard it. Kennedy shot. The young man sat there so idly, so relaxed, so leisurely, he didn't mind one bit me listening, he had no eyes for me. As if the news was just what he expected. As if it suited him fine."

"What did you find out there?"

"Senator Kennedy of New York had won the primary in California. Was making a victory speech at the Ambassador in Los Angeles. On the way to the press conference, in a kitchen corridor, he was shot in the head from behind. 1:15 A.M. California Daylight-Saving Time. 4:15 our time. Lay on the ground, his wife kneeling beside him. The business with the rosary. The last rites. Unconscious in the hospital. Then all over again: Robert Francis Kennedy, Senator from New York—"

"In the subway there was something in the air, and yet there wasn't. Maybe today's being the hottest day of the year was why everyone looked so apathetic, was avoiding everyone else's eyes, was so silent. It was probably no greater tragedy than life itself is for many New Yorkers. Then at Grand Central I saw a TV set in a window, the picture on, no sound from the speakers. On the screen there was always just the one crooked word, as if written by a finger in the dust: Shame. As soon as I got to the bank I phoned the school."

"Gesine, would you go to school on a day like this?"

"I'll let you have a note for Sister Magdalena."

"For tomorrow too."

"D'you want to take the rest of the week off?"

"You're not bad as a mother, Gesine."

"Oh yes I am, I guess I was silly. Felt I had to talk to you."

"And so you had. I needed you. First I was mad at the bank for not allowing personal calls, and then at you for obeying. Now I feel better; you did try."

"And at home too."

"By that time I was at Times Square. The crowds there! When someone left, his face was dark with rage as he pushed his way through the others. Once I was almost knocked off my feet."

"Listen, under Times Square I saw so much courtesy, it must have played hell with the train schedules. A young black, black leather jacket and Afro hairdo, stepped back for a fat white bookkeeper. 'After you, go ahead!' he said to the bewildered white, who had probably been bracing himself for a swearword. 'After you, brother,' said the black. 'Brother!' In the subway!"

"I don't know anything about that. In Central Park people were behaving as if it was a holiday. What I heard was: the fine weather, Tonia's varicose veins in one so young, summer sales in Herald Square, team politics in New York baseball. On Broadway the same thing. The music was playing in the supermarket as on any other day, and my cashier was crabbing about customers who didn't have change."

"That would have made me furious too."

"I was furious at you, Gesine! Because you told me this was normal for this country, John F. Kennedy, Martin Luther King, and you were right again, Robert Francis Kennedy."

"The Ferwalters didn't know either where you could be."

"I was moving around town by myself."

"Buying newspapers, one after the other."

"Not as choosy as you, I'll take the *Daily News*."

"Can I pay you back?"

"I paid out of my pocket money. Pocket money is for personal needs, right?"

"At lunchtime I didn't stay in the bank, I went across the street. Twice more during the afternoon I went downstairs, always sure you'd be standing outside the building, waiting for me."

"I was!"

"Mrs. Lazar just looks so severe. She can't keep it up for long with kids. She would have taken you to me."

"It wasn't because I was shy! It was because I was mad at you, I knew you'd be expecting this of me too! For ten minutes I admired your precious lobby and then I ran off to be sure you wouldn't catch me in your conceit."

"About myself?"

"Conceited about yourself! Who else could comfort me but my mother! And that I needed comfort! Just suppose I wanted to cope with it alone? As if you knew me, inside out!"

"I don't even know what you've bought for supper."

"Nothing! Nothing for me. There's a T-bone steak for you. And some green beans."

"No supper for me."

"Gesine, you've been working, you must eat. Tomorrow you have to go back to the bank. Do eat. Or can you stay home?"

"Tomorrow I have to work."

In the end there was not much left of knowledge inside out; where her mother was planning on reconciliation, Marie was bent on agreement. She showed the strain required to achieve an acceptable tone of voice while discussing the shopping and washing the dishes; how she longed to disappear behind the curtained glass doors of her own room. However, she did need her mother for one more thing. She was listening for the click of the elevator cables, and the moment the bell rang she was at the door. And what were two moving men carrying late that evening into the Cresspahl apartment, an apartment that for seven years had been immune to American television, what good now were the educational, economic, and maternal considerations? A television set was trundled in over the threshold by the muscular pair, and a mother was needed to sign the rental agreement. Marie ordered the set to be put in her room, she paid the $19.50 herself. Pocket money is for personal needs.

Undoubtedly she is embarrassed at this breach of one more agreement; she hastens to turn down the volume of the set when the news is interrupted by commercials. If I tell her that outwardly her love affair with a politician has all the earmarks of one of my own, it will take a long time for her to believe me.

## June 7, 1968   Friday

Along the south side of 96th Street, starting at West End Avenue, workmen are painting the curb, some thirty yards of it, as far as the Number 19 bus stop. The men are using hand brushes fastened to broomsticks with two pieces of string. They are working away unhurriedly, not without satisfaction in their expertise, soon they will be taking a break. Dave Brubeck, Take Five. The yellow paint shines in the sun, immaculate and fresh. Life must go on. But we know one child who cannot understand this.

I wonder if Marie knows that these television tubes have a way of imploding when, as she is doing again today, she sits in front of the set for ten hours with her schoolbooks?

At the kiosk the newspapers are once again stacked up higher than usual, alongside the plywood fence around the burned-out building there is a further supply, it is hard to tell how many. The line-up starts south of the newsvendor, people coming from the north are oblivious and do as they always do, snatching the top paper and holding out the money with the other hand. This morning the crippled fingers are already busy with other money, the papers have been divided up into those for free sale and those for preferred customers, be sure and take your place as fifth in line.

"Not you, my dear!" says the old man, severely, as if in rebuke. He's willing to talk to you today, Gesine. "Don't ever stand in line here again! Are we friends or aren't we?"

Customers in the line-up hear patiently, indeed approvingly, that the old fellow is on special terms with this person and even speaks of it openly. Today the display of emotions seem permissible, even of entirely new ones.

In the subway there are fewer people waiting on the platform, even though it is a workday, they manage to get on the train almost without crowding, and whom have we here? A heavyset old Negro, his spine bent with rheumatism, is offering his seat to some white woman. "It's not easy for you either," he said. Can this be New York?

Under Times Square the city looks more familiar, so dense is the brew of humanity. On Lexington Avenue people are walking shoulder to shoulder, as if they were all in a procession. Here the sunshine has shrunk to a sliver. At some of the store entrances there are signs saying they are closed, other stores display placards announcing a temporary closure for the following day, thus still contriving to draw their customers' attention to themselves. In a side street a young West Indian girl winks, she is wearing an elegant shirt, from Bloomingdale's at least, and shows off her heavy eyebrows and skinny legs, she has a business to carry on too.

From the entrance to the cafeteria to Sam's counter is a distance of twenty yards, a glance toward the door is enough for Sam to shout to the kitchen: "Large black tea!" so that two minutes later he can hand over the bag. Meanwhile he wants to know how things are going. "How about me! I'd like to, but I can't," he says, meaning the required emotion that he is unable to produce. "Man, Gesine, what a day this's going to be!"

For the bank is working. Our ostensibly revered Vice-President could not let it rest at a simple directive; in a memo he explains the obvious: This is Friday, regular payday for most wage earners in the city, all checks must go out before the weekend. For all departments, De Rosny. He might have added: Furthermore, I have the support of the Chamber of Commerce in this matter. Obediently the employees on the lower floors will be counting bills, weighing bags of coins, checking accounts, or clicking imaginary money on bookkeeping machines through the four mathematical processes; on the sixteenth floor people are blatantly reading the papers. They are working hard, these people who allow their employer two weeks' grace in which to pay them, they have long since turned to the center page, where the Kennedy reports are carried over from page 1. Mrs. Lazar's job is to defend the department with her very life, she scarcely looks up, she feels obliged to whip the pages back and forth in an irritated, schoolmarmish manner. Here we have Henri Gelliston, who regards the banking business as the sole science on earth; now, with a look of astonishment, he is absorbing the headline: White House Plane Flies Body from Los Angeles. In a minute he will learn that the hearse was blue and that even while boarding the plane Mrs. John F. Kennedy would not yield precedence. As far as Wilbur N. Wendell is concerned, the entire financial business of South America might as well suffocate under his spread-out *Times*, he has to study a photograph of the cemetery personnel taking measurements for tomorrow's grave at Arlington. Tony, Anthony, who is so intent on making everyone forget that he was born in an Italian slum of this city, our man with the studied perfection of manners, is sprawled right across the desk in his effort not to crease the paper and, like yesterday, his diary is closed on the first page of a newspaper with which he otherwise would not even clean his shoes, the tabloid *Daily News*. It is as quiet in the executives' lounge as in a reading room, apart from one minor detail the sight could serve as an advertisement for the New York *Times*. De Rosny must know why he is not making his rounds this morning; he might get a shock at the industriousness of his subordinates.

All the papers now have to eat their words. Ruthless was something he really had not been. If when young he had fought more recklessly than wisely, the *Times* is now ready to forgive him, since he had not done so for a low or selfish aim. It still does not credit him with a full regard for due legal process, it sees him as a warrior, a big man who at his death was still growing. What is De Rosny to do now with his innumerable stories about Bugs Bunny, the crazy cartoon figure, the inventor who could deprive his neighbors of health and property with his motorized hammock? De Rosny will simply have to dream up a new target. Do you want to bet on Richard Milhous Nixon, who can produce such beautiful tears?

As if there were no homework to be done. Not all Czechoslovakians, after all, waved at the Soviet troops marching in for maneuvers. Their numbers are probably greater than expected, and they also have heavy equipment; the load limits at the bridges had to be raised from thirty to seventy tons, something one is glad to do for dear friends. Such flexible bridges might have given the Interior Minister food for thought, but actually he was worrying about his own Secret Police, which acted as if they were still taking orders from Stalin. Make a note of that. According to recent reports there have been as many as 30,000 cases of internal-security officers arresting innocent persons on trumped-up charges.

The one who by three in the afternoon can no longer stand such preparations for a trip to Europe is Miss Cresspahl. Marie does not answer the telephone in the apartment. It may be the best sign. If she can't hear the phone she is far away from the box, from the newscasters' voices, doing her homework at Pamela's, with Rebecca in the park where the ice-cream vendor rings his bell. If you don't want to think that, you can believe the child is at St. Patrick's Cathedral. What good will that do her, since the coffin is closed? That makes no difference to her, she may still want to walk past it and lightly touch the flag on the casket. She shouldn't be standing there alone. There should be someone to receive her. Miss Cresspahl leaves early, she can't notify anyone, even Mrs. Lazar has already left.

At this hour the line starts on Lexington Avenue, at 47th Street. It is so densely packed that anyone walking beside it has to do a balancing act. At the angular plate-glass biscuit that is the Chemical Bank it is too soon to expect Marie. No doubt she tacked onto the end, but earlier. She is not outside the Barclay Hotel, nor outside the Waldorf-Astoria. How yellow the General Electric building is, frenzied Gothic with a crown full of holes surrounding a water pot. The stationary people accelerate the sense of pace irrationally. Business is going on merrily all around, buttons being touted that say "In Memory of a Great American. Robert F. Kennedy. 1925–1968." One might buy one of these, for Marie. Fifty cents each. That probably means a hundred-per-cent profit. Here is another entrance to the IRT, 51st Street, the next station is Grand Central, from there it's twenty minutes to get home. The people are hardly dressed in mourning, that man could go aboard a yacht just as he is, this woman you would expect to find working in her back yard. Here we have a mailman who has got stuck once too often in the procession, now even the phone booth is occupied. "I'm forty-five minutes behind schedule!" he says to those around him, and they smile at him and nod. That's the way things are in New York when something has happened. He too was merely looking for sympathy. Where is the line heading for? Now it is snaking around the block of the Seagram Building and curving south along Park Avenue. Seagram is handing out plastic cups, although not with whisky, water is good enough for publicity. There are no tears in evidence; although conversations may not be cheerful, there is a certain liveliness. Here again the commemorative buttons are being peddled, now they cost a whole dollar, maybe because of the high-class environment of the Embassy Club and the rear of the Chemical Bank. What profit percentage? Here a trash basket is being stormed by two den mothers making paper hats for all their Cub Scouts. Such splendid towers of commerce, and at their feet the populace is scattering plastic, paper, cans. Whenever someone collapses the line bulges out toward the curb, here two girls in skintight pants are leaning limply against the pillars of Union Carbide. The fainting spells are due less to the muggy heat than to the exhaust fumes from the cars. For other New Yorkers are driving along Park Avenue out into the country, to the ocean, though, in a gesture of mourning, with their headlights on. Here it takes an hour to travel one block, unless one is walking freely beside the line-up. The police have set up gray barriers to protect those waiting in line from queue jumpers. There are many children among them, almost every third person seems to be a minor; but this must be about the fifth thousand, it would be easy to miss Marie. No one is talking about the occasion itself, not even about Thursday's amendment to the gun law. Hitherto mail-order houses were free to mail out pistols, revolvers, hand grenades, mortars; as of now they are restricted to rifles and shotguns. Including the kind of rifle used for the other Kennedy. Bankers Trust, the command center of Colgate-Palmolive, the headquarters of ITT. At the corner, before the line coils west into 51st Street, a backward glance was still possible at the Pan-Am Building, where the Kennedy fortune is administered. At Madison Avenue police actually formed a cordon to enable the line to cross the street. It was at this corner, during one cold winter, that Miss Cresspahl had walked up and down carrying a picket sign, outside the Archdiocese of New York, the palace of Cardinal Spellman, the lover of war.

This is the beginning of the final stage, the soft-drink vendors are becoming aggressive. One of them feels he is being stared at by a noticeably ragged beggar in the line, he'll teach him to envy him his success, for a while he holds out the bright cans in such a way that they pass under the nose of this thirsty fellow, until he turns away. Again and again a Puerto Rican or a black stands out among the whites, roughly every fifth person is dark-skinned. These are the people who felt they were meant when this millionaire spoke of them. What did they expect of him? Of these, most of the women are not carrying their shoes in their hands, the men have just barely loosened their ties. At the cathedral the police are in holiday mood, moving lightly among the TV juggernauts, chatting at ease over their walkie-talkies, waving to the helicopters. The true ruler is a cameraman, hovering high over-head with his equipment in a seat shaped to his buttocks. This close to their goal, people are now beginning to offer resistance to anyone trying to sneak into the line, perhaps not as viciously as on unholy days, more likely with allusions to the dignity of the occasion, preferably in a preachy tone. Outside the northwest entrance to the cathedral, men in uniform with wordless directives chop off five or six heads at a time from the serpentine queue. Inside, something golden, brilliantly illuminated, is discernible. If Marie has gone in, she must have wanted some Catholic person with her. She must have wanted to go through the proper motions of genuflecting, making the sign of the cross. But she is not here either, she does not emerge from the south entrance after fifteen minutes, the probable duration of a walk past the coffin, and yet her mother has seen her often, and still sees her, as she walks away past the gray wall of 50th Street and the weeping women in the hot light from the west.

Marie has never left the building. When the phone rang, she had just gone down to the basement to ask Jason for advice in adjusting her TV antenna. She has watched the whole route, starting at Lexington Avenue, up and down Park Avenue, all the way to the cathedral and past the coffin. To do this she did not have to be there in person. She was not there, yet she has even picked up the rudiments of how to make the sign of the cross. She was there with TV. It was inevitable that she could not be found today either.

## June 8, 1968  Saturday

A day in front of the TV set. But we will not spend it without super-vision. When Mrs. Cresspahl telephoned D. E., Mrs. Erichson had to bring him back from the car, as he was just about to drive off, in response to Marie's telephoned request in fact. The child wants a referee too.

> *Get her back to me, D. E.*
> *To you?*
> *Away from the Kennedys.*
> *Hasn't she inherited this obsessive reveling in grief from you?*
> *If it's from me, take it away from her. Get her out of it.*
> *No strings?*
> *Get her back to you, D. E.*

By eight thirty he has arranged his long bones in our apartment, on one of the Salvation Army chairs, his back to the sun-filled park, immune to any suspicion of insufficient attentiveness. Beside him there are a tin containing eight ounces of tobacco, three pipes, a variety of implements, and now he orders a quart of tea; he is getting ready for a protracted session. His clothes look more like the weekend in the garden to which he had invited us in New Jersey, right down to the sneakers; with his expression of somnolent gravity he gives a good imitation of a professor who is willing to face one more bothersome examination. The language spoken is American.

With his preparations he succeeds in disconcerting Marie; his role forces that of the organizer on her. She moves the set this way and that in front of him, with apologies for the distorted picture; he nods solemnly. He may be qualified to teach physics and chemistry; he is incapable of improving the performance of this kind of apparatus. "The tube is overworked," he observes, a rebuke implicit in his factual diagnosis so that Marie nods, abashed. She cannot prove that he is being facetious, yet her piousness is somewhat impaired. She is now sitting beside him, he could put a consoling hand on her neck, her arm, he is free to do this; he holds back severely, out of respect for her mourning, and makes her question her own behavior by reflecting it. She had expected nothing but silence from him during the programs, soon she cannot stand it.

Around nine o'clock she sucks air in through her teeth, as if in sudden pain, for there on the screen is a scratchy, distorted picture chopped up into its own shadows; it shows the widow of the day, in the act of crossing herself. The face appears bright and clear in the bedeviled surroundings. D. E. looks at Marie in astonishment and explains nonchalantly: "The grid, you know." She nods, innocent and tractable. The grid. I see.

Mrs. Cresspahl would have burst out long ago, against her own intention but wanting to make a point: This Robert Kennedy of yours, he had Martin Luther King's phone bugged, that's the kind of attorney general he was, just so you know! Now she is prevented from making further pedagogic mistakes, besides she finds amusement in glancing sidelong at the couple sitting stiffly in front of the box. She forgets herself in sudden glee, she smiles, from gratitude or elation. She receives an indignant look from D. E., as if there were nothing to laugh about, and obediently withdraws, taking the radio with her, into the one room whose door can be firmly closed.

WQXR, the voice of the New York *Times*, transmits on 96.3 megahertz, now it is going to show its educated readership how a Grand Old Lady behaves at the death of a murdered adversary. Calmly, reliably, she describes a banking business, of good repute, recommending its services to the public. Not only does our worthy Auntie Times earn a little pin money by advertising on behalf of others, she also promotes her own merits over the air by referring to the in-depth reports she will be selling tomorrow. It is undoubtedly her channel, she mentions her name, it is she in person. Auntie Times is not prepared to accord her liquidated enemy so much as one iota of sympathy or condolence, undeterred she continues to honor the dollar, she doesn't get anything for nothing either.

In the other room D. E. hasn't yet invited the child to visit a mortuary in New York where other dead are lying, their sharp noses pointing upward, equally Catholic but with no prospect of a funeral in the most elegant church on Fifth Avenue; but he is already playing a game with Marie. Each of the two participants wins a point for being the first to recognize the function of the V. I. P.s being conducted before their eyes through the checkpoint and into the cathedral. They tied for the Secretary-General of the United Nations and the President of the auto workers' union, the President of the United States, and the former chief of the C. I. A.; Marie took credit for almost all the others, from Robert Lowell the poet to Senator Eugene McCarthy; only with Lauren Becall does D. E. claim to have been quicker; she hasn't caught on. After that they start guessing the colors in the procession, since these do not show up on the set, they surmise white for the seminarists, they go wrong with the brown of the monks, the olive green of the army chaplains, the crimson of the monsignors, the purple of the bishops, they agree on the scarlet of the cardinals. Meanwhile Marie, simply by imagining the colors, has gained an insight into the finer details of the production. D. E. is allowed to compare one meaning of "service" with the other; she joins in an estimate of the costs.

She will not yet go so far as to make jokes with him, but from time to time their eyes meet as they used to, conspiratorially, in secret complicity, as when the voice of the surviving Kennedy brother breaks toward the end of his eulogy. Although she still wishes to respect the tearful tone, D. E. anticipates her mounting suspicion by commenting on the motto of the deceased:

"Most men look at things as they are and wonder why.

I dream of things that never were and ask why not."

Once he has explained the source of the lachrymose quotation from George Bernard Shaw, together with a history of Fabianism, he is free to add: "Even when they borrow they take the best."

She then proceeds to look more suspiciously at the eight half-orphans bearing bread and wine in gold vessels to the high altar; nor does she care to defend the water sprinkled on the coffin to invoke God's purifying grace from Heaven, nor the swinging of incense to carry the prayers of the faithful up to God. All too often has she had to recite this in school against her will. Gradually she recognizes what is going on in the cathedral as a private ceremony that is depriving her of the dead man, and when the slow movement of Mahler's Fifth Symphony is played by thirty members of the New York Philharmonic she cannot yet put into words how the Kennedys behave when they borrow; she admits the thought with a painfully amused sidelong glance. Again the cheerful stomping of the "Battle Hymn of the Republic" disturbs her composure, she cannot defend herself against D. E.'s reminder that the tune was lifted from that other song,

John Brown's body lies a-mould'ring in his grave,

about the ambushing of Brown, the slaves' friend, at Harpers Ferry in Virginia, the plagiarism bothers her, as does the implied decomposition of the body; added to this she would like to think of it as a lesson such as she would be unlikely to receive from Sister Magdalena; the puzzling over it dries up the corners of her eyes. Soon she is arguing with D. E. over the placing of dead Catholics in relation to the altar, the feet toward the altar and the head under the stars of the flag, she proves to him, so that in the end she is obliged to cry out: "But they're carrying him out of the cathedral head first!"

To begin with, the only amusement she permits D. E. at the behavior of the other Mrs. Kennedy, the widow of the President, rigid and silent she stands for almost four minutes on the top step, can you all see me? never mind if the motorcade gets hopelessly behind schedule, she wants her share of the limelight, and Marie finally does say, half embarrassed, half annoyed: "That's just what she'd like. She's just inviting someone to shoot!"

Her store of reverence has had a hard time surviving the news item from London inserted into the program. That a man has been seized at Heathrow who is suspected of the murder of Martin Luther King, that they have caught him after such a long interval, that they have finally caught him but on this day of all days, just right to tie in with the spectacle of her senator's funeral—it's too pat, too calculated, it looks to her like a trick on the part of grownups who think kids are dumber than they really are. The tailored effect bothers her and, although she may not actually doubt the truth of the report, it does seem impaired by its timing. "They're trying to distract us!" she says, furious; she has been distracted.

Moreover, she is wantonly unfair and criticizes President Kennedy's widow for her desire for still another bullet and enhanced fame; President Johnson has long since reached Washington from the cathedral in New York; the train bearing her senator's coffin is still standing at Pennsylvania Station. The TV commentators are so hard put to it that they allude to the train that carried the body of Abe Lincoln, they reminisce about the history of the station, one of them gets onto the subject of the renaming of Idlewild.

"Which I undertook solely to keep New York clean," says D. E. incautiously, immediately apprehensive; she nods pensively, her lips pursed. Her dead Kennedy is not to be separated from the staging of his last journey, the family represents him, this is the way he would have liked it. "No," says Marie. She would vote against the name Kennedy Station.

Her stubbornness persists for a while, the set is not turned off; her agitation has gone. The course of events has become predictable. Many more times will she see the observation platform of the last car and the coffin lying on six chairs, many more times will the camera in the helicopter show her the two trains, only she still has to face the American character of the spectacle. There are three trains, the first to intercept any explosives (one reporter hastily corrects his slip of the tongue, "dummy train," to the official term "pilot train"), the third a unit with two diesel engines for repairs and the consequences of a new crime. But the ones who do get hit are not the 1,000 famous friends of the Kennedys on the funeral train, they are two spectators in Elizabeth, New Jersey, who are struck and killed on the tracks by an express train traveling in the opposite direction. The intrusion of the commonplace disappoints Marie, but D. E. refrains from exploiting the first signs of boredom, it is two o'clock before he uses Annie's prewarmed bath thermometer and some outlandish science to prove to her that an implosion of the set must not be prevented. It is Marie who presses the button, and to please D. E. she takes him to the Olympic Swimming

Club at the Hotel Marseilles. She watches him as they leave the flat. His expression as he says good-by to Mrs. Cresspahl is casual, not triumphant.

Broadway is hot, as hot as if it were being roasted from below as well as from above. A predictable crowd is dawdling along occupied with its own affairs, it is only the heat that has swept the sidewalks on the east side so clean. Fearless of TV cameras, the Upper West Side goes about its business, women in curlers are out shopping, young men in T-shirts discuss the day in the shade of the marquee outside Strand Bar, carry bags of washing into coin laundries. No matter what the TV stations may have shown of Fifth Avenue, with flags at half-mast and solemn crowds along the route of the cortege, here it is Saturday as usual. Very few stores cover their displays with black-framed photos of the Senator or with funeral ribbons, scarcely one is closed; Mrs. Cresspahl gets her four bottles of spring water (the water from the faucet is revoltingly brown from deposits in the mains, washed up by pressure changes since kids all over town have been turning fire hydrants into street showers and adults have been sitting at home for three days in front of their television sets); she has no difficulty finding what she needs at the deli for a proper lunch, necessitated by D. E.'s presence. And Marie swallows much of her grief with black bread from West Germany and pickled herring from Denmark. She would have regarded a hearty appetite as shameless, now she is not even aware of it, for D. E. hasn't finished one second ahead of her. We're thinking of handing the child over to you, D. E., you're obviously qualified for the job.

By three o'clock sections of the morning broadcasts are being repeated on television, since the train does not pass the cameras often enough and the crowds on the platforms along the route to Washington merely produce the same waving, shouting, and flourishing of placards. Marie knows the younger brother's eulogy by heart, knows in advance the point at which his voice begins to break. Meanwhile the train has reduced speed so often for the benefit of the sightseers, has been so plagued by defects, that it is hours behind schedule, and one more of D. E.'s calculations proves correct: tired by her swim, Marie nods off, in the midst of the discussion about whether the broken brake shoe of the last car would be called *tormosnoi bashmak* or *tormosnaia kolodka*. She is so far away in sleep that she has slid down until she is now lying on the sofa, she does not hear the hollow ringing of the locomotive's bell on TV coming to an end, or the sound of the closing door.

Riverside Park seems no emptier than usual, the New York *Times* may offer statistics to prove this. Mrs. Cresspahl is not looking at the desiccated paths for acquaintances, she is searching for secluded nooks; sure enough, before reaching the underpass leading to the promenade along the Hudson, she finds some overgrown steps where she can lean against Professor Erichson's chest and weep to her heart's content with total disregard for propriety. Some people caress another person, with rhythmic strokes down one shoulder blade, like a disconsolate horse; this one simply holds tight, seeking no more contact than desired, does not speak.

*It's an infection by mass hysteria.*
You *haven't been infected, Gesine.* You're *not hysterical.*
*Because it's the third day I've been at odds with my own child.*
*You'll get her back, Gesine.*
*Because she might have got her sentimentality from me.*
*Don't you know? You're not sentimental. She's just fallen a bit into American ways.*
*I'm not bringing her up properly.*
*Jakob would have approved. So do I.*
*You could tell me now, D. E., as long as it's not out of pity.*
*Just believe it.*
*I believe it.*

In the evening, faithful to the four-hour delay, television has also arrived in Washington. The position of the coffin is indicated by the flashbulbs being shot at it by spectators; the darkness is all-enveloping. The family's stage-managing requires that the deceased shall pass the Senate buildings in which he had occupied offices. Welcoming cheers that die away in embarrassment. Sharpshooters on the roofs, plain-clothes police everywhere. The body has to spend four minutes taking leave of the softly lit figure of Abraham Lincoln, appearing doubly in his chair, so distorted is the picture. And once again: the "Battle Hymn." President Johnson in the first car behind his defeated opponent, surrounded by Secret Service men. The moon draws veils over the throng, it cannot light up the black water of the Potomac. When the coffin is unloaded, one of the dead man's sons insists on helping to carry it, so has to grasp it at the head end. At first the bearers go off in the wrong direction, walking more or less toward the eternal flame, have to turn off at an angle across the rise. After the final service John Glenn folds the flag with brisk precision and hands it to the new head of the Kennedys. An official car has brought the deceased's cocker spaniel from his home, Freckles in person. The previous widow tries to assert herself once more against the Senator's widow, making the most of the occasion she busies herself and her children with the placing of posies on their own gravestones. The other relatives kiss the casket of the most recently deceased, leaving it to stand on the grass. Again and again strangers kneel beside the African mahogany, touch it with their lips, pray. Marie sits with her legs drawn up on the bench, holding her hand to her mouth, merely surprised at a ceremony described by her mother as being quite different in Europe.

The voice on the air says nothing about the relatives not staying for the interment. Apparently the New York *Times* has been taken aside during the day by one of the young nephews, who has pointed out the unseemliness of its behavior as well as the consequences for future business; now it assures its customers of its good taste by means of dirgelike classical music and subdued readings of the news. A station on the next channel closes its transmission with a commercial on the dangers of smoking.

Television switches to seascapes, underscored by mawkish singing, then to a photographic portrait, presented as being all that remains to us. The eleven o'clock news is sponsored by Savarin coffee. The commercial shows the expert surrounded by coffee workers who anxiously await his reaction to the brew. He likes it, and folkloristic delight spreads over the Indian faces. The expert takes himself off in his genuine South American train. A co-sponsor of the news is the cockroach exterminator Black Flag, Kill & Clean. If Marie has her way, we won't be buying these things, for a while. Now live music is played, continuously, interrupted by a photo of the deceased that seems to be hanging slightly askew. He has his hand up to his chin, in conversation; he looks younger than three days ago.

At one A.M.: THE GREAT GREAT SHOW, a fairy tale from prewar Hungary: The Baroness and the Butler. Anything not to put off the viewers.

On the chair next to Marie, D. E. has borne up steadfastly, roughly two and a half ounces of tobacco have been well roasted in his pipes, the third bottle of red wine has been opened, he doesn't want to be the one to give up. Hardly has Marie become aware of the transition to the normal program when she asks if she may switch off the set. She trundles it over to the apartment door, its cord wound up, ready for the rental company to take away.

"D. E.," she says, "what do we have to do so you'll stay with us tomorrow?"

"Drive with me now across the Hudson and all the way into the New Jersey woods to where my log cabin is."

"It's a deal," says Marie, looking at him tenderly, amused, in happy anticipation. She leans against his chair, arranging his gray hair this way and that. He has earned her gratitude.

In D. E.'s car, before entering the New Jersey tunnel, she turns toward the back seat. The place is dark enough, her mother won't be able to see her expression.

"Thank you for letting me have this," she says.

"Who, me?" Mrs. Cresspahl is startled out of her doze, for a moment she thinks there is someone else beside her.

"Yes, you. For letting me watch TV. That's what I'm thanking you for."

## June 9, 1968   Sunday

is the official national day of mourning, just as yesterday one was decreed for the City of New York; Marie was not interested in a trip to Arlington Cemetery to check out the TV reports at the fresh grave. What she wanted was a drive to Culvers and Owassa lakes, to the Delaware on the Pennsylvania border, and beyond Little Swartswood Lake to the rustic manor D. E. calls his log cabin. In Arlington they may be making pilgrimages with flowers to R. F. K.; along our route we saw people like ourselves out for a Sunday drive, stalls with eggs and cherries for sale in front of farms and woodland paths, people strolling about in the little towns, busy coffee shops, children beside tinkling ice-cream trucks, shores covered with colorful sunbathers. Marie watches us without contempt for the fact that we are spending all the early part of the evening in D. E.'s shady garden, idly chatting, without a worry in the green twilight; she appears as if by chance at the bay window of the kitchen, where she is advising Mrs. Erichson on the preparation of dinner, infrequent glances are meant merely as a reassurance that she is not going to disturb us. She speaks German to D. E.'s mother, although with an American "Granny" slipping naturally over her lips. "Why are we preparing such a big dinner, Granny?"

"How far have you got, Gesine?"

"Yes, help me. I can't get Cresspahl away from the Soviets. 1947."

"You should tell Marie about them."

"D. E., she gets it all wrong."

"She can't even think straight about today's Russians."

"She's a convinced anti-Communist. She believes the school to that extent."

"A confused anti-Communist, my dear. In her collection she has a poem copied from *Pravda* of June 7, written by that fellow, what's his name—"

"That one. I know who you mean."

"You know the one."

"I've read about him in the New York *Times*. He came to see R. F. K. in November '66—"

"—I can never get enough of the name Kennedy."

"—while he was still alive. It's part of history. At the time of the vote on a citizens' control board for the New York police."

"The vote of fear."

"Senator Kennedy had just cast his vote, and who should ring the bell on the fourteenth floor at United Nations Plaza? A Soviet poet, and for three hours he slouches on a sofa high above New York, conversing with this representative of American imperialism, and what kind of communiqué do they publish? One has 'faith only in those politicians who understand the importance of poetry.' "

"The Senator from New York: 'I like poets who like politicians.' "

"And much comforted the poet wended his way home, reduced to a scarecrow, his breast swelling with pride."

"Now I've got the name. Eugene."

"Yevgeny Yevtushenko. Right?"

"He has struck again. Maybe it's meant as an act of friendship for the dead man, not even Marie feels quite sure."

"Let's hear it."

" 'The price of revolver lubricant rises.' "

"You anti-Communist."

"That's what it said. And:

'Perhaps the only help is shame.
History cannot be cleansed in a laundry.
There are no such washing machines.
Blood can't ever be washed away!'

And:

'Lincoln basks in his marble chair,
Wounded.'

What does Abe Lincoln do at night? Wasn't he at a theater? Listen to the Yevtushenkos' Eugene:

'But without wiping the splashes of blood from your forehead,
You, Statue of Liberty, have raised up
Your green, drowned woman's face,
Appealing to the heavens against being trodden under foot.' "

"Do you believe that?"

"Marie even wonders whether he believes it himself."

"D. E., I tell her things she doesn't want to hear about. About the Twins who ruled in Jerichow longer than any other Soviet commandants before or after them. They behaved as if they were gentlemen, very high class. Refined. Superrefined. They could very well have belonged to the Plessen family. Aristocratic landowners, and they administered Jerichow the way the Plessens used to. Breakfast together, not before nine, each waited on by his own servant, linen and silver on the table, punishment for the slightest mark. At ten, departure for the town hall, to govern. They kept the Mayor in a file room, where he was permitted to sign papers, his office was used by them as they sat side by side even at his desk, Germans had to keep a distance of three paces, just as at one time the day laborers had had to do in the presence of the noble family. Even-tempered, never in a rage, never any alcohol. Never walked a step in town on foot. They were not brothers, that was the only thing Jerichow knew about their private lives, they did not even look alike, rumor worked away at their nickname and could never figure it out. When they caught one of their subordinates hobnobbing with Germans, they had him taken away like a mass murderer, the beating did not begin until they were behind the fence. Terrible beatings. If one of the Germans came with a complaint, Mina Ahlreep for instance, and did not know the first name and patronym of that kind Soviet person who had shot down her fake clock from the gable, the slanderer found herself spending the night in the town-hall cellar, without proceedings, to give her time to remember the name. They did not bother to explain this to her, and next morning she was turned out of the building without a word. That's how loathsome the Twins found the Germans. Their arrival put an end to the all-night parties in Louise's parlor and, while she did demand compensation for the broken furniture and the ruined parquet floor, she did not know the regimental number of Mr. Draan. Pontiy had sometimes carried candies in his pocket for the *dyevushki*; the Twins did not even say *idi syuda* and used to shoo children out of the way like chickens. They had had the Kommandantura fence raised by two feet and, although they never received anyone at the villa, put up a triumphal arch outside it that had to have its lettering renewed by Loerbroks the painter for every Soviet holiday, as well as for the anniversaries of major victories in battle. If Loerbroks is not dead yet, he can still produce a portrait of Iosif Vissarionovich Stalin from memory, although in three colors only, mind you, and in Format A2 of the German Industrial Standards, this being how he had to do him over every Christmas. Stalin got the spot at the top of the arch: in the changing mottoes farther down and on the pillars there were constantly renewed allusions to the Army and the Army only, so that the four grammatical cases of *Krasnaya Armiya* were more firmly engraved on my mind than those of any other words. After work, still wearing their crisp uniforms and freshly ironed caps, the two Wendennych gentlemen, the Demwies Twins, would ride their horses out to the Rehberge, some nearby hills, on such occasions without their adjutants. From 10 to 11 P.M. we could listen in to phonograph music, Tchaikovsky, Moussorgsky, Glinka, Brahms. Those are not the kind of Soviets Marie learns about in school, and she doesn't want to hear about it."

"Cresspahl wasn't held indefinitely at Fünfeichen."

"She pictures it like a prison cell at Sing Sing."

"If she had a more accurate picture she wouldn't let you go to Prague."

"That reason has only existed for the last six months."

"It is a reason."

"Whereas you never told a lie even as a child."

"Always since then, when I was allowed to. And enjoyed it."

"I want Marie to see the Russians as they are today."

"The ones who were eighteen in 1947."

"I'm not going to help the school! Haven't I told Marie how Cresspahl got into the hands of the Soviets? I found that hard enough. All we need now is the Fünfeichen menu and she'll distrust Socialism for the rest of her life."

"You wouldn't be giving that Sister Magdalena ammunition. Marie would be better prepared."

"She's much too young!"

"She certainly knows all about the rapings that take place in New York."

"That's what we get for letting you study physics and chemistry. You regard truth as an absolute value."

"Marie would know more about you. She would understand why you want to make one more trip back to the other side. No, not that. She might suspect something."

"D. E., women's fashions aren't the only ones. It's not considered chic to disparage the Soviets. I don't have such reasons."

"So when is Marie supposed to catch up on this lesson?"

"When she's fifteen. . . ."

"That means she'll be told about the year 1953 when she comes of age. We won't be allowed to tell her about your death till she's on her own deathbed."

"Cresspahl concedes. Erichson wins on points. Your concern for that brat is downright ridiculous!"

"I owe her that much. In a minute she'll bring me a beer. The stories you know!"

"You tell her about the camps. You do it in such a way that all she gets out of it is justice, respect for the law, humane execution of the law."

"Then you."

"School in 1947. In the Grade 7 classrooms, Iosif Vissarionovich was now hanging a lot higher than the pictures of that Austrian. In that way a faded square became obvious, but no one could expect the new leader to be anything but tall. Only that the title had been expanded. Wise Leader of the Peoples, Benevolent Father of the Peoples, Generalissimo, Preserver of World Peace, Creator of Socialism, Guardian of Justice. Light Still Burning in the Kremlin, Guarantor of a Truly Human Future. There's something wrong about that guarantor."

"It's correct."

"Never once have I seen a portrait of him looking straight at the viewer, he's always squinting down to the side as if someone had stepped out of line or sneezed. As kids in school we weren't allowed to discuss him like that, either his physiognomy or any other human attributes; someone told on Lise Wollenberg, she couldn't help laughing at the parting in the Voshd's busy mustache, the scare was punishment enough for her, she got an E in Russian and an E in deportment. She had every reason to watch herself. The Cresspahl girl also wanted the subjects of the Leader of the Peoples to give her back her father, that meant she had two strokes against her. Could that have been carelessness? She diligently learned the new history of inventions, somewhat as Marie learns religion, knowledge for keeping on tap only. It had not been that feudal character Drais von Sauerbronn who had thought up the bicycle while looking at some Chinese drawings, it had been a Russian peasant who was released from serfdom for having cycled from the Urals to Moscow, 1,500 miles. According to that, even Russian feudal overlords were more benevolent. It was not Marconi who had been the first to send signals without wires, we have a Russian to thank for wireless telegraphy. The withering defeat of the Kuntze-Knorr brake by a Russian one was taught in belletristic style: the revered Moscow scholar demonstrates some braking tests in a tunnel to his German colleagues, and while his system is gently bringing the train to a stop, one of the foreign duffers groans: Kuntze-Knorr yis finyished! The first motorcar was driven in Russia. Mind you, the Party did not invent the airplane, but a tailor from Minsk or Tula did; likewise of Russian origin were the pharmacy, the crane, your Caran d'Ache crayon, the telephone, all the components of the railway from *stantsiya* to *passashirskiy* and *pochtovy* cars. However, the student who learned all this was entitled to English lessons from Mrs. Weidling, who was not arrested until the fall of the following year."

"You forgot penicillin."

"Such a docile student, in an essay entitled 'Looking Out My Window' she writes about what she sees from her window, about the green Russian fence crowned with barbed wire, above that the roof of the Kommandatura villa, beyond the open gate an American truck with bulletproof mesh over its headlights, and if the student craned out the window she could see around the corner of the brickyard to the east, that is where the sun rose, as *krasniy* as the Red Army. It was quite a popular ending, the Cresspahl girl had been genuinely out to flatter, this essay was returned unmarked by Mrs. Beese, who kept her in after school. The essay had to be rewritten, looking out onto the schoolyard, where there was nothing whatever to be seen. Mrs. Beese did not divulge the lesson to be learned from this, the Cresspahl girl was supposed to discover it for herself. Eight weeks later she handed in a résumé of a Russian short story in which she casually quoted 'the fierce nature of the Russians,' 'the Russians in their fierce nature,' she was simply thinking of the story in which a Russian estate owner keeps a wild bear in a room and locks up unsuspecting guests with it, she must have been blind in her assiduousness, with this essay she was sent to the school principal. A Social Democrat, a teacher since 1925 and again since 1945, he was so horrified at the obtuse child that he could not even explain the disaster. He went in person to the school secretary, borrowed some nail scissors, cut out the five or six words, returned the exercise book. 'That really won't do, child.' Whether the hole was to be struck over with a corrected text or blameless white was a decision that transcended his powers, it was too much for him, and he gestured like one who is sufficiently occupied with his own drowning and now you come and ask him the time."

"I don't believe it."

"You see? And yet you want me to tell this to Marie?"

"Is it true?"

"His name was Dr. Vollbrecht. The one who nearly didn't get appointed principal. In his inaugural speech he was supposed to welcome the Red Army as the bringer of true human culture, his wife had been raped by twenty-one armed Red soldiers. They kept him for three days at the courthouse in Gneez, then he let it be known in the town that he had been away for family reasons, finally he admitted to the arrest but only that it had been 'in error.' Then he gave the speech."

"No. You're pulling my leg. I'd do the same. You can't tell me the New School is disavowing Pushkin."

"You see? Marie would be only too glad to believe that. She would have an additional advantage."

"That it's true."

"That it happened, and that I was there."

"That's tough."

"Right, and what am I supposed to do about it?"

"Erichson concedes. Cresspahl is the winner, and not only on points."

"Why don't you write to young Vollbrecht? He's an attorney in Stade, the post office there will find him."

"No, Gesine. I wouldn't dare."

And what was the reason for the big dinner? D. E. stood up after the meat course, squeezed a napkin between collar and neck, the way fine folks do, and made a speech for Marie. Originally he had once again wanted to marry the Cresspahl family on this particular day, but business had prevented him and he promised not to mention the irksome affair again until September. As a substitute he could offer an amateur play, rehearsed for two hours, a production with several parts, the cast consisting of a prince by the name of Dubrovskiy, a guaranteed untamed bear . . .

"Will September be all right for us?" asks Marie.

---

### June 12, 1968   Wednesday

Rain. Rain. Rain.

The Soviet Union is having trouble with its socialist brothers and sisters in Czechoslovakia. At one time it had among them a man it could trust, a major general who last December attempted a military coup against the denigrators of St. Novotný, although he failed. His backers may have forgiven him for failing, also for crossing the wrong frontier. They barely resent their lost friend for proving to be a bigtime thief (clover and alfalfa seed valued at $20,000). But that it should be a Soviet general to whom he was indebted for his passport to travel abroad! That went beyond a joke. It would be acceptable had it been only the New York *Times* that told the tale. Let the world know about it. But that the people of Prague should find out via a reprint in the daily *Lidova Demokracie*, that really takes the cake, and the ambassador in Moscow is handed a sorrowful letter. It would be a sad thing for amicable relations. Be prepared for the consequences if the appropriate authorities of the Czechoslovakian Republic fail to take immediate measures against their own news organs! Alfalfa and clover seed indeed! It may be true, mind you, but must the papers pounce on it?

"Your Soviets weren't all that amusing," says Marie. She is to be told what they were like, she has been promised; a reconciliation is involved. The promise has been made by our Professor Erichson, to whom truth is something concrete; why did Mrs. Cresspahl feel such relief at each delay? Why did she want to postpone it, at least until the fall, preferably for a whole year?

" 'My' Soviets."

"In your Soviet Mecklenburg. You were in the same place with them. You met each other. You know them."

"I was twelve. In 1946 I turned thirteen."

"Gesine, name me a child in Mecklenburg who knows nothing about my country."

"You can have a whole class of Gneez schoolkids."

"Couldn't I tell them about what's acceptable in New York, from Harlem to the Hudson?"

"It would be only what you've seen. What you know. Only what's real for you."

"Real for me."

"They'd never believe you, right from the start."

"Gesine, I do want to believe you."

"You think I have a secret ax to grind, but you say you won't doubt me. How is it ever going to work?"

"I have an ax to grind too, Gesine. Oh I do. Indeed I do."

"So I'll admit that Cresspahl had a rough time in Soviet hands. Sometimes. Worse than I wanted to tell you."

"Starvation?"

"Starvation too."

"Physical abuse?"

"Injuries of various kinds."

"It happened to him by mistake, Gesine."

"It happened to him."

"The Soviets were the conquerors. They were soldiers, foreigners. Why shouldn't they have made a slip of the pen now and then? They may have misunderstood something in the foreign language, more than once."

"Some of the interpreters had learned their German from the Nazi occupation and had to go through Polish before arriving at the Russian."

"Gesine, am I being a bad relative if I don't care to hear all this about Cresspahl in detail?"

"It isn't exactly a water-butt story."

"Gesine: for a while he wasn't there."

"He wasn't there. So for a certain length of time he couldn't help me, whereas I absorbed the earlier times solely in my life with him. In words, but even more in knowledge conveyed by mood, look, facial expression. I had Jakob's mother, she was a stranger in Jerichow, she couldn't bring home much more than the hospital and its environment. As for Jakob, I had to share him in yet another way. And just as he didn't take along kids on his business trips, so he didn't make himself accessible to them either. For the surviving Jerichow families I was the daughter of the mayor who had been arrested; they were more likely to have a word for Hanna. And in Gneez there was nobody at all who wanted me as a dependent. What you'll get now is nothing but a young teen-ager's I-was-there, plus the confusion introduced by hindsight. Will you settle for that?"

"What else have you kept from me?"

"The disappearance of Slata."

"I'd almost forgotten about her. You led me past her on purpose!"

"Slata went to meet the first Soviets to arrive in Papenbrocks' hall as if she wanted to be taken away from that house, away from such a family. The Gneez commandant kept her not only as an interpreter, she was his assistant; he would have allowed her to visit the Papenbrocks. She never got around to that. Louise had treated her too long as a servant, Albert had merely looked on, not helped her. So in Gneez hardly anyone knew that a Nazi *Sonderführer* had carried her off from Russia to Mecklenburg as his fiancée, with a child, and to parents-in-law who were obligated both to the Air Force and to the Nazi Party by financial profits. She was known as the Angel of Gneez. She had been in the country since the fall of 1942, it was impossible to lie to her in either High German or dialect; many people felt they had to thank her for returning unscathed from a Soviet interrogation, their innocence more or less established. And yet she was a stranger, she could favor no one but sick women, starving children, or a refugee who had stolen some potatoes out of need and not to sell. With a disgusting meticulousness she helped her boss, Y. Y. Yenudkidze, 'Triple Y,' to supervise the Gneez business world, the mighty Johannes Knoop was obliged to surrender his wagon for transporting wood, to hell with export-import; in these educated circles her erstwhile future relationship was preserved as a moral defect, a snare for the future, to be kept on ice for the time being out of deference to their partner

Albert of Jerichow; when overcome by rage they referred to her as a floozy and, believe it or not, a traitor.

"The Angel of Gneez did not live in the barracks on Barbara Street (which were protected from the Germans by an eight-foot fence): during the day Slata left her son Fedya with Mrs. Witte, in the requisitioned City of Hamburg Hotel, where she slept on the top floor, which was still furnished as Alma's private apartment, behind two doors (apart from the main hotel entrance). Sometimes she would spend the evening downstairs, in what had formerly been the dining room, in the company of officers from the Kommandantura, also functionaries of the German Communist Party. Then Slata would understand very little German, especially unintelligible were the efforts at conversation on the part of a young fellow who, five paces away, kept his mocking, confused eyes on her, his expression deliberately gloomy, as if he were not the future district chairman of Gneez. No. Even Cresspahl's petitions, with which he tried to circumvent K. A. Pontiy at a higher level, went no more swiftly through Slata's typewriter, although under the Nazis he had had more to say to her than to pass the time of day, about a Hilde Paepcke, for instance, who wore her hair under a scarf just like she did, evidently someone he also liked. In the eyes of a twelve-year-old the District Chairman was a callow youth, but she wouldn't have minded being like Slata someday."

"I like the way you look in those old photos, Gesine. Even if I say so myself."

"But she was blonde, Marie. In those days that was considered pretty. She was grown-up; she had my worries behind her, how to hold one's bosom, how a girl gets pregnant. She was tall, willowy almost, yet impressive. The way she stretched out her arm, or bent her knees to lean down, I loved to see that. They were such flowing, harmonious movements. She had a small mouth, quite full. I was at cross-purposes with the language because she said my lips were 'pouting.' Slata nodded with her eyes when she listened. On the street she would pass me with a closed-in expression, she chose not to recognize me; yet I saw the invitation to meet her eyes, to playfulness even. Then it would seem to me after all as if we had exchanged smiles and said: Hey there. How about it, eh? Hey there yourself."

"Such an important person. And you tried to do me out of her."

"Then she disappeared. She was gone from my life. Once, when again there was no midday train to Jerichow, I went to see Mrs. Witte, unthinkingly, remembering the days when I used to have lunch at the hotel, my mind wasn't on Slata at all, but Slata was all that Alma could talk about, though she had lost the power of shaping words. She merely pointed around the room she had given up to Slata for a bedroom, I followed the movements of her crippled finger, anxious to reassure her, set a bedside table back on its feet, swept up some broken glass from the rug, hung up some dresses, tidied Fedya's scattered bedclothes, was on the very point of hurrying off to Jerichow, on foot, to warn Cresspahl, but had to go to Alma's kitchen, put on a kettle, get tea out of the can marked 'Salt,' all in obedience to her helpless breathing and panting."

"It was all a mistake, Gesine."

"It was all very sudden. Y. Y. Y. had driven up to the hotel as he did every morning, whistled cheerfully up at the front of the building; only he had brought along four armed men and had to whip up his anger by stomping up the stairs. That's how much he had changed since the previous evening, but she had not."

"Did they beat her?"

"Because she offered resistance. Her child had a fever and was supposed to stay in bed."

"She was the wife of a Nazi, even if not in the eyes of the law, she had set fire to villages in the Ukraine."

"Triple Y knew all about that when he made her his confidante. He'd forgiven her."

"She had a son by that Robert Papenbrock."

"He spoke Russian better than German. He was no longer called Fritz. Answered to Fedya."

"Her name was found in Cresspahl's files."

"Yes. That wasn't why they picked her up."

"Gesine, you didn't want to tell me this because of your ax to grind. You think I'm going to misunderstand the Soviets again. But I do understand them."

"As long as they don't beat people up."

"Gesine. I don't like that kind of punishment. I don't like it when a person betrays his country. You're trying to tell me it's acceptable. First Cresspahl, then Slata."

"Tell that to Slata."

"Right. She came back. It's possible to try to explain it to her. It's already been explained to her."

"She did not come back. Fedya survived the trip to the Soviet Union, he died there in camp."

"Gesine, run the tape back to Alma Witte. I want to erase all I said. I want a chance to think about it. Next time warn me. Say: Stop."

"The result was, Mrs. Witte had lost something. And that was Fedya, who learned to call her, rather than Louise Papenbrock, Granny. He was only three, she could still carry him in her arms. Who's my little darling then, who's my chickabiddy? She lost the mother of that child. The mother could easily have turned the tenant relationship into one of dominance; she was reserved, a shade too independent, occasionally almost a daughter. The young thing had accorded her the respect she was entitled to. That suited Mrs. Witte down to the ground. When someone like the proprietress of the City of Hamburg spontaneously praises Miss Podyeraitska's politeness, she draws a wide swathe through the opinion of the locals, especially when she hints at further virtues. The Angel of Gneez.

"Alma Witte had also lost what the locals call pride. You have to be more than capable to maintain a hotel in a Mecklenburg country town in second place after the Archduke, well ahead of all the others. Her hotel had been patronized by the judiciary, the high-school teachers, the Reichswehr officers of good family. When she walked through the dining room in the evening, the men rose to greet her. If a stranger wanted an introduction to her, he would do well to bring along one of the established guests for the purpose. On one occasion she had requested the staff of the Mecklenburg Reich Governor to make less noise, without waiting for their compliance; their corner had subsided into the usual moderation. Commissioner Vick, not from the Gestapo but from the Kripo, the Criminal Police, because I am an honest National Socialist! had to mind his p's and q's or she would have refused to serve him. The Soviets had turned the building into a hostel for functionaries of the new administration and for transient Party officials, yet she called Mr. Yenudkidze a gentleman; in the evenings she had sat with them in the dining room like an honorary chairman; revelry of the kind that took place at Louise Papenbrock's was unthinkable.

"Whether Mrs. Witte felt genial or humble behavior to be appropriate, it always was appropriate. It was just that her sense of propriety depended on acceptance, recognition, response. Such partnership had been wiped out by the assault in her home, she no longer trusted in the exchange of like manners, mutual agreement on traditional forms. The Alma Witte of earlier days would have got herself up in her Sunday best and presented herself at the town hall to request the commandant to clear up the incident, diplomatically considering she would have to let the faux pas go by the board or insist on an apology. Now they had not waited for the door to be opened, they had broken down the frame and smashed all the rare frosted glass. They had ignored her dignified protests and, in defiance of all good manners, dragged guests out of her home. They had punched her in the chest and not even held out a hand to help her, with all her sixty-five years. Alma Witte submitted nothing in writing to the Kommandantura, neither a petition for the pardon of her young friend nor an application for damages. She was not even allowed to feel satisfaction over the fact that Y. Y. Yenudkidze was now spending his free evenings at the Archduke Hotel, now known as the Dom Offitzerov; he felt no embarrassment on her account. People in town invited her comments on Slata's departure, she declined with sorrowful dignity, as if refusing a course at the dinner table; once again she was drawing an exaggerated swathe of Soviet aura after her, whereas actually she had just wanted to avoid venting her grievances. From a child she could demand that a shameful sight be forgotten. For that I did not need to be obedient. For me she was a very old woman, why shouldn't she have bouts of illness? I hoped she would get better."

"Gesine, you liked her, too."

"There have been lots of people in my life whom I've liked."

"Gesine, mightn't it have been pity?"

"Pity for what? If she had cried, I would have followed suit, naturally. I couldn't be a child who felt pity."

Gesine, might it be that I'm jealous? Of Slata? Of a proprietress of a City of Hamburg Hotel in Gneez?"

"Stop."

"No. No. I have to know."

"Mrs. Witte was never the same again, except outwardly. It wasn't the manners of the Red Army that were her undoing. It was her own doing. Once in the spring of 1946 I had to ask her to put me up for the night, when the evening train to Jerichow had also been canceled. She gave me permission to stay, offhandedly: one did not enter Alma Witte's home with a request or an objective, the formalities of a social visit were necessary. She made me sit down in her restored salon and embark on a fitting conversation about the canceled train, whether it had been sabotage or requisition, about the district administration of Gneez, about Cresspahl. For she certainly hadn't become nervous. Besides all this, she was giving me an education in the upper-class niceties of conversation, replies in complete sentences, clear enunciation, euphemisms where appropriate, the whole truth where necessary; she seemed perfectly all right to me. Unhurried, every inch a lady, about nine o'clock she walked downstairs with me into what had once been the lobby, she had heard some noise there, she would put a stop to it. It was nothing but a Red Army soldier who had lost his way, at the station two girls had caught his eye, a couple of young teachers, guests of this establishment, young chicks new to town, they need only have preceded the young drunk to the Kommandantura, where he would have been given a thorough dressing-down and a safe bed for the night.

Now he had fallen down in the hotel vestibule and was brandishing his pistol in the half-open door facing the reception desk, too drunk to shoot, in other words blind, but still attracted by the company of the young ladies who had so inexplicably disappeared at this point into a house wall. That's where I saw Alma Witte's crippled index finger again. She was pointing at the thrashing figure in the vestibule, as she had once done at creases in a tablecloth, spots on a knife, cigar butts on the carpet, that must be cleared away, cleaned up, discreetly removed. Now there were no servants to jump to her orders; now, again, she could not speak. Standing around the great personage were two experts in education, one almost qualified woman judge of the People's Court, from the dining room Comrade Schenk slowly emerged, a man to all appearances; but not one of these could grasp what Mrs. Witte's trembling finger conveyed. And it was a female person who crept along the wall to the vestibule, gently closed the banging door, and from cautious knees turned the key in it."

"He might have fired."

"He took his cue from the door. The door was shut. The girls were gone. All he wanted to do now was sleep."

"Why didn't any of you report him to the Kommandatura?"

"Someone would have had to leave the hotel by the rear, down a wobbly ladder from Mrs. Bolte's apple storeroom into the yard, over the wall and onto the street, maybe right into the arms of another of those straying characters. Comrade Schenk forbade it, for the sake of the public weal. Thereupon Mrs. Witte immediately forbade it again, pointing a highly indignant finger at him for daring to lay down the law in her hotel. She was not vindictive. The drunken youth would have got a terrible beating at the town hall and, after Triple Y had waked up, another portion for reminding Slata's protector of her apartment. No, Alma Witte hadn't become nervous, or vindictive. But her pride, that she had forfeited. Before it grew light again the dazed sleeper took himself off, and before anyone in the house had risen Mrs. Witte had scrubbed the space between inner and outer doors twice. That's the way she was."

"And the person who locked the door, that was you, Gesine?"

"I stood there, unable to tear my eyes away from that crippled humiliated finger. Over and over again I forced myself to think: Don't laugh. Oh don't laugh! Why aren't you laughing, Marie?"

"You know many more stories like that."

"Many."

"You're convinced I'll make wrong use of them."

"That's what I'm afraid of."

"Wait and see, Gesine. Just wait and see."

### June 13, 1968   Thursday

The Czechoslovak Communists have submitted a new travel law to the National Assembly, all that is lacking is an acceptable wording for the exceptions. Those excepted are persons facing judicial proceedings, persons on active military service or about to be drafted, bearers of state secrets, experts of especially high qualifications, and those who have been convicted of damaging Czechoslovak interests on previous trips. All others are to be entitled to a passport for travel abroad and, without an exit visa, to travel wherever they like and for as long as they like, their country will welcome them on their return. Let us hope the Soviet Union is not made sorrowful again when it reads about this in a Prague newspaper or in *Freiheit*, published in Halle in East Germany.

The weather. Fair and mild is the forecast for today; cool tonight.

"Gesine, may I lay a trap for you? Yesterday I was clumsy. Today I'm going to catch you."

"May I lay a trap for you too, Marie?"

"I know yours. You won't see mine."

"Mary Fenimore Cooper Cresspahl."

"And Henriette. Ready?"

"The tape's running."

"Gesine, did the Soviets behave more ruthlessly where you were than the British did in India?"

"They behaved like occupying forces. Theirs was the land, they administered the power, and even with the glory they saw to it that they got their share."

"But the losers weren't all equally scared of them. The ones who had something to lose. The middle class. What you call the bourgeoisie."

"If they were scared of the New Order it wasn't because of their place within it. That was fenced in."

"That was kind of a pudgy finger, Alma Witte's. All white and trembling. Very bourgeois."

"No. Take just the people in Jerichow, they weren't the Alma Witte type. They genuinely wanted to surrender everything, starting with their own sense of identity, if in exchange they could only hold onto their money, as a means of increasing their property and, in turn, their money. The Soviets didn't take that away from them. The same as in the old days, potatoes, grain, milk, continued to be routed via their stores, even the green Soviet fence went through their account books, they were still making a profit on the labors of others. Not even Papenbrock had been relieved of his granary, his manager was looking after that for him, Waldemar Kägebein, who had turned out to be right after all with his Aereboe's *Manual of Agriculture*. For receiving, storing, and shipping the grain he charged a fee which not only appeared in Papenbrock's books but was entered at the bank. If Louise was allowed to charge no more than 43 reich pfennigs for the bread, she simply added bran to it until she could make a profit on the price. I don't get something for nothing either, she used to say. She could comfortably think to herself: And I haven't had to give up much either."

"Just her husband."

"He was replaced by a trusteeship. Just as under the old laws."

"Wasn't she in danger too?"

"If Albert came back and she hadn't looked after his property, let alone had frittered it away; then she believed she would be in real danger. Mind you, the Soviets might invite her too for a joy ride to God knows where; she intended to survive that with the consciousness of her innocence (just as she also expected Papenbrock home daily, vindicated, pure as the driven snow). Besides, hadn't she shown the Red Army her good will, her hospitality in fact, when Mr. Draan's cronies ruined the parquet flooring her parlor with their dancing? The only thing that could happen might be an accident; for that eventuality she held Horst's widow in reserve; although of inferior background, from the shoemakers' town, she was nevertheless a daughter-in-law, destined to take over the administration of the inheritance. Why should this chain be broken?"

"Her aristocratic friends had run away from the Soviets."

"They found that a positive relief, your middle class. For the time being, the conquerors' punishment had struck the others. How could she carry on a friendship that had become impractical, meaning: bad for business? Friendship for its own sake, for display purposes only? There was now no point in flaunting an alliance with the Plessens, the Oberbülows, in fact she had no trouble remembering things that indicated hostility: a greeting ignored or perfunctorily returned, the lack of an invitation to the Von Zelck double wedding in 1942; in those days she would never have deplored the fact, by so much as a critical nod in the direction of the Von Lassewitzes, that a German landed aristocrat was keeping forced laborers in his stables, foreigners though they might be; now she tucked her chin firmly into her collar and alluded with pious severity to justice. In one of the Papenbrock attic rooms lived a family called Von Haase, deported from southern Mecklenburg, removed more than the prescribed twenty miles from their estate. Louise needled them in the kitchen when they came to get water, their daughter Marga had only to show the slightest defiance for Louise to call after her: 'I bet your mother used to beat prisoners of war too!' She had no proof of this beyond invention. She wanted these people out of the house, the uncomfortable memories; she would have shut her door in the face of any Bothmer on the run."

"And denounced him."

"You don't trust me. You think I'm twisting my story against her. Just to cast aspersions on her."

"You hate her."

"Marie, there was nothing about her for a child of thirteen to hate. I avoided her because that was more or less what Cresspahl had wanted, and now Jakob too. Did I know why? Can you hate an order?"

"That wasn't my trap at all, Gesine."

"She wouldn't have denounced him, it might have got around to the neighbors that she was being more helpful to the Soviets than necessary. And there was something else she shared with the Jerichow householders: to a limited extent they wanted to remain in the nobility's good books. The situation might change again."

"Back to what it was like before? But they'd lost!"

"The Soviets, astonishing conquerors that they were, didn't introduce their own economic system into Mecklenburg, those communal estates under state administration, their famous kolkhozes. They faithfully kept to the agreement with the Allies, the Potsdam one, and took away the land from anyone owning more than 250 acres, while taking everything from the Nazi leaders of course, and reformed the land. They did this earlier than agreed, but did they do it in the Communist style? Socialist production is large-scale production, you'll be learning that one day; the Soviets gave away their acquired land in small lots, many of them twelve and a half acres, to farm hands, unlanded laborers, displaced persons from the eastern territories, even old farmers got something, and the town of Jerichow, believe it or not, was given aristocratic fields to cultivate, and even a piece of the Gräfin Forest. In confirming so much property, in providing the Mecklenburg world with such quantities of it in terms of concept and reality, they did not give the impression of intending to stay indefinitely."

"But they must have done it with clenched teeth. Merely to honor their agreement?"

"You don't credit them with that, Marie."

"Ah. That was your trap. Right, Gesine?"

"Not yet the spring of the trap door. The thing was that they had put their signature to a promise that the German people were not to be enslaved, and they did not depart from it. They kept their Communism to themselves. Sometimes they assumed an appearance that pleased even the most solid citizens. They spoke to the Germans through their own newspaper, they might have called it the *S. M. A. News*, the *Antifa Review*, *Red Front Freedom*, but they used the name *Tägliche Rundschau*, *Daily Review*, *Front Line Newspaper for the German Population*, by June 1945 the words Front Line had been dropped. Nor was it a random title, it had once been the name of a Christian paper with fiercely nationalistic leanings, the Soviets appropriated it from the loot they had pocketed from the Nazis, all strictly legal. Papenbrock would have approved of this procedure. The bourgeois concept of property counted for something with the Soviets."

"Maybe they still needed your bourgeoisie for a while for their economy. But they didn't admit them to positions of political power. That would have been like promising to cut off their own arm."

"Just don't ask Sister Magdalena about the Potsdam agreement."

"You must be kidding."

"As to their plans for their share of the conquered people, the Soviets couldn't have made them plainer than by their leader's prophecy: painted on a bed sheet, it hung outside town halls or was inscribed in red letters on the front wall of school auditoriums:

HITLERS

COME AND GO

BUT

THE GERMAN PEOPLE, THE GERMAN NATION

REMAINS

Nicely centered, as is the wont of lettering artists. When you have that facing you for hours on end you keep trying to translate it into Latin, with *et* or perhaps more elegantly *atque*, it looked so classical, as wise as the Leader of the Peoples working nights in the Kremlin, a genuine example of his style yet in a disguised voice, for it wasn't one of his tricks of dialectic, it was simply history as a series of waves, Hitler as a recurring type notwithstanding the growth of the international workers' class, a promise of eternity for a state that was identified solely as German, thus including a Mecklenburg streak. It was an outright education in irony, just the thing for bourgeois minds."

"They didn't believe it, Gesine."

"When the Soviets were using cotton cloth for it, cotton they could have been sleeping on? Your middle-class citizens pursed their lips, they enjoyed demonstrating their cleverness. Their native cunning. As announced, the Soviets handed over the administration of their conquest not just to Germans, to opponents of Hitler; predictably, they sent relations, German Communist émigrés, trained for this German state in Soviet schools; predictably, they were accompanied, in line with their theories, by representatives of that class to which alone they ascribed productivity and historical strength and which, moreover, was entitled to an equalization in both income and power; to no one's surprise, the Communist Party arrived. It was their turn now."

"Arm in arm with bourgeois parties. Under the eyes of K. A. Pontiy."

"These were left behind in Jerichow by that commandant as a souvenir. After Cresspahl's arrest—"

"Stop."

"In the fall of 1945 Pontiy was no longer the Russian potentate, his orders became more detailed every day, now they dealt with what had been British Mecklenburg under the same plans as applied to the rest of Mecklenburg; with a sigh he abandoned his statistics. He would have liked to do it by decree. On Remembrance Sunday he summoned Bergie Quade, together with Köpcke's wife, to appear at the villa at coffee time and, believe it or not, they were served coffee. They were also allowed to sit down, in the brown leather armchairs, facing the corner of his desk; they tried to live up to this by sitting bolt upright, their knees decorously together, anticipating a discussion of their unorthodox bookkeeping. What was suggested to them was the

founding
of a regional group
of a Party
of German Liberalism
(or: of Liberality) and
Democracy;

Bergie's mind was still dwelling on visions of a complaint about the removal of the former mayor, Mina was encased in an almost new dress, let out at the back with two gussets, acquired for the sake of the widowed Mr. Duvenspeck; she had recently been feeling like a woman again. Now they missed their cues, whatever they said, we're only women, you know, I'm only taking my husband's place, you know, just in the business, you know, a political party's only for folks with an ax to grind, you know, you've still got our husbands, haven't you, and what will the neighbors say, Commandant!"

"Liberalism. Isn't that something to do with the gold standard?"

"Not at that time. What it did offer was stimulation of the economy by the economic self-interest of the individual, unrestricted competition, protected but not interfered with by the state, international free trade, laissez faire, *laissez-aller* . . ."

"It must've been an interpreter's error."

"Oh, they were willing all right! It was a gift, why ask whether they deserved it or not? Whatever they imagined under the name of this party, it sounded like the past, like the days before the war, before the Nazis. They did the right thing, they asked for time to think it over, they made bashfulness their excuse, because of the speaking in public. Bergie couldn't get it out of her head that Pontiy's assistant Draan might have been her son, she felt she would have no trouble bamboozling him. Mrs. Köpcke licked her lips, she had been chosen because she was a woman. And if the Soviets were going to offer cake for good behavior, she could cut herself as good a slice as any man. Each intended to palm off the top spot on the other, but that did not yet interfere with their close friendship. There was only one snag, and that had to be removed, the neighbors' ignorant talk about sucking up to the Soviets; here they had learned something from the reputation for which Cresspahl had to thank them. In this connection they both remembered K. A. Pontiy's briefest reply, the approximate offsetting of their political activity against the expedited return of their husbands from Soviet prison camps; wasn't that a sufficiently honorable reason?

"It took time to bring this home to the good citizens of Jerichow; Duvenspeck, although manager of the gasworks, was one of those most easily persuaded to accept it. Unexpectedly, Böhnhase emerged as the founder of the local Liberal Democratic Party of Germany, Böhnhase the tobacconist, formerly of the German National People's Party, sentenced in 1942 to seven years' imprisonment for the offense of bartering tobacco goods for bacon, yet not recognized as a Victim of Fascism, ready nevertheless to serve as a pillar of anti-Fascist Liberalism, consulting hours during business hours, the rationing of tobacco no argument against the Party, the abolishment of smokers' ration cards an argument in its favor. Both Mrs. Köpcke and Bergie had to admit that they had underestimated a masculine appetite; besides, Böhnhase had been away from the trough too long. They joined his party, no longer chief offenders, merely fellow travelers, they attracted others, Plückhahn the pharmacist, Ahlreep the jeweler, Hattje the general storekeeper, tinker tailor soldier sailor, the local Establishment so to speak, faced as they were with the Big Brother state. Bergie would have given a lot to see Papenbrock's expression."

"Did Louise have to join too?"

"It was voluntary, Marie. Permitted. Desired. In place of her husband Louise joined the conservative party, which called itself a union; like the Liberals, it aimed at being democratic but, in contrast to them, Christian. That's how K. A. Pontiy came to voice his public

 expression

 of my respect

 for the cause

 of the equal status

 of women,

for, although Pastor Brüshaver did not generally preach atonement for German war crimes, even in the 'social' sense, he believed that party politics were incompatible with a spiritual office, all that was needed being his call to an 'honest self-reappraisal,' and Pontiy was content with a chairwoman—"

"Louise Papenbrock."

"Käthe Klupsch."

"She was the laughingstock of the town."

"Käthe Klupsch was incapable of laughing at herself. What she was best at was the forgiving tone in which she referred to people who went over to the Communist Party or to the Farmers' Mutual Aid, merely in order to acquire a new residence permit or to become entitled to a plow or even a head of cattle from the reserves of the land reform. When asked how things were going, Swenson, Otto Maass, Kägebein would reply to one another: 'Coming along very nicely, thank you!' In public it sounded better when Käthe Klupsch announced: 'We've joined forces not for any advantage, for the sake of the cause.' "

"Whatever your trap was, Gesine, you've smashed mine."

"Mine was simply meant to demonstrate that sometimes you're mistaken about your ruthless suppression by the Soviets."

"I wanted to prove to you that you can convince me. That at least a gang like that has got its just desserts. Now they're on top again."

"What do you call a double trap like that, Marie?"

"I don't have to tell you."

"Your American is better."

"A double cross, that's what it's called."


On one occasion we believed Herbert H. Hayes, when he looked up the weather of Easter 1938 for us. Let us hope the New York Weather Bureau does not employ him anywhere but in the archives. In the forecasting department he would be a cause for concern. Today was

not "fair." It might deserve the term mild, although only for the per-
sistent rain that carried on for hours.

## June 14, 1968   Friday

The Czech trade delegation is back from Moscow. It has brought along
gifts. The Soviet Union will increase its deliveries of natural gas to
three billion cubic meters (100 billion cubic feet). The Kosice steel
mill is to receive two million tons of iron-ore pellets each year, though
not before 1972. Is it possible that our sanguine Vice-President De
Rosny had the wind up? No, the Soviet Union has refused a hard-
currency loan, modest though the requested sum was, $350 million,
only seven eighths of the debts to the Western market. All the more
happily, all the more speedily, will De Rosny obtain a larger sum. That
trip to Prague, we'll not get out of that. Marie knows this, she doesn't
want to talk about it.

The *Times*, that prim and proper aunt, curtseys. She apologizes.
She has made a mistake. In that Soviet poem about the dead Senator
from New York it should not have said that Abraham Lincoln basks
in his marble chair. The correct wording should be that the marble
Lincoln rasps. Marie could use this for her Kennedy file. She does not
want to hear the name for a while.

"And what are you not going to tell me about today?"

Before Christmas 1945, Erwin Plath trotted once more through
northwest Mecklenburg, the area committed to his care by the Socialist
Party in Hanover. One goes to some trouble for a guest; Plath got his
meeting in Jerichow, twenty minutes standing in the brickyard drying
shed, within comfortable sight of the Soviet Kommandantura, so that
he did not shiver only from cold. It was bitter enough for him to have
to admit to an error before instructing his audience on the new Party
line; they heckled him relentlessly, they did not even respect his status
as a courier. There were fourteen men present plus two women; of
these he knew two to be former registered members, of two others he
was willing to believe it, for eight he could imagine neither a past nor
a future in Social Democracy, in one case he thought he must be
dreaming. Hadn't he been expelled in 1938 with full illegal procedure?
Furthermore, they refused to give their names, which means we have
to be satisfied with initials for all of them, only W. can be interpreted
as Wulff and B. as Bienmüller. P. was Plath and wrote himself Plath
and came from headquarters, the important delegate Plath. They quickly
put him in his place. "In all my life," P. was still saying nineteen years
later, "I've never experienced a Party meeting like that!"

W. The meeting is open. It is resolved: This is not a meeting. Regarding the agenda it is unanimously agreed: There is no agenda. This takes care of the function of recording secretary. I ask that the election of the recording secretary be approved. Now bugger off.

P. The Party regrets the erroneous directive of August of this year.

S. Do we have a chairman? We have no chairman. Permission to speak can only be given by the chairman.

H. You've got us into a fine mess, Comrade. If the Soviets now know the name of any one of us, we've got you to thank for it.

P. Who's been found out?

L. None of your goddamn business.

P. The Party admits that the attempt to capture secret spheres of influence in the Communist Party has failed. Comrades who applied for membership in the Communist Party have been called upon to form their own local of the Socialist Party. That was wrong, I'm not ashamed to admit it, I'll say it again!

K. Say it again, Mr. Comrade. Like in school!

P. Among comrades there's no Mister. Who're you anyway?

L. None of your goddamn business.

P. We must bend every effort to create a strong organization of our own Party as a counterweight.

W. We're not in Krakow here. In March '33 the Communist comrades in Krakow sent all their papers to the Regional Crime Department. That's where the Soviets probably found them.

P. That is irrelevant.

L. None of your goddamn business.

S. They don't know a thing about us. We didn't send any parcels to the Nazis or any to the Soviets.

H. But there's one man they do know. That's your stupidity, you nitwit. That's your fault.

P. Is it you, Comrade?

H. You can call me Mister.

P. Needless to say, the Party will do everything to cover up for that comrade.

K. Permit me to ask: Have you anything to cover him with?

S. Right, he can run away by himself. For that he doesn't need the help of any gutless Party shit. That'll make us one less.

P. How many are there of you anyway?

L. I move that it's none of his goddamn business.

W. Since we have no meeting, no agenda, and no procedure, there's no way of proposing a motion. The motion is passed.

P. The most important thing, in case of a union with the Communist Party, is to create enough leverage within the Unity Party. If it should ever come to that.

S. If the Party in the British Zone unites with the Communists, you're free to come back.

P. There must be no weakening of the Party. Your case is different. You've still got to found a local section!

H. Register it, you mean. Inform on ourselves, that's what you mean.

P. Well, do you have a local station? Do you represent it?

L. None of your goddamn business.

H. That's what you'd like, to have something to report.

P. Boys, I've worked my way across from Ludwigslust to Gneez. Everywhere local sections of the Socialist Party are at work. We're kept informed of everything going on in the administrations, from the regional level right down to the districts!

S. Then those fellows can have a nice chat with the Communist comrades about us being Social Fascists. All about that alliance with the Nazis. What happened to Social Democrats who emigrated to Soviet Russia?

K. Are we about to have the privilege of receiving an explanatory word from headquarters?

P. Perhaps you won't have to unite at all. In that case, all the more reason for you to be there!

A. It's only the Soviets anyway who want the Unity Party. We can forget about that.

P. Boys, you just don't know what's going on in the world.

B. If you call us boys just once more. If you use that word just once more.

P. You haven't the slightest idea! Oh, how the Communists lost ground in Austria on November 25! And what do the Social Democrats look like now! In the Soviet Zone of Austria! 4 seats for them, 76 for us!

K. Next thing, you'll be comparing the successes of the Social Democrats in the Hungarian communal elections with the defeat of the Communists.

P. That's right—I almost forgot! That's how you're going to look, too!

A. Go ahead and help out the Soviets!

P. Only an independent German Socialist Party in the western zone will be in a position to support you.

B. How come Cresspahl ever got that way? To have such a high opinion of you?

L. None of his goddamn business! None of his goddamn business!

W. The minutes have been read and approved. We will now proceed to the vote. For. Against. Abstentions.

H. We're going to hold you responsible each time someone's cover gets blown. Whether it's in the next half hour or the next year.

S. You wanted something to report, didn't you? How'll that do?

W. Resolved that there be no minutes. The meeting is adjourned. There has been no meeting.

"What d'you have today that you're not going to tell me about, Gesine?"

"A death. Stop?"

"You're completely emptying out your Jerichow. Soon I won't know a soul there."

"Warning was no longer in Jerichow. Because he had helped out on Griem's land, he was allowed to call himself an agricultural worker and participate in the drawing when Gerd Schumann passed bits of paper around in a hat obtained from the Von Zelck manor specially for the occasion. Warning drew ten acres of moderately good land, an hour by wagon from town, almost uncultivated. Not that fall, but next year, he might at a pinch have made a living off it with his wife and their two young sons. But unfortunately his work in the fields had not taught him much more than to obey orders. On his return from the Dreibergen prison he had had to tend the cows owned by the town, a job given him for his wife's sake. He no longer told stories, leaning comfortably on a pitchfork handle, when a cow next to him lowed, no one discussed stories with him any more. He had become hard-working, eager, for fear of another trip to Dreibergen. After the war his wife insisted on their own acreage: he would have done better working under supervision. Christmas 1945 he was picked up by the N. K. V. D., no one paid much attention. He was still under a cloud because of that business with our Lisbeth, so neither his arrest nor his release aroused much comment in town."

"If he gets shot, you're all to blame."

"Peter Wulff took the blame himself. He had wanted to help the browbeaten fellow back on his feet when he took him along to a meeting of former Social Democrats with Erwin Plath; he immediately regretted it, for Warning thanked him effusively for such a show of confidence, for his reinstatement in the Party, he actually spoke of happiness. That's no way to talk. He hadn't meant it that way. He had meant it to be an experiment."

"They needed him as a stopgap."

"Right. But Wulff would have entered him in the rolls again, no, would have agreed to regard him as a comrade, because he behaved quietly at the meeting, sanely, and above all held his tongue. Wulff was no longer alone in his feelings when Warning refused to utter a word about his interrogation by the Soviets, come what might; perhaps the fellow really had firmed up at one spot. Wulff trusted Warning, the more so since Warning had assured him, with a twisted smile and an embarrassingly solemn handshake: 'Nothing'll happen to you fellows.' On New Year's Day Warning went and hanged himself."

"It was a crime to insist on silence from a person like that."

"Warning didn't enlighten the Soviets on the mood of the Jerichow Social Democrats. He even withstood his own family; his wife knew nothing about the arrest beyond the four days it had lasted. He didn't even tell her or write her why he could no longer face life. All she had to go on was the paper in his shirt pocket, a new summons to the Gneez Kommandatura, 'because of a formality.' "

"He hanged himself where the meeting had taken place. So they would believe him."

"Yes. In the brickyard shed."

"If he didn't betray anything, someone must've betrayed him!"

"Yes. In that way he left a legacy. Of his sort."

---

*June 15, 1968   Saturday, South Ferry Day, Public Library Day*

---

You must take a scientific view.

Before the fight starts, the public is given details of the contestants, weight, previous victories, etc.

Prague team:

ČESTMIR CISAŘ, born 1920. Known for his very short haircut and forthright speech. Note: wears glasses. Graduated in philosophy from Charles University in Prague. A clean slate during the Soviet purges! 1956 served as secretary of the regional committee of the Czech Communist Party in Plzeň, 1957 returned to Prague as deputy editor of its *Rudé Právo*, 1961 became editor-in-chief of its monthly journal *Nová Mysl*, known to sports fans as *New Thought*. May 1963 appointed to the Secretariat of the Czech Communist Party, in September already demoted for a tendency toward cultural dialogue and listening to other opinions. In his new post as minister for education and culture, began to remodel the Czech school system while remaining faithful in principle to the Soviet-designed education legislation of 1953, loosened up the curriculum, reduced instruction in Party matters, and did not appoint a monitor to look over the shoulder of every teacher. Too popular both with students and with professors, he received from St. Novotný not the supreme punishment but the post of ambassador to Romania, in other words, a training in Romanian cultural policy. After Novotný's resignation, summoned to the Secretariat of the Central Committee, put in charge of education, science, and culture, mentioned as possible new president of the Republic, recently entrusted with delicate missions on behalf of the Party chairman, for instance: persuading the press to deal gently with the Soviet brothers. Stated occupation: journalist and philosopher.

Moscow team:

FYODOR VASSILYEVICH KONSTANTINOV, in the opposite corner. Born 1901. Since 1952 in leading positions of the Communist Party of the Soviet Union. Author of the textbook *Historical Materialism*. Was permitted to celebrate the second anniversary of Stalin's death with an article on "J. V. Stalin and the problems of Communist Structure" on the inside page of *Pravda*, known to sports fans as *Truth*. Author of the sentence: "The productive forces continue to develop even under conditions of imperialism" (*Voprossy Filosofiy*, 2/1955). Since December 1955 head of the Department of Agitation and Propaganda in the Central Committee of the Communist Party of the Soviet Union. Since 1962 director of the Institute for Philosophy at the Academy of Sciences of the U. S. S. R. Stated occupation: Professor. Philosopher.

Cisař enters the first round with an address at a public meeting in Prague. The occasion is the 150th anniversary of the birth of Karl Marx; in it Cisař casually remarks that Leninism was a monopolistic interpretation of Marx's views. That was on May 5.

Konstantinov, in the best of form, quick of wit and nimble on his feet, had already countered by June 14 with massive blows, to be lifted from *Truth* as follows:

This puts Cisař into the ranks of a Menshevik like Yuli Osipovich Martov (Tsederbaum), 1873–1923, Russian socialist, co-founder of *Izkra*. Tsederbaum.

Among the contemporary revisionists it has become fashionable to interpret Marxism, Marxist philosophy, Marxist political economy, and scientific Communism differently, in a non-Leninist manner.

With the industrial and economic successes of the Soviet Union, Leninism has become the banner of the world's Communist movement.

Revisionist exponents of reform seek to discredit Leninism and demagogically preach a "rebirth" of Marxism without Leninism.

Communists have always considered, and still consider, Leninism as not a purely Russian but, rather, an international Marxist doctrine. And this is the reason that Marxist parties of all countries have originated and developed its basis.

Turn your eyes to the finish, but don't neglect the timing!

For where, during this fight, are the First Secretary of the Czech Communist Party and his prime minister? They are staying in Budapest, negotiating a twenty-year friendship pact. What else do they say? They declare the immense importance of their alliance with the Soviet Union.

Referee to the telephone!

Where, on the other hand, one might well ask, are the delegates to the Czech National Assembly? They, with their President Smrkovský, are staying as guests of the head of the Soviet Communists, Leonid Brezhnev, and though they may all be carrying *Truth* with Mr. Konstantinov in their jacket pockets, the Soviet News Agency is only allowed to report a "warm and friendly talk" and express confidence that the visit "will help further strengthen the fraternal friendship and cooperation between our countries."

Does Fyodor Vassilyevich Konstantinov have any option other than to lose? Than for his trainer to throw in the towel? On points?

They too must look at it scientifically.

## June 16, 1968   Sunday, Father's Day

The third Sunday in June, set aside in honor of fathers.
Because someone is a father.

Endowed by Nature with standard equipment, they look upon
Their exception as a merit.
Proud of their procreative ability.
If there is any guilt, it wasn't theirs.

Children are a necessity.
So that a father can send himself, even if only a part
of himself, on into the future.
Which they need neither know nor fear.
They want to be there.

That's how much fathers love themselves.
Nor shall their property lie around on the earth, they see
to it that they can supervise it.

A name is to remain, a rank, a right to power.
Whatever, a legacy.

Hoping to be looked after in their old age.
Frightened of being alone.
To die observed.

A child, a pawn of marriage.
See the Civil Code.
An object, a child.
For playing, for playing with.
Paternal authority.

Duties of a father.
See the Civil Code.
Searching around in the victims, whether they are truly
represented in them. To be like them.
They want to be the measure, whether filled or broken: the
character is to be theirs.
The children are to be better off than the fathers.
What the fathers do toward this betterment.

If children want nothing?
Not the place of consciousness that knows its end to be
the goal, not even themselves?

In Europe fathers stagger along with one foot in the gutter,
wearing paper hats, tooting, yelling, beer in their throats,
in their own honor.
Father's Day.
Among them boys who have not yet got a girl with child,
they'll get around to it someday.
In honor of the father.
Nature's wisdom.
Continuation of the human race.

Fathers know why.

---

*June 17, 1968  Monday*

---

The United States wants to release some Czechoslovak money. No,
not the gold to the value of $20 million that belongs to that country

and that the Americans wish to be applied as compensation for property nationalized in 1938. The amount in question is only $5 million owing to some 10,000 citizens from Social Security and railway and military pensions, earned while living in the United States. It belongs to them, but their new government has first to put in writing that the sums will actually get into the hands of the recipients at a reasonable rate of exchange. "We are not thieves" is what the Czech Communists are required to say.

Once again a Soviet poet has expressed his feelings, Voznesensky by name. He does this not for the sixty-six-year-old doctor who was shot to death and robbed while making a house call Friday night in Brooklyn but on the occasion of a less common death:

Wild swans. Wild swans. Wild swans.

Northward. Northward. Northward.

Kennedy . . . Kennedy . . . ;

he laments the loneliness of the roots of apple trees on Kennedy's balcony on the thirtieth floor, resorting, in the opinion of the New York *Times*, to poetic license as well as suffering a lapse in memory. Mrs. Kennedy lives on the fifteenth floor; moreover, he is struck by the resemblance of the dead Senator to Sergei Yesenin.

"You're right, a week has passed," says Marie. "Could you leave me in peace a while longer with that name?"

"Vesógelike. I'm sorry, I mean."

"You wanted to test me. Right. I'd have done the same."

"In the IRT, remember, the ventilators are mounted in pairs. Now they've removed one from each pair. It makes you start sweating, as if your whole body were cr—"

"Gesine, I'm silly, I know. It'll heal. One day it'll be all gone."

"If only you'd have a good cry!"

"You also hold it against me that I got over Martin Luther King's death in a few days. But you see, I didn't know that much about him."

"What was it like the day before yesterday on the South Ferry? The first trip all on your own?"

"Smooth gray water. I wanted to punish you. I succeeded."

"Yes. No. You had to make a start there one day without help."

"Gesine, is it because of my Mecklenburg blood that I can't manage a reconciliation by will power alone?"

"Let's wait a bit longer."

"O.K. Now tell me something that won't concern me in any way."

"Louise Papenbrock?"

"She doesn't concern me in any way."

"Do we do it with trap or without?"

"Without."

"Your great-grandmother didn't feel really comfortable in her new political importance. Sometimes she had actually to support herself by defying her unruly son-in-law Cresspahl, who had advised others as well as herself against all this parliament business. Flying in the face of this didn't turn out quite right, that didn't help her much when trying to fall asleep. For the first time in her life she was registered with a political party, she suspected tricks in its goings on, she felt above asking questions. How she would have loved to follow Pastor Brüshaver in everything! And it was precisely from him that she had to endure vexation, enough to make her shudder in private. She had joined this Christian Democratic Union, the C. D. U., for Papenbrock's sake, following an imaginary order, she had merely wanted to keep a place warm for him in it. But Papenbrock, so it seemed to her more or less, had kept business and politics strictly apart, at the office and certainly at the dinner table, whereas she had brought politics into the home!

"Pontiy's unit had gone off in disgrace, she had got rid of Draan's parties (she had not regarded Second Lieutenant Vassarion as a political figure); secretly she tried to reinstate the big parlor as part of the Papenbrock property and may have earned a few square yards of floor by spending four days on her knees in it, scrubbing. It seemed to her that the room would be easy to hide, unsuitable as it was for housing refugees; moreover, the current Kommandatura did not insist on entertainment with dancing. Oh how sour she could look when obliged to pretend to a good heart, to eagerness to make sacrifices! Her smile often slipped off her face when she had to open up the double doors again so soon for her friends from the Union; not only they, but children too had known about this noble salon, the three-foot-high oak paneling surmounted by the Von Lassewitz fauns and nymphs, the raised stucco hunting scenes, the deep recess at the end consisting entirely of plate-glass doors, everything suffused with the green light from the garden. (One child had wondered why the grownups used a room like this only for special occasions.)

"Although there were very few meetings of the Jerichow Union, almost each occasion grated on Louise's *amour-propre*. There was that Klupsch woman sitting up front, that old biddy, presiding over the meeting; Louise begrudged her not the work but the place, she would have liked to bang on the table herself. In her own house. That Klupsch woman had more fat on her than her bones wanted to carry, yet it reminded Louise of her own stoutness in the midst of all the emaciated, shabby figures around her. How many people realize that a person can get fat on grief! The Klupsch woman was then entitled to read out the newspaper, the *Neue Zeit*; sometimes a copy would contrive to find its long way from Schwerin to Jerichow. The Klupsch woman was entitled to decide who should speak when. Kägebein, her employee, then had something to say about the temporary allocation of town land as garden allotments for refugees, and he had never asked her permission. Then Mrs. Maass, to the satisfaction of her husband, referred to the injustices in the expropriation of large land holdings; Louise had also felt that some compensation was called for, now she could only nod. She had meant to indicate that she was not to be overlooked, so her signature got onto the telegram in which the local section of the Christian Democratic Union of Jerichow advised Colonel Tulpanov at the end of December 1945 that it was not up to him to replace the chairman of their Party according to his whim. Now the attention of one Colonel Tulpanov, of the Soviet Military Administration in Berlin, was drawn to one Louise Papenbrock and to the fact that she had been troublesome. As for Brüshaver, she could not lean on him at all; he just sat there and, what was more, in the front row, like a guest. He spoke too, of course, but about German faults, about honest improvement. Louise was inclined to forgive him, he had had to come up with such thoughts in the Nazi camp; but how come she kept feeling he was referring to her? Would he dare do such a thing? It was the same when he stood in the pulpit preaching about virtues like friendship and that they didn't count unless they were transformed into qualities. Did he mean . . . Louise's reserve in her relations with the Von Haases? He couldn't know about that. He had no right to say that to her. Many times she would have liked to call out to all seventeen persons present at the Party meeting: What about me? What do I get out of it? Are you going to pay me rent?"

"Was there someone taking notes again when Brüshaver spoke?"

"Not in church. In Papenbrock's parlor, yes."

"Then their power was restricted to talking."

"So for talking they were given the room the Communist Party could not fill. In the group that met at Krasemann's, at the Rifle Club, it was regarded even more as a game of hide-and-seek with the Soviets. For it was not only Duvenspeck (German Liberal Democratic Party) who expressed his conviction that in Liberalism the freedom of each individual was compatible with the freedom of every other individual, hence had to be restricted by it. When one Sunday in October the Communist Party had people rounded up to burn down the estate manors 'which were a disgrace to the countryside,' although that certainly applied more accurately to the laborers' cottages, Stoffregen the local historian, just released from working on the dismantlement of the railways, gave a subtle lecture on the influence of Italian and English architecture on secular buildings in Mecklenburg, 'which last Sunday we were allowed to see for the last time'; in the minutes there was merely a reference to the urgency of the potato harvest."

"Whereupon Stoffregen was arrested. Oh, Gesine."

"No. Stoffregen made a name for himself through this, that's the way they wanted it. People like Duvenspeck, on the other hand, and Bergie Quade, though as housewife or civil servant they claimed to have been hitherto nonpolitical, were needed for jobs on the Anti-Fascist Women's Committee, or as administrative advisers, and perhaps it made them feel more important when they could apply for a permit not merely as individuals but could start with: As a representative and member of the Christian Democratic Union . . ."

"What could they apply for?"

"Whatever they liked. The removal of Fritz Schenk from his post as mayor, the construction of a power line to Jerichow . . ."

"But what did they get? What were their limits?"

"I can tell you one of them. They had got together as private associations, they were appointed, not elected, to public office, but they did have one mandate that had been imposed upon them by everybody, there was no getting out of that. It was to increase living quarters. An imperative mandate, you might call it. After all, you're Mina Köpcke, six days a week you've been chasing around after your workers, Sunday morning has gone on bills and bookkeeping and taxes, now you're sitting after supper on the sofa, Duvenspeck is there too, in his shirt sleeves, you wouldn't mind taking off your blouse, well, unbuttoning it at the neck anyway, Duvenspeck is a bit tight, that suits him quite nicely, now fill my glass up, right up, Eduard, cheers Edi— and at that moment the oldest child of the refugee family comes into the room, as arranged, mind you, stands by the stove to warm the pillows for her brothers and sisters, a ten-year-old like that sees more than you think, the kids will lose all their respect for you just because they can't find a place to live, the Liberal Democratic Party herewith proposes that the lot of the displaced persons be improved and requests the Soviet Kommandantura to allocate living quarters from the reserves of the occupying power at Jerichow North airfield."

"That was the limit."

"Yes. Their idea was to pull a fast one on Pontiy's successor, surely he could see the empty buildings for the former civilian employees at the airfield, all those broken windows. They promised to have the living quarters restored by the honest craftsmen of Jerichow. They proved to him: for only one company of guard personnel an airfield like that is too big. If not a single plane flies out of there, the strategic value must be—shall we say: Nil. Doesn't that make sense, Commandant?"

"What kind of a commandant was he?"

"I never knew that one, never even saw him. In Jerichow he was known as 'Seatwarmer' because after three weeks he moved on. But I know his answer, I can imagine his despair at these mad, crazy Germans, buzzing around in a fellow's brain like bumblebees, without the slightest idea of territorial tactics, so close to the border with the British, they're the people who're supposed to have almost defeated us? It was a brief answer, given with the last remnant of patience, I can also detect an imploring note rising on the last word to rage. Now guess."

"The commandant regrets . . ."

"No."

"The Red Army refuses to brook any interference in matters which . . ."

"No."

"Get out."

"No."

"There is no such airfield."

"There—is—no—such—airfield!"

---

### June 18, 1968   Tuesday

Brezhnev had tears in his eyes. In the two-hour conversation with the Czechoslovak parliamentary delegation on Friday, things turned out differently from the way Professor Konstantinov would have liked and the Soviet News Agency knew. It is true that a representative of the People's Party, an outfit with Catholic inclinations, reported on the conversation, but he is a member of the Czechoslovak National Front; it is true that he talked about it to that tiresome *Lidova Demokracie*, but anybody in Prague could buy that issue. Brezhnev denies that his country is trying to intervene in Czechoslovakia's democratization. He is disappointed at much of what the unleashed press there is spreading among the population, the Soviet Union's feelings are hurt; it does not intend to intervene. Leonid Ilyich is prepared to justify himself before any international tribunal! He also concedes that mistakes have been made, even if he omits to say what mistakes. Leonid Ilyich, First Chairman of the Communist Party of the Soviet Union, wept.

---

"Socialism was intended for you, Gesine. They made no secret of that, right from the start."

"Socialism was intended. But not a prepackaged one. The Germans were supposed to make their own."

"What's German, Gesine?"

"The German brand of Socialism was to be something special. To a large extent specific. In February 1936 the Communist Anton Ackermann wrote to the Germans: Individually, the

outstanding features

of the historical development

of our people,

its political and national characteristics,

the special traits

of its economy

and its culture

will find exceptionally vigorous expression."

"What were those German characteristics supposed to be? The way the judges dress? How many doors a bus has? What color is used for military uniforms? Blue for the Navy?"

"A German military setup was prohibited. Weapons, buildings, literature. Nothing doing."

"Maybe that you were supposed to do it in German. Not in Russian."

"Yes. But imagine how people like Stoffregen, as local historian, went to work drawing up lists of things German! What was German about the state, German about the people—"

"Gesine, when are you going to show me one person who enjoyed it. Who was in the driver's seat. Who did it of his own free will. A person like that. Who knew what was going on. Who was happy about it. You must know someone."

"I do know someone. Imagine yourself to be twenty-three years old—"

"By all means, Gesine. By all means."

"—in the summer of 1946, you're the district councilor for Gneez, you've gone over to the Communists not for the sake of a bit of bread but from the Eastern Front, you're the founder of almost every third local section in the Gneez area, you're allowed to carry a weapon, you speak to the Russians in their own language, à la Moscow, you have a room in the City of Hamburg Hotel, not with breakfast, mind you, but in winter Alma Witte is obliged to heat it for you—"

"His name's Gerd Schumann."

"So that's what you're called now, that's the name you've been given, you've even got used to it, it lacks a few hollow places where you can fit in smoothly, where you feel it to be individual, where it can belong to no one else. You mustn't change it now, for the time being you're to keep it, you've spent too long going around the villages with it, people wouldn't recognize you; but who has the forms for a different name, is permitted to stamp them and sign them? You do. You don't bother to exert this power, you wield enough as it is."

"He has everything he wants."

"You're one of the very first, the Soviets took you along in the Initiative Group North, you weren't with Comrade Sobottka on May 6 in Stettin, you were still studying administration in Stargard, but you were there in Waren on the River Müritz when the Sobottka group elected itself as the regional Party leadership for Mecklenburg and Western Pomerania, you haven't missed the bus, you've proved your worth. You owe nothing to anybody, you worked for it: it is also to your credit that by now no one is without shelter in Mecklenburg, although the population has doubled, 52 per cent are displaced persons from the east, they now have a roof over their heads, you've put them to work, they can now feed the occupying power, the friends, they have enough to eat themselves, you yourself receive bread for your labors. Where at one time 2,500 estate owners exploited the soil, you have helped to settle nearly 6,500 new farmers, it was your Party that saw to it that 36 large bridges weren't left in ruins but were repaired, the canals are open again, except for the lock at Bolter; among your achievements are 539 trucks in running order, 243 tractors, 437 automobiles, 281 motorcycles, a section of railway, 11 scheduled bus lines . . . all this has been got rolling by your Party. That's what you have wrought. Those are your worries."

"He can't have any others, Gesine."

"Oh yes you can. You can have worries about the Party. The Red Army sends you to Mecklenburg, a little knowledge of the local dialect would have helped. You have no idea what people may be saying to each other, possibly right to your face. In a rural area you would have preferred to know the acreage needed to feed a farmer's family of four, how much milk a cow can actually yield, that the locals still measure the land in rods. It was the same sort of thing with the other comrades in the Initiative Group North, they came from Silesia, Bavaria, the Ruhr, they were miners, mechanics, some of them had known nothing but the Party from the inside. One had been waiting in Sweden. In Sweden! The Party came to your aid, it sent you along the coast from village to village, soon people weren't laughing at you any more, you even proved to them that 12½ acres can be enough to feed a family, not the 37½ set by the Party line back in 1932; let's hope the other comrades got along equally well. You know the reasons for it. The German émigrés living in the Soviet Union could only produce cadres, and not even enough of them, and certainly no technical or agricultural experts; take what you can get. Those whom the Nazis did not kill off in their prisons and camps are broken, sick, exhausted people; you must make do with them too. You have to talk them out of the silly ideas they've dreamed up, away from the Party. They come to you with demands for Socialism by violence, for total expropriation, for large-scale agricultural production, you mustn't spoil anything, they have to find out for themselves that we can't entrust the administration of Socialist estates to the same managers who served the agrarian capitalists. One of them, a camp inmate since 1939, argues that after the brown strait-jacket he doesn't want to put on a red one, you explain the special German method. They demand from the Party the unrestricted seizure of power by the working class, you gently point out to him that Socialism can only be made with the existing human material, with the farmers, the lower and middle classes, and certainly with the working class in the lead; that's precisely why the Red Army has removed the major estate owners, the major military leaders, the major banks, and major industry. Sent them away. Others fail to understand why Mecklenburg is to lose its proletarian centers in Rostock and Wismar through Russian dismantling; and it's you who have to tell them that the workers built war planes at the Heinkel and Arado works, warships and rocket components at Neptun, flying boats at Dornier, you raise the question of restitution first in moral, then in political terms. When they ask you to intervene in arrests by the Soviets, you can only silently shake your head and indicate that, where security is concerned, the Soviet friends can trust only themselves, and justifiably so. Someone else has understood about the dismantling but not about the Rasno-Export or Techno-Export stores where the Soviets are buying up gold, gems, porcelain, paintings, the last remaining possessions right down to wedding rings, in exchange for cigarettes at the precise black-market price; you ask him who might own such things, would he? When they ask you about the years from 1935 to 1938 in the Soviet Union, about émigrés who never came back, for a few moments you're too young; then you ask about the harvest. You have your own load to carry. You have to tolerate, you have no option, a mayor of Gneez of whom you know, from a prisoner's statement, that during the Nazi time he persuaded comrades to defect, that is, to volunteer for the Wehrmacht; with his tobacco store he survived, they call him Senator, that Social Democrat. And as if that were not enough, you must for the time being admit members of the bourgeoisie to the administration, the only requirement being that at least they were not in the Nazi Party, that they had been locked up for refusing to give the Hitler salute; only too often it is more important that they have some knowledge of business. The President of the Mecklenburg–Western Pomerania Regional Bank is Dr. Wiebering, a bourgeois anti-Fascist; mind you, the Vice-President is Forgbert, a Communist, he has yet to learn the banking business. Will he? As for yourself, you're floating a bit; although each procedure crosses your desk, you sign the permit, a copy of each decree is filed, what did your deputy, Dr. Heinrich Grimm, do after being thrown out of his job as district councilor by the Nazis? He claims to have behaved decently. What does that mean? Who is this Elise Bock through whose hands and typewriter pass almost all your files, who does she associate with, why won't she join the Party? Yet you would rather trust her than all those people who now come running to you with their applications for membership, talking about their good will, giving the special German road to Socialism as their reason, they don't have the faintest idea about the Party, somewhere in this district of Gneez you have to find an empty building in which you can train them, quiz them, prepare them for the Party, you're not allowed to refuse them membership. You're not homesick for Mannheim, the Allies having smashed the place to bits anyway. Except that down there in Baden people wouldn't look at you so oddly just because of the way you speak. There's plenty to do for the Communist Party down there too by the Neckar. Your place is where the Party sends you. You could think of a better one."

"Don't try to tell me he's sorry for himself, Gesine."

"You're twenty-three! You want things to be perfect. You want the Party to be pure. Now you're faced with nothing but confusion. Muddle. Piddly details."

"That I can understand. It's like in a Russian film we saw the other day. Where the Red Army soldier loses his Party book. For him that was worse than . . . if you woke up tomorrow in a hotel room in Mongolia and found you'd lost your passport. I can understand him, I think. And if he can't cope with the Mecklenburg dialect right away, let him stay with Russian. With the friends."

"That's what they were called. It's all right for you to call them that."

"To dance at the Dom Offitzerov! Kind of a privilege."

"You haven't got time for that! You arrive at the office, you're intent on getting rid of the ten-day-old pile of reports and stuff, when Triple Y phones you. Mr. Schumann, he says. The night before last they had been almost on a first-name basis. He may have forgotten. What else does he say? Asks whether you've been to the station. Have you been to the station, Mr. Schumann? Finish. End of conversation. You're driven to the station, your pistol in your coat pocket, there's bound to be a ruckus going on there. What you actually find is a freight train full of displaced persons, deportees, from Pomerania, from Poland, they're sick, infested, now the town is faced with typhus again. These few hundred can infect 40,000. It takes three days of your time to have the dead buried, to turn the Barracks of the People's Solidarity into a hospital, to commandeer the doctors for night duty; your Social Democratic mayor stays away another few days on his official visit to Schwerin. Does Triple Y ever come to inspect, to intimidate the stretcher-bearers a bit? On the contrary, the railway station and the surrounding streets have been declared Off Limits for the Red Army. What does Yenudkidze say on the fourth day? Good boy, he says. You don't lose faith in him, you don't mentally equate yourself with him; you wish he were friendlier in telling you certain things, not so condescending. You realize that there's no way of avoiding the union with these Social Democratic jokers. Tactical reasons are reasons. This business of the People's Front has to be. You report to Triple Y on the trouble with the bourgeois parties; you do it humorously, with amusing details, you don't complain. You manage to convince the new farmers to trust in their property, you remind them of Count von Gröbern, who described to the Prussian Diet the three oxen he needed in his fields, two to pull the plow and one to drive it; at last the people believe that you want to bring them justice. In Wehrlich they invited you to the celebration after the drawing, you danced there. A woman hugged you, not out of gratitude, a spontaneous expression of her happiness. It made you blush, the men helped you out of your embarrassment by slapping you on the back, and for a whole afternoon you weren't an outsider. Then the Soviet Military Administration sends you people from its own Central Agricultural Administration, well-fed, well-dressed gentlemen, one wearing pince-nez, and at a public meeting, a licensed meeting, they demonstrate that in terms of climate and soil quality Mecklenburg is the best area for the cultivation and propagation of seed potatoes, sufficient for the needs of half Germany, if only, of course, 1,500,000 acres of estate land remain in large, undivided sections. This demolishes three weeks of propaganda and persuasion. The people no longer believe you. They ask each other whether they are really working the land for themselves. This is the fix the Red Army has got you into with its People's Front, Model 1936. Suddenly you see that the bourgeoisie was merely allowed to talk, the land is distributed, will remain distributed.

With a bit of patience you puzzle out the kind of supercunning variation being played before your eyes; you mentally apologize to Triple Y for everything, almost everything."

"He was having fun with the bourgeoisie."

"You can only laugh at the bourgeoisie. They play hide-and-seek with you, and you with them. They think they're so smart when, after someone has moved away or died, they manage to fill the job of tenants' spokesman with one of their own people, you turn him around, then warn him, and finally reward him, and hey presto the Party finds out all it needs to know about what's going on in a building, or at least no less than before. In the elections for block monitors, the bourgeoisie gets nowhere. You fail to understand any comparison of such jobs with the building wardens of the Nazis, you weren't here in those days, that's all in the past; on the other hand, you can ask who else is to collect the fees for the ration cards. They imagine their meetings are secret; you laugh yourself sick over local historian Stoffregen, who enumerates the things that are Mecklenburgish in the new administration and thus could lead to sovereignty for the region, later to union with Denmark. In Rostock a Dr. Kaltenborn appears who tries to prevent the dismantling of the Ernst Heinkel works by proving that the British do not regard Heinkel as a war criminal. In Bützow, where an oxygen factory that has been dismantled in Peenemünde is being rebuilt, the former owners turn up from the western zone and offer their services, provided you don't bother them with a second dismantling: after a while all you can do is shake your head at the ingenuity of such people, who don't even find out where they are. Let them think you've been Russified, that you're a babe in the wood of German culture; one day even you notice how often the Party slogans appear, nicely centered, on house walls, you put a stop to such childishness, not angered, with your sudden burst of laughter that stretches your ribs, they like that. The day will come when they will like you."

"The one thing he can't accept. Slata?"

"Well, after all, you're twenty-three—"

"Then I don't want to be that. She goes steady with a German, he defects to the Soviets. Maybe both at the same time."

"If Triple Y didn't mind, why should you?"

"It's not wholesome."

"Slata may have told a wholesome story. She hadn't run away with the British. She had waited for her own people. How do I know?"

"Right. How do you?"

"You have to suffer insult as well as injury. In your own Party there is talk that you would have taken Slata if he had brought you

Triple Y. You know what they call it, careerism. They don't think of you the way you do. But that's what matters to you."

"You can't know that."

"He had a photo hanging on his wall. It showed Triple Y, Yen-udkidze's adjutant, his political adviser, and, standing behind those three, a young woman, blonde, sporty, the only one not smiling."

"She shouldn't have shown it to you, that Alma Witte."

"She did it to show me he was brave. So I wouldn't make any silly remarks when he walked past us. She too wanted to educate me. She wanted me to realize that someone like that can know unhappiness just like any ordinary person."

"That's why he stayed on at the City of Hamburg Hotel."

"Almost under Slata's room."

"But he had power?"

"No district council of Gneez ever had so much power at his disposal. It grew every week with the notion held by others that he had all of it. It gave him a kick."

---

## June 19, 1968   Wednesday

This morning the blind beggar on Lexington Avenue (my days are darker than your nights) has set down a yellow pail for his dog containing clear fresh water. By evening the edges of the pail are soiled, and the water is full of grit. Extra-smart passersby have tossed their coin donations into the water.

In the main concourse of Grand Central Station, as part of the vast welter of sound made up of footsteps and jumbled voices, there is a lesser sound, much more familiar, growing inordinately in the passages leading to the shuttle. It comes from a man who is removing the subway tokens from the turnstiles. The tokens rattle against the gray metal, the pail scrapes along the ground as the man walks on. A squat, wide-mouthed pail, like the ones we used for watering the horses.

In the evening a thunderstorm hangs suspended above the river. The flashes of lightning make silhouettes of the park, sometimes they light up only the far shore, with stabs of colored white. Some, the very brief ones, hardly perceptible, etch sharp grooves in the brain.

As children, sheltering from a thunderstorm in a grain stook, we used to think: Someone can see us. Someone can see all of us.

## June 20, 1968   Thursday

Wakened by a flat cracking in the park, similar to shots. People standing at the bus stop across the street are unalarmed. Behind them children are playing war.

Our newsstand at 96th Street is covered up. No papers, on account of death in the family. The old man really should have made clear whether he himself was the deceased. The weekly stock in trade, too, is covered with a much-weathered plastic sheet. Customers keep coming up, are taken aback, as a rule stop just a few steps away from those stacks which look like grave mounds and make off on a curve of embarrassment. Nobody tries to steal anything. Whoever may still be harboring remnants of sleep expects the hand-lettered cardboard to read: Closed out of respect for . . . whom?

In the subway underpass a boy in a skullcap is walking past a whisky poster; someone has painted Fuck the Jew Pigs across it in neat cursive script, twice for good measure. The boy carries his head as if he hadn't noticed it. One New York *Times* left at Grand Central. Weather partly sunny, partly cool. Put on record: a picture of Heinz Adolf Beckerle, former German minister to Bulgaria, indicted for complicity in the deportation of 11,000 Jews to the extermination camp of Treblinka in 1943. Because he suffers from sciatica, he is lying on a stretcher, clothed in a middle-class outfit between pillow and blankets; two Frankfurt policemen carefully carry him up the stairs to the courtroom. Frankfurt on the Main.

Sometimes one manages one's ultimate awakening at the water fountain that faces the passage to the Graybar Building. Two gentlemen happen to be hanging out there today; they take turns bending over, raising their heads high like chickens, trying to numb their alcoholic pangs.

The beggar at the doorway has a red pail for his dog today.

Some thirty people can testify to the fact that Mrs. Cresspahl entered her office at 8:55 and left it no earlier than 4:05!

This deferred lunch break taken at a quarter past four had been the one and only slot that Boccaletti, the hair stylist, had been able to find in that whole week for an appointment for his Mrs. Cresspahl. Seated in the waiting room were the other regulars, among them the two ladies who take pleasure in addressing each other with tender solicitude, each content in the shared certainty that the other is, after all, a good deal worse off than she. There were signs of this as far back as our escape, you remember, at Marseilles? Mrs. Cresspahl would have liked to hear more of this German, but Signor Boccaletti calls her over with greater urgency than usual. He isn't trying to gain time for the customer next in line; he wants to complain about the long way to Bari, where things work differently. He flings two hands full of lather into the air; only then can he exclaim: "Signora, uccidere per due dollari? Ma!"

(Giorgio Boccaletti, Madison Avenue, is requested to communicate by the agony column of the *Times*—discretion guaranteed—the lowest amount that would make it worth while.)

Delays on the West Side express track. The P. A. speaker promises, in a growl that turns gruffer with each repetition, that the dawdling local will stop at all express stations; there is no way to fit a human being to that distorted voice, and how could a local help stopping at those places anyway! As for actually getting aboard, it took the third train to do it, and that had too little air for breathing.

For ten minutes I stood in front of a poster exhorting the public to Support Our Servicemen. Underneath there was an SOS in Morse code, below that a photograph showing a white soldier administering plasma to a black one. At the left, under a red cross: Help Us Help. According to Amanda Williams's reliable sources, the secret significance of this poster is: The Americans are in a state of extreme crisis in Vietnam.

A little later two black women performed an almost simultaneous movement around their vertical axes, moving their neighbors along with them, so that I could stand averted from the poster.

On Broadway, a black man, drunk perhaps, tottered into a delicatessen and saluted the owner with a word not in my vocabulary. "If you don't like to hear that, why don't you just get lost!" he shouts. He staggers on between the glass cases and makes an inflammatory speech, but that has moved well beyond anybody's comprehension. The proprietor, slightly crouched, his hands on the cash-register stand, watches the enemy from under his brows, with no anger.

At home, Marie has flowers. There had been a dozen peonies to begin with, for six dollars. "A Puerto Rican woman with her small child, nine years old, was there; the girl wanted the same kind of flowers; her mother repeated again and again, 'But they don't last, child!' So I waited for the girl at the door and let her have six of them. Do you approve, Gesine? Talk to me!"

"Approve, Marie. Why flowers in the first place?"

"It's Karsch's birthday today, that's why. Do they take out your memory too in the bank, or what? It's Karsch's birthday!"

## June 22, 1968 Saturday

In České Budějovice there was a bishop who had spent sixteen years out of office, suspended from his diocese—that is, under house arrest. Last Sunday he was allowed to celebrate mass again in his cathedral of St. Nicholas, in the presence of three representatives of the secular authorities, who conducted themselves with extreme courtesy. The very next Tuesday the police telephoned him about a man who had lost a large sum while counting money at an open window of a train compartment. Would he mind if the guardians of the law were to bring the unfortunate man over for a while in order to receive from the bishop the kind of solace not available in a police station?

A request of this sort from the state power that had him deported in March 1951 (then too by a detail of three men) the Bishop of Budweis in Bohemia accounts a most heartening portent for his future in the C. S. S. R.

The second autumn after the war, Cresspahl's daughter had stopped bidding Pastor Brüshaver the time of day. She eschewed even the effort of pretending to have failed to notice the man of the cloth. She did see him all right; who could overlook him? He wasn't lean from last year's hunger—the Nazi camps seemed instead to have remodeled his whole body to a frame of small-boned frugality; the trousers and coats of 1937 flapped to his cautious, almost stiff movements. For the time being Gesine did not choose to be ostentatious about her refusal to greet Brüshaver; she actually let on that she recognized him, as one passes by something familiar that is of no further use. Just as Brüshaver formerly used to get on without pride or severity, so now he tried nodding for a while—he first, he the elder! Then he fell back on simply looking at the child, without reproach, without a puzzled expression, which merely enabled her to top it all by denying acquaintance outright in such an exchange of glances.

Jakob as a rule soon noticed when Cresspahl's daughter had a bee in her bonnet; but he didn't really manage to talk the bee out of it. Jakob was not satisfied with himself as head of the family.

The household had shrunk; three souls was all he had been able to report to the census, adding Cresspahl, Heinrich, in the column headed "Resident but absent." The N. K. V. D.'s Sunday job in September had had its effect, and even more the rumor that tried to trace all tracks back to the mayor who had been taken away. By late September all refugees had moved out, even the teacher from Marienwerder, who preferred to rough it with two other families far off in

the Wehrlich forester's lodge, and to look after her little son herself as
well, rather than spend any more time in the vicinity of such dangerous
enemies of Soviet power. The Housing Office did not make up for
these departures; even the new batch of Sudeten-German resettlers was
told in time by the refugees already assimilated in Jerichow to beware
of the lone house on the brickyard path, opposite the Kommandantura,
the site of countless house searches, a dead loss for future prospects.
Left to themselves as though in a haunted house, Gesine lived in her
little den, Mrs. Abs in Cresspahl's big room, Jakob on the other side
of the hallway. In the back part they used only the kitchen and, on
occasion, one of the pantries to put up Mr. Krijgerstam or business
people who were like family. Only in the evenings did this amount to
a household: at breakfast Mrs. Abs prepared lunch for the two others,
then the door was locked until everyone got home from work or school,
with no one in charge. After that you could sometimes see light at the
place where Cresspahl used to do his writing; that was the child doing
her homework. Mrs. Abs carded sheep's wool, and Jakob, on evenings
without overtime or business appointments, watched the two others
stealthily over the edge of his Russian dictionary, head of the household,
dissatisfied with himself.

His mother had handed over to him both the official status of
administrator and the external management even before Cresspahl's
disappearance, as soon as he had declined to join the land lottery. No
matter how much he had disappointed her, the farm property was in
any case to have been his. She did not want any further discussion of
the point; even attempts at explanation or extenuation were too much
for her. Her cooking job in the hospital kitchen left her just barely
enough strength to see to supper and a modicum of cleanliness. It had
been his decision to stay behind, with a child virtually without parents,
in a house that wasn't theirs, in the Mecklenburg countryside, with no
more than a few square feet of garden of their own; let him administer
it. He was old enough to do it. Let him take the responsibility. Moreover, she was preoccupied with waiting for her husband. She talked
neither of Abs nor of Cresspahl as of vengeful judges expected to return
and show him up for his bad stewardship. For his part, he thought of
her as resigned, though not content. That other person's child, this
Gesine Cresspahl, was inscrutable to him. She had shaken hands with
Brüshaver at the grave of Amalie Creutz. Just because their function
there was that of assistant mourners? Dutifully she had accompanied
her father to the first service held by Brüshaver after the war; it was
only the fourth time she had been in St. Peter's since her christening—
same as Cresspahl. What made her stop? She was only thirteen years

old; what could a child like that know about the good or harm in the Protestant community?

For that matter, he saw her make distinctions. It might be contempt that she showed for individual adults. It might be that she wanted to make a point. When for instance she returned by the same train as Dr. Kliefoth, they would have shared the same compartment and walked on side by side past the end of Station Street, as far as the corner of the market square; they didn't have to talk, the old man and the child; they obviously belonged together. Allies. From former times? Jakob wouldn't know. This Kliefoth was a university graduate like Brüshaver, a person to be shown respect. For him she dropped almost a sort of curtsey; Brüshaver she left behind like an empty shop window. There was one person, Louise Papenbrock, her true natural grandmother; rather than meet her she would cross to the other sidewalk. This might well derive from habits formed in her father's time, inscrutable as always. But Heinz Wollenberg was allowed to stop her. Just because she rode to school with his Lise? With Peter Wulff she stopped on her own; with him she had talks. Jakob was permitted to see this with his own eyes; she talked about it. Usually it was about news of Cresspahl. At such times Jakob kept his mouth shut and his eyes on the Cyrillic column in his little book; he had doubts of the man's return. (In his opinion Cresspahl was dead.) If she needed comfort, she could go and get it from the person whose office it was. To him she wouldn't give the time of day.

The latest thing the inscrutable Cresspahl child had got up to was black marketeering. Johnny Schlegel had been able to unload another two bags of wheat flour when the wagon returned from the town weighing station, all aboveboard and in good faith, even though Kägebein at the Papenbrock granary might have to charge some additional shrinkage loss to the Red Army. Or to himself. Or to nobody. Whatever might have happened to those two bags in the bookkeeping way, Jakob was thinking, in reality they had stood in the back pantry for some two days or so. Out of the blue, this Gesine forbade the bartering of the wheat. Because half of it belonged to Hanna? Her share would be forwarded. No. Because Gesine was the only one entitled to make decisions about her property? He was perfectly willing to consult with her. She told him what he could do with his counseling; she would not have this sale. He figured out for her that she had 6,000 marks sitting in those two bags—but perishable ones. Here were eight tons of coal briquets. This could get her a winter coat—sewing thread, lining, a dependable tailoring job—and a fortune left over. He knew somebody who would part with a pair of winter boots in her size—

used, to be sure—for 560 marks, with a 10 per cent discount if traded against wheat flour. This was on an evening in the winter of 1946, when he was expounding to her the proper commercial utilization of her harvest's yield; the stove was already stoked with coal from butter (four pounds per hundredweight); the lamp was already burning the oil he had laid in for the winter (a dozen and a quarter eggs). He displayed little zeal in going through these figures, for that type of transaction would cost him a good deal of time, not to mention the distances; however, he would gladly make this his contribution toward paying tangible rent for this house. He was even confident he hadn't used a didactic tone—he certainly hoped so; all of a sudden this child jumped up—you try to make her out—clutched her notebooks as if they were about to be torn from her by force, ran off. Jakob was left with the slamming door and a headshake from his mother, whose veiled derision, however, was aimed at him, and with two exclamations from Gesine that frightened him. It wasn't because of their injustice, only because he didn't comprehend them. Are children like that?

Jakob didn't understand it. Next morning the child apologized. Held her breath while chewing. Asked if he had really meant it. What, accepting her apology? Why, there was nothing to that. No. The business about the plan for the winter. What such a child does at this point is stand facing the window, resist so stubbornly being pulled closer by her pigtails that the older one finally lets go and promises, in a dignified, distinctly reserved manner: As you wish, Gesine.

*Vilami na vode?*
*No, not written on water with a hayfork. As you call it.*

This was on the Sunday preceding the provincial election, so that they had plenty of time to draft the plan by which the wheat was to be converted into supplies sufficient until early next year. For a long time Jakob felt uneasy at these conferences, because of Gesine's tractability. It gave him the feeling that he was cheating her. She approved whatever he wanted to invest in, whether shoe soles, virgin wool, or coal igniter; he would have preferred an occasional protest. He was all the more shocked by her stipulation, the only one he had blindly accepted: not only was the list of commodities to be agreed on between them, but she was to be consulted about every trade route, every partner.

Jakob had learned that the children in both the Jerichow and the Gneez schools engaged in trade with the food-ration stamps that should have been turned in for their school meals. This Gesine, though, wanted to know about every shoemaker he threw out a line for, every stray lawyer who drifted up, even when they had long passed the volume of 200 pounds of wheat flour. She found out too much. She got involved in deals that were dangerous, and not only for a child. This is not the way you have children learn from your example. This is not how one heads a household.

Why did she want it this way—who was to figure that out?

His mother might be right when she felt that this Cresspahl child was in need of religious instruction. Gesine had stubborn convictions on that score, he was by now quite aware of that. How to talk her out of them?

## June 24, 1968   Monday

The outcome of the election for the Mecklenburg Assembly on October 20, 1946 is known. The Socialist Unity Party got 45 seats, the Christian Democrats 31, the Liberals 11; Farmers' Mutual Aid was able to send 3 representatives to Schwerin; not enough votes fell to the lot of the Cultural League for a Democratic Renewal of Germany for it to be represented.

In this new campaign, the campaign director for the district of Gneez had made his rounds with a feeling of uncertainty, perhaps because of his defeat in September. Moreoever, the mood had changed. To be sure, the honor this commission conferred had come his way once again, but this time more than just towns was at stake; his nose dive could be all the steeper. He drove this kind of fear out of his mind, having once recognized it as self-serving. A kindred sensation remained, the moral certainty of something impending that could spoil everything. It sat hunched on his neck, similar to the premonition of a blow. A sudden assault he felt ready to ward off—his record that way was well known—but what would he do in case of a catastrophe? To outward appearance all he showed was fatigue; inside he felt weak. It was not due to the many replays each and every day—the replays were all right; represented truth. What could it be?

On driving into Jerichow he thought he had got a glimpse of it. It was the last day before the election, and it was his first appearance in this windy village that claimed to be a town. It might be a guilty conscience, nagging him for having shirked this Jerichow. Here Slata had lived for three years, in a capitalist merchant's house, destined to be the wife of a murdering Fascist arsonist; he didn't want to see the house, not to mention such putative parents-in-law of Slata's; far be they from his gaze. The man—Papenbrock was his name, wasn't it?— was bound to have been lining his pockets, engaging in interzonal trade under the eyes of the Red Army, cozily protected under its New Economic Policy; he'd take much pleasure in dealing with the fellow when a new page was turned. He resolved to avoid by all means asking about these Papenbrocks. There was, admittedly, a private element in such a resolution; perhaps it was enough for the moment, or until the ballot count was completed, that he not confess such a weakness to anyone but himself.

He stood with his back to the window of Papenbrock's denuded *comptoir*, incognito, for without car, chauffeur, or leather coat he thought himself sufficiently unrecognizable. The woman who squeezed out of the door next to him was Louise Papenbrock, who used to be able to send a maid on such errands. Now she had to walk down Town Street in person to alert the comrades—the Liberals too by the prompting of Christian duty, for they had once again been denied a list of candidates. Even Alfred Bienmüller learned within the hour that a stranger had arrived, car and chauffeur and leather coat parked behind the freight shed.

This evening's lecturer was walking down Town Street at leisure for the time being, like one who was hoping to give himself a treat in a strange environment by some purchase, but didn't have anything definite in mind. Nothing could ever occur here of what he feared in secret. Moreover, the object of his fear was unknown to him, which made the sensation as such unscientific. The Mayor here was of his own party, though the two assistants were Christian Democrats, which meant that the town had not received the full allotments on its ration cards in the last few weeks, to be sure, but certainly almost half of the printed matter. That would certainly help. His friends had also made use of a feature of bourgeois democracy by which a French conservative grants amnesty to political enemies, or a German Social Democrat sends flowers to the daughter of a war criminal, both then assured of rightist votes. Here it was merely the dialectic in reverse: no flowers, arrest instead of amnesty. Gerd Schumann, for instance, had become weary of Ottje Stoffregen's acid comments. So Ottje, this very day, was unbolting rails on the track from Gneez to Herrnburg and carrying them off with his delicate teacher's hands for dispatch to the Soviet Union. Nor did they economize on paper; almost every shop window, every yard gate sported a poster of adequate size.

As he read the first one, he was sure that his worries had fallen into line and reported themselves ready for action. A damnable hole, this Jerichow. If only he had never set foot here. The handbills invited the public to tonight's political demonstration and bore the signature of Alfred Bienmüller on behalf of the German Socialist Unity Party,

the S. E. D. The text began with a personal description: Gerd Schumann, member of the German Army, after desertion to the Red Army
admitted to the National Committee for a Free Germany, twenty-three
years old, district councilor. There were countless handbills, all exactly
alike. At the brickyard he turned around, and there he found Town
Street's name for the first time, on a sign by the cemetery wall. It was
certainly the main street, but it did not bear the name of Generalissimo
Iosif Vissarionovich Stalin. It was an old-fashioned sign in black letters,
the words white on blue, so complete and appetizing, as if it had spent
years wrapped in wool in a drawer.

The speaker of the evening hurried back to the market square. It
was still called Market Square.

That's where they had placed him, right there. The location permitted an almost complete view of the façade of the railway station
("Everyone in Jerichow has to go to the station some time or other.")
He could make out his chauffeur on the steps. He was flapping his
arms against the cold directly beneath the bedsheet that carried in black
paint the slogan:

FOR IMMEDIATE MERGER WITH THE SOVIET UNION
VOTE FOR THE SOCIALIST UNITY PARTY (S. E. D.)!

It wasn't exactly centered.

He fell out with Bienmüller after the first few sentences. As district
councilor he was accustomed to being asked into the parlor for a bite
to eat or a little drink. As comrade Socialist campaign director, he took
it for granted that people would agree with him. This Bienmüller carried
his muddy workshop yard with him. A heavy truck crank dangled from
his left hand as though it were weightless, he kept his felt hat on so
that very little of his face showed, and there, hard to believe, he was
bending down to his work again.

"That business at the station—that's provocation! That's worse
than at Gneez, where they sent out postcards with such things as
'Eggheads, Vote for the S. E. D.! Come, come, Latin scholars!' "

"Well, well."

"And you claim to be a comrade!"

"Isn't it what you want, laddie? Don't ye look to t'Soviet Union?"

"I demand that we look into this with the commandant!"

"We haven't but one. We have two."

"That's where you'll explain your posters, friend."

"Nah, they won't let me go there wid the Djeep. Orders from
occupation forces, that be."

"You, Comrade, aren't going to be mayor here for long!"

"Nah, that's for sure. I be the third as 'tis."

The speaker of the evening, on his hurried march to the Kommandatura, was brought up short once more by the sign in Peter Wulff's window. He was vaguely acquainted with this name. He had once had his file card pulled from the records of the old Social Democratic Party, the S. P. D., in Gneez. Member until the banning of the Party in 1933; courier services, illegal actions (volunteered), arrested during Mussolini's visit to Mecklenburg (Bützow-Dreibergen); 1939–1940 at Sachsenhausen concentration camp, declared unworthy of military service; not yet a member of the S. E. D. (united). Sloppy record keeping, probably. He was a man close to sixty, tall but bent, as though he had been a stevedore carrying heavy loads, dirty white in the face, still fair-haired. In the half-light of the hallway he looked merely massive, soft, but outside, to one's surprise, he proved forceful, much more aggressive than Bienmüller. Peter Wulff had in fact immediately taken a spade from a hook and gone into the yard to dig. (He who digs and keeps digging hasn't a hand free for striking a blow.)

"Morning, Comrade."

"Red Front's what we're saying."

"Red Front, Comrade."

"Not your comrade."

"But you are a member of the Socialist Party, surely!"

"Been."

"Your name is in the card file. All you have to do is vote for the merger."

"That must I give a thought to."

"Yes, why don't we take counsel together!"

"Nah. Bring me Cresspahl is all."

"What on earth is that?"

"Our mayor."

"Is Bienmüller not approved of? Is he to be withdrawn?"

"Cresspahl is who we'd wanted. Now you've got him. Bring him. Questions ye can ask in commandant his office."

"That's what I'll have to do, Mr. Wulff."

"Or go to that Slata; she knows it too."

The district councilor must have announced himself at the Kommandatura with a little too much urgency, being the district councilor, and possibly might not have been quite polite enough when the gentlemen did not care to receive him. It might have been wiser politically, when all was said and done, to conduct the dialogue on the administrative level, as suggested by the comrades of Wenndennych, who had all sorts of low-level complaints concerning the provisioning of their bailiwick with food, fuel, building materials. The district councilor, a friend of Triple Y, may have taken the wrong tone in the course of berating subordinates for the mistakes in their political work among the Jerichow people. This in no way justified their having his pistol taken away from him. His memory retained that moment as a pantomime sequence; while he had been distracted by the Jerichow guessing game—which of the twins had the political and which the military say-so—an orderly had spun him, with a dreamlike regularity, on his own axis, unraveling him first of belt, then of holster, then of the artillery. They gave him the army decree about the possession of weapons by German civilians to read, in German, while he kept pleading that he, after all, knew the Russian language, perfectly, spoken and written too! They had him conducted to the brickyard path, with the firm assurance that the request to prosecute would be transmitted to the Soviet Military Administration in Russian, in any case, but only on Monday because of the election.

Later he seemed to remember trying to find accommodation in a house diagonally across from the Kommandantura, which stood curiously aloof, making him feel that it was at a great distance from this town. All he wanted was three hours of quiet before the start of the rally. He could not face people again so soon. But this was denied him by a child, a girl, at most thirteen years old. She kept answering him in two sentences, now joined together, now separate, in Low German or upon request in the standard language: "It's no good."

"How come?"

"Droeben sunt de Russen."

"What's that got to do with it?"

"It's no good. Over there are the Russians."

Finally he gave her up as feeble-minded, a phantom. That's the kind of thing one is apt to imagine in moments of emotional stress. There are such illusions.

By six o'clock the market square was crowded. Next to him on the town hall balcony stood Mayor Bienmüller, and they were framed by the Wenndennych Twins. The rally began late by half an hour because the people in charge insisted upon a listing of his key points, dated and signed in the presence of witnesses. How are you supposed to make a speech under such conditions? Timidly he began with the harvest, industrialization; he was still far from his accustomed élan, that swelling of the chest from inside, as he made mention of the Bolshevik Leonid Borisovich Krasin, the expert on explosives and bank robberies under the tsars, the representative of the young Soviet Russia in London and Paris, who had had time before his death, while in command of an icebreaker in 1929, to free an icebound German railway ferry from Warnemünde. Then he put to use the two weapons the Party had bestowed upon him to avoid a recurrence of such an embarrassing result as that of September. The market square was rather quiet when he repeated the slogan from the election manifesto of October 7: Our Party stands for the protection of property acquired by the workers' own labor.

Then came the gimmick that experience had taught him was sure to draw applause. For the production of it he saw in good time to the proper marshaling of intonation, pause, and volume; those words coming directly from Berlin, from the very mouth of the German Communist Party—the statement about stout resistance to the Soviet Foreign Minister and his recognition of the Oder-Neisse Line: Our stand must be determined by *German* interests. *Russian* foreign policy is conducted by Molotov.

"Need we say more," cried the speaker of the evening; "our Party conducts a *German* policy!"

At that point one of the twins had to take his arm. It had escaped his notice that beneath him on the market square some people were crying. Someone had fallen down too.

The conclusion of the rally was supplied by Alfred Bienmüller, as mayor and local chairman of the Socialist Unity Party. The guest speaker, as an emissary of the district, did not understand everything; his mental confusion persisted. Moreover, Bienmüller, with his brand of High German grammar, slipped easily into Low German cadences.

"You had a good laugh at me," said Bienmüller. "We told you, we did, that a humane great power like the Soviet Union don't ruin people just for territorial gain, dint we? Seems to me, seeing that even the Swede dint . . . sure thing, Mr. Duvenspeck! Laughed at us, you did. Wouldn' believe us, you wouldn'. Now you've heard it, you drivelspouts. You also remember who you heard it from! Now let's see that it won't be the only happy thing in store for our refugees that they are allowed to go home again; let's give them a little help for a happy time. Seeing we haven't helped them with another job. You shut your trap, you, will you? 'Nother thing needs saying. There are rumors going around here. We know who brings them into the world, too, and *we* are to pay the alimony. That's not right. They say that if too few Socialist Unity votes are collected in a town, the people get less on the coupons, less coal and less of all that isn't there. As truly as I have all this written here on a piece of paper, as truly as I am now going to tear that paper to bits before your eyes, so truly is that untrue! That's not what we want to be elected for! Look at us—go ahead and look, and then vote! That have I now said by the Party's mouth, that I say as mayor. Quiet! I will allow no . . . The meeting stands adjourned."

This is how the district councilor of Gneez lost his election. In the whole of Mecklenburg his Party received 125,583 votes less than at the rehearsal in September. He would have liked to blame this on Bienmüller's concluding speech but had to refrain for scientific reasons. For lo and behold, in the town of Jerichow his Party received a percentage of votes equaled only by two or three other Mecklenburg communities: over 70 percent.

His revolver was not returned to him. That stood for a loss, after all, which feeling could take hold of. Still, it fell short of the real thing. What had he been afraid of—answer me that?

These days when a leading member of the Czechoslovak Communist Party finds an anonymous letter in his mail that reviles him as a Jew and threatens "numbered days," how does his Party paper, the *Rudé Právo*, react? It prints the letter in its entirety, and he is allowed to reply to it just as openly. What is he allowed to answer? That such anonymous letter writers reveal their own character by taking the tone of 1952. What was 1952 about? he asks. That was when Rudolf Slánský was executed in the name of the people. We learned about that in school.

## June 25, 1968   Tuesday

The elections to the Mecklenburg Diet of October 20, 1946 produced three results.

1. During the night of October 21–22 the Red Army emerged from behind its fence and paid visits in Gneez. It parked large trucks so quietly in various parts of the town that the ensuing events went virtually unnoticed. Where the patrols entered a house or flat, they pulled out complete families. To reproach them with cruelty would be inappropriate, since the soldiers were helpful to the evacuees in the packing of luggage and carried any object desired, from a kerosene lamp to an oak sideboard, down the stairs and were careful in loading them into the trucks. This happened repeatedly in some houses, and not at all on many streets. Toward morning, when eyewitness accounts in the town were exchanged and the resettlers had long been traveling in passenger trains toward the new eastern border, the supposition was voiced that the town had sampled yet another whiff of the Soviet Russian national character, a new example of impulsive, even arbitrary action. This version must be contradicted. A comparison of the elim-

inated addresses showed that, though widely scattered through the town, they all had two things in common: the deportees had all possessed residence rights for at least five years, and thus they had the status of citizens and by no means that of refugees or resettled persons; second, the male heads of households had without exception worked in the Arado factory, at Gneez Bridge.

The Arado factory had been in a special category of war industries because, for one thing, it had been producing rocket parts for the Peenemünde testing installation. The other matter, its manufacture of prototype parts for the AR-234 jet bomber, that great hulk sporting four B. M. W. jet engines—we'll keep that under our hats. Any conclusion to the effect that the dismantling of the plant and the rounding up of the labor force followed logically from the rules of war must be rejected as rash. The idea could not have been to render a moral service to Great Britain, damaged as she had been by rockets from Peenemünde. After all, the victorious Allies had each reserved its own zone of oc-cupation for dismantling and confiscating industries by way of repa-rations, and the British—this should be emphasized—had during their provisional administration of West Mecklenburg confiscated construc-tion blueprints of the Arado factory as war booty for their own use. Further: this gang of capitalist hijackers had not shrunk from encour-aging members of the factory's staff with scientific training to join them when they were forced to exchange their Mecklenburg territory for the British Sector of Berlin.

Moreover, no dismantling work went on at Gneez Bridge the night of October 21–22, for under decree No. 3 of the Soviet Military Admin-istration of June 25, 1945, the machinery, assembly lines, cooling facilities, etc., of the local Arado factory had been dismantled and removed to the Soviet Union on July 5, right after the Red Army's entry into Gneez. In this context, the public cannot be warned enough against warmed-up horror stories to the effect that in the courtyard of the Gneez post office hayforks had been used to heave telephones onto army transport, and other work descriptions of the kind. The disman-tling of Gneez Arado took place under the surveillance of a university teacher and engineering graduate, attached, with the rank of colonel, to the Soviet rocket troops, that is, with the utmost care. A proof of this is the method of stock-taking: after the written entry each machine was photographed three times: once at rest, then being operated by its trained worker, and finally in rear view, again with the worker attending it, who had to appear in the picture from the tip of his feet to his hair part. In this connection one should recall that the carpenters of the town had worked up their entire stock into custom-made boxes and had received orders to spend two days making wood shavings, not as waste but as the chief product.

The Arado management in Gneez had been stripped of authority in early August. People with bourgeois interests bring up as a counterargument that the remaining workmen did not abandon the plant but produced primitive tools from waste material and in September started to supply the population with rakes, spades, stovepipes, cooking pots, frying pans, metal combs, rulers—or at least carried out repairs of such objects. This calls for a refutation in the sharpest terms— namely, that the origin of the material used in a great many cases could not be established by the People's Police (aluminum sheets for rabbit hutches!); that the plant, situated in a country town as it was, carried out every imaginable kind of blacksmithing except work on horses; that the manager, who had been elected in an illegal and arbitrary way—Dr. Bruchmüller of the Christian Democratic Union— had not been cleared of the suspicion of having made away with what tools and trade goods were left in the Arado factory before the second dismantling last November; that (we're coming to the fourth and fifth points) a large part of the production went to fill private orders; and that the currency circulating under S. M. A.'s auspices was boycotted by the members of the former Arado factory at Gneez Bridge through contracts stipulating payment in kind. Solely on that account, the deportation of former employees might be looked upon as just punishment, and permission for families to move as a unit, as an indulgence, since there can be no question of fact in regard to the above, not to mention disregard of the Fascist capitulation terms. The term Ossawakim, current among the population, is to be fought as hostile propaganda that has seeped in from the western zones of occupation. Whoever allowed the interpretation of this Soviet acronym as "Special Authority in Charge of Dismantling" to leak to the outside should have his head torn off. (Whoever runs at the mouth to the effect that the meaning was quite a different one actually—i.e., Ossoaviachim—

Promotion
of Defense,
Aviation,
and Chemistry
of the U. S. S. R.

should have more torn off than just his head.) Any further inquiries from the Free German Trade Union Council are to be uniformly met by the response that five-year labor contracts have been concluded with all displaced families and that now the Soviet Labor Organization would look after their interests. Copies of such labor contracts would be forwarded upon request. The small scope of the present review of these matters permits us to subject the tactical discernment shown by the Soviet Union and the Red Army to a friendly appraisal.

If our friends had undertaken such a vitally necessary measure during the preparations for the election, the Soviet Occupation Zone would have yielded a result similar to that of the vote counts in Berlin, where the Social Democratic Party under the American and British bayonets is still able to open its mouth wide, and where it received 63 seats out of a mere 120, whereas we could barely scratch together 26. By this time even Comrade Schumann must have seen a great light about why he had been shivering in his boots these last few weeks. Sure—if only! The Red Army, you see, did not invite these Gneez citizens to the Soviet Union during the election campaign, or one day before the election. No, it did so one day after the election. The comrade district councilor can talk so convincingly of a debt of gratitude to the Soviet Union, but when it looms there straight before his eyes, he doesn't recognize it. In sum, since the summons to the election had placed the securing of peace and friendship with the Soviet Union above all else, it is a fact that the former employees of the Arado factory at Gneez Bridge also turned in their ballots and voted as they did.

2. The census of October 1946 sustained a kink. Ossawakim had its impact not merely on people in the town and district of Gneez, but also in other Mecklenburg armament plants of potential or strategic importance, and, further, in the other regions of the Soviet Zone, such as Carl Zeiss and the Jena glassworks, the Siebel aircraft factory in Halle, Henschel in Stassfurt, the A. E. G. factory in Oberspree, the Askania works of Friedrichshafen in Berlin, etc. The census was to determine who was at home the night of October 29–30, and also what profession he claimed for himself. This is how the undertaking failed to register a type of migration that is undetectable by statistical means. Furthermore, the result suggested that for natural reasons fewer specialists in heat-resistant glass or electrical measuring equipment (G. E. M. A., Köpenick) were to be found in the Soviet Occupation Zone than in the zones of the Western Allies. Here one must call upon other sciences than sociology. In the town and district of Gneez, Ossawakim had spread the conviction among the peace-loving population that the Soviet Union (after the lapse of a full year) considered the demilitarization of their Germans concluded, and that the census of professions also proved that Soviet interest in specialists for war was no empty delusion. Local rumor had it that anyone who volunteered for the Red Army as a mercenary in the war against Japan could be sure

of clothing "like new" in quality, firm footwear, and regular meals. In this matter, people's expectations for the future might be summarized in a Low German phrase, which in itself symbolized a dual result. It meant: Just take me where I can register!

3. The Gneez district councilor was kept thirty-six hours in a prison cell in the cellar of the Gneez town hall. The cause was a quarrel that had its inception in the pistol that colleagues of Triple Y had taken from him in Jerichow. In the course of events, Comrade Schumann unexpectedly, and inexplicably even to himself, requested Slata's address (just in order to write to her). Y. Y. Yenudkidze was known as a calm commandant, with no streak of malice, let alone given to impulsive action. He had the young man delivered to such an address. Sixteen years later, in the spring of 1962, the young man of that phase would attempt to explain to a woman that this was the end of his education, the final turning away from private desires, the complete merging of the self in the Party. It would not be a woman he was married to, still, he would mention neither Slata's name nor her whereabouts. He *is* married. It would happen on an evening in the palace gardens at Schwerin, after a concert. He would no longer have the same name. His surname would resemble his father's except for two letters, but for a first name he would be called exactly what his mother wanted. Two days after the election to the diet of 1946, seven days before the result of the census, he was called to Schwerin. There his name was waiting for him. Personnel Division at the level of state administration, Security Department at the level of the Central Ministry. He never returned to Gneez. I have never seen him again.

"But I, if I came along to Prague, I would see him," says Marie. She would see him. I will recognize him.

We've been waiting all day for the black rain that is finally hanging over the Hudson. By noon the air was quite dense with moisture. Perfectly dry people acquired a second skin of perspiration as soon as they left their air-conditioned homes. The upper edges of buildings shimmered. Ten blocks away Lexington Avenue lost its contours; it was a moot point whether after twenty blocks it would have quite melted away. Now, at nine in the evening, the rain from the north has arrived, in the middle of it come two lightning flashes, they stab your eyes, short-circuit something in your brain.

"The rain of New York is something I would miss," says Marie. (Children take rain along on a journey.)

## June 27, 1968   Thursday

In the fall of 1946 the Cresspahl child with a lot of belongings had just about moved from Jerichow to the chief town of the neighborhood, to Gneez. Her residence was Jerichow. That's where she figured in the official lists for purposes of registration and assignment of living quarters; that's where she got her ration cards (Group IV); that's where she had the appointment with her father in case he returned from Soviet arrest or any locality from which a return was conceivable. But Gneez was where she went to school; quite frequently, Traffic Control would combine the noon train to Jerichow with the evening one, and should no coal be available for that one either, she would sleep at Alma Witte's until the next school morning, in the room from which Slata had disappeared. To Jerichow she would come back in the dark, as it were into the dark.

Gneez was a large town. For a child born in Jerichow who has taken an expanded roadside village of a town like Jerichow for the predestined, if not the only possible, kind of world, Gneez is a town of which larger ones are inconceivable.

On the Jerichow-Gneez spur line, twelve rate-book miles long, with four regular stops and one flag stop, the train, scheduled to take forty-one minutes, at that time took about an hour. It was made up of three coaches of that third-class type where the transverse compartments have exit doors alternating between left and right, plus two or three boxcars for delivery to the town of Gneez of the potatoes, beets, or sacks of wheat gathered at Jerichow. These cars as a rule returned empty in the evening, and as soon as the train had passed out of sight of the Soviet control officer at Engine Routing, the People's Police swung out of the open boxcars and came shinning back on the long running boards to the passenger coaches, where they might at least get a little warmer playing skat. Yet in the morning, rain or frost, they sat hunched on the boxcar edges alongside the fruits of the soil, their 98K carbines placed at an angle, implacable enemies of irregulars, thieves, and black marketeers. Had the Gneez District Council been able to supply its need for rolling stock from the coastal area, even this largely single-track line would have been dismantled for the Soviet Union, as second tracks had been everywhere in its occupation zone. As it was, though, this line was in service on a regular three-times-daily schedule, and the Cresspahl child managed to attend high school in Gneez, as mandated by the Educational Reform Act.

The milk train from the coast approaches Gneez in a bulging

westerly curve, which is apt to make the pointed spires of Lübeck appear gathered in a semicircle, as if in a stereopticon viewer. At the Gneez Bridge station, abolished then, the line still aims south-southwest, and the rising sun brushes the windows. At the Gneez station the Jerichow train is aligned almost exactly east-west, and might, with a little marshaling, be dispatched to Hamburg or to Stettin. Now that both cities on this classic line were shut off by borders, the train never got beyond Platform 4. Gneez had four platforms.

They had an open plaza there that took up more space than all of Jerichow's market square; it was lined with buildings just like a market square. On the right you would find the outsize steel gates of the loading ramps; next to them the three red-brick stories of the town hall, which flew the flag of the Red Army; straight ahead the Princes' Mansion, rebuilt to become Knoop's Storage and Moving, crossed hammers on the opaque panes; at the left, along the track going off to Bad Kleinen, bicycle sheds and the bay set back into the sidewalk where the out-of-town buses used to stop and start. In the center of this unbelievable spaciousness they had laid out a veritable park, a square of lawn; now, to be sure, trampled black, with bare trees here and there. Straight through the square, though, a lane made for the great showpiece, cynosure of one's first view, a four-story building of gray stucco, its columns and fluting rising clear to the elegantly rounded hip roof: a palace, the Archduke Hotel, erected c. 1912 to the design of an architect who had believed in a metropolitan future for Gneez. Not only did the building encroach on the Rose Garden with restaurant and a three-story wing of rooms, but it also bulged one and a half times as much into the street in front, its bottom floor expanded to a café picked out by graceful stucco garlands, an almighty gateway to the reception halls, and a more subdued one to the Renaissance Film Theater. Only then, fifty yards down the street, did this colossus yield the frontage to low-story small fry, white-painted middle-class houses with retail stores and bars in their feet.

This was Railway Street, which had borne an Austrian's name for a few years and was now again named after the building to which it led and from which it came. The archducal name still perched on the hotel's roof, in proud black letters fastened to wire gridding, and just as the mansion had formerly deterred small-time salesmen, so these days it was reserved for a superior quality of custom by a red-and-yellow tin sign on the semicircular forward sweep of the registration desk; a sign that to most Germans was illegible, but was conjectured to mean Officers' House, but only for officers literate in Cyrillic.

Such was Station Square in Gneez, extant token of a prosperous rural town's resolve years ago to create an enduring monument, not by a swagger of ostentation, but by modest presentation of what was available. Of more than this the citizenry of the new century was not inclined to boast: the overall soundness of their situation was to be plain to the eye. The square had been the site of political demonstrations since the 1914 War, and it was here that the Red Army had established its civil government.

The square was guarded round about by lanterns; they didn't have to shine—what if their panes were shattered by stones or shot out? Still, they stood loftily in stiffly gesturing pairs, they remained candelabra, black-lacquered ones. In almost every space between them a pole, with the red banner, had been erected, or a lettered sheet rigged up, by which means the Red Army held discourse with the locals in their own language in black letters.

Anyone who found the Dom Offitzerov too grand and unnerving could find a narrow path straight ahead, alongside Knoop's edifice of hereditary proprietorship, and might be genuinely shocked by the difference between the doorless railway frontage of the Princes' Mansion and the grand façade that commanded the southern aspect, with its opulent balcony bays, figures in niches, and a serene sweep of ornamental stairs. There had been a park there once, which had been slowly devoured by an exurban settlement, which had burned down once every century since the fifteenth, until the Social Democratic Party of 1925 projected a medium-income public-housing development there, with lots at reduced cost, subsidized mortgage terms, and a salutary dislike of haste. Hence six of the units were completed only in 1934 and 1935, and hence Gneez-Neustadt was ever after featured in picture books as an example of the flowering of Mecklenburg under National Socialism. This was scarcely a town. It was a field strewn with separate red houses, each by itself in a fenced garden plot, the whole organized into groups of six by frugal asphalt lanes under the patronage of the Honorable Company of Musicians. It did not prove possible to restore the name of Mr. Mendelssohn-Bartholdy on the customary enamel sign, but it did figure on two others, carved in oak. This has been the "new," "good" quarter of town, offered to employees of government, the parties, white-collar workers transferred here, but now thickly settled with refugees, children's homes, and personnel assigned by Soviet authorities. Only when, bearing left after left, one had wandered through this pattern of squares did one find oneself at the tail end of Railway Street, an inconsiderable square that had once comprised the widened city wall, the Lübeck Gate, the guardhouses not mentioned by local chronicler Lisch, and a jocular representation in bronze of the creature to which Gneez owed its nickname. Now, though, all the square had to offer was a bridge over the town moat, a low-lying, almost stagnant watercourse as wide as a man is tall. Here began Old Gneez.

On maps, Old Gneez resembles an early mathematician's attempt to make from odd-angled bits of wood a polygon approaching a circle. The raw disk, articulated by fine veins, was split down the middle by Stalin Street, on which two horse-drawn vehicles could pass each other without moving over, an artery for shopping, strolling, through traffic. Almost everything east of this thoroughfare, down to the Rose Garden, counted as the "old," "good" quarter, collective address of people who could document ancestors in residence there as far back as the French occupation of Prussia, or of refugees, as the case might be. To the west, the side streets might show isolated stuccoed structures to begin with, but they betrayed their nature by decaying half timber at the sides; they stood convicted by the cottages sloping low behind them, the small farming businesses, the craftsmen's yards. These were houses built not just for one family but for parties out for rental income on top of it. Anyone passing through the Danish Hedge quarter could tell by the doors. Factory-made, hardly any carving or legends on the beams. Laborers, you see. They were glad of any place to lay their heads down. So it was, on the west side; what could you do about it, eh? For that matter, there were such crooked walls in the quarter that the odd door was hardly noticed. That's how quite a few houses had escaped pillage. They also had got away more easily in the matter of having refugees billeted in them. But even the Soviet regime had been unable to eradicate the social boundary marking the "decent" quarter: Stalin Street.

Stalin Street, whose former name came from its orientation toward Schwerin, crept toward the market square for a hundred yards to the south, vanished there on the cobblestoned pavement and resumed existence at the opposite corner as Schwerin Street—less grandly, however. There was the Bulls' Corner, Bleachers' Lane, Cooper's Path. That's where the child occasionally visited in a house with a stately entrance and narrow story of living quarters with servants' rooms above it. That's where she sometimes watched Böttcher at his carpentry. She liked to watch that. The Chapel of the Holy Blood stood diagonally across Schwerin Street. This had once been one's way to school.

But the market was unforgettable for a child from Jerichow. It may well have had an area similar to the one at home. But for Jerichow things did not go beyond one market, which could be recognized as the model for the spectacular public square of Gneez by the station. The houses here often showed four rows of windows on top of each other, each of its own dimensions, in separate upward-scalloping façades, behind whose apex there was not mere air but an unquestionable window to an attic room that existed. They so proudly kept at some distance from one another; they left elbow room not by necessity but out of self-respect. There ought to be no dearth of that. The roofs had their backs turned from the market; like hair partings above faces, they are all meant to be different. In the gables hung pullies; in places a solitary gap had been promoted to at least half a wheel with spokes, or coats of arms had been painted there, from interlaced initials to a burning circling sun. (On the south side, a house will turn to the market the broad side of its roof with a mansard finished in masonry; you don't find this on any picture postcard of before 1932.) Here you had the Court and Council Pharmacy. You find houses here that speak of history not only by their worn bricks: in this hall the citizens of the town rendered their contributions to Frederick II's war of 1756–1763; commemorating the French occupation: arson and pillage by the Vegesack Division. Here is where Frederick IV, King of Denmark, spent the night from December 19 to 20 in 1712. On the market square stood the post office, the former palace of the counts of Harkensee, its Doric columns courteously retracted. On the west side a generously proportioned house has its forehead drawn up so high that the roof must keep to the horizontal for a while before it bends down in the back. In the front there are double doors sized to the golden mean of two, three, and five. They are approached from two sides by a staircase leading up to the next floor. This notwithstanding, it stands in a row with others; it does not demand a greater space. That one was once the town hall. The staircase had once been meant to show respect to authority, to the elected first among equals. The cellar underneath was to retain its view of the market. It had been too modest for twentieth-century pretensions. For all their grand ideas they still hadn't been able to get away from the thick-mopped lindens surrounding the market square, keeping close to the line of houses; they had just gone on growing. The candelabra were not going to grow. Station Square might suffice for the modern era as a drawing room, but the market square was Gneez's front parlor now, as ever.

The town did not end there; south of the market there was almost a third of it still to come, the "ducal" quarter, laid out somewhat more spaciously by court architects between the pincers formed by tree-lined avenues following the former fortress walls: police jail, District Council Office, palace theater, cathedral yard, the classical high school (which had been converted into a Soviet army hospital), and the esplanade, probably over a hundred yards long between the public swimming pool and the housing estate Little Berlin on the municipal lake. At the corner of the cathedral yard stood Alma Witte's hotel; that's where the child from Jerichow sometimes spent the night.

Town of Gneez. First mentioned in the tithe register of Ratzeburg in 1235. In 1944, c. 25,000 inhabitants; 1946, just under 38,000. Chief town in the district. Industries: sawmill (Panzenhagen) and canning plant (Möller & Co., a branch of Arado). Remainder: craftsmen's shops; trade insignificant—with one exception. Environment: forest on all but the south side; on the east a ridge of hills 294 feet high, reforested under the gracious sponsorship of Duchess Anne Sophie of Mecklenburg. At that site, the last witch burning, in 1676, hence the sobriquet Smoekbarg (Mt. Smoke). Next to the municipal lake, Warnow Lake, Rexin. Rail connections to Bad Kleinen, Herrnburg, Jerichow.

Ever since the Cresspahl child had been transferred to the Gneez Bridge school, she could have turned right directly from Station Square, walked down Warehouse Street and across the bridge to the school in the Lübeck suburb. If she wanted to learn more about the town of Gneez than her homework required, did it perhaps have to do with the free time she had to fill until the next train was due?

She wasn't a stranger any longer, to the point of taking notice of houses first and people second. She remained a commuter student but in effect had moved to Gneez in many ways.

She would enter the houses. She would talk to the people, on business, and she had a good deal more time to give to this than Jakob had. She inquired of Böttcher the price of a churn; she compared that figure with Arri Kern's ideas on the matter: Böttcher was awarded the business.

In the new good part of town, the station suburb, she had to visit a Russian officer's wife who was Controller of the District Council Office. The German landlords tried to oust at least this particular intruder by offensively inadequate service. Thus they gave Krosinskaya no bed linen and spread it among the neighbors that her kind could hardly have been used to any. Krosinskaya did not have a husband in the barracks on Barbara Street; hers lay six feet deep near Stettin. This meant that she would actually have had to buy sheets and covers. She bought liquor. Once, she took her clothes off in front of the child from Jerichow, down to her silk slip, seemed to push up an invisible weight with both arms, and asked if she was still beautiful. The child put her age at forty, accorded her the attribute she wanted, not at all untruthfully. The only thing was that everything about Krosinskaya was a little too large, too heavy, from legs to bosom. Krosinskaya was a meticulous payer. Her German hosts struck her as funny. They wouldn't give her any furniture—what of it? So she lived in bed. On the bare mattress cover she spread sheets of the army paper; on the daily *Krasnaya Armiya* she spread her supper, sausage and bread and onion separately, ate with a knife. In other ways she was quite fastidious.

Another Soviet family, employed at the railway station, trained their little boy to hate Germans. He would kick over Granny Rehse's mop bucket and treat her in every way like a coarse scullery drudge. Granny Rehse would have liked to show the seven-year-old tenderness; the way it was, she did not understand him. This was the Shakhtev family. They didn't buy liquor, but traded liquor for records. It was to be Beethoven's music, and cheaper than you could get it at Krijgerstam's Razno-Export. They produced the liquor amid querulous protests, berated the German child as a Fascist brat, weren't above threatening denunciation on occasion—all this with pointedly good manners which precluded any kind of intimacy. Mrs. Shakhtev had been a physician in peacetime. Her darling child, Kolya, had been looked after by a nursemaid at home.

The child from Jerichow had to settle down at Gneez. When she moved to the Bridge School on September 1, 1946, the homeroom teacher, Dr. Kramritz, was struck by the signature, Abs, on the old report card. Kramritz had asked only out of curiosity, but she was panicked into the truth. Mrs. Abs was neither her stepmother nor her aunt, nor anybody entitled to sign her report cards. The Cresspahl child had no legal representative.

Late in October she heard about Control Council Directive 63. There were to be "interzonal passports" for travel to the western zones. The frontier was open again. Whatever might be tying Jakob to the Jerichow gasworks and to Cresspahl's house, she didn't know what it was. One day he might go west. Think up a funeral over there, a deal in nails, and the People's Police will give you the travel paper. Mrs. Abs would not stay without him. Cresspahl's child had to wait.

In Gneez you could see what was happening. From one day to the next, Brigitte Wegerecht had stopped coming to school, without an excuse either to Dr. Kramritz or to her friend. Then she sent word from Uelzen (British Zone).

Unexpectedly, rooms turned up empty in Gneez overnight, entire apartments. Leslie Danzmann scattered a fairy boon of room assignments over the refugees. You could find families again who lived all by themselves behind a door of their own. When Dr. Grimm was to take over the District Council Office as senior administrator, upon forceful representations by Krosinskaya, his family took a trip to attend a christening in Hanover, not a surprising thing for so staunchly Lutheran a family. He discussed the work load left behind by Gerd Schumann throughout one lengthy evening over wine in the Dom Offitzerov; next morning it turned out that he had swum across the lake near Ratzeburg. That man knew what he was doing. Brigitte's mother, nee Von Oertzen, might have complied with the last will of her husband or the wish of her brother. Would the Cresspahl child have been justified in blaming Jakob's mother for doing likewise?

Jakob still went visiting often enough at Johnny Schlegel's. He had a love affair there. That Anne-Dorthy was prettier, smarter too, than younger girls such as Gesine. She might be a countess and all that, but here was something that Gesine Cresspahl knew—she wasn't thirteen for nothing: such love relationships are for life. There could be no doubt. If Anne-Dorthy was called to Schleswig-Holstein, Jakob would follow her there too. Then the Cresspahl child would be rid of the custom-sanctioned educational responsibility that the Abs family had lent her.

Children who are alone in the world are taken to a home. There wasn't one in Jerichow. The consolidated home for children was in Gneez.

---

### June 29, 1968  Saturday, South Ferry Day

---

The Rawehns, Elite Apparel for Ladies and Gentlemen, had been conducting their store on the market square of Gneez ever since the days of the French. At one time they had been loosely connected with the famous Ravens of Wismar. Even in the fall of 1946, a winter coat was to be turned out along lines of design deemed fashionable by the House of Rawehn, the more so if the customer was merely a craftsman's child from Jerichow, in charge of an old woman from even farther away, a refugee person. Mrs. Rawehn, a short, buxom woman still under forty, neatly and impregnably done up in her city suit, was far from high and mighty in her conduct toward this Mrs. Abs and her protégée, who promised payment in wheat. She mustn't give offense to well-to-do customers. Moreover, it had been a long time since she had had black worsted cloth of this quality in her hands. It had probably lain in a drawer since 1938, a French drawer, for all one knew; she wouldn't have minded laying in more of this than one and half yards, double width. Not to mention the tartan lining fabric. But how this Gesine Cresspahl looked at her! It was enough to make you look into the mirror! Crouched as she took the measurements, she did look at her reflection, her whole body taut, her dark chestnut hair swept upward and fastened in tight strands in what they called the "All Clear Coiffure," meaning "everybody up out of the shelters." So how she looked could not have been the reason. Likely as not, it was merely that look of defiance, almost, that girls are apt to have at that age.

The girl was thinking of a coat reaching below the knee. At Rawehns' children wore short coats. The girl wanted buttons covered by a placket. She had brought along eight large horn buttons—were those of a size you could hide? The girl wanted a stand-up collar; fashion decreed an Eton collar for children, half covering the shoulders, corners rounded. The girl would have preferred no belt in the back. "But that'll ruin the pleat!" Helene Rawehn cried out. "Everybody will recognize this as our work. What are the people in Gneez to think!"

It did not escape her notice that the thirteen-year-old was now and then looking for support at the face of her companion, who had such a hollow look about the eyes. She received glances that were to console and encourage, but Helene could not discover anything that spoke of expertise in tailoring. For that matter, the old woman hardly spoke at all. Mrs. Rawehn gave in about the belt in the back. She would fasten it with buttons at the side seams; it could be taken off at will. She would turn over the hem by an inch, seeing that the child seemed to want to wear the Soviet style. The coat was supposed to be ample for two years of growth, but Helene did not give an inch in the matter of the visible buttons, the style exhibited in the windows, and the Eton collar; with these, to her, the expertise and honor of the Rawehn (Raven) clan were at stake. Actually the child rarely balked at the fittings (on Sundays after a discreet creeping approach through the side alley and rear door so the Soviet ladies, who were waiting in the salon with the English magazines, might not have their appetites pricked by such cloth, and the truth was that Mrs. Rawehn did not cheat the

child by even a pint of flour, and what's more, she sewed the button-
holes with her own hand. She would have been delighted to put the
finished coat in the window as an advertisement for the firm, provided
these had been peaceful times. She had worries enough of her own,
about the husband who was missing near Kharkov, that Heini, that
skirt-chaser, that love-crazy fellow. Why shouldn't the child too push
out a lip in times like these?

The child was unhappy with the coat. Not because it served the
planned purpose so poorly. Slash pockets, once they tear, need coarse,
obvious seams. Patch pockets you can easily reattach, and it won't
show. She didn't want a coat with a collar named after small boys;
someone might grab her there and by the back belt. She had to move
so much among crowds nowadays, one's buttons seemed to pop all by
themselves; if she'd had a placket, she could have kept them on. She
had planned this coat to be more than just to live in: it had been
destined as a durable shelter for the journey on which the Soviets might
someday take her—as they had called for her father. Now Gesine
Cresspahl owned a black overcoat that had nothing but contemporary
elegance.

Ask Countess Seydlitz; she will want to be knowledgeable in this
case too and prognosticate from the successful marriage of the parents
that their child would come to maturity well ahead of the norm and
develop a sense of identity, of the place where its ego might want to
be rooted, to the point where it is sufficiently aware of itself to let the
world know about it. Marie Luise Kaschnitz, however, has witnessed
and can tell how a child can be injured by a perfect union between
the parents. They make common cause against it, don't let it see
them separately, deny it a choice of disparate avenues to loving. Hold
it fast in the inexorable plight of being, even at thirteen, hardly
more than the child of parents, defined almost exclusively through
them.

Yet the one child as well as the other can run back to the parents
when the world refuses to understand them or hurts them (there is also
Big Brother—"just you look out, he has cleated boots"); they are snug
under parental protection, not at a loss for self-understanding. After
all, the elders only set right what such children cannot yet do for
themselves, it is they who teach them how to stay invulnerable even
when things are out of joint.

The child Gesine Cresspahl had been left by her mother as long
ago as November 1938; she had been betrayed at age four and a
half. Her father, indispensable not only on this account but also as
her ally in the English secret, had conducted the mayor's office at

Jerichow to the displeasure of the Red Army—was it the matter of abortions or insubordination?—at any rate he was in Russian hands now, unreachable, less in charge of the child every day, because he did not see what she saw. In her house lived a woman from the island of Wollin, whom she craved as a mother forever, but she could hardly entreat her: Adopt me! She was helpful, and, more, she accepted help and was happy with the strange child if some afternoon a stove was already lit when she came in. Another thing I learned from her: Now you can have children of your own, Gesine.

There was Jakob Abs, Abs's son; he made her his little sister. Whatever time he didn't need to work he gave to his business affairs. First priority, though, he gave to a girl; she was not too young for him and was a creature whose beauty no dream could dream up; her name was Anne-Dorthy. It wasn't only to see her that he was going away, but away from Jerichow too. He studied his Russian out of a book of railway terms *(zheleznodorozhnykh terminov)*; from the gasworks he was headed for an apprenticeship with the railway, and that railway would carry him away from Gneez to Schwerin and, one of these days, out of Mecklenburg altogether.

Those were the people left to her.

What is such a Gesine Cresspahl to do now, when she is to turn fourteen on March 3, 1947 and cannot rely on a single person in Jerichow and environs? Will fear make her so blind that she will run after people just because they are there, in search of her father's whereabouts? Or it might have been her own fault: she saw herself as alone vis-à-vis the adults; not, to be sure, in open hostility, but still, without any hope of help from them. Why didn't she think of herself as an ego, with wishes, with a future, which had merely to be kept secret for the time being.

The child that I was, Gesine Cresspahl, half-orphaned, at odds with the surviving relatives for the sake of her father's memory; on paper, owner of a farmhouse near the Jerichow cemetery; on her person, a black overcoat: she must have resolved one day to give the adults the necessary worldly due, while smuggling herself away and into a life that would allow her to be the way she wanted to be. If nobody told her, she simply had to find out for herself. Courage is not a great deal of use there.

Strangely enough, school presented itself to her as a path to the outside. Her father had taken her out of the school in Jerichow because the teacher, Stoffregen, was given to hitting; also because she might unwittingly betray him to the Sudeten German Gefeller, Principal of the school and Nazi speaker on the district level. So her father had hidden her in the Gneez Bridge school. From this the child worked it out in her mind that he had seriously advised her to pursue advanced studies. This being so, she had no choice but to put her nose to the grindstone and march forward straight to where school gave out, to that fairyland that was called graduation and permission to make a choice. No, she wasn't exactly courageous; she was afraid. She started on a policy of lying. For entering Grade 7 at the Gneez Bridge school, she had had to turn over not only the transfer papers from Grade 6, but also a curriculum vitae. This was a school under the administration of the Red Army, and her father wasn't on good terms with the Soviet authorities. Or vice versa. That part she couldn't know, but another part she had learned. She put him in her curriculum vitae, describing him as a master carpenter, self-employed; she made light of his share in the construction of Mariengabe air base, fobbing him off with a construction worker's job, had something to say about liberation by the Soviet Union, and pretended that he continued to live, work, and reside in Jerichow.

Whoever might one day examine the official curriculum vitae of this Gesine Cresspahl will be forced to posit several persons of this name. Or possibly a single one who was a different person every year and became a stranger to herself from one day to the next.

Zeal calls attention to itself; she decided in favor of diligence. Just as in the old school she had been able to deal with the poem "John Maynard" by recitation, answers in class, tests, in the new school she now supplied the teaching staff with the desired description of present-day life in Mecklenburg.

To wit: the building of the anti-Fascist democratic constitution. I. Definition: the first word, a modifier to be used only in compounds, expresses opposition. It is here directed against a form of government the symbol of which was the bundled rods of the lictors in ancient Rome; against suppression of the people through the concentration of power in the hands of the few. We don't have this sort of power in Mecklenburg. Democracy, a combination of the Greek words for people and ruling (*dēmos* and *krateīn*), denotes the exercise of power by the people themselves. We see in the district of Gneez how the exploiters and robbers were chased away by the people or were forced to seek housing and jobs at least thirty kilometers from their estates. The people themselves consist of the workers, the peasants, the lower bourgeoisie, the middle bourgeoisie, in this order. (This bit was awkward for her because she had a rather unfortunate ranking, being a craftsman's child.) All this taken together amounted to a constitution.

II. Application: an example of this is offered by the reform of schools.

In Physics she would write upon demand: Aleksandr Stepanovich Popov, Russian physicist, born on March 17, 1859, at Bogoslovsk, in Perm, died on January 13, 1905, in what was then St. Petersburg; in 1895 he invented the telephone. (She believed this, taking no further interest in the origin of the anecdote; up to age sixteen she would think of telephones only in the context of authorities and a few select middle-class families, favorites of the authorities.) Even in her senior-year graduation exams in June 1952, the answer would still have been correct. With no particular purpose—certainly not looking for any-thing—she opened the encyclopedia inherited in 1950 from the Papenbrocks and happened upon the place where Alexander Graham Bell's life is described. Even long after this she wished there were another reason for forgetting the year 1895, for retaining an anticipatory attitude toward Edinburgh in Scotland.

In 1947 she was taking third-year Russian, still with Charlotte Pagels. The subject was the derivation of Mecklenburg words from the common Slavic, the language from which the modern Slavic languages, like Russian, were derived. Fine. At the close of the class, Cresspahl raised her hand, with the shyness for which the child had been noted, and asked for permission to say something about Gneez. Might it not well be derived from the Slavic word for nest—*gnezdo?* How that A rang in the class record book! (This sort of thing hurt her with the other girls in the class, even with Lisa Wollenberg; she had to make up for it, on the strength of the location of her house opposite the Kommandatura of Jerichow, with stories about a Lieutenant Wassergahn. Finally Lisa came to her aid. "Oh yes," she said. "The Cresspahls at one time were practically occupied territory!")

Just no peeking, aside from the curriculum; any such glance could send you into a tailspin:

*Fold little hands,*
*Bend little knee,*
*Meditate on the S. E. D.*
*It can give us more than cabbage and flour:*
*More of what the Chairman and his Deputy devour!*

When a class of schoolgirls is left to itself toward noon, sitting freezing in their overcoats at 50° at most, what crazy song-and-dance routines they can produce, shrieking, vaulting the tables like maenads:

*Eat less sugar?*
*Wrong, wrong, wrong!*
*Eat* more *sugar,*
*Sugar makes you strong!*

Until Fifi Pagels came rushing in, totally unmindful of the black-market prices for sweeteners, merely feeling injured in her dream of well-behaved children of c. 1912, and exclaimed, "You wicked, wicked children!"

In February 1947, in Dr. Kramritz's class, they were studying the new Mecklenburg constitution, which the diet of the previous year's election had adopted. I. Citizenship of the country resides in all its inhabitants of German nationality. The members of the civil service are servants of the people; they must at all times prove themselves worthy of the people's confidence. II. Fundamental Rights and Obligations of Citizens, Article 8. The freedom of the person is inviolable.

*Persons who have been deprived of their freedom*
*Must be informed at the latest on the following day*
*By whose authority and for what reasons*
*The deprivation of freedom has been ordered.*
*Without delay they are to be given the opportunity*
*Of voicing objections against the curtailment of their freedom.*

Dr. Kramritz was the tenant of two rooms in Knoop's Princes' Mansion. When Knoop returned in March from his deprivation of freedom, this was the first thing his sincerely concerned mother had heard from him since February 3. Even to trusted friends Knoop would let out no information about the place of detention or the events that had figured in the missing freedom. What he liked to reply, with an inscrutable smile, in leisurely, unctuous High German, was: The charges were struck down, just like Emil.

*"Would you have gone to England for the Soviets, Cresspahl?"*
*"For you, Gesine, yes. That's what I wanted to ask you as soon as they released me to join you."*
*"That's not far away now. Then I'm going to say the wrong thing again."*
*"Do it for me, Gesine."*

## June 30, 1968 Sunday

The Abses got me into Pastor Brüshaver's preparatory classes for confirmation for only two hours; that was enough for him to show me the door; I had to take dancing lessons, two afternoons a week, at the Sun Hotel behind the District Council Office; this was in springtime 1947, because in the wintertime there would not have been enough fuel or daylight. I would lose the time for homework, get back to Jerichow, disgruntled, on the evening train. But my long face had no effect on either Jakob or his mother; the child had to get what was proper for her. Dancing lessons.

This is what they saw in Jerichow, what Jakob saw in his education course at Gneez: some middle-class avatars and values were to be rescued. To them I was a middle-class child, regardless of my father's disappearance and the fact that one of my uncles was guilty of an unmentionable crime; it almost seemed as though they had taken me on commission to install a high-class education. In Jerichow as well as in the main district town they saw high society unscathed, except for those caught with weapons in the Soviet Union or in the files of the Nazi Party or with titles of landed nobility or with overly lucrative business relations with the former Reich. Or on unsigned slips of paper. The others were left with the belief that they would yet be needed; they themselves were sure of this. Whether one of them traded in shoe heels or weighed the butter ration for the workmen in slivers of twenty grams each, they all felt certain that the supply system for the population would function even worse without them. No one in our school class had said so aloud, but almost from the beginning we thought of ourselves as divided into natives and refugees. The grownups expanded this distinction to long-established gentry versus alien trash; admittedly, this was in part because the decorative wood carvings of the Sudeten Germans and East Prussians hurt their business. Those aliens had had to leave behind almost all their property, whereas when it came to the right people in Jerichow, plundering Soviet man had not nearly managed to find all the articles of gold or oil paintings that at some time of greater distress they might barter at the Razno-Export of the Red Army for cigarettes, which in their turn could be converted into butter or a good-as-new Bleyle tricot suit that was left in the possession of a refugee boy. These members of the upper crust had seldom lost sight of each other; even Gneez was small enough for that. Now they tended to make contact again—in conservative parties, for instance—where they discussed the laissez-faire state or a future merger with a

Scandinavian country. Even Mecklenburg, in its identity as an auton-
omous *Land*, had been left to them by the revolutionary Red Army.
The disturbing addition of "Lower Pomerania" was done away with by
the law of March 1, 1947, so that those people had less of a say from
then on, and that could really be counted as a gain for Mecklenburg.
The Land, or State, of Mecklenburg. In Article I, 1, Paragraph 3, of
the new constitution the state colors were decreed: blue, yellow, and
red. These were the traditional ones—who would fight that?

They showed what they thought of themselves in other ways too.
Johannes Schmidt's heirs in Jerichow would end up letting the Socialist
Unity Party have its loudspeakers for election campaigns without a fee.
Wauwi Schröder did the same for musical and electrical needs, but
this was in Gneez; he had two shop windows—one of them up to
February 1947 displaying a gold-framed sign that proclaimed in dec-
orative writing:

> We take pride in making available without charge
> to the Red Army and the Party allied to it
> our amplifiers to serve the anti-Fascist cause.

There followed an additional reading:

> The microphone unaccounted for since September 19
> we regard as a free token of our good will.

To this add two medium-sized azalea pots. After the next great
rally, which was held in connection with the Moscow meeting of the
Council of Foreign Ministers on April 24, Wauwi disconnected his
microphone along with the remaining cables and replaced the writing
in the shop window with the latest dictum of the ranking functionary,
to the effect that the Socialist Unity Party would continue to oppose
any change of the borders. This section of public opinion gladly advocated the return of the refugees to the territories beyond the Oder
and Neisse Rivers. Anything to be back among themselves.

They found each other in a province they took to be theirs by
birth and tradition: at the cultural events. Accepted table manners,
nuances in forms of address, apparel fitting rank—all this was understood. And how could anyone decry a paint dealer's commercial spirit
if he practically never missed a program of the Cultural Society, even
one devoted to the interpretation of a poem by Friedrich Hölderlin or
the like? The old families of Gneez had collected items of Mecklenburg
culture and lore, not merely the five volumes of Lisch or the *Yearbook*,
but also glass, silhouette art, chests, portraits of dead-and-gone mayors,
and views of the cathedral antedating the inexplicable incident of the

summer of 1659. At one time in the distant past they had nearly collected enough money to give a commission to the experimental sculptor Ernst Barlach; he was to depict in bronze their somewhat embarrassing heraldic beast in as dignified a pose as feasible. Because of Barlach's controversies with the Nazis of Güstrow and Berlin, nothing had come of this in the end. Gneez was not Güstrow. They had placed those of Barlach's books out of favor with the Nazis a little farther back in the display cases. Such poems, for one thing, had been in high fashion in 1928, simply indispensable for one's self-respect; for another, their market value in the future might well be negligible on a short-term basis only.

The Church also "belonged"; religion was assuredly part of established decorum. At the evening organ concerts the cathedral was more tightly jammed than for Church services. Senior Minister Marjahn's sermons were certainly edifying and innocuous, but should he happen to let himself go just a mite on a major holiday, his ears were bound to ring later with the tongue-lashings of dutiful matrons who, aprons tied over their Sunday best, were late pulling their geese out of the stove, or found themselves with a delinquent carp on their hands. In the starvation winter of 1946, these ladies had survived. If Dr. Kliefoth's apartment was cleaned out, then this was his bad luck in the first place. What was more, in 1932 he had elected that one-horse town Jerichow to live in, over the middle-class community of Gneez, which could boast no fewer than two town chronicles spanning the centuries. Still, one would probably have to accept him, with good grace or bad, into the old elite. Ph.D., senior high-school teacher, lieutenant colonel in the Army, oddly respected by the Soviet authorities. But he didn't come forward.

The Cresspahl child, while a commuting student from Jerichow and a ticklish sort to associate with because of her father's arrest, was judged with pleasure to belong to the elite families. This Cresspahl, after all, had been appointed mayor by the British, not the Russians. What a dressy black coat she wore. She knew what she owed to herself, didn't have her tailoring done by refugees, but at Helene Rawehn's on the market square. And just as etiquette demanded at this stage, she attended dancing class.

"Mr. Yenudkidze," they addressed their commandant, even to his face. They weren't going to be found wanting in good manners. He possessed that quality too, unfortunately. Politeness was what they now intended firmly to commit him to.

There were exceptions; they were characterized in terms of the proverb about the traces left on someone by what he has touched. Thus

Leslie Danzmann had a dim future prophesied for her by the Knoops, the Marjahns, the Lindsetters when she went so far as to get involved with the new dignitaries. Leslie Danzmann, old Mecklenburg family, English grandmother, widow of a navy commander, a lady. Arrived toward the middle of the war in the bay area of the district of Gneez, rented one of the most contemporary houses close to the sea, lived absolutely *comme il faut* as lady in charge of the household of a gentleman who had had something to do with the Reich Air Ministry in Berlin. No compromises. Class. Then the people who still played tennis had drawn attention in Gneez; Leslie Danzmann, too, was drafted into the Labor Service, assigned to the Labor Office. Force majeure. After that, did she have to seek out the Russians again and apply for work in their administration? The fact that someone owns nothing except a defunct pension and has never been trained for a respectable job, such as piano teacher or doctor's wife, what kind of an excuse was that? To be sure, she too had spent some little time in custody, in the Cresspahl affair; funny thing that, wasn't it? Had she taken due warning from this, though? No, our fine Danzmann had gone and offered herself to the Russians again. To the children one says: Don't you go too close to that. Now she was in the soup, dismissed from the Housing Office and straight into the fish cannery. She surely might have got the idea that Comrade Director of the Housing Office was inviting her into the Party. Can't she think of any other answer than: But what are the neighbors to think of me, Mr. Jendretzky? As far as the neighbors' opinion was concerned, she wasn't far off the mark; but she up and blurts that out. As if one didn't drill it into the children: Watch your tongue. Now she comes early every workday on foot from the coast, by the milk train to Gneez, stands at a stinking table till evening, cleans flounder, boils fish stew. No, she didn't complain. In that regard she still belonged. What the language of cannery women must be like could easily be imagined by a housewife of some worldly experience. The word they use for the female genitals one knows. But a lady of breeding does not use such language. When a woman, a married one, lies down, on her own, with a man, what goes on then they talk of as . . . They are workingwomen; what do you expect? What a horrid word, by the way. Apropos, if you think of it a mite deeper, by chance it isn't so poorly chosen. That kind of word never crosses my lips, Mrs. Schürenberg! Leslie Danzmann had it coming to her. When a girl has herself raised to middle-class standards and wants to live like that and have things come to her only when she wants them to, then she mustn't go where she can be booted out and into the fish cannery! And did she display any neighborly feeling, this Leslie Danzmann? She was right close to the fish where she worked, after all, couldn't she bring some along now and then, as a little attention? No, she didn't. If she spoke of her work at all, she praised the proletarian women. They were supposed to be so good-natured. Helped her, she claimed. There was one, Wieme Wohl, from the Danish Hedge quarter, notorious all over town, who had more than once said before the handbag inspection: "You, Danzmann, come here, here's an eel for you. Tie it around your belly. If you can't stand that, let me do it for you. It's only for ten minutes, Danzmann! Now don't you be so high and mighty. . . ." Danzmann had remained firm. "It's nothing to do with pride," she said. "It's not mine, you people! It does not belong to me, after all!" The women had talked to her. Leslie in the end was willing to believe that fish, and especially eel, never made it to the retail shops, but went to the controlled outlets of Red Army and Party. She had no problem with that; she could see that. Then she had persisted with her "but it isn't *my* eel." That's what happened to you if you let yourself drop through the meshes of decorum and property rules!

Cresspahl's child did not like to go to dancing class. She did so in obedience to Mrs. Abs.

On those afternoons she was in Gneez with Lise Wollenberg. At the lessons they were the fair one and the dark one from Jerichow to the boys from out of town. The class was taught by Franz Knaak, a member of a Hamburg family which had produced the local dance pedagogues, all but one, since 1847. This one was fat, liked to speak French, the nasals; he was so proud of his mechanical good manners that he managed, with languid brown-eyed gazes, to make light of his comprehensive corporeality. For a start, he taught them old German dances, Kegel, Rhinelander, all with references to the heritage of our fathers, instead of something Russian, say. It took universal and almost vehement pleas for him to stoop to the Schieber, a tangolike shoving motion; he then demonstrated it in such a slimy way that one might conceive a disgust for it for life—or so he hoped. He wore something in the nature of a cutaway suit, shiny at the neck, and holding up the tails with two fingers each, he would embark on the mazurka, for example, with a feeble springiness of step. What a strange monkey, Gesine thought in private. But she noticed clearly enough that Lise, merry long-legged Lise, followed Mr. Knaak's leaps with an oblivious smile; Lise was so informed about everything. "How do you think you'll get a husband if you don't learn to dance!" she had said, and down the long side of the room the mothers were draped on worn plush chairs, Mrs. Wollenberg among them, and dabbed at their eyes. She couldn't see that. That wasn't how she wanted to get a husband. She already knew one; he took another girl dancing.

Her coat was black because she wanted to wear mourning for her father, not, God forbid, because she thought he was probably dead, but in remembrance of him. It was the decent thing. She knew that. But it was a thing that it was unseemly to talk about.

On dancing-school evenings she almost always met Leslie Danzmann on the platform. She greeted her, waited for the train at a great distance from her, never got in the same compartment. Leslie may have imagined a new humiliation for herself, this time from the smell that emanated from her. That wasn't it. The smell was appetizing, if anything. The Cresspahl child meant to punish this Danzmann woman. She had been released, her father hadn't. She hadn't brought her any message from him. She might even have betrayed him.

### July 2, 1968   Tuesday

In Hesse, Federal Republic of Germany, Dr. Fritz Bauer died, attorney general and one of the few in office who from the beginning considered the crimes of the Nazis properly subject to judicial prosecution, and acted upon this opinion. He was particularly after those who held out clean hands in token of innocence, all ink spots washed off, from Eichmann down to the concentration-camp doctors. Without him, there would not have been a prosecution of the Auschwitz case from 1963 to 1965. She had thought up many draft letters to Mr. Bauer, child that I was, but sent none off. All of sixty-four years old, dead.

The Gesine Cresspahl of the Soviet Occupation Zone had started a diary early in 1947.

It wasn't one, properly speaking. (Just as the present one isn't, for other reasons: here a scribe makes an entry in her behalf for every day, commissioned by her and with her permission, but not for the ordinary day.) That one she writes herself; omitting whole weeks, however. It was not born out of a New Year's resolution. To be sure, it was to forfend forgetting, but for the sake of another, not for herself. It hardly looked like a book, more like a flimsy brochure. Jakob's mother would have shied away from touching it; Jakob wouldn't have got past the first line. She knew very well why she had to protect it. It used to lie now between these, now between those pages of Büchner's *Economic Geography of Mecklenburg-Schwerin*. That book is a dissertation, fat enough for a dedication to one's parents, yet slim as brochures are: more than a few slips of paper can hardly be inserted there. The slips contain no dates; thus even a second look might not betray a diary. Few complete sentences were to be seen in that adolescent handwriting, merely words set in successive rows, in the manner of a poorly designed vocabulary list, with much crossed out. One word that was still legible was jagged. Occasionally, she forgot what she had meant to perpetuate. This word is found one more time. It conveyed the recurrent idea that the face of the pupil Cresspahl must surely strike grownups who talked with her like a jagged knife-edge—just because this is what it felt like from inside. But what are we to do with jottings like "Ya kolokolchik" or "Packard? Buick?" They are simply lost. And not only were there Russian words, crossed out or left standing, but also German ones hidden in Cyrillic transcription. That is lost and gone; nobody can catch it any more. It wasn't much of a diary; but it was to be that for Cresspahl. If one writes down something for somebody, surely he must come. If someone is dead, can he read?

"Ya kolokolchik" is not crossed out, so at the time it was nothing private. In that case, "ya" can also mean "I," surely, as writing it in Russian suggests; somebody here thought up a kind of abbreviation. Kolokolchik—what could Jakob have done with a little sleigh bell? Could this be a name for Anne-Dorthy, who still hadn't called him to join her in her Schleswig-Holstein? One would hope not, for in name-calling, of all things, she would not like to enter into a contest with a girl whom Jakob preferred to her. Had this meant herself perhaps, the bell that was too little?

"Rips." An entry for black-market operations, a material, or rips in it? Can't be pains in the ribs; the inescapable daily dealings with Jakob hurt in another place. No. Rips was Bettina Riepschläger, substitute teacher for German at the Gneez Bridge school, little older than the schoolgirls of Grade 7-B, and trusted, two months after her own school certificate and a quick course in education, with humanities courses; a cheerful girl, devoid of any desire for professional dignity. In her class we did anything we felt like, and she did the same. It often looked as though *she* were talking out of turn. The student Cresspahl wanted to prove to her that she had no intention of exploiting a certain shared experience in the vestibule of Alma Witte's hotel; she liked best just to look at her. Bettina had had her thin light hair cut in the tousled fashion. She caught strands a little over a inch in length between her fingers and thus combed them. Blond, experience had taught, was Jakob's color, contrary to darker tones. Today she probably knows that the fashion originated with that film from the Hemingway novel, in which the Spanish rebels had cut a girl's hair off; that Maria, however, is supposed to have been dark brown. It would be better if Jakob remained without knowledge of such a cornflower dress, which fell into all the proper drapings; of such beautifully full-grown legs; of this carefree light voice, which could make the transition from a tone of comradely friendship to a firm one that could announce rejection and yet safety. It could happen that Bettina acted exactly her age, nineteen. "Kinnings," she might say, and then we were children for a while. Lise Wollenberg once cried because she was afraid that Bettina might walk in the schoolyard with someone else; Lise had already begun to place her feet the way that Miss Riepschläger did. She was from Ludwigslust. This teacher very seldom used the contorted expressions of Dr. Kramritz; the anti-Facist–democratic constitution or the leading role of the party of the working class occurred only as though they were self-evident, because they were there. In her class we wrote essays like "My Best Friend." Cresspahl from Jerichow had slid even more deeply by that time into her indissoluble need for privacy, so she didn't care to name any best friend and took refuge with a dog. There was no dog; it was neither the one belonging to the Kommandantura nor Käthe Klupsch's chow chow; she had made him up, from his anatomy to his conduct. She ventured to assert that said Ajax fearlessly kept his place at the edge of the military swimming pool, however much she splashed him in swimming by. For this and many other reasons, he was the student Cresspahl's best friend. By way of a mark, she received the question, in discreet red writing, "A little on the sentimental side, perhaps?" She was greatly pleased. She now considered this Bettina one of the most rational teachers of her whole life, and there was something about her that she wanted to tell Cresspahl. Rips.

Shkola, school. In this regard, the diarist had her reservations, even worries. For there were few teachers like Bettina, who was "off" after school just as the students were. The likes of Dr. Kramritz thought themselves respected, even venerated, merely because it was quiet in their classrooms; but he was hardly talked about. It was an established thing that life in Gneez had little in common with his elucidations of the Mecklenburg constitution. His stiff knee had fallen to his lot in precisely that war which he now described as the nation's guilt, instead of his. It looked wrong, though, when he pressed his wire-framed glasses down harder on the bridge of his nose; he seemed to be arming himself then. His punishments were all permissible under the school rules; he enjoyed his authority. The refugee children were afraid of him. Gesine Cresspahl was repelled by the trace of a scar on his nose. Still, he was able to force the class to recite the desired material. It was different with Miss Pohl, math and geometry. She was one of those teachers who remain "Miss" throughout their career, although she was past fifty and past maidenly grace in any section of her frame. Intensely russet hair, crew-cut; full in the cheeks and chin. Always in that same green huntsman's suit, occasionally with hat to match. We called her bust the *Vorwerk*, or outwork, the term for a tenant farm at the edge of a manor estate. Refugee from Silesia that she was, she didn't know the word. She was angry with the world for its share in Germany's losses; that's what was hidden behind her perennially sullen look. She didn't care. Once a child had failed to master a problem in arithmetic after two explanations, in this lady's book he was simply deficient in mathematical sense, and was given up in this subject; and what if he could not be promoted now because of this E + ? (Gesine Cresspahl achieved recognition from her for an essay about the soil properties and economy of China; this error persisted into the next spring semester.) Mrs. Pohl, Miss Pohl might well have practiced her profession as a chosen vocation in the past; now it was a job for her, the prerequisite for residence permit and ration card. This far she would give full measure, but anything beyond she declined. The student Cresspahl still believed in escape through learning; time seemed to run through her fingers with this kind of instruction, and she often had a sense of things omitted, things missing. What of this she meant to tell Cresspahl at some point came from her memory of his helping her once before, in 1944, with school. In school. Against school.

"Antif." for anti-Fascist, -ism. This item gave Jakob one of his heavier evenings. For Cresspahl's daughter did not come running to him with trifles, certainly not every trifle, even less "running." Admittedly, she was younger than your countess named Anne-Dorthy, but she had long left off being a child. Jakob might well think she was taking from him what he owed her as the man of the house; on the other hand, she wouldn't have known whom to ask those questions she learned in school as answers. She had a hard time with the term anti-Fascism. Hadn't Fascism been something Italian? Jakob had to confront this assignment by a re-education course of his own, like she had had in school. He looked pretty resigned to the task of turning these matters over and over, once again, behind his hard broad forehead. They often sat on the steps in front of Cresspahl's door, with the view of the fenced-in Kommandantura. Neither saw much of the marching guard or the picture of Stalin in the triumphal arch. Like Cresspahl, Jakob was able to switch his eyes to long-distance viewing. Unfailingly, it struck her again that his temples looked so firm and his forehead was joined so seamlessly to the curve of his skull. Why was it that he had his hair cut so high up his head and so short, when a few days later it again looked like a pelt? If one likes a horse's coat, one . . . Also, she couldn't quite come to terms with the slight shift of the folds at the corners of his eyes; it looked so taut, so alive, as if he was aware of all his movements. At that point she realized she hadn't been listening properly. Jakob had long been busy pointing out to her that the Nazis with their "National Socialism" had seized a term from the socialists, possibly two; that a prefix like "anti" must by no means, for that reason, be used in the vicinity of Socialism, and that there was no reason why she should not adopt "anti-Nazism," provided she thought she'd be understood. "Yes . . . no," said the Cresspahl child. Conversations have a way of ending so incredibly abruptly. She thought it was an ugly word. "A turdy word for a turdy thing," said Jakob. She gave up then. She had known the whole time that he'd soon get up anyway, stretch comfortably above her, and dismiss her from his great height, smiling, solicitous, like an adult to a child. "Forget that Bettina, nih," he said, halfway into Mecklenburgish, and soon he had passed under the walnut trees and was on his way to town. That, she resented; that, she would put down in her diary. Under Antif.?

---

## July 2, 1968   Tuesday

"One-legged, bicycle." She had seen a man who could manage a bicycle with one leg.

"A. in Gneez." She had been unable to give up that child. Alexandra returned in her dreams and was alive (and bearing no resemblance to a certain Hanna Ohlerich, who had slept side by side with her for weeks, after all, in a fever they shared). Alexandra in a foreign country, her hair in a scarf, so that two bright arcs stood out over her forehead, said in Ukrainian: "Here, Gesine. Hold this young man for a minute." And didn't Gesine find she had Fat Eberhardt Paepcke in her arms; nor was he dead, only sleeping and dreaming like she was. (At Gneez a freight train had passed through in March full of people from Pomerania who had been kicked out by the Poles. Gesine had made it to their stop with half an hour in hand, dashed from car to car and pestered the tired, dirty people on the straw with questions about the Paepckes from Podejuch. Exactly as in the dream, she knew that they had died two years ago last April; as in the dream, she couldn't afford to lose time and ran to the next sliding door, confused by shame, by hope, almost crying, her speech much slurred.)

"White bread." Three exclamation marks. This referred to Dr. Schürenberg's manful resistance against the Communist occupation.

Since officially there was no white bread, he would call for it on many prescriptions.

"R. P." Robert Papenbrock. A stroke between the two letters had turned it into the formula for *requiescat in pace*. However, this helped little to lay the incident to rest; it had been her doing, anyway, rather than a chance happening. The memory of it returned so sharply and painfully, she flinched as if from a blow. Jakob's mother tried to talk her out of it, she talked so quietly, so consolingly, right into her dozing off. Next morning it was unforgotten. How can something that began as clear, cold, and clean as a wet-honed knife turn into a fear of guilt?

R. P. had been sitting in Cresspahl's kitchen one evening. Gesine returned from the detested dancing class that was so indispensable for higher breeding, and had meanwhile progressed far enough in finer etiquette to have a sixteen-year-old beau, the boy from the pharmacy, waiting by the front door for further talk about tango steps and the graduation ball. In the kitchen a stranger sat at the table. Since Cresspahl's disappearance this house had seen few strangers or guests; she wished hard that this might be Cresspahl. This hope wore away in minute glimpses, faster than anything can turn into words in the mind. This man's shoulders, averted from her, were rounded not from age but from indolence. His whole body was too long; even from behind she knew that he would be ruddy-faced and healthy-looking. For another thing, Cresspahl would surely have risen at the sound of her steps, or turned around, said: "Well, look . . ."

She was barefoot again at this point, no one had heard her steps on the floor tiles. At the table with the stranger sat Jakob and his mother, not with any air of intimacy but polite enough, a little insecure, as if for all their good title to their places they still felt they must defend them. The man gave just a casual glance upward when she stepped to the table, seeing nothing there but a child. "Hello there," he said, condescendingly, intrusive with kinship, very much at ease. "Out," said Cresspahl's daughter, age fourteen.

This was weeks ago, and still she kept persuading herself there hadn't been any hatred. She had merely looked at him. She had memorized his face: a round skull of the Mecklenburg type, on the meaty side. Big eyes of that blue which is to proclaim honesty and wavers so quickly. Full, pampered lips. Such propriety, such a blithe state of nourishment. In a suit of re-dyed uniform cloth that fitted as if made to measure. Since the rubber boots did not harmonize with the splendor, he had probably meant to pick up leather shoes here.

He still had not risen. "Out!" she screamed. "Thou shall get out of here!"

She was sorry about the thou when he was out of the house; she should not have got so familiar with him. Then at last it dawned on Jakob that she didn't want her own uncle, a brother of her mother, Louise Papenbrock's favorite child, in Cresspahl's house. Oh dear, he hadn't even got a beating! With a crooked smile and the shrug of one caught *in flagrante*, Robert Papenbrock had oiled out of the kitchen, fearful of a youth who had nothing going for him but greater strength. He had made threats about burning the house down. That was the only time, and Jakob saw to it that the guest had a little fall, with his face fetching up on the sharp threshold of the back door. She hadn't even wanted to turn him over to the Kommandatura for trial and sentencing; what's more, she had been too much of a coward, and her escort from the dancing class was still standing by the side of the house. The eldest of the Papenbrock clan had moved slowly southwestward, at a dignified saunter, until Jakob upon her urgent request hurled a stone after him. How peacelike the high green grain shoots, how peaceable the low sunlight. The rock didn't properly hit the target, just the left kidney.

The Abses had agreed to hear everything, until midnight. For it took her all that time to get her narratives from the life of Robert Papenbrock straightened out, from his desertion all the way across the Atlantic in World War I to the circumstance of his having sat here at this kitchen table. She became more than a little confused from her own vehemence: Cresspahl had not immediately promised Papenbrock he would be tossed out, at that time elder bushes still stood there, but there was barbed wire in them; before that he had managed to get Lisbeth indicted; that was my father's wife; this Party speaker had in America recruited Nazis, had turned whole villages when special SS officer in the Ukraine; he had even abducted Slata and was responsible for her arrest. Voss flogged to death with steel rods, no, I have to ask Cresspahl about this! "Yes," said Mrs. Abs. "I wouldn't have done otherwise," said Jakob. "Yes."

For an evening this worked well enough. Then she woke up with the icy doubt that was proof against any invention.

She needn't harbor any fear of this kinship. He wasn't going to set the house on fire. He was in too great a hurry. That is how he got himself into a line of Soviet guard posts along Dassow Lake and had to swim for a number of hours with a considerable flesh wound in one of his fat legs. In his letter from beyond the zonal border, from Lübeck, he called himself "shot to a cripple" and testified to the genteel breeding of the House of Papenbrock by the solemn concluding sentence: Wherefore I hereby disinherit you.

Perhaps it had been the right thing. But she had been an obstacle to this man's seeing his mother one more time. To be sure, he hadn't tried to meet with her, had preferred to enter Jerichow by a back door. Certainly. She had had right on her side. Other arguments could be brought against that. Whatever Cresspahl's decision was going to be, she must be the first from whom he would hear it. R. P., R. I. P.

But Cresspahl sent no word, didn't come, was in "Siberia" or dead. His daughter was well prepared for the man who had been in prison with him, the woman to whom he had called greetings to take to a house in Jerichow. For these she carried around, in her coat as well as dress pockets, some stationery and an envelope. It would come to her at the proper time what was the first, the most important message she would have to send him.

## July 5, 1968 Friday

In Bonn yesterday, once again a court was in session in the case against that Fritz Gebhardt von Hahn, of the Department for Jewish Affairs of the Foreign Affairs Ministry under the Nazis, accused of complicity in the death of more than 30,000 Bulgarian and Greek Jews. For the defense, there appeared a witness who had also been employed in a senior position in the Nazi Ministry of Foreign Affairs, Monitoring Division.

He gave his Christian names, was known as Kiesinger. Profession: Federal Chancellor. That silver-haired species enjoys the West Germans' trust. With the likes of these the Social Democratic movement collaborates in a coalition government.

When did he join the Nazi Party? Right away, in 1933. "Not from conviction, but not from opportunism, either." What possible motives were left? He was not asked that question. He claims not to have had anything to do with the Party until 1940, besides paying his dues. At that point he was sufficiently trustworthy to supervise the evaluation of foreign broadcasts. When enemy stations reported the extermination of Jews, Mr. Kiesinger simply took the position of incredulity, left the matter out of the summaries prepared for his superiors, so that the Nazis were left in the dark about what they were doing. (This made it possible for Mr. von Hahn not to find out what exactly happened to the Jews whom he sent on their way.) In the same way, colleague von Hahn was unfamiliar with the expression *Endlösung*, final solution, until the end of the war. Only late and slowly, very gradually, the disappearance of yellow-star wearers and the tales of soldiers on furlough from the front bred the idea that there was something untoward at work there. That "something really ugly" was in progress concerning the Jews. Officially he took cognizance of nothing. Under oath. Leaves the courtroom without handcuffs.

In Soviet Germany, in Mecklenburg, the Soviet Military Administration on February 26, 1948 decreed the end of denazification as of April 10. Of the guilty it was said that they were in detention or that the Western Allies were giving them shelter. The Americans in particular sported sheltering wings in this regard: thus did Dr. Kramritz instruct his Class 8-A of fourteen- to fifteen-year-olds. Former National Socialists were now being specially invited to join in the "democratic and economic reconstruction" provided they "atoned by honest work." Whoever was at liberty had his innocence attested thereby.

Atonement clearly came in a variety of forms; how could a child recognize them all so quickly?

The Arado factory in Gneez had now been expropriated in due written form. Heinz Röhl had even lost his Renaissance Film Theater by legal process, on the grounds of ticket miscounting at the time when the Soviet power unleashed its captured Ufa films upon its famished Germans. This being characterized as a profit motive, it netted him aggravating circumstances instead of extenuating, as he probably expected from his experiences under the Republic. But for all this, an economic tsar did exist in Gneez; he dwelt beyond the reach of laws, in the style of Frederick II. We almost forgot that one! According to prescription, he was a former National Socialist, this Emil Knoop, who had manifested himself in the town with a quiet radiance and subdued hosannas; with him people presently ran out of comparisons. Lo, I bring joy unto you. At first he had a hard time with the reputation he had left behind him. His father had always been thought of as a businessman of some prominence, also a respectable citizen, this Johannes (Jonathan) Knoop, who could be forgiven such little foibles as raising carp and running a hunt in somewhat gentrified style. Trading in coal, hauling, import and export traced their origin to 1925. In the matter of getting close to the proper people in Gneez, the youth Emil was often enough in his way. Take 1932: it was a moot point, after all, with which group a businessman had the moral duty to affiliate himself. Johannes would have liked best to throw in his lot with the right-wing German National Party. But the youth Emil used to run off to the shooting practices of the Hitler Youth with his father's entire gun cabinet. This was an anxious year. An expensive one, too, for Johannes now had to contribute to both sides. And though one might grant that

Emil's political sagacity became fully manifest by 1935, the fact remained that what he had learned best of his father's business was the
quick dip into petty cash, and that his teachers had evidently pushed
him through school certification exams in a wheelchair. Then the Nazi
Labor Service was to reform him, but on his return he left a pregnant
girl behind in Rostock. What a time it took until the girl came to see
that life as Mrs. Knoop in Gneez would be nothing but torment! He
further learned from his father how one cuts a figure in Gneez, complete with sports car and silk scarf around his neck. But this, along
with quit-claim and alimony payments, was more than the firm could
carry. He had to enlist in the antitank outfit at Magdeburg at so early
a date that he became a reserve officer candidate, then in 1939 went
to the Polish war as a corporal and returned from the Russian one as
a senior lieutenant. Not straight to Gneez. The British in June 1945,
at the port of Kiel, let him loose on the civilian population because
he could prove to them that he had never had anything to do with the
Nazi Party except for letting them dock his officer's pay for Party dues.
For his training for the black market in Belgium, for his practice in
all occupied countries (except Italy), it was certainly better to belong
to the Party. Whatever it was that still kept him away for a while from
his loving family, in a bank in Hamburg that is said to have looked
like a true counting house of yore, he may have infused his amateurish
business sense with a little scientific stiffening. Early in 1947 he took
over Gneez. Shows that people did move here from the west, too! The
coal trade he left to his father. His aptitude for the transport business
became obvious in more ways than one, for he brought with him a
nearly factory-new American vehicle, a sort of truck for which you
could get sufficient spare parts in Mecklenburg. He hardly did any
hauling in Mecklenburg. He spoke sparingly about his undertakings,
one clearly could not drag much more out of him than that he assisted
the S. M. A. in conducting business. He had, to be sure, said rather
loudly in the Café Borwin one time: I've got to get the Russians everything, from tank to horse—all befuddled. He did know what he was
doing, though, for when one evening he was negotiating in the Lübeck
Arms in Jerichow, the waiter came charging up, white as a sheet, and
whispered: Mr. Knoop, Karlshorst headquarters on the line! Sure, said
Emil in his easygoing way: "They can't do without me." Sometimes
they were able to, though; then he would do a little time in the cellar
of the Gneez courthouse. He reformed that place in a matter of days,
procured the keys of other cells, had food brought in from outside (from
Mrs. Panzenhagen, whose cooking he preferred to his mother's), got
hold of a record player with jazz music of the thirties, with the result

that he became a little too much for the guards, it seems, and they released him after six weeks (with feverish apologies). Johannes Knoop became more and more transparent with apprehension. Gneez received a demonstration of Emil's brand of filial devotion: by the autumn of 1947 the old couple were living in Hamburg, not in Pöseldorf exactly, in fact quite far from the posh Inner Alster, in the country, you might say. As to letters, they probably wrote to him rather rarely. Granted, the old man had been put in charge of Emil's old bank, but Emil seemed to have forgotten it. To each his own business methods, traditional or acquired. Emil's main office was in Brussels. And why not? Didn't the Soviet Union have a trade agreement with Belgium? Emil's office in the Soviet Sector of Berlin was called Export & Import, the one in the British Sector was a room in a dentist's offices and made do without any sign. The fact that Emil had to be frequently absent from Gneez helped his legend grow in greater comfort. A foreign truck-trailer rig that stops before Papenbrock's and the Red Army's silo, loads the contents to the last grain and makes off toward Lübeck and the border crossing has some evidentiary force. Emil was soon respected, almost popular, among the decent citizens of Gneez. Could he not have lived like Louis the Last among the Belgians? And yet he worked his fingers to the bone for Mecklenburg and the S. M. A. Did Emil parade his financial successes? No, he always wore the same hat, pretty greasy by now. Didn't he evince Christian compassion, in case after case? There was in Gneez a Mrs. Bell, who lived in one room of her own house in the Berlin quarter. Divorced in 1916 with a comfortable settlement; always the wealthy lady who dealt with difficulties over the telephone. Now that she had been deprived of the phone, the world was too much for her. Emil called on her and installed her at his private line. He had needed a woman to keep his house, anyway. Do you think Emil wore gold rings on his fingers? No; if he could really be happy about something ("like a kid"), it was, instead, that, in addition to the white ("personal") *propusk* or pass, qualifying one for long-distance travel orders from the Central Travel Authority, including border-zone traffic, he, Emil Knoop, had been granted another one, the red one, authorizing travel over the entire Soviet Zone, including border-zone traffic!

Wasn't it a hoary lesson from experience: let the Army once get a good-for-nothing by the short hairs and he'll come out of it with a lifelong sense of what's what. You can tell by his short haircut, for one thing. Short, black, and neat. Nor did Emil ever buy a round for everybody in the place; he only paid for those who were worthy of his love. Nice and relaxing to hear him tell stories—not anything to do with his business, but with his life: how in September 1939, near Cuxhaven he shot down two Viscounts and provided for the crews' interment with military honors. How in what he called Bridgehead Vistula Delta he discovered that a concentration camp named Stutthoff had been maintained there, calling for a slogan to be painted on his truck: "Stutthoff Remains German." Personal reminiscences, you see. And now they finally knew what the weather had been like when he skippered the crossing of the Baltic to Kiel on May 9, 1945: the sea had been calm that day. What was the use of envying a lucky stiff? His interzonal pass was always in order, he could depend on being exempted from local transport pools; the Rationing Board not only recommended him, they even attested to the legality of his fuel sources. No one envied him his chauffeur or his 275 lbs. of weight on the hoof. He had such a restful effect. Nobody felt like getting a close look at his black, boxlike briefcase; it was too full of dangerous currencies. When he really happened to fall on his face, smuggling horses to Lower Saxony or having beer barrels of "uranium" confiscated at the border, he'd laugh himself silly telling about it later. He was thought of as a sweet guy. One time he returned to Gneez from the great world of the steel trade when the potatoes on the state-owned farm hadn't been dug yet. He promised fifty marks for every basket turned over at the truck. By evening the trucks were full to the rim, and he threw a party for the workmen. The potatoes came in very handy indeed; he also took the small stuff. And how he shed tears when Dr. Schürenberg gave him an idea of the diseases that affected the schoolchildren. The Chinese Beggars' disease, is that what they had, from eating orache leaves? Emil simply couldn't cope with that, he had to have a triple brandy, instantly. What? They suffered from scabies? Under his very eyes? Dr. Schürenberg did not disclose to him that the name stood for the ordinary itch or mange; he described their avitaminosis or deficiency in vitamins. The children got their ankles all bruised by the sharp edges of those wooden clogs, time after time, and this led to inflammations of the lymphatic vessels, horrible pains in the groin. He had seen Cresspahl's daughter ("That's another fine man," roared Emil, in tears) at the station, she could only walk stiff-legged, it hurt her so much. "Cresspahl?" said Triple Y, the town's commandant, Y. Y. Yenudkidze. They were gracing the Dom Offitzerov, guests of Triple Y. "I swear!" Emil exclaimed, sobbing. This was shortly before Christmas 1947. "An orange to each child," said Dr. Schürenberg. For he had been to college and had in mind to abolish in one go this unheard-of prestige of a common tradesman. "And to anyone who works, a salted herring!" sobbed Emil. Gneez spent the next few weeks in a state of some breathlessness. Emil could always beat a retreat with the truthful plea that he had been as full of the right stuff as ten sheep bloated on horsetail. But it happened, and on time. The salt herrings came. The oranges were distributed in the schools and children's homes and hospitals. The trucks it took were provided by Triple Y, because Emil had a "liquidity" problem, the notice having been so short; and Emil's part was to see that the articles were pilfered in sufficient quantities in the port of Hamburg. Gneez had long learned to believe in Emil.

Thus did he atone.

And was innocent, because he went about free, a child could see that; and did see him in splendor on splendor. For this man, the Communists in March 1948 provided the *National-Zeitung*, addressed to former members of the Nazi Party or other "patriotic" thinkers, so that he might come to feel at home in their Germany; and when their People's Police three weeks later confiscated all press publications licensed in the West and paralyzed their distribution, they permitted Knoop and his like a discreet subscription to the West Berlin *Tagesspiegel*, the *Daily Mirror*, sent in envelopes. This was to counteract any whiff of residual coolness. At the time of his fall, nine years later, he had to take leave of a flock of boathouses, a pheasant-breeding station, and the first "Hollywood" swing in all of the district of Gneez; but for Cresspahl's daughter it came too late. She could comprehend, at a pinch, that the Communists had allowed him to help them out on the level of commodity circulation, for as long as they still had to learn from him and the Soviet Union; and she probably felt sorry for him as he was led away, past blanching government secretaries in his reception room; but it was too late. Too long had she had to feel ashamed for her hand in that bag of oranges.

## July 7, 1968   Sunday

Haven't we been saying, continually and steadfastly, that the New York *Times* was a maiden aunt? Hasn't this been our word for it throughout?

We can prove it by yesterday's performance, her dissertation on the penetrating effect of the American Way on the economy, politics, and culture in that portion of Vietnam which this country means to save from Communism. Everything has been taken into account, thoroughly checked, and readied for instant consumption: the South Vietnamese within reach of U. S. Army broadcasts imbibe from their TV screens "The Adams Chronicles" just as greedily as "Perry Mason"; the students read the contemporary classics of literature from New England and Pennsylvania; Coca-Cola has found entrance there; the

home is torn apart, the family broken up by the insane income structures, by the forced separation from soil and house and village; the
songsmiths sing antiwar numbers in U. S. style; the middle class is
angry about the loss of its influence in politics and administration,
soured by the new status symbol, money (bar girls make five times the
salary of a university professor): only 6 per cent of government ex-
penditure is covered by direct taxes, a once self-sufficient rice country
has to import rice, the land reform has foundered; the infiltration of
French-style bureaucracy by the American variety spoils the home-
grown one: all the consequences of the American war are at least
mentioned, not even the religious bickerings are omitted. Just one
blessing of Western civilization, venereal disease, though also an
"Uncle-what-did-you-bring-me" gift, the New York *Times* passed over
in silence. A maiden aunt.

We are able to prove it by its presentation of today, those 800 odd
lines about the brutality of American police. Sternly and like a physician, she bends over the culprits and asks what could be at the bottom
of this: is it because otherwise the citizens won't testify? Because citizens
take a swing at the police, too? Because cops enjoy other people's pain?
Because they are chock-full of contempt? Because they are afraid?
Because they are ashamed of their low educational level? Because the
Police Academy does not prescribe a psychiatric examination? This is
followed, for deeper monitory effect, by the telling blow that it had
been a policeman in New Jersey who had acquired the forty-year-old
Smith & Wesson in contravention of the mandates of the law; that it
had been a second policeman to whom he sold the shooting iron in
just such a culpable way; and that only then did it come into the
possession of that person who shot and killed a young girl in a ladies'
room in Central Park. She is going to straighten out the police forces
of the nation or know the reason why, this maiden aunt.

A person of such stature should be able to feel sure that only
appropriate opinions are circulated about her, her in particular—leaving aside, of course, the ill-bred definitions that come from Moscow
and its suburbs. This kind of noble simplicity and quiet grandeur she
cannot muster. At the risk of raising doubts about her poise, she prefers
to play it safe and herself disseminates what is to be thought of her.
Hence we have read on an aged enamel sign at Woodlawn Cemetery
that she is "indispensable to informed conversation"; in the subway
that "to keep up with the times you need the *Times*"; also the alluring
solace that "you don't have to read it all, but it's nice to know it's all
there"; in bronze and marble we have read that she is the Diary of the
World; today, though, "one of the nicest things about the New York

Times is: it can be delivered to you" (this with a sketch of the *Times* in the act of delivery).

All right, then, whom have we there?

A senior citizeness; not exactly maidenly, but chaste. A maiden aunt.

A short person. What wrenches her head forward, the gout or that the posture is better for peering over her pince-nez? Jet-black dots for eyes, square glasses. The lips are curved up at both corners to form a delicate semicircle, far from frivolity or a vulgar grin. Controlled amiability. Not a wrinkle anywhere on her face.

On her head she wears a mound of thick ringlets, which fall over her ears. The traces of hair curlers are clearly in evidence.

A chubby person, to judge by the round shoulders, which are covered by a black knit woolen cape with a few broken stitches, or by the ballooning taper of her dress, whose lower part forms a narrow oblong bell with the upper. (We had imagined her more on the gaunt side.)

Her attire is dignified, a white dress with a geometric pattern and a broad ornamental border down the middle and at the ankle-length hem, where, however, some threads hang down loose. (We had felt sure she would be more neatly turned out.)

There she stands, her bulky body erect and taut, her little feet turned neatly outward in little high-heeled boots. Her limbs may seem stringy with age, skinny, brittle; her left hand has a firm grip on a heavy roll of paper. Beneath her right hand, though, and its straightened middle finger rests the carved grip of a cane, which she doesn't need for support, since she has planted it in front of her at an angle, almost with some unexpected coquetry. That is her posture. That's what she looks like, as presented by herself.

Hello, Auntie Times!

---

### July 8, 1968  Monday

For a week, we are told, the workers at thousands of factories and collective farms of the Soviet Union have been holding demonstrations, in the middle of harvest time, and condemning, so we hear, the "anti-Socialist and anti-Soviet elements" in the Czechoslovak Republic. The newspaper *Mlada Fronta* professes puzzlement. This very thing, *Pravda* shouts back from Moscow, puts the journalists of *Young Front* among the "Irresponsibles." Furthermore, the First President of the Czechoslovak National Assembly has received letters from Moscow, Poland, and East Germany. Josef Smrkovský has kept the wording to himself, has to discuss it with the Presidium of his own Communist Party; still, he acknowledged receipt with the assurance that the C. S. S. R. would tolerate no interference by other states in her internal affairs. "Interference." That's all it is.

In May 1948 Cresspahl, stark naked, was lying in a water butt that had been set up in Johnny Schlegel's flower garden. Johnny sat on the bench next to the butt, as idle as if the workday had already ended. It was early morning. The cats had sense enough to avoid the site of this spectacle; the stupid chickens held their heads low and swerved and wondered why they mispecked so often. The chickens were about the only ones who kept up a conversation. Every hour or so Johnny would knock on the sill of the open window behind him. Then Inge Paap, nee Schlegel, would come with a bucket of hot water and put it down at the corner of the house, keeping her back to the two and not once turning around. Johnny with his one arm was able not only to carry the heavy bucket, but to handle it in such a way that the water ran out over Cresspahl in a gentle swoop, only sprinkling his head.

Since Johnny was no less excited than his guest, he had a very hard time keeping silent. He did not care so much about the time, he had allotted the work due on the farm and really was quite unwanted there. He must be getting old to have his mouth itch like that. This Cresspahl, after all, for the moment knew nothing but that his daughter was still in Jerichow with the Abses, and still in the old house. Couldn't he find some kind of question to ask, after all those years of absence in the Soviet Union? Johnny cast dignity to the winds and said, as if he were making some calculation, that this must have been a somewhat long journey for Cresspahl, all right. . . . Cresspahl admitted that on the long trek from Wismar here he had found himself at the north end of Wohlenberg Inlet, and there heard on the west wind the bells of Klütz. How had it come about that the people of Klütz still had their bells?

"They say what they've always said," confirmed Johnny, a little uncomfortable now, after all, and possibly giving a sigh, too. Cresspahl lost no time taking this personally. For the bells of Klütz recite

> Sure is, true is
> That the 'prentice dead is
> Who lies in Fieken pond.
> He never lied
> Nor cheated nor stole
> Our Lord God received his soul
> In Mer-cy, Mer-cy, Mer-cy!

and it might be plausibly thought that Cresspahl had played that 'prentice over the last two and a half years, falsely accused, now situated at the bottom of a pond and without the prospect of rehabilitation at the hands of a Lord God; but he wanted to make it clear that he wouldn't stand for the slightest utterance of pity. That's why Cresspahl observed, not without a little malice, that Johnny's barnyard stank.

Johnny promptly took a deep breath and roared. For it had been all of an hour that the boy Axel Ohr had been busy behind the barn trying to burn, with the aid of old straw, a pair of underpants, male, a kind of undershirt or camisole, also felt boots and a black rubber coat. So far he had achieved only thick smoke instead of fire, and Johnny lit into him fiercely, spanning the ninety yards between them with ease. Now Axel Ohr had to carry the smoldering matter on a hayfork around the corner, where the wind tore the smoke away. Axel came slinking across the yard, shyly stepped up to the corner and asked as a favor for permission to bury the stuff rather than burn it. Both the naked man and the clothed man looked at him in amazement, almost with contempt; so he turned back, shoulders slumping in hopelessness, ashamed at having presumed to tamper with an order from Johnny. He was a frightful dictator, was Johnny. Take the fact that Axel Ohr was forbidden to put his hand to hard work for the rest of the day. Here came Inge with a fresh bucket.

Johnny had let that sigh escape him more because of the conditions of the time than anything else; he felt himself a little unjustly punished. So he said merely that he didn't have a crock of beer about the place, but he wouldn't feel any poorer for serving up a glass of schnapps. This put him one up over Cresspahl, who actually shrank into his shoulders at the memory of the sip he had been made to take a while ago by way of a proper salute. "Or maybe a cigar?" Johnny followed up his advantage generously, quite the good host making up for a bad stench with a good one. Cresspahl moved his head in indecision, prompting Johnny to deposit his nobly rolled herb on the outer lath of the bench and excuse himself for a while to see to things in the kitchen and bring Axel Ohr the kindling, which the boy would hardly have thought of on his own. When he returned, the cigar lay in the same place, more or less, hardly damp, but Cresspahl's face was even paler than before, if that was possible. What was wrong with the man's stomach, that he couldn't eat!

Then they turned out the bath broth and carried the tub off in the wake of the sun, which had meanwhile left the windows of the parlor. The chickens made a monstrous fuss. Now there were three buckets of fresh water at the corner.

Johnny came up with the bench under his arm and made casual mention of his obligations to Cresspahl. He spoke of his Gesine and her notable abilities as an agricultural worker, both in wheat and in potatoes. Two bags of wheat she still had coming to her, but he was going to pay her off in part in smoked meat. What did Cresspahl, as the person responsible for her education, have to say about this? Cresspahl inquired about the date. Because the morning before, in the Schwerin jail, there had been such a rush about signing papers, and he wasn't able to read small print yet. Johnny went off and returned with his schoolmaster's spectacles on his nose. In his hand he had Cresspahl's release paper, from which he read first the date, then the whole. The naked man now wanted to have another go at the cigar. Johnny Schlegel told him about the master of Cresspahl's house, about Jakob. He was learning how to hitch up railway cars at Gneez station, yet he didn't want to sell his roan horse. Couldn't Cresspahl have a word with him about this sometime, man to man? Jakob was a man of the world, after all, in other ways, with grownup love affairs; here on the farm he had a thing going with a certain Anne Dorthy until she gave preference to her titled clan in Schleswig-Holstein. Johnny was in a position to go on from there to love tragedies of quite another kind that had occurred before his eyes; men were like that. He had quite missed (men are like that) Gesine's sufferings over Jakob's visits, and Cresspahl would spend several years surmising in Jakob a somewhat private distaste for nobility. Now Johnny fell to concocting a lie about a canister of kerosene supposedly being held by him for Gesine. They had perjured themselves for each other a couple of times, these two, one more now apparently would not matter.

Axel Ohr took up a position ten paces away and reported successful combustion. He had also washed, to Johnny's elaborate astonishment; Axel Ohr wished himself elsewhere, where he wasn't "the boy" on the farm. True, he sometimes doubted that what Johnny in a given case inflicted upon him in that menacing tone of his was really punishment. This runaway city child, sixteen as he was, should have realized that he had been as good as adopted by the Schlegels, and on the side had learned almost everything that Friedrich Aereboe had to offer in his treatise on general agricultural business management, even a thing or two more. Just ask Axel Ohr about the wrinkles in the computation of total assets! Now he stood there, awaiting an extravagantly repulsive commission. He was to ride to meet the noon train at Jerichow station. "On Jakob's roan?" he repeated, blushing, afraid he might have misheard. "With Jakob's horse?" Johnny washed out his ears thoroughly, while Axel waited for the catch. "Young'un . . . !" said Johnny, serious, threatening. He was able to behave so wretchedly in High German! The catch was that Axel was to pick up a girl there, even if only a fifteen-year-old one. Chances were that she would want to hold on to him on the horse. The thing was that Axel had not quite got the hang of girls, even if he had known this one for years as Cresspahl's daughter. That was Johnny, he'd spoil everything for you. Resentfully the boy went off to saddle the horse.

Now Johnny put Cresspahl through a quick course in the things Cresspahl had missed since the fall of 1945, from the establishment of Soviet joint-stock companies in Germany to the provincial Diet election and that Gneez high-school teacher who last May had had to go to jail for two years for having written glowing recommendations for former students bound for schools in West Berlin: the student Piepenkopp has demonstrated a firm character and maturity, that sort of thing. This was communicating with the enemy of peace. This man has driven young people into the fangs of the enemy of world peace. Johnny had had Richard Maass make him a book with blank pages, in exchange for good-quality rapeseed oil, and almost every day he noted something down in it. He read to Cresspahl about the Communist coup in Prague; the German Socialist Unity Party would like to see the Germans do the same. People like you and me. Jan Masaryk, the Czech Foreign Minister, had voluntarily jumped out of a window. Did Cresspahl know of anyone here who would jump out of a window, in Mecklenburg at any rate, so things would go the same way here as there? Then he explained to him what "free peaks" were. This was a new name for surplus harvest yields, which after delivery of the proper quota could be freely sold to the Economic Commission at a higher price. Cresspahl was inclined to detect in this the innovation that an agricultural enterprise was for once allowed to operate with a profit. Yes. In principle, certainly. But since Johnny had had to say good-by to such patrons as Colonel Golubinin, the V. K. A. had been coming to the farm. The People's Control Committees. They produced forms to do with "surveillance of production and product destination," then increased one's quota by their own lights. What connection did a post-office person like Berthold Knever have with *triticum vulgare*, ordinary wheat, not to mention *triticum aestivum*, winter wheat, sown in summer? So that some farmers had to buy back at free-peak prices wheat that they still owed as part of their quota. No, not Johnny, he co-operated with the other people on the farm commune-fashion, you see. It was just the progressive, you have to admit, precisely the advanced features of Johnny's management structure that were a thorn in the side of the Gneez District Attorney. Man lived longer than a cow and didn't learn a thing

. . . Cresspahl demonstrated that whatever he had missed during the gap in his life, he had learned something, too. "Is that book in a safe place?" he asked. Johnny nodded in his pride, unconcerned. Five years later his book proved too carelessly hidden, and since he had the gall to pass it off as a novel, he didn't get off until 1957. For the time being he was sitting on a bench beside a naked friend and cautiously adding fresh water for him.

"Here's your seahound!" said Johnny Schlegel as he led Cresspahl's daughter to the butt, which was now topped off with two boards. This was quite wrong, for Cresspahl had no mustaches, his skull was tower-shaped; furthermore, in Mecklenburg they call a seahound, a seal, someone who merrily gets away with risky pranks. Cresspahl had not got away with his. It did fit a little, because of his shining gaze, as from an incalculable distance. "He won't bite you," said Johnny, and the Cresspahl child wished devoutly that he wasn't going to leave her alone with this man. At first she saw only the ears, which protruded so wrongly beside the lean, narrow face. They had cut his hair clean off, and the stubble of new growth looked dirty. The head between the boards looked cut off, in part because the arms were hidden. She didn't know where to look, she felt like crawling down a hole with embarrassment, she was near crying. Johnny by that time had long vanished from his own yard.

"I have brought you something," said the stranger in her father's voice.

Johnny made a noisy scene with Axel Ohr in the hall. It was about Axel's having released the roan into the pasture in his thoughtless way. It dawned on Axel that for the conveyance of this Cresspahl to Jerichow he was to get the roan once more, as well as the rubber-tired carriage. The precious rubber coach, which was such fun for a horse that it ran by itself in front of it. He was going to drive like a young king. Well—a viceroy. Not on the way there: Anyone with eyes in his head (though hardly a girl like Cresspahl's daughter) could see in the dark that she had got her father back broken, outright sick; this required driving at a walk. But on the dashing return drive—Axel Ohr could already see it before him, the whip planted picturesquely on his left thigh, behind him the road swirling with dust between the animated flood of green wheat and, on the right, the sea. Axel Ohr prevailed upon himself to believe in his good fortune, for that day.

*"You didn't cry, Cresspahl."*
*"If only I could have cried, Gesine."*

*July 10, 1968  Wednesday*

Now the Communist Parties of Bulgaria and Hungary have in their turn written to the one in Prague. (Romania is keeping out of this; she interprets the principle of nonintervention exactly in the sense in which the Soviet Union claims it for herself.) The letters run pretty much the same way: all of them accuse the Czech Central Committee of not having proceeded energetically enough, either against the "revisionists" in its own ranks or against the "counterrevolutionaries" outside the Party, all of whom were misusing press, radio, and television for the dissemination of truth about the past and the present. But Alexander Dubček and Josef Smrkovský do not care to make an appearance before a tribunal of their colleagues; they are quite prepared to hold conversations with one partner at a time. Meanwhile, two Soviet regiments remain in the C. S. S. R., although the maneuvers were terminated on June 30. They are short of repair shops, they explain. They can't get enough rail freight space, they complain.

The blue workman's overalls that Cresspahl had borrowed from Johnny Schlegel were indubitably clean, for Inge had washed them. Cresspahl put them on just a few hours a day. As if he had not got clean enough in the half-day's bath at Johnny's, he would still often sit in a tubful of water in the kitchen when we were out of the house.

"Now he was fearful. As I would have been. I swear."

"Marie, he was sick. His water cures . . . We had trouble keeping him from going straight to the town hall that first night, to register, with his confidential certificate concerning his absence. The former Cresspahl would have summoned the Mayor to his house. For Berthold Knever, like it or not, held the office now for a change, risen higher than ever Lichtwark the postmaster had, and grown quite fidgety and badgered under his honorific burdens. Knever would have come as though under orders, vaguely conscience-stricken. He was pleased, if anything, that Jakob held out the certificate and demanded a food-ration card for Cresspahl, without the personal verification the law called for. Knever stood for quite a while with his back to Jakob, sighing; he was the first who accepted the return of his former superior with some discomfort. Jakob, you must know, when he was telling something could be suddenly overcome by laughter in his throat, as though he were adding to his own amusement the pleasure he meant to give his audience. With Jakob you could tell very easily when he was glad. Cresspahl remained apprehensive that he might have infringed regulations—as if authority were in the right simply because it was set up as the law."

"Stir-crazy."

"You are not to get at the books on the top shelf, you hear."

"I know it from the New York *Times*."

"It wasn't so bad that I always came upon him sitting, wherever in the house he happened to be. Mutely and politely he would sit at Lisbeth's writing desk, at the kitchen table, on the milk bench. A certain spasm or tic in his walk had remained with him, he had not been self-conscious about this handicap with Johnny and Inge, Axel Ohr was allowed to see him climb from the carriage; but I wasn't supposed to lay eyes on him like that."

"I would have been proud of that. As a daughter."

"His daughter was worried instead, until the limp gradually waned. And another bad thing was that he hadn't let Axel Ohr drive along Town—I mean Stalin—Street to give the burghers of Jerichow an eyeful; that we sneaked in from the west, so that he remained a rumor for a time; that he waved Jakob off whenever he invited him to go into town, however casually. That sometimes when I sat bent over my homework I felt his gaze, as though he could never get used to the fact that my face changed with my movements, grew softer around the eyes, that my hair hung down quite straight and yet curled in a tiny wave above the braids. I had never been scrutinized like this by anyone."

"I have, Gesine. And I know by whom, too. For you, though, he didn't behave Mecklenburgish enough."

"Now I have learned it too, this single-parenting."

"That's what I meant, Gesine. But he had lowered himself in your eyes."

"Oh, nonsense. I was embarrassed, insecure. Would not talk to him without being asked. I already felt guilty about having taken dancing lessons at a time when he was in prison camp or dead, perhaps. Not to mention the reception I had given Robert Papenbrock."

"What sort of a grade did you get from him?"

"Hanna Ohlerich had pretty unexpectedly been removed from the house. Cresspahl showed no interest in this. I told him about it one time, as much as I could make myself tell, and lied, too, in my predicament. He nodded. My breathing came so hard I had to turn my head away, he was watching me so fixedly in that new way of his. For the Robert Papenbrock business I asked Jakob in as my witness, but by Jakob's narration of it Cresspahl's relative had left the house of his own free will, after a few words about the weather. When Cresspahl learned the truth he was almost glad. He gave thanks to Mrs. Abs for the dancing lessons. With Jakob he proceeded cautiously; to him he felt he owed a debt difficult to pay. As to my behaving like a solemn goose toward Brüshaver and old lady Papenbrock, this was swiftly taken care of; Brüshaver simply gasped when Cresspahl's daughter greeted him first, and deferentially. In my battle with Brüshaver about religion I was vindicated; I went to confirmation voluntarily."

"You passed."

"By the skin of my teeth. With Jakob, Cresspahl could talk more easily; Jakob was the shrewder physician. For I trotted out Alexander Paepcke's aunt Françoise, who as a member of the Mecklenburg Diet had had the house at Althagen released for her use, that worthy elder; Cresspahl's daughter was afraid of the future that was now to come into being, you see; the filling in of the past inescapably confronted her with her losses. But Jakob—wouldn't you know it?—had kept the *Handbook of the Mecklenburg Diet*, first electoral period, up to date in his own way. Starting on page 64, the membership was tidily checked off, those at any rate who still had the right to a seat; some had their biographies crossed out, or their arrest by the N. K. V. D. was noted, a flight to West Berliin, West Germany, a suicide. This gave Cresspahl an idea of the neighborhood into which he had been released."

"You were jealous of Jakob."

"I merely sat there, placidly content. Anyone who talked as he was doing wasn't planning to leave Jerichow for Schleswig-Holstein."

"What on earth made you stay? Cresspahl had friends in Hamburg, in England!"

"He didn't have his Mecklenburg affairs in any kind of order yet. Admittedly, he had lost all his property, real estate and cash, in the service of the Soviet power; but for my sake he wanted to wait and see if they would honor the entry of my name in the real-estate register or would confiscate the house on top of the rest. He wasn't healthy; he would lock himself in, half-days at a time, when one more wife came visiting a person who had miraculously returned to life from 'New Brandenburg,' asking for news of a son, a husband. Of his Hamburg friends only one had been heard from, and he wasn't a friend but a Party member of long standing, Edward Tamms, who stood in need of a whitewash letter from Cresspahl. In Hamburg they weren't finished with the denazification process yet. As to England, he didn't begin to get up the courage for that. There, Mr. Smith had perished in a German air raid in 1940. No Arthur Salomon was living who might have put in a good word for Cresspahl; in 1946 notice of his death was sent through the law office of Burse & Dunaway. And where would he have gone but to Richmond? In Richmond the town hall had been damaged

by German bombs. True, in the British Sector of Berlin there was a
hydraulic engineer to whom Cresspahl had once sold an Alsatian dog
with excellent papers; Gesine had met him last summer on the village
street of Ahrenshoop, and with him he would have been welcome to
stay for a week. He was too handicapped for that."

"When did Cresspahl recover?"

"When he managed one day to write a letter to Mr. Oskar Tannebaum, furrier in Stockholm, and thank him for a parcel. Written
all in one go. This was in mid-June 1948."

"Now you could leave."

"By now the Soviet Military Administration in Germany had barred
traffic between its zone and the Western ones by rail, car, and on foot."

## July 11, 1968  Thursday

At the end of the school year of 1947–1948 the women teachers of the
Gneez Bridge school were in agreement that Cresspahl, Class 8-A-
Two, would bear watching. Only Miss Riepschläger, in the pardonable
distortion of her youthfulness, excluded herself from the common concern. "She has her father back, Gesine may tie herself into knots with
joy as far as I'm concerned," said Bettina Riepschläger in her simplicity.
The older, more experienced pedagogues were willing to grant the child
this for the first two days, for a week at most, but felt it was open to
suspicion when such a reversal from a gloomy to an open, even confiding manner endured so long. Mrs. Beese and Mrs. Weidling got
into each other's hair over the psychological theories in which they
had been trained at different times and at different institutes. Mrs.
Weidling was thinking of some dictation she had given that involved
grammatical tidbits. At the time she did not realize that her voice in
the heat of elegant articulation tended toward gobbling, if not owlish
croaks; thus the English word *usually* came out with all but five students
in fantastic shapes, but those five had their seats around Cresspahl,
who on the other hand had not made herself conspicuous by whispering. How could such a timid child all of a sudden jeopardize her
promotion into senior high school? Further: during recess Gabriel Manfras and Gesine publicly (!) wrote on the blackboard what each had
understood; Gesine wrote "usually," well and good, Gabriel wrote
"jugewelly," then crossed out Gesine's version. The former Gesine
would have compressed her lips, turned on her heel, defiant, abashed.
The present one, though, went running after Mrs. Weidling, holding
the student Manfras by the arm (!) and asked in a tone of cheery
camaraderie for a decision on the correct spelling. Now, have you ever

heard the like? Mrs. Beese asked whether Cresspahl had been given a demerit in the class record book. No, no fraudulent assistance could be proved against her, answered Mrs. Weidling, once more aghast at her memory of the student Cresspahl's confidential inquiry, as they went on alone, as to whether she got such tidbits from the B. B. C. She too listened in now and then. Was it conceivable to conclude a pact of secrecy with a child? "Severity, first and last," said Mrs. Beese dreamily.

Gesine merely felt that she had waked up. Abruptly the nail-biting before decisions was gone, whatever was done was done right, from the outset. She saw no reason why she shouldn't one day use a wooden attaché case as a schoolbag. Upon demand she would explain to anybody the roll-top lid, the three drawers—but not the secret compartment, the place of manufacture, its provenance from the storeroom of a prison; why, she happened to be the daughter of a man who could make this sort of thing with his hands. It was only right for her to offer her confidence to Mrs. Weidling if she was going to reciprocate. (She had occasion to regret for some time the abrupt disappearance of the tidbits from the English bill of fare.) Even in Miss Pohl's class the brave studying, the dogged persistence had turned into a willingness, a thinking along as if for fun, a joy in comprehending; she kept her countenance when La Pohl backslid into her former misconception of the pedagogical Eros and made peevish remarks like: Yes, Gesine, only a bit late! or the one about two minutes before closing time; all this was likely to do was put a twinkle in Gesine's eyes. Not only had she reached a B + level in Mathematics but her grades in nearly all subjects entitled her to senior-high-school entrance, and to top it off, a head of family valid in the eyes of the law could sign her application. (Expressly in the matter of Mrs. Abs's contested signature, Jakob had brought an action for award of guardianship through Dr. Jansen; she could now pitch that straight into the town moat of Gneez.) The future had arrived, and she had been in time to meet it.

She was wary of exuberance. She was among the first in her class to report to the office that Emil Knoop in his indefatigable patriotism had cleared out and made available for the plebiscite. When she got there, Mrs. Beese was on duty, and since it was the time before the noon train they stood facing one another alone against the background of those windows that picked out piece after piece of Stalin Street's crossed hammers on white glass. On impulse she decided that Beese was approachable, after all. As for the constitution of Germany as an "indivisible democratic republic," that sounded all right to her, especially if "a just peace" was going to be added. But what she had learned in school about elections did not seem to square with ballot lists open to public view and the consultation of children in such a matter. She wanted to know if this was really all right. "I have personal knowledge of your identity," said Mrs. Beese grimly; she was missing lunch that day. Gesine mentioned her inadequate age. "You just sign there!" Beese spat out, disdainfully and yet encouragingly, and the child understood it might be useful for admission to senior high. So she scrawled her name for Germany's unity, appeased the teacher with a curtsey, and skipped happily across the rippled tiles of the vast hall to the searing-hot white street of Stalin.

Granted, the student Cresspahl had her father restored to her: did it quite escape her what manner of father he was now? He was in pretty poor condition for working; his earnings could hardly be expected to take care of school fees. Yet her bearing was alert to the point of gaiety, as though she quite approved of the state of things.

Cresspahl, hard to believe, had been released upon conditions beyond the obligation to register. He was to set up a woodworking plant, for instance, with the machines confiscated from him, and run it as manager. Even the telephone, once seized as part of his business property, was reinstalled for him by technicians from Gneez in the interest of the other, the people's, economy, and moreover with the old number, 209. The hitch was that the machines he had driven into a drying shed of the brickyard in April 1945 were not to be found there. Right by the Kommandatura, under the eyes of a Soviet military policeman, behind two-inch door timbers and a virginal lock, they had vanished—from the planing lathe and plate grinder down to the most minute saws and clamps; the shed had been virtually clean-swept. There stood the noble Wenndennych Twins, nonplused, the itemized lists from the Soviet Military Tribunal in Schwerin in hand, brought to shame in front of the expropriated German, whom a judgment of their own army judiciary absolved from guilt in this offense. Since for professional reasons they disbelieved in ghosts, in late May 1948 investigators from the Economic Commission entered numerous workshops north of the Gneez-Bützow line. In a carpenter's shop at Kröpelin they found a groover; in the Floodline Abattoir of Wismar, now a "people-owned" ship repair yard, a crude-oil engine as well as purchase agreements whose antecedents had a way of sinking into darkness just before reaching a certain Major Pontiy, a certain Lieutenant Vassarion; a way of doing business that is, under nocturnal circumstances, effected by a handshake and not sealed by a sufficiency of written documentation. Cresspahl received furious letters from colleagues who at the time had paid in labor or goods for the items of equipment the District Attorney's

Office of Gneez was now having hauled off to Jerichow. Under the circumstances he rested content that the machinery tracked down by mid-June did not come to enough to start production, and offered not the least resistance when the postal service took out his telephone again, after half of the brickyard had burned down one humid Sunday morning. This not only restored the honor of the Red Army to its pure radiance but also relieved him of the impending trusteeship. The Wenndennych brothers had ordered the tardy fire brigade away from the more brightly blazing main gateway and toward Cresspahl's yard, with the result that it kept his daughter's house out of danger but was unable to save the prospective workshop. The District Attorney's Office found enough half-fused scrap iron in the wreckage to satisfy them and waived an interrogation of Cresspahl after he had regretfully referred them to the Kommandantura as the competent agents in the affair. For that matter, what could he have said? The commandants, polished and fragrant, had entered his presence with impeccable apologies and had even accepted coffee, in a severe standing posture, having called his attention to the smoke in the air. The *Volkszeitung* reported the misfortune as due to a plot by unscrupulous elements hostile to world peace and in the service of American imperialism; in Jerichow there was talk of Cresspahl's experience with fire since November 1938, and never again did the twins pay a cozy visit to Cresspahl, just as they notoriously kept the Germans at a distance from their residence and persons.

Gesine didn't mind. For one thing, she would have received no harm from the fire, because she had been moved for that night from her room into Mrs. Abs's at the other end of the hallway. For another, she did not seriously hope for a return of those times when Cresspahl had hoisted on his shoulders a desk, an oak top with two cabinets attached, had walked right through all of Jerichow with it and up the stairs to the precise spot in Dr. Kliefoth's study where the piece was to stand. Now Cresspahl was hardly up to supervising a workshop. She watched him fork potatoes into piles, those, that is, which Jerichow's nimble fire brigade had not squashed or trampled; he had a stiff grip on the hoe, moved slowly, his head bowed. Yet there had been a time when he could make an interior door with nothing but an ax. But now he was back. She didn't have to have everything at once.

They were sitting on the milk bench behind the house; it was morning. Not only was there no school that day, but she could also sit next to Cresspahl as long as she felt like it. What if he didn't notice that the uprights of the bench had begun to rot and needed shoring up. Before them in the meadow grass, shaded and wet with dew, stood the oldest of the cats on stiff legs, watching a baby blackbird fallen from the nest, half-fledged. The cat set down two legs in front of the two hind ones, it didn't even take the trouble to creep. The screaming mother bird was in such a hurry that she dropped out of the tree like a stone, in the springy rebound already jerking her head high against the fiend, offering herself up for sacrifice, ready for suicide. The cat gave her a sidelong glance, gray and dispassionate, and walked toward the chick, unmoved by the blackbird's shrill laments. It was going to dispose of one after the other. Gesine wondered if in former days, too, she would have got up and removed the dumbfounded cat from its victuals; now, at any rate, she returned with the predator under her arm, accepting the fact that the beast thought she had lost her mind. She sat back down next to Cresspahl, keeping her grip on the cat, which gradually acknowledged stroking but clung to its suspicion. What kind of new ways were these? At that point Gesine saw Cresspahl put away the stone that had been meant for the cat.

Those are the unprofitable ones among the arts, they bring neither turnover nor profit. In the last week of June, Cresspahl's daughter saw how much trouble people could have with money saved. Obediently, zealously, she recited in school for Dr. Kramritz opinions about the West German currency reform that he did not share and that troubled her as she voiced them: the surviving leaders of the Fascist war economy were mainly concerned with the rescue of the decaying and crisis-ridden capitalist economic system, aided and abetted by the leadership of the bourgeois parties and the Social Democrats; in stark contrast with the currency reform as carried out in the Soviet Zone. But she was immune to the frantic chaos into which the people of Jerichow and Gneez were plunged by June 24; so was Cresspahl, so were Mrs. Abs and Jakob. After the devaluation they had a grand total of 224 marks left in their four savings accounts; only Jakob and his mother had the stipulated 74 marks per head that could be exchanged at the post office for certificates with pasted-on coupons. But many owned amounts in excess of that, which up to the 27th were still worth one tenth of face value, and to own sums above 5,000 marks was even risky, redolent of profits from armament deals or black-market trans-actions. Miss Pohl was observed storming up and down Stalin Street in Gneez past emptied display windows; by Saturday she had a genuine antique china object from which punch might have been ladled had it been intact; also a nonrepairable electric heater: the power restrictions occasionally prompted the trading citizen to let go of electric appliances. Many hearts went out to Leslie Danzmann, who had planned to pay back to Mrs. Lindstetter, wife of the District Court President, those

200 marks she had borrowed a week before for the purchase of a pound of butter. The august beldame rejected the payment and even refused to go down to 2,000 marks in paper money. When her humanity was appealed to, Mrs. Lindstetter clothed her revenge in the following resolve: Well, there's no help for it; we'll have to go to court about it, my dear! For Christmas, Gabriel Manfras would be given a violin from the Johannes Schmidt Heirs House of Music, an instrument of guaranteed and decade-long unsalability, though he didn't know it at the time. Mina Köpcke, given in a worrisome degree to the Inner Life and the practice of religion since that ugly altercation with her husband over the gasworks manager, Duvenspeck, now expanded the range of her sentiments to the arts and acquired for 3,000-odd marks two genuine painted pictures (in oils), a landscape of birches in early spring, with a brook in high spate that abruptly broke off on a diagonal course, and a stag whose posture suggested embarrassment. Pennies and other coins of low denomination were virtually unobtainable, since they retained their face value for the time being. About old Mrs. Papenbrock it is seriously asserted that she rounded off her bread prices downward. What really happened in those days is that she curtailed her bread output below the legal minimum, and that Miss Senkpiel offered the rounding off—upward. Mrs. Papenbrock once overcame her disdain of her son-in-law and sought counsel from Cresspahl because all balances on her accounts had been canceled one day before the promulgation of Decree No. 111 of the Soviet Military Administration, a circumstance that the embarrassed gentlemen of the town bank did not care to explain to her. Cresspahl assured her against his better belief that the Soviet power confiscated the assets only of living defendants and spared her his opinion that she mustn't even dream of Albert's release. She did not fail, though, to forget her offer to lend him the amount by which he was short of the per-capita quota; her double chin gracefully extended, she turned about, almost exactly on her heel, did not offer him her hand, satisfied with the disappointment she had anticipated, but for which adequate descriptive terms would have failed her. (This was the first time she had been in the house since 1943.)

Even past Sunday the old money had not been starved out, it chased people around with its useless offers, made them flap like fish on dry land. Everyone in the house was distressed on Jakob's mother's account, for such housing developments as Jakob had declined after the war were now having their equities devalued by a 1:5 ratio only, which meant that the Abses would have had to make payments only until 1955 instead of 1966, for a property that Mrs. Abs had wanted merely in order to receive her husband with something in hand. She knew that such a responsibility was probably too much for her, but it was the thought of Wilhelm Abs's uncertain life on or under the earth of a Soviet camp that never left her. She kept it to herself, alone in her room, praying with unseeing eyes, tears unavailing.

On Monday Cresspahl received two small postal packages containing currency notes, payment for bills of 1943 and 1944; he was not permitted, however, to postpay the 30 marks by which he had been short of his personal exchange quota. Berthold Knever, unexpectedly resubstantiated at the parcel counter of the post office, found that the days passed a little more swiftly during the currency reform, allowing him to turn his thoughts away from his worries once in a while and to exert a measure of authority over Cresspahl by adopting a snappish tone—no longer a dusky bird but one dusted with gray. Then came Jakob, who gave him trouble. Jakob didn't shout, of course, he only needed to look at the Mayor with his brooding, wondering gaze and at once got Cresspahl's certificates, with the coupons in place, in his hand, without a receipt. Emil Knoop, unmindful of more urgent concerns, again arranged for the cut he had allotted to himself, although it took many private visits to the Soviet quarter of Gneez. His calculations led him to the overwhelming probability that the soldiers and noncoms must by this time have spent practically all their month's pay, and the officers and employees of the Military Administration their fortnightly salaries, so his benevolent idea was to go partners with them in using their unrestricted exchange quotas, be it for a 5, 4, or 3½ per cent levy. His advances to the commanders at Jerichow he came to regret as a misstep, for when these gentlemen had him shown to the street, he had to anticipate a denunciation and future loss, even if only of time. Perspiring, a little on the portly side after all by this time, he stood in the sun in front of Cresspahl's house, again omitting a visit to his "fatherly model." What was he afraid of? Never, though, and nowhere in Jerichow or Gneez, were to be found those enemies of peace with their suitcases full of the old currency to whose evil machinations the whole monkey business owed its rationale. Cresspahl's daughter was spared all this, was spared any part in the turmoil. They didn't have anything. They had nothing! In your head this may feel like a brisk merry wind.

Meanwhile, not only Mrs. Weidling and Mrs. Beese were confused by thoughts of the western sectors of Berlin, which the Soviet Military Administration was just then cutting off from both rail and water connections, to whose people it would not supply potatoes or milk or electricity or medicine. There was much talk about World War III, and some about the prospect of the Soviet Government's offering

Britain, at any rate, what had at first been the British-occupied territories of Mecklenburg in exchange for British rights in Berlin. The child Cresspahl was observed twice during these days frequenting the Renaissance Film Theater at a ticket price of 8.50 marks a time, but was by no means reduced to that confused and intimidated condition that had been so characteristic—not to say comforting!—to the teaching eye. Why, the girl didn't even bite her lip any more when she had no reply to a pedagogically grounded question. Promotion to senior high was granted her; but still, what a regrettable instability of temperament had to be noted against this student!

## July 12, 1968   Friday

Friday. Thirty-nine days to go. Not even six weeks. Whatever the employee Cresspahl may do, there will be the twentieth of August. She may go to the Atlantic shore once more, push up the windows another thirty times, do the fall and winter shopping with Marie, get into D. E.'s bed whenever she feels like it; she will use up another two tapes "for when you are dead"; Marie shall have her crayfish soup; perhaps a dream will remain with her into the waking stage; altogether and throughout, she will be in the thrall of an illusion of life. In reality she is sliding on the slippery ice of time toward the appointment De Rosny has made for her with the Obchodný Banka. If she is granted travel by boat, she will depart from New York about August 12; if by plane, on the 19th. On Wednesday she starts work in Prague. *Pravda* mentions Hungary. This may suggest tanks. And if they go in by air?

It is almost quiet in Cresspahl's office. The telephone has been dormant since the start of work. Sometimes a wave of chatter sweeps through the door from Henri Gelliston's calculator. From immeasurably far below comes the gossamer-thin yowl of a truck. Alarm system damaged. The pedestrians, one may assume, are walking in suspense to the source of the noise and leaving it behind with indifference. Here someone is writing a private letter; you will come to regret it.

My dear Professor, it runs, I hope you will forgive me; I approach you upon the advice of a friend, and because I distrust New York analytic practice—the proverbial shrink is reason enough—and am aware of diagnosis at a distance being misdiagnosis ("so drop the idea!"). . . . She would still like to know whether she ought to think of herself as psychically disturbed, since for professional reasons she faces a change in her situation in life that is profound enough to justify executing a will and making preparations in case her psychic condition should become dangerous. Curriculum vitae attached . . . What a lot you are giving away!

The handwriting alone. What you trace there are large, continuous, round shapes which drive sharp tangents downward—what has been called a tulip hand by someone. On closer inspection you see that the letters in their middle sections, while fluent, are not completed to make the prescribed circles or ovals; they are open, and the upper as well as lower extremities are stunted (simplified). The latter especially do not develop beyond vertical strokes. Still, if one can think in terms of tulips, then these are tulips stylized on short upright stems. A mature handwriting. But what will another discover there, and what will he make of your using black ink?

". . . and when it comes to absurd actions in my life I know only the usual sort, including my reaction to the death of the man who was the father of my daughter. Generally, I would think of myself as normal. The exception: I hear voices.

". . . can't say when it started. I assume it has gone on since I was thirty-two, but I don't recall any triggering cause. It isn't that I will this, and yet I get back, sometimes almost totally, into past situations and speak to the persons of that time as I did then. This takes place in my head, without any direction of my own. Persons deceased speak with me, too, in my present setting. They remonstrate with me, for instance, about the upbringing of my daughter (born 1957). The dead do not persecute me; we can generally come to some agreement in such imaginary conversations. But are they? Are they illusory? I also speak with dead persons whom I know only by sight, who may have said as many words to me as a child as are needed for a greeting or for handing over a piece of candy. Now I am drawn by such people into situations at which I was not present and which I could not conceivably have grasped, be it with an eight- or a fourteen-year-old mind. So I hear myself speak not only from the subjectively real place (in the past), but also from the place of the now thirty-five-year-old self. On occasion, the self's situation in the past, that of the fourteen-year-old child, changes in the hearing to that of the partner of today, which surely I could scarcely have occupied. Many of these imaginary conversations (which truly happen to me) generate themselves from trivial elements, from a tone of voice, a characteristic intonation, a hoarseness, an identity of roots between English and the Low German of Mecklenburg. These scraps suffice to produce in my consciousness the presence of a person of the past, her speech, and thereby a setting much before my birth, like that of March 1920 on the rented estate of my grandfather, when my mother was a child. I hear my mother, the other people in the room, not merely as a listener, but in the knowledge that all this was directed to myself, all that which toward the end of the vision proves to have been addressed by the people of then to the me of now.

"Where living persons are involved, absent or present, this tendency of my consciousness can also be misused—as a faculty, I mean. I am able, for example, even when my daughter is silent to reconstitute her thoughts from mimetic details and to answer them (in my mind). This works even during the worst quarrel; although I have no proof that my 'transmission' reaches her. Thus the child is rarely safe from me; almost totally at the mercy of spies. My only excuse is that this happens outside my volition.

"Not only with my daughter, but also during everyday mundane talk, in the office, in the subway, with colleagues or strangers, along with what is actually said runs a second strand whereby the unsaid gains expression—that is, that which the interlocutor suppresses or only thinks. The volume of this second, imaginary, strand sometimes crowds what is 'really' heard at the moment to the periphery of attention, though it never blanks it out. I again feel distrustful of the term imagination here, for although I certainly do not rely on the authenticity of what I heard merely extrasensorily, the latter often enough turns out to be more correct than something I knew. It is possible that I am doing this interpolation of another acoustic strand in my partner's speech merely in order to strengthen my own sense of self, but this I find doubtful, since again and again I 'hear' the most derogatory things about myself from persons whose sympathy I particularly crave. While I concede in a general way that such sympathy may always contain its own negation, I am incapable of projecting this possibility on friends or even acquaintances.

"Ailments: None. The second acoustic band does not cancel the first, least of all in conversations with persons whose discovery of a weak spot would be bound to affect professional reputation. When I try to tell my daughter about her grandfathers in Mecklenburg and Pomerania, the interjections of the dead sometimes cause me to pause, but no longer than it takes a thorn to rip a triangle into a dress (or else the child, considerate beyond her years—just eleven—conceals her terror at those times and allows herself no gestural reaction). Such automatic dialogue transmissions bring about a state of marginally reduced consciousness, from which I can will my way out; considerably faster by the child's calling to me (not car horns outside the window or the like), but then in a flash, immediately. Is this an illness? Should

I readjust my professional duties accordingly? Should the child be protected from me?"

" 'They talk with me.' You have snitched on us."
"You! Where have you kept yourselves?"
"Have you been waiting?"
"But you dead as a rule are . . ."
"Quick with the mouth."
"At your post."
"We had things to do."
"You tell me about it."
"We haven't anything."
"Never did you say: We are all there. Now no one wants to talk with me."
"What do we have to do with the future?"
"What is . . . this is not meant for me, Marie asked it: What is . . . lasting?"
"We."

---

## July 13, 1968   Saturday, South Ferry Day

Dear Anita Rodet Stütz—

Greetings first. Since you wish it, I am writing to you, repetitiously, about our dealings with the person we address as D. E., who two days ago paid you a visit as a Mr. Erichson, with fringed asters in his hand, just as we charged him to do.

If there is a living together involved, it is one with intervals, he beyond the Hudson on the flatter ground, we on Riverside Drive in New York City; it is one at distances, on a visitor's footing, for a day and a half each time. Coming to visit, though, makes for plentiful partings, salutations full of dialogue. For all that, he is cautious, shuns surprising us; even though coming by appointment he will call from the airport—wondering if his visit is still convenient after all of ten days. Then we report looking forward; to news, too. For when this one has gone on a journey, he has found something.

You suppose: presents. Those too, almost everything D. E. brings back from his excursions we have liked. For Marie, the clever revolving sphere whose scales show the temperature in Fahrenheit as well as Centigrade, atmospheric pressure in millibars and millimeters, and relative humidity on top of it; she has been recording her measurements since June and needs no New York *Times* for her weather. Only during the first years with him did we suspect him of an intention to ingratiate himself by filthy lucre; by this time we know and like, both of us, the casual, the worried look by which he tries to assure himself that he has really thought of us precisely enough during his absence. (Seeing that one of us assesses the atmosphere in the American manner, while the other is still caught up in the European habit.) Presents from abroad.

We are more eager for other things. Such as the pleasant moment when the automobile of the U. S. Air Force, in mufti trim, sets him down in front of our yellow stump of a house, within five minutes of the announced time. (He argues a queer sort of axiom by which a person can manufacture punctuality, providing us with two kinds of fun: one because he manages to do it, and the other because we can make fun of him.) What we have been waiting for is a time just after handshake and embrace, which I inaugurate with the invitation, practically the entreaty: "Tell us, tell us!" And Marie has had time to clap her hands and speak Mecklenburgish and shout: "You are such a good liar!"

News. Where he has been. What he has seen, what happened to him. Such as in London that Irishman, whom the city has sunk in the earth, at the handle of a lift in the underground, who sings in his ever nocturnal mind of a Johnny, I hardly knew ye, too slowly but credibly saddened, with pauses during which he warns his freight of citizenry against the sliding gates. He too enters D. E.'s narration, with his curly mustache and undersized bass voice; we can hear him and would like to visit with him. Or the furious biddy in Berlin, who in her evil screech called upon him to emigrate to the peaks of the Ural Mountains because he was crossing, in your country, a totally empty roadway against a red light, as Americans will, and because he does look a little like a student, with his fluttering hair. (Is West Berlin like that, Anita?) We also take for genuine the insatiability with which he interrogates us about school, about the city. Did we fool Sister Magdalena with accomplishments in the *imparfait* of *connaître*, so that against her grain and favor she had to mark the record with the letter that stands for excellence? What news did we have of Mrs. Agnolo; what has Eileen O'Brady said to us; has James Shuldiner haunted us again, baring his heart to us on the narrow benches at Gustafsson's? What dress you wore, what kind of vegetable grew on Anita's balcony, whether you still see us next to the pot in which a certain Anita was boiling up rancor against U. S. Southeast Asian policy? On and on this way, back to front this way, and athwart and free of guile. As though we, each in his place, had lived a piece for the other, preserved it and brought it home, each for the other's delight.

You will say that things are this way only between people who . . .

Yes. (With one exception. We leave a certain blank. As I wish he worked elsewhere, so he would like to keep me from a mission that looms before me. [Version for the mail censorship.] It is not much help to know that he bears the burden of an oath and that for me, too, the obligation is imposed from outside, rather than being a design of my own, as it ought to be, after all, in the fairy tales of the life that is not an alien one. We have to settle this by listening to one another up to the point where advice would turn into instruction. We manage. He knows that I know. Should he recite what disturbs me about such missions, I'd have to agree on the spot. And sign my name to it.)

Reservations—I admit to them. And could hardly think of a single one that would scare away my spontaneity.

What he had been in London for (besides the other thing) was to complain in Moorfield Eye Hospital about the tasseled sorts of veils that have lately come between his eyes and the streetlights. At our breakfast table he transformed himself, napkin thrown over his shoulder as a white coat, into a titled British specialist lecturing to us with senile exultation as well as meretricious compassion: This, it is to be feared, Mr. Erichson, sir, is a matter of age. . . .

Now you—I can hear you say: If someone up and admits to what is a strike against him, a physical weakness, after all, instead of resting his case with his advantages . . .

Just so, Anita. He is not afraid of confiding. We laughed, was all.

Here we have somebody who refrains from changing us. Oh, he would like to abolish, for our benefit, the rule that this country allows employees no more than two weeks' vacation in the entire year and not a single day for one's household. D. E. would offer me machinery that would clean the wash and dry it and deliver it to the table ironed. But given the fact that this household can make do with the communal apparatus in the basement of No. 243 and wishes to inspect, moreover, what in the way of fish and fruit it trades its money for, it follows that D. E. can have only one of us this Saturday. When the other then suggests to him they should survey once more by ferry all the water between Manhattan Island and that of the Estates General, then she may take his careful nods for a deliberated assent, beyond a mere favor.

You see, Anita: I let him have the child. (With one limitation: flying; only once did I let them fly without me as fellow passenger. A superstition. Which is respected.) The child will go with him. When Marie invites him, it may be that for once she wants to talk over with a man what strikes her as incomprehensible or irrational in her mother; I follow along with that thought, untouched by fear. The latest addition to their repertoire is a burlesque routine where one takes his turn to say (confidently, despondently, or pleadingly): "God knows." The other (gloating, appeasing, neutrally informing, "next, please"): "But he won't tell." Also available with the appendix (in a knowing, conspiratorial tone) "Will he?"

With him you too would play this game after a while. (It was Marie who brought this bit of inanity home from school, from her strictly religious school.) About you he let it be known that you had spunk, he was going to go rustle a horse or two with you.

Marie may occasionally forget the injunction to telephone home every two hours from wherever in Greater New York. When she is with D. E. the ring comes trickling in on the dot, cf. axiom above. (Why, what did you think, Anita? They haven't a pay phone on the harbor ferries?)

In the basement Mr. Shaks (much obliged for the postage stamps) insisted on helping with the old-fashioned machine and having a talk. This supplied us splendidly with every sort of humidity reading, but especially with news of Mrs. Bouton. What, have you never heard of Thelma Bouton? Works at a jeweler's at 42nd Street and Fifth Avenue. Early yesterday in comes a man with a shoe box, locks the door behind him. She asks him what he wants. He shows her a bread knife. Armed beggary. She whacks him over the head with her broom. Man, did that guy take off! All this time I felt uneasy, restless. When I got back to the apartment, I saw wha for, firrst crack. It is not the weather for jackets with pockets in them, you see, so D. E. set off in nothing but shirt and trousers. On the table sat, abandoned, two pipes, a tobacco pouch, and the poking gear. I felt so sorry for him!

You now opine, Anita, that this is the way only with someone who . . .

Yes. And when I had trundled across Broadway with our shopping cart ("granny wagon," they call it here), I missed him. For at the end of my rounds I happened into Charlie's "Good Eats" to reward myself with iced tea, and there I read what the New York *Times* had to communicate that day about the difference between kosher caviar (from scaly fish) and caviar from sea owls, alias lumpfish, which have only a spiny skin. III Moses 11: 9, 10. This is to make me ever mindful of what sort of a city it is we try to make our way in. As I strive to imprint this on my mind, my glance slides off the edge of the paper to my neighbor, well known to me by sight. An old man, an away-looker, an aside-stepper, he always holds his neck as if he'd just been hit. One of those whom they . . . I thought: a victim. Sad to say, there is also the verb to victimize. He cut slices off me with his corner-skewed interest in my hand, the *Times*, or my nose, Heaven knows which; I promptly rose from the stool and simulated, for Charlie's hospitality's sake, a sudden indisposition. This is how things stood, and how urgently I wished for someone at my side to walk down the steeply sloping street with. 96th Street, you know, in a hot noonday may looked deserted— the only live thing left seems to be the TV screen transmitting the movements of tennis players from some basement.

At home I caught the first phone call. Marie had a win on points to report. The South Ferry, heading south, has Governors Island to port, and Marie had been instructing D. E. about the malodorous U. S. Navy there.

ERICHSON, taken aback: But I thought nothing but Coast Guard was stationed there.

CRESSPAHL, Socratically: And under whose orders is that gang?

ERICHSON, confidently: The Navy's and the President's. But only in wartime, surely.

CRESSPAHL, mildly, lessening a triumph: Use your head: Vietnam. U. S. Navy. Ships. Naval guns.

ERICHSON, embarrassed: Your round, ma'm.

Second phone call: Marie has privately encumbered this gentle-man—advanced in years, after all, near forty—with the time difference between Berlin and this eastern seacoast, has taken an exhausted man along a footpath past the ferry dock, down Bay Street. Half-shaded Riverside Drive reads 75° F; over there it must be close to 90. The suggestion is an honor, seldom granted to me by Marie; will he be in a state to appreciate it? Bay Street is a three-hour-long ribbon of dust, wafted across by the brackish smell of the water between the piers and warehouses, lined with weathered timber structures, sheds, gas stations, rotting industries, and those shacks promising beer with blue or red neon snakes. If you ask me: what she is looking for there is an America out of my father's youth. But it is true, if a wind rises there it has had a long run over the bay, and in the hazy distance there is the promise of the tracery of the Verrazano-Narrows Bridge, a span of almost 13,700 feet, growing as you watch.

"With you, Sir Doctor, to be walking / Is both an honor and a gain." Marie sounds quite excited in her latest position report. Well, it's just that south of Stapleton D. E. requested a detour from his guide lady, just a few steps up Chestnut Avenue, and she granted him the favor because he made up reasons to do with his professional prepa-ration. But there, at a corner of Tompkins Avenue, they now found waiting for them the house in which Giuseppe Garibaldi awaited his return to the Italian revolution between 1851 and 1853, a candlemaker for the time being and noted as yet only on account of his fellow dweller Antonio Meucci, because the latter claimed to have invented the telephone earlier than Alexander Graham Bell, the kind by which Marie flings a line of words over to Manhattan Island. Hitherto she knew only the Garibaldi who is a fixture on Washington Square in his copper sulph . . . his verdigris, his saber firm in its scabbard; Marie has even been left in ignorance of the fact that he draws and lifts it every time a virgin passes by at his feet. Why don't you work out how often he does it per day, Anita?

(In a city like this one, Anita, I felt I had to explain to the child at age ten what-all it is that men want from women, as a precaution, you see, against one of them wanting to force Marie to it. She looked sullen, incredulous; refrained from questions, until the end, when with a kind of indignation she demanded a confirmation: "You and D. E., you . . . you too?" She lacked the word for the activity; I intend to spare her this another eight years. How do you do that in New York City?) This is as far as I got when

Earth had by this time veered to such an angle with the sun that it put on those false, venomously glaring stains and hues and slicks that serve to make manifest unto us the decline of the planet each earthly day; at seven thirty I received an invitation to dinner. Can you guess, I wonder, with what counter-question I accepted? You are right. What dress I am to wear.

You are saying, Anita: You do that for somebody whom you want to . . .

Quite right. It was to be the "yellow and blue raw silk," it turned out; and then I had to look for them so deep in old Brooklyn, I had to search the city map and the subway network folder to boot. Darkest BMT territory, let me tell you. There I found the two among Chinese, in a private dining room rather than a restaurant, D. E. must have known them not since yesterday or the day before. (Since I keep my secrets to myself, how can I deny the same to him?) And as always when he is the giver of hospitality, the host people made a fine old fuss about "che bella signorina," "carina," all wreathed in exclamation marks, except it was in Chinese, of course, if you care to translate it for yourself. And I got a hand laid on mine and another on my cheek. For what was I wearing over the "yellow and blue raw silk"? A man's coat from Dublin, with a folded tie in the breast pocket, and what lost articles I was bringing along in my briefcase you will probably have divined, fondly devoted Anita and friend of the house.

You are saying: Let a man, I mean if he sees this sort of thing . . .

And hears, Anita. It went like this:

"We chickened out. From South Beach we took the bus to Bay Bridge."

"Great weather for ironing."

"I know, you prefer to tramp around in the decaying wastelands of Staten Island."

"Do you know what a fig tree on Staten Island indicates? You probably think, the season."

"At 96th Street and Broadway? At Charlie's? But he lives up in the hundreds."

"Chopsticks for me. Are you game to eat with chopsticks?"

"Did the Germans waste that . . . person?"

"It was a German woman."

"That people should be alive who remember their grandparents in Italy!"

"Barely living, that's all. Formerly German."

"God knows why."

"But he won't tell, will he."

"By the name of de Catt."

"Tell us, tell us!"

"You are such a good liar!"

Meanwhile, the host family sat at the neighboring table and did as we did. It was all the same who passed bowl or cutlery to whom, we or they. We were at home there. We were guarded through the crack of the kitchen door by a ten-year-old boy who watched with military severity whether we were treating his parents with due respect. Marie was eager to draw him into conversation, but unfortunately he allowed his dignity to bid him overlook her entirely. D. E. would have been happy to stay with the Chinese into the night (if only to get the boy to join us at our table), but we gently brought Mrs. Erichson to his mind so that with his filial duty he might also recall the mail that gnawed away his time in New Jersey. To take care of him. And when we were taking leave in front of the three garages below our house on Riverside Drive, one of the mechanics, the middle one, Ron the blabbermouth, let out to D. E. that he could take his car anywhere now, not to worry, it would go to San Francisco again and, all in the day's work, to Tokyo; a lady, you see, had stepped in in the afternoon and reminded them specially of the needed servicing and checkup. Yes. Unless he was mistaken, it had been the very lady here with the gentleman, now that he made her out properly.

So he who laughed last was D. E., on his way to the West, alone, in his high-and-mighty Bentley. Still laughing, alone in the night. For he well knows at what time I throw back my bedcovers, and what I find under the sheet. It is Král's *Guidebook to the Czechoslovak Republic* of 1928. So that nowadays I might find my way about there, should the mood ever take me; take notice then, Anita. I would manage with the help of J. Král, Assistant Professor of Geography at Charles University in Prague, for D. E. has secured his assistance for me.

Dear Anita. That's the way things are with us. Under, over, beside, between what I wished for at fifteen and untutored. But I am thirty-five.

---

### July 15, 1968   Monday

---

The Soviet Union informs us by *Pravda*, truthfully, how greatly she is astonished by the "morbid interest" taken by the West in her war games in the North Atlantic. She complains of reconnaissance aircraft of the North Atlantic Treaty Organization in the area of the exercise, of the presence of a British destroyer. By this reasoning, the person who could not care less about what the Soviet warships are doing there with their Polish and East German brethren is in good mental health.

The Soviet authorities have stopped the withdrawal of their troops from Czechoslovakia. Since yesterday they have been deliberating in Warsaw with their Polish, East German, Hungarian, Bulgarian friends about the C. S. S. R., in her absence, and when the official press declares vital a "decisive counterblow against the reactionary and imperialistic maneuvers" in that country, it would seem a good time for De Rosny to give up. On the contrary, though; he chimes in with Tito, in whose opinion nobody in the Soviet Union could be "short-sighted" enough to use force against the Czechs and Slovaks. De Rosny is a Titoist.

With Tito we had to be uncommonly angry. Right at the ceremonial matriculation into Fritz Reuter Senior High School this was presented as one of our main occupations, and often that fall we marched in a column of 400 seniors through Gneez to the town hall with banners on which we demanded the removal of Tito; this was accompanied by singing something about the skies of Spain, which spread their stars over our infantry trenches. There was no mention of the cold in that song; now the word Spain chills me. We had to stand for a long time in the cold until the market square had been saturated with columns of demonstrators (the people from the Panzenhagen sawmill were invariably late) and the three up on the town hall balcony could start their addresses. Whenever one was finished we shouted our complaints against Tito in chorus, and should gladly have been as enthusiastic as Lise Wollenberg, who just that morning in Contemporary Affairs had given me a wink as she recited Comrade Stalin's five articles of wrath against Tito, one of which, the false primacy of agriculture, I had to whisper to her. For she was my friend.

That's how she referred to me. When two girls have spent one hour every schoolday in a train for years and more time on the way to it, after a while they will either ride in the same compartment on good terms or separately on bad ones. The Cresspahl girl did not have the pluck for open enmity at this time. The Wollenberg girl and she had been almost the only ones who found themselves reunited in the waiting room that Grade 9 proved to be; and Lise was a favorite with many teachers, blond as she was, girlishly abashed as she was able to look in moments of peril, drolly confidential when ingratiation was indicated. Cresspahl would have found it hard to put into words what actually disturbed her in Wollenberg. When it came to that, she herself secretly thought that a Yugoslav might know the economy of his own country more accurately than the wise Leader of the Nations in the distant Kremlin, and upon command called him the Marshal of Traitors; we all lied, for our parents' sake. Lise overdid this perhaps, in the way she had of looking around her, indulgently smiling with her gentle lips, as though she were telling us invitingly: It won't hurt our grades . . . it's all a joke; come on . . . we're pulling a fast one on Kramritz . . . it makes no difference. . . .

The error had been committed irrevocably when once again the same worktable was chosen in Class 9-A-Two. That proves cohesive even in the time spent on outside things. She remained at my side while the students of the higher classes took inventory of us girls of Grade 9 in the matter of potential, willingness being taken for granted. Recess was like a marketplace. But one time it was I alone who was asked to step aside by Messrs. Sieboldt and Gollantz, of Grade 11; they already wore long pants. The gentlemen wanted to know what the Jerichow people were thinking about the blowing up of barracks and about shelters for refugees. I had hardly drawn breath, flushed with the honor awarded me, when Lise sputtered forth: the explosions had been like parachutes rising from the ground, she now had understood a little more about the atom bomb . . . this was word for word what I had told her. Sieboldt and Gollantz left instantly. At my protest, Lise said it had been she, after all, who had been addressed, and what did a word matter? Gollantz stopped me one more time, alone, he was concerned about the choice of a spokesman for our class, so it would be represented in the Student Government, which was headed by Sieboldt. I made the mistake of telling Lise about it. Her only problem with it was that the gentlemen had not approached her, and she consoled herself in the grownup way she sometimes had: ah well, they leave school two years before us, and where would that have left us? (Us!)

She was well aware of how pretty it looked when she tossed her long fair ringlets next to one who meant to keep her dark braids still. This meant that Wollenberg was in the vicinity of Cresspahl when she received invitations to walks, to the movies, and accepted for us. Up came Gabriel Manfras, who had come ashore in 9-A-One, Pius Pagenkopf, Dieter Lockenvitz . . . and she had sworn that we were inseparable, so that I had to tag along like a chaperone. Sometimes I looked at her sideways when some bright scene was projected on the screen, hordes of horsemen storming across a steppe to retrieve or fetch his dumb Sukhra to good Takhir: in chorus with the others around us, at the top of her voice she cheered the extras on, like those who at Kolberg in April 1945 staged the Final Victory. She was able to forget herself so completely. She was wholly a creature of the moment.

With the boys she was tart and scornful to the point of inscrutability. They had to address themselves earnestly to me; even Lazymouth Manfras found a lot to say about interior terminal moraines as exemplified by the Gneez municipal lake. A *trois* with almost every one of her gallants, I managed to make myself scarce under a tenable pretext. The next day Gabriel Manfras was even more introspective than we were used to seeing him. Pius Pagenkopf, a tall dark boy, oldest in the class, this Pagenkopf after being alone with Lise bowed his head low over his notebooks for days in order to be sure to avoid the sight of her. Lockenvitz, a shy, lanky, bespectacled top-of-the-class, sagged to a C in many subjects after he had declared his feelings to Lise. And all three of them found a separate private occasion, when early in November new I. D. cards were to be issued to everyone over fifteen, and asked me to juggle prints when I went to Stellmann with Lise. I told her about it. She laughed, tickled deep in her throat; she giggled when she got herself ready for the occasion. A lot of encouraging gentleness found its way into that passport picture. She gave me one, which I let Pius have. But at one point Lockenvitz dropped something from his wallet; it was a passport picture of Lise Wollenberg. Before her eyes he slipped it into his jacket, in the place where the heart lives and operates; she burst out laughing, jerking her head high like a colt. Of Manfras it was said that he had Wollenberg in a 7″ × 11″ blowup standing on a curio cabinet at home, and the shot was not made after the I. D. photo, either. One day Pius Pagenkopf, walking past the first row, took Lise's I. D. picture from his shirt pocket, tore it up, and tossed the pieces onto her table. She gave quite a complacent smile and later asked if he wanted another. What was I to say when she explained her behavior to me by the "absurdity" of the boys? Neither Pagenkopf nor Lockenvitz was absurd; nor could one say this about Gabriel.

We all wanted Pius to be our class spokesman, and he would have been if only Lise had not shot off her mouth about a serious type of boy able to defend us in storm and stress. Pius drew his dark eyebrows together like someone with a toothache and crossed the name Pagenkopf off the list. Lise was by no means struck dumb, she now pestered Lockenvitz. He hung back for a long time, he was a refugee and would have a difficult time against the natives; for her sake he accepted the candidacy, on the third ballot he made it. He had to live that down for a long time, because, when in December student self-government was banned, the members of the regime-sponsored Free German Youth, the F. G. Y., elected him president of our group of classes; he had after all been our spokesman. We would have a day off, whereas he would have to go to meetings of the Central School Chapter Authority (Z. S. G. L.), where, you guessed it, he found both Sieboldt and Gollantz. We didn't unfold the notes he sent Lise during class, he was quite sensitive enough; he saw her laugh out loud, as if highly delighted that he was embarrassed, and we got furious with him. At one point she sent a slip of paper his way that had no writing on it. It was silly, for a while he let his wistful glances take a rest on me (and he owned an I. D. picture of me, of which I had given a single print away, to Lise). She worked it so that a passage in our 1949 Class Day paper certified Lockenvitz, the friend of her youth, as one who "loved all women, whether blond or brown."

"We." With her I was to enter my name as a member of the Society for the Study of Soviet Culture, which subsequently became the Society for German-Soviet Friendship. Dr. Kramritz had mentioned the profit and boon of "social activity"; this was one of the lesser ones available. There could be no doubt that old Wollenberg had advised his daughter to do this, he felt in need of more safeties than membership in the Left Democratic Party of Germany . But Cresspahl waved it aside, though he might have found this additional protection useful. Being almost an English schoolchild, I favored the British as it was and berated them soundly when they crashed an Air Bridge plane in our neighborhood and lay in Schönberg Hospital. To have Lise, all by herself, step up to a desk with a stranger sitting at it—I felt it couldn't happen to a better person. I had taken her as far as the door, just to keep her in a tolerable mood.

Jakob had thought it unwise to have this Lise now know about my distaste for Soviet culture, my distinct disinclination; he turned his head back and forth slowly, his kind of headshake for matters of principle. I realized the harm only when he suggested: you'd better keep on the right side of her.

For Jakob's sake I forced myself to say thank you when Lise gave me an old dress because she now got fashionable ones from the new government stores. Jakob's mother, after all, was glad to have me neatly dressed under my black coat. Cresspahl or Jakob would look into my face or notice the least little scratch on my hand, but they didn't have an eye for worn collars. That Lise wanted to brighten me up like a shabby backdrop really put the lid on it; but I was spared an open breach. For after the Christmas vacation Heinz Wollenberg at last did find it beneath the dignity of a businessman to have his daughter ride the dirty, cold train both morning and noon; for people of Wollenberg's caliber the Housing Office found a room in Gneez for Lise, at a "relative's." By this time, moreover, the food-ration cards were valid only at their place of issue; in Gneez one could often find sugar or coal starter fluid when there wasn't any in Jerichow, so Lise could bring some on weekends.

Now that we went to school by different ways, my place in class had to change. When we met only in school hours I was able to march a few rows behind her in our parades and watch her from a distance. There she was, flinging her legs and belting out devoutly: "You DO have a goal before you / that KEEPS you from error in the world . . ."; there she was, skipping and merrily shouting the slogan against the Greek Government, the paeans of jubilation over Mao's victory at Suchow, of hatred against the renegade Tito. We had parted company.

She did have a goal before her; today she is a tax consultant in the Sauerland region of the Federal Republic. Her dress—green organdy with large woven-in dots—would have suited me for that Class Day, for birthdays; all I did was try it on.

---

### July 17, 1968  Wednesday

Because Cresspahl's foolish Gesine balked against a life in England, he had to take steps to set her up in that Mecklenburg of twenty years ago; as custom and decorum dictated, he inquired of the guild master about an interview. Willi Böttcher agreed so hastily, so readily to visit us in Jerichow, we couldn't help thinking that he wanted to keep the former convict out of his house, and out of the sight of the people of Gneez. He came on a Sunday, in a black suit, not perspiring in the September heat, sat down hesitantly, preferred for a long time to talk about the weather, his sly, good-natured face looked squashed. When I came with the coffee and he humbly entreated me not to go away, me, a schoolgirl of fifteen, I became certain of it: this man had come to confess, and for that he needed someone in whose hearing Cresspahl would not use rough language. "Heinrich," he said heavily, and sighed. What use was it now to beg for fine weather?

Cresspahl had really asked about professional prospects for craftsmen, but if Willi entertained preoccupations, why not talk about them first?

Now it was Cresspahl's Gesine whom Böttcher addressed, on whom he called for witness, whose visits to his workshop were to be enough testimony to what he found so hard to utter. But Gesine had watched him at work because she missed her father; all she had seen there was a lot of business. Turnover.

"Damn turnover!" Böttcher scolded all of a sudden, as if it meant bad luck, and trouble on top of it. "True, at that time . . ." He looked at me; I sent the glance on to Cresspahl, who returned a nod to Böttcher, relieving him of saying aloud: "when they nabbed Cresspahl . . ." The firm of Böttcher had to keep going from its share of confiscated furniture, which the Red Army stored with it by way of reparations, but later preferred to barter back to the natives for tangible value; and then there was the mechanical production of wood cubes for automotive gas generators—this had been the mainstay of the business, the butter, you might say. He couldn't afford to keep up the reputation he had acquired even beyond the Mecklenburg border with his standardized lines of furniture; at any rate, he had stayed with mass production. Until early in 1947 it was the watchtowers the Soviet authorities were ordering for their new prison camps; he had shipped them to places all the way to the Polish frontier. *Ptichniki*—birdhouses. This had been comfortable work, because the Soviets did not demand designs, both parties were at one in the exact image they had formed of such towers. Only the height was prescribed in each case. Since this was honest Mecklenburg toil, it had its price; each roof, for instance, was timbered with sleeve lining, as if to last a minor eternity. Normally the towers would have cost 900 marks; they were billed at 2,400 marks, the money had to be divided among so many people. The Soviet partner took it for granted that Böttcher must receive an appropriate share of the yield, and settled it through Price Administration, Internal Revenue, and the commandant of Gneez. Gesine had seen this, hadn't she?

His glance was so imploring; for a moment, as if in a dream, I felt sure I had seen a watchtower in Böttcher's yard, with a guard and a Kalashnikov. Reprieved from a nightmare, I thought back to the tower beneath which I had crept through the Gräfin Forest, and nothing could have happened to me, for Jakob was with me. It was Cresspahl who had lived underneath such towers.

*"Would you not have made them things, Cresspahl? I'truth not?"*
*"Not if you were in stockade between 'em, Böttcher. I'truth not."*

In honor of this article of Böttcher's production the two had a drink of schnapps—a single one. The bottle remained standing between them, a memorial to Böttcher's role in Cresspahl's imprisonment. But the matter was now erased between them; he took a little more to sit on than the edge of his chair, presently leaned back. It was true enough; to his embarrassment the factory was minting money. His workers were happy about the incoming orders; he let them have the scraps for home heating before they had a chance to steal them, continued to negotiate for them bonus rates for night work, also special ration cards for heavy work. Then came the picket fences for Heringsdorf and other chicken feed, but in 1947 he undertook the interior furnishings of Russian ships in the shipyards of Wismar and Rostock. They are still plying the seas, those cabins and bunks of his—shoddy work is not in Willi's book! What he did do, though, was allow for one hundred per cent cutting wastage (30 to 50 per cent would have been justifiable). Under these circumstances, complete nursery furnishings for the director authorizing billings found their way into a handclasp instead of an invoice. When later he had to equip the buildings for marine supply services, especially the so-called bazaars, he got into temporary difficulties, being deficient in expertise where the black-marketeering of groceries was concerned. At that point Emil Knoop returned to Gneez and helped him in his need.

What followed was the sort of serenade to Emil Knoop's ballooning fortunes that Cresspahl's child might have sung too. She was angry, to be sure, recalling the starvation winter of 1946–47, when milk and honey flowed at Böttcher's table. And yet, what did it profit Böttcher that he could drive a Mercedes, that the Soviet guards at the free port of Stralsund raised the boom because his glum, sagging face was sufficient identification, that he lived high off the hog with canned goods from Denmark? For one thing, he always had one leg in jail ("I have made my peace with that," he said dejectedly, yet as if he looked forward to it in some way). For another thing, the conferences with the Soviet gentlemen turned out so wretchedly boozy. At Stralsund a waiter had intuitively diagnosed his state and could be relied on to serve him water instead of Richtenberger liquor. ("That money belongs in your pocket," said Willi Böttcher, dolefully, a dignified man with bitter religious disillusionment in his past.) But he couldn't bribe all the waiters on the Mecklenburg coast, and so it happened that during a nocturnal leak between Rostock and Gneez he fell down a steep embankment, while his Soviet business partners, oblivious, drove on without him, in his Mercedes. All night on the wet ground. No—holding his liquor was not Willi Böttcher's forte, all of Gneez knew about that as well as Cresspahl. Didn't have the gift. Always spent half the next week in bed. And then the wife! The old woman! Old tartar!

One must hand it to him: clearly Böttcher too had had his pack to carry, said Cresspahl mildly. His daughter was enraged by Böttcher's easy geniality, but then, grownups simply were incomprehensible. We have told each other this or that, so now let's bury the hatchet. As if Cresspahl had told about Fünfeichen concentration camp!

Some strand, though of Böttcher's business was always held in Emil Knoop's hand; if Böttcher balked, something went wrong. Willi had made some wall paneling for the Gneez Kommandantura. The invoice was endorsed by Price Administration and by Internal Revenue; Triple Y would probably have made payment by Whitsuntide 1948. But in his chair sat a deputy, behind him the 3' × 3' picture of Goethe from the Gneez high school, and flatly refused payment on any terms. Willi went to the reception room outside Emil Knoop's office so early that he was second in line. Emil was practically airborne on a trip to Ostend; there was just barely time for a scrap of information; the deputy commandant had left a furniture allotment with a sewing machine that had a damaged base, but he had designs on a young woman on Rose Garden Street and wanted to give her evidence of his sentiments. Willi Böttcher cast his mind back to the workmanship of the Middle Ages and handcrafted a new sewing machine base plate for him, with all the care a journeyman gives to his test entry for the guild, with inlaid centimeter ruler and ornamental bands. Now the deputy paid for the eighteen square yards of wainscoting, had Böttcher sign for it, scooped the money off the table, returned it to the cashbox, locked it very ostentatiously, pulled a new receipt form out of his drawer, asked for a second signature, and handed the money over. . . . By evening the negotiations had moved to Böttcher's workshop, where the deputy sat on Böttcher's planer, only slightly sozzled, and dispensed words of wisdom: You Germans, you think we are all dumb. . . . (Oh PLEASE, Mr. Deputy, how can you think . . . !) But we are better grafters than you.

Cresspahl let his eyes rest on his guild master, whose word had once been law in the craft and the bookkeeping of their trade around Gneez, who now had to make double entries of every receipt if he didn't want to be escorted to the penitentiary by Internal Revenue agents. A change of venue seemed called for. Where, Cresspahl asked, did Emil's power and glory have their limits? "No place, nohow," Willi declared peevishly. Though their conversation once more succeeded in steering clear of the painful topic of Cresspahl's absence, it now sounded for all the world as if he were unburdening himself to his younger colleague.

The latest news about Emil Knoop dealt with the saluting drill given by him to a Soviet guard at the green fence around Gneez's Barbara Street, in full sight of German passersby, Soviet military personnel—why, even the commandant, Y. Y. Yenudkidze, who gave the spectacle his expert attention from the comfort of his private villa's upper floor. Emil corrected the docile Red Army man's hand grip, he shoved and squeezed his feet around; ever more briskly was he saluted by Soviet Man, almost up to the standard of the late Greater Germany. In a strident crow, he erased cosmetic flaws: So must you do! Look here: Zonk! Zonk-zonk! Zonk! until the the present-arms routine had firmed up, and Emil for his part passed the guard at the salute on his way to his conference with Triple Y. Without Knoop, everyone knew, nothing worked. The people who talked of a twin to Knoop might actually be right. For how could he be on trial in Hanover because of a load of blue basalt that had been spirited away, and at the same time be negotiating in Jerichow about the razing of the brickyard at the township's expense? Oh yes—say what you like. You won't get your hands on him. He is about to go to Moscow; not with a delegation, by himself! As a guest of honor!

"*Reckon I'll lay my hands on him.*"
"*He has double receipts from the Tax Office; we're sheep droppings for him.*"
"*Willi—what if he had to help you?*"
"*Don't feel hurt, Cresspahl. You've been away a long time.*"
"*He has a friend, hasn't he?*"
"*Friends he has.*"
"*One friend: Klaus. Your Klaus.*"
"*Yeah—Klaus. We think of him all day. How the old woman frets*

*herself. Is he still with the Russians, is he dead there? Is he alive? If he isn't, I'd think of selling out."*

*"Then think of him in truth, just once."*

*"Cresspahl, you would . . ."*

*"He has a friend in Gneez who's thick with the Russians, and now he's going visiting . . ."*

*"Emil! Emil Knoop!"*

*"If he can't get his friend out from Moscow—"*

*"Cresspahl, I won't ever forget that. Come by day, come by night, you shall have what you ask for. Whatever you ask for, Heinrich!"*

*"If he can't pull that off, he's good for nothing. Then he's through in Gneez."*

*"I've done nothing to merit that from you. And I won't ever forget it."*

*"I'd rather you forgot it right now."*

*"What?"*

*"You know nothing. You keep your muzzle shut."*

This kind of operation Cresspahl was capable of by this time. His daughter took it for a sign of convalescence, she welcomed it. The firm of Knoop delivered to Mr. Heinrich Cresspahl a load of Finnish board timber, from which he constructed a workshop behind his house, a large room on stilts at a right angle to Lisbeth's bedroom; and when the State Museum at Schwerin asked whether by any chance he undertook restoration work, it might be that Knoop had in all innocence written them a letter. Then came the people from antique shops. Cresspahl had realized what fate had been prepared for the crafts in Mecklenburg; but he felt he would have a living there for his lifetime. It was his last retreat. From that time on he worked only by himself.

Emil Knoop never realized who his challenger was; in his good-natured way he had intervened at Schwerin on Cresspahl's behalf. The search for Klaus Böttcher he carried forward in the sporting spirit that had become his usual frame of mind. It is true that he returned from this trip to Moscow alone. It was Christmastime when I saw on Station Street a ragged young man staring obliviously at the people who were thrusting forward to form triple lines, shivering with cold, because in the Renaissance Film Theater *Die Fledermaus*, part of the Soviets' cinematic spoils of war, was being shown, with actors who, as he, like we, had probably learned in the meantime, had been minions of Fascism. I found it hard to explain this to him as I took him to his parents; and I first had to see a man of almost thirty cry before I understood why Böttcher had been so anxious to have a good reputation with the

Soviet authorities, even when it injured a fellow guildsman, and what had prompted Cresspahl to take such a conciliatory stand. And then I humbly took back my thoughts about him, "from the heart," as one says because one is ashamed.

Still nothing but allusions from "reliable sources," no wording of the collective letter from the allies of Czechoslovakia.

## July 18, 1968   Thursday

The New York *Times* has read the letter of the Warsaw Pact comrades to Czechoslovakia and communicates from it the following demands. "Decisive action against rightist and other forces inimical to socialism." O.K. already! Agreed.

"Control of the press, radio, television by the Party." Because they had asserted, "without foundation," that Soviet troops in the C. S. S. R. constituted a threat to national sovereignty. If that is not supposed to be so, well and good. But let these media bring to the people what they observe.

"We are not coming before you as advocates of Yesterday who would like to interfere with your effort to make amends for your mistakes and weaknesses, including infractions of socialist legality." If you keep that thought, all right.

The New School taught us to rank one another by paternal status. Just as the student Cresspahl was the daughter of a craftsman, so Pius Pagenkopf had attached to him a father who occupied a position of leadership in the Socialist Unity Party of Germany and high office in the provincial government of Mecklenburg. Backward middle class and progressive intelligentsia, how could they sit at the same worktable from January 1949 to graduation?

Pius . . . called on to decline this adjective, he had got stuck once. As a nickname, he must have preferred this to a High German translation of his surname (Horsehead). He was also the only Catholic in our class. Pius . . . if only memory would serve our requests! Of Jakob I retain an awareness of his closeness, his voice, his calm movements; all I have of Pius is the memory of a snapshot. We were nineteen and eighteen then, displayed against sparse April reeds at Gneez municipal lake. You see a spare, lanky boy with a bony head, squaring his shoulders as if to strike back at something, annoyed by the camera. He is holding a lighted cigarette, like a grownup. And the snapshot tries to convince me that Pius's face had always been so finished. As to the small girl next to him with her hair in braids, my only memory of that moment is that her father meant to forbid her to smoke, because she is hiding her smoldering contraband in her cupped hand. With all that, we look like a well-adjusted married couple and knew one another far more thoroughly than our fathers cared to notice.

At the start of Grade 9, Pius was nothing much more to me than Mr. Pagenkopf's son. As director of the Internal Revenue Office in Gneez and a Social Democrat, he had been dismissed in 1933 and compelled to eke out his 75 per cent retirement pension with a job in the freight section of the railway station (taken into "protective custody" during Mussolini's visit to Mecklenburg). In view of this, the people of Gneez were inclined to consider it equitable in 1945 when the British appointed him interpreter to the town commandant. But they held it against him that he accepted the mayoral chair under the Soviet occupation, and the Social Democrats in particular held a grudge against him for speaking in favor of the merger with the Communists, and more so lately for aiding the Soviet administration in the provincial capital. The Pagenkopfs, a family of three on paper, had again been inhabiting a four-room apartment, since 1945; that aroused resentment in a severely crowded town, and on top of that Pius's father put in such rare appearances in Gneez that even his son's girlfriend knew him only from pictures taken of speakers' stands or newspaper articles on the Party's New Face or the Yugoslav conspiracy. About his night life in Schwerin people had it from reliable sources that he could take his pick there of striking women, younger and also nimbler conversationalists than Mrs. Pagenkopf; she was a peasant's daughter with a primary-school education, which was why he had to smuggle her onto the IN listing entitling you to ration cards for the intelligentsia. It was obvious that with such a father Pius would lose no time raising his hand at the constituent assembly of the Free German Youth, and with such a father at his back he could simply wave aside his election to various F. G. Y. offices as one more "social activity"; Comrade Pagenkopf saw to that for his son. Who would thenceforth be surprised to see Pius, after the opening of the new government stores, wearing a freshly laundered shirt, at 100 marks each, every three days, and leather shoes, the pair priced at 210 marks? He did keep up the appearance of an upper-middle-class person. The son of such a father might permit himself strolls with a retail merchant's daughter (middle class), but that he paid visits to the daughter of a Cresspahl did border on arrogance surely, which explains why she was not half taken aback when she found him at the door in December 1948, at coffee time on Sunday. Presently she thought she had seen through the pretext.

Warning had been given of an impending class test in Mathematics. If someone feels wobbly in math, he may surely look up a classmate, even if she lived in distant Jerichow. Now he stood before her, a plausible smile of recognition at the corners of his mouth, constraint in his eyes, because someone might after all run way with the idea that he had wandered around the market square of Jerichow merely to run into, say, Lise Wollenberg, rather than because he had trouble locating the brickyard path (straight ahead, take a right at St. Peter's). "Dobry den', Gesine," he says cautiously, almost entreatingly. She too knows Russian, she asks: "Kak delá, gospodin"; she takes him into Cresspahl's room, "sadites," the next thing is "na razvod," to work! so that he would believe at last that he is being believed. The feeling involved here was hardly compassion, more urgency, just as the sight of someone's wound demands a bandage. Apprehension, though, was present too, and with it the thought "O my far-off homeland!"—which is a straight translation from the Russian and roughly equivalent to our "Stop the world, I want to get off" or "O brother, we're in for it now."

But Pius did nothing halfway. At the end of Geometry the question stuck in my throat, and Pius answered it. We reached an accord about our fathers, the younger one, who lent his services to the Russians, and the older, whom the Russians had put through the mill; the two had permitted us to do this, each for himself. Cresspahl commented merely that she hoped Pagenkopf Senior stuck only his own head in the lion's mouth. All that was lacking now were a few snippets of paper and the community spirit generated by Mrs. Habelschwerdt.

La Habelschwerdt ("The Cleaver") had received her school certificate at Breslau twenty-one years ago, and, as luck would have it, signed up a senior schoolteacher to marry. When he was reported missing "in the East" and she was left with half-grown children, she had taken training as a beginning teacher, surrounded by quite young girls, and now taught us Mathematics, Chemistry, and Physics. The boys in the class sincerely rated her "acceptable" (meaning "fit for a new husband"), her legs were rated A minus, considering her forty years. Her nickname had been incurred by overly harsh reproof, which strained her narrow voice. As the dependent and, by now, the relict of a politically compromised person (Nazi Party member), she was perhaps excessively anxious to render beyond question at least the admission of a son (middle class) to the New High School. She also wanted to safeguard her teacher's salary; she had absorbed the teachings of the New Pedagogy overzealously and possibly understood some of them less than accurately. Thus she slammed her steel ruler on the table (repeatedly, as one might hit a vicious dog) when a week before Christmas a cloud of handmade confetti blew into the aisle from Pius's place; thus she called to him over all the thirty-nine intervening heads: "You of all people should give proof of community spirit here!"

"You of all people" . . . in an English or American school this would probably have become her nickname. Eva Matschinsky was admonished as follows: you just don't let all your stuffing flop on the table, Eva Maria! You of all people . . . La Habelschwerdt was bewildered by our laughter, she had forgotten about the youthful abundance of her own bosom. She had merely been reminding us and Eva that as a barber's daughter (backward middle class) she had to make up for her social origin at least by exemplary conduct. And Pius (of all people) should seek a uniformly agreeable public image, as was fitting in view of his father's standing (progressive intelligentsia). And because of Pagenkopf's eminence she acquiesced with a sigh in Pius's refusing her, the homeroom teacher, an apology! I alone knew the truth: it had been Zaichik who did it.

With him, Dagobert Haase (Rabbit, or Zaichik in the conquerors' idiom), Pius, had taken a worktable at the beginning of 9-A-Two, because of their shared way to school from Grade 1 on. Not a friend, a habit. Giddy, intrusive, quick-witted, usable. But Zaichik could not drop the note-passing business. When it came to the ship-sinking game right under Mrs. Habelschwerdt's nose, Pius had cured him of that. But when a slip of paper is passed from the right, it is considered a breach of solidarity to shake one's head, and unfortunately this note had been addressed to Pius himself ("Eva already wears a . . . ; Eva sinned in a Ford"). Pius had torn the message into small bits and left them on his open book. The teacher approached, the book was slammed shut, and the telltale cloud among the chair legs testified to Pius's lack of community spirit. Now it might be that Pius lacked such spirit where the community of teacher and taught was concerned, but if such a sentiment in a person counted as a virtue, indeed, a public virtue, then to have it disputed because of another's offense was an injustice. The worst part was that Haase/Zaichik made no use of the honor code to which a member of the Free German Youth dedicates himself: he failed to set things straight. Pius dissolved their tablemateship and now stood alone. The one to whom he expounded all this in a state of multilayered uneasiness was also on her own.

Thus began the first coed study team at Fritz Reuter High School in Gneez, two years before the official introduction of such a thing, and it was a scandal. For one thing, seats in the classroom were exchanged at the start of the school year, never in the middle, except by action of a faculty member. Second, the odd student left over in the pairings had to sit alone, or if worst came to worst, a boy and girl side by side could be tolerated somewhere in the front rows. And anyway: Cresspahl's daughter was approaching sixteen, and Pius was barely seventeen! And besides, the table to which Pius had moved with me stood in the farthest corner of the room, hard to get a good view of from the teacher's place, and since Pius had ceded me the chair near the window, he also screened me from view down the aisle. The school might be termed New—abstracting from most of the faculty and the furnishings and the building—but this remained an offense against propriety, youngsters like these, of opposite sex, at the same table. Unheard of, that's what it was.

"Angelina, wait a while . . ." was the mocking ditty aimed at us before the start of the first class after the Christmas holidays; there was a lot of anticipatory giggling around us, for the Principal, Dr. Kliefoth, was expected; he was thought to have old-fashioned ideas, and indeed a corner of an eye twitched when he caught sight of us, as though a fly had attacked him there. He tested the class in his own manner. He started with Matschinsky, jumped to the Cs when the Ws were due, added some Ps, and then relaxed against the back of the chair, hands in his lap, sending first a stern glance sideways from under his beetling brows. The rigid white brush of hair on his skull was quite motionless although the heat was by no means up yet in the pipes. It was Pagenkopf's and Cresspahl's task to translate, taking turns, that letter from E. A. Poe's "The Gold Bug," which unfortunately begins with "My dear" and contains locutions that might have fit into a love letter. We had to struggle with the foggy light of the ground-glass lamps and were in no mood to giggle. Lise Wollenberg, made rash by her rancor, willed herself into a fit of laughter and reaped from it a demerit written into the class record book for creating a disturbance during instruction—a ticklish thing for one already handicapped by her bourgeois background.

For each of us he recorded an A. Kliefoth was hard to classify, middle class and militaristic, but as principal he was also progressive intelligentsia; after his tacit approval, what could La Habelschwerdt do to us? As luck would have it, she found the change actually recorded in the Principal's handwriting on the class seating diagram; we saw her whip upright. Never again would she be able to convict Pius of a shortage of community spirit, and by the following year she invited us to afternoon coffee: the two of us together.

When the singing and jeering had started around our new table, Pius had contracted his eyebrows as if from pain and tightened his lips as he used to when he was standing under the horizontal bar, collecting himself for his leap. That man mastered every challenge in his life by tenacity. Since he stared so arrogantly into space, as though our mere intention sufficed for success, I lost my self-consciousness and became confident that this was going to be a good time and would end well, Supposedly, after Mrs. Habelschwerdt's sighs, we nodded to one another like two horses long in harness together; after which we counted as a couple in love.

Because of our fathers, it remained incomprehensible for a long time that the Cresspahl girl walked home from school with a Pagenkopf and did her homework with him, or that Pius sacrificed half an hour's sleep in order to meet Gesine at the milk train from Jerichow. We didn't wear our contract on our sleeves, even to each other. The Cresspahl girl got over the hump by arguing that custom demanded one should walk with *some*body. How matters stood between her and Jakob she was afraid by now to inquire. And Pius always had somebody now with whom he could pass Lise Wollenberg by as if the matter of her passport picture had been properly settled only when he tore it up.

### July 19, 1968   Friday

"It's all going to come down today." (Robinson Eagle Eye)

"It's all going to come down today, Gesine. And don't smoke so much!" (Mrs. Eileen O'Brady)

"Let it all come down today, my gardener has made a bet with me." (De Rosny)

If only it would all come down today, all the heat that is hanging over the city, making the mornings pale, the days hazy, so that the high-up cornices flicker, and standing still in the sun becomes unbearable because the blaze of the concrete strikes through one's shoe soles. Last night the dirt in the air left only a small broiling hole for the sun. When you have swum eight blocks through hot liquid air, the air conditioning at the bank feels like a blow to the heart. If only everything would come down today.

All of it did come down today; it's been four hours and we're still telling each other where it caught us. D. E. claims to have stood at the edge of his mother's lawn after lunch, hose in hand, nose up and probing the air; whereupon he stowed the gear away, for cool, dry air was on its way to New York overhead. He prided himself not a little on his nose, and in this complacent attitude, with an exuberant flourish of his claret glass, is how we'll remember him. The white-collar worker Cresspahl watched the beginning of it, neglecting her official duties: the light between the glass skins of the office slabs around her was toned down and excessively clear; all angles were honed to a sharp edge. Then, at a quarter past four, you heard the first thunderclap. Marie feels sure that she saw the lightning that went with it in the broad descending swatch of 96th Street, which ended in the dim window of the river. When the first fat drops burst at her feet she was at "Good Eats," and Charlie waved her inside, old customer that she was, but pressed against the Broadway side of his windows stood a gentleman who lacked the change for a cup of coffee; he surrendered, shoulders sagging, to the sluices flooding the sidewalk. At the bank's palace, too, the rain gushed down in a dense flow, and from the sixteenth floor you could hear the car tires sloshing on the wet pavement. At a light in New Jersey, D. E. stopped next to a pedestrian striding along as if on parade, a piece of cardboard held over his half-bald head and never mind that the rain blackened his suit. Along Broadway, Marie saw a black dance, a big carton on his shoulders, heaving it high every few steps, never jolting anybody. Then the fire trucks started wailing on Third Avenue. Torrents now swept down on D. E.'s windshield, but if he has promised arrival at six, he is on hand at 1800, and more power to him. On Lexington Avenue, on the other hand, the pedestrians behaved as though it were more important to keep walking than to keep dry; rain evidently generates less solidarity than snowfall or heat in this country of ours. Twenty minutes had now passed since the start of the coming-down, and a men's shop had its window sign ready: Umbrella Special. But Mrs. Cresspahl maintained her dignified progress beneath the New York *Times*, folded to form a roof. The beggar established on this side of Grand Central Station, who when on duty gives people a fright with his uncovered double leg prostheses, had taken time off and was now leaning against a wall inside the Graybar Building, trouser legs turned down. When Marie stepped outside, she learned a new kind of breathing, which D. E. was able to explain to her now in terms of the plunge of relative humidity by at least ten points. In the subway it was still stuffy, only one fan in two was operating; sullenly the riders stood jammed together, regardless of the fact that they had come through yet another week of New York, anyway. By a quarter of seven the rain was so weak it could barely manage a dribble, but it had at least wiped away the clump of fog that hid the Jersey side so that we could make out the waterfront again in its gloaming. Then the thunder trampled back and forth over the Hudson, unable to leave its waters. Now it is quiet; the asphalt mirror of Riverside Drive shows us the treetops in the friendship they maintain with the sky. From the park comes a squealing bird call, like that of an injured young animal. A seagull? Yes, Marie has seen the seagull above our

treetops; there it is, sawing into the wind, and the wind bears toward
the house.

## July 20, 1968  Saturday, South Ferry Day

At the table elaborately set for breakfast (American version for D. E.),
across from the festively sunlit park, the New York *Times* got between
us; we all but slid into a quarrel. Twenty submachine guns of U.S.
manufacture have been dug up under a bridge between Cheb and
Karlovy Vary in five army packs or civilian knapsacks bearing the date
1968. Also thirty handguns with ammunition to fit. In the vicinity of
the West German border. And *Pravda*, Moscow, had managed to
broadcast this yesterday morning before the Czechoslovak Ministry of
the Interior had even been able to announce the find. To such as
Professor Erichson it promptly becomes possible that such arms caches
can be had all over the country for the finding, and that the Soviet
Union could justify any sort of military incursion by Sudeten German
"uprisings"; so if you ask this expert, he would think landings of airborne
troops most likely. But there was a woman at this table who was to
travel to that area in four weeks' time and would prefer to have it
painted in somewhat brighter shades. Then came Marie's glance, askance,
dumbfounded at the unheard-of idea that in our family someone could
be prohibited the expression of a thought. Both looked at me as if to
say "Here is one who is run-down, she needs an outing." That they
can have, but on the way they are to listen to the Pagenkopf story, as
a warning, as a promise, whichever way they want to take it.

"Kann denn Liebe Sünde sein?"—Can love really be a sin? This
song, unctuously croaked out in a smoke-roughened baritone by a Nazi
actress and put back into service to divert the Germans' attention from
hunger, this time courtesy of Sovexport—who do you think was the
target of this ditty at Fritz Reuter High School, starting in January
1949? Cresspahl's daughter and Pius Pagenkopf, that's who, to drums,
fifes, and a brass band. We were the Couple.

Lise Wollenberg too believed it. She had taken the niece of Mrs.
District Court President Lindsetter to her table, a small-framed blond,
who despite her tender flesh was called Peter because she had been
wearing her hair short ever since the start of the Soviet occupation.
This looked intriguing alongside Lise's long ringlets. Of me the Wollenberg wench would say: with that kind of father, Cresspahl was well
advised, of course, to make up to the new regime.

But Mrs. Pagenkopf was no upper-class lady, smart of dress and
hairdo, activist slogans on her lips; she looked bent, stoutish, work-

worn to me, as frugally dressed as Jakob's mother. She pulled in her shoulders as if there was much fear still left from the swastika years, and new worries very much alive because of her husband's "conduct" at Schwerin—this loaded word showing how the good people of Gneez necessarily interpreted Mr. Pagenkopf's political activities. She was too shy to go on stage for a public discussion at the end of the film at the Renaissance Film Theater. But she did read the first page of the *Volkszeitung* and would have been capable of spelling out to the comrades what had happened to the S. E. D. since the first Party conference in January 1949. (She actually advised us on articles for the underground resistance.) The neighbors interpreted her laconic manner as her revenge for those times when the Pagenkopfs had been people one had better keep away from. She referred to me as "thy Gesin," in a tone of fond reproach; she rarely addressed me directly. But since Pius had chosen me, she presently found a little rhyming phrase: "Röbbertin his Gesin." For that matter, I would have had to shout to talk to her. Since her loss of hearing had become incurable, she turned to everybody but Pius her right ear instead of her eyes; who knows if she ever looked into my face. One got the impression that Pius's mother lived in the kitchen and manifested herself most distinctly in the perpetually polished windows, the waxed floors, the carefully groomed sausage sandwiches Pius would bring from the kitchen with the tea. Yes, there was tea. And there was butter on the bread, for the Pagenkopfs had three ration cards, and this household would never have wanted for the fifty-five marks per pound of margarine at the special shop. The sandwiches were spread liberally; I never went hungry again in the East after 1949. In this Lise was right; I was plugged into one of the delights of the ruling class.

As for Jakob, I meant to keep this Pius away from him; wasn't I breaking faith with him, even though I had to accept his going with other girls? A few weeks passed, and I saw Pius in conversation with him, the rangy aristocratic boy in a courteous pose before the thickset fellow in the greasy railway outfit. I was in Jakob's keeping every inch of the way.

Pius and I were a recognized pair; from the shared classroom table we went together to the Street of German-Soviet Friendship to the Pagenkopfs and did our homework in the parlor. We had no choice, since the maidservant that Helene Pagenkopf had once been had crowded the main living room with flower stands, whatnots, spindly little tables, easy chairs, leaving barely enough clear space around a piano, the contribution of Pagenkopf Senior. Since we left the house again together, we were a couple.

The teachers got used to this. When the Physical Education lummox couldn't locate me, word about the workout schedule was sent by way of the student Pagenkopf. It goes without saying that Pius accompanied the student Cresspahl to the pool, conveying her swimming gear on the carrier of his bike. Like her, he joined the swimming club called Trout, since his father had requested some "social" visibility from him. Because in a dual relationship, in a couple, each partner must look out for the other, Pius had ascertained that children exceptionally gifted in a sport were rewarded by transfer to special schools, there to receive more training in their form of athletics than knowledge of useful subjects, with the result that after their tournament victories they would be in a rush to enter a profession, yet would have fallen behind the majority. This duly noted, the performance of the freestyle ace Cresspahl sagged almost to average clockings. There was little evidence to bring against her, for the other teachers reported steady performance by this student; the Physical Education lummox hit his stopwatch on the head when he accused Cresspahl of giving too much of her attention to Pagenkopf. Nevertheless, he exempted me from his exercises, since he didn't like to interfere with couples. We must have been to his liking, as a pair.

KLIEFOTH: What is all this fuss about, Mrs. Habelschwerdt! It's precisely at the table that the two are safe from . . . the drift of your esteemed apprehensions!

The world finds it charming when there are similarities between the partners of a pair; and I grew to be a little more like Pius by becoming a member of the Free German Youth, as he had. Because his father had felt compelled now to request from "my son's girlfriend," too, some civic activity. He may have been a little short of this currency, for my membership booklet with the rising sun on its cover soon proved insufficient: I had to procure in addition the slim oblong one that showed a black, red, and gold flag stuck aslant into a circle, diapered on the Soviet one. By now this stood for Society for German-Soviet Friendship, and Cresspahl, after perusing the telegram from Stalin printed below my name, promptly raised my allowance by fifty pfennig, "for the next ones." It was small wonder, then, that at the start of Grade 10 Pius was voted president of our F. G. Y. class chapter and I his deputy. We held these offices until graduation, and they were noted in our school certificates.

As a couple we rode to the unlicensed bathing spot on the south bank of the Gneez municipal lake; without the others we swam diagonally across to the boathouses Willi Böttcher was now putting up in the water for the progressive intelligentsia. Together we came swimming back to the rest of the class, and obviously we had been talking the whole time. When I happened to be there without him, they sometimes sang to me the old question about whether love could be a sin, but the old embarrassment had been driven out of me by Pius, and they learned to inquire about him through me. We were, after all, the ones who dried themselves off on the same towel—the Couple.

When two have been a couple for a long time, they go to the movies according to the state of their purse and the film's allure; when two are still far from being a couple, one has to pay for the other's ticket and in the course of ninety painstaking minutes test the possibility of becoming one. If only one of a couple is present, a seat is kept for the other; next to Pius, "Save that one for Gesine," and as you come in they call, "Here is your husband!" That applies to F. G. Y. meetings, the theater trip to Schwerin, potato digging during harvest service. When one of a couple is on card-checking duty, Gesine will take Pius's dish along with hers and bring him his school lunch. A couple has more time than other people: these two can spare themselves the promenading, at least two afternoon hours up and down Stalin Street, spent in tremulous reconnaissance for the object of one's longing; a couple already has each other.

One thing I want to tell you, by the way: Pius is as little Catholic as she is Lutheran.

In early 1950 we registered together for track-bed maintenance with the East German State Railway, because this time Pagenkopf Senior had requested a civic activity that was discernible at least to the eyes. The couple poked about for three weeks in the road metal of the run-down track beds of the Gneez station with shovel and pickax. In the snapshot one can see "my son's girlfriend" shoveling, while Pius, amiably leaning on a stick, is looking into Jakob's camera, a knit cap on the back of his head. The reward, the material incentive that is, was a free ticket to a destination of one's choice. But a trip *à deux* was removed from our grasp because Cresspahl needed my coupon for a trip to "Berlin." So Pius went to Dresden by himself, via East German Wittenberg for the sake of his father's reputation, and back via West Berlin for my sake. For if one member of a couple travels, he or she brings home a present for the other. Gesine Cresspahl, Class 10-A-Two, owns a ball-point pen.

The lead-off game was pretty poor stuff, but now it's Fritz Reuter High against Grevesmühlen, and again the center forward is Pius. You see, two minutes before the starting whistle, here comes Gesine. Over there, in that empty patch in the bleachers, the one with the pigtails, who is now folding her long skirt about her legs. Who is now sitting up straight, for Pius to see her. Why should these two wave to each other? He's seen her long ago. She doesn't applaud him either, you know. He knows. They are a couple, after all.

Yes, but can love be a sin?

In the winter, the power cutoffs disturbed us in diagramming benzol chains or explaining the societal motivation of Lady Macbeth. Then Pius might sit down at the piano and play for me what he had been taught in eight years. (He had thoroughly drilled himself in Schumann's "Reverie"; I once heard his rendition from the street on a dusty, languorous summer afternoon; dreams involving Lise he kept to himself.) But often there was total silence behind our dark windows. Early on, Zaichik broke in on us with his Eva Matschinsky, on the pretext of bringing us candles. Then they saw Pius return to the piano and the Cresspahl girl calmly go on smoking: they must have thought us uncommonly clever. Worse for them, they had lost an overt cause of their visit. He had told me of his elder sister's death from typhoid fever, I had told him about Alexandra Paepcke. We could certainly claim that we knew this or that of one another.

One time, when I was sixteen and the rail service to Jerichow was interrupted, I spent the night at the Pagenkopfs, in a room by myself. I did not wait for Pius.

Pius would have refused me any information about the amended second line of the song about that Angelina who still had to wait.

We were careful never to take each other's hand.

In the summer of 1951 we were touring on our bicycles. At Cramon Lake, diagonally opposite the village of Drieberg, we stopped for half an hour's swimming. While changing, I was clumsy or he was, and our feet touched for a breath's length.

Pagenkopf and Cresspahl spent the vacation together. They bicycled to Schönberg, to Rehna. Pius spent two weeks with the Cresspahls, after all, and these two weeks they went to the beach from Jerichow every morning. Whose business is it what those two do when they are alone! They are a couple.

---

### July 22, 1968   Monday

---

To come right down to it, what is it that threatens men's civilized life on earth? Above all else it is that bomb, which produces heat by nuclear reactions—so argues one of its inventors and he would now like to see the Soviet Union get along with this country, in this as in other fields of hygiene. Such an active thing, the remorse of scientists.

Another, expert in mathematics and philosophy, sounds

impatient. The Chairman of the Soviet Council of Ministers should give public assurance to Lord Bertrand Russell and the world that the Red Army in the C. S. S. R. will refrain from acts of violence. Just so we have something to go by for the future. Those vexing uncertainties, don't you know.

Actually, the Soviet Army concluded its war games in Czechoslovakia three weeks ago, and still keeps troops in that country. Their army newspaper reports from Moscow what they busy themselves with. They are looking for new bagfuls of American arms, and once again they have found them, three of them.

The widower, the crusty old bachelor Cresspahl was surrounded from late summer of 1948 on by as many as three women. One of them you know, a fifteen-year-old you can guess, the third one will surprise you. Regrettably and by way of advance mourning, the first wore some article of black at all times, a collar, a scarf, or whatever; the second—what do you know?—was called a fast piece behind her back; add to this the Brüshaver woman, the Pastor's wife, coming to visit as once upon a time. Her lips set ever in resolute lines, her spectacles stuck at an outlandish angle on the top of her head, a careless part in her now lusterless ash-blond hair, this is how she stepped among us; careful not to be caught looking around like a stranger. However, the one-time path between Creutz's Landscaping & Gardening and the manorial villa was now out of bounds even to her as part of a Soviet reserved area; so she had to come in public sight, from Town Street along the brickyard path, overcoat over apron for decorum's sake, and easy in her manner from the first visit. But Cresspahl was glad to have her see him busy himself in the kitchen with his daughter and Mrs. Abs, in the shelter of a family as it were, and turned a cool shoulder by asking what we might do for her.

She went at it as only a woman knows how, snatching something out of thin air; quite at random she went on about how "men" were eternally fussing and posturing and generally "carrying on." This was hard to contradict, and taking what she meant to be a reasonable tone, she added an invitation to Cresspahl to have a look at a window in the parsonage that leaked rain water, making puddles on Aggie's waxed floor. Thus she reminded us that we used to know her as Agatha and that Cresspahl's profession was carpentry and cabinetmaking. This furnished the beginning and brought up the dictates of etiquette; because Gesine forgot these in her pride, Mrs. Abs offered the visitor a chair and a tin mug of roasted-rye coffee. She lost no time praising it.

Not a word about the absence of the Cresspahls, of the Abses, from her husband's sermons, not a word about Gesine's arrogance; we owe thanks for that, Mrs. Brüshaver, ma'am. Directly, the next morning, Cresspahl cleaned one of his carpenter's rules, oiled the joints, pocketed it, and actually went halfway into town among people, for the first time since three years ago October, since May of this year. Went out on a job.

It was a window frame on the upper floor of the parsonage. Aggie went through the motions for Cresspahl, showing how she braced herself against the frame while polishing the panes, the heel of her hand breaking almost inch-deep, through what looked like flawless enamel paint, into rotten wood; it was not staged, either. It turned out that up to two thirds of the frame could be scraped away with one's fingers. Aggie wanted an explanation, since the window had been renovated as recently as 1944. A craftsman safeguards his professional discretion and refrains from appraising someone else's workmanship. In 1944, Wallschläger had been in power here, that shining light of the ministry, the proclaimer of Nordic leadership. If someone had it in for him, all he needed to do was to use the softest of softwoods, black poplar it would seem in this case, make one or two ducts in it with a nail guide or screwdriver, hide the whole thing under paint, and move away from Jerichow in good time. For the rain, driven by the westerly winds and the sea breezes, will separate the frame from the sill within the year, stealthily wash out the mortar, and will soon leave nothing to hold frame and masonry together but the wallpaper inside. By that time it's too late for any repair; we are dealing with a total loss here, which will require more than eleven pounds of tobacco on the black market. "I'll have to patch it up," said Cresspahl consolingly. "An emergency dressing for the winter," he promised, and Aggie calmed down, seeing him measure the window as though it might be saved. His keeping the sabotage job from her counts for me as the second step of Cresspahl's return to life with people instead of against them as decreed.

Now just you try to find, for the reformed currency of East Germany and reasonable words, some cement in Jerichow or Gneez to slap over the masonry and bandage the rest of the frame, just a paper cone full! You'll sooner see a sack of flour cross your path. In addition, we are short of a big hunk of beech or stone oak, $5'' \times 6'' \times 3''$, to say nothing of sodium silicate or synthetic resin to weatherproof it. Anyone looking for these has to scout around, must at least offer conversation, and when he comes to inspect the barely covered scar in the wall he sees Pastor Brüshaver standing in the yard, bent over the flower beds he is spading, but with an upward glance suggesting that he knew you. Subjects to take up then might be the times when the Pastor had to make an appointment to speak to Mayor Cresspahl in the town hall about permission to hold an assembly (divine service). Or later, when it was May and we had a new constitution, whose Article 44 sanctions religious instruction in nondenominational schools, when Brüshaver found his charges waiting in front of a locked door on School Street, and the District School Commissioner in his communications behaved as if to an upright Communist: the Lutheran Church was redundant among the social groupings, and its pastor in Jerichow an irksome petitioner rather than a comrade in anti-Fascism. Potatoes need loose soil, Pastor Brüshaver. Hoe once before the sprouts show. When they've reached four inches, hoe and mound them; mound again when the plants are as long as your hand, (it'll do your waistline a power of good). Then Brüshaver, for all his Greek and Latin, had to inquire, and Cresspahl enlightened him: Jist summat folk say . . .

Neighborless. Teasing. Aggie Brüshaver now brought the ration cards to the house, neighborhood volunteer for Jerichow South that she was ("because *someone* had to do it, and because from me they get only the accounts and no certificates of conduct"). When Cresspahl tried to refuse vegetable fat and bacon Aggie had diverted for him from Swedish Aid, it was pointed out to him that she was guided by medical need, not charity, and that a patient of sixty-one had every reason to comply with the orders of a registered nurse. She had noticed how my father held his head, and soon I came upon her vigorously massaging his shoulder and neck muscles, and felt jealous that he had never asked his daughter to do it. "Surely I am the obvious person for that," said Aggie when he thanked her and she gave him a pat to indicate he could put his shirt back on. One time Jakob was with us for the weekend, and she came and fussed and bridled, pretending to be lecturing him harshly. Jakob had gone to St. Peter's at Easter of 1949 for the sermon dealing with the Resurrection, and she reproached him for having sat through it all with his arms crossed, even though it happened in a rear pew. "As if you were considering an offer!" she boomed; after a while Jakob nodded as if in agreement. And because I can hear her still, I have a chance to see him once more. Brüshaver had now been functioning for three years without teeth; they had been knocked out for him at the Nazi concentration camp at Sachsenhausen. Finally Aggie overcame his distrust of "German doctors," and he appeared with yellowish plastic structures in his mouth and kept chewing on nothing, like someone combating a bad taste. "Say sixpence!" my father demanded, and they would practice synthetic speech with each other like little boys. I once noticed Jakob's mother stretch her lips as she watched those two, it looked strained, as if it hurt; she had tried for a smile, furtively. When she meant to speak severely to Aggie, she addressed her as "young woman!" Those two had reached the stage of confidences in the hospital. And whereas one set may have pardoned me from a sense of Christian duty, the others could find it in their hearts only because I "belonged," by residence, shall we say.

The Gesine Cresspahl of 1948 meant merely to tolerate the neighborhood. For one thing, she now was a university-track senior-high-school student by profession and had settled the matter of God for herself in a way she thought wholly original; for another, she was able to sustain her unbelief by the simple means of recollecting the prayer by which a Lutheran chaplain of the U. S. Air Force had besought God's help for the crew of the plane that would drop the first atomic bomb on an inhabited territory. She credited Protestant theology with sufficient tactical and strategic judgment to recognize a conventional ravagement of the city of Hiroshima as sufficient, given the war situation as of August 6, 1945, 9:15 Washington time. The student Cresspahl was aware of the reason why the New State with its New Era liked to schedule its parades, meetings, and work details to coincide with religious holidays and celebrations. She counted herself out in this competition. The Church was no longer her business, anyway.

"The pagan girl can hardly live in peace / If other pagans find some fault with her." Look at this Jakob, who is bringing a rain-soaked cat into the house, carrying the dripping bundle before him by its ruff, until finally he drops it with the finding: Wet as Jonas! Only then does he become aware of Cresspahl's Gesine waiting and lets an idle glance glide over her, as though she lacked the knowledge of Biblical whales. Listen to the pronouncements of Heinrich Cresspahl this summer; English and evangelical is their tenor: Don't preach in Jerichow, and the staunchest faith in the state Lutheran Church (to take her word for it), but adherents of the faith in her house, she feared, would stir up the ill will of Albert's jailers. She wrung her hands with those qualms, she wailed and yowled faintly: people were always singling her out like this, demanding more from her than from others. . . . Brüshaver engaged the rear room of the Lübeck Arms, now called a rathskeller. Lindemann, the tenant, sent word that assemblies were subject to registration and permitted on an equal footing with club meetings. The Jerichow Mayor's office prohibited the use of secular premises for religious propaganda. (The Mayor was the one after Bienmüller, Schettlicht, the pop-eyed agnostic from Saxony.) Brüshaver suspected behind this a policy statement of the Red Army, and felt delicate about testing this with the Jerichow Kommandantura. How could he have any idea that the Wenndennych Twins would have ridden roughshod over

Comrade Schettlicht! Finally Jakob ran out of patience, and the German State Railway pushed one of its workshop cars onto Papenbrock's now Federal rail spur, arranged with benches as for a conference and equipped with a stove, for which the gasworks donated a barrowful of coal. Wherever Jakob worked with people they were willing to do him a service, and he was, for them, as is the way among friends. In this vehicle, under the light of stable lanterns, Cresspahl's daughter held out until Christmastime.

She tried to act the modest child, ready to atone with a will; in addition, she was prepared to find it equitable that she was hardly praised for her fluent recitation of the main Articles of Baptism. Water by itself is not enough, to be sure. On the other hand, she had to admonish herself to sit still and did her best to avoid scrutinizing Brüshaver's face, for it seemed to smile perpetually. What did it was twisted muscles and strained tendons, which pulled at the corners of his mouth and rigidly fixed the folds near his eyes in the involuntary semblance of a grin. He also pretended that the fourth finger of his right hand had always stood out so pertly from the palm, stiff hook of a bow of pain that forced his shoulder downward. When he lifted the book between index and ring fingers before placing his thumb on it, casually as it were, the hand seemed artificial, nasty. He could not help groaning when he had to use his lower arm; it would hurt you just to watch. Religious instruction is carried on in the catechizing mode; there was no shelter from Brüshaver's impaired voice, which turned something exceedingly grainy round and about in his larynx as if every sound meant an injury to the tissues within. Gesine argued desperately to herself that these were his souvenirs from six years at Oranienburg and near Weimar, to be weighed against the virtues of an official certificate or I. D., which by now had his comrades at the town hall, at the District School Commission in Gneez, and at the District Council Office raise their hands as if to shoo something away. The trouble was that she couldn't always retain control of herself; and it was certainly foreign to her intentions when she heard herself say, through a droning in her ears as if she were talking under water: the matter of omnipresence, she knew it by heart and would recite it if required to, but to believe in it—she couldn't bring it off. This said, she ran so blindly to the door of the platform level that she almost tumbled from the high steps, ran down clammy Station Street into the dark abyss of the market square, hid in the ruined lightless telephone booth, shaken by racking sobs, afraid of the twilight in which everybody would see her.

Cresspahl remembered the winter of 1944 when she had sought refuge in that same booth from school and authorities, and came to her rescue by suppertime. He led her off like a child, one arm around her shoulder, and the route they took spared her the lights at home and the look of Jakob's mother's dark, lens-enlarged eyes; they went into the humid low-lying thicket, where only hares and foxes could hear, untroubled that the bodily presence of Christ in the Communion service struck her as cannibalistic. This was the last time that he held and guided her like a father; of his consolations she retained the one that absolved her: You gave him a chance. You gave it a try, Gesine.

The following afternoon she saw Mrs. Brüshaver enter the yard. On winged feet she retired into the Frenchmen's room, which Jakob's mother, with her sense of decorum, had had rearranged for us as a place to have our meals in. In her hiding place, as fast as she could think, Gesine scraped together arguments against the emissary of the Church, weapons in case of discovery: Aggie had stopped as early as 1937 instructing children in the Christian faith. Did she doubt what her husband proclaimed as articles of faith? As for Cresspahl, she urged him to have himself hung upside down before an x-ray screen in order to get to the root of the pains in his neck; Aggie let her husband live with a case of Dupuytren's disease, hard ropelike scirrhous tumors in the palm; there was surgery available for this. She was a nurse, but turned her back upon her husband's troubles with yet another bureaucracy and went off to the Jerichow Hospital; she also left him to deal with all that paperwork of the parish. Is that a prescription for Christian matrimony?

Aggie answered her through the closed door, she thought herself alone with my father in the hall. Despondently she asked him, as if she were pleading for forgiveness for herself: What if the child turned out to be right, Cresspahl?

The sun hung in the westerly haze, already one quarter gone from the earth; its low rays filled the room with a viscous, blood-colored light. I had never found myself in such an ominous red vapor before.

In March Cresspahl installed a new window frame in the parsonage, made by hand out of a rail tie so intensely permeated with creosote that dewdrops would sit on it without seeping in. In the meantime the Brüshavers had found a section of crumbling wall a yard wide, running along the chimney from the attic to the ground floor, donated by means of a few chisel blows into the copper flange in 1944 by opponents of the state Church of Mecklenburg. This was part of Brüshaver's inheritance; the Pastor of Jerichow lived in an undermined house.

A week after Palm Sunday in 1949 there was a christening at the Brüshavers. Aggie ("with me everything grows like that") had yet another child, a boy, Alex.

Persons who dispute the omnipresence of Christ are neither worthy of Confirmation nor equal to the duties arising from godmotherhood, that goes without saying; and Cresspahl's daughter learned, without envy, that in addition to Jakob's mother another child in the Confirmation class had been designated to watch over Alexander Brüshaver's conduct as a Christian. This was a girl from former East Prussia, who was able not only to recite but also to trust in that omnipresence bit. She was Gantlik's daughter, and her name was Anita.

---

### July 23, 1968   Tuesday

---

Enter Anita.

No "little Anita"; a rangy girl with strong shoulders like a boy, almost athletic of build from the work in the fields that had been exacted from her in the village of Wehrlich for nothing but her food and a bench with a straw pallet under a dripping thatch roof. This was because she wasn't a local child but a refugee one, with almost no possessions to back her, without a mother, and with a father who had left her behind in her rural serfdom and kept the pay he earned with the Jerichow police for himself, as if he wished ruin and a wretched end on her. This is how matters stood, and when the child came to town for Church service and Confirmation class, one and a half hours barefoot, she came past her father, her gaze impassive and free of rancor. How does such a child, without a guardian or anyone to stand up for her, get away from day labor to the country town of Gneez, into higher education, into an apartment in the best neighborhood by the town moat, in a three-story house with water running out of the wall and light from the ceiling?

When she entered Grade 9, the rumor was there before her and gave her a nasty welcome: "the Russians," it claimed, had helped her to this. The truth about that is that the lord commandants of Jerichow, the Wenndennych Twins, arranged to detour to Wehrlich when they wanted to travel the countryside as ruling Muscovites, and let this Anita, a fifteen-year-old child, sit by their side to translate for them what these Mecklenburgers might try to say. It is also true that the Comrades Wenndennych allotted her compensation for her services as if she were on their level, that is, a coupon for a bicycle, a Swedish import, the prize exhibit of the government store on Stalin Street in Gneez. The citizens of Gneez called it the first bicycle in Mecklenburg for which "the Russian" had paid in cash; and while they were about it, they talked of Anita as the Russians' sweetheart. Thus Anita was enabled to commute punctually, from September 1, 1948 on, by bicycle to Fritz Reuter High School and back, ninety minutes in the morning, ninety minutes back to Wehrlich, over unpaved country roads, against the rains and west winds of this dank autumn. All she had to do about the bicycle was lock it; it was safe from vandalism, for although the Russians were far from being social assets, as avengers they were redoubted. It was a bicycle with white tires that had TRELLEBORG impressed on their sides. It is true that Messrs. Wenndennych also asked her about her personal well-being and took umbrage at her habit of doing her homework in the former municipal library under the patronage of the Cultural Society because she lacked a home and her brute of a "host" could at any moment send her from her books to clean out a pigsty. The Jerichow Kommandatura secured from the one at Gneez a change-of-residence permit and the allotment, out of turn and as an exceptional favor, of Mrs. Weidling's sitting room. A dangerous boon, another blot on her escutcheon; regardless of the fact that Mrs. Weidling had been hauled in last November by the Kontrasiedka, counterespionage, on account of her carefree wartime journeying in German-occupied territories with a man in a black uniform. This was clearly not done in order to provide Anita Gantlik with a whole apartment for herself, but that is how it was distorted. And we were present when Anita was for the first time called upon by Baroness von Mikolaitis, who was allowed as a favor to sell her Baltic origin to us in the form of instruction in Russian. Anita rose humbly, dropped a hint of a curtsey, and gave the fluttery old lady a longish reply. That was all we could make out after as much as three years of Russian instruction. It sounded like: The Russian word for railway station, ma'am, voksal, is derived from the amusement park near the Vauxhall station in London; Tsar Aleksandr II Nikolaevich also had one erected in his city of Pavlovsk, Voronezh Region. . . . The word *voksal* was certainly mentioned. Such fluent, unpressured, unstrained speech coming from one of us was a novelty to the Baroness; and it also exceeded her own capabilities. Simply in self-defense she found fault with Anita's stressed o's. Anita made them sound short and less rounded, while we applied some Mecklenburgish lengthenings; she said thanks for the correction, in Russian.

The following week she reported to Mikolaitis that she had produced her "o" in front of native speakers (this in Russian), and that it had received their blessing as Moscow standard articulation. If she sounded helpless, suppliant, she was not simulating; she was asking the instructor for a decision. The end of this affair was Mikolaitis's inviting Anita to private lessons, but with the idea of herself learning the flow of speech from her. She struck the pose of a Solomon; she was a coward. Altogether, we found little to emulate among the adults. Incontestably, three or four times a week a crackle came from the loudspeaker above the blackboard, and Elise Bock, school secretary as of old, transmitted the summons: Gantlik to Principal's office. Anita would take leave of the subject specialist in German or biology, give a sigh or two, drop the regulation curtsey, and gather her notebooks together as if parting forever. Two periods later, sometimes after 3 P.M., she was back in her place, having interpreted for Colonel Yenudkidze at the town hall; given the fact that Slata had left. A modest young girl, in her well-worn black suit she entered the school as if joining a celebration. She spoke in a low voice and with downcast eyes. She may have worn her dark chestnut hair in braided loops about her head under the impression that this was the fashion in the city.

A broad, compact forehead, behind which worrisome things went on this fall. She was awkward, to boot, borrowing the notes covering an hour's missed class from Dieter Lockenvitz, our top student. Lockenvitz's white hair stood up with hurry and distraction, and what with his urgent cogitation he overlooked this girl's urge to sit down at his table for a minute and have him point here and there among his lines and formulas; for her private benefit, for him to take notice of her for once. When Lockenvitz stood at the board and tried to force algebraic successes—for in math his laurels grew only sparsely among clumps of blackthorn—her eyes, wide open, were fixed on him, she clearly vested hope in him, longed to be able to help. I trembled a little for her, she would have been a welcome morsel for Lise Wollenberg's big mouth. But only Pius and I saw what was going to waste there in the way of desirable things. If she had one happy day that winter it was when she was able to force her father to register her as a resident of Gneez and then make himself scarce by return train. For the first time she was alone in a room, behind the ice-cold glass with a view of fog and freezing linden tops, in strange parts, but by herself.

*Because, let me tell you, Gesine, my name wasn't Gantlik at all. Was he your stepfather?*

*Oh, utinam—had it only been so, Gesine! That he had been a stranger without any right to me.*

"Anita" *is a false name, too?*

*That was because my mother had seen a film set in Spain, in 1933, and heard a hit tune. "Juanita"; I forgive her.*

*But never your father.*

*When he is good and dead.*

*Our gentle, vindictive Anita.*

*We were settled by the Memel (but its name there was Niemen) under our good Polish name, of which "Gantlik" is the stub. Come the Germans and offer us the blue I. D. card, German People's Census, Group One, for Persons of German Nationality of Proven Merit in the Nationality Struggle—all this because of one grandfather from West-phalia. He up and joins the German Nazi Party, my weakminded father, because it tickles him to see German tanks flatten a Polish village. Applauding the Germans, and all of us get involved, Mother, siblings. Gantlik.*

*Without a German passport the Germans might easily have pressed him into forced labor in Germany proper, Anita. Without his family. This way, you received ration cards, could go to school.*

*A German school.*

*A school. And you could go to the movies.*

*"The City Mouse and the Country Mouse." "Quex, Hitler Youth."*

*And your mother was able to go to a café with you, to a restaurant; she could go shopping in the stores.*

*And my father, as a citizen of the "Empire" under his German pseudonym, he got compensation for the farm, was given a new one near Elbing (Elblag). When the Red Army caught up with us in January 1945, we were able to document in writing that we were Germans. My mother, my brother and sister, we buried them in an open field. My father, the German, he couldn't stand up for a child of eleven.*

*You pray, Anita, I know. There is one line there, the one about forgiving.*

*I do that. I forgive the three Russians who worked me over, I forgive all Russians, wholesale and retail.*

*Never your father.*

*Gantlik—before he dies. This was his war. He did that.*

*Then you were curious about the Russians. Because they took out their revenge on an eleven-year-old child.*

*I was, Gesine. Still am today.*

*D'you know what we used to say when Triple Y had you summoned out of class? "Anita is off to donate blood." Because it always had to be you. Because you used to come back so exhausted.*

*That was Pius speaking.*

*Pius was a good man.*

*None better. In those days I used to hide that business about the*

*Niemen and the Memel because I was afraid you might call me "Volks-deutsch" behind my back. Or "Teuton by Right of Conquest, Female."*

The student Gantlik rid herself of her father by having the Red Cross trace a sister of her mother, a widow with two children who was having a thin time in the Ruhr District, and to whom the names Gneez and Mecklenburg were redolent of fleshpots. She was installed on paper as the head of Anita's household by the town moat; Anita's earnings became the mainstay of the budget. Immediately after the separation of the western zones from the Soviet one she began blustering in a dreary whine about the sacrifice she was making for her niece Anita, being in a country whose money bought less of everything from butter to a wristwatch. She conveniently forgot that Anita had secured her a roof over her head, that Anita contributed to the common cash out of her honoraria, that it was Anita who made herself responsible for the education of her two boys, around eleven years old. Her father still found mention when we had to recite our genealogy to the school to document eligibility for educational grants-in-aid (twenty-two to thirty marks). "My father is a laborer," said Anita, in as East Prussian a voice as she could manage; and wrote it down accordingly. Later the questionnaires became more sophisticated and proscribed generalities. "My father knocks off rust at the Warnow Shipyards in Rostock," Anita testified.

Were we destined to become acquainted, to be friends? Not on your life. From the working team of Cresspahl and Pagenkopf, Anita borrowed neither paper nor pen; perhaps she felt a distrust of such a matrimonial show among students, or possibly meant to show it respect by reserve. It was Pius who in passing put his elaborate set of compasses and other gear on her table, because she was equipped for a homework assignment in geometry with nothing but a homemade protractor without a degree scale. Pius thought it was time to make Lise Wollenberg eat a little more crow; also, it pained him to see anybody drudge. When Anita returned the things next day, she said her thanks with a sigh that came right up from her boots; but ignored the student Cresspahl, who was sitting next to Pius. Whereas I was afraid she might take any word from me as condescension, she didn't want to seem to take anything for granted. Because she felt like a stranger, unwanted, an intruder . . . a refugee.

Anita, the alien corn, found a patch of meadow with a path leading through reeds on the south bank of the Gneez municipal lake, and fancied herself protected from the natives. What a shock it gave her when loudmouths from all four Grade 9 classes turned up at her habitual bathing spot, not yet trampled down. She immediately covered herself with her towel, embarrassed because she was ahead of things in the development of a bust; what remained visible were long, slim thighs, firm calves. "Beautiful legs," said Pius as we swam across the lake to the boathouses. "Lively legs," I amended; "early learnt, ne'er unlearnt." Upon our return we found her besieged by youths from Grade 10 who craved to borrow her towel, praised her wide-spread wavy hair, offered her cigarettes: young turkeys in the mating season. In her embarrassment Anita said something disdainful and tremulous about the mental state of people who in school learn the structure of the human lung by heart, only to muck it up afterward by inhaling tobacco smoke. We, Pius and I, looked around for Lockenvitz, although we knew he was away at a meeting of the Central School Chapter Authority. But the person who was eminently visible at the edge of the group of bathers, with a cigarette between her fingers, was Röbbertin his Gesin. . . . What course do you have in such a fix but to blink arrogantly into the May sun and take a thoughtful pull on the cigarette from Dresden, twelve pfennig apiece, after all, and real imitation Lucky Strikes?

This had been one chance at a rapprochement, and it sank like a stone in the municipal lake reeds. What was Anita supposed to see in this presence but another slur? Yet we felt deeply sorry for one another. She pitied me because I had bothered the Pastor of Jerichow with a show of sincerity; her oblique look of concern for me, noticeable only in the light of the Confirmation railway car—my memory has kept it faithfully. I pitied her because she thoroughly understood the work she turned in in the Natural Sciences (Mathematics: A; Chemistry: B; Biology: A) and yet unerringly came out with a god who is present in the molecule, the atom, and the sparrows he shoots off the roof with nuclear weapons. Anita, a resident of Gneez, every Sunday took upon herself the journey to St. Peter's in Jerichow merely because the Canon of Gneez supported the secessionist Pastor Schwartze of the Mecklenburg Church at Ludwigslust and denounced his very own Bishop Dibelius (West Berlin) as a warmonger; also an "instrument of American aggression," "Atom Dibelius." Dibelius had spoken of the administration of the Soviet Occupation Zone and its Department 5 as a "quasi-state," also of "arbitrary power stepping across all law," of "inner falsity and hostility to the Gospel of Christ."

Brüshaver wanted to throw in his lot once more with his Martin Niemöller, member of the council of the Evangelical Church in Germany, co-signer of the Stuttgart Declaration of War Guilt, and author of the proposition that all occupying powers should withdraw from rump Germany and rely on the United Nations to keep the peace there. That's why Anita was absent when on Sunday mornings we raked the municipal park areas or spaded up a third of the schoolyard for a Michurin garden; in her basic black dress she stepped before Brüshaver, probably also called on the Wenndennyches in the Kommandantura, since unlike us she was never once reprimanded for unauthorized absence. And was called by this time Anita the Red, because her swimming under the spring sun of 1949 had bleached her hair, bringing out a reddish tinge.

Anita could have stayed with the Brüshavers as a member of the family, but she was afraid of seeming to intrude, and especially of being pitied. Moreover, Aggie was no more than a nurse, however registered; Anita needed someone who was bound by the like of a Hippocratic Oath. Had she trusted me, I would have been there instantly with Jakob's mother. That aunt of hers from the British Zone, she let Anita do the housekeeping for her, hence the laundry too. They shared a bathroom, but that woman lacked the sense to ask a sixteen-year-old about her menstrual cycle. Otherwise Anita saw nobody in the world but men. So she went to the Gneez Hospital, Station Street, at the corner by the town moat, in the hope of passing through the works and emerging anonymous. What the works did for her was this: behind those frosted-glass windows with their prewar border of vines she was told of the cervical gonorrhea bestowed on her by the Red Army when she was eleven. She had almost forgotten that act of vengeance, by persistently keeping it just out of the focus of her thinking.

The isolation barracks in Schwerin, to which Anita was moved posthaste with an infectious-disease certificate, she later described as a camp. She lay there caged together with youthful and not so youthful ladies who had incurred such internal complaints voluntarily, even for payment. The physician in charge, a woman, she remembered as lean, bitchy, a "Nazisse" or she-Nazi; she could imagine her without difficulty with a swastika on her gown. For Anita was snapped at as if she were to blame, because a quite different guilt had come to light here. That paragon of medical experience accused her of negligence. She had been detained in Poland when the children around Jerichow were officially directed to report for V. D. examinations (over the signature of H. Cresspahl, Mayor); evidently the further course of the infection was all but symptom-free, except for a modicum of flux. The diagnosis described an advance of the infection to the top of the uterus, with endometritis specifica as the result to date. They congratulated Anita on having got away without pain—"And stop making such a fuss!"

She was addressed formally because she had been promoted to

Grade 10. But the treatment with short-wave radiation and a sulfa drug that stained the urine red seemed dangerous to her. She escaped from that facility and made her way eastward by night via forests and footpaths. One person, though, Triple Y of Gneez, had been missing her, and from Gräfin Forest down to the badlands uniformed men in his service and pay were on the lookout for precisely such a girl, one who crept along by herself, unarmed, and claimed to be Russian. Alone in his jeep with a child who would not give information in his or any other language, he bethought himself of a boon companion, Dr. Schürenberg, and gave him a fright by knocking at his door after midnight. Schürenberg at that time still had the right to place selected patients in the municipal hospital under his own care; and Schürenberg it was who finally notified the Principal's office of the senior high school. And who was the third person with whom these two had sung and caroused in the Dom Offitzerov? It was Emil Knoop, the Man with the Heart of Gold ("by weight, Yuri, by actual weight!") and he brought the antibiotic penicillin back from Brussels and Bremerhaven. Here one man acted according to his duty, which enjoined help and silence upon him in any case; another acted diplomatically, for Comrade Yenudkidze detected under the turf of Stalinist foreign policy the growth of an East German state; and come the time when the Soviet Military Administration would have to withdraw step by step out of the town hall of Gneez, a magnanimous gesture on leave-taking would be just as well. As for the third person, Emil, for a little thing like a refugee girl he wasn't going to make too much of the laws and regulations that described such imports as a contamination of the anti-Fascist German people's movement by the drugs of Anglo-American imperialism (with fine disdain for the fact that penicillin was being synthesized by the Western process and produced in the south of the Soviet Zone for the use of the higher echelons of Party and Security). You could learn a good deal from Knoop; all of it illegal, unfortunately.

The entire summer vacation of 1949 Anita spent in bed, initially in four-day stretches only because of the four injections given her weekly, later according to orders from the physician in charge, because of malnutrition. We traveled by water, traveled in the Black Forest, passed under Anita's windows, and forgot her. Before her bed of rest in visiting hours there appeared the Twins of Jerichow, the commandants Wenndennych, to present chocolate creams and a volume of poems by Aleksandr Blok. Triple Y came with his suite, brought red carnations and persuaded himself to interpret the word cystitis on Anita's fever chart as tactfully as did the students Pagenkopf and Cresspahl, who had been prompted—no, delegated was the term—by their Free

German Youth unit to call on Anita at the start of the new school year. She looked at us incredulously, wide-eyed, not recognizing us at once: so inflexibly was she prepared to be alone and remain alone.

Her aloneness had begun when she made her peace with the prospect of reaching at best the Havel River by going east, never the Niemen. For one school year she stayed behind in the 10-A-Two classroom while we were receiving the benefit of physical education. If only she had trusted Aggie Brüshaver—but she regarded her as one enjoined by Christian wedlock to tell her husband, a man, everything.

"Anita the Red"—this name stuck with her. Because she continued to go and help Colonel Yenudkidze with his German language—in the Barbara quarter by now, behind the over-man-high green fence. What were we to think but that she sided with the Red Army? The Deputy President of the 10-A-Two F. G. Y. group had the hardest time trying to get rid of at least three copies of *Jungen Welt (Young World)* among her fellow students; Anita used the *Krasnaya Zvezda*, the Red Army newspaper, for Contemporary Studies class, from a subscription she shared with Triple Y. Her garrulous aunt complained about Anita's recent practice of locking a certain room in the Weidling apartment both on leaving and when she was in, because she feared for her record player in the presence of her healthy, boisterous young cousins, Gernot and Otfried; and anyway, what could Anita listen to, allegedly without company, behind a locked door? Tchaikovsky records, every time. And the Red Army station, Radio Volga, faintly audible from the Potsdam region. She was insatiably curious about the Red Army and Russian workers and peasants.

What she would have to say about the latest news from the C. S. S. R. I would surely agree with. The leadership of the Czechoslovak Communist Party has turned down a meeting with the Soviet comrades plus hangers-on on their territory, but accepted one on their own soil. As if the contest might be less than friendly over there.

"Red Anita"; this was due in part to ethnological prejudice and error. For while Anita was still contributing more than her share to her aunt's housekeeping budget—to maintain her in the household and herself in the apartment—she did keep a certain amount for purposes . . . shall we call them private? Yes, if we mean secret. In the first place, she had to pay off Emil Knoop for the cost of her medication at a rate of exchange of six to eight East marks for one of the "West" ("Only death is free of charge," Emil had remarked in his good-natured way, failing to notice her sharp start at the word). At length, assuming a businessman's stance, he gave her employment in helping with his correspondence with the Soviet Army in Germany, where Yenudkidze's assistance gave out. The credit thus accumulating with Knoop she left untouched, even when she had to cheat her hunger with oats and sugar, roasted together without fat. Then again, she might amaze Helene Rawehn, Elite Apparel, Market Square, Gneez, with pure wool and raw silk material and strike awe into the male youth of Fritz Reuter High School with adult suits, tailored, with narrow skirts a hand's width below the knee and sweaters like those worn that year in France or Denmark; to be expected in Mecklenburg around 1955, with luck. Next to Anita, La Habelschwerdt seemed threadbare, shabbily dressed; but how do you ban a student's appearance that is unexceptionable except for elegance? At first we thought this was meant to enliven and stimulate Dieter Lockenvitz; but he was precisely the one she avoided. But she appeared at class celebrations, she accepted invitations from the twelfth and eleventh grades, declining to dance, however. A gentleman who escorted this lady to her house would start for home not unthanked but without a handshake. Anita received propositions that were way out of line; asked for a nocturnal walk around the municipal lake, she inquired so baldly into the young men's intentions that they could not help but recognize as an impertinence what was to have hovered as a lovely dream over the proposed promenade. "What for?" Anita asked, unmoved, businesslike, lifting her head with a slight jerk, her lips pursed, obviously well aware, for her part, of a whereto and wherefor. She wore her blouses buttoned up to the top, with a narrow velvet ribbon tied in a double bow, and yet it happened that "Bitter Rice" was shouted in her wake, in allusion to an Italian film enjoying a very different sort of notoriety. The earlier Anita had worn knee socks; Anita cured used only nylons, seamless.

"The Red Croptop." She had had her hair cut while still in the hospital. What was left of the braids was a short, close-fitting plumage which came down to her forehead in an artfully premeditated crisscross effect. At her nape Fiete Semmelweis, Jr. had left two slender opposing strands in such a way that they emerged in a startling russet from the outer brown and dovetailed against and across one another with every slight turn of Anita's head.

### July 25, 1968   Thursday

In order to leave nothing undone to keep the Soviet troops from marching to the defense of the Czech border, Prague television is showing them everything that already is standing in readiness there of domestic armor, dogs, and barbed wire. The West German Government is preparing to move the maneuvers planned for mid-September near this frontier, at Grafenwöhr and Hohenfels, to the area of Münsingen and the Heuberg, 120 to 150 miles farther off. To enable the Red Army to move away untroubled toward their home stations in the east.

Before the end of the 1949–50 school year Dr. Julius Kliefoth was relieved of his office as principal of Fritz Reuter High School. His students had to make do without an official explanation; were they to suspect Kliefoth of "conduct not conducive to learning"?

Kliefoth was stubborn. Invited to the Supervisory Authority in Gneez to accept a food parcel, allotted him to ensure that at least a head of a civil service office would be suitably provisioned in the midst of famishing children, he had begged to be spared favored treatment. He was supposed to have used the term bribery in his indignant amazement. A year later, in March 1949, the German Ministry of Popular Education had approached him via official channels, and by order of the Soviet Military Administration decreed him an increase in salary and purchase coupons beyond the ration card; also special loan terms in case he intended to build a home of his own. This was to keep men of his caliber from choosing to build a cabin in the western zones. Kliefoth would gladly have gone to England for ten days. When it was pointed out to him that his living in a sublet room on Field Street in Jerichow was incompatible with his rank in the school system, he refused to move into an apartment all to himself on Cathedral Court in Gneez. He came to work on the milk train, often rode home in the evening on the bare wooden seats of the unheated compartments and could feel fortunate if he had been able to find kerosene for his lamp. Now, the Mecklenburg Ministry of Popular Education lacked any contrivance by which to remind him of favors received. Kliefoth's a tough old curmudgeon; yet he must give in, come the end.

The Mecklenburg Ministry of the Interior also was disappointed in Kliefoth. On May 15 and 16, 1949, he was summoned to the Gneez town hall, where a vote was to be held on the Third German People's Congress. It was a historical performance in that it evaded the word election in an exemplary fashion and came down to a single alternative. The question asked simply whether a voter was for peace or against, take your pick. His yes for peace, however, took him to a consolidated list, a bloc made up of the existing parties, so that someone's rancor against the Communists over, say, the strangling of West Berlin, would automatically injure the electoral standing of the Free German Youth, and a preference for the Party of the Soviet Union, since for the last three days it had let food and work materials back into town, would as inevitably help the Society for German-Soviet Friendship. Kliefoth was a civil servant; in his innocence it escaped him that the authorities wished to take advantage of the confidence instilled in the middle-class voter that this affair must surely be aboveboard if our Julius was supervising it, this respected man with book learnin' an' all. Kliefoth certainly kept up a starched front, feeling himself bound by a formal official assignment. On the first day his polling place was run like a classroom. He inspected the approaching voters like candidates for examination, greeted the awkward ones with encouraging mouthings, obliged by speaking Low German. In his bailiwick things were to be run in such a way that the voters of Gneez would step before the ballot box of their own free will, known to him personally or producing a valid I. D. card, and the municipal police had no duty but to show outsiders the way out. Kliefoth leaned his head back to look at each person approaching his table instead of merely raising his eyes to them; an effort that toward evening took more and more time. If he looked stern it was because the dignity of the proceedings precluded smoking. He was the picture of a civil servant discharging a duty imposed on him by the Government.

During the morning of the 16th, instructions arrived from Schwerin marked "Blitz telegram—rush to desk," signed Warnke, Minister of the Interior. This directed Kliefoth to declare valid any ballots found unmarked in the box; the large preprinted YES was to suffice. If there was writing on a ballot, it was to count as valid for the choice indicated, except where the text was evidence of a state of mind "hostile to democracy"; whatever that might be. By dint of such numerical legerdemain, peace plus the consolidated ticket attained a rate of approval of 68.4 per cent, 888,395 persons, but 410,838 had done such odd things with their ballots that their NO allowed no conversion. The report of the Gneez Electoral Commission lacked the presiding officer's signature; Kliefoth had taken a leave, for "philological reasons." For the historical record he had to revise this to read "an attack of physical weakness." How could an aggressive and Party-minded minister like Warnke approve of an official who took almost an entire Monday off on his own say-so and insubordination?

"Dismissed because of his past," Lise Wollenberg opined, with her notorious inclination to gloat. But when the Soviet authorities in their Decree No. 35 declared "denazification"concluded in their zone of occupation as of April 10, 1948, Kliefoth had not even once had to interpret his curriculum vitae before a special jury—unlike Heinz Wollenberg, Kliefoth had evaded Hitler's party as early as 1932 by seeking the bucolic purlieus of Jerichow, and after the outbreak of war had gone into hiding in the Army. To be sure, the Red Army wanted a written report from him about what misdeeds had taken place under his responsibility and Hitler's supreme command when he was a captain on the staff of the II Army Corps in the Demyansk encirclement, and continuing to his last rank of lieutenant colonel. What he had to say must have convinced the military government, for in 1945 they accorded him a blameless discharge and in 1948, in May, they recommended him to "their" German administration, Ministry of the Interior, as a teacher of tactics in the professional training colleges of the newly established German People's Police, or VOPO. The ministry lured him with two salaries, one civilian, one military, and with a double pension: Kliefoth excused himself with a medical certificate, citing the eight teeth he lacked from the full set of thirty-two one ought to be able to deposit on an army's table. They had offered him retroactive payment of his Army pay to boot, back from May 1945. One refusing such abundant munificence may well gather a modicum of wrath over his head.

There was also talk that he had been letting the reins drag; we know who took them out of his hands. For this fall of 1949 was a season of meetings in Fritz Reuter High School. Out of the Third People's Congress (where Kliefoth had indeed stepped on a toe or two) a German People's Council had constituted itself, and out of this a People's Chamber, which on October 7 declared the territory of the Soviet Zone a German Democratic Republic, and its inhabitants citizens of this state, complete with constitution, government, and, for the time being, the traditional eagle on black, red, and gold. All of which was to be observed by solemn rites in the assembly hall, to last two teaching hours or an entire half-day. Kliefoth for each of these hours requested of "one of the younger colleagues" the favor of expounding to the youthful audience how these events between Mecklenburg and Saxony looked against the background of developments elsewhere in the world, whether they would advance or retard them, with particular attention to China. Kliefoth appeared to slumber behind the red-draped table on the dais, the narrow skull with its brush of white hair inclined forward, hand on chin; actually, though, he was calculating how much of the prescribed curriculum was lost in the time given to such performances and saw the afternoon melt away in teachers' conferences discussing curricular repairs, for which he was personally responsible to the Board of Popular Education of Mecklenburg. When at last he rose to adjourn the meeting his shoulders sagged, the claws of the Picasso dove painted on a panel behind him seemed to touch the back of his neck, and he appeared bowed down by the cares of office. Yet there had been a time when he could speak in a tone of confident authority, looking forward to his return to work. "In this spirit, then . . ." said Kliefoth resignedly; he certainly sounded fatigued.

Kliefoth's professional Waterloo came over the subject of Iosif V. Stalin (born 1879); others are positive that it happened over the business at Christmas 1949.

1949 minus '79 yielded the Biblical, the magical age of seventy for the distant Generalissimo Stalin. And just as the citizenry of the young East German Republic sent close to thirty freight cars full of presents on their way (on the remaining rails) to the Genius at the Helm of the Soviet Union, the German People's Best Friend (amid some embarrassment over the delay in supplying a planetarium for Stalin's own city), so the students of Fritz Reuter High School of Gneez, Meckl. delivered their burnt offerings under Loerbroks's portrait of the birthday child (members of the arrangements committee: Sieboldt and Gollantz; responsible for the contribution of 10-A-Two: Lockenvitz). Julie Westphal, her eyepits narrow with an adamant spirituality, her forehead screened by a cast-iron fringe, her bosom quivering in a jacket of mannish cut: this durable maiden on the wrong side of fifty had had herself refurbished in Güstrow in the art of musical direction. Under her baton a female choir of members of Grades 9 and 10 sang the favorite song of the birthday child, which with its nostalgic longing for a certain lost Suliko, intoned by sixteen-year-old girls' voices, was apt to cast a pall over the celebration. Guided by Julie's choreography, students of Grade 11, in regulation blue shirts and blouses, stepped solemnly forward and back, raising and waving flags; in the meter and tempo prescribed by Julie, the future graduates recited in chorus what the somewhat younger audience repeated as their vow to the Architect of Socialism, the Lenin of Our Days, the Teacher of Vigilance in confronting the Agents of the Enemies of the People, and whatever other items of personal description Dicken Sieboldt may have gleaned from the dailies of Stalin's Party in Germany. As guest pianist they had the benefit of Cantor J. Buck of the cathedral, who transmitted a Tchaikovskian sentiment; a winged austerity flowed from him, handsome Joachim, unarmed by either intuition or warning. As the concluding item, the new national anthem. Director Kliefoth was present as master of the feast, his grayish-green four-in-hand hanging from a worn collar as usual, in his workaday knickerbocker suit, the baggier and saggier of the two he owned; his frugal lips displayed a dry champing and the discomfort of a man who is abstaining from smoking out of respect for the occasion. Mission accomplished.

This had been December 21, and for the 24th 10-A-Two had

been authorized to give another festive performance. This one we owed to Anita. That little foreigner, from "East Prussia," had been dissatisfied with the information we could supply about the person after whom our school was named; what she found out about his writings was couched in the formulas that Mecklenburg children used to fend off questions. After her diffident inquiry we rehearsed the description of the Christmas celebration from the seventh chapter of Fritz Reuter's *From My Roving Days*, and performed it for our parents as a narrative with staged episodes. What parents were available. Custom would have dictated that Anita expiate her proposal by mounting the stage in person, but we were sufficiently embarrassed to designate the student Cresspahl, alas, for the role of the Vicar's wife, Mrs. Behrendsen.

There was no dearth of rustic youth; the Vicar's wife had real gingerbread cookies and apples to distribute. The melancholy Franz of the original we had dropped in favor of the coachman Jürn; Pius did Jürn and the narrator and had the last say with his ride through the village, the sounds of song coming from the poor peasants' huts, and the final consolation in homely Low German: ". . . and on high Our Lord had lit his great fir tree with the thousand lights, and the world lay beneath it like a Christmas table which Winter had neatly covered with his white snow sheet, so that Spring, Summer, and Autumn might place their gifts on it. . . ."

That Dr. Kliefoth thanked the participants and wished them, as well as the guests, a "happy Christmas holiday" proved to be the last straw. Because he could have kept us from doing it. For at least a week he had had on his desk an order that banned school celebrations in winter except in honor of the Generalissimo, or possibly for the Soli manikin, whatever that was. Furthermore, the expression "winter holiday" was now decreed for him to use as the official designation of this recess in the school's operation; that is what it has been called in Gneez and Mecklenburg ever since.

In school Gesine Cresspahl saw her principal for the last time when he substituted for one of his younger colleagues, serving in the map room. He had difficulty handling the long poles with their heavy windings. There was a thin line of foam on his lips after an hour of Latin with the seniors. He recognized her at once when her turn came and she asked for the physical geography of South China; but he looked at her as though her emphatic greeting had come as a surprise. Alert serene eyes in steeply rising cavities, surrounded by multiple folds: an owlish gaze. And because Kliefoth disappeared in the middle of the school year, without a school assembly for thanksgiving and farewell, it was, at one point, too late for a torchlight procession in his honor, and at another point such a gesture was judged inopportune, the technical equivalent for a simpler term. Because it would have meant a twelve-mile trip for his students from Gneez to Jerichow, where Kliefoth was spending his premature retirement, alone with Messrs. Juvenal and Cicero and Seneca. The tales circulating about his ample pension income also served to soothe a sixteen-year-old conscience. But the student Cresspahl was on her guard in Jerichow, her home town, and studiously avoided the path leading to the garden plots, where Kliefoth planted 900 square yards of land with potatoes and tomatoes and onions and carrots, as he had learned to do as a child in Malchow-on-the-Lake. As if she had her doubts that he would fill her hands with red currants.

## July 27, 1968   Saturday

Awakened by the silence; it was capacious, it contained bird song. Sleep was aware all through the night that the alarm clock was muzzled, and it set waking time for the hour when the squadrons of cars have rallied to Riverside Drive and the first children are led into the park. The dream presented a wood thrush, showed a migratory thrush, set its sights as high as a tanager. All were rejected, for all these are busy by this time with the upkeep of the nest and the raising of their offspring. What was singing there was a wren, known as *Zaunkönig*, fence or hedge king. A cheerful little king on the grilles of the park on the far side of the hot quiet traffic lane, in the temperate shade of the stately hickories . . . the walnut trees that had been present in the dream like an oleograph in Pagenkopf's hall. Woke up on my own.

A quarter to ten; greeted by the framework of a breakfast: tea is waiting on the hot plate, two eggs are in attendance under their quilted caps, only the napkins are still empty of rolls. The New York *Times* is here, but who is missing is Marie, or any word from her. The young lady is absent on a secret errand.

It is announced that Edward G. Ash, Jr. of Willingboro, N. J., U. S. Army, and David A. Pearson of Tonawanda, N. Y., fire fighter, U. S. Navy, have been killed in Vietnam.

The British Communists are shirking any word of reproach to the big Soviet brother, but they have the crust to find dandy the way the Czechoslovak Party is sweeping away the "injustice of the past," how it insists on socialist democracy—and what do they serve for dessert? "Only the Czech people and its communist party have a right to determine how to deal with their internal difficulties." This involves, for starters, 32,562 people in Britain, abstentions deducted.

Antonio (Tony the Crouch) Corallo of the Mafia got his in Federal Court at Foley Square: for attempted bribery of a water-department employee, three years in prison. But the maximum sentence would have been five years as well as a $10,000 fine. So, assuming good conduct . . .

A man of thirty-four from Astoria (we nearly moved there once), Vladimir Vorlicek, yesterday entered the firearms department of Abercrombie & Fitch, bought $5.50 worth of shotgun shells, surreptitiously loaded a shotgun—such stuff apparently lies around there without any safeguards—and blew his brains out. He had arrived some time last year as a refugee from Czechoslovakia. There is another No vote.

"Good morning, Marie! What a beautiful child she is! Are you visiting? What a classy dress you are wearing, blue-and-white-striped, to go with blond braids, and silk ribbons on bare shoulders! A fashion plate!"

"Good morning, Gesine."

"Something is troubling you, young woman."

"As you see."

"But nobody is to be troubled here! It is a holiday, the sun is out, we could go and take the South Ferry right away. What do you say, Marie?"

"It's just . . . you sometimes like to have hardboiled eggs for breakfast, Gesine. When they've been left to cool overnight."

"What if I do? I can get along without them today."

"I meant to get some ready last night, and when they had been on the fire for some time I started to read, and went off to my room with the book in front of my eyes. Then there was a bang, and it made me think of Robinson Eagle Eye's jalopy and its shot muffler. When I finally noticed the stench, the saucepan was sitting on the gas with its bottom black and warped, and the eggs had exploded all over the place. Right up to the ceiling."

"You did a good job, though, cleaning up."

"Danke."

"Is German the language of the day, then?"

"O.K."

"In that case you should say Stielkasserolle, cooking pot with handle, even though the natives fantasize a 'pan.' Oh, I am sorry. Vesógelieke."

"Here you are. The nearest thing in . . . Kasserolles I could find on Broadway. Aluminum like the other one. With my own money."

"The old one had long been worn out. Amortized over four years. Tell me, fellow student, would you like a lecture about amortization law? The domestic exchequer deliberates, approves, and allots."

"Make if half . . . And what do you charge, roughly, for an hour's German lesson?"

"Lessons in Current Events. I charge an insalata di pomodori e cipolle. Puoi condirla?"

"Coming up, coming up!"

"Current Events or Contemporary Studies were a new subject, in that under the Nazis it would have been called Weltanschauliche Erziehung, Ideological Education. It was offered to 10-A-Two of the school year 1949–50 by a new head of Fritz Reuter High School, a Mrs. Selbich, barely out of her twenties, we had heard; acting principal. If she had her eye on confirmation in office, this kind of teaching could well count as successful experience."

"Selbich. Selbich."

"Dr. Kliefoth used to do that with us."

"Good grief. An outsider. A young one. A successor. Tough break."

"That shouldn't keep sixteen- and seventeen-year-olds from having an open mind. They shouldn't hold it against the new Madam Principal that the dignity of her office prevents her from personally closing the classroom door behind her, causing her to give the nod to the weakest person for this service, Mrs. Lindsetter's niece, Monica (Peter). We were willing to make allowances because she stalked instead of walking, as if her feet hurt her ('like no woman you've ever seen,' Pius whispered); because she stood erect like a commanding officer facing troops on parade; because surely she couldn't help her new growth of fair hair hanging down lankily—except that she could have brushed it for half an hour every morning. Class 10-A-Two rises and turns its collective gaze on the shirt worn by the specialist in Contemporary Studies. To go with a brown skirt she wore the blue shirt of the Free German Youth, complete with shoulder boards and arm patch. At this point, Kliefoth would have performed a gesture of 'at ease,' sure of having everybody's attention; this lady inspected us rather a long time before saying 'Sit down.' 10-A-Two derived small edification from the preceptress's first question, asked in a hectoring tone, as to why we were without exception in plain clothes instead of sporting the proud blue shirt of the F. G. Y. Pius looked at me as if expecting advice or a cue. I jerked my head, signaling 'go ahead!' This kind of communication between us had become precise and quick by now; it eluded the pedagogue's eye, or couldn't be proved. I knew that Pius would tease her, and since I had recognized her I had hopes of her as partner in a game. Pius raised his hand, received a curt nod, rose, and said in an exaggerated version of Mecklenburg dialect: 'The blue shirt, that's our garb of honor. We only wear that on festive occasions.' A similar mistake was made by the Wollenberg girl, who would have avoided it if Mrs. Selbich had not looked familiar. Lise barged on, unasked and without standing up, and in a confidential tone quoted from the dress regulations, commenting: 'But then, it's a pretty rare thing for someone to have a black skirt for everyday wear' (gazing at the brown-skirted hips of Madam Principal). But Bettina had changed more than her name, she had lost her sense of humor, she spoke differently, in a hard voice, as if to threaten us, as if we were dirt. . . ."

"It was the Riepschläger girl?"

"The Riepschläger girl, married and divorced Selbich, demanded 'Silence!' in a manner as blustering as it was clumsy, and called for the First President of the F. G. Y. for Class 10-A-Two. Well, this brought up Pius again, and while she was at pains to intimidate us with the verdict that shameful conditions had been allowed to spread, that the entire basic attitude might call for a checkup—"

"Bunch of pigs, as the Wehrmacht liked to say?"

"While she was trying to do that, Pius involved her in a circumstantial discussion of the enormous expense we had been to at the District Office for nothing but a shirt apiece, which we certainly wore to rallies, street marches, and year-end meetings, but declined to use even on potato-digging details;

*Our blue shirts are black with sweat,*

he quoted, and as for the girls in the class, they all had complaints about the clumsy footwear that belonged to the uniform. 'I am putting you on warning that I may revert to this matter again,' the transformed Bettina announced, as though she had the authority to mete out punishment. The former Bettina would have gained dry land by the smiling injunction that every hour with her must be thought of as a festive occasion. All might still have turned to sweetness and light."

"What a course like this can do to a person!"

"And the failure of a marriage. And a Party candidacy. And Heaven knows what."

"Had she messed . . ."

"Dropped everything. Upset the applecart. And for the first time Pius shook his head when I told him something: that in elementary

school Bettina had been cheerful and unassumingly friendly, a person
to confide in, for whom students did good work just to keep in her
good graces. Pius made a face as though he had to learn me by heart
all over again from the beginning, and troubled wrinkles crossed his
forehead."

"Lise Wollenberg, though, on the next day you had Contemporary
Studies with Selbich turned up in a blue F. G. Y. shirt."

"In a black skirt, though in private shoes. It wasn't long before
Lise had it all down pat about the employers in capitalist West Germany
trembling at the sight of the freedoms the workers have acquired in the
German Democratic Republic and are going to bring with them one
day on their way west."

"Kliefoth had to make that kind of prediction too."

"A Julius Kliefoth speaks as his spirit listeth. He had evolved for
himself the kind of epistemological therapy that makes it the teacher's
duty to put at the children's disposal whatever the present offers. When
Austria was to get her peace treaty all for herself, or Indonesia independent status, he required in the first instance elementary essays in
economic geography, and in the second expected at least some population figures. The fact that the Bulgarian politician Traicho Kostov
confessed to his intention to assassinate Dimitrov and associate his
country in a sisterly accord with Yugoslavia, then denied both and was
nevertheless executed in December 1949, was received by Kliefoth as
a news report. He held press conferences with us; with him we were
allowed to ask, like news correspondents: 'Is it true that . . . ?' (England
has accorded diplomatic recognition to China? We could have tripped
him up a thousand times, but the thought of his astonishment, the
warp of those tasting lips, was enough to keep us in check. We had a
pact with him.) The newspaper method led him to those he had been
allowed to subscribe to until the war broke out: one at a time for a
three-month subscription, from the French *départements* and the English counties in succession. How nourishing, he would stress, this
kind of practice was for one's mobility in foreign languages, one's
awareness of current affairs. (Facing him were children who knew
intuitively what he was missing and who had learned that having a
West German newspaper in one's possession meant a demerit from the
school, and showing it to others meant jail.) And if Zaichik insisted
on learning the foreign term for Düsenjäger, Dr. Kliefoth would write
to his academic friends at Saint Andrews or Birmingham; the word jet
he explained to us as best he could as equivalent to Düse, nozzle, a
technical term; fighter we learned to understand as fighter plane, a

weapon in readiness. We were in the know when a staff officer on familiar terms with such planes from the Eastern Front commented: 'Frightful thing, that.' "

"Did Bettina believe what she wanted the kids to recite in Contemporary Studies?"

"I hope so, for her sake. Because if, on top of everything else, she had her doubts, who would want to be in her shoes? If that was part of her burden, she must have sensed in our silence the mixture of compassion and mockery for Dieter Lockenvitz as he stood at the map stand in the front corner, preparing to report tidings of joy anent the decline of the West German economy, confronted with more than two million unemployed. He writhed; he shuffled his feet; he tried to hold onto the map stand, while Bettina supplied a running review: 'You've got the right idea, but you don't know how to handle it; you twist and turn as though you wanted to view a ball from all sides!' "

"Not bad. She is pleading."

"This was a last surviving hint of the former Bettina, who wanted to persuade a boy nearly her own age: 'Come on, we are the same kind of people; why couldn't two buddies like us come to agreement . . .' The only thing was, Bettina had developed some blind spots. She didn't have eyes to see that a student might be agonizing over the news of January 1 to the effect that food-ration cards had been abolished in the neighboring territory so evidently doomed to decline and fall; also because he didn't dare meet the eyes of those two in the southeast corner of the classroom. Only recently he had debated with them whether the much-vaunted model of May 1950 for collective labor contracts with the state employer, with its implicit agreement to planning imposed from above, was not obviously by-passing any code of workers' rights; also, whether a woman who gutted fish at the P. O. E. (People's Own Enterprise) Freshlicanned had a proper grasp of such ideas as an individual's share in plant ownership or in the value of labor. Bettina should have realized that student Lockenvitz's speech was stumbling over what his thinking brought up."

"And that you all lied like an American President—that isn't worth mentioning."

"Since when has the school been an institution to which we confide more than the prescribed subject matter? I'm sure that with your Sister Magdalena, too, who wins any such argument is a foregone conclusion."

"All I mean is, I wish you had been the winner once."

"I did win once. By the length of a bathing suit."

"Tell me about it. Tell me. You fib so beautifully."

"Now comes the era of successes, the man in charge had said last April, yet sometimes coal failed to arrive for running the evening train to Jerichow, where my bathing suit for swimming in the Baltic waited. When I woke up at the Pagenkopfs in the morning, I went off with the suit I kept for the Gneez municipal lake and did a few hundred meters there, mostly in the company of Pius, who would have preferred to sleep longer but exacted the virtues of a chaperone from himself. When we ran out of time for the detour to Helene Pagenkopf's laundry line, we would take the wet things to school with us. It was May, the windows were open; on the sunny sill the things would get dry by the fourth period. Keeping my face toward the preceptress, I sometimes reached out and felt the material, which had the fragrance of fresh water about it."

"And the Selbich woman had it in for you."

"Perhaps because the sight of me reminded her of a time and an occasion when she was in better shape. When she caught me with my forearm on the window frame, she called on me and in her rage made all sorts of remarks about people who paw swimming things, in the process getting herself entangled in the circumstance that when one changes for swimming one is naked for a moment . . . 'and this while you are being told about the personality of Comrade Stalin, the wise leader and guarantor of the world peace camp!' "

This 'you' was plural, was it?"

"It meant Pius and me, although the Gneez lake furnished separate dressing rooms, and enforced their use. Pius had instantly half risen from his chair."

"What a spectacle! Tall powerful youth assaults helpless new teacher."

"He would have been plenty sorry! I held him firmly back by his jacket with my right hand and worked my lips as if I were telling him something. If he understood it, it was the name 'Kliefoth.' " For Kliefoth had resigned his position in the school service on account of an incident in 1939, when he was trying to move a tenth grader back from dangerously thin ice; the student had been in uniform, and brought an action against Kliefoth: "You have insulted the Führer's coat of honor, Professor sir." Bettina similarly was wearing her heraldic blue that day, an attack on which might actually have cost Pius his graduation. In his stead the student Cresspahl got up, left Pius behind with his thwarted chivalry, and strode steadily toward Bettina Selbich, without any sort of permission. Bettina started to panic and called, "Sit down!" and presently: "Gesine, stop it!"

"As if she had recognized you all of a sudden."

"Baut if there are advantages to being in the tenth grade, one is that the students are supposed to be addressed in the grown-up third plural, *Sie*; I could afford to ignore this lapse. The other one was that students must not be touched."

"Ah, to be in the tenth grade at last."

"I planted myself right in front of her, as one girl before another, gave her my most gracious look, like . . ."

"Your kindliest one, Gesine."

". . . pursed my lips a little and showed her the least little tip of my tongue."

"Unseen by others."

"Unprovable. She alone had taken in what I had communicated to her, as from one woman to another; she was quivering in her blue shirt as I walked to the door and out. She screeched, our Bettina."

"A tenth grader can afford to ignore that."

"And proceeds, every inch a queen, to the Principal's outer office, where she borrows from Elise Bock a sheet of paper and an envelope, besides accepting the offer of a cup of coffee from her. What later rumor turned this into is that F. G. Y. member Gesine Cresspahl lodged a complaint with the C. S. C. A. of the F. G. Y. . . ."

"What sort of beast?"

". . . with the Central School Chapter Authority of the Free German Youth against F. G. Y. member Bettina Selbich, Madam Principal (Acting). In actual fact I hid in the map room, thus adding to Bettina's burdens the fear that I might have run out into the street; punctually at the start of the next period I stood behind our table. Pius smiled the way Jakob sometimes did: relieved, just a hint in the corners of his eyes, looking upward from under his brows."

"Saying his thanks."

"Forgiving me for having messed up his male-protector act. We were anxious, though, for in Madam Principal's office there was a cabinet full of radio equipment and a microphone, so she could ask me to report to her over the loudspeaker in our classroom. Things might have turned pretty ugly."

"She didn't say peep."

"But what did say peep, and more, was the rumor mill I have mentioned. Rumor had it that Mrs. Selbich had dealt Cresspahl's daughter a resounding slap in the face, which forced her to consult a dentist. Rumor insisted that after the departure of the student Cresspahl 10-A-Two had become unruly (the girl had her partisans, of course), so that Mrs. Selbich saw herself obliged to place her chair on the teacher's table and to climb the resulting structure with the aid of a

second chair to gain a vantage point for surveillance; a fine display of
Riepschläger calves and thighs. (Unfortunately for Bettina, the report
in this instance claimed no more than she had done; Pius swore to
this.) The alleged complaint changed wondrously into an action filed
with the District Attorney's office for student abuse. It was reported
that Mrs. Selbich had attempted to undress Cresspahl's daughter; neither Pius nor I gave out a scrap of information. But in town I was
saluted and made much of at every step, just as I imagine they used
to cheer a popular reigning princess, and in Jerichow the saga of schoolgirl grit defying school authorities had already preceded me. I went to
get the milk at Emma Senkpiel's; she went to the back room with my
can and returned it to me heavier than usual. (Twelve people watched
me weigh the free allotment, all looking like gleeful conspirators.) So
it cost a few marks extra. At home Jakob's mother found a dozen eggs
in the milk; and the egg coupons were redeemed with margarine in
the three ten-day periods of May."

"Gesine, you're fibbing. Those are the eggs that blew up on me!"

"Much obliged to you; I might have forgoteen about them."

"Now for the complaint."

"Dicken Sieboldt intercepted us the next day at the unapproved
bathing place; he used to walk up to me publicly in the schoolyard.
He had an air of secrecy about him, something circumspect. He talked
with everybody until he had me to himself and could take me aside.
He had a lot of praise for me, he being chapter secretary of the
C. S. C. A. of the F. G. Y., because I carried Elise Bock's sheet of
paper, bare of writing, in my coat pocket, along with the unaddressed
envelope. 'That's a thing for my mother's son,' he said, quite the
competent, duly briefed functionary; he did not enlighten me as to
what mischief he was prepared to pull off. He behaved as if in the
middle of his neat agenda he had received an unexpected assignment,
impossible but rewarding. They called him Dicken because he had
something bull-like about him, menacing to the stranger who found
himself in his paddock without warning. For him I was 'Cresspahl his
Gesin.' He disliked vagueness, and he knew his reputation."

"Gesine, is this going to be a murder-most-foul story?"

"Don't worry. But the thing was, Granny Rehse, whom Bettina
Selbich in her new magnificence had seen fit to engage as a cleaning
woman, gave notice; Bettina had to do her own cleaning in her Cathedral Court apartment. The landlord gave her notice; her complaint
won out, but the prevailing tone on staircase and landing was very
different now. Say, a garbage can happened to be left in the dark in
such a place that Bettina took a little spill."

"You are mean."

"Aren't we? And Jakob, two hours away by rail at the Güstrow Locomotive Engineers School, had long been friends with Joche by that time; Joche was glad to be his lieutenant. So Bettina didn't have much luck traveling by rail. The conductors always looked at her ticket more suspiciously than at those of other passengers, who then tended to move away from her. The railway police would walk casually through an entire train, only to pounce upon Bettina and examine her personal identification, hers alone, with open suspicion; how could they be personally acquainted with someone who had immigrated here from far-off Ludwigslust! Bettina became disorganized: between Schwerin and Gneez she misplaced her ticket. This led to a deposition at Gneez's main station: what impression did the passenger make? Distracted. Are there sufficient prima facie grounds for considering her capable of the offense (fraudulent acquisition of transportation services)? Premeditation is suspected."

"Central Station."

"Yes indeed. Branch line to Jerichow."

"How was she to know that a railwayman was registered with the Cresspahls at Jerichow!"

"This Ariadne thread was unraveled for her by someone else. Someone who had something bulky about him."

"Oh, you, my far-off homeland!"

"The Chapter Secretary at Fritz Reuter High School had some concerns of F. G. Y. administration to discuss with Madam Principal, a fellow member. Overburdened as he was by his office and his preparation for senior-year finals, he could make such appointments as this only for the late evening hours. He was observed several times in Cathedral Court at night."

"Oh, you, my far-off homeland!"

"We had an ally within the teachers' conference: the Physical Education lummox. Who never failed to wink at us when he came across his erstwhile star swimming with her Pius (we were the Couple). Thus intelligence reached us that it had been suggested to colleague Selbich at the conference on grades that she raise the student Cresspahl's customary B for conduct this year. She apparently sat stock-still in her seat for a while. And indeed, this student had not allowed herself to be caught in any breach of school regulations throughout the year, and she graduated from Grade 10 with an A in conduct."

"And was Bettina once bitten, twice shy?"

"Mrs. Selbich overlooked the table in the rear corner of 10-A-Two whenever she could. After all, she was serving a three-week term of sitting over that page in the class record book which she had had to substitute with her own hand for the original one, where she had inscribed something pretty dashing before reason returned to its throne and she tore it up before the eyes of the class."

"I'd feel sorry for her now."

"So would I. For she began combing her hair during class, involuntarily, I am sure; the Ripeschlägers had raised their Bettina differently. Two years earlier she would not have tolerated a thing like that, neither on our part nor on her own. She only caught herself holding her wide-toothed comb when she was already passing it through her hair—which by the way derived little benefit from the attention."

"You and your bathing suit and Comrade Stalin."

"One of these (the bathing suit, I mean) now hung at Loerbroks the painter's, who had become our janitor. For all to see it hung there at the end of the schoolyard. The Cresspahl Memorial Site. Bettina may have wished it lay on the ledge of one of the windows of the 10-A-Two classroom."

"Comfort her!"

"We were obedient. She explained to us the decline of capitalism in general (miners' strike in the U. S. A.) and in particular (every West German jobholder works for about one month for the cost of military occupation). We repeated this on demand and had a hard time stifling the question about the per-capita deduction from East German workers' wages to pay for the Soviet occupation. Contrasted with the above was the rise of Socialism, the pact between Stalin and Mao, a development credit of $330 million. If someone wanted to know why this kind of transaction was couched in dollars, he concealed this desire. And Bettina combed her hair. Zaichik derived an instance of the decay of the British Empire from the liberation of India; while we still seemed to hear the engine noise of the British planes that helped to break the blockade of West Berlin. Gabriel Manfras expatiated on the Soviet gift of work norms, quantity of work units, or time norm; with an air of quiet ecstasy, it seemed. Bettina Selbich praised the vigilance of Soviet battalions, the trial of ten priests in Czechoslovakia for high treason and espionage in April 1950, jail sentences ranging up to life; Anita thought of the troubles that had befallen Pastor Brüshaver on account of Herbert Vick's will; she obeyed Bettina's call and disgorged for her what was wanted. Bettina combed her hair, her head to the converted! Don't mock the afflicted! And Gesine is to translate this for him into contemporary German, as though she were too uneducated for Luther's. Jakob's mother allows him to tease her about her special Old Lutheran quirks, at least spiritual matters get ventilated this way. But this fall she goes to Brüshaver's church for the first time, and takes Holy Communion from him. In October the daughter of Johann Heinrich Cresspahl, born in 1933, well known to the parish office, appears in the chancel of St. Peter's in Jerichow and craves a second admission to instruction preparatory to Confirmation. So that she might enter once again into the enjoyment of her elders' approval. The little coquette.

With the arrival of the warm season, Pastor Brüshaver went for a walk with his charges to instruct them in a meadow in the wood called Gräfin Forest; under the vast vault of the Church they were too few to keep each other warm. He had been trying to borrow rooms in Jerichow for that one hour on Saturday afternoons, from the Quades to the Maasses (strictly excepting the Cresspahl house). But the good townspeople complained of the dirt tracked in on their sacred floorboards by the soles of fifteen-year-olds. Right after the war Mrs. Methfessel had indulged herself with such notorious Nazi rhetoric as the "community of fate" in which her husband and Brüshaver had encountered each other; now she hit an embarrassing snag in her recalcitrant scion "Lurwig," who chose the Pastor's tutorial hours to practice dribbling his ball against the parlor door. Mrs. Albert Papenbrock had the largest parlor bowed, with tugging movements. Triumph of the World Peace Movement! The British have had to suspend the bombing of Helgoland. We sat in front of her in the hot light of June, the fragrance of linden blossom wafting up to us; somewhat less than attentive, because there was nothing to be learned in this class but a mode of behavior. Bettina once more bore out the younger Seneca's dictum—*Non vitae, sed scholae discimus*. Of one student, at any rate, it is certain that she mused about a time when travel would be permitted again to the vicinity of Helgoland. One way or another, the way to inquire into our obedience, our patience, this neophyte teacher had pigheadedly barred to herself. What, tell *her* anything? You're crazy. We deported ourselves with excruciating politeness in her classes, you could hear a pin drop; it was soporific. That was when I first wished I might never have to go into teaching and be trained and made over from a Bettina Riepschläger to a B. Selbich. I know that after no more than three such lessons I would have stumbled out of the class in tears, without dispute or discussion. She persevered, though, you must hand it to her. Now make a wish, Marie."

"I wish you could sleep as long as you need, and want to, every night. Tout à vous."

## July 28, 1968 Sunday

Topple Bettina! That is Marie's goal. But the leader and preceptress merely stumbled in the summer of 1950, though repeatedly; she could be riding for a fall.

We certainly made an effort. Bettina as homeroom teacher of 10-A-Two did let Pius register our candidates for the trip to the Whitsun Rally of the F. G. Y., but she insisted on examining them; mainly in view of the superadded condition that they keep their distance from the western sectors of the city. Pius she passed without any fuss; he was our first president, after all, not to mention his being the son of the deserving Comrade Pagenkopf in the district capital, who by way of the District School Commission could make an unprotected apprentice teacher eat dirt any time he pleased. The second class president, Cresspahl, it is hard to credit, gave homework assignments as an excuse, not mentioning a paternal admonition. The latter had to do with the fact that in early May the tenor of official sloganeers had still been "Free German Youth to Take Berlin by Storm!" Heinrich Cresspahl called to mind the teachings about the world that Gesine had brought home from the New School. According to these, the West had rashly picked up precisely where the Weimar Republic had gone off the rails and crashed; he remembered police in their bulbous black helmets hurling themselves at demonstrators with truncheons, even firing at them. He did not wish to have a "storming" child in the street, nor did he look forward to receiving back a daughter brutalized and broken. He all but begged her, offering her an excursion to Berlin on her own in the summer vacation. Gesine reserved the option of forgoing that treat. She acted the role of the dependable child resigned to paternal solicitude, the little show-off (in part because it was still a source of comfort to Cresspahl to have someone listen to him and pay attention to him). The real reason, of course, she kept from him: it was conceivable, was it not, that Jakob would remember his filial duty at Whitsuntide and pay a visit to Cresspahl's house; an event that this Gesine was minded to await in a deck chair by the milk bench behind the house, making believe, for Jakob, to be reading for school.

The student Cresspahl thus was a no-show. Gabriel Manfras declared in a restrained manner: we must show everywhere how sincerely we stand for peace. Being what he was, he took in Bettina (as well as the rest of us). Lise meant to use the opportunity to shop in West Berlin, and she made no bones about it, either to us or to Gabriel, who was somewhat disconcerted to listen to her parrot his formula in

a proximate and sprightly version. Anita was shrewd: she made her
excuses, citing interpreting duties for Triple Y and Emil Knoop. In
fact, she wanted to make some money working with Emil's calculator.
The student Matschinsky, Eva, might well think herself duped. She
wanted to go along in order to be near Zaichik. This Rabbit, Dagobert
Haase, dreamed of joining the visitors to the automobile exhibition in
West Berlin, but gave himself airs with a sham curiosity about recent
buildings in the "democratic" sector. Now Eva hemmed and hawed
awkwardly. Dieter Lockenvitz hewed to the same line as Zaichik, only
with a finer blade, talking about the relative autochthony of the superstructure as an expression of indigenous form in the new Berlin
architecture. Since he managed to remain serious and, what is more,
to quote from the work of I. V. Stalin about Marxist linguistics, what
could Selbich do to him? (She had never been to Berlin, we thought.)
Eva did get her permission, possibly because Selbich felt a need to
ingratiate herself with 10-A-Two. Where the former Bettina would
have smiled, and Eva's joyful anticipation been refreshing, today's
Bettina dismissed her with a disparaging "Ah well, you simply haven't
the awareness."

Pius signed up with more than the prescribed equipment (blue
shirt, toilet kit, fighting spirit); he traveled by resolution of the working
team Pagenkopf/Cresspahl. Accordingly, Gesine paid a visit to Horst
Stellmann on Jerichow's Stalin Street and requested a "rapid" camera.
Stellmann dug up a Leica from his hindmost drawer, much moved by
the thought of how accommodating he was ready to be with Cresspahl's
daughter. She, however, wanted a less conspicuous item, one that
might pass the newly introduced luggage inspections at Nauen and
Oranienburg without raising a suspicion of illicit dealing with West
Berlin. Horst at length produced a bellows camera that was more
modestly priced, with 300 marks' deposit instead of 2,000, and that
could be raised to the eye and put away in nothing flat. How astonished
he was when he caught sight of Cresspahl's daughter on the Whitsun
holiday on Town Street, poles away from any vigilante conduct in
Berlin.

Pius returned on the Tuesday after Whitsun and reported delays
in train movements, which were suggestive of indifference on the part
of the railway personnel toward the transport of young human freight
in the interest of peace. Also, accommodations on straw in a business
school at Berlin-Heinersdorf; a brawl with students from Saxony over
nocturnal theft; five hours of slouching march up to the reviewing
stand, which contained the Caretaker and the head man of the F. G. Y.
Honecker was his name. Almost thirty-eight years old now, he had

once weighed a takeover of West Berlin by his outfit against bloodied heads on the friends of his youth. To make up for it, he had announced something unheard of about potato bugs. Irritable reaction on the part of Berlin inhabitants to the free rides allowed the blue-shirted guests on municipal transport. Zaichik and Eva had made it to the exposition halls at the radio tower. Dieter Lockenvitz had set out for the Congress of Young Fighters for Peace at Landsberg Avenue station on the belt line, to be opened by the poet Stephan Hermlin; he claimed afterward to have lost his way, and remained absent, undiscoverable. Pius knew what Gesine was waiting for, but droned on and on with his narration; the two of us behaved at times like a married couple fond of teasing each other. At last she climbed down a step from her dignity and asked: "Have you got her?"

Pius had her, in his camera box. The youthful yet confident Madam Principal who is in charge of the delegation from Fritz Reuter High School of Gneez—how could he go and lose sight of her! She made his task easy by falling into a helpless panic at the bashful earnestness with which Dicken Sieboldt, in Berlin too, made for her blue blouse, as though he meant to disclose his admiration at the same time to her and to a public forum. This bemused her, allowing Pius to follow her as if invisible, until he finally came up with her in Palace Street, Berlin-Steglitz, U. S. Sector, West Berlin. In front of a shoe store: she was just a young thing, after all, was Bettina. When she became aware of Pius and the camera at his eye, it must have dawned on her in pain and suffering that she could not accuse a single student from Gneez of a detour to West Berlin in betrayal of Peace as long as one of them was in possession of a photograph convicting Madam Principal and senior F. G. Y. member of having succumbed to capitalist seduction with regard to circulation in the streets of divided Berlin.

## July 30, 1968   Tuesday

The Soviet Politburo, untraceable for the most part since Saturday, emerged yesterday morning, nine men strong, into the light of day from fifteen green sleeping cars, which were dragged by a red-yellow-and-green diesel locomotive into Czechoslovak territory, into a sugar-beet and wheat-growing area, to Cierna. The procession was headed by Leonid I. Brezhnev, who was greeted at the brick station by Alexander Dubček and fifteen of his advisers. Kisses? Embraces? Nothing of the sort. Three and a half hours of deliberation, then each delegation, nicely by itself, withdraws into its train for lunch.

No communiqué, unless we scrape one up for ourselves from

*Pravda*, which instructs the hosts, in the name of the whole truth and nothing but the truth, that their country depends on the Soviet Union for almost its entire oil needs, for 80 per cent of its imports of pig iron (border crossing Khop-Cierna), 63 per cent of synthetic rubber, and 42 per cent of nonferrous metals. Moreover, the Soviet terms of payment, we learn, are more favorable than those offered by the West, where favoritism and discrimination are rife, as we know.

For another source, we may lend a well-disposed ear to the New York *Times*. That gallant beldam with her compulsion to pluck this flower truth out of this nettle bluster opines that a Soviet invasion of Czechoslovakia would be a disaster for the French Communists. But she also infers from the ban on travel to the C. S. S. R. that the Soviet Union has imposed on its journalists that its own propaganda blasts have been given the lie. And what if the Soviet Government was anxious to protect its reporters, valuable trained personnel after all, from a future where visitors to Prague might have a hair or two harmed on their heads?

On the first schoolday after the Whitsun excursion those returning from it received their welcome; it also applied to those who had stayed at home to compose a love poem to Comrade Stalin, to B. S., or to a girl who had caught their attention as they peeked through the imperfect screen of a gooseberry hedge to where she was sunbathing. Many at first failed to notice that welcome. Gneez as well as Jerichow was so pasted up with posters, what would strike them about handbills of standard business size that had been plastered over the plate-glass front doors of Fritz Reuter High School and in stripes along house walls at eye level? The leaflets depicted members of the Free German Youth in formation; the blue color was registered by the viewer as familiar to saturation point, and so was the query directed to the F. G. Y.ists as to what they were marching for. The desired answer was so inescapably hackneyed that Pius had given up on reading the rest and comfortably forgotten about the whole business; so had Gesine. An equation with two unknowns, with three, is a challenge to the youthful Free German brain which may well deflect it from another topic.

Right into the middle of mathematical exercises under the tutelage of Mrs. Gollnow broke Bettina's voice over the P. A. system, hoarse, despondent, with the brittle harshness of desperation. All students, bell signals notwithstanding, are to remain in their classrooms. Responsibility for surveillance is to fall upon whichever faculty member is now in charge.

Evening fell, the dusk of late May, before the last of the students were let out into the street. The police—Section D of the Criminal Police—began the interrogations in the two senior classes, which meant that six hours passed before it was 10-A-Two's turn. To start with, Mrs. Gollnow saw the period to a tidy conclusion by fulfilling the day's program. Later she offered oral tutoring, and finally fell to telling what she called little tales from her life; what it had been like at Leipzig University; her correspondence with the writer Joachim de Catt, who used Hind Limb as his pseudonym. The windows were wide open, there was plenty of air, but toward noon the 10-A-Two classroom felt like a prison; a jolly one, for a short time. For Mrs. E. Gollnow, to general satisfaction, drew the veil from her initial, revealing it to be Erdmuthe; she would rather pass for a first-rate person among us than suppress her craving for pride's sake: she was a smoker and admitted it. Next: a vote on the right to smoke in a room designated for education; inventory taken of available smoking wherewithals, and distribution according to pure Communism: to each according to his need, not his merit. But toward two o'clock the *Turf* cigarettes

*Thousands under Russian leadership.*
*Thousands,*
*I am telling you*

had run out, and so had the hit-or-miss imitations of U. S. brands, and private fear had crept up to one's throat, not least because Gollnow had once and for all banned all conjectures about the quarantine. Something must be up out there that concerned the student body as a whole. Was the town on fire or what?

Toward three in the afternoon, rolls were distributed from the school canteen by a fiercely uncommunicative Loerbroks, who was guarded by a civilian unconnected with the school; dry bread without water or soup, you got sore swallowing it. Mute guesswork, bewildered (or scornful) looks of inquiry, shrugs of helplessness; it soon became difficult to remain confident. Those needing to use the restrooms were let out upon giving two knocks on the classroom door, but were escorted by a male or female officer, who refused to communicate with the students. With 10-A-Two, they began by the seating order (did the Principal's office have a copy of the seating chart?) instead of alphabetically. Thus Gantlik came before Cresspahl, Wollenberg before Pagenkopf, and no one returned. Cresspahl was the last to wait there in the company of Mrs. Gollnow, who had run out of comic turns, instead whispered something like "good luck," as if this student might stand in particular need of it. A searing, famished expression had entered Mrs. Gollnow's eyes.

Gesine was in luck, in the corridor her eyes lit upon a single raincoat, forsaken among countless empty hooks; she picked it up as if it were hers. In a pocket she felt paper, was even able during her wait outside the Principal's office to read some of the print. Elise Bock was to play escort and sentinel; she watched the student with appeasing sympathy and had already snatched the scrap away when the call to her phone had barely tapped the bell. Shadow of trees behind Elise's back.

*That was a neat job, Anita. Thanks, and thanks again.*

*The Criminal Police people first checked out 10-A-Two as a whole, with B. S. always in the thick of it. But they are after you.*

*Racking my brain about the cause of it finally numbed me.*

*They wanted to know if perhaps you resented the state. Because of the shitty deal its builders gave your father. Fünfeichen and all that garbage.*

*Forceful and to the point, our Anita.*

*Seeing that things happened in a rush then. They also wanted to know whether you absented yourself from the All-Germany Rally so you could take a secret trip to West Berlin—*

*Where I know no one except an Alsatian sheepdog.*

*—and collect handbills there that show free young German people marching behind and under barbed wire.*

*So that's what it buys you, that office I hold in the F. G. Y.*

*They don't care two cents about that; if anything, it'll add to their suspicions, Gesine.*

*Which is why you went into hiding behind printed letters.*

*Go ahead, guess some more, but later. They are after your hide. They want to know if you've got somebody working with the railway.*

Into the Principal's office, the place of interrogation, stepped a student, her head lowered, her braids feeling heavy; she barely raised her head to her F. G. Y. comrade, Selbich, who stared straight at her from behind her desk and over clenched fists and jerked her head to indicate the visitors' corner. A set of overstuffed furniture, confiscated with the rest of the Bruchmüller household goods; on it a son of Mecklenburg with the Unity Party's badge in his lapel, looking almost too tired for a labor of malice; next to him a man Bettina's age, a boy who would have had Lise Wollenberg throwing jealous fits if he had chosen another at a ladies'-choice dance; a gentleman. Material of elegant cut clothing his chest, and over his knees creases that had come fresh from under a hot iron. Stern and mocking his gaze, which said: Don't worry, we'll get you, too. The student said, "My name is Gesine Cresspahl, 10-A-Two, born . . ."

"There are grave things, very grave things we have to take up with you . . ." began this man of integrity and good will, the kind uncle, who disliked punishing, unless it were appropriate or needful. An upraised palm stopped him dead, as if he were on strings. ". . . that we have to talk about with you, young lady. This will make it quite clear to you that we proceed here in due form. You get it, tenth grade and all that sheep crap. Do you happen to know where might be the street of the Siblings Scholl in Schweree-en?

"If that is all, Mr. . . . [no name offered]. From Schwerin Central Station you take a right turn onto Wismar Street, that is southward toward Stalin Street, go on as far as St. Mary's Square, today Lenin Square, where you find the Dom Offizerov and to the east the passage to the palace, enthused about all over the country. Behind that, Kaiser Wilhelm Street, nowadays Street of National Unity, branches off to the right, southward again, and it leads to Graf Schack Street, both right and left. That is the shortest way, I think. Graf Schack Street is a household word to a young native Mecklenburger; that's where you go dancing, at the Tivoli! The street has only twelve numbers; it was the site of the local health insurance building, part of the Mecklenburg Social Insurance Center, and No. 5C was the residence of Pastor Niklot Beste, member of the National Consistory after the war, from 1947 Bishop of the Lutheran Evangelical Church for Mecklenburg. Graf Schack Street is part of the original suburbs of Schwerin. Adolf Friedrich von Schack, born in 1814 at Brüsewitz near Schwerin; member of the Munich School of poets from 1855, elevated to count by the Emperor in 1876, died in Rome, Italy, in 1894. His long poem 'Lothar' . . .

*Blest!! O childhood's blissful season,*
*The dawn of life, with gold bedewed!*
*A light we fail to sense with our poor reason,*
*A parting glimmer of infinitude*
*Surrounds thee yet!*

Anyone who knows his street knows all its ins and outs, whatever its name may be. On the left, eastern, half you have a view down to

Castle Lake. In the new Mecklenburg it was renamed after the Scholl siblings."

"Will you shut up, Gesine? She is making fun of you, Comrades, this brat, this . . . bitch!" screeched Bettina Selbich; she practically had her whole blue shirt loose and fluttering by raising one fist. The local interrogator's partner was up in one leap, sending a whiff of fruit smell over to the accused, who sat there as subdued and conscience-stricken as she knew how. The foreigner busied himself around his comrade colleague. "Your nerves, dear madam, it has been a hard day, a blow to our World Peace Movement, please compose yourself, out in the hall if you prefer . . ."

After this the atmosphere changed to the point where one might imagine that tea had been laid out on the low table with the crocheted doily, that tea cakes were constantly being offered to the lady under constraint, a glass of sherry too, if she cared for one. So the student knew about the Scholl siblings? That they were students in the Nazi era, Hans and Sophie, and were executed at ages twenty-three and twenty-two at Berlin-Plötzensee for having distributed leaflets at Munich University. "Excellent," the Sovietnik opined, glazing at his German apprentice as though he meant to encourage him to learn these data, but without much confidence. "And we," he said, with a touch of delight, clearly with amusement: "we have come from the M. S. S. from Siblings Scholl Street in Schwerin. We are concerned about those leaflets that arrived last night at the Gneez station and were turned over to a total of four distributors. One of these ministered to your senior high school; would you like to have been the one, Miss Cresspahl?"

What followed was an exchange of verbal strokes, today I would say a squash game, but with your skin at stake (skin is always on the outside, as a friend is fond of saying). The only good point was the changeless tempo, breath-taking though it was, which outpaced the Mecklenburg minion as Achilles did the tortoise; which meant several times, because an infinite series nevertheless approaches a finite terminal value, outside of math as well as in. Someone had seen to it that on the extended leaf of the cabinet stood a microphone from People's Own Enterprise Radio Technology.

And what, if you please, does M. S. S. stand for? Ministry of State Security. Many thanks. You're welcome, no trouble at all. Was the establishment of the M. S. S. overlooked in the curriculum of Contemporary Studies? To one's best recollection, yes. The historic date of the statute of February 8, 1950? Perhaps because of the excitement over the Peace Rally in Berlin. Responsible for the omission was . . . teacher's name? That nin . . . that was Bettina Selbich. It isn't as though we didn't know all about it, all we need is corroboration from you, young friend Cresspahl.

She claims an alibi, based on her arrival by the milk train at a time when the school was already gift-wrapped in subversive papers. Since the gear has broken on her bicycle, and replacement could not be had for coupons or money (that little device separating a driven shaft from a driving one, trademark "Torpedo," for Miss Cresspahl, you can get one at any bicycle shop in West Berlin). Shopping trips to West Berlin are denied; but that friend from way back, Pagenkopf, seems to approach that place of ill repute without a shudder. Pagenkopf is well aware what he owes to his father's position in the chairmanship of the Unity Party for the State of Mecklenburg. And to himself? The First President of the F. G. Y. class chapter does have an awareness.

Occasional overnight stays at the Pagenkopfs in Gneez because of quarrels with her father? Not at all, by agreement. Political agreement too? My father tries to comprehend the message of the present. With Miss Cresspahl for his preceptor? My father is taciturn by nature, also too gravely weakened for long conversations. Grandmother is a member of the Liberal Democratic Party? Not an illegal party. Grandfather in detention with our Soviet friends? No indictment has been brought. A brother-in-law of Cresspahl's is a civil servant with a Western ministry? At odds with the family. Cresspahl himself a prisoner, most recently at Fünfeichen? My father refers to this as a checkup; trust is a good thing, surveillance is better: a quotation from LENIN. Excellent— and now a quotation from STALIN! "Never in the world has there been as powerful a party as our Communist Party—nor will there ever be." Your grade in Contemporary Studies, Miss Cresspahl? B. We'll have a discussion with our colleague Selbich. If you please, your first thought on noticing the leaflets! Visual advertising, if it annoys the viewer, defeats its purpose. Any criticism of the use of visual advertising, such as why smooth paper is available for it, but only wood-fiber stock for notebooks? Or that material is more plentiful for propaganda streamers than for consumer textiles? Oh no, nothing like that. The leaflets were blocking the light on the main staircase, you see. Why leaflets rather than pasted posters? Because of the format. Your second thought, if you don't mind? The form of address. "Young friend." No— "F. G. Y.er." On the model of biker, miler. To Mecklenburg ears it may sound childlike, or South German. The Red Bikers of Munich? No; modes of locomotion or gymnastics ought to be kept apart from the demanding name of a youth organization which . . . Worth considering; to be submitted to higher authority. All right, quickly now, the birth date of Comrade I. V. Stalin? December 21, 1879, new style, at Gori near Tiflis, Georgia. And why Rome, Italy? Because there is a Rome near Parchim, about 400 souls strong, Mr. Inspector.

The advance of darkness calls on us to honor a regulation; about two gentlemen and a single lady at an interrogation. (He, he! bleated the Mecklenburger.) If a light might be turned on? Always at your service. Thanks. Everybody look pleasant, please. We are going to recruit a female witness. Madam Principal? Oh, what next! Let her answer the telephone. The first interrogation in my life; how different reality is from one's dream! We now welcome Mrs. Elise Bock; and you bring us coffee, colleague Selbich, but at a trot.

About the student Gantlik. Member of the class F. G. Y. chapter; on the office staff of the local Red Army commandant. The student Lockenvitz claims to have lost his way in Berlin. In a strange city. Social background of the student Lockenvitz. Something to do with agriculture in Prussian Pomerania. About the attitude of this young comrade to the Government's policy of turning his homeland over to the Poles? "To People's Poland" is how Lockenvitz puts it. About Jakob Abs, officially registered with Cresspahl, Brickyard Path, Jerichow, courier carrying leaflets from West Berlin. Posters to paste on walls. Traveling by rail on a free pass. After graduating with honors from Locomotive Engineers School at Güstrow, registered for a course in Elements of Dialectical Materialism. The third thesis of that doctrine? Transformation of quantity into quality. Railway worker Abs's private life? Handball. His plans for the future? He is a grown man; why would he discuss things with a seventeen-year-old girl!

The student Cresspahl comes to class in a white blouse. Blue shirt only on festive occasions. Turns up in school in a petticoat, dragging in fashions of the decaying empire. Quite wrong: a petticoat is a ladies' underskirt. Regrets hereby expressed for the mistaken suggestion that the friend of Bettina's youth had appeared in class in an underskirt. No—out of vanity in a full, slightly stiffened skirt, made with the help of illustrations in the democratic press. The student Gantlik has been found guilty of Protestant leanings. Well, she has been very much absorbed in Max Planck; the physics of this is above the student Cresspahl's head. Planck? The one who figures on the reverse of the West German two-mark piece? Never had Western currency in my hand; never seen any, hide nor hair. Any feeling on the part of colleague Selbich for the graduating senior Sieboldt? Known only from hearsay; a mere appearance of infatuation. On both sides? The Principal was too young to have any influence on exam grades for graduation. The Principal seemed to have somebody in her bad books. If only I knew why. A hypothesis, perhaps, in confidence? It is herself. Psychology, is that it? And now, quickly, let's have the third thought upon seeing the criminal postings on the school wall, of fellow members of the F. G. Y. behind barbed wire. Barbed wire? Never saw it.

Here the student Cresspahl fell silent for the first time. Here she was testifying truthfully for once and felt unsure. What begins, what goes on, when one's consciousness unexpectedly realizes a percept that nine hours earlier it had shrugged off? An afterimage? In the anonymous message of warning, barbed wire had been only a word, now the twisted strands with their braided-in barbs were a mental image, and underlying it the tone of voice from the evening broadcast of the B. B. C.: barbed wire. From last night's puny feeling of weariness over yet another spate of posters, how could the resolve arise to testify to the barbed wire, as vividly as if it had been conceived in the morning?

After earnest self-examination, the student Cresspahl began to confess, but came to a halt.

She thought of Kurt Müller. "Kutschi," chairman of the League of Communist Youth in Germany in 1931; sentenced to six years in a penitentiary for "preparation for high treason" in 1934; thereafter kept in the Sachsenhausen concentration camp. After the abolition of Hitler's battalions, chairman of the Communist Party in the State of Niedersachsen; in 1948 vice-chairman of the national C. P.; in 1949, member of the Federal Parliament. Protected by his parliamentary immunity, he undertook a journey on official business to the republic of the German Sovietniks and was listed as "missing" on March 22, 1950. Two months later, the Ministry of State Security had confessed and admitted the arrest of Kutschi Müller on the same date. This present evening, too, he was spending behind walls and wire; if the members of the F. G. Y. marched for anything, it was, among other things, for this armed wire.

She thought of a boy in 10-A-Two who was arrested because of a hit song. Slightly soused at a class party, he had amended the dreamy image in the first line of a sappy piece of mush that ran "when at Capri the red sun sinks into the sea." Instead of "sun" he had sung "fleet," from reckless high spirits, and probably under the illusion that his office as chairman of his class chapter would shield him like a bulletproof vest. Little Paul Möllendorff, it was, and his oral dexterity had if anything hurt instead of helped his case in the courtroom. Four years in the penitentiary.

She thought of Axel Ohr. Axel was eighteen, anyway, and he had wanted to join the All-German Rally of Free Youth, with a parcel for luggage that looked like bundles of newspaper. Inside that he had six and a half pounds of electrolytic copper, which he planned to sell in the out-of-bounds half of Berlin in order to buy baling twine for Johnny Schlegel's agricultural commune. Johnny had got away unscathed because Axel had dreamed up this little contribution in the privacy and silence of his mind. Axel was threatened with the full rigor of the law, which meant five years in the penitentiary. There certainly was a law against exporting nonferrous metals; but it could be of little help in bringing in the grain harvest. Axel sat in the cellar of the Examining Judge's office; wire with spikes surrounded this dungeon. When the New Free Youth marched in those blue shirts, they marched for this, among other things.

F. G. Y. member Cresspahl repeated, after earnest deliberation, that no barbed wire had come to her notice at the time. Asked for the goals of the F. G. Y. on the march, she made the desired reply. She was admonished to scrutinize any visual advertising in future with a vigilant mind (she had pleaded matutinal somnolence) for the sake of dialectic utilization of the mischief she had herself invoked. And it won't hurt to keep your ears open, get me? "Vas slushayu, I obey," said the student Cresspahl, which was a sweet morsel for the interrogator to swallow, though also a sour one because he was equally proud of his nationality and of his skill in concealing it. Barking a laugh like a man angry at himself, he replied with unexpected rudeness: "Do svidaniya"; promising her another meeting.

Waiting at the portals of the institution for secondary education were almost all the students with whom Cresspahl had ever exchanged a word or traded a smile. Close to seventy had felt like waiting it out and making sure of seeing this child restored to their midst. People shouted hurrah as in the old days when cheering a capable young reigning princess. There was singing.

Lise Wollenberg had gone home.

And the student Gantlik, visible just a moment ago at the bridge over the town moat, absented herself hurriedly when she had seen enough. She continued to consider it unwise for the time being to show even a speck of evidence of a connection, an alliance between her and the student Cresspahl. Oh yes, you do talk like that, Anita.

We concurred almost unanimously in the emotional verdict that Bettina had flung herself at the neck of the investigators from Schwerin, but had bullied and threatened the students in her charge as if we were some vicious breed of vermin, lepers, disease carriers, keep your distance; yet at the same time she had seemed ready to bite us. Perhaps we made room for her too eagerly when she came marching up with the two gentlemen in leather coats. The wind had gone out of her a little; we heard her keen at leave-taking: "And this had to happen in my school, of all places, Mr. Commissar!"

On us she now pounced vehemently with the order to bring water and scrub brushes from the janitor's premises and remove the remnants of the handbills from the school wall. (The school's front door, two mighty hunks of oak wings, of prewar make, c. 1910, had been hoisted out of its hinges and carted off by the Gneez Criminal Police.) Thus it befell that the young dandy from Siblings Scholl Street in Schwerin had to pry himself one more time out of his glistening, black-cherry-colored automobile (People's Own Enterprise Eisenacher instead of Bavarian Motor Works A. G.), in order to reprimand Comrade Selbich and keep the throng of putative culprits from studying even the remaining small print as they scratched at it.

And once more he singled out the student Cresspahl for a parting word. He planted himself before the younger person in a pose of good fellowship in his made-to-measure, easy-to-clean suit and let it be known that his name was Lehmann. (To this day I would recognize him by a too hastily repaired harelip. Let him fret from boredom in Leningrad or Prague; why should I disturb him.) "A noteworthy surname," he added, revealing himself to be one of the imperial potentates of the New Mecklenburg.

After this, one may wonder if Betteenkin still accomplished the leap from interim to tenured principal. Anyone worried about this, of course, embarks on the long summer vacation of 1950 with a somewhat heavy heart, restless practically, ants swarming all over his brain as he goes to sleep.


"Three times you could have nailed her during the interrogation," says Marie; she is complaining.

"Bettina got her fingers rapped, for starters. And we had promised one another: only in an emergency."

"If that wasn't one, tell me of one!"

"Coming up! Coming up!"

---

## July 31, 1968   Wednesday

---

The New York *Times* chooses to show us a helicopter from which dangle four cases of supplies for front-line positions of Marines near the Demilitarized Zone in Vietnam. A shot in the style of propaganda companies, devoid of news value.

The Masters of the Kremlin and the Hradshin at Kosice are keeping secret what they may be discussing in the clubhouse at Cierna. Those

from Moscow are supposed to have beaten it to their green train at
10:30 P.M., somewhat upset. However, in order to give us at least some
information, Auntie Times describes the parlor coaches of the Czechs
as painted blue, unlike the Soviet ones.

*Pravda*, the organ of Soviet Truth, prints the East German impression of the quiet daily life in the streets of Prague, along with current
conjectures about events behind the façade; it just shows you. It also
treats you to a facsimile of a letter from ninety-eight workers of Auto-
Praha who request the Soviet troops to extend their stay in the country.

And a city councilman of New York has spent a week in East
Harlem, in the guise of a writer; he now professes to know what life
there is like. He hasn't seen any rats, but the point is that he doubts
that rats could stand it in one of those houses on 119th Street between
Park and Lexington.

Staff news from the first half of the high-school year of 1950–51
in Gneez, Mecklenburg:

First, to initiate the new term, a stiff-legged man climbed the
podium to the lectern facing the assembled students (blue-shirted) and
introduced himself as the new principal, with all the powers thereunto
appertaining, and wearing in his lapel the enameled depiction of clasped
hands: Dr. Eduard Kramritz. He pressed his wire-framed glasses (gold-
plated wire now) into the sores on his nose and proclaimed: "Some of
you already know me." Applause. "The rest will get to know me—
with a vengeance." Applause.

Assuredly, Bettina Selbich was not to blame for the posted query
to the members of the F. G. Y. as to why they marched. But at a
vigilantly conducted teaching institution such heckling questions don't
come up in the first place; can you follow that, Comrade? Also, the
District School Commission had received letters, from the typewriter
of the councilor, since transferred, and from the hand of a Dr. Julius
Kliefoth, both showing the marks of a classical education and remarking
on the moral maturity required in one called upon to exercise a solicitous surveillance over the education of "the souls of young students."
(By this they meant us; Kramritz as principal must have dealt them an
embarrassing surprise.) The Unity Party showed some generosity in
that it did not separate Bettina from the service; on the other hand, it
extended her waiting period as a candidate by a full year.

Changes in the teaching staff: Dr. Gollnow is going into retirement, two years past the due date. Her place is assumed by Eberhard
Martens—soldierly bearing, fair hair cropped recruit style, known as
"the Evil Eye." Serving an internship in German in co-operation with
the members of what is now 11-A-Two; Mathias Weserich, M. A. in

language and literature from Leipzig University: another spastic, a little
more mobile at the knees, whose greeting took the shape of a bow from
the neck, enhanced by a mouth stretched open almost to a rectangle
and crammed full of chalk-white teeth. Colleague Selbich's new employ: specialist in German, also Contemporary Studies. Applause.

As for Erdmuthe Gollnow, she had been visited at the beginning
of vacation by the students Gantlik (by herself), and Pagenkopf and
Cresspahl (together). Tight bun, kindly gaze into the cups of apple-
blossom tea; grandfather clock, curio cabinet, sofa framed by curving
wooden edges. Anita had got stuck in the etiquette of a visit; it was
from her two schoolmates that Mrs. Gollnow learned later that Anita
too had probably meant to plead with her to stand still and put out her
hand when the salver holding the office of the principalship was carried
past her. The old lady sighed a good deal, said her thanks for the trust
reposed in her, but declared herself too frail. (She was in better shape
in terms of health than Alma Witte.) "Ah," the latter would croak, in
bouncy tones: "Ah, to be sixty again!"

When the assembled teachers moved meekly to the right side of
the platform, it was mounted by the Central School Chapter Authority
of the Free German Youth, who seated themselves behind the red-
draped tables, a wall of cloth. (This, Marie, was to avoid the risk of
undignified leg movements interfering with the reverential mood of the
youth fanciers down on the floor.) Beneath the claws of Picasso's ruffled
dove, Lockenvitz and Gollantz surrendered their offices, to prepare for
transition to Rostock University. The officers for minutes and treasury
resigned, pleading an overload of work in view of impending senior
finals. By a vote of 288 to 34, Dieter Lockenvitz, 11-A-Two, is elected
the new secretary to organize the school chapter. By 220 votes and a
lot of abstentions, Gabriel Manfras, 11-A-Two, becomes chairman.
Up front, Young Comrade Manfras!

We would never have thought that Gabriel had it in him to
perform as an orator! Yet what a far-carrying voice this reticent child
launched from his throat all of a sudden. One might guess that he was
making up for the silence he had kept from the first hour of school to
the last, from the class visit to the theater to the class party; that we
had taken him for a shy boy was instantly forgotten. The meeting now
proceeds to the election of a presidium. Nominations, please. Dr.
Kramritz, as friend and partner of the F. G. Y. school chapter. Acclamation. The Physical Education lummox, because he rakes us over
the coals politically as well. Genial laughter. Then, inevitably, the
members of the Central School Chapter Authority. For first member
of the Honorary Presidium I submit the name of Comrade Iosif

Vissarionovich Stalin, a shining example to us for his mighty labor for peace; his daily care for the improvement of the proletarian capital, the opening of the Great Northern Seaway, the draining of the Colchis swamps; not least, for the completion of that work of genius on Marxism and problems of linguistics. Frenzied applause, quick to subside. Further nominations: the President of the People's Republic of Poland, Boleslaw Bierut, for the peaceful encounter of our two nations at the Oder and Neisse Rivers; Comrade Mao, liberator of the Chinese People's Republic, partner of Comrade Stalin; the writer Thomas Mann, in memory of his late brother Heinrich, recipient of the National Goethe Prize, who by his journey to Weimar evinced that realism which shines forth from every buttonhole of his writing! Further, the author of *The Socialist Sixth of the World*, the theologian ostracized in his own country, Hewlett Johnson, the "Red Dean" of Canterbury! The public who have stood up to applaud are requested to go easy on the bleachers. Youth Comrade Manfras has the floor to present an appraisal of the world peace situation, "and likewise in Gneez."

Gabriel looked at us like a stranger, clasped the front edge of the lectern with his right hand, propped the knuckles of the left against the lower rear edge, gazed down into his script, was ready and able to make a speech. (There stood a child who had been tipped off that he would be nominated for election and accepted; who had a paper all prepared to read.) Youth Comrade Manfras began tidily, the first of September the Day of Peace, thus we too pledge. The criminal incursion of North American troops and their South Korean mercenaries into the northern republic, whose leader we all . . . Let the West Germans who groan under the yoke of capitalism fear war; why, they are buying swarms of sailboats to escape in, they hoard gas and stand in lines before the consulates of South America; we, by contrast, enjoy security under the newly elected General Secretary of the newly founded Central Committee of the Unity Party, Walter Ulbricht; and the infamous use of the sobriquet *"Sachwalter* Ulbricht" (Caretaker Ulbricht) reflects pitifully upon anyone with access to a German dictionary. The vigilance of the Party, as it was demonstrated in the unmasking of those leading comrades Kreikemeyer and Company, co-conspirators of the American *agent provocateur* Noel H. Field and his abhorrent marital triangle—this vigilance will also . . . The decay of the British Empire at the side of the U. S. A. can only . . . The species-degrading interview of the West German Chancellor with the organ of high capitalism, the New York *Times*, his proposal for the rapid establishment of a new German military force, will inevitably . . . We adjourn the assembly with the song "We are the vanguard soldiers / Of the pro-le-tar-i-at."

In Gabriel Manfras's panoramic survey of the world, he had more than once injected the word diversion, and the Latinists among us had thought at first what an old-fashioned chap he must be. But when he poured into the mix those people with the glue pot and their curiosity about the goal of F. G. Y. marching and called them American "diversants," this fractured at least the grammatical link for the listener. Only after the song did we have a chance to find out from Anita that there actually was such a Soviet word, *diversiya*, but it didn't mean diversion or anything like it, it meant sabotage, an attack, an assault. From the side? No, frontal, or all around really, said Anita with some embarrassment. If only she had realized at last that her work with Triple Y had long impressed us as a job!

As for Gabriel Manfras, we now had a notion how he had spent his summer.

Dr. Kramritz, too, had undergone a course designed to hone him to a fine political edge; meanwhile he had sort of lost track of his family. Misplaced his wife. Which led him to make a proposition to colleague Bettina Selbich, who by that time sported a skintight blouse of non-blue material and a manner that was graceful with humility. He explained that in case of a divorce he needed to know where to turn for refuge. Rumor in its wish-fulfilling way inserted a slap in the face at this point; the eyewitness Klaus Böttcher reported a couple in tears on the forest path that winds its laborious way around Mt. Smoke. At this point, though, Bettina's landlord won his suit for eviction against her; nowhere but in Danish Hedge could she find a single room. The sequel was that she was commended by the local Party for moving closer to the working class, and that she walked in fear of Wieme Wohl. The complete apartment at Cathedral Court, three rooms with kitchen, basement, bathroom, was taken over by the reconciled Kramritz family, with its view over the parish meadows down to the rows of poplars lining the municipal lake. *Kaderschutz* is what it is called, protection of trained personnel. If you want it, you make your choices accordingly.

The news about Thomas Mann's signing of the Stockholm Appeal, the declaration calling for a ban on the atomic bomb regardless of ownership, had eased our minds about our own. A year later we had to hang our heads in shame:

> *This "document" is not new to me . . . in that it is part of a photomontage which purports to show myself in the act of signing the Stockholm Appeal in the spring of 1950 in Paris. I am shown on this occasion wearing a suit which I had taken to Europe with me in 1949, but not in 1950. The picture also shows the black*

*mourning neckwear I had tragic cause in May 1949 to add to my*
*wardrobe. To find out how this came about is neither feasible nor*
*interesting to me. What I do know, and what I have truthfully*
*stated, is that I did not sign my name to the Stockholm Appeal*
© Katja Mann

Kreikemeyer and Company were German Communists living in
French exile as internees. Kreikemeyer in 1942 was helped to escape
by Field, representing American Unitarians, and became the leader of
the illegal German C. P. in Marseilles. Seven year later, Willi Kreikemeyer was appointed Big Chief of the German railway; he was Jakob's
general director. In May 1949 he had gone out on a limb for his party
when the railway workers in West Berlin went on strike to secure
remuneration in the currency of the city in which they lived and bought
food. On May 5 Willi K. promised them payment in West German
marks, then retracted his pledge. One person was killed in clashes with
the police, a number of injured were added to the load he bore on
behalf of the Party. On May 28 he promised payment in West German
marks up to 60 per cent of wages, and, in addition, to refrain from any
reprisals. Late in June he broke his word again, lest his party lose face,
and decreed for 380 railway workers dismissal without notice or reas-
signment to places in the East German Republic whose very money
they had disdained. Willi Kreikemeyer, adherent of a party and its
statutes that claimed to respect the profession of a religious faith, promised Jehovah's Witnesses twelve special trains to take them to a conference in Berlin in July 1949. He took money for the order, then
canceled the trains; all this for his party. Now it has been accusing
him since late August of having furnished addresses to the American
O. S. S. Jakob went about woebegone that summer of 1949; a loyal
member of the F. G. Y. is bound to recite this kind of thing on
ideological training evenings. If I had raised an objection, he would
have come at me with the question: And what school do you go to,
Gesine?

When the Carola Neher Club had finished researching her life
(and death), I commissioned, with D. E., a curriculum vitae of Willi
Kreikemeyer; the three scholars, for all their canniness with registers
and sources and cross references, could establish no life for him since
August 1950.

As to the Federal Chancellor of West Germany, Bettina Selbich
alerted us to the illuminating similarity between his name and that of
the President of Columbia University, former commander of Allied
forces in Europe: Eisenhower—Adenauer. Contemporary Studies.

When it came to the President of the North Americans, we were encouraged to make Harry S Truman the butt of our ridicule because he fraudulently used his middle initial to simulate the status of a true American, while in fact the S stood only for itself, not a name. There was also Truman's former employment as sales clerk for neckties and other haberdashery; it was suggested that we should adduce this, too, as evidence of his inferiority. Contemporary Studies.

On October 13, 1950 the East German Republic observed for the first time the "Day of Activists," and Elise Bock was awarded the title of "Deserving Activist" as well as a handsome amount of money. A last salute from Triple Y, who was now free to return home. The administration of Gneez had been turned over to the Unity Party; his successor was a military commander who moved out of town into the woods around Mt. Smoke.

On August 15, the Government of the East German Republic (a fine corporate person, that) ordered up some operation involving ballots referring to the People's Chamber and the administration of land, district, and municipality. It counted 99 per cent yes votes, plus another 0.7 per cent.

In the summer of 1950 began the political trials at Waldheim; on November 4 it came time for the executions. Cresspahl did not wear any crepe for the person he might recall had been his father-in-law. The child Cresspahl still remembered compassion for Albert Papen-brock, because of the time when accepting sweets was forbidden to her; sadly he sat under the beach umbrellas of the Lübeck Arms in Jerichow, having to gulp down a large sherbet entirely unaided. Gesine Cresspahl wouldn't have had the courage to confront Mrs. Selbich wearing black crepe on her sleeve; the latter had developed a great facility in applying to Principal Kramritz for demerits. Thomas Mann's family suppressed his letter to the *Sachwalter*, the Caretaker, in the collection of letters issued pro tem. In actual fact he wrote to Sachwalter Ulbricht in July in part as follows:

> *Some ten trials took place in an hour. No defense counsel was admitted, no witness for the defendants allowed to testify. In handcuffs, though none but a few were being sought for real crimes, the accused, the guilty before any trial, were brought into Court, and the Court, by rote and rule, pronounced prison sentences of 15, 18, 25 years, even for life. . . . Mr. Premier! Perhaps you are not aware what revulsion, what indignation, often simulated, but often deeply felt, these trials with their death sentences—for they are all death sentences—have evoked on this side of the world; how*

*conducive they are to ill will, how destructive of good. An act of*
*mercy, sweeping and summary, as the mass sentencing of Wald-*
*heim has been in only too high a degree, would be such a blessed*
*gesture serving the hope for détente and reconciliation—a deed of*
*peace.*
       *Use your power . . . !* © Katja Mann

But the Sachwalter needed his power for the arrangement of such
rituals of jurisdiction, as his wise leader and preceptor, Stalin, had
shown him in Bulgaria, Hungary, and Czechoslovakia. Why should
he restore their honor to a few useful dead when of the living in his
country only some 51,000 found the courage to mark their ballot sheets
with a No; only as many people as lived in Gneez and Jerichow.

Klaus Böttcher was sitting in his father's kitchen, cooling his feet
in soapy water. In comes his wife, Britte, and reports: Klaus, three
gentlemen are here, all in black suits; they want something from you.
Klaus scrambles out the window, dangles from the sill high above the
shop yard, drops down, takes off barefoot over the fence, the town
moat, the wall, on and on in the direction of West Berlin. In Krakow
he has to go to ground with a carpenter colleague, his bare feet were
bleeding so fearfully. Britte follows her husband's thought processes,
she gets a phone connection to Krakow. "You can come back, Klaus,
they had all come from the university, they wanted to share in ordering
a boathouse from you, you klutz, Klaus!" Britte said tenderly. When
questioned about the sense of guilt in his behavior, Klaus would say,
newly embarrassed each time: "How shall the hare prove he's not a
fox?"

In December 1950 Jakob's mother applied for an interzonal permit. This was a piece of paper constituting official authorization for a
trip on her part from Jerichow to Bochum, West Germany. If she was
correctly informed, a remnant of the Wilhelm Abs's family lived there.
In the Abs clan they wrote each other at most in the event of a death,
or a birth perhaps, and then a fortnight late. She was old, of course,
and wanted to come as close as possible to the event she feared. Jakob
made time for the commuting between authorities—Cresspahl's daughter lacked the necessary kinship—and so it took well into January before
they had assembled:
     a certificate of registration with the police,
     a report on any police record,
     a handwritten curriculum vitae (the fourth draft),
     proof of the political or economic reasons for the journey (here
         Cresspahl and Jakob invented an inheritance in the Ruhr district

for her, and Dr. Werner Jansen, attorney in Gneez, produced
on his magic typewriter, when his staff was absent, a district
court's notice of delivery bearing a West German date line),

a statement in support of the journey by the Unity Party (this was
shunted by Mrs. Brüshaver via the O. d. F. to the C. D. U.
of Schwerin),

a statement by the Internal Revenue at Gneez confirming that the
applicant is leaving no tax arrears behind.

After that, all she had to do was to have all these documents translated
into Russian. Forty-eight marks was what Lotte Pagels charged for this,
including the mistakes the job contained (courtesy of Krijgerstam).
Anita, you would have done it for nothing, admit it! But since Anita
looked past the student Cresspahl, how could the name Abs be a clue
for her?

And how useful she might have been as an interpreter with the
Sovietnik in Gneez town hall who advised the town administration in
the sovereign German Democratic Republic. It wasn't a lot to ask of
Gesine that she should brace herself and take the initiative in approaching Anita with a request. But Gesine was against such a journey;
and Mrs. Abs seemed to her carefully enough equipped; and people
sometimes went away and stayed away; shyness was another pretext she
used. If the application were to be turned down, it would be her fault.

All the time until December, Aggie had busied herself with what
a Federally examined and licensed R. N. considers no more than her
duty. She had worked on Dr. Schürenberg, District Medical Examiner;
Schürenberg summoned Cresspahl, examined him credibly, and attested his incapacity for work; this put him on a retirement pension.

In 1950, New Year's Eve was celebrated in Cresspahl's house for
the first time since 1937. There was no carp to be had, but Jakob
brought crayfish. For the first time we were being something like a
family in Cresspahl's house. Gesine watched from afar as Jakob's mother
scrubbed the live creatures off in cold water with a birch brush, then
took them to their death in boiling water. While the family's churchgoer
was off for the service, Gesine stood by the pot, eyes now on the clock,
now on the recipe, scooped off the floating fat, added wood to the fire,
let the broth cool, ladled out the "butter" of the red roes—distracted,
though. For through the window Jakob demonstrated to her for half
an hour how a young man of twenty-two shaves in honor of a social
evening. Let the traditional carp be missing on New Year's Eve—the
joking was there. Cresspahl drew closing lines in his last professional
books. Four of the party confessed their resolutions for the coming
year; four times Jakob refilled Gesine's glass.

*Jesu, let me gladly end it,*
*This my freshly entered year.*
*Thy strong hands' upholding lend it,*
*Ward off peril and its fear.*
*Lastly, in Thy mantle furled,*
*I shall glady quit this world.*

"Och, stay with us just yet, Mrs. Abs."

"Nah, I've had it. Such engines, such out-worn tracks, such a salad of signals, let the devil drive it. Happy New Year, Gesine!"

"Happy New t'you all."

---

### August 2, 1968   Friday

The *Times* would have been so glad to report that the Soviet and Czech delegations had had a meal at the same table, had broken bread together. But she, too, is given only the communiqué mumbling about an atmosphere of complete candor, sincerity, and mutual understanding. They are planning another session tomorrow at Bratislava, but this time with the leaders of Poland, East Germany, Hungary, and Bulgaria. Could it be that these will wreck whatever the U. S. S. R. may have agreed to sign at the rail junction of Cierna?

And what had the weather been like this July? The New York *Times* has ascertained it and informs us: too hot for the time of year. About the 16th we must have had a somewhat miserable time. That Tuesday—we could have done without half of it. But don't wish your life away.

Anyone who sends his memory back to his school years in Gneez and the German period in 11-A-Two will inescapably have it come back at him with "Schach! Schach!"

The practice teacher from Thuringia involved, Mr. Weserich, had actually been encountered by the Cresspahl-Pagenkopf team before the end of the summer vacation, and a slight acquaintance resulted. They came upon him on a bench in front of the dressing rooms at the municipal lake. It was at an early hour, when he could hope to be alone, and he was adjusting the screws on an aluminum frame at his left knee, where the rest of the leg was missing. Again his lips formed a square, he seemed in pain; we were petrified.

Yet it was he who started an apology. "There we are," he said calmly, prising himself upright and away from the bench. "For Führer and Reich; I believed it, too," he added, leaving the sequel to us, full of confidence in our diplomatic skills. Thus he came already equipped

with a reputation when the demoted Madam Principal Selbich introduced him to our class in the sour way she had. "We are going to read
*Schach von Wuthenow* by Theodor Fontane," he announced, leaving
no sort of doubt about his intentions. How terrified we would have
been had we comprehended them!

We had German four hours a week; Weserich related to us the
century of Fontane's life from May 5, 1789. He began with Count
Mirabeau, the Deputy of the Third Estate, he laid out his traps openly:
we overlooked them. He told us of Fontane's childhood years, his
sojourns in England and France, he read to us from his family letters,
*car tel est notre plaisir*. Clean High German, freely assembled from
memory while his gaze was absent. On September 11 he had the
effrontery to request our first impressions from our reading of the work
by Fontane mentioned earlier. Out of the blue, from one week to the
next, gleaming eyes full of joyful anticipation!

Anita raised her hand, she was ready to sacrifice herself; he overlooked her, but smiled to her, to her alone. We others, some thirty
souls, were allowed to expostulate that there was but one copy of this
book, in the Cultural Society Library, while our home shelves offered
only items like Fontane's novel *Effie Briest*; and attempted to talk him
out of his plan. The end of this round was that he paid us compliments,
praised our resourcefulness, and promised a return engagement of his
inquiry on September 18. "We'll see each other often enough, of
course," he held out to us.

In order to propitiate this person, we passed the hat among thirty
students to collect whatever typing a hundred and thirty printed pages
came to with Elise Bock; the mimeograph stencils Pius saw to by a
visit to the F. G. Y. District Office. ("Thou shalt not muzzle the ox
when he treadeth out the corn," he confessed, but only in the privacy
of his teamship.) But before the pages could be run off, Anita had to
use her pull at town hall to obtain an authorization and certification
of "unexceptionability" in the matter of Multigraphing a text. On the
18th, there we sat with our piles of rough spotty paper, and Zaichik
the Hare enjoyed his entrance in advance.

"There's an old chestnut for you!" said Zaichik. "Who gets a girl
pregnant must take the oath!"

The guest teacher rendered thanks for this instruction in Mecklenburg folk wisdom. He was right, what spoke out of Zaichik's mouth
was the spirit of the sturdy peasantry of Gneez (and of the expelled
gentry), although he failed to realize what conjectures he was inviting
about his parents' marriage or his own relationship with Eva Matschinsky; who shrank in her seat and blushed.

There stood Dagobert Haase with his artless and slightly chubby corporality, grumbly and defiant was his manner, like someone who obeys but feels he doesn't have to. And spoke: "All this is maybe a hundert fifty years back. A cavalry captain has a girl friend, he wants to marry her perhaps. Sudden, like, he falls for her daughter, twenty years younger, but because folk crack jokes about the pockmarks in her face he wants to duck the consequences. The King orders him to marry her; so he ends up doing it, but shoots himself after lunch. His name and the child he leaves to her."

Zaichik executed an accommodating half-turn to allow us to read in his face what he meant: Ain't it the truth?

Mr. Weserich thanked him for this summary of the plot. Might the student Haase be prepared for an additional question?

Zaichik dropped his head, playing the silent martyr. Upon demand he named the protagonist, "like the title"; the daughter, "someone called Victoire"; the mother's maiden name . . . "can't call to mind."

"The address of the Von Carayon family?" this Germanist asked past Zaichik, expressly to spare him, and when the student Cresspahl could name only the city of Berlin, we had the privilege of returning to the beginning of the novel: "In the drawing room of Frau von Carayon on Behrens Street, a number of friends had assembled for her evening reception."

We were instructed that persons of rank at that time . . . "but it may perhaps be an idle undertaking to ask for the year?"

"1806," ventured Anita, and was asked to confess her reasoning. "Because the people in the book discuss the 'three-emperor battle' of Austerlitz as something quite recent; and that happened the previous December, on the second."

"Resuming, then, persons of rank at that time carefully selected their addresses, expressed their self-esteem, pointed to themselves, by the situation of their residence. Thus it was—unfortunately!—unavoidable for him to equip us with the information that Behrens Street ran one block south of Unter den Linden, the Rue de la Paix of Berlin; that the Carayons enjoyed a stroke of good fortune in that theirs was a house on the corner with Charlotten Street, a short walk from the Opera, the Lustgarten, or pleasure park, the Palace. Behrens Street— named after the armorial bear of Berlin, as a widespread notion has it, but in fact named in honor of the engineer Johann Heinrich Beer, to whom Berlin owes Französische Street and, after 1701, Jerusalem and Leipzig Streets. Very familiar, these, to every accredited Berliner, by personal experience also to the members of 11-A-Two, for whom they might ring a bell, though quite a different bell, only as from September

11. And if one cared to weigh the fact that the author of our narrative would eschew a mere coincidence, why did he draw the name of an architect of the seventeenth to eighteenth century right into the first line? Perhaps in order to invest the past of the story with an aura of an even older era? Intelligible? And are we at all inclined to be heard on the subject of the subtitle? *A Story from the Time of the Regiment Gensdarmes?*" No? Was it really for such a resolute silence that a young practice teacher found himself spending whole class hours expatiating on the onomastic descent of this regiment of cuirassiers (which wields a straight épée in place of the lance) from the cavalry troop of Charles IV of France? In view of the author's French background? *Gens d'armes, au Moyen Age, soldats, cavaliers du roi?* Since the hour for whose intriguing elements he felt obliged to us was coming to an end, he took the liberty of suggesting that by Wednesday we should at least have tried really to *read* the first two pages.

11-A-Two spent close to three weeks on the first six pages of the novel. If you looked searchingly at Mr. Weserich because of this waste of time, he would not take it to heart. We began to look forward to his outbursts of comic despair when we had actually failed to find in the clear-enough phrase "in England and the Union states" a reference to the United States of America, or when we knew no more about the antecedents of Mr. von Bülow, Adam Heinrich Dietrich v. B., than that he was arrested for being a writer. Was it conceivable that in the whole town of Gneez you couldn't dig up more than a single encyclopedia, which moreover had been lent out for years?

Nobody could accuse Weserich of pettiness or pedantry, and we showed him good will. Against the Latin quotations we had been armed by Kliefoth and on occasion would translate one ourselves *(hic haeret)*. After a while Weserich recognized that a knowledge of Latin might admittedly be helpful in the learning of French but could by no manner of means replace the teaching of the language itself. He wondered about this, he disliked to give in; should he challenge on this score the intellectual fathers of the school reform, who had replaced French with Russian? Henceforward he had us submit utterances in Fontane's second language for translation; never less than three at a time, on that he insisted. "Time is running away from us!" he exclaimed, and we were on the second chapter. On the other hand, we did on occasion look up in the dictionary things like these: what an embonpoint was and a nonchalance, what a gourmand excels in and what a gourmet; we inquired among old people if they remembered seeing a Sinumbra lamp, a wreath-shape oil lamp that cast very little shade. When our knowledge pleased Mathias Weserich, causing him to feign surprise and incredulity, we did him the favor of falling for this and enjoying it.

Two of the weekly periods went by over the mystery of why Fontane placed titles over his chapters, unlike *Under the Pear Tree* just three years earlier and *Count Petöfy* one year later than *Schach*. What is a "superscription"? Its place is at the head, but why do paintings carry their signatures at the bottom or side? It points to what follows. It is an act of courtesy to the reader: at the end of the chapter he is to take a breather and then know beforehand where the journey will take him, to Sala Tarone, to Tempelhof, or to Wuthenow. Yes—and it is to make our mouths water? Such writers do exist; we are dealing with Fontane. A chapter title is a milestone on the road: Wayfarer, twelve miles farther lies Jerichow village. It is the signboard of a town, the stranger reads "Gneez i. M." there and is not greatly enlightened at first; once he enters the town he knows where he is. A title as warning; as an ornament to accompany the old fashions of Berlin in 1806. That may well be, but what, ultimately, is a superscription?

At the "Italian Wine and Fine Food Shop of Sala Tarone" in Charlotten Street we hit a snag: the gentlemen have to squeeze through a row of closely set barrels, and the cooper enjoins caution. "It's all full of tacks and nails [*Pinenn und Nägel*] here," he said. In our class we had a boy named Nagel. We could have behaved like grownups, but the next day he was named Pinne Nagel. He took it stoically, happy deep down that he too now had something personal, a nickname. In future, his comment about tricky calculations or uncomfortable quarters was "It's all full of Pinnen and Nägel here." He survived, Pinne Nagel, and works as a jaw surgeon in Flensburg.

But our Mr. Weserich wanted to be instructed on what a *Pinne* was. How it differed from a Nägel he grasped only when he had served up the story of Little Erna, the perennial heroine of Hamburg anecdotes, about Grampa lying in his coffin and Erna's mother fixing his cap, which kept slipping, with a little carpet *Pinne* for the sake of decent appearances. It was the same sort of thing with the Low German passages during Schach's visit to his home territory. Weserich actually behaved as if these were Chinese to him. We translated for him why *de oll Zick*, the old nanny goat, was always butting *Mudding Krepsch*, Ma Krepsch, in the place where she had her *Wehdage*, her woe days; we put it in writing, since he asked us to. One day he arrived with reproaches: we had concealed a word from him, right in the early part, in the fourth chapter. We were contrite and promised amends. It turned out that it was about Aunt Marguerite in the story, who "spoke the Berlin speech of the time, which operated almost entirely in the dative case, with a pruned mouth," with no quotation marks to single out the offending term. We had behaved as if this were a universally intelligible word! This was it, then, and he asked to have it demonstrated to him. He stood before one girl after another (we had gulled him to think only girls pruned) and watched her lips move from a preset front and round position; then thanked her. We dropped curtseys, gathering up our below knee-length skirts at the sides.

We had already got to Wuthenow, page 122 of our copy, chapter 14; we had had enough of Schach (the character, because he had spoiled for us the boat ride on the lake with his lachrymose shirking), when we were invited by Weserich to lecture (without a script) on how we had become acquainted with Schach. Forty-five minutes' worth of deliberation, right to the bell. Then the weeks frittered away on the beginning proved a rewarding investment: we found the last line of the first paragraph, in which he figures *in absentia*, also nameless. The assembled gentlemen, v. Bülow, his publisher Sander, and v. Alvensleben, converse with their hostesses, the Carayon ladies. Bülow is looking for a quarrel. He quotes his Mirabeau's dictum about the state of Frederick the Great as a fruit already rotten before it came to ripen. In his sermon he preens himself as if casually with the apothegm *nomen et omen*. Not with the *est* that we learned at school, but with *et*, which placed the name and its significance into closer, more poignant, meaning and proximity. After Bülow's emphatic pronouncement, "Europe might have stood a little more seraglio or harem politics without major damage . . ." who has his name announced in the middle of that sentence? The captain of cavalry Von Schach, the Shah between two women; his antagonist is already here, he will have the last word to the end. Fontane and the discipline of names. Fontane and the art of introducing characters.

A list of characters: Josephine, Victoire, Schach, Aunt Marguerite, the King, his much sighed-over Queen Luise, Prince Louis, General Köckritz, the innkeeper at Tempelhof . . .

A list of places, sites of action: the Carayons' drawing room, the tavern with the *Pinnen*, the coach ride, the (invented) church at Tempelhof, the villa on the Spree at Moabit, opposite the western *lisière* of Tiergarten, once an animal park (our consultation of dictionary and encyclopedia should by now have led us to the place where a reason for the choice of the word *lisière* might be found); the military parade at Tempelhof, the bed scene, Wuthenow-on-the-Lake, palace and park at Paretz, death on Wilhelm Street. Get it? Written anonymous opinion poll about the virtues of the locales. The lake came in first; by this time most of the students were again from Mecklenburg, the kids from the Niemen and Silesia took potluck. Pius showed me that he had checked Paretz. The student Cresspahl found her favorite image in the swans which came sailing up in wide-open file from Charlottenburg Park.

Another ugly incident: Schach rambles on about the Prince, his gracious lord; he loves him *de tout mon coeur*, as he tells Victoire. But Louis, he goes on, with all his adventures in love and war, is still "a light that burns with a robber." We had put a word over on our German teacher! Now he stood there entirely unaware of what a robber on a light was in this North Germany! "We agree that we have deserved punishment and request an ample measure of it," as schoolchildren used to be made to say. It is a light with a wick that produces excessive soot, which steals the candle wax away. When candles were still made of wax.

Anita had spared herself the curtsey by which we had meant to tease Mathias Weserich. She had all she wanted, had seen to it herself. A habit had gradually taken hold in the class of turning toward the left rear corner when Dieter Lockenvitz was called on; Anita, too, liked to watch him talk. Mutinously, her eyebrows rose in apprehension. The student Lockenvitz disliked some details of a narrative laid in the period of the Regiment Gensdarmes. In the fourth chapter, in the Tempelhof churchyard, hazel and wild-rose bushes grow so luxuriantly that they form a dense hedge "notwithstanding they were still bare." For this "notwithstanding" a student would get a red mark. In the chapter *Le choix du Schach* one finds something like "Certain understandings arrived at, twilight presently separated the party . . ."; was this a misprint or was there faulty grammar here? What annoyed (*aigriait*, we were now able to think of it) this student most was Fontane's habit of presenting utterances in direct discourse both in the subjunctive and in quotation marks. Weserich kept the boy in good humor by interposed questions, although he regularly conceded his points anyway. But Anita, now faced with the official necessity of choosing a tablemate and offered a chance to gaze at this Lockenvitz hours at a time and from close by, chose instead a girl, Peter (Monica), who was weak in Chemistry and Math.

When Weserich once stopped at Lise Wollenberg's table instead of pursuing his aimless ambulations among us, we were offered an enactment of the phrase "she hangs on his lips." That's what she was doing, and she would not have been greatly taken aback had he politely ushered her out of the classroom and offered her his heart and hand. But Weserich must have had some experience of girls who toss their heads up like colts and whinny when they laugh. It was only in the seventh month of our collaboration on someone from the Regiment Gensdarmes that he delivered a speech, for her alone.

"My dear Miss Wollenberg!" he began.

"You look at my mouth as if something was missing there. You mention the color of my teeth in a voice loud enough to reach me. I have the honor of informing you that no hair will grow around my mouth because the skin there is a transplant. My teeth have an unnatural look because they came from a factory. Are these all the questions you have? Would you like to let me know where in this story about a captain of horse, Von Schach (you may recall), you surmise the narrator to be?"

"Nah," said Lise, straining for the aplomb of cheekiness. We felt sorry for her, the big blonde child, caught in the temptation to play fast and loose with an adult ("and with the monstrous maketh sport"). But we did not begrudge Weserich his counterattack, considering the embarrassments Lise had caused his colleague H.-G. Knick.

Something quite different for a change. Who is the narrator? How does he proceed in his role? Has he been present at all events? Would those involved have wanted or even tolerated that? When are they free from observation? When they write letters. Once they are written, the narrator communicates them to us. What does he refrain from telling us? Why are we left to guess about the stolen hour of love from nothing but two instances of the familiar pronoun *Du* being used? Good taste or tact; or strong savoir-faire? Lockenvitz, for your collection we donate to you a dandy term which will take you on wings of the morning, yea, even unto the school certificate or beyond: the authorial narrator.

He knew where the ice was thin, our Mr. Weserich, and kept away from it. Bülow, staff captain but also political essayist, confesses his abhorrence of taverns and restaurants in the subjunctive of quotation (to student Lockenvitz's distaste), saying that in these he felt that the "police spies and waiters were strangling him." There were such places in Gneez. For a long time now, birthday parties had rarely been held outside the house. Well might Weserich wear an ingenuous mien; he came from Thuringia. In his first scene with Schach, Bülow talks of the ineluctable marriage between state and Church; all Weserich had to do was to remind us offhand always to remain within the time of the narration. When Victoire in her bounty writes her friend Lisette a letter in which "your new Mazovian home" is mentioned, Weserich knew that he was facing a child who had lost a home in those parts; there was discussion of the claims Victoire makes on the course of her life as they emerge from the letter; but how could the teacher have any idea that Anita too thought of herself as a person "cut off by Fortune with a shilling"? The silence that answered the mention of an infantry regiment called Möllendorf most likely escaped his notice altogether.

If we take the narrative impulse to spring from the variety and energy of the relationships between the characters, what do we do on having placed Aunt Marguerite in a central position?

As required by the curriculum of the New School, our Mr. Weserich paid due attention to the element of social criticism. Two hours of discussion were given to the concept of honor, the attitude toward it: dishonorable actions. Understand? A government inspector like Gogol's, traveling the realm in search of ideological failings, would not have set off any panic sitting in on a class or interrogating us in Weserich's absence; our teacher's career would not have suffered. Fontane had supplied the novel with salt on which the Regiment Gensdarmes runs a sleigh ride on Unter den Linden, in the middle of summer; upon the question what the gentlemen intended to do afterward with the soiled but precious condiment, the gentry replied from the full sense of its authority: mainly, it must not rain. If it doesn't, the stuff will still be good enough *pour les doméstiques*, for the servant class.

"*Et pour la canaille*, the black masses," someone says; for the people, known as the populace or mob. Weserich impressed upon us that the idea had come from the youngest sublieutenant; we thought we knew a good deal about seventeen-year-olds.

Meanwhile, much water flowed over the dam. Marlene Timm, inevitably nicknamed "Tiny Tim" despite her average stature, received official permission to go abroad for a visit with a clan of aunts in Denmark; she was much marveled over and sat among us as merely a guest. Axel Ohr was to be taken care of by his five years' penitentiary sentence. Jakob indeed had not got the chance to drive more than a few engines; for disciplinary reasons he was transferred to signal stations between Gneez and Ludwigslust, meanwhile collecting credits from courses at the College of Transport Technology in Dresden—which might as well have accepted him as a full-time student. Jakob's mother was refused the trip to West Germany. Heinrich Cresspahl, of the brickyard path in Jerichow, suffered a cut in his pension because of faithful declaration of income derived from the healing of chests and sideboards. His daughter did actually go to Berlin, to get carving tools for him, the kind with retractable blades. Oskar Tannebaum sent a "petticoat" from Paddington, which according to Cresspahl was a railway station in London. In the town hall of Richmond, the town once envisaged for Cresspahl, the second version of Picasso's dove of peace was on view in November 1950. The Americans got it in the neck in

Korea. The seasons came and went; we were still reading *Schach*. Schach!

We had found out that he remained invisible over a hundred and thirty pages; on purpose, as we were willing to assume for Fontane's benefit. Almost everybody calls him "handsome"; therefore vain, opines Josephine de Carayon. Bülow derides him as His Majesty, Captain Von Schach. Victoire finds something of the solemnity of the consistorial councilor about him. His actions occasionally give him away: when he poses as the mentor of his regiment and denies it; when at the Prince's he gives a needlessly nasty report of Victoire; when he cravenly hides in the entrance hall from Mama, at Wuthenow from his duty; and altogether behaves so as to tempt Josephine de Carayon to pit the worth of her own family against his imaginary Balto-Slavic nobility. We all found his shirking blatant yet unfathomable; Anita had the final word on this. She stuttered at first, stumbled over a word; we took this to be nervousness, common enough among seventeen-year-olds. "The business about getting her pr-pregnant," said Anita; "I can go along with that." What were we to think of this but that her tongue had tripped? Even while talking, Anita was apt to pursue her thoughts in the isolation in which she lived. "But that he doesn't try harder (and has to have his king order him, and his queen, too), to be a good human being!"

This had come over her against her will or wish; she braced herself against our laughter at the old-fashioned term. We were embarrassed on her behalf; we were proud of her. Had it been Eva Matschinsky—who knows?—we might have laughed; in Anita's case we looked straight ahead; I saw nods of agreement.

And no one outside our class has ever learned what Anita's concept of a man's honor was.

"During the military reforms two years after this, the Regiment Gensdarmes was disbanded, for that matter," said Zaichik in order to shorten the silence. He had learned to eat crow, our Dagobert with his old chestnuts.

An hour's worth of deliberation about the *beauté du diable, coquette, triviale, céleste*, and fifth and last *la beauté qui inspire seul du vrai sentiment*. (The only girl not at ease here was Lise.) Then about Alexanderplatz in Berlin and who was it named after; and how it is that a so-called nobleman may get involved with a pockmarked girl after his prince and gracious lord has transfigured her for him, so that he can see a *beauté du diable* in her.

And is it Von Bülow in the end who pronounces the judgment

of the author? No, he's nothing but a pumpkin head. (Please, would the class enlighten their teacher on pumpkin heads?) For argument's sake. We've run into this before: the omniscient narrator. Here Lise Wollenburg found evidence for the conclusion that Bülow had to be treated as separate from his inventor: because of the finest white linen "in which Bülow by no means excelled."

We were coming to the end. We could tell because Weserich took us back to the beginning, with a festive air: to the title. We were forbidden on principle to consult Fontane's letters ("statements of intention do not constitute evidence about the work"); he quoted one of them to us, the one of November 5, 1882, which ponders titles for the novel: "1806; Before Jena; *Et dissipati sunt*; Counted, Weighed, and Cast Away; Before the Decline (Fall, Ruin)." What reasons could 11-A-Two in April 1951 offer to Mr. Weserich for the choice of the definitive title?

"Because a person's name is always the fairest announcement"; this came from Lockenvitz (he owed it to Th. Mann).

"Because nearly all the others imply a judgment, anticipate the reader's own. Fontane wanted his readers independent!" Weserich instructed us, and now we were to start on the joy and delight of reading a novel by Th. Fontane of the year 1806 once more and afresh.

But we spoiled that for ourselves. Lockenvitz, he was the one who messed it up. We were accomplices. Lockenvitz, now a member of the working team Pagenkopf-Cresspahl, asked us casually whether we thought Mr. Weserich himself would pass muster if examined. It is true, we gave him permission, but expected he would once more complain about Fontane, the first sentence, for example, the hiccups one might incur from a present participle there.

What Lockenvitz came up with, right after the Easter lambs, was a journal from the half-capital, wearing a colorful wrapper; *Form*, it was called, or *Sense*, the message of East German state culture to the rest of the world. In Issue 2, pp. 44–93, the incumbent expert on the socialist theory of literature had written about Fontane's *Schach von Wuthenow* that, viewed ideologically, the novel was a "fortunate accident," that the implied critique of Prussian values was "unintentional," was "unconscious."

Lockenvitz had requested permission to read this near the end of German class, in order to spare Mr. Weserich any possible embarrassment in front of the class. Weserich listened, his mouth forming that rectangle as though he were listening for a receding ache. He said his thanks, borrowed the expensively printed journal, stalked out of the room on his single leg. (When the stump of the other incommoded him, he had occasionally cited that verse about the knee which roams the world alone; it is a knee, that's all.)

For one week he was out of town. Practice teachers may go on professional trips just like other teachers, thought 11-A-Two. But the one who came back found us repulsive.

*Schach* was canceled. For the rest of May and most of June he rushed with this class through Fontane's novel *Frau Jenny Treibel*; we finished the school year with two weeks in hand. Weserich still heard us out when we broke into his speech with ours; he nodded as at something expected. He banned what he called jokes. The stove was dead; the egg broken; the dish eaten.

Lockenvitz was abashed, crushed in spirit. Whether or not he had actually hoped for a duel between a high-school class in Mecklenburg and a Grand Dialectician, things had gone awry. He made an effort, he asked for permission to add a point about Count Mirabeau, after whom Victoire de Carayon called herself Mirabelle: after the death of this revolutionary, vouchers had been found proving payments to him by the French royal exchequer; the removal of the soiled ashes from the Pantheon surely must have been known in 1806?

"Thy Herwegh is another of the kind," said Weserich dryly. (Herwegh receives rather merciless treatment at Treibel's hospitable board.) "Puts himself grandly at the head of the workers' rebellions in Baden in 1849; but when things took a bad turn he fled across the French border, disguised as a day laborer!"

The familiar address "thou" that was implied in Weserich's "thy" choked Lockenvitz rather than gratifying him. This child of contradiction, we saw him swallow; he lowered his eyes, sat down without a word.

Lockenvitz wrote a twenty-page essay about *Schach von Wuthenow*, without command or counsel, and sent it after German teacher Weserich to his vacation address. Only years later could he feel pride again in the discovery that Fontane nowhere allows Schach a first name; a custom of the nobility, certainly, yet a comment on the person. Our Weserich had resumed studies at Leipzig University; for a while he lacked the time for correspondence with a high-school student in Mecklenburg. Mathias Weserich's dissertation on *Schach von Wuthenow* was printed at Göttingen, across the border.

That he used us as biologists use guinea pigs, we had known then, without indignation. We had also run swimming races with him, 100 meters with stopwatch, without cheating him by holding back on our speed. You could tell by his shirts that no woman took care of them. And perhaps grownups were like that: once a shot has hit them in the mouth, they keep out of the way of another. He had owned a single suit (gray summer cloth), and this is what he wore with a handkerchief in his breast pocket and a tie every day; as if he owed us the respectable getup. And he had taught us to read German literature.

## August 3, 1968   Saturday

The New York *Times* still has not been able to find proof of any luncheon shared by Leonid Brezhnev and Alexander Dubček, but thanks to the transatlantic time difference she is at least in a position to report that the two embraced one another this morning at the Bratislava station. Auntie Times has learned that Brezhnev's disposition has been softened by written appeals received from the leaders of three Communist Parties—the Yugoslav, the Italian, and the French.

But the spectacle of the East German leaders threatening the Czechs and Slovaks with lip-smacking references to the overwhelming military might of the Soviet Union—that is too sickening to watch.

The helicopters are allowed to fly again from the tower next to Grand Central Terminal to the city's airports. A Douglas Clipper 8 has crashed near Milan; fifteen dead. We too are due to fly soon.

Charlie in his "Good Eats": he surely isn't the type you associate with leisure-time sport after two hours straight of frying and cooking. Do they let you into a club with such raggedly cut yellow hanks of hair? His customers wear their shirts outside their trousers, they come in loud lumberjack-patterned checks and not without smudges of dirt. This morning, though, these gentlemen razzed each other about their golf handicaps, and clearly meant it.

Here is the part of America we are going to miss: Marie ordered one of those meatballs in a jacket with a slice of onion. What does Charlie shout in the direction of the hot plate? "Burger takes slice! Do it special for my special lady, mind!" And Marie looks down into her lap as blushing as behooves her. And proud, because she is part of the scene.

A message on the stairway to the subway:
### RADICAL
is a state of mind.

And as if it were a breach of etiquette to break and enter a house whose owners were two hours by car out of town, we spent the time from morning to early afternoon on Jones Beach; thanks to the Blumenroth family, for this state park seems to be accessible only to people with cars. Mr. Blumenroth, baked red under his thin frizzy hair, may have enriched the Cresspahl household by a new locution: "There is a reason for everything!"

This mindless adage he uttered upon deeming his vigilance adequate for Pamela's games on and under the rubber mattress. When she had drifted twenty yards offshore, Mrs. Cresspahl went to the rescue with him. (Once, in the Baltic, she had swum after a ball for three hours, out of stubbornness. It put wave after wave between itself and her until it drifted off to Denmark.) Pamela for a long time found it difficult to adjust to the confiscation of the mattress as something grownups will do; her father took even longer to shed his air of stupefied reasonableness, such had been his fright. It took a while before he resumed the sidelong glances that were to remind us of our sessions at the bar of the Hotel Marseilles. Mrs. Blumenroth was hard put to it to overlook her husband's antics. And to forestall his remark on the subject, she uttered it herself: that bosom you can certainly be proud of, Mrs. Cresspahl.

"Thank you," she replied, in the approved American fashion of acknowledging, not deprecating, flattery, and found it tiresome for a change.

What do we know about Mrs. Blumenroth?

Born in 1929. "I am from the Carpathians." Yes, the Germans came for her. She wasn't allowed to take anything with her. Her clothes, yes.

Arrival in New York, 1947, marriage, 1948. Her fear of having been sterilized. Pamela, 1957.

Harsh Hungarian accent on a cracked voice. She knows that her voice was gentler in her childhood; hence her preference for whispering.

She admits to one defect: an incapacity for lying; unless by conscious resolve, for which an occasion is yet to arise.

Her black hair is perhaps dyed. Very short, cut to form heart-shaped swatches; one sharp end drapes the forehead. A face with few wrinkles, its expression timid rather than welcoming. When she feels like laughing, what emerges is invariably "ha-ha!"

"I am fussy, nervous." In younger years one would have had the patience for children.

Once she nearly laughed. Her husband brought in a new bed, and the visitor was to test it, sit on it. Mrs. Cresspahl's verdict: quality merchandise. Mrs. Blumenroth: "Ha-ha!"

Keeps a very tidy household. Everything cleared away promptly.

What she found irksome about the postwar era for a woman used to comfortable circumstances and with a sense of propriety was the way one could slide into a false, insecure position.

Persistently striving for a well-groomed appearance; always in fear of the roof collapsing on one's head.

"At my age my back can't help hurting."

She would take in a German child as a foster daughter.

*Voilà*, Pamela—a companion for Marie's further life.

She is standing there, her chest pushed forward, a short neck tilting her head back. She widens her lips, everything is thrust backward and down as if her head had grown onto her rib cage. Her whole face laughs. Marie beams at her friend's expression.

Marie is pursuing plans and objects; gets excited. Pamela behaves as if she were the second eldest. A "girl" in the European sense.

She is going to turn out a nice, sensible woman. Short on intelligence, but unerringly right-minded. We want to see all of this. We want to go to Pamela's wedding.

---

### August 4, 1968   Sunday, South Ferry Day

---

"Gesine! You listened to the record of variations for the pupil Goldberg till after midnight. The Quodlibet twice!"

"Vesógelieke. I am sorry. The people upstairs had a party going, so I wanted my own racket."

"Fooled you! You thought I wanted to quarrel with you! The music gave me happy dreams."

"Marie, I'd like to bet you that we won't quarrel till after the end of October."

"Want to bet that I'll win?"

The communiqué of the Soviet Union and its protégés from Bratislava: you can turn it every which way, but it contains no more than what they've always been reciting, from the achievements of Socialism to the West German thirst for revenge. It winds up with a unanimous mild endorsement of national self-determination, without any mention of Czechoslovakia. The U. S. S. R. promises to withdraw her last 16,000 soldiers. Censorship remains abolished; freedom of assembly and association continues as before. A single concession: the Prague leadership has requested the newspapers to refrain from printing articles voicing opinions that might vex the allies. Articles containing facts are apparently permitted.

On the next-to-last day of October, a part of the trial of Sieboldt and Gollantz was held in the assembly hall of Fritz Reuter High School in Gneez. Principal Kramritz had instructions to have a paper placed

on Elise Bock's desk for the names and signatures of those who wished
to testify in this trial. These volunteers were all handed postage-paid,
preprinted, and machine-numbered postcards, without text, representing their invitations. But whoever came to the assembly hall on
Monday afternoon with nothing but the F. G. Y. members' booklet
was promptly turned away by the two uniformed females at the check-
in table. They wanted to see the personal I. D. card, perhaps motivated
by distrust of the administrative practices of the F. G. Y. District Office
(stencils and mimeographed materials unaccounted for). Also, documents issued by the police are harder to forge, and if forged, easier to
trace. At another screening, Bettina Selbich turned back everyone wearing a lumberjack flannel shirt instead of the blue shirt—on grounds of
"deficient awareness." Thus in the end the assembly hall was occupied
by few students, but many watchdogs from out of town.

The assembly hall was remembered as a space dark with oak, lined
man-high with paneling, with benches as sturdy as pews and a ceiling
of wooden coffer work. Now it was a hall for displaying the colors of
flags. In this regard, the F. G. Y. made a poor showing; its colors were
outnumbered two to one by the red of the Unity Party, sometimes with
the clasped-hands emblem, and by the black, red, and gold of the state
flag, now equipped with the farmers' emblem, a wreath of corn sheaves
open at the top, and the workers', a sledge hammer. (Contemporary
Studies with Selbich: "The eagle, that buzzard of bankruptcy, we are
proud to leave to the reactionary forces in West Germany!") The front
wall, above the red-draped judges' table, is given to Picasso's dove of
peace, second version. The décor stamped the affair as an official
procedure, not some sort of club meeting. Manfras and Lockenvitz,
the ranking functionaries, this time sat on the bench of 11-A-Two (as
they'd better). Silence, as at a funeral service in full view of the coffin.
When the school building was completely encircled by the blue of the
People's Police, the armored personnel carrier from Rostow drew up
to the portals. A platoon under arms escorted the accused up the six
spirals of stairs to the hall. As they passed through the doorway we
could hear clicks and knew that their handcuffs were being taken off
that moment. Sieboldt and Gollantz showed us straight, almost rigid
backs and an intentionally lackadaisical gait as they were conducted to
the platform and took seats between four constables. Two boys, age
nineteen and twenty, dressed in the Sunday suits of their late fathers.
Impassive faces, which refrained from the slightest distortions of greeting, even those they might have managed unobtrusively by eyelashes
and corners of the mouth. But they gazed very searchingly to check
who had come for their leave-taking. Later, the presiding judge realized

his mistake and ordered them to look aside. He was a garrulous man, fussy as an aunt, helpless: how could you possibly . . . this is a dreadful thing . . . such depravity in the flower of youth . . . that's what he talked like. The District Attorney was also handicapped by a bourgeois education, with a penchant for nasty innuendo, which to him was subtle irony. Not a word about the defense attorney; except that he too wore the button of the state Party in his lapel. The prosecution thus had brought their own lackey, who for our benefit referred to them as the Honorable Court. It was cold in the hall; from the long windows came the pale radiance that occurs only in October.

"Oh, the way things are arranged, Dicken Sieboldt will have a fat chance to tell you what the flyers said!"

"The student Cresspahl had come to see him and Gollantz one more time. As one goes to a person one will never see again."

"To pay last respects?"

"When you are seventeen you may feel like that. But we knew the verdict, after all. Though Father Stalin had reintroduced the death penalty on January 13—the utmost protection for society—these two would be given only twenty-five years. The usual."

"For a few flyers."

"And Pius gave me the ultimate proof that we were friends. Because of his father, the Pagenkopfs were considered in agreement with the Sachwalter's regime; they of all people got something dropped into their mail slot. And one time in June, Pius waited for me to ask him for the table of logarithms. What I found in there could have been slipped in accidentally. When he turned it in to Section D, true to the duties of a vigilant friend of peace, he need have no scruples about swearing that he had not shown the picture with barbed wire and imprint to a soul. After I had finished reading, a glance hung between us such as life has to offer you perhaps three times, if you are fortunate and things have gone well."

"You dry yourselves with the same towel! You sleep wall to wall! But you trust each other only when you have the power to send him to the penitentiary."

"From that moment on I had another brother."

The former students Sieboldt and Gollantz had been indicted for private and conspiratorial visits to West Berlin. This was the site of the East Bureau of the Social Democratic Party of Germany; there resided the Investigating Committee of Jurists for Freedom; there operated the League to Combat Inhumanity. These groups, so East German courts claimed to have proved, were responsible for a bridge blown up, a bar set on fire. For my part I believed Jakob when he told of the discovery in Rostock of a railway car that had been diverted from Saxony with forged freight papers; the butter in it now meant a shortfall for the people of the city of Leipzig—assuming it was still edible. But when it came to that, Sieboldt and Gollantz had disclaimed any intention to vent other people's anti-Communism on their own relatives and neighbors by causing even greater disorder in food distribution than the East German authorities managed on their own: they had gone to West Berlin with something they had thought up themselves. So much the worse, opined the High Court. It was true that they had accepted a picture of youth marching in formation behind barbed wire from one of those societies that were all registered with district courts in West Berlin, but they had done so on condition that it was combined with their own text. So much the worse, opined the High Court. While the defendants were merely badgered to admit to the infamy of those statements, at least two students knew them just about by heart: the slogans Peace and Struggle for Peace were mere camouflage for the consolidation of Soviet tenure in Central and Eastern Europe; since the Soviet Union had also come into possession of an atom bomb—by thievery—offensive preparations had begun by reinforcement in manpower and equipment of the People's Police, by campaigns among members of the F. G. Y. for joining the camouflaged Army, by the appointment of one of its leading officers to the Vopo's central body. What are you marching for, members of the F. G. Y.? This was what the students Sieboldt and Gollantz had worked out. Aggravating circumstances! Disparagement of the World Peace Movement in conversation—by the assertion that in French newspapers Picasso's peace dove was depicted as armed with hammer and sickle, that the British call it "the dove that goes bang"—would you translate for us this monstrous insult to the world-wide wish for peace? *Die Taube kommt mit'm Knall*, but make it a little less unbuttoned; where on earth could you have picked up such things, for Heaven's sake?

"Gesine, you reckless child!"

"I did feel a little edgy." But Dicken Sieboldt answered in genial tones: "It's in the air," and glanced at the air above Gesine's head, where the assembly hall's balcony hung, barred for the day and studded with armed men.

"If he had suspected you! One thought that you might have betrayed him, and he would have dragged you down with him!"

"But things were carefully designed to deal with such situations in that democratic German country. If Cresspahl's daughter tells her classmate Sieboldt about a transmission of the B. B. C., it is his duty to report her. If Sieboldt seems pleased by some news that has come to him from his classmate's mouth, it is her duty to report him. With the Sieboldts, denunciation would have caused them to repudiate and cast him out forever. Like that. And if Cresspahl's daughter had been lauded for the arrest of a neighbor's child, he would have deemed her unworthy of any further glance or word."

"Listening to you, it all sounds pretty easy. But *someone* denounced those two."

"Gollantz was openly considered to be engaged to a certain Lisette von Probandt, a girl in his class. The two were 'the Couple' of the season; they were watched by the kids of the ninth grade the way the kids of the earlier ninth had watched Pius and me. If a girl is put under arrest and given the third degree . . ."

"So there was something Sieboldt had to forgive Gollantz for."

"And Gollantz was urged by the High Court to confess himself led astray by Sieboldt. But Gollantz stood his ground, so as to be given just as many years as his friend."

"This obnoxious Statue of Liberty, see how her arm is dropping? You watch, they are going to close it to visitors, because of dilapidation!"

"Elementary, my dear Mary."

The defendants were repeatedly ordered to show greater contrition. When they were bullied, threatened, abused, they appeared quite content, as if any other treatment would have been disappointing. As if they had expected it. And the blue-shirted children before them dimly realized what was sufficient, for these two, as reasons for joy, for that tight serenity that stiffened their backs in the face of twenty-five years of forced labor

for sabotage:
Attempt to maintain
reactionary student self-government,
a relic
of the pseudodemocratic heritage
of the Weimar Republic
by means of
fraudulent usurpation
of high and highest ranks
in the Central School Chapter Authority
of the Free German Youth;
for espionage:

Reconnaissance
at the vulnerable flank
of the Peace Movement
of the Republic;

for terror: because they had undeniably undertaken, you see, to spread in the town of Gneez and in their high school an opinion different from that expected by the Ministry of the Interior (which they persisted in calling the Ministry of War); for illegal association (Sieboldt with Gollantz). Not to be caught short, a Mr. Kramritz popped up and sputtered about the "fraudulently obtained school certificates"; in fact, they had secured admission to university study by work in the subjects of examination. Then a Bettina Selbich was heard from, mindful of the nocturnal visits of the F. G. Y. functionary Sieboldt, and she spoke haltingly; had her victim wanted to talk, it would assuredly have passed his lips that "a gentleman takes his pleasure—and keeps silent." He spared her, and if it cost him a struggle, this was how he meant to think of himself later, anyway. Manfras, too, took the floor with one of those "personal position statements" required by the young tradition of "democratic jurisdiction." His indignation, the tremor of rage in his voice, were understandable to the defendants; to us too. For when the F. G. Y. school chapter was about to send its protest against the murderous incursion of U. S. troops into peaceful Korea, they had tricked him. Made him lose face. Injured him in his political conscience.

"Of the c. eight million people who go about earning their living in the neighborhood of this ferry, the *John F. Kennedy*, a few are bound to recall that it was the other way around."

"We did too. Because when we were summoned to a general school assembly toward noon on June 26, Bettina's efforts at the rostrum to construct sole responsibility for the imperialists was distinctly edifying. To ask us to affirm a lie by acclamation, to demand a yes vote for falsehood—this was a matter for derisive fun to children who knew how to use a radio. And who had been delegated to confer on wording outside the door of the hall? Who returned with a mosaic flawlessly assembled out of the costume jewelry of newspaper prose? Sieboldt and Gollantz. And whom did they thank for his dauntless help in the composition, whose skill with words did they commend for the succession to leadership of the F. G. Y. at Gneez's high school? Gabriel Manfras. They had chosen him for the task of reading, in accents of passion, from the town-hall balcony to the people drawn up in squads below a text that seemed unobjectionable; but now he had been maneuvered into the position of accomplice to a forgery and tainted by the commendation of his political work by skeptics of the peace campaign. There was reason for anger here; the defendants could appreciate that."

"A word in conclusion."

"Sieboldt and Gollantz thanked the High Court for its efforts, again denied, each for himself, any consciousness of wrongdoing, and voiced a final scruple: possibly it might have been more appropriate under the circumstances had they been allowed to attend the afternoon's events in the garb of honor of the Free German Youth."

"I could never do that."

"You could, Marie. Some people get like that when everything is behind them, and before them twenty-five years in the clink. Never to be able to ride through New York Harbor on a ferry. To have lost a girl. Never to wake up except from blows struck against the length of iron rail. To know that one's sole luggage will be the reminiscence of a mere nineteen or twenty years of life."

"If I were Lisette von Probandt and had a memory, life would revolt me."

"The twenty-five years turned into a mere five. A West German chancellor paid a visit to the Soviet Union. With the remaining prisoners of war, Sieboldt and Gollantz were released into West German custody. They took up the study of law together in Bonn and Heidelberg; in 1962 they were appointed to the Foreign Ministry, and soon there will be an embassy where we will go to visit them."

"So the Soviet Government has educated two civil servants for the West Germans."

"That's called cadre development! And our Lisette—she waited out her seven years. She married her Gollantz, and Sieboldt visits them as godfather."

"Forgive like that—I could never do it."

"You'll be able to. You'll learn."

(Sunday, too, is South Ferry Day if Marie declared it so.)

### August 5, 1968   Monday

On Czech television, Alexander Dubček as head of the Communist Party announced that the conference at Bratislava had yielded the country further space for his liberalization policy; it fulfilled "our expectations" (not "all our . . ."). They say he made an effort to conceal his party's satisfaction.

In Florida yesterday, in the proper weekend spirit, a man accompanied by a child of about two rented a Cessna 182 in order, as he said, to take a look at the neighborhood. Then he pulled a revolver: the plane had to go to Cuba.

Over southeastern Wisconsin yesterday, a Convair 580 collided with a small private plane and took the wreck of the loser with three dead jammed in it all the way to the landing strip.

We too are due to fly soon.

"The student Lockenvitz."

(Because you want it, Marie. Only what I *know*.)

"Early in 1950, we had invited him into the working team of Pagenkopf and Cresspahl."

For selfish reasons. We hoped to learn from this overgrown, weedy, famished boy how he was able to think in Latin. "Eundem Germaniae sinum proximi Oceano Cimbri tenent, parva nunc civitas, sed gloria ingens," he had casually quoted when the term Obotriten-Adel (nobility dating back to a Slavic civilization of the tenth century) was mentioned. "This sweep of Germany [it said] is held by the Cimbrian, now a small tribe, but immense in renown."

Social background, father's profession: farmer. In the questionnaire of 1949: M. A., agrobio. 1950: Director of Municipal Gardens, Parks, and Cemetery Plantings of . . . [no fear—I am suppressing the name of the town; actually, you pronounce it regularly in its Polish form, and only Anita understood it, if anyone] . . . of a major town in today's People's Republic of Poland. Middle class.

Political provenance, party affiliation of parents before 1945: None. Before 1933: German National People's Party. Imperialist. Insists that his father had kept aloof from the Nazis. But how did he purport to excuse the fact that he had spent his fifth school year in a National Institute for Political Education? In 1944 his father had been confronted with the choice of either being drafted into the Army or producing some other token of devotion to the Hitler state. The fees charged by the N. I. P. E. schools were a heavy financial burden. They were distinguished from the neo-Teutonic Order "castles" of the Hitler Youth by less emphasis on physical prowess. Take his glasses: steel frame, which in hot weather sent rusty trickles down his nose.

But why did the Soviet authorities take away his father, who had been neither Army nor Party, with the result that in February of 1947 he was "last seen lying dead on his bunk"? (Thus stated a witness; Lockenvitz's mother hoped for a pension. The pension—cf. husband's social position in the past—was disallowed, provisionally in 1947, definitely in 1949. Claim for educational benefits for student Lockenvitz approved.) On the questionnaire in Contemporary Studies, Lockenvitz stated: My father had a quarrel about the rent with the owner of our house, and a false charge was laid against him. When he felt he could trust us he added, asking for our silence: "That's when the Soviet Army headquarters was in our villa."

Arrival at Gneez: at age eleven. That unnamed city in the east was to be defended, and so the father sent his family with the relocating German Army toward the Western Front. The unnamed city now lies in ruin. Mother's profession since 1945: garden worker. Son's class: proletarian? No: white-collar worker.

First habitation in Gneez: opposite the cemetery, with Mr. Grave-digger Budniak, in a single room. Since 1949, two rooms near the dairy. From March 1951, an apartment created out of soldiers' barracks in the Barbara quarter, which the Soviet authorities had vacated (blowing up a third of them). In the plaster of a barracks' gable you could see the outlines of the Nazi eagle and the circle surrounding the swastika on which it had squatted.

An only child. Peasant kinfolk in the father's place of birth, Das-sow-on-the-Lake: there he spent vacations, was paid in kind for harvest labor. 1948–1949: worked twenty hours a week in a bicycle repair shop; he needed the money for books. (The town library closed at five thirty; but one can read till midnight.) From 1950, deliverer of express mail for the East German postal service for the district of Gneez: for this purpose Anita had all but forced upon him the Swedish bicycle he then rode (not that in his scatterbrained state he had realized that at her price this was a gift . . . ). He earned twenty pfennig per kilometer, plus fifteen pfennig if it rained. Whether it had rained depended on Berthold Knever, the postmaster. One time, a woman at Old Demwies had waited so avidly for that letter with the red sticker and the address crossed out in red—signaling a safe departure for the West—that she gave him an egg. But often he spent his afternoons in the sorting room doing nothing but waiting for express mail; and with homework.

A sensitive child. With a name like that. A nickname: Dietchen, Dieterkin (bestowed by Lise Wollenberg) Lockenvitz, and then, really, to have locks all over one's head, long unruly waves, and end in a sort of vitz or fits or misfit. Lockenvitz bowed his head and pressed his lips together as if coming to a decision; but consult GOETHE here:

> "For a man's proper name is not at all like a coat, which merely hangs about him and can be pulled and jerked on him if necessary; rather it is like a perfectly fitted dress, nay, like his very

skin grown onto him all over, which cannot be scraped or scuffed without injury to himself."

Such a child would rather have this kind of book in the house, ready to hand at all times.

A disadvantaged child. More important even than furniture in all those moves was a framed photograph of his father, an enlarged passport picture clearly showing the crimped metal fasteners. Mrs. Lockenvitz, though, had been only thirty-five years old when her husband "was seen" for the last time; from what he left behind she took only the charge to get the boy as far as the doors of a university. (His father had studied agrobiology.) That explains why, after the 1949 carnival, you could see in the window of the Mallenbrandt Pharmacy an eloquent photograph of the festivities: a young woman, her breasts squeezed together by her bodice. Therefore a child feels ashamed. A sixteen-year-old who is whipped by his mother because upon her receiving a nocturnal visitor, male, he takes his father's picture from the wall and hides it; and the child makes her feel ashamed. At a time when electrical gear was in short supply, he had fastened above a window a bell from the sleigh that had remained behind in the east; he had put it within reach by means of pitch-treated sack cording, all because he was so eager for visitors. Now he unscrewed it, and ignored knocks at the door.

A young man who is adept in the way one enters a room containing a lady; who is schooled in the manner knife and fork are handled, now that a third plate is carried in from the kitchen for him by Mrs. Pagenkopf; who because of good manners persists in thanking her for every snack, with a servant's bow from the neck; who refuses the offer of a second sandwich—merely because it is proper, and although he continued to be hungry for a long while. Until we convinced him that at this house there was no listener at the door (who, the proverb claims, hears what he's hated for!). It took a long time.

It pained him to lie. If the school demanded it, so much the worse for the school; and he was at pains to let the teacher involved know. Bettina Selbich observed him uneasily as he declaimed for her the seven commandments of the Stockholm Appeal:

I vow
to stop railway trains,
to unload no military cargo,
to withhold fuel from such vehicles,
to disarm mercenaries,

to forbid my spouse and children any service with the country's
armed forces,
to refuse to supply my government with food,
to refuse to work in telephone exchanges or traffic control—
in order to prevent a new war.

Bettina had the feeling that there was something objectionable about
his recital. He had let her in for many humiliations in the past; she
decided to give it a try and ask for the source of the text. Anita addressed
the air in front of her, saying in a resigned tone: "In *Pravda*, first week
in July."

(*We thought she wanted to keep you from harm. Or did she slip
papers containing copies from her Russian readings into your workbook?
Was this perhaps what went on?*)

With us his approach was cautious. Zaichik would come calling
with Eva—they had tired of memorizing nitrates and nitrites and sent
inquiring glances toward Pius's music cabinet of People's Own provenance—and when he had given his nod as host, they did close the
windows, but without hesitation tuned in the station in the American
Sector. They broadcast a hit parade on Fridays there. Bully Buhlan
sang to Zaichik's edification and delight: Yoop-dee-doo, oh, yoop-dee-
doo, you can't take a wall and ram your noodle through!—
This should have reassured Lockenvitz. For we had been apprised
of the ban on western stations in Contemporary Studies by Bettina,
with the following elucidation: Musicians who for opportunistic reasons
decorate Mr. Adenower's road to war with their offerings are devoid,
once and for all, of the humanism that might inspire their interpre-
tations of Mozart's and Schubert's immortal symphonies!
Lockenvitz held back until Zaichik and Eva had left, then remarked: from such a lyric out of Berlin-Schöneberg one might, at any
rate, draw a sociological inference; the people over there have to pacify
their population, wean them from their demands. Thus spoke Lockenvitz for their benefit as he had heard them talk in school. Pius looked
at me, his forehead in irregular folds, and hoisted his shoulders up as
if nonplused. We pussyfooted around each other like diplomats! Pius
had another try. What was Lockenvitz's preference in music?
Lockenvitz had an occasional yen for syncopated music.
This meant early American jazz, which had just been promoted
by government decree from a music of decadence to one that was
progressive inasmuch as it had developed from workers' songs at a time

of openly practiced slavery. Conversation by prescription is what this boy went in for.

Then the East German Government fulfilled what it had announced to its youth at the All-German Rally. On June 23 it transmitted to the governments friendly to it this warning: American terror planes had dropped great quantities of potato bugs over the territory under its control, in order to injure socialist agriculture. In late September the students of 11-A-Two, heads searchingly bowed, began to patrol the potato fields around Gneez to discover and harass *Doryphora decemlineata*. Shamed and embarrassed by a state authority that expected them to believe that canard about an agrarian attack and to proclaim their faith by joyous action. You ought to write an entire book, Comrade Writer, about those afternoons, so infinitely did they drag on, so infinitesimally did the earth lurch over against the sun in an easterly curve.

And Lockenvitz was revealed to us, at least as the son of an agrobiologist overcome by memory, when he said: "Ha! Those wily imperialists! The potato bug or Colorado beetle hibernates about eight inches deep in the soil, to emerge as soon as the temperature rises above 10° Centigrade. Which means early May. What is the date of the All-German Rally? End of May. So the bugs arrive on schedule, obediently the females deposit their eggs in bands of twenty to eighty, each totaling up to 800; after seven days the larvae are hatched, and after the pupa stage, the bugs need just another fifty days and they are ready. This means July!—not June 23. Not at Whitsun. Listen, you two: if we have potato bugs here in Mecklenburg, they must be the descendants of those first sighted in southwest Germany in 1937! If they thrive here, it is because the land reform cut down the hedgerows, because in the hedges were birds' nests, and in *those* sat the destroyers of this quarantined pest! And because, along with the estates of the nobility, pheasant breeding died too!"

"We," the boy had said. We had arrived.

Now he would do this sort of thing also with our entertainment in mind, as when he recited, for Bettina S., with carefully dosed hyperbole, and, apparently unconsciously, divagated into labyrinths of cogitation. . . . Those six-legged heralds of the U. S. invasion! But our country is prepared. We have the pheasant, after all. A game bird of low profile living in bushy terrain, also in cabbage fields. Eats caterpillars, worms, and beetles, pests in general! A bird that is vulnerable to poachers, since it is a poor flyer. But what people hunt is its worst enemy, the fox; hence the pheasant's great proliferation. Historical research traces the economic brutality of the American aggressors back to the Lend-Lease agreement of 1941. Under the pretense of aiding the heroic fight of the Soviet Union with arms and food supplies, they used the packing to smuggle into the country 117 different sorts of insect pests and weed seeds!

Bettina in her confusion was about to enter a new A for him, but inquired for safety's sake: since these facts dating back to the war were absolute news to her, and since she planned to use them at an agitprop meeting in the provincial capital, she wondered if she might ask the student Lockenvitz where he got this from?

"Any time," he said; "from the *Literaturnaya Gazeta.*"

*(Believe it or not: Bettina trotted over and asked the Russian specialist whether by any chance this was an émigré journal.)*

Seventeen forlorn Colorado beetles were found by the student body of Fritz Reuter High School, 400 strong; nine of these were ladybugs. Lockenvitz, wishing to do the duty he owed us as a friend, asked us if we knew that a wanted list was posted at the distribution window of the post office, and that almost every day a few letters would go to spend the night with the Stasi, the State Security Police.

This Lockenvitz we can now ask about the meeting with the poet Hermlin in Landsberger Avenue. Lockenvitz had barely stopped short of lying: on a streetcar, bound for Grünau, he had gone as far as Schmöckwitz by mistake, was invited into a house there for discussions about art in Mecklenburg, about the sculptor Barlach; tea and red wine. Lockenvitz borrowed a pair of shoes from Pius—his own had been waiting for repair for four weeks. Airily, he communicated to us his thoughts: our socialist achievements—you have always to presuppose someone from whom they have been lifted, who now stands on the sidelines and sulks. What's been holding up our American shoe-resoling plants?

This Lockenvitz of ours we picked when 11-A-Two had suddenly to delegate some member for an F. G. Y. training course at Dobbertin near Goldberg. At first we sat on our hands when we saw Manfras vote against his own removal from home and school curriculum; and when Lise Wollenberg used her ballot to take revenge for neglect and to punish him on general principles for being descended from outsiders. Then Pius, as was his privilege as chairman of the class chapter meeting, asked how the candidate felt about such an excursion. "As secretary for organization of the Central School Chapter Authority, the Z. S. G. L., one has to strive continually for progress in the knowledge of theory," he answered, like someone agreeing to sacrifice himself for us. Second vote: unanimous—as was considered chic.

In November 1950, he departed; in January we had him back; things had gone badly. Like start, like end: failure.

Literally. In November, the Ministry of State Security collared a brother of Mrs. Lockenvitz in the shipyard of Wismar; indictment: sabotage, espionage. Mrs. Lockenvitz tried to beat a son on his way to get training in the mental processes of a ministry such as this. He pinned her arms down and with an expression of quasi-medical scrutiny stated that she seemed to him hysterical; sidetracked by curiosity, she inquired about the symptoms of this disease and was dissatisfied with his answers. Now he sat there far from home and had to repress even his wish to return to Gneez and the apartment in the Barbara quarter.

How his stint with the Dobbertin workshop ended, Lockenvitz kept to himself. What probably happened is that one of the instructors wanted a more satisfactory answer about the third basic law of dialectics; this could net you an unfavorable final grade and a bronze badge instead of a gold one for "superior command of subject."

For his first question to Betteenkin, our Mrs. Selbich, was this: If, by the doctrine of dialectical materialism, quantity by its inevitable growth is bound to alter its nature and change to quality, how does this work out in a comparison between the brain of Turgenev and that of an elephant?

(LOCKENVITZ, in the period preceding course work at Dobbertin: children should be spared this. When in 1946 I answered the doorbell at Budniak's house, two men were standing there who asked for Mrs. Scharrel. Mrs. Scharrel lived on the second floor and was in black-marketing, professionally. Mrs. Scharrel: "Just you tell 'em I'm on my way to Wismar!" This was hard for me to do. But you obey grownups, don't you? The first time, you forget; with luck. In 1948 the catechism teacher asked who among us had never in his life told a lie. I raised my hand because no one else wanted to; magic! I had parked a second lie alongside the first. By now the mechanism works pretty well, of course. But children should be spared this.

The child Lockenvitz, after having worked through the Old Testament for a second time, requested an audience with the Canon of Gneez Cathedral and neatly explained to the Comrade Pastor why he would henceforth stay away from the meetings of the Young Congregation. This is mentioned lest there be any doubt what manner of fifteen-year-old he was.)

He was uncompromising. Introverted. Lost the zest for teasing

Betteenkin; lost ground in Latin; lost weight. In one's memory he sits, in a blue shirt that seems all empty folds, obsessed with reflection behind his poorhouse spectacles. Then came January 12, 1951, when at Dresden an eighteen-year-old high-school student was sentenced to death, for "instigation to boycott" and attempted murder of a VOPO (with a pocket knife); in Gneez, the Kripo, the Criminal Police, in uniform, entered the Renaissance Film Theater, bent on discovering who it was who muttered or laughed at every appearance, in picture and sound, of the Sachwalter, his clownish Saxon dialect, who incidentally considered the sentence appropriate; even after it had been reduced to fifteen years in jail. This provoked the female partner of the Pagenkopf co-operative to the careless remark: "If it is really true that this statesman is such a thorn to the Americans, why have they failed in three years to knock him off?"

Luckily for all of us she asked this in the great outdoors, one evening on the Gneez skating pond. Lockenvitz only skated figure eights, alone and in silence, for a few minutes, then he rejoined our circle by an inside curve and let us have the benefit of what he had learned to opine. The ice was gray in the darkness; you had to keep your eyes fixed on the track. Sometimes you heard a blade grate; the night constantly widened around us, and with it Lockenvitz's hardened, almost adult, even-toned voice:

"Formerly, when the commanding duke fell in open battle, it was damaging to the morale of the army. Today this would only produce a need to close ranks. The result is uncertain in any case: the successor may turn out to be even more aggressive. You have to guess at the strategy he might be contemplating; before, you knew whom you were dealing with. Almost any such single person is expendable, no matter how much power he concentrates at the time—unless he combines charisma with the requisite ability, a rare combination (our soulmates in Moscow excepted of course). Deduction: the machine is running today; it'll keep running. Second: even war today isn't yet a free-for-all without rules, where each side may cheerfully do its worst. Certain norms or rules are invoked at the summits, precisely because they are occasionally (and surreptitiously) infringed. One such tacit rule forbids the assassination of the opposing leaders other than in open battle. If rules of this caliber are consciously and flagrantly violated, this chills trust in the validity of all limiting agreements. The result may be a retaliatory attack with nerve gas upon the offending capital. Hence: fear of the negative effects of an infraction of a major rule upon the perpetrator himself. And that's why everything stays as it is."

"Grammarian," he had said when 11-A-Twos a year ago had to announce their choice of profession. "And what are you choosing now, young Comrade? Historian?"

"Teacher of Latin," said Lockenvitz grimly.

This was the January when in Germany's West the High Commissioners of the Allies assembled on the Petersberg with the Federal Chancellor, his assistant, and two generals to deliberate on whether Germans should be armed again.

It was the January when the East German People's Police sent recruiters to the high schools, who arrived with the blue shirt under their uniform jackets and talked with the boys of 11-A-Two as one youth comrade to another. They promised training with rolling, floating, and flying equipment. Lockenvitz arranged with Dr. Schürenberg for an appointment exact to the minute, performed twelve knee bends in the hallway of the Villa on Prince-Electors' Esplanade (vulgarly called Dissectors' Parade on account of the density of physicians there); he repeated this exercise in front of the doctor's desk and received a slip of paper attesting to vegetative dystonia.

To lend credibility to this with the school authorities, he applied for exemption from Physical Education classes. Henceforth he left school when the gym lummox chased us over the vaulting horses, spun us around the horizontal bar; he would stroll outdoors by himself. At handball and soccer games he would squat behind the goal, elbows propped on knees, chin resting on two flattened hands; he would watch, but drop from the moon when a girl asked him the score.

At the start of the school year 1951–52, when he was nominated for a second term as secretary for organization, he declined the candidacy; grounds: need to improve scholastic achievement. (But really— what did he have to do but to summon us for marches, actions against potato-bug bandits, assemblies; once a month, to report to the F. G. Y.'s Central Council on those preprinted forms that we had undertaken such-and-such actions or gestures in the interest of peace; how many members of the school chapter had taken out paid subscriptions to the journal of the association, *Young World*.) He was an A student in Latin, English, German, Contemporary Studies, had Bs in the rest of the subjects, except for a C in Chemistry, which irked him like a tick.

Christmas 1951 he found a bag hanging on his mother's door, filled with ginger cookies, walnuts, a pad of inkproof linen-stock notepaper, and a pair of gloves that owed nothing to machines. A freshly laundered gym bag it was, with a drawstring, the kind girls used.

Lockenvitz went to see Gesine Cresspahl with the idea of thanking her.

Gesine was annoyed with herself that she hadn't thought of this first; she had to assure him of her innocence.

*(If only you had known it . . . it came from Annette Dühr of 10-A-Two. She was so pretty, so arresting to look at with her hazelnut eyes, her deep-brown braids, and a face that invited confidence. Later she worked as a stewardess with East German Airlines, which helped entitle her to take training with Pan American. On her return, her picture made the front page of* Berliner Neue Illustrierte. *Here was a girl who liked you and wanted you to like her. You could easily have found her by taking a walk across the schoolyard and back, her gym bag prominently showing in your hand. When Annette holds out a hand to you, however discreetly, she has a right to think you high and mighty when you happen to have other things on your mind than girls. But it would have gone better with you had you wanted to find her.)*

Lockenvitz would now join our homework team at the appointed time and leave immediately after completion of the assignments in Math or Chemistry. Once, Pius asked me to question him about how he imagined these sciences to fit in with the talents of a woman. I rejected the idea, I was afraid of Lockenvitz's mother; not for anything did I want her to hear that he was in love with an unresponsive girl. Lockenvitz probably meant it as an apology for his guarded manner, as a present, when he brought along a note purporting to explain what kept him aloof from us:

> "Between events and their unbiased apprehension people insert a quantity of concepts and purposes and demand that what happens should conform to them."

We urged him to palm this off on La Selbich as a critique of the discipline of Contemporary Studies (originating in an "imperialist" country), the more so as she would never hit upon the author (G. W. F. Hegel, 1802). He tossed his locks off his forehead with a peevish laugh, as though he had outgrown playing games with Betteenkin.

Pius and I kept our mouths firmly shut when on a November afternoon we saw him step out of the house where Bettina S. had had an apartment bestowed on her for loyal endurance.

Zaichik—we were not on speaking terms with him for six months. He wanted to start a correspondence with girls of a socialist British household, in partnership with another boy. Lockenvitz did him the favor, even wrote something to Wolverhampton for Peace's sake and the censorship's. Then he found out that Zaichik had smuggled into his envelope, by way of introduction, a snapshot of Pius, because he judged Pius to be more attractive to a maiden's eye. Actually, among the girls of 11-A-Two, Pius was rated merely "intriguing," whereas Lockenvitz was "our handsome young man." Let us hope that it eased his heart that we sided with him in such a momentous thing.

Lockenvitz was the first in our school to wear glasses with a Plexiglas frame, demonstrably acquired on Stalin Street. (Opticians were a protected species in all of Mecklenburg, armored against deep probing by tax authorities; they indulged themselves in virtually metropolitan window displays. Almost no optician was ever hauled into court in Mecklenburg.)

Lockenvitz did not wear a Canadian-style jacket.

When it came to vacations, each of us took off decently separated, Pius, Cresspahl's daughter, and Lockenvitz likewise.

One factor in his calculations, if such they were, had been neglected by inattention. Vegetative dystonia does not mix well with bicycle touring.

For he rode a bicycle like a healthy person, twenty-five miles per hour was routine for him. He would have taken half an hour to Jerichow! But he push-biked it into the yonder on weekends. We could only hope that nobody would start wondering.

Matthew 16:26. Oh shiyit!

Dear Marie, this is all I *think* I know of Dieter Lockenvitz.

---

**August 6, 1968   Tuesday**

---

If we want to get through this day in one go, we will need numbers.

I.

If somebody lives in New York and his place has been broken into, he may wait till he mildews before his insurance payment comes. But if he has paid his premiums under a plan devised by De Rosny, he can submit a list of missing objects on Tuesday, certified by Precinct 23, and will receive precisely a week later by office mail a cashier's check; hard currency, cashable from Manhattan to Leningrad.

Just as De Rosny's bank wants to make a profit even on the insurance carriers of those he calls "my colleagues," so an in-house travel agency is to derive a profit from the sums that the colleagues can afford to put into vacation travel. Anyone entering this room on the eighteenth floor without the five-stroke emblem of this money institution across his heart, without the name tag, in a white linen suit like a passerby off the street, has it pointed out to her first that these premises are not open to the public.

"I am aware of that," replies Mrs. Cresspahl, pleased. Here for once she is not known as "our" German, "our" Danish lady. The girl behind the counter has her head covered with a beehive of blond hair; her lips are compressed, something must have gone wrong for her this morning. We would have liked to show her the cartoon from the current *New Yorker* that we clipped for D. E.'s delectation. Under a sign saying SERVICE WITH A SMILE stands a butcher in an apron, who is handing a customer the bag with her purchases, looking serious and questioningly baffled. The woman before him jerks her nose high with anger, her mouth is creased with indignation. The caption hints at what she wants to know: *"Well?"* (How about that smile?)

Quite unlike other sales transactions, this one is marked by questions, terse, snappish ones: Corporate I. D.? Social Security number? Department? Department head's extension?

Here employee is pitted against employee. I think we'll pull a little rank on this young specimen. We too find it hard on many a morning to produce the grimace of sham affability, but it was from people like her that we learned it, by explicit demand. Let's teach this one the road to Mandalay—that is, a way to the ostensibly revered Mr. De Rosny's telephone without giving his name away. Here, a unique attraction, please move on: a chance to see an employee's expression run the gamut from embarrassment, to panic, to gestures of humility and submission, to cordiality. "I am ever so sorry, madam; my apologies."

Then we both felt a little ashamed and settled down to deliberate how you cancel a reservation for two to Frankfurt/Main on August 19, evening; also a rental convertible in which we had meant to start for the frontier crossing at Waidhaus in the Upper Palatinate Mountains— hello there, Czechs and soldiers! The date, the time, may remain as it was. But now we'd like to take the trip with Scandinavian, or it could be Pan American, as long as the plane gets to Copenhagen in the morning. Our friend Anita wants it that way; I doubt that you know her. There ought to be a hotel, surely, near Kastrup, on the beach, which takes people in early in the morning, until early afternoon perhaps. For catching up on sleep, you ask? Yes, "sleeping in" was just what we thought of; we understand each other now, don't we? If the hotel dining room tends to be crowded, we would like a reservation for a table for four. Although we are only two, yes. Thanks for your attention. The thing is, we like to have our lunch in private. For 1600 or thereabouts we need a reservation on a flight to Ruzyně. But really, even an American travel agency should know this—the airports in the Communist countries! It's near Prague. Prag. Praha. You say this means a stop at Schönefeld near Berlin? A transit through East Berlin doesn't bother us too much. And what do we do about the rental car, have we forgotten about that? Circumstances have changed; we don't consider that feasible; "impractical, but grateful for the thought," as the actress said to the bishop. You want to send a Telex to a Communist country to arrange for a car to be reserved there on the twentieth at 2000 by the people that TRY HARDER? Like yourselves? You know what? You are going to get a picture postcard from us. VISA? We have it. International driver's license? Ditto. The invoice is to go to the bank? Absolutely. Linen too hot for 75° Fahrenheit? You'd be surprised how cool it feels. Try to get some at Bloomingdales. No, *we* owe you thanks!

II.

More than an hour before the department stores on Fifth Avenue get overrun by lunchtime crowds, Mrs. Cresspahl is standing in a luggage department in the role of customer. It was to have been Abercrombie & Fitch, but that was where a man from Czechoslovakia shot himself on Friday two weeks ago. We would have known the floor as the elevator passed it. About the store she is in now we would say: things are perhaps 3 per cent cheaper here.

Is it the suit, the handbag of crocodile leather, the shoes from Switzerland? Or can one tell from the customer's hairdo that a Signor Boccaletti has made it his charge? Whichever, there approaches the department manageress in person to attend to this lady. (There go the younger salesladies' commissions from the transactions to follow.) She wishes a good morning, calls the radiant mess outside the windows a sweetheart of a day, and what could she possibly do for us?

"Hello. We need two large suitcases; here are the measurements. They should look as shabby as possible. Please."

"I beg your pardon? You are looking for shoddy merchandise in a house like ours?"

"As if they were made from a worn-out rug. But stabproof, each with two wraparound straps and locks that tell even the casual observer that they can be opened with the bare hands."

"I *think* I am beginning to see what you mean."

"These might do, actually. Unfortunately, they won't do unless your exquisite bazaar boasts in addition two aluminum housings that fit into them with hair-breadth snugness."

"I see, I see!"

"That's just what we want you to do. We were witnesses to the travel preparations of a gentleman named Professor Erichson, which appealed to us. We are modeling ours on his to some degree."

When the customer requests delivery to Riverside Drive, not the most impressive address, the full-figured woman betrays a certain hesitancy on noting the open checkbook. Make up your mind, dear lady. We look her straight in the eyes; she has the choice between an intake of over $200 and an act of distrust. The bank on which the check is drawn is two blocks away. If the woman prefers to call the institution, we have to accept it. She has the right to demand the employer's address; ask Mrs. Lazar about our credit record; we might be mired knee-high in suspicion of fraud. She decides to smile, of all times at this crucial point in our negotiations. Is this justified in terms of drama theory? Evidently it is, for what does she say to us? "I can tell by your face. You would sooner break a leg than swindle an old woman! Believe me, I know about people. . . ."

And because this is true, we give her a special look as she comes striding into the store's restaurant, every inch the supervisor, who may set her own mealtimes; only to change into a good-natured woman, somewhat run off her feet, who tells about her insomnia; no pill does any good. She is a Mrs. Collins and lives in Astoria, Queens. What a coincidence! Another thing she had meant to say: a week ago to the day, a gentleman came into the store, in one of those South American hats; he bought luggage just like you, Mrs. Cresspahl. You know, spending four decades advising customers on suitcases, you get so you . . . Exactly. For some $600, paid in cash. The next day he asked for me, because he liked the service he'd had. . . . Nothing compared with mine, Mrs. Collins. And introduced himself as the impresario of a female ballet troupe; they exist, after all! You bet they do. What he wanted was a present for each of the dancers, a reward, a premium, whatever; it came to $2,000. How great it is to make a sale like that! How happy one is to honor a credit card! We too, Mrs. Collins, we never take more than three tens to New York streets. The next day the credit card blew up on me. Ripped off. A loss of $2,000. No one likes to go to management with that. You see, Mrs. Cresspahl, I just wanted to fill you in because we gave each other such a long look a while ago; can you forgive me?

III.

The New York *Times* has examined people's wallets in New York and northeastern New Jersey. Assuming an average wage of $3.02 for a factory worker in that area, he had to slave in June one hour and forty-four minutes for a rib steak in a restaurant.

The conference at Bratislava has swept the Moscow papers clean of their daily pablum of suspected counterrevolution, anti-Communist conspiracy, etc. What does *Pravda* give us to understand? Only that the imperialist "enemies of Socialism" are to blame for the fact that such a discussion came about in the first place.

At La Guardia Airport a runway has been opened for STOL, short takeoff and landing. What do you bet that D. E. will not take us next Saturday to look at the thing?

IV.

When Mrs. Collins came running back into the restaurant, she had a message. Would we be so kind as to call New York such-and-such number? Thank you, Mrs. Collins.

But employee Cresspahl was angry nevertheless. She had informed no one in the bank where she was going this Tuesday morning to buy luggage; for a moment the idea that someone might be following her was intolerable. That she might be under surveillance!

There is a remedy for that. Turn your mind to all the English equivalents to the Czech adjective *hrozný*: frightful, terrible, gruesome, appalling, dreadful, fearsome . . . And which proper name resembles it in sound? *Hrozná doba*, the time of terror. *Hrozná bída*, cruel misery. *Hrozná zima*, fearful cold. *Hrozné počasí*, awful weather.

The moment she arrived at *to jsou plané hrozby*, these are only blanks, fired to scare, she can think without rage and speculate that somebody may have entered her office and consulted her calendar. There it is, the hour and the name of the store. In whose time was she out shopping? In time she has leased to the bank business, for which a per diem and expenses will be paid her, moreover; thus speaks Anita. Anita, this is how compliant a person becomes as an employee.

V.

The address was "good," a pleasant location on Park Avenue in the thirties, a lawyer's offices. We know Mr. Josephberg from the parties given by Countess Albert Seydlitz; he is a man with whom one can go off into a corner and speak German, about Mr. Tucholsky, who was his client in Berlin, about Tilla Durieux, who unfortunately kept marrying other people than Mr. Josephberg. For once, contrary to the classic saying, posterity does not tender wreaths to actors. When D. E. heard the name he formed another connection for us: this man, ennobled by emigration at the very outset, in February 1933, became D. E.'s attorney. Since then he has been ours, too. Anyone trusted by D. E. we trust too.

"Is it ready?" asks Mrs. Cresspahl in a telephone booth in Grand Central Post Office. "Should I come right away?" "Mr. Josephberg requests your presence urgently," affirms his secretary on a formal note, as if she had blanked out my appearances with Marie in her office. Or was this meant to be sarcasm? Because one had better be present if one has to give a signature? It's just a short subway hop under Lexington Avenue. The cause is good, too. Since the time Anita told me of an American school in the south of West Berlin, we have been putting together a codicil to the Cresspahl will.

Anyone undertaking a journey ought to leave behind a last will and testament. Hereby I bequeath my entire estate to my daughter, Marie Cresspahl, born on July 21, 1957, in Düsseldorf, daughter of Jakob Wilhelm Joachim Abs, railway inspector. The number of my life insurance policy is . . . Marie is requested to retain until her twenty-fifth birthday those of the books from Mecklenburg that were published before 1952. I assign guardianship in matters of her education to Mrs. Efraim Blumenroth.

This was quite sensible, and it was wrong. Mrs. Blumenroth lives on Riverside Drive, so Marie would have kept her school, her home environment; children survive in the Blumenroths' care, even if they lack a mother of Jewish descent. How would it occur to me that Anita is ready to do without traveling for Marie's sake! Now we have finessed it this way: guardianship over education is assigned to a woman in Berlin-Friedenau, tried and found true over twenty years. Legal guardian of the child, however, is D. E.; he has to check, personally, four times a year whether the child is acceptably prospering. This is what I was on my way to sign, glad that it was ready.

VI.

"Are you feeling well, Mrs. Cresspahl?"

"Yes, many thanks, Mr. Josephberg."

"Heart, circulation?"

"I had no idea you were switching to medicine, Doctor! All right, I suppose. A little run-down, perhaps."

"Forgive me if I can't speak to you today the way I used to in our previous pleasant table conversations."

"Let's get it over with, dear Doctor. Am I being sued by someone?"

"It's worse news than that, Mrs. Cresspahl. Forgive an old man the liberty of putting into words what he believes he has observed about your life."

"Go ahead."

"This is the worst news since your late father's demise."

"Go ahead!"

"According to a testamentary disposition by Dr. Dietrich Erichson, you are the first person to be notified in case he dies."

"He is dead."

"He died in a plane crash near Vantaa Airfield in Finland. On Saturday. At 8 A.M.."

"What kind of plane was this?"

"A Cessna."

"He has no license for a Cessna!"

"Both the Finnish and the American police have identified him beyond a doubt."

"In such a case one burns up."

"Indeed. According to a medical opinion, Mr. Erichson may have lived five minutes beyond the impact. Without being conscious of his situation."

"Broken and burning, in full consciousness!"

"Yes. Please pardon me, Mrs. Cresspahl."

"This sort of thing would have been reported in the New York Times."

"The government that employed the deceased expressed the wish to have the news suppressed."

"How do you identify a person who was burned to death?"

"By the teeth."

"Why not a bullet in the chest? An injection? A stab with a knife!"

"The deceased was evidently under orders to leave tangible evidence of his dental condition behind."

"Why am I learning of this only today?"

"Because the American investigating commision had to fly from Washington to Helsinki first."

"Ten hours!"

"Because the gentlemen deemed it appropriate to release the news only today."

"A photograph!"

"There are no photographs of the site of the accident."

"There are official photographs, taken by a commission."

"If you give me a formal assignment to this effect, I shall be glad to contact . . ."

"I believe it now."

"You are the heiress of Mr. Erichson, Mrs. Cresspahl. His mother
retains habitation rights until her demise. Besides real estate and monetary assets, there are some copyrights . . ."

"No."

"If you wish me to, I will undertake to notify Mrs. Erichson."

"No."

"Allow me to express my sympathy, Mrs. Cresspahl. Please be
assured that these coming weeks I shall be at your side. . . ."

"Could you request Mrs. Gottlieb to accompany me to my office?
Without letting her know what . . . you told me?"


VII.

The office, the only place in New York to be alone, with the door
closed. Whatever one does or has done, when someone has died, it
turns into a reproach; playing with water and flirting at Jones Beach.
When there was a thunderstorm, Jakob's mother would set a lighted
candle on the table and pray. When we drove through Minneapolis,
we neglected to look closely at the bordering wall frayed by the broad
noon light and the plane of light beyond it, taking it blithely for the
famous river. And why not, since anyway, no doubt about it, we
planned a vacation in Finland for next year. He intended to fly across
the Alps with us; we had an appointment in Rome. According to
Protestant belief, God is able to see what is written on airplanes. The
quarrelsome din of car horns on the streets of Manhattan; how could
there possibly have been a time when one felt nostalgic for sounds that
betray nothing but bad manners? Also, the diagonally ascending planes
offend the eye accustomed to order and the perpendicular. A child,
comfortably sitting on the floor, its back propped sideways against the
wall, is seen lifting something, then letting it down with two connected
sounds, almost like musical notes. A rhythm in which a tired body
senses itself, without volition, merely as a synapsis function in the
brain, with a feeling of utmost despair, senselessly plangent with the
two sounds that draw each other in the wake. A heavy pendulum,
impeded in its swing just before the rupture, the pauses lengthening
unjustifiably. In my time you flew to New York in eight hours. Sometimes, when I arrived at Hamburg, on summer afternoons, from Copenhagen, the obstructed light in the passport room felt like home to
me. When I take pleasure in something, D. E. hugs himself. Gesine!
people say, with an adjuring stress on the second syllable, as if trying
to catch me with the name; D. E. does that differently, I like to hear
that. Big Marie is day-ed, Lit' Marie a-waits D. E. "My Daughter";

once. And the white sphere, not unlike a cherry bomb, which perilously travels toward the closed eye, dizzying the gaze and setting the brain vibrating with it, but sometimes pleasantly as birds fly, white middle-sized ones—seagulls perhaps. There are people who take flying with equanimity only because the situation comprises the unexpected crash, yes, watch out, and the end of life—at this moment (as at every other, potentially) it poses the demand for definitive settlement of one's personal affairs, including one's demise. Those who take such an attitude cite philosophical motives.

D. E. was flying to Athens, deep beneath him a teensy patch of prepared ground in the midst of an unbounded surface of water; "we going to hit this, I wonder?" I can see the point about helicopters; at least one likes to hear one's own crash. Returns from a trip and all of a sudden knows, on top of everything, something about the Gothic origin of the churches of Prague buried under the Jesuit Baroque. He certainly has been there. Took a look on my behalf. "Jan Hus and the Symbolic Function of the Chalice to the Utraquists," the advocates of the Eucharist in both forms. The idea: to be on a flight over J. F. K. and not to leave the airport; the child that I was. In English: "I expect to die very soon; would you permit me to make arrangements that would keep you cared for? At least on behalf of the child?" Supine, he saw the white sky recede, brushed by singed treetop fronds. You are poor at suffering, D. E.! You convert everything to cause and responsibility, and by this reckoning you pay; then you put the people behind you. "Why am I to suffer, Gesine?" A bus has a long breath. Airplanes grind air, don't they? Today I am the cat that waits for the missing host, someday, like myself, scabby, tunneled by pus, limping and blind in one eye. DOES THE AIR OF MANHATTAN MAKE YOU UNHAPPY? US TOO, IN SPADES. A year ago the telephone dropped the old exchange signal; since April 1967 the nine has been followed by a full-bosomed, purring ding-dong note. Those variations for the pupil Goldberg on Saturday evening turn out to have been the dirge for D. E.

VIII.
"Would you free the line, please, Mrs. Cresspahl? We have an international person-to-person call for you."
"This is a test. This is a test."
"Anita! You are calling me at the bank, you know."
"I have something to talk over with you that would be too risky with Marie around."
"Roger, Anita."
"Helsinki airport, Roger?"

"So I am told."

"Is it yours?"

"If I believe it, it is mine."

"Would you like me to go to Helsinki?"

"There are no remains."

"But a fatality."

"Anita, he traveled with a sheet of instructions in four world languages: 'to be cremated at the place of death without singing, address, sermon, or music whatsoever.' So he wouldn't cause me unnecessary trouble by his death, you know."

"Tell me what I can do."

"Come to Prague in two weeks' time; I'll be on vacation there."

"Ty znayesh—say no more."

"I need your advice."

"Does Marie know?"

"If I tell her, she'll go to pieces."

"Let me think about it till tomorrow morning. Can you hold up until then?"

IX.

"Well, Mrs. Erichson!"

"Evening, Wes."

"How's Mr. Erichson?"

"He is fine. Away, I'm afraid. But fine."

"What can I do for you, Mrs. Erichson?"

"A drink."

"Most certainly. But what kind of drink, that is the question."

"Something to pick me up, Wes."

"Mrs. Erichson, with all due respect: could it be that you need something different to pick you up?"

"Anything."

"I'll get you a taxi, Mrs. Erichson."

X.

At Riverside Drive, how could it fail, there is airmail from Finland. A map of Mecklenburg Ducatus, the Duchy of M., Auctore Ioanne Blaeuw excusa, where artlessness reigns in geography and Muritz Lacus is blithely combined with Calpin Lacus, but Fleesen Lake still awaits discovery; where the duchy receives a kindly yellow griffin in its coat of arms instead of the vulgar ox head. But the Mare Balticum is beyond doubt, two Hanseatic caravels ride it full of spirit, and next to the gilt-framed colorful wind rose over the Bight of Wismar you can read how it should be called in truth: Oost Zee. In the upper right we have to conjecture Finland.

Putting your make-up on until Marie arrives and then sitting still there with the view from the window—perhaps you can go through with it.

We are still in time, just barely. On WRVR, 106.7 kh, "Just Jazz" is beginning. D. E. has asked us to tape this for him; there is no way we could forget that.

## August 7, 1968   Wednesday

The person scratching at the door is our Robinson Eagle Eye, who is bringing two expensively wrapped parcels, with the visiting card, sincere greetings, and the home address of Mrs. Collins in Astoria, Queens. Yesterday morning I was still alive. Behind Mr. Robinson appears Marie, in high spirits and looking forward to the unpacking of the suitcases. Now the lying begins.

"Why are you wearing sunglasses indoors, Gesine?"

"We have workmen in the bank. Got bumped in the eye."

"Did you see Dr. Rydz?"

"No, another doctor. I'm supposed to go easy on my eyes for three days or so."

"Are you in pain?"

"Yes. And under medication."

"I have been wondering. . . . But you are tired?"

"Go on, ask away. Slow, that's what I am."

"Is it going to be an evening as usual?"

"Shall we do something else?"

"Yes. I'll do the cooking, though it's your turn. I have an idea there was more to be said about that August 1951 when Cresspahl wanted you out of the way, in Wendisch Burg."

"In July, State Security searched Cresspahl's house. The pretext was that he had begun to make a lot of money with his work, more than his pension amounted to. Actually, the state could not get it into its head that it could victimize a person a second and a third time, and still this Cresspahl would keep on the right side of the law. The other business began earlier."

"Is it something to do with Jakob?"

"With Jakob too. Because something worked reciprocally: as I have liked many people, so a few have liked me."

"I happen to know one who is traveling on Scandinavian . . ."

"On Finnair."

". . . and is looking forward to you."

"And to you. Because you are even prettier than I."

"Gesine! The Papenbrock hair!"

"The widow Papenbrock—she had a sulk on against the house of
Cresspahl. Because when the state's sovereign might after Albert's death
confiscated his town mansion and warehouse, the old woman waited
for our invitation to move in with us. For that Cresspahl wouldn't raise
a finger. It would have meant Church authority infiltrating the house.
Off she went to Lüneburg, where some of Albert's real estate was left.
Because we were in hopes of a final parting, we took her to the Hamburg
line. Her feelings for me were less than benevolent, but she said unthinkingly: 'At least you have our hair.' "

"And your breasts, set so nice and high."

"Well, well, Marie. Not that subject! My bosom was at best a
conjecture among the young gentlemen of 1950; none ever saw it bare."

"They must have wished they could."

"In that way I was unaccommodating, and it hurt my reputation.
When somebody dreamed up a romance with me and didn't get anywhere, he invented one and peddled it around."

"That's just like weed."

"It grows back. One boy had a literary vein; he pushed a slip of
paper into my pocket with a quotation that went more or less like this:
'Not that Gesine had suddenly become a sensitive being of delicate
feeling. She remained as she was, assertive and fainthearted, greedy
and cowardly, longing for all of the "higher and finer life," as of late
it may also be seen in the cinematographic theaters': it took me forever
to solve that one! It was a Gesine in a novel."

"A pity, I feel."

"Have a look among our cookbooks. There is one of the year 1901,
published in New York by Appleton & Co.; *European and American
Cuisine* is the title, and it was written by the principal owner and
President of the Brooklyn Cooking College; what was her name?"

"Gesine Lemcke. Don't like that, one bit."

"Other children have the same name as you."

"I wish you could have your name to yourself."

"It was given me because Cresspahl had once meant to flee over
land and sea with Gesine Redebrecht of Malchow. Yours comes from
Jakob's mother."

"One thing is true, actually. You were assertive. You are."

"That's easy when Jakob watches over you as though you were his
sister."

"No kisses after the dancing lessons?"

"With that, too, I waited."

"Is this meant to teach me something?"

"You want me to tell you a story. There were other admirers who wished to be known to me even if somewhat vaguely. One of them was my classmate for four years. In 1951 he wrote on the blackboard: 'Effi Briest, very pretty to my mind, because there are many e's and i's in it; those are the two superior vowels.' Fontane."

"You knew who it was."

"And given the sad fact that I had to withhold what he desired, I intend at least to withhold his name. Altogether, I think I am going to be imprecise about names from now on. For when Cresspahl had wang . . . arranged a Danish deal for Knoop, Gesine too was invited to the toasting of it on a boat, a yacht in Wismar's harbor. We don't want to cause trouble for the fellow because of his unpatriotic dealings with Communist Germany, but I owe him thanks for a sailing cruise to Denmark."

"Past the East German coast guard."

"They hadn't any 'wall' floating in the sea yet in 1950. A Danish sailboat could and did do anything, even smuggle a girl aboard. Provided Cresspahl knew about it, provided the proper terms between yougn lady and aging man (about thirty) were maintained, without kisses on the cheek, I had nothing against learning navigation."

"Gesine, you had a vacation in Denmark at seventeen! That's why you showed me Bornholm!"

"One had to keep one's mouth firmly shut, though. But a Mecklenburg sailor, once he has one too many, likes to boast, and to hell with him. So here was another opportunity to get me into trouble; it was nothing but dumb luck that the Kripo didn't get wise to it."

"There was that boy who lived on top of the pharmacy."

"No name. But I had a hard time trying to sell him the line that it was strictly his business if he went mushy over a girl who thinks herself long spoken for. They took you to be their personal property, the young gentlemen."

"Assertive."

"I may have exaggerated. I liked to go dancing, because of the movement . . ."

"And because one likes to do what one is good at."

". . . not because of the hands on my back. If two boys got into a fight over me, I kept out of it. I wasn't some piece of property or chattel, after all. The truth is that I never gave anyone reason to hope. Those pained glances—I couldn't stand them."

"And the overnight stays at the Pagenkopfs."

"And Lockenvitz's coming to Jerichow, when he was still able to show kindness, and staying till morning. It wasn't unusual for me to spend nights under one roof with three men."

"Pagenkopf, Lockenvitz, Cresspahl . . ."

"And Jakob. Yes, quite right: we keep him in a separate category. But it was Jakob who wanted to defend my good name on Town—on Stalin Street in Jerichow. I know only that he came home bloodied; next morning found me packed off on a train to the distant southeast of Mecklenburg, to visit the Niebuhrs. Klaus was stunned to see me manage an H-class yawl like a man! Luckily, he got himself tied up with the Babendererde girl (the teacher branch)—Ingrid, that is. The other Ingrid; you are thinking of Bøtersen. The three of us spent four weeks on Upper and Town lakes in Wendisch Burg; then Cresspahl sent word. I promptly found out what everybody in Cresspahl's house tried to hide from me: Jakob was serving eighteen days in the cellar beneath Gneez District Court for assault and battery."

"I once had a boy fight for me too."

"Is it a gratifying feeling?"

"If somebody insults me, I'd rather straighten things out myself."

"You see? And Jakob had a police record for several years."

"How about later—did he go on having fights?"

"Don't worry, Marie. Both of us had learned our lesson. I stopped going out to dance, except to school events. I am inclined to term my conduct with gentlemen since 1951 little short of flawless. I was once offered a private railway car! One of those provided by West German Railways!"

"The kind Hitler had, was it? Fibbing, Gesine!"

"Hitler wasn't moneyed, you know. Filched from the state. You may as well believe it; a real live millionaire led me onto the mountain, showed me the treasures of the world, and said: All this is thine. The mountain was Platform 3 at Düsseldorf Central Station, and the all-this-is-thine was a railway car in which Hitler may have taken his fits for a spin. A misbegotten sleeping car, sort of."

"You and a millionaire."

"If you are a well-to-do citizen of the U. S. A. and not at odds with your government, they may, by all means, let you go into the forest near Mönchen-Gladbach to take a look at how your army works for the defense of Western Europe."

"Instead of which, your eyes come to rest upon a secretary with Papenbrock hair, who conducts herself modestly and nicely at her desk, is a skilled typist too, wears a supersmart jersey sweater; to her he offers—

with permission from her superiors—the modest dwelling on wheels in which he is compelled to travel through Federal Germany because U. S. railroads are in a bad way."

"Envy is an undesirable quality for a bank, Marie. A message from De Rosny himself."

"I wouldn't have minded looking at the thing."

"What was there to see, do you think? A four-room apartment strapped for space, a cupboard like that on a sailboat, train telephone, Telex."

"Paintings on the walls. Framed. And seven guest rooms.

"One; mostly occupied by the valet, who also does the cooking when the chief gives a dinner party. For the rest, a double bed. After half a year of gallivanting, that was to be the price, you see."

"Would he have married you?"

"After two years I would have been certain of a severance payment. He still commutes daily from Munich to Hamburg or back. For a treat, they may haul him through the Ruhr instead of the perennial into Frankfurt and out of Frankfurt. From Wunstorf they can connect him to the express to Regensburg. He forgave me, by the way."

"May I ask a question about Taormina?"

"With him I really liked to travel; there was real conversation to be had at the table. He also gave himself the air of wishing to understand that I do what I feel like instead of obeying my hormones or glands. He made a good deal too much out of a night spent at Taormina, in separate rooms."

"And then came the one you had waited for all this time."

"Then came Jakob."

"You were—twenty-three at the time."

"And a half. Since you talked about the handsomely high-placed bosom, let me give you a little warning. These days it is thought a bit ridiculous for a woman to allow herself so much time. I am sure you would not like people to laugh about your mother."

"But my dear lady, I beg of you. All my conversations with you are held in absolute confidence! And please feel entirely at home, although I shall now retire. You may play the variations for the pupil Goldberg as long as you wish, and the Quodlibet twice."

---

### August 8, 1968   Thursday

---

To be the messenger of death.

On D. E.'s route to New Jersey the threatened buses are already in service: the lower deck as a whole is higher than the driver's seat;

smoking prohibited. The windows are stained so deeply blue, the landscape is hardly visible. In its place, memories. "Oh, you can't buy memories," Esther once exclaimed. And you can't get rid of them either.

The bus emerges from the tunnel south of Hoboken. Years ago, D. E. took the child and me to a cider shop at the waterside there. Men were eating clams from stoneware bowls, tossing the shells into the sawdust on the floor. Marie studied him earnestly, her hospitable friend. For she was still a child at the time, who did accept a piece of candy from a strange lady on the bus but handed the wrapper back to her after finishing with it: "to keep our city clean." How she enjoyed it when he demonstrated to her the jerk of the wrist she could use to whang her shells against paneling. "Whack!" said D. E. I do suppose he had fun with us.

It is a testy Mrs. Erichson who is opening one wing of the double door to D. E.'s solid farmhouse. Rigid her expression, rigid the smooth white hair standing out from under her black riding cap. Black are coat, jodphurs, boots, the bow at the shirt collar. She has already had a visit today, from a couple of gentlemen in sports coats who half pulled something on a chain from their pockets and quickly dropped it back in, making believe they had really shown it to her. They craved to see D. E.'s study, perhaps rummage a little in it; she showed them the door. Now she is out of sorts and a little anxious. In a foreign country one should defer to emissaries of the authorities; what do you think, Gesine?

She heard with relief that she had acted according to her rights. Reluctantly, for she had meant to go riding, she ushers this next visitor of that day across the hallway, opens the door to the kitchen, allows herself, in some surprise, to be led into the living room and safely lodged in an easy chair. This is to safeguard her against a fall when the news is broken that her only son, the center and pride of her old life, purportedly and by hearsay has lost his life in northeastern Europe in a flying machine he has known for four years how to control. She is sitting as if ready for execution. Next is the blow, the crack in the neck, the sagging of the body which diminishes it.

"You believe that, Gesine?"

"I shall. I must."

"Burned and buried and now nothing left?"

"That's the way he wanted it."

"Now you can put me under the earth too."

"You will live for a long time yet. You were on your way to put the fear of God into a horse. And you must keep an eye on his things."

"I have mail from him, written on Sunday!"

"Postmarked."

"Written, you see?"

"I see. But there is your son's lawyer, he says—"

"Did you bring the probate paper, Gesine?"

"Leave that be, please!"

"You will let an old woman keep the house."

"You can keep it forever."

"Gesine, are you pregnant?"

"Not I."

"Are you now sorry you aren't?"

"How could I bring up a child without him?"

"Little Marie, how does she bear it?"

"I don't dare tell her . . ."

"Could you come and live with me?"

"We must go to Prague."

"He's been dead such a short time."

"He would have wanted it so: get the work done."

"Yes. That's how he is. And when will you be through with Prague?"

"Marie has to go to school. Why don't you come to New York?"

"That is so far away from him. What, you're leaving?"

"The cab is waiting outside. I must catch the bus. Marie is waiting at home. Can't you come with me?"

"No. I'm going riding."


Early in 1951 Robert Pius Pagenkopf enlisted with the Armed People's Police at the Aero Club in Cottbus. He was the only one to do so of the 370 upperclassmen of that time. Lately many had left after Grade 11, the completion of which many parents still took for the equivalent of the abridged-curriculum diploma of old. These decided to go to West Germany, mostly without much of an idea that compulsory military service was waiting for them there with open arms. Pius took his stand on the other side. Since we merely pretended that we were a couple, he had made this decision by himself.

Pius's first commitment was for all of three years. A cold glamour hung about our table, a goodly portion of which devolved upon the student Cresspahl, as she sat through the last school year alone in 12-A-Two, in a much smaller room on the third floor, one of fifteen, alone at her table, with a view from the window of cathedral and courtyard. We tried to persuade Pius to stay to the end of senior year. Even his father had qualms, the deserving official with the Party administration at Schwerin, much though his son's new "societal activity" could be made to redound to his credit. One could lose a son that way. Helene Pagenkopf kept weeping for weeks. When Pius took the woman in his arms and stroked her shoulders, you could see how tall he had grown. Six feet, and a few inches above. When we talked to him of the advantages of a final documentation of competence in humanities and natural sciences, he smiled because we still believed in such things. As if the science of equine dentition could be of help to a student in later life. What physics he might need in years to come, the Air Force would equip him with. The student Lockenvitz envied Youth Comrade Pagenkopf the tactical skill of his scheme; not so much the career itself, which was closed to him because of his eyesight. Nevertheless, he exhorted Pius to consider the value of the Great Latinum diploma, recognized by universities the world over; Pius would look stern, keeping his off-black eyebrows rigid, as if he felt intruded upon.

Pius's decision seemed to gild the study goals of the New School so uniquely that he might have taken it easy in his studies and still in his school-leaving certificate received the grades of his status in January. But laxness and Pius were incompatible phenomena. Pius stuck to the lesson plans and thus kept the student Cresspahl to the habit of study—the form learning should take in youth. Where we differed was that he knew his future, and this widened his perspective far beyond school.

In one of the ninth-grade classes of 1951, the F. G. Y. sponsored a contest among sellers of its newspaper, *Young World*. The prize was won by a smart little tyke who deposited his pack with Abel the fish seller, on National Unity Street, a procedure that rendered the business unprofitable but avoided molestation of and by passersby. The incident kept the school talking all day. Pius shrugged and made you feel like a child next to him. In 11-A-One there was a boy named Eckart Pingel, who proclaimed in Contemporary Studies: In the Soviet Union you will also find the biggest pigs! Now he was to be demoted in his class standing; Bettina Selbich advocated disciplinary proceedings. However, Old Pingel wasn't just any old father; he was foreman at Panzenhagen's sawmill, proletarian nobility. The tale circulated among the workers of Gneez that Pingel's Eckart was to be kicked out of his school just because he told the truth. This was why he could talk his way out of it in front of the teachers' conference by adducing Soviet advances in the breeding of the common domestic pig. Bettina threw this alibi straight back at him; but now he was able to give a reading from the textbook his class had ferreted out for him. To be sure, Eckart Pingel forbore frequent mention of his scientific discovery, but he was known to have hit upon it first, and wore the fact like a decoration.

Pius laughed too, but merely by pushing air through his nose for a snort; it sounded derogatory. Peel by peel his belonging to us fell off him; he looked at us from some distance; he was almost an adult. There were evenings he spent in the Danish Hedge; without telling his mother, true, but without making a great secret of it either. After that his body aroma changed, and to his silent, eyebrow-raising astonishment his friend Cresspahl began to expand her morning toilette to include scent. Further, Pius frequented bars where the railway men of Gneez congregated, including the Linden Tavern, where once in a while the women conductors danced on the tables. For the convocation concluding the 1951–52 school year, Gabriel Manfras suggested that the school chapter of the F. G. Y. should "delegate" Youth Comrade Pagenkopf from its midst for service in the Armed Police. Pius examined him attentively and endlessly until Manfras, who lacked the toughness for such service, flushed for once. Pius was "bidden farewell" by students and faculty.

He went to Cottbus for recruit training, was enrolled as an airman, promoted to private first class and then noncommissioned officer; at one point he signed his rank as *Fahnenjunker*, the outdated cornet of older armies. Mrs. Selbich was preserved to 12-A-Two as homeroom teacher and given the occasion to suggest to the student Cresspahl that she might read to the class from his letters so that all might have the benefit of Pagenkopf's edifying patriotic example. Cresspahl felt tempted, for Pius reported how the postal censorship was organized "in our outfit." Private letters had to be handed over unsealed in the guardroom by the recruit: this makes him circumspect as to what his pen should bring to paper. Another thing to be learned: the comrade noncommissioned officers regale each other with the contents of incoming letters, supplying gusto and footnotes; this makes it awkward when the writer is not the mother but some other female. Even a mother can make it a wretched business—for instance, by voicing her curiosity about her child, unmasking the "child" as a mother's boy.

When you listen to the long-termers, it is worse here than in the Regular Army, Pius confides in writing; contrary to service regulations, he sends his mail by a civilian route. Gesine would have liked to make this the subject of a public reading, presented as an example of Stalinist vigilance. But she suspected that Betteenkin would grab the letter from her, once she had brought it to school. It contained, among other things, terms of address like the Russian word for little sister (Pius was eighteen months older); she denied exchanging letters with him.

Gesine had an awkward time with her own letters to Cottbus. She had to steer clear of her customary mode of address, to avoid adding the weight of his nickname, aggravated by guardroom humor, to his neck: to her he simply *was* Pius; to his mother Robert and Robbing. Also, how could she tell, in a letter subject to scrutiny, that three "bourgeois" boys from Gneez had been sent to take a course in socialist reorientation; naturally they distrusted one another. But once in their allotted room in Schwerin, one of them covered the keyhole, the second blocked the window with his back, while both helped the third look for the microphones. In complete harmony, sworn buddies, they returned to Gneez after their four weeks' stint, to be appointed revenue officer, dairy manager, and personnel chief at Panzenhagen. An entirely new network of relationships (though known in essentials) was drawn over the town, making it occasionally irrelevant that one had known a person for twenty-odd years: how could Gesine write of the above without messing up Pius's record in Political Education forever and a day? This is why she was relieved when he wanted to hear from her again about what happened to a fishmonger named Abel who moved to England: everyone calls him Able there; when he changes his shop sign to Ebel, they call him Eebel; patiently, he changes to Ibel—and so forth. She takes this to mean that he was again being tutored in English and hence would be able, in case of emergency, to move over into civil aviation. Another news item was equally unsuitable: the entire Pingel family—evidently from animosity against the school after Eckart's demotion—had decamped westward. She liked it best when Pius came on a visit, walked around the municipal lake with her, and had brought her something. For Cresspahl had meanwhile found time and strength to bethink himself of parental authority and had issued a warning, laced with threats, to tobacconists from Jerichow to Gneez forbidding them to sell his daughter anything smokable. Thus it came about that Pius would arrive with cigarettes from China, brand name "Temple of Great Joy." (Men in Pius's squadron could volunteer for service in that People's Republic.) There is a snapshot from one of these visits, our only picture.

In 1953, Gesine Cresspahl moved to Hesse, in West Germany, and was concerned that she might have lost Pius, too, by this removal. It was not unreasonable to be afraid that Pius had learned to disapprove of such freedom of movement; nor could one doubt that correspondence with people in hostile countries was forbidden him. But the old friendship proved rustproof, as the proverb promises: Pius now addressed his letters home to "My dears," and this included Gesine, or Helene Pagenkopf would have kept the messages in her son's handwriting rather than passing them on obediently to Röbbertin his Gesin. In 1954, Pius prolonged his term of duty, became a professional officer, advanced to lieutenant by Christmas; and Gesine complained to her Robertino—the form of address she had wrested from her maiden soul—what troubles she was having with her English in an American-occupied province. Meanwhile, Pius had brought the two Soviet Moo-Oxen well under his control, the YAK–18 as a trainer, the YAK–11 for real, and was able to return from the U. S. S. R.; stationed at Drewitz, rank squadron leader (acting). Gesine sent the aging Mrs. Pagenkopf a miniature shaving set that might come in handy for a young man. Pius was now flying the MIG–15, in formation, but one time singly, which was the reason he was transferred to Parachute Training Command. Gesine took this for a demotion and thought of Pius as "grounded," as they called it where she now worked. This may happen to you for reasons of health or as a punishment. So she was glad to hear he was unharmed—even though he had taken his fighter on a swoop beneath the autobahn bridge across Greater Zern Lake. Eventually his regiment forgave him; first lieutenant in Merseburg.

In January 1956, the Sachwalter of East Germany admitted that he was training young men to fly for purposes other than their amusement: those flying clubs of the Armed People's Police now belonged to the National People's Army, the N. P. A. As if a people, all by itself, lacked the "national" element. Six months later the Air Force of the Red Army, now known as "Soviet," asked around among its subordinates in the G. D. R. which pilots they might be able to spare: they had drawn lasting attention to themselves by their flying performance. The file card of Comrade Pagenkopf (for this title had become his) was pulled from the registers of Gneez and elsewhere. His personal data were now bound into the "most sought-after passport in the world," the one with the emblem of the Soviet Union. Gesine sent a few announcements of the birth of a healthy baby girl in July 1957; Pius gave the child a Russian *matryoshka*, a doll in a doll in a doll, with directions for use: the innermost, which is impossible to open, is called "the soul" in that country.

Major Pagenkopf started in yet another basic training: with the MIG–21 A, B, and C, so as to ready himself for the MIG–21 D, an all-weather fighter-interceptor (known to NATO as Fishbed). Gesine, too, went through a training course, severe and thorough, at a Düsseldorf bank; Pius tackled an SU–7 ("Fitter"), a heavy fighter-bomber, suitable for nuclear assignments. In the snapshots he always stands by himself now, a young man in a tailored suit meant to look British, an arrogant, remote look about him; to a junior lieutenant, a model; to an East German officer, a V. I. P. Because the Air Force of the G. D. R. is subordinated to the air defense forces of the Soviet Union;

it was given no Fishbed. About Pius as one cleared for access to state secrets: he gave it as his opinion that the Caucasus bore less resemblance to Grunewald Park in Berlin than Göring had asserted, an air marshal of times gone by. Gesine was in a position to understand that he was now being instructed also in the history of World War II; at present, one could conjecture, it was the Battle of Stalingrad. Gesine was shipped off to the U. S. A. in order to learn the more advanced tricks in the proliferation of money; unmoved, Pius asked "my dears" for Marie's adventures with the American tongue. When jet fighters sent supersonic booms over West Berlin to intimidate the population, Pius was not among the pilots: he was a test pilot, a precious commodity, saved as "cadre" substance. Medical examination every four weeks, rest periods in the sanatoriums reserved for people from cabinet members on up. And impossible to reach. Anita, for all her skill in journeying, long looked for him in the Soviet Union and never laid eyes on him in his lifetime. He now could slur the o like a Muscovite. Gesine was given the royal heave-ho from her first job in Brooklyn; Pius tested the SU–9 (Fishpot) for any needed modifications—a fighter with a maximum velocity near Mach 2; withheld from the N. P. A. Perhaps this was why he eschewed visits home. When he had come home, rumor knew of his appearance at his mother's at midnight, in 1962. When President Kennedy was assassinated, Pius wrote a letter that was to comfort one Gesine in New York City. For form's sake, deprecatingly, he mentioned to "my dears" a short marriage to a Masha, a Marie. This one was alone for good. . . . Did this man ever come to a sense of his true self in the midst of his jobs? The latest involved a TU–28, a long-range ultrasonic fighter plane; he controlled a flying machine over 100 feet long, with a wingspan of 66 feet. Colonel Pagenkopf. Would you like to bet that the k in his name came out much like a g in Russian voices? And because he had gained the affection of his Soviet superiors with his contributions toward the improvement of their airborne weapons, they sent a welded casket to Gneez, Mecklenburg, in December 1964, instead of burying him where he was. Nothing short of industrial-grade equipment would have opened it. Pius got to be almost thirty-three.

(For the technical descriptions thanks are due to Professor D. Erichson. He procured these data on more than two-year-long travels in negotiations with intermediaries in the confidence of the U. S. and West German air force commands [among whom we have been requested to call no special attention to a Mr. B.]; this at times and on occasions when he would no doubt have preferred to take a rest and, say, a glass of tea. Our thanks to you, D. E.)

We owe a report on Pius's obsequies to our schoolmate Anita Gantlik. With her assortment of documents, she, the Protestant, traveled to Gneez to take part in the Roman Catholic observance which the socialist parents had compromised on. According to this source, then, the delivery of the materials for transubstantiation was announced by two bell-metal strokes. There was mention of our brother (formerly: servant) Robert Pagenkopf. To whom is now vouchsafed the viaticum or stirrup cup which he had long been without. For the other side, too, it was an article of faith: "this is My body, this My blood." Pius's mother stepped forward to take Holy Communion; Old Pagenkopf stood stiff like a post, conscious of guilt. Whereupon it is announced that the Catholic rite of burial is beginning. That we know all about. Coffin invisible until the chapel. Lots of kneeling. Looking forward joyously to Pius's union with God. "Angels will usher him into Paradise." Parting, with incense, at the grave.

No military presence. Casket without the colors of the Red Army or the National People's Army. It bears a brass plaque with the full name. His address in Eternity.

Noticed among the mourners were . . . The wreath legends read . . . That Gesine in New York might really have hit upon something more intelligent than "Robbing his Gesin." Oh, it is to be taken as a dative? "To Robbing—his Gesine"? Fancy that, now. An elaborate Mecklenburg luncheon, in conversation with the priest.

Two death notices to be delivered.

As for our work, we figure in the New York Times, page 1, column 3: the C. S. S. R. desires loans to an amount between 400 and 500 million dollars for the purchase of industrial equipment. De Rosny: I can't wait.

At Riverside Drive a troubled child is waiting, wanting to commiserate: "There is a cable here and I opened it, I am afraid. It is from D. E. in Finland. He's been in a crash. He doesn't give his address, the scatterbrain! One would like to write to him, after all. Signed: Eritzen."

This is Anita's hand. Comrade Writer, see that you appraise it properly!

Handwriting of student Gantlik, Anita: no distortions; excellent; particularly in telegrams.

"Any improvement with your eye problem, Gesine?"

*August 10, 1968   Saturday, South Ferry Day*

A derelict known only as Red climbed to the mast top of the Fulton Street lightship. He wanted to speak to Mayor Lindsay. The New York *Times* shows us in three photographs how he plunged to his death; she gives the brand of film and the shutter speeds. By way of practical hints for the rest of us?

A British passenger plane crashed yesterday in Bavaria. Forty-eight persons on board, no survivors. We too are due to fly soon.

In Hitler's school we were warned against the stunted shadow of a man wearing a "plutocratic" hat: Enemy Listening In. In the New School we learned to warn each other: Youth Comrade Listening In.

At first we had viewed the loudspeakers in every classroom with suspicion, since all they seemed to do was replace the hand-carried memos by which school announcements were made until 1950. If they also housed devices for transmitting sounds in the other direction, they might be of use to supervise a teacher at his work; we thought them incapable, though, of sorting out the voices of thirty pupils in recess conversations. For that you would indeed need a human being.

In Contemporary Studies class we had been instructed about the criminality inherent in Hitler's language, as exemplified by the term *Untermensch*, subhuman. In recess Zaichik said casually, enjoying the recollection: "If I've ever seen such a one, Fiete Hildebrandt was it." He meant the former "agricultural night surveillance officer," Friedrich Hildebrandt, installed by Adolf Hitler as Party boss and chief Federal administrator of the good State of Mecklenburg. Pius informed us, his voice implying approval, that he had been shot in an open field near Wismar in 1945. The Cresspahl girl contradicted him: sentenced to death by an American military court in 1947 and executed at Landsberg-on-Lech in 1948. She knew this from her father, who actively kept track of the postwar fortunes of gorgeous peacocks like Fiete. For Cresspahl, the mere name Hildebrandt had been a daily threat as recently as five years ago; Wallschläger, that shining light of the Church, had included the Special Commissioner for the Defense of the Realm of 1945 in church prayers. At the teachers' conference of June 1950, there was a discussion of the fact that 10-A-Two showed a deplorable interest in information of the kind the state media withhold from the East German people as unhealthy: a treasonable concern for the fate of criminals. We looked around at the other children in the class; who among them kept his ears cocked and turned our relaxed chatter over to some authority?

Who found it in him to deliver teacher Habelschwerdt to the knife of transfer for disciplinary reasons, by secretly quoting her silly phrase about the students' community sense? This had admittedly been a pedagogical goal of the school under Hitler, at least in name. But anyone who had had to recite this for years surely had a right to a slip of the tongue once in a while. That Mrs. Habelschwerdt was now wasting her gift for natural sciences teaching arithmetic at Niklot Elementary School—did she owe it to one of us, one with whom we went swimming, shook hands on occasion?

Gabriel Manfras was the last to occur to us. How plausible could it be that the First Chairman of the F. G. Y. school chapter would waste time and effort on denunciation? Also, we felt a need to treat him gently, which got in the way of our discernment. Gabriel Manfras was stricken with a mother who still threatened him, five years after the war: "Our Führer will return, and he will judge you." Gabriel was haunted by the memory of the crowd lining the road among whom he too had waved and shouted "Heil," quivering with fervor, when Hitler's man in Mecklenburg staged a political rally with a ride through Gneez. That sort of thing one wants to step away from; so we accepted the hideous earnestness with which he now espoused another brand of Socialism. We smiled only slightly when he reported on his successes as People's correspondent; when the initials G. M. figured as by-line for a report to the *Schweriner Volkszeitung* about a skating or skiing contest where the U. S. A. took first place—the latter item was lost by G. M.; in his version of events the Soviet Union attained a "prestigious second place."

The student Cresspahl could still call to mind the time in Jerichow's elementary school when she for once had felt like being noticed by this close-mouthed, glumly brooding child with the ruler-drawn side part in his hair; merely by way of a joke and for her own fun she told a story exemplifying Soviet Darwinism and ignored the implications of being within hearing of Gabriel Manfras: the Soviet scholar Michurin lectures on insects. He shows his listeners a flea on his right hand and orders it to jump to the left hand. The flea complies, and does this repeatedly. Now the professor removes the flea's legs and orders it again to jump. The flea refuses. Professor Michurin has scientifically proved that amputation of legs in fleas causes deafness. . . . Gesine Cresspahl laughed, from pleasure in this inversion of logic, and because she enjoyed other children's laughing with her. She should probably have given more attention to the labored grimace of disdain that the Manfras child forced onto his face.

Surely the student Lockenvitz was concerned only with a fine grammatical point when he auscultated the name of the German People's Police to establish whether there was a possessive or an accusative relationship between the members of the compound, *Volk* and *Polizei*. Who possessed whom, and who stood against whom? Did the folk own its police, or were the Police there to police the folk? His interest was semantic when he translated the concept of *res publica* as the "cause of the people" and sensed a tautology in the expression *Volksrepublik*. Even the question why the term was granted to China and Poland but withheld for the time being from a possible German People's Republic—even that question was to harm him later. Thanks to Manfras.

By hidden paths a book circulated at school by the title of *I Chose Freedom*. It was the work of a defector from the Soviet Purchasing Commission in Washington, D. C., and it reported compulsory spying on colleagues, institutionalized fraud in industrial production, brutality during interrogations by the state police, concentration camps and forced labor colonies in the Soviet Union. This Viktor Kravchenko had had to sue a French Communist newspaper for slander; it had called him a lying troublemaker in American pay; a Paris court had judged his evidence convincing. When Dicken Sieboldt lent this book in confidence to Cresspahl's daughter, he simply had to credit her with good sense about passing it on. Lockenvitz criticized the language of the account, or at any rate its translation into German, whereupon Pius decided to forgo reading it and had the contents related to him. At this point, Gabriel Manfras arrived with a confiding air, nudged the talk to the enemy's arguments, that it was necessary to know them, and were they contained in a book called . . . ? Gesine disclaimed any knowledge of such a book—among other reasons because it could painfully injure Gabriel's image of the Soviet Union, where man's heart pulses so free in his *shirokaya natura*, his expansive nature. She thought the contents of the book might start a conflict with Gabriel, with results offensive to him; and she wanted to spare the child that.

On the market square of Gneez, the new one, a loudspeaker mounted on a pillar tootled all day, from morning, when the sleepy workmen stepped off their trains, to evening, when they deserved some respite. Or there resounded the plaintive call: We don't want to die for the dollar! "All well and good," said Pius, broodingly, "but why is it that at the Leipzig Fair all business is transacted on a dollar basis?" Manfras hurried to carry this to the specialist Selbich, but Pius was almost a soldier now, rallying to the defense of the Republic; it wouldn't be easy to trip him up. So she pretended that the question had been put by "someone" in 11-A-Two and expounded to the class the exigencies, inescapable for the time being, of the world market; laboriously, driven into corners by the student Lockenvitz with references to the self-sufficiency of the socialist camp. For the work team of Pagenkopf & Co. the policy spy and sycophant Manfras stood unmasked, he who was ready to do even filthy jobs for the good of the Unity Party. We could protect ourselves from now on, but how to warn the others? A notice on the board in block letters would have brought uniformed men down on us, or, worse, plain-clothes agents. We confined ourselves to surreptitious nudgings and casual but meaningful throat-clearings when someone among us let himself go too openly about a foreign general and marshal who had troops under arms in Mecklenburg. A discreet nod in the direction of Manfras, who sat nearby with his head down, faking math notebook entries—and the impulse was squelched.

Hünemörder came back to Jerichow and Gneez from the Lüneburg region, faithful to his vow that before he did so the riffraff around Friedrich Jansen and Friedrich Hildebrandt would have to be smoked out of Mecklenburg. He had brought a few pounds of tacks and nails with him from the West, planning to open a hardward store in Gneez; he had figured it all out in his economics-trained mind. What he now needed was a sales clerk, and he learned to his surprise that Leslie Danzmann was available. Mrs. Danzmann, the lady? Why, yes; after losing the job with the Housing Office, she had also lost the one with People's Own Enterprise Freshlicanned. Again and yet again accused of embezzlement and unlawful appropriation of eels, etc., prevented from presenting evidence in defense, she had, in her pride, given notice. Seeking help from the Christian Democratic Union in Schwerin, she was aided once more by her reputation in the past and was permitted to help out in the reporting of lawsuits by the *Neue Union*. Her column "Courtroom Glimpses" made her name briefly familiar in nearly all the towns of Mecklenburg; then what had been entered in the files about her life and career caught up with her. Now Leslie Danzmann was available, at whatever wage was offered. Relieved, with warm homespun phrases she dealt with the lines of buyers squeezing up against Hünemörder's shop window, which held the scarce merchandise. After two hours of free trade the People's Police got wind of this, entered the scene in pairs and led Leslie off, handcuffed to Hünemörder. What Hünemörder drew for his attempt to sabotage the people's economy by distributing quota-regulated commodities remained unknown, because the proceedings took place in the capital; Emil Knoop, who presumably was to run the supply line, had just taken ship to Belgium—by this time Knoop even had lighters crossing the borders with his cargoes. Leslie Danzmann was detained in the cellar of the District Court for a few days, without disclosure of charges and occupied with the cleaning of cells and passages. According to her, she was released at the exact hour she had finished putting the premises in order. This was another misadventure that was visited upon Danzmann by way of civic instruction; but what profit would she derive from it in terms of social awareness, asked the Cresspahl child in a circle of intimates, noticing too late the encouraging expression on Manfras's face as he approached.

Betteenkin was furious. The brooch on her blue shirt quivered ("Her front is where the brooch sits," another saying that had been mischievously brought to her notice). But she had to let it go at a vague threat against people whose compassion for individuals of a reactionary middle class . . . The student Cresspahl smiled purposefully. She knew of a photograph, and so did Bettina, which showed the preceptress in languishing commerce with a specimen of the middle class.

The Colorado beetle rebellion brought matters to a head. 12-A-Two had been ordered into the fields to learn how to differentiate between *coccinellidae* and *rodolia cardinalis* and *leptinotarsa decemlineata*, but there were three absences. Whether by appointment or by negligence, the students Gantlik and Cresspahl had preferred a stroll to Mt. Smoke, perhaps because they were positive that the rest of the class was out of town. Zaichik had made it known that he was to unload coal into his aunt's cellar. All three received written summonses to plead their cases before the teachers' conference. There the student Haase was confronted with the fact that after the stacking of pressed coal—economically defensible—he had found leisure to visit the Renaissance Film Theater, instead of mounting his bicycle and flying headlong to join the potato-bug detectives! While we were waiting in the classroom for a possible *consilium abeundi*, verdict (or notice) of dismissal, Zaichik confided to us who had got him in the soup; in front of the picture palace he had come upon the student Manfras, who had been excused for political service. (A photograph exists of this penitential bench which shows Zaichik with his coat collar fastened to the hook of a map stand, neck slewed sideways and arms slack, as if in the process of being hanged.) A repentant Anita was saved by her contract with Soviety authority. A repentant student Cresspahl had a guardian angel flying circles over her head: he had photographed Bettina in West Berlin. In Zaichik's favor was the fact that by way of the filmic work of art *Council of the Gods*, he had at least allowed himself to be enlightened about the imperialist conspiracy; for the rest, a severe reprimand. He thanked the conference for its indulgence.

The act of communication was undertaken by Anita. It was unusual for the student Gantlik to step up to student Manfras's table between classes as if she had an urgent message for him; that's why the class quieted down and everyone noticed the furious twitching of the two reddish arrowheads of hair at her neck, heard her voice vibrate with passion like an organ. "Anybody who drags our personal conversations, what we tell each other in strict confidence, things about our families and private life, into the Principal's office and to the Party is, he is . . ."

What was the worst condemnation to pass Anita's lips? He is a bad person.

Gabriel kept his face still, features vague, tried to look attentive, and gave a nod from time to time, like someone who is willing to endure even this for the sake of political necessity.

Since then we have been reminded of him when *Les Lettres Françaises* are mentioned, or the slandering of a revealed truth. This in turn brings back the appearance he presented at the festive rally at the conclusion of the school year 1951–52; he stood behind the red table of the Presidium and thoughtfully sang along with the choir what had been imposed upon us in July 1950 as both statement of fact and confession of faith:

*The Party, the Party*
*Is always in the right!*
*Comrades, hold high the cause.*
*For life was ours where the Party was;*
*It gave us peace and peaceful might,*
*And sun, and wind, and she gave it free;*
*Oh, Party, we live through Thee!*

We are certainly aware of the finding by an East German court concerning people like you: the term informer is not an insult but denotes a profession, since it is one of the duties of a house warden to supply the political leadership with information about the population.

You can be sure that we remember you. It was you who turned our class 10-A-Two into an intimidation chamber. We have you to thank for the fact that school from eleventh grade on turned into a long-drawn-out struggle against fear. So enjoy yourself. For she has granted you almost everything, the Party, sunshine and never a headwind. It began with enrollment into her slate of candidates in 1951. It continued by her promising you admission to Humboldt University in Berlin a year ahead of time. She gave proof of her confidence in Youth Comrade, now Comrade, Manfras: he was permitted to complement his studies in Marxism by visits and stays at the British Center of West Berlin. There is one limitation, and we find it well deserved. Since he is a cottager's son, not a farm laborer's, he falls short of proletarian nobility, and this leaves him still excluded from those meetings near the Werder Market every Tuesday, where decisions are made about East German policy, domestic and foreign. Which disability makes Comrade Manfras try all the more zealously to interpret such resolutions. Anita eyes him on occasion, for a few seconds, on the TV screen. For this he is abundantly rewarded—he gets it free, as our love song to the Party mentioned; he may walk into the State Bank and help himself from the foreign-exchange coffers to anything he happens to need for untrammeled travel to the countries of his opponents. His English is reported to be international now, with overtones of British. A country house on Müggel Lake, car, and shopping privileges in West Berlin—everything provided for. His one dream, though, is to be taken into the diplomatic service. But there is an inbuilt barrier, almost insuperable if not noticed before age thirty-six. In his columns reporting on the high society, such as it is, of his country (which belongs to the likes of him), the telephones "shrill madly," though that piece of equipment predictably and invariably does merely what a spurt of current has trained it to do. He also has trouble with participle/gerund syntax; he will hardly earn an honorary Ph.D. for such descriptions of characters as this: "Raising roses on her balcony, the coffee-brown wife of the Secretary . . ." However, we may be mistaken. He may end up as an embassy counsellor; let us hope somewhere else but Prague.

"Two questions," says Marie.

"Granted, your honor."

"You gave Pius a general's rank at one point."

"It's been three and a half years since he . . . But when I think of him as though he had gone on living, he is a general by this time—major general at least."

"On the other paw: you think you have your Bettina Selbich well in hand."

"One twist of the arm, and she is free—is that what you are saying?"

"You were both between the devil and the deep blue sea. Admittedly, you took a picture of her marveling at West Berlin—illegally."

"However?"

"The person who had his eye to the viewfinder was there too—when it came to producing proof."

"Good heavens. I am so glad you are only telling me *now*!"

At home on Riverside Drive, the daily cable from Helsinki is waiting. Today it says: Patient temporarily unable to drive. Signed: Eritzen.

## August 11, 1968   Sunday

Over the Ashau Valley near Tabat in Vietnam an F-100 Sabre Jet fighter went into a dive and fired cannon and rocket bursts at U. S. troops. Eight dead, fifty wounded.

Over West Virginia a two-engine Piedmont airliner attempted an instrument approach to Charleston airport, elevation 950 feet. Crashed in flames just before the landing strip. Of thirty-seven persons on board, only five survived. We too will be flying soon.

Before that, Marie would like to have a children's party, but without a note of farewell. Because my best friends are Pamela, Edmondo, Michelle and Paul, Steven, Annie, Kathy, Ivan . . . and Rebecca Ferwalter; we have an appointment with Rebecca's mother on a park bench to negotiate the kosher part of the menu.

She is eying us with plain reluctance as we approach, propped on her bare, fleshy arms, and attempts to look gratified. Mrs. Ferwalter is back from that portion of the Catskills she calls Fleischmanns. Rebecca has found a boy named Milton Deutsch there, whom they call Moshele (Moses). Moses Deutsch loved Rebecca a lot and beat her up; Rebecca would come to her mother for a good cry and go out to meet Milton anyway the moment she saw him from afar. Mrs. Ferwalter says, vows in passionate anger: never will she seek a place where Milton Deutsch might be encountered!

Conversation on a park bench.

"Will the Nazi Party come to power in Germany?"

"Few people wish for that in Germany."

"What can those Nazis want, anyway?"

"A change of the borders, for starters."

"Do the Americans have a right to mix with this?"

"If the Government in Washington sees fit, it'll do it."

"My dear Mrs. Cresspahl, leave that to me. I will bring Passover cookies; they come in all colors with a thick icing; children like them at a party; they taste like marzipan. The last time we baked them at home was in '44. Our village belonged to Hungary then. Transports had been coming through since 1941, and people were taken away in the country. In May 1944, everybody was rounded up. I had a Catholic passport, giving Catholic for religion. The Germans looked at me and ordered me along. The Hungarians and the Germans, they were twin souls. They were all soldiers. Excuse me, what are Schwaben?"

"Inhabitants of a South German province, I should think."

"Were the Schwaben more for Hitler than others?"

"No more than the others."

"These were Schwaben."

("Transylvanian Germans?"

"No. Those were anti, you know.")

"We got to Auschwitz. I spent eight months there. Most went straight to the Krematorium. Many of the Aufseher, the supervisors, are still walking the ground, and you'd be surprised where. As we are talking here now, I have talked with Mengele.

"I was *selected*, detached, to the Magazin as Einweiserin, store and issue clerk. In the kitchen, two girls carried baskets behind me. I divided the margarine up and dropped it into the cauldrons. The girls fished the margarine out again right away and tossed it into buckets of water to harden it. A good woman was my Chefin there, Mrs. Stiebitz. She looked the other way."

" 'May we put that aside?' "

" 'It's yours, but look sharp.' "

Mrs. Ferwalter now explains what a *Block* is, using beveling hand movements; it has houses standing like this. In one block there were girls, thirteen-year-old children. After hours she carried buckets of soup to them. Once she was stopped on the way by a Jewish Kapo: You are stealing, you bitch.

"And you pay for yours, right?"

The Jewish Kapo threatened to put her on report, and the next morning she was indeed called out of ranks, after hours of standing, and accused of resisting a Kapo and also of theft. Mrs. Gräser, the head of the women's camp, said: "You are going to be shot now." Called a *Posten* over, a guard.

Mrs. Gräser had grown fond of a girl and used her as her right hand, a girl named Frances. Frances said: Come, they all do that. If you really like me, do me a special favor and let her live. She does a good job in the kitchen, you know.

The sentence was commuted to one hour's kneeling on sharp gravel, holding up two stones in raised hands. It took many weeks for her knees to regain their normal shape.

"Mrs. Stiebitz kept silent during all this. You have to understand that this was 1944, and the Germans were fed up; they had had it.

"When we had got there, there was just nothing. Then trees were planted, like for a park. Those who lived to see that had turned into animals.

"On arrival at Auschwitz we were entlaust (you know, some kind of disinfection) and our hair cropped to the skull. The hair grew back, of course, and Mrs. Stiebitz liked to say: how pretty. Which it was. Yes—the Selektion was like a beauty contest. Even Mrs. Gräser once said: you could try out for beauty queen.

"At my Bestrafung, my punishment, they cut a trench through my new-grown hair. I went off and had the rest of it cut off. I was twenty-one.

"We worked in two shifts. The day shift was so-so. What was bad was the night one. In our corner seven crematoriums were at work. At the end of the night shift the sky was red as fire. I used to hear the people scream: Help! Help!

"You will understand, Mrs. Cresspahl. You are a woman, you see.

"From Auschwitz we were taken to an ammunition plant in the West, perhaps in Germany. I saw a sign saying Geh-len-au. It was quite a small camp, for Frenchmen.

"We saw the British parachutists being dropped. We were herded to the station and locked in boxcars. The inhabitants of the place looted the stores. The train pulled out. Half an hour longer, and the British would have been there. They took us to Mauthausen. In Mauthausen I was liberated.

"In 1945 Mrs. Stiebitz went into hiding in Austria. The camp people got clothes for her and an American paper [she drew a very long rectangle in the air with two fingers] so she could return to Germany.

"The first few days after liberation [May 9th] we lived on a farm. Good food, real milk, last year's red apples [this in housewifely accents]. But we were afraid; at the neighboring farmyard SS were in hiding. They might come out, after all, and start it all over again. At Mauthausen one of the supervisors picked himself one of the fifteen-year-old girls every night.

"The Jewish Kapo who had caught her with the soup buckets turned up after the war in an office building in Tel Aviv, Israel. I am going to report her! Until a friend advised: 'Why do you want to take on all this trouble? Running to the court and back, procuring testimony, signatures.' So I let it go.

"Everything was rationed in Israel then; the townspeople went foraging in the countryside. This Kapo enters a kitchen through the back door and calls. The farmer's wife, who has gone through Auschwitz, is sitting in the front room; she recognizes the voice, cries out. Everyone piles out on the street, detains the fleeing Kapo. She drew a year in jail.

"Another girl who was brought to trial in Israel was from my home village; she mistreated everybody except me. She had become a Kapo at Auschwitz. In those days you could get off if as many witnesses testified for you as against. I up and spoke for her. She is an old friend; she is a wicked person.

"But God has punished her. She married a man who treated her shabbily; she is divorced.

"The really wicked thing was that the Germans compelled the Jews to kill one another. Shove your relatives into the fire alive."

(Rebecca has had a fall.) "My child, I have waited for you so long, eighteen years!"

(Rebecca is to have a bite of roll for consolation, showing fish an inch thick between the halves.) "You see!" (Since Rebecca is being stuffed with food, she is on the chubby side despite her delicate frame.) "If only my child ate like yours!

"We left the C. S. S. R. legally, with passports. We were allowed to take all our household goods along. 1948. It took eight or ten days to get to Tel Aviv.

"Because my brother had got sugar on the black market—it was rationed—he was sentenced to half a year in jail: the sentence to begin the next Monday. He didn't feel like waiting for that, went to Bratislava and over the border to Vienna. The police went into action on Monday morning. So that's how we are in New York with the Almighty's help.

"And is it a deal that the cookies I bring to the children's party, Mrs. Cresspahl?"

---

## August 12, 1968    Monday

---

The New York *Times* wishes to prepare her readers for an anniversary: It will be seven years tomorrow since Walter Ulbricht, the East German Sachwalter, or deputy, had the border between his part of Berlin and the territory of the Western Allies blocked by a wall, in order to keep his citizens from moving west, and those of West Berlin from coming for visits. Certain exceptions are permitted, such as a death in the family, or when the legal retirement age has been reached. "On my birthday I was happy," wrote a woman from *democratic* Berlin to her daughter on the other side, "to have become older. Now it is only five years till I can visit you." The Wall is manned by two East German brigades and three regiments in military training, in all about 14,000 men under arms.

On October 7, 1951, the East German state holiday, selected households in Gneez, Mecklenburg, also two in Jerichow, received the same mail, without sender's address. The envelopes, the paper, were of standard size, but stained, with little fibrous blisters, easily torn; the kind that government offices use for notifications. The texts were written on the same typewriter, whose keys for e and n were out of alignment. Anyone who cared to copy this information by hand (like Cresspahl's daughter) before turning the missive over to the German People's Police in token of his Stalinish vigilance, was able to compile an interim case on the role of justice in Mecklenburg since 1945.

(The distributor assumed some acquaintance with abbreviations and acronyms on the part of his readers. They should have no difficulty reading Z as *Zuchthaus*, penitentiary; S. M. T. as Soviet Military Tribunal; F. T. for *Ferntribunal*, trial *in absentia*. He could further take it for granted that a person of reading age in Mecklenburg would have no trouble expanding the letters Z. A. L. to *Zwangsarbeitslager*, forced labor camp, and verh. not into *verheiratet*, married, but *verhaftet*, arrested, arr. The writer was evidently in a hurry or could not get at the rickety machine very often:)

1945

Professor Tartarin-Tarnheyden, L.D. of Rostock, b. 1882, arr. Nov. 20, 1945; sentenced by S. M. T. to 10 years in Z. A. L.

Professor Ernst Lübcke, Ph.D., b. 1890, natural scientist, on Sept. 8, 1946, arr. by Soviet officers, abducted to the U. S. S. R.; missing.

Fred Leddin, b. 1925, student of chemistry, arr. Sept. 20, 1947; sentenced by S. M. T. to 25 years in Z. A. L.

Hans-Joachim Simon, student of natural sciences, arr. Sept. 27, 1947; missing.

Herbert Schönborn, b. 1927, law student, arr. Mar. 2, 1948; sentenced by special court of M. V. D. (Ministerstvo Vnutrennykh Del, Ministry of the Interior) to 25 years in Z. A. L.

Erich-Otto Paepke, b. 1927, medical student, arr. Mar. 8, 1948; sentenced by S. M. T. Schwerin, to 25 years in Z. A. L.

Gerd-Manfred Ahrenholz, b. 1926, chemistry student, arr. June 23, 1948; sentenced by S. M. T. to 25 years in Z. A. L.

Hans Lücht, b. 1926, medical student, arr. Aug. 15, 1947; sentenced by S. M. T. Schwerin, to 25 years in Z. A. L.

Joachim Reincke, b. 1927, medical student, arr. 1948; sentenced by S. M. T. Schwerin, to 25 years in Z. A. L.

Hermann Hansen, b. 1910, Catholic university chaplain at Rostock, arr. 1948; sentenced by S. M. T. Schwerin, to 25 years in Z. A. L.

Wolfgang Hildebrandt, b. 1924, law student, arr. Apr. 3, 1949; sentenced by S. M. T. Schwerin, to 25 years in Z. A. L.

Rudolf Haaker, b. 1921, law student, arr. Apr. 1949; sentenced by F. T. to 25 years in Z. A. L.

Gerhard Schultz, b. 1921, law student, arr. May 6, 1949; sentenced by special court of M. V. D. to 10 years in Z. A. L.

Hildegard Näther, b. 1923, student of education, arr. Oct. 8, 1948; sentenced June 9, 1949, by S. M. T. Schwerin, to 25 years in Z. A. L.

Jürgen Rubach, b. 1920, student of education, arr. Feb. 8, 1949, by S. M. T. Schwerin; sentenced to 25 years in Z. A. L.

Ulrich Haase, b. 1928, student of Germanic philology, arr. Sept. 22, 1949; sentenced by S. M. T. Schwerin, to 25 years in Z. A. L.

Alexandra Wiese, b. 1923, applying for admission to Rostock U., arr. Oct. 18, 1949; sentenced Apr. 1950, by S. M. T. Schwerin, to 25 years in Z. A. L.

Ingrid Broecker, b. 1925, student of art history, arr. Oct. 31, 1949; sentenced by S. M. T. Schwerin, to 15 years in Z. A. L.

On Dec. 17, 1949, an S. M. T. at Schwerin sentenced eight defendants, including two women, to up to 25 years in Z. A. L.

Jürgen Broecker, b. 1927, applicant for admission to Rostock U., arr. Oct. 21, 1949; sentenced by S. M. T., Schwerin, on Jan. 27, 1950, to 25 years in Z. A. L.

On Feb. 17, 1950, an S. M. T. at Schwerin sentenced one Helmut Hiller and eight others to a total of 375 years in Z. A. L. for alleged connections with the East Bureau of the S. P. D., the West German Social Democratic Party.

On April 16, 1950, an S. M. T. at Schwerin sentenced the senior high-school students

Wolfgang Strauss
Eduard Lindhammer
Dieter Schopen
Winfried Wagner
Senf
Klein
Olaf Strauss
Sahlow
Haase
Ohland
Erika Blutschun
Karl-August Schantien

to a total of 375 years in Z. A. L. The same court passed sentence on the chairman of the Youth Council of the Liberal Democratic Party of Mecklenburg, Hans-Jürgen Jennerzahn.

Horst-Karl Pinnow, born 1919, medical student, arr. Apr. 2, 1949; sentenced May 1950 by Soviet F. T. to 25 years in Z. A. L.

Susanne Dethloff, b. 1929, applicant to Rostock U., arr. May 4, 1949; sentenced May 1950 by Soviet F. T. to 10 years.

Günter Mittag, b. 1930, medical student, arr. early June 1950; tried by S. M. T., sentence unknown.

On June 18, 1950, the senior high-school teacher Hermann Priester of Rostock, sentenced to 10 years in Z, was so brutally beaten in Torgau Prison by People's Police Sergeant Gustav Werner, known as Iron Gustav, that his thighbone was broken. When he was unable to stand up, the VOPO cursed him as a malingerer and crushed his pelvis. Hermann Priester died of his injuries later in June.

Gerhard Koch, b. 1924, medical student, arr. July 13, 1950; missing.

On July 15, 1950, the Güstrow District Court lodged in the Zachow Hotel sentenced nine high-level officers of the Raiffeisen rural co-operative affiliate at Zachow to a total of 84 years. Among them was Arthur Hermes, b. 1875. Hans Hoffmann, L.D., was included because he made efforts to move the assets of this famous farmers' self-help organization from Mecklenburg to Göttingen (two tank barges, five tank cars). "Sad to say, he succeeded in this." Included also, Prof. Hans Lehmitz, Ph.D., b. 1903, natural scientist, member of the Unity Party: 15 years in Z.

On July 18, 1950, the Greifswald District Court sentenced additional members of the co-operative to penitentiary terms.

Friedrich-Franz Wiese, b. 1929, student of chemistry and member of the university committee of the Liberty Party, arr. Oct. 18, 1949; sentenced July 20, 1950 by S. M. T. Schwerin to 25 years in Z. A. L.; on Nov. 23, 1950 sentenced to death by S. M. T. Berlin-Lichtenberg.

Arno Esch, b. 1928, law student, assessor with the provincial committee of the Liberal Party, arr. by Soviet security personnel in the night of Oct. 18–19 as he was leaving the Party's Rostock offices. Opposes capital punishment. "I feel closer to a liberal-minded Chinese than to a German Communist. . . ." "In that case I wish to state that we do not have the freedom to make decisions here. I request that this statement be included in the minutes." Sentenced to death July 20, 1950 by S. M. T. Schwerin, in accordance with Para. 58, Item 2, of the Penal Code of the Russian Soviet Socialist Republic, for preparation of armed insurrection. While being held before trial, he was mocked for his pacifist convictions. The death penalty was reintroduced long after he was jailed. Executed in the U. S. S. R. June 24, 1951.

Elsbeth Wraske, b. 1925, student of English philology, arr. Apr. 11, 1950; sentenced by S. M. T. Schwerin, July 28, 1950, to 20 years in Z. A. L.

On Aug. 8, 1950, an S. M. T. at Schwerin sentenced Paul Schwarz and Gerhard Schneider, both members of Jehovah's Witnesses and on this account kept in concentration camp under Hitler, to 25 years in Z. A. L. each for "anti-Soviet activity."

Siegfried Winter, b. 1927, student of education and most popular handball player in Rostock, arr. Aug. 16, 1949; sentenced by S. M. T. Schwerin, on Aug. 27, 1950, to 25 years in Z. A. L.

Karl-Heinz Lindenberg, b. 1924, medical student, arr. Sept. 16, 1950; sentenced Oct. 12, 1951 by Greifswald District Court to 15 years in Z.

On Sept. 28, 1950, the Schwerin District Court sentenced the high-school student Enno Henk and seven others to prison terms up to 15 years for alleged distribution of pamphlets.

Alfred Loup, b. 1923, student of education, arr. July 3, 1950; sentenced Oct. 31, 1951 by S. M. T. Schwerin to 25 years in Z. A. L.

Gerhard Popp, b. 1924, medical student and chairman of the C. D. U. university chapter at Rostock, arr. July 12, 1950; sentenced Oct. 31, 1950 by S. M. T. Schwerin to 25 years in Z. A. L.

Roland Bude, b. 1926, student of Slavic philology and member of the university chapter leadership of F. G. Y. at Rostock, arr. July 13, 1950; sentenced Oct. 31, 1950, by S. M. T. Schwerin, to twice 25 years in Z. A. L.

Lothar Prenk, b. 1924, student of education, arr. Mar. 24, 1950; sentenced Dec. 9, 1950 by S. M. T. Schwerin to 25 years in Z. A. L.

Hans-Joachim Klett, b. 1923, medical student, arr. Mar. 23, 1950; sentenced Dec. 12, 1950 by S. M. T. Schwerin to 20 years in Z. A. L.

On Dec. 18, 1950, an S. M. T. at Schwerin sentenced 14 former VOPOS to death for "anti-Soviet agitation and formation of illegal groups."

On Apr. 27, 1950, the Schwerin District Court sentenced a defendant named Horst Paschen to life imprisonment for "agitation for boycott in conjunction with murder of a coast guard."

Joachim Liedke, b. 1930, law student, arr. June 1951; sentenced to 5 years in Z.

Gerhard Schönbeck, b. 1927, student of philosophy, arr. Sept. 6, 1950; sentenced Aug. 22, 1951 by the Güstrow District Court to 8 years in Z.

Franz Ball, b. 1927, student of classics, arr. Jan 18, 1951; sentenced Aug. 22, 1951 by Greifswald District Court to 10 years in Z. A. L.

Hartwig Bernitt, b. 1927, student of biology, arr. June 29, 1951; sentenced Dec. 5, 1951 by S. M. T. Schwerin, to 25 years in Z.

Karl-Alfred Gedowski, student of education, b. 1927, arr. June 26, 1951; sentenced to death Dec. 6, 1951 by S. M. T. Schwerin.

In the same proceedings:

Brunhilde Albrecht, b. 1928, student of educ., arr. June 29, 1951; 15 years in Z. A. L.

Otto Mehl, b. 1929, student of agriculture, arr. June 29, 1951; 15 years in Z. A. L.

Gerald Joram, b. 1930, medical student, arr. June 29, 1951; 25 years in Z. A. L.

Alfred Gerlach, b. 1929, medical student, arr. June 29, 1951; death.

Above the entrance to the courtroom of the Soviet Military Tribunal in Schwerin, the words LAW MUST REMAIN LAW have been fastened. On the dais, a court consisting of three officers. Present besides the accused: an interpreter, guards, and overlifesize pictures of Stalin and Mao. Accusations: contact with the Free University of Berlin; manufacture and dissemination of leaflets; possession and circulation of antidemocratic literature. The sentences rest on Article 58 of the Penal Code of the Russian Soviet Socialist Republic, Paragraph 6: Espionage; Paragraph 10: Anti-Soviet Propaganda; Paragraph 11: Formation of Illegal Groups; Paragraph 12: Failure to Report Counter-revolutionary Crimes. Karl-Alfred Gedowski in his closing statement: In order to decide in favor of one ideology, one must also know the other.

Gerhard Dunker, b. 1929, student of physics, arr. Dec. 24, 1951; missing . . .

The author of this solicitous correspondence could arrange the ways and means as circumspectly as he liked and see that his letters bore different postmarks by mailing them in Stralsund, Rostock, Schwerin, Malchin, Neubrandenburg; but he gave himself away by his selection. He was indifferent to the fact that Peter Wulff was accused of having cheated the state (which did not exist before 1949) in the years 1946–48 of a total of 8,643 marks in income, business, and sales taxes; in which matter in the consent proceedings at the Internal Revenue Office in Gneez in May 1950 he long refused to pay the 8,500-mark fine. He was duly sentenced, according to Para. 396 of the Tax Code, to a 7,000-mark fine and three months in jail. This Wulff ought to have been listed in the chronicle. Because it involved economic policies, the author also ignored as too petty the case of farmer Utpathel at Old Demwies, who went to the penitentiary for two years because of arrears in the delivery of his quotas of meat, milk, wool, and oil seeds; this though he pleaded his advanced age (seventy-three), the inferior quality of the seeds supplied by the state, the total loss of his herds to the Red Army in 1945, the cattle plague of 1947. The local court at Gneez conceded these "objective difficulties" with the retort that as a progressive farmer he should have mortgaged his agricultural enterprise and procured cattle on credit in order to fulfill his obligations to state and people: for deleterious treatment of a major farm unit (42 hectares of farmland), confiscation of property; for an economic crime as defined by Para. 1, Item 1, Number 1 of the Penal Code, Economic Section 2, two years in the penitentiary. Now Georg Utpathel's farm stood untended, open to the inroads of neighbors. This sort of thing was evidently a bagatelle to one who felt more closely concerned about punitive court proceedings against higher-education institutes, who considered worth reporting only purely political and ideological punishments. Here is how they will catch him, said Jakob, along with his copiers; and he took such notices away from Cresspahl's daughter, ostensibly in order to discuss them with his friend Peter Zahn. In fact, the bulletins were in safekeeping with an unknown third person in the railway union headquarters in Gneez; it was he who sent Cresspahl's daughter her property after Jakob's death, in an envelope bearing a Dutch postmark.

For the time being, the nameless court reporter (who never used a Gneez mailbox) kept his involuntary subscribers up to date on the harassment of owners of taverns and hotels on the Mecklenburg coast under the aegis of Project Rosa; this was for the sake of variety. Perhaps it also was to avoid monotony that he inserted among the case histories this comment by the Soviet News Agency TASS about the death penalty: "it bears a profoundly humanistic character in that . . ." Then again, he showed his preference for senior high students, telling us about Dicken Sieboldt's removal from the Neubrandenburg penal facility to an unknown location; and a preoccupation with undergraduates in Mecklenburg, as if he planned to apply for admission: the State Security office in Rostock, he noted, had appropriated the "People's House," diagonally across from the university, and constructed cells in the basement and on two floors; the interrogators threatened their victims with "kinship liability," Hitler's infamous *Sippenhaft,* and beat them up when they felt like it. Or he would focus on the future of Mecklenburg students; or explain to his customers how the Bützow-

Dreibergen prison got its name from the three hills at the southwest corner of Bützow Lake, on which the facility at one time was to be erected; or he would tell us about the first warden of that establishment after 1945, the journeyman mechanic Harry Frank of Bützow, who passed himself off as a privy councilor until he eventually had to hang himself in a cell in June 1949; or about the hit squads terrorizing the overcrowded jail that was named after the VOPO lieutenant Oskar Böttcher. By their tone they were dispassionate, those accounts that came to our houses; only once did the compiler give way to anger and · concluded his report with an appeal: "Mecklenburgers! All we are famous for by now is the rutabagas, known as Mecklenburg pineapples, that are fed to our political prisoners. Does that satisfy us?"

After Christmas, beg pardon, the winter holiday, the following were arrested in Gneez and near Jerichow: the students Gantlik, Dühr, Cresspahl; Alfred Uplegger, in 10-A-Two at the time, evaded capture. The gentlemen in leather coats came to his farmyard just when he was busy with a long-handled ax at the log-splitting stump. "How shall the hare prove he's not a fox," he staunchly quoted to himself and swung at them. Because of grievous harm done to the body of the state he had now unexpectedly committed a real crime—he could see that without coaching—and he ran to West Berlin as fast as he could. But there was one who had been in jail since the start of vacation: the student Lockenvitz.

On January 3, 1952, Jakob paid a visit to district headquarters of the People's Police in Gneez to ask the whereabouts of Cresspahl's daughter; he could afford to speak calmly because he figured in their files as a violent character. Given the fact that even a man in navy blue uniform dislikes meeting such a type on a hostile footing—for example, at night on unfrequented paths between garden plots—it stands to reason that the people in the precinct gave him a rational argument: they would have given him a hint long ago if they had known anything beforehand; "surely you know your Hannes, Jakob!" Jakob took a leave from work and braced himself for long waits in the lobby of that villa in the composers' quarter in the cellar of which local State Security sorted out the short-term deliveries until they were ripe for referral to Siblings Scholl Street in Schwerin. Promptly two of our gentlemen opened the door for him; carefully they went over his documents with him—I. D.s from the labor union, the F. G. Y., the police, the Society for German-Soviet Friendship, Social Security, the old Federal Railway—before he could finally state his case. Saddened, compassionate of bearing, they advised him to call on VOPO district headquarters, the competent authority for missing-persons cases. In this office, they went on, the name Cresspahl was unknown even by hearsay. . . . "Why, we keep telling you, Mr. Abs, you may believe us . . . !"

The door to the lobby was ajar; Cresspahl's daughter could hear Jakob clearly, until he took his leave in the disgruntled manner of a citizen who had come to check on something and had his own credentials scrutinized instead. The student Cresspahl was standing there on the parquet floor her second day, three hours per day, strictly held to immobility. The interrogators desired the suspect to focus straight on a nail that had been driven in the wall four inches above average eye level. On it hung, in a gilt frame, a tinted photograph of Marshal Stalin. Talking without orders was frowned on in this house; talking at the gentlemen's demand, urgently recommended. While Jakob was standing in the lobby, the prisoner Cresspahl had trouble breathing because of the gloved paw being held over her mouth. When the outer door closed behind him with a sigh and a satisfied smack, the orders were resumed: lift your head! stretch your arms! keep the palms level! At the end of the three-hour stretch of this, writing exercises were regularly scheduled: write a new version of your curriculum vitae and have the discrepancies with yesterday's discussed. Jakob's appearance had furnished a new weapon to the interrogating staff; what do you do with the question whether you, the high-school student Cresspahl, were having a sexual relationship with that railway man? This was followed by more standing gymnastics, consonant with the resentment now felt against foolish Gesine Cresspahl, who on a murky Wednesday morning in January boarded the milk train to Gneez, taking a compartment by herself, with the result that at Wehrlich station she could be manhandled to the back bench of a Black Maria with a minimum of fuss. And now let's have a brief appraisal

of the Criminal Doings
of the Enemies
of Socialism;

we even convicted the Acting Premier of Czechoslovakia, that Rudolf Slansky. By your leave, Youth Comrade Cresspahl! Raise your head! Stretch out your arms!

She scored only one single slap, near the end of the ten-day investigation; she had really blown her top that time. When on the evening of January 12 she came back to Cresspahl's house, she received a hug from Jakob; it was a remarkably expert job, as though he had made a habit of it with her.

That had been Saturday. The next day at lunchtime, Anita came over after church; another first. We both started talking and said in unison: "Look here, I have something to tell you! (In confidence)."

Guard duty in Dr. Grimm's former villa had been so meticulously arranged that neither girl had had an inkling that the other slept on the far side of the same wall, was fed Mecklenburg pineapple from a bowl, lay down under a filthy blanket and the emanations of all manner of sweat. They were at one in their apprehension concerning the person to whom they owed such quarters and treatment; the interrogation had chiefly sniffed for the antecedents, utterances, and habits of "our handsome young man," Lockenvitz. We felt offended in our notions of masculine toughness and grit. We readily appreciated that he had wanted to gain time at some cost to the backs and palms of three unwitting girls; but a disappointment lingered. Until Jakob played Solomon for us, saying: may the Powers preserve us from the impatience of women! Did we have any hope of ever getting a husband? Consider, won't you, what must be done to a person before he will let harm come to a girl!

Anita liked it in my father's house. There was Cresspahl, who squared his shoulders for her sake at the welcome and looked into her eyes as he thanked her for the acquaintance. There was an old woman who said grace before the meal. There was a young man who pulled out her chair for her, served her food, entertained her with narrative discourse; you could also get an answer to a straight question from him.

The third member of our sisterhood of crime we recognized in a Physical Education class, which was held jointly with 11-A-Two. Annette Dühr walked stiffly; she probably had had to stand longer with straightened knees. She had been seen leaving something at the door of the Lockenvitzes' apartment and had found less belief than we had. Her watch crystal was broken. Her back had blue welts on it, from beatings. She was missing one tooth. She looked past us in an imploring manner: she wanted to be excluded from our club.

One female felt left out. Lise had been hidden in the bookbinder Maass's attic as soon as two turned up missing in 12-A-Two. The moment State Security might seem to be coming for her, Mrs. Maass would have taken her into Gräfin Forest at night, to a car by which she would have been rescued to the safety of Berlin; now it was all for the birds. As if she were no earthly use, an unproductive Lise Wollenberg.

As for Gabriel, by this time nobody would take a piece of bread or a word from him any more. Beset by his own school class, implored by the Dühr family to secure an intervention of the Central School Chapter Authority in favor of the missing girl, he had concluded that such suggestions were evidence of a grave lack of confidence in the socialist state. "Our security organs know what they're doing; no more than what is necessary. In such a case you swallow your questions; you simply help them!"

Manfras quite possibly chafed under the indifference the girls had shown him since the summer of 1951; in languishing poses we sang at him, point blank to his face, until the predictable blush was obtained: Don't look at me like that, big maan, / Too well you know it, that I caaan / Refuse you nothing, nothing thaan . . .

Another person arrived from Cottbus after curative treatment: Pius, summoned to Gneez for a deposition. "Temple of Great Joy" he brought and a reproof: actually, we had never been shown any denunciation of us in Lockenvitz's hand and signed by him. The gentlemen conducting the interrogation had proceeded on an intuition that the culprit must have suborned accomplices. And who would type willingly and well what a young man might ask her too? The girls, that's who. "And you of all people, Gesine! He tried to protect you!"

(That reproach was merited. For after the Easter vacation of 1951, which was to be called spring vacation from then on, Dieter Lockenvitz had stepped out of the working team of Pagenkopf & Co. Simply faded out, without an explanation. Questioned in class about whether there had been a quarrel, he had let it be known that he was in love with Gesine Cresspahl, couldn't help himself; and to witness, day by day, the favors enjoyed by his rival, Pius, was just unbearable. After that Pius and I gave him the bird in public, a questioning crooked index finger tapping against a temple, but left him his fiction. He had figured out that no one could impute connivance between the student Cresspahl and himself at least for the past eight months—or with any of his transgressions.)

Lockenvitz's trial was held in District Court in the morning of May 15; though the trial report was to mention a public trial, no public was to be in evidence. Here the students Gantlik and Cresspahl had seen to timely redress by the criminal act of elegant bribery of the court employee Nomenscio Sednondico (I-know-the-name But-am-not-telling), which N. S. notified class 12-A-Two via Elise Bock so punctually that even before the start of the proceedings in District Court an unruly swirl of young citizens in the pride of their blue shirts demanded entry; shouts were heard: "Friendship prevails, friendship prevails!" or "We are the defendant's school class!" Among the intruders you could see colleague B. Selbich, obliged to follow the exodus of her subjects in order to gloss over their blatant rebellion. We owed it to her arrant cowardice, in fact, that we could see him one more time, the one-time high-school-student Lockenvitz.

It was obvious that State Security had tried out on him what his bulletins accused them of. But for their miserly ways they might have been able to cover up this or that trace behind a pair of glasses of the kind they had smashed. As it was, he was led in with his face bare, acting blind, stumbling; he hung in the prisoner's chair as if even this were beyond his strength. Though he held his head in a listening pose, he avoided looking at us. Because he had had to part with his upper front teeth, there were difficulties of articulation.

MANFRAS testifying: The defendant's work in the Central School Chapter Authority—it was practically sabotage.

(Whatever work had come up in the management of Free German Youth, it was Lockenvitz who had dealt with it; Gabriel's part had been the annual addresses, the Surveys of the State of the World. Now he accused himself of lack of vigilance, as something-or-othered by the Great Comrade Stalin . . . )

WESTPAHL testifying: Since 1948 Dieter Lockenvitz has assisted in building up the library of the Cultural Society; in cataloguing, in the ordering process. He was familiar with the premises. How could I suspect him of leaving a window open with the idea of climbing in at night and using the typewriter?

MRS. LOCKENVITZ testifying: My son is an uncommunicative child. He can't have got this either from me or from his father.

SELBICH's testimony: not forthcoming. (Afternoon visits in the Rose Garden, Gneez.)

The state attorney must have skipped instruction in German during his training to become a people's judge. Wild flailing about in the grammar, raucous voice breaks in the mis-stressing of foreign terms.

The defendant's attempt to obtain a high-school certificate by fraud. (It would have been of a caliber you get once in a decade [except for Chemistry]. The defendant had been destined, you see, for the times when a person would be rewarded according to his abilities.)

The monstrous ambition (mis-stressed) of the defendant to publicize court sentences that the judicial archives of the sovereign Republic kept under lock and key in the interest of the state! Collecting subversive information.

Terrorism. (This rested on the fact that he had also directed his correspondence to the District Court judges in the new Mecklenburg, in order to disconcert and intimidate them if possible.)

Motion by the prosecution to have the defendant's mother arrested in the courtroom on suspicion of complicity. (Gerda Lockenvitz, born 1909, garden worker; for neglect of parental educational duty and active complicity, two years in the penitentiary.)

The corpus delicti, a bicycle of Swedish (foreign!) manufacture, is confiscated and forfeited to the state.

(Completely omitted was any mention of how a child originally a newcomer to the region had found access to confidential files and records of closed trials. Those circumstantial reports on the events of June 18 and July 20, 1950, and December 6, 1951, were grist for the mill of cross-examination. However, the court maintained the fiction that the details of Lockenvitz's one-sided correspondence were unknown to anyone below the bench; a possible implication that this child had a mind to continue protecting his sources.)

Question: Do you confess your hostility to the first workers' and peasants' state on German soil?

Answer: I confess endorsing the basic identity of the German and Old English possessive cases. I confess endorsing the administration of law in the open marketplace in Germany.

Penitentiary, fifteen years. And since the Soviet authorities had waived their interest in this isolated transgressor, he was spared the journey to Moscow by the Blue Express, in the hitched-on prison car camouflaged as a vehicle of the German postal service. And likewise he forfeited the privilege of learning practical mining in Vorkuta or logging in Tajshet. And so he also missed the Soviet amnesty of 1954, which annulled the verdicts of military tribunals. Since he had been sentenced by a German court, he served two thirds of his sentence.

In September, the interrupted correspondence was resumed:

Gerhard Dunker, b. 1929, arr. Dec. 24, 1951; sentenced June 17, 1952, by Güstrow District Court to 8 years in Z . . .

At first 12-A-Two knew where Lockenvitz had been taken: to Bützow. Two classmates were allowed to select a job for him, since he had let it be known what firms placed orders for convict work:

People's Own Enterprise Rostock Shipping Concern;

P. O. E. Güstrow Garment Works;

P. O. E. Registry of Deeds, Schwerin;

P. O. E. Wiko Wickerware Manufacture;

P. O. E. High Voltage Installations, Rostock;

Messrs. Wiehr and Schacht, Bützow.

They had a fair idea of his menu and were able to compute from the data they had from him an hourly wage of 94 pfennig. At the end of the month, after deductions for tax, social-security insurance, and prison dues, these earnings left him with 15 marks, just enough for two pounds of butter and four jars of jam. They knew the allowable content of a package they would be permitted to send him at times as a reward for good conduct:

1 lb. of shortening,
8 oz. of cheese,
8 oz. of bacon,
1 lb. of sausage,
1 lb. of sugar;

the rest of the prescribed 6.6-lb. maximum weight to be made up of fruit, onions, brand-name biscuits in original wrappings.

Anita demanded such a parcel from herself only once, and that one came back to her. To do this legitimately, the sender would have had to live in the same jurisdiction as Lockenvitz and be related to him.

Thanks to his own reconnaissance work, we were able to imagine him with an inch-and-a-half haircut, in secondhand VOPO uniform drilling; saluting N. C. O.s by removing the cap and eying the passing dignitary from two yards ahead to two yards in his wake, while "assuming a soldierly stance"; marching in formation, sleeping—never alone—a shit bucket next to him. We withdrew from him.

Had we, by any chance, expected to hear in his final plea an apology for our ten days of investigatory detention? To believe Pius, Lockenvitz had had no reason to think that anyone had been hauled in but himself. Jakob said: "He has still to learn it, that sitting in the clink!"

After the administrators of East German justice had disciplined Lockenvitz, they began to doubt, starting in the summer of 1952, that the practice of secretly arresting citizens and holding them incommunicado sufficiently intimidated the remainder. Perhaps the publicity campaign of this high-school student had helped to motivate the organs of justice to publish their judgments in the provincial papers, thus delivering the deterrent in print.

Were we troubled and awed to watch a boy of eighteen, for whatever kind of truth, and be it a proven fact, risk a future from which he had reason to expect admission to higher education and, with luck, free choice of a profession? The memory of Lockenvitz causes a faint flutter in one's thought; birds flushed in the dark.

From Gneez they wrote to us that his mother had returned to town as soon as she had served her two years. She tried to wait in Gneez for her son; but that canon whom Anita had moved all the way to Jerichow to avoid, took the trouble to fulminate against her from the pulpit, using such words as the Bible offers for the casting out of profligates. People say that she is waiting for him somewhere in Bavaria.

From 1962 on we could have looked around for Lockenvitz. But his schoolmate Cresspahl preferred to wait and see whether Anita would tone down her threat of 1952: "If ever he should cross my path in the subway and offer me a seat—I would remain standing."

We sold him down the river, the student Lockenvitz. Anita's is the last word: we are guilty before him.

## August 14, 1968   Wednesday

Yesterday morning at five past nine two gentlemen entered the Union Dime Savings Bank, dressed in ordinary street clothes ("more or less like a police lieutenant," ventures a member of the police); they brought with them a revolver and a cleaver. As they stood in the street with $4,400, bank employees shouted "Stop thief, stop thief" after them and no taxi would stop for them in the thick of morning traffic; thus they spent the rest of the morning at the 17th Precinct. (One of them had just been released from Sing Sing in June, after serving a sentence for exercises in the discipline of bank robbery.)

The East German Sachwalter has departed Karlovy Vary so incensed over the refusal of his Czechoslovak colleagues to put the muzzles back on their press that he has his own press keep silent about his whereabouts these seventy-two hours.

The citizens of the C. S. S. R. have delivered forty pounds of gold and valuables, estimated at about $20 million, to the Development Fund of their Communist Party. The Party, however, would rather have them cut down their coffee or beer breaks, limit waste, work harder. A workman, in a letter to the labor union paper *Prace*, asks what for—when young people have to wait ten years for an apartment and pay 40,000 crowns ($2,500) for it into the bargain. New machines is what we need! And some sort of feeling that work has its rewards!

The permit for leaving high school—testimonial of maturity for higher education—the Secondary School Certificate: the student Cresspahl acquired it several times.

Once from the teachers, in the form each saw fit to give it.

In Latin, from a hunched and timorous ancient, who with a display of absent-mindedness glossed over the fact that in 12-A-Two his favorite disciple in grammar, the adeptus Lockenvitz, was missing indefinitely, and the girl students Gantlik and Cresspahl had been absent for some ten days, all without the obligatory excuse slips from home. He gave himself away by not calling on them in class until sometime in February, when they might be expected to have caught up with the others. He drew back somewhat if his Marcus Tullius Cicero elicited the comment that possibly this castigator of corruption in the state might himself have satisfied his requirements of ready cash;

or, worse, if one dwelt on the propagation of Latin by the Christian missions in Western Europe. He had once got his fingers burned, badly, on matters historical: transferred from Schwerin for disciplinary reasons. He would have fluttered away in a heart attack had a class delegation appealed to his own tested and true moral sense for instruction on the bad habit of memorizing and reporting what fellow students might be saying on inspection tours of a gasworks or a brewery. His heart yearned for retirement and the leisure it would afford for the composition of a most private and original monograph about the Schelf Church at Schwerin. Whoever quietly held his own with him on the ablative absolute would receive an A for his school-leaving grade; appreciation of considerate treatment.

An A in English was received by the graduating senior Cresspahl from Hans-Gerhard Knick, who had learned this language with the aid of records and thought he spoke it after traveling to Berlin, still in short pants, in 1951 to the World Festival of School and College Students and playing translator to a group of girls from Britain inclined toward Socialism, who treated him with indulgence. When Gesine, owing to her preoccupation with Dreiser's *Sister Carrie*, slipped in a "conductor" in place of a "guard," he at first ventured upon a correction, but soon gave her up. This student further enjoyed a modicum of protection because she intended to go on to university studies of a subject he was in such need of reviewing, and, second, by a legacy from the Free German Youth Lockenvitz, who had known Mrs. Knick in their lost homeland as a well-to-do bourgeois daughter, not a scion of workers and peasants, as would have been fitting for the mother of a language teacher who hoped to be accepted as a candidate by the Unity Party.

There was a B in Russian on the final grade sheet for G. Cresspahl, chiefly because of her participation in a conspiracy to be of assistance to a young people's teacher by the name of Von Bülow in advancing in this language to the level of teaching competence. She was sufficiently cowed by her descent from the gentry to be worse confounded by the behaviorist psychology purveyed by her training courses, so dissimilar to the demeanor of a 12-A-Two in Mecklenburg. It followed that instruction in Russian was administered by Anita. A victim. For the curriculum prescribed Stalin's essay "On Dialectic and Historic Materialism," which teems with "Furthermore . . . thus can . . . thus it may be . . . thus ends . . . thus transformed . . . thus must . . . Moreover . . ."; this was followed by the same author's disquisition on "Marxism and Problems of Linguistics." V*as slushayu*, Yes SIR. None of us would have been able to buy even a pair of nail scissors in Kiev or Minsk with this prose. At the end of the school year 1951–52 this

Eva von Bülow went to Hamburg, where she is now an interpreter in the German-Soviet steel and shipping trade.

In Music there is a B, earned under Julie Westphal; because the student Cresspahl was content to remain in the second-string altos, thus gaining free time when the first-string choir practiced for the summer tour of Baltic resorts; and, later, time for unsupervised vacations. Another reason for the mere B was that candidate Manfras had reported to this specialist Cresspahl's description of one of her scholarly dicta as *dumm Tuch*, twaddle. This referred to Julie's verdict that the song "Der Mond ist aufgegangen" should disappear from the musical repertoire of democracy because of the prayer it contained for the quiet sleep of the sick neighbor: such solicitude undermined the ideological vigilance of class-conscious man, in that the neighbor might very well be a camouflaged enemy of the people, whom it would be a transgression to let sleep in peace. A third reason: that the student Cresspahl, to be sure, listened to and recited what Mrs. Westphal dispensed about the cosmopolitan, reactionary nationalists and enemies of the Soviet Union such as the composers and musicians Paderewski, Toscanini, Stravinsky; but thereafter petitioned the teacher for a demonstration of these disgraceful properties in the works of the proscribed composers: just a few bars at the piano, Mrs. Westphal, so we get an idea of . . .

In Biology/Chemistry, an A from an undersized elder, a male. He was a wimp like the one for Latin, only on the bloated side, an ellipsoid. Under him we received in tenth grade that element of instruction which is to explain to children the sexual needs and abilities of the human being. At which point this drooler, who thought of himself as a lady-killer, had thrown a sop to his thwarted libido by reciting to the boys, winking, index finger erect by his eye, a Goethe line, "the thought alone will lift Him," followed by the verses:

*When you're aware*
*of Him hanging there,*
*so loose,*
*so big*
*in his trouser leg,*
*You've a dirty mind,*
*and I like your kind.* (Heinriche Heine)

(Where a girl student of 10-A-Two knew that from or got to hear it? Guess! Your closest answer is: osmosis.) The ellipsoid was still disporting himself before us, reveling in examples of e-vol-u-tion in nature. In the year of the Lord 1952 he served his pupils the canard that a type of infantile paralysis was caused by eating bananas; the same fairy tale had been handed to children in 1937, another period when bananas were unobtainable. That he might indeed worship that figure and Stalin's favorite son Soviet biologist Trofim Denisovich Lysenko, the members of the Biology/Chemistry class deemed incompatible with this teacher's academic descent from Heidelberg University. Dutifully we recited to him that it depended entirely on environmental conditions whether plants would pass on acquired characteristics or not. That they could do it was, for better or worse, the sum total of our knowledge in a special field. This was why Anita on a tour of inspection of a seed-growing and hybridization farm approached the man in charge with a question about Michurin and his fosterling Lysenko. Here was a chaired professor, a multiple doctor by merit and by honor, a holder of the National Prize, who had deemed his continuance near his experimental fields more important than the triviality of their appropriation by the New State. To such a man Anita addresses herself with modesty and a tone of respect that cannot escape his notice. He may have brought back some stored-up anger from a meeting in Rostock or a session of the Academy: incensed, stern as a privy councilor, he laid it out for her, her alone, that a fixation of genetic properties by the somatic detour might at best occur once in a trillion years—for otherwise the doctrine of evolutionary progression of life forms would collapse. "You won't find any Lysenko beds in this place, young woman!" We were standing close to her, saw her cast down her eyes and flush. At such moments we missed them, the gentlemen Pagenkopf and Lockenvitz; they would have done something, each in his way, to keep a girl in their class from being hurt. Fortunately, the Comrade Professor himself realized in time that here the school, not Anita, had to be ashamed. He walked her away on a little stroll with his arm around her shoulders in order to tell her something about productivity appraisal and certification of seed grains, and about the circumstance that a small country's agriculture cannot afford chancy extravaganzas in genetics. We stood in a group around our specialist in biology, ignored his embarrassed babble, and hoped that a comforted Anita would return to us. "Hail Moscow and Lysenko!" said the student Gantlik (when no Youth Comrade Manfras was near); that afternoon helped her to renounce a fancied choice of profession.

An A in Mathematics and Physics came to both Gantlik and Cresspahl from Eberhard Martens, dubbed "Evil Eye" because from his N. C. O. past he had retained a hypnotic gaze that searched for transgressions. A teacher who carried on instruction long after it should have dawned on him that only three members of his class had grasped the notion of function as a prescription of conjugacy. With us his manner was constrained; our stiff courtesy was a riddle to him. We had heard him tell stories, in broad Mecklenburgish, cozily confiding: "I hardly sweat; all that marching in Russia cured me of it; the others were always drinking; there's only one occasion when I sweat . . ." For another instance, we had heard him tell, in a man-to-man talk with the subject specialist H.-G. Knick, of a startling encounter on the streets of Warsaw in 1942: "A female coming my way, she bats her lashes till I notice; her bosom is out of phase, you might say, with her gait; so I go to work on her. Would you believe, the little brute had cross-laced elastic from garters to bra . . . technically it was Rassenschande, crime against the master race, I suppose." Evil Eye attempted to leave the East German Republic in 1954, but baggage control at the border found what looked like private photographs of Heinrich Himmler and that SS general who had ordered the Warsaw Ghetto razed and the survivors driven to their death. Two years in the penitentiary. To this teacher we showed a specious compliance until graduation.

As for the subject specialist in German/Contemporary Studies, we might have tried a light-hearted manner with her; but as a rule we abstained. For in the ninth grade of 1952 there was a girl named Kress, half of the student Cresspahl's name. When asked who Comrade Stalin was, this child voiced the conjecture that he was the President of the Soviet Union. "Sit down! F!" screamed Bettinka, and in the same breath: "Your whole family is suspect to me!" Since she was seeing the student Kress for the first time and remained unacquainted with her family, one person in 12-A-Two knew what it really was that released all this rancor.

Grave of mien, we recited to her in German class stanzas from the poem "The Raising of Millet," which the writer Bertolt Brecht had published the year before:

20
*Joseph Stalin spoke of millet*
*To Michurin's pupils, spoke of dung and parching wind.*
*And the Soviet people's lofty harvest leader*
*Called the millet grain a child grown wild.*
21
*Millet, though, was here arraigned in vain;*
*When the moody steppe-daughter was tried,*
*In Lysenko's far-off sheds she testified*
*What was born to her and what was bane.*

Her thoughts possibly dwelling on a differently defined shed in which the student Lockenvitz, he too far off, was interrogated about what was bane to him, Anita interpreted for Mrs. Selbich the poetic goals of those lines. They looked toward the scientific basis for the Marxist concept of societal development, the shaping of man by his social milieu as well as the inheritance of virtues so acquired (including the points of difference from the environmental theories of Marx's contemporaries; strictly avoiding at the same time the term sociology, which was still taboo then as an expression of imperialistic pseudoscience).

"The Raising of Millet" was further embellished by a setting to music, which could be sung with a comic lengthening of the last a vowel in each line:

*Tschaganak Bersiyew, the nomaaad,*
*Son of the free wilderness in Kasakstaaan . . .*

What could Betteenkin see in this but a somewhat childish outburst of exuberance within the framework of the curriculum?

By the same author we studied in Mrs. Selbich's class the work called "Herrnburg Report," a poetic memoir on the reception accorded the returning West German participants in the All-German Rally of 1950 by their police at the border crossing of Herrnburg. The Interior Ministry of Schleswig-Holstein had decreed that the young people be registered by personal data and employer and given medical examinations because they had slept on straw. The returnees fought back with stone-throwing and fisticuffs and bivouacked one and a half nights in an open field, until they gave in and held out their I. D.s to be stamped "Processed" or "In Order." This episode had blossomed in the poet Brecht's hands to their having "planted" the F. G. Y. flag on the roof of Lübeck's main railway station and prevailed; this came with the following poetic findings about two party chairmen in the Federal Republic:

*Schuhmacher, shoemaker, your shoe doesn't fit,*
*No way can all Germany walk in it.*
*Adenauer, Adenauer, show us your hand,*
*For thirty pieces of silver you sold our land.*

This was performed at the Third World Youth Festival of the F. G. Y. in Berlin, and the girls from Britain with their socialist

consciences who surrounded our H.-G. Knick (in knee pants) were
bound to find *awful* what he translated for them:

*Germans hunt Germans down by decree*
*For crossing from Germany to Germany.*
*. . . Roadblocks and fencing—*
*What is the use?*
*Look at us dancing*
*Gaily across.*

For the absurdity of it, we suggested a performance of the same
choral work at Fritz Reuter High School in Gneez (Herrnburg being
in our neck of the woods, after all); Bettina S. was overjoyed at her
pedagogical success. But Julie Westphal lowered the boom on the plan;
she had an inkling of our astonishment at a poet who was able to wax
indignant about West German police controls since he was immune
for the most part to the East German ones. But the school achieved
its pedagogic purpose all the same. By only presenting to us Brecht's
potboiler work, with the National Prize rewarding it (100,000 marks),
it kept us away from his *A Hundred Poems*, which came upon the
market that same year of 1951; we had every reason to suspect these
to be a can of worms too.

Anyone willing to part with a copy, however much used, of Bertolt
Brecht's *Hundert Gedichte*, with dust jacket if possible, is requested to
name his price to Mrs. Gesine Cresspahl, c/o Statni Banka Česko-
slovenska, Praha 1.

In the matter of denouncing the cosmopolitan enemies of the
people, Bettina had her work cut out for her. Of Rainer Maria Rilke
she knew that he had been a lyric poet alien to the people; Stefan
George she called a stylite. But what to do about Jean-Paul Sartre?
The student Cresspahl suggested that this person had published a book
called *L'Être et le Néant* in Paris in 1943, under the Nazi German
occupation. She got an A. Oh, how we missed Lockenvitz!

He had still been with us at the class excursion to view Barlach's
works, rode along to Güstrow with us wearing a suit, because the student
Cresspahl wore a Sunday outfit, her father having indicated this to be
seemly for a visit with one deceased. He, Barlach, had been so plagued
and tormented by the Mecklenburgers, Fiete Hildebrandt always in the
lead, that he died, at Rostock, in 1938. He had wanted to be buried
at Ratzeburg in West German Holstein. When Bettina was through
with her "interpretive" applesauce, we stepped a second time before
the hovering angel in Güstrow cathedral, before the figure of the Doubter,

and the young woman of ill-omened 1937, in order to study them in silence. (Lise Wollenberg proved not above trying to fasten the name "Fettered Witch" on her former friend Cresspahl, on the strength of a dubious resemblance *en face*; whereupon she found herself on occasion stared at, precisely by boys, as if she were demented.) With a set of reproductions showing Barlach's "Frieze of the Listeners" Gesine Cresspahl moved to Hesse, to the Rhineland, to Berlin, to Riverside Drive in New York City.

Our excursion had been in September; in December 1951, an exhibition of Barlach's works was opened at the German Academy of Arts in Berlin, N. W. 7. The following January, a teacher of German and Contemporary Studies in Gneez began to learn from the S. E. D.'s newspaper what Betteenkin had misinformed us about four months earlier. The Unity Party had sent their official art expert to the Academy, one Girnus, well versed in the elitist practices of Formalism; he was willing to concede in the deceased's favor that the Nazis had treated him as one alien to their kind. But Barlach had manned a doomed outpost, had essentially been a retrograde artist. Untouched by the breath of the Russian Revolution of 1905. Wove a halo around a world of "Barefooters." What, by contrast, did Stalin in his work *Anarchism or Socialism* say about the world of the barefoot pilgrims? Barlach's orientation toward a decaying social stratum—so Mr. Girnus—barred him from access to the great progressive current of the German people. Insulated himself against it. That was the whole secret of his self-chosen increasing isolation.

We dutifully composed an essay in German class about the whole secret, meticulously distinguishing between the utterances of a certain N. Orlov in the newspaper of the occupying power, trying to disparage a West Berlin daily:

*Daily Survey! Latest Issue!*
*Waily Survey: Bathroom tissue.*

and certain thoughts of Ernst Barlach's (now promoted to a Formalist) about the three-dimensional world of the sculptor's intuition being bound up with "the most solid concepts of the material involved, stone, metal, wood, firm matter." We lied like troopers; we were working for senior finals.

Since their visit to Barlach's house by the lake island of Güstrow, the students Gantlik and Cresspahl had come to a mutual agreement, a clandestine understanding. Both had taken their distance from art criticism as dispensed by the subject specialist Selbich, found one another on the ridge of Heather Hill, where a slope begins, well known to the children of Güstrow as a sledding place in season, but opening to the eye, too, a sweeping view of the island in the lake and the gently rising land beyond the water, sparingly set with backdrops of trees and roofs, radiant, for the sun had just managed to oust some somber rain clouds: a sight that I pray may be with me in the hour of my

*We don't care a hoot if you find this a bit overcharged, comrade writer! You are going to write this down! We are still able to withdraw from your book this very day. Up to you to figure out what kind of things we keep in mind in case of death.*

dying. We confided to one another thoughts about people's inescapable need for the landscape in which they grew up as children and learned about life. We told each other how much we liked one another. For the remainder of the school year we continued counting as two—strangers to each other; but we were friends.

Anita very nearly forfeited her high-school certificate. Member of the Free German Youth that she was, she had now to avow her approval of the resolution of the Fourth F. G. Y. Parliament of May 29, 1952, which stated that service in the barracked People's Police was an honorable duty for all members. She who had sworn only two years before that she would refuse a job even in a telegraph office that was war-connected, was elected to march like those F. G. Y. girls in Leipzig with carbine slung over the back, whereas the boys carried theirs shouldered. A future was being readied for Anita where she could acquire the sharpshooter's badge of the F. G. Y. by scoring twenty-one rings in three shots for class one. Anita sat in the class chapter meeting with head drooping, no movement from the copper ducktails at her nape, and kept stubbornly silent. Who knows whether she was still listening when Gabriel Manfras spoke up in a mildly menacing vein about a balance between scholastic achievement and the caliber of political consciousness that must needs go with you on your assault upon the fortress of Higher Learning.

The student Cresspahl, who presided at the meeting, admonished herself with what sounded like indignation: "I could slap myself! Here we are talking about the Stockholm Appeal and obligatory military service and don't even notice that Anita is ill. You are feeling sick, aren't you, Anita? Go straight home. A vote on student Gantlik's indisposition. For. Against. Abstentions: none."

So it came about that the Fritz Reuter school chapter of Gneez was able to wire its approval of militarization to the Central Council of the F. G. Y. in Berlin—unanimous approval, which was held to be chic. And so Anita moved to West Berlin as soon as the document recording her scholastic achievements had been handed to her.

Apart from this, was there cheating during the senior finals? Oh yes; there is a legend about English texts hidden in a rotten pew in the assembly hall. But here I should in fairness fall silent, since most of those participating or implicated still live where they acquired the certification of their abilities.

My first final had been my last visit to the student Lockenvitz, on May 15, 1952.

The second one dated from June 25 and contained these general appraisals:

G. C. has been a conscientious, dependable student, who did her work independently and thoroughly. Her initiative made her a model to her classmates.

Societal participation:

G. C. has been a member of F. G. Y. since 9/10/1949. She has performed useful organizing work. She consistently and successfully endeavored to gain full understanding of problems of ideology, Weltanschauung.

License No.: Zc 208-25 3 52 5961-D/V/4/ 59-FZ 501.

There it was again, *Weltanschauung*, the banned term. Mrs. Habelschwerdt had had to do penance for a verbal misstep. New School, old terms. From now on let anyone who has to, or wants to, try to toe that crooked line.

The third final was held at Jerichow.

In the last days of June, Cresspahl's daughter was riding home on the Rande Dike after a swim in the Baltic, at the odd time of about 5 P.M., when retired senior teachers of English and Latin stop working in the garden plots behind the New Cemetery and proceed homeward in order to brew their tea, a habit they adopted during their student years at the universities of London or Birmingham. There she saw an old man striding along in a torn shirt, rake and hoe over his shoulder; and the former senior-high-student Cresspahl gave him the time of day as shyly as her feelings prompted her. He responded as he used to two years ago; pretended to be appalled when the child was about to get off the bicycle and accompany him part of the way. He would not hear of it; instead, he begged the young lady's pardon for his unseemly attire.

To be quite sure to escape from her sight, he sent her ahead to town, with precise instructions about what she was to buy in the former Papenbrock bakery in the way of crescents, Silesian crumb cake, and "americans." When she presented herself in his two rooms on the market square in Jerichow, Kliefoth had shaved and donned a black suit, and stood at the door like the young lady's most obedient servant. It was his visitor who eventually had to eat up the delicacies to the last crumb, while she rendered confession covering two years of school. He sat at the table, upright and firm of gaze. He felt comfortable; you could tell by the way he held the cigar away from him and watched her with a certain benevolence. The girl student was unsure of a good outcome.

"Iam scies, patrem tuum mercedes perdidisse," Kliefoth said eventually, a challenge in his voice.

"You will soon realize that your father has misspent your tuition money. What you have learned in that school, Miss Cresspahl, is poor equipment for a life in the quest for knowledge."

Half of the summer vacation of 1952 Cresspahl's daughter still spent at the seaside. But from early afternoon each weekday she had to report to Kliefoth with a bag of baked goods and receive instruction by means of a book, one of whose maxims read: "It may be fairly said that English is among the easiest languages to speak badly, but the most difficult to use well" (Professor C. L. Wrenn, Oxford University, *The English Language*, 1949, p. 49).

On her departure for the university she received as a gift, as a reliable instrument of instruction, Gustav Kirchner's *The Ten Principal Verbs of English, in British and American Speech Forms*, Halle (Saale), 1952, and she moved with it right to the other side of the world.

This teacher the student Cresspahl went on visiting as long as she still occasionally returned to Mecklenburg. And always she had to eat cake before his eyes, since this was one of his fixed notions about young ladies.

He gets an annual report by letter from us every year, and seven more if we feel like it.

The student Cresspahl once asked him in passing what it was like for ten-year-olds in the year 1898 at Malchow-on-the-Lake in Mecklenburg. He sent thirty pages in a script like embroidery.

"The ten-year-old country boy of '98 could be myself; but we town boys kept our distance, you realize, from those agemates left behind us, those also-rans or 'land moritzes,' local corruption of 'land militias.'

"Now, how did the ten-year-old get from the country to the town? I know only one case of a bicycle being used (then still called a velocipede, Low German *Vilitzipeh*), and that only in dry weather. Of the boys from the manor estate only a coachman's son and the District Governor's walked with me, the latter having already marched the three miles from his manor. Residents of lakeside localities (like Petersdorf,

Göhren, Nossentin) used to come to town mostly by boat. To be continued. 20.9.63. Kl."

All this merely because I wanted to know how my father might have grown up. Yet what does Kliefoth complain of: he can spend an entire week on Robert Burns's poems, and still let one slip by him.

We send him, via Anita, the cigars and tobacco that are his due by his need and his merit (as Brecht in East Germany meant to see to a fresh rose every morning for the poet Oscar Wilde), which is why his letters invariably begin: "Admonishing finger raised against the spoiling of a useless old man . . ."

He signs his letters with a logogram of his name, as though he were grading a paper.

His invocation is "Dear, revered lady and friend Cresspahl."

If only we had deserved it.

My third final: that is to count and last.

---

### August 15, 1968   Thursday

An airline clerk at J. F. K. may be called N. PODGORNI or at any rate wear a nameplate to this effect on his uniformed chest, suggesting that he must be used to outlandish incidents, and he may have been working for one and the same company for six years—this morning he gazes dubiously upon two ladies named Cresspahl, who wish to travel to California with no luggage but what they may be carrying in their coat pockets, including, who knows, a weapon to shoot with; he would really have liked to frisk the two. Go suck an egg, Mr. Podgorni, and good-by, sir.

What are we up to in San Francisco for a day? We wish to make our approach by air over Golden Gate. Marie is to see the big wheel that pulls the streetcars by cables over the city's hills; the boxy Spanish houses on the hillsides, radiant with whiteness in the sun-browned foliage. Perhaps we will once more at the main post office come across the beggar who six years ago gave thanks for a quarter with the acknowledgment: "You are a real lady, that's for sure." We are in need of a window seat at Fisherman's Wharf. And why do we rate all this? Because Marie faces a return flight to New York City toward 9 P.M. Because we must brace ourselves again for a flight over great distances. And why do we want to do it? Because in New York strangers' voices barge in on the telephone line, Italian as well as American, asking for a Professor Erichson. Because at any hour a cable from Helsinki may be delivered informing us that somebody is impeded in his speech. Would the two ladies with the name starting with C please be the first to enter the passenger cabin? Let us welcome the sisters C. aboard our 707 for the flight to San Francisco.

"The idea is to get used to partings," conjectured the younger of the travel party C., after she had during the steep ascent taken the measure of her real estate on this earth, the island of Manhattan and the orange two-decker boats in the harbor. "I would never go away for good from where I am at home!"

"That's easy to say for someone who has any number of institutions of higher learning at home, and a Columbia University around the corner."

"Gesine, would you advise me to go to college?"

"If you would like to consider a matter and scan it for all its corners and edges, and see how it is interrelated with other matters, or follow an idea through to the point where all its ramifications are present in your mind, simultaneously; if you would like to train your memory so that it acquires dominion over everything you think and remember and wish to forget. If you seriously want to lower your threshold of suffering. If you like to work with your head."

"And if all you had learned in life was how one milks a cow or boils potatoes for hogs?"

"The business about lying would be just as bad, and so would one's guilt toward others. But memory would be less acute—more comfortable, I think. 'Be dumb and working . . .' I could go for that. If you repeat this to anyone, I'll deny it."

"If you had stayed in Jerichow, you would have been married in St. Peter's; three marks for wedding decorations, four marks for choir and organ play, without the embarrassment of solo singing."

"All the truth in that is that I'd like to be buried there. If you can get the community to open the old churchyard one more time. It doesn't have to be a grave of my own; Jakob's will do for me."

"Because the earth is imperishable."

"Yes. Out of superstition. So deposed on earth, today's date, 30,000 feet above Chicago."

"You have to have Mr. Josephberg draw this up. If we crash, we die together after all."

"With luck."

"D. E.'s going to arrange that for us."

"D. E. can cook, D. E. can bake. The third day he steals the young queen's child. And there will be / the end of me."

"Of him, Gesine. Rumpelstiltskin."

"The leave-taking in 1952 was like the first one in 1944. Cresspahl took his daughter to the front door, leaned against the frame, spoke a final word to her. Tie a scarf round your neck. As if the trip was only to the Gustaf Adolf School in Gneez rather than to Martin Luther University on the Saale River. Only that he smoked as a little man bakes."

"Come, my grandfather was quite impressive in stature!"

"De lytt man—by that they meant in Mecklenburg the poor man who heated his oven with brushwood and sticks; the well-off used beech logs. They make for a fine, even smoke."

"When someone is about to lose something . . ."

"He will smoke hastily."

"Now about your dowry."

"My dowry was a rented room on Court Moat of Halle, five minutes on foot to the Saale; Jakob had arranged that for me. Those railway workers got around. Thither was delivered a chest with a compass-rose carving on the lid. Heinrich Cresspahl, Esquire, master cabinetmaker, retd., at Jerichow, had equipped his daughter for a life on the Saale River with a suit for the winter, two new dresses for the summer (Rawehn's, Elite Apparel, on the market square in Gneez). Dr. Julius Kliefoth had contributed, in the German originals, Fehr, *English Literature of the Nineteenth and Twentieth Centuries, with an Introduction to Early English Romanticism*; Keller and Fehr, *English Literature from the Renaissance to the Enlightenment*; Wülker, *A History of English Literature from the Earliest Times to the Present*; the *Columbia Encyclopedia* of 1950; a Muret-Sanders English-German dictionary of 1933. From Jakob's mother there was a Bible, with an inscription on the flyleaf: Acquired by barter for a hare, 1947. God Bless G. C. in Foreign Parts. There was also an account at the Postal Check Office, Halle/Saale."

"I call that pretty bold, not to have your scholarship remitted to you by the state."

"No scholarships for a student from the reactionary middle class."

"Your father paid taxes, didn't he? And you had been given honorable mention for your performance in the state youth outfit!"

"For Cresspahl, the state was someone he didn't have a contract with; this entity merely had a lien on his labor. He didn't care to receive from it a present of tuition assistance for his daughter. He transferred to her account 150 marks a month, 30 marks less than the youngsters with a proletarian pedigree could call for at the Office of the Dean of Students on University Square 8–9."

"That would have made me angry."

"Marie, I could make ends meet. I was able to buy butter."

"Mad at the state, I mean."

"Look left and right before crossing! Any day I could lose what the Seminar for English Philology (6) was offering in the fall semester:

History of American English

Modern English Syntax (with seminar)

English Language Laboratory

History of English Literature during Industrial and Monopoly Capitalism (with seminar)

History of American Literature during Imperialism.

"To get all this, the Division of Humanities student Cresspahl turned up on time for the obligatory courses in Russian, Pedagogy, Political Economy; she took tidy notes in Social Sciences, recording among other items that Trotsky in his vanity had once offered to die for the Revolution, with the stipulation that three million party members should watch him do it. No objection was voiced by this student when the university was given a banner showing Picasso's dove of peace (third version) by the Communist Party of France; she too applauded at the solemn ritual. Even had she been taking biology, she would not have mentioned that pigeons are quarrelsome by nature, destroy each other's nests, and are a plague on any house they attack with these nesting places."

"Such a taciturn child—didn't it draw attention?"

"The Cresspahl child had learned something from her friends Pagenkopf and Lockenvitz. Were she to walk a tightrope, she would spread nets underneath first. Asked for one of the most significant sentences in American literature, she dutifully recited the dictum by J. L. Steffens (1866–1936) about his visits to the Soviet Union:

I have seen the future, and it works.

Add to this the ability to know and produce at the right time what expression is used by Britons when they mean Kommode—that is, chest of drawers—and you are in a pretty fair way. The other anchor to windward she owed to Pius's example: 'societal participation.' At Martin Luther University it was sufficient for the time being that she register for a course in lifesaving. Heavily dressed, with a weighted backpack, she swam fifty meters underwater, took an upturn for air; how could a watchdog suspect that this compensated for her disgust at the bathrom on Court Moat, which she was allowed to use only once a week for a shower? A student like her, who has to fit in an additional fifteen hours a week for English alone, lacks time for holding offices with the young German Frees. And if they offer her one once, she has the upper-level swimming certificate under her belt; she'll be seven steps ahead of them in no time, devoting two hours of her week to a club the Ministry of the Interior founded in 1952 to teach young people telegraphy and shooting."

"Gesine, you're fibbing."

"The authority that Pius Pagenkopf intended to assume as commander of an armed flying machine was now claimed by his friend by means of a small-caliber rifle. She planned to deliberate at leisure at whom she would finally level the gun and squeeze the trigger so the shot would go home."

"You don't even have a license to carry a gun!"

"Since when have I needed a piece of paper to shoot?"

"Oh, you fighting-trim amphibian, you!"

"Envy, my dear Mary, is an unpopular quality; even in a bank. Although bankers, we are told, have human feelings too."

"I give up. I believe it."

"As you wish. I'll say 'cheese' if you like."

"Something about Saxony."

"About three or four people in Halle. The first two considered themselves a couple; they charged 25 marks for a furnished room in the second-best area. The female party worked for the manager of a People's Own Enterprise; she had slid off, if slightly, from the marital path, into the job of learning her boss by heart. Her day matched his mood; once she proudly reported that she had straightened the manager's tie in the nick of time before a conference. I had pictured things differently at the People's Owns; since then I have an uncomfortable suspicion of what it took to become a management secretary in the East Germany of those days. The man who was merely her husband felt forgotten, neglected; he fell into the habit of knocking at the sub-tenant's door, preferably in the evening, for a discussion of wives short on connubial understanding, who run to meetings and conferences until the small hours. The student Cresspahl left the slopes of the Reilsberg after less than two months and moved near St. Gertrude's Cemetery in Halle. The sign in the forehead of streetcar No. 1 identified its terminus as Happy Future; the house near the streetcar stop was mean, offering toilets for four parties halfway between landings. The residents were wary of the stranger, partly because she was awkward about the local vernacular, partly because her clothes looked as if she could buy more than their own food or clothing ration cards allowed them. The landlady made an effort—she needed the twenty marks; she polished the window, swept out the mansard, which Anita from a single description recognized as "Schiller's death chamber." On January mornings the water in the basin was frozen. That was when I resolved that my child, should I ever have one . . ."

"Thank you ever so kindly."

"That it would grow up unfamiliar with sublet rooms, in a room of her own, with running water and a shower."

"How happy I am to have you! How I am going to miss you!"

"A tua disposizione, Fanta Giro. Do we order champagne from this indigent airline?"

"What good is a frugal life? I want my steak well done, through and through, if you please."

"The fourth person in Halle was of the tribe of Gabriel Manfras."

"A sniffer for states of mind."

"Meanwhile my file had been transferred from the District Office of Gneez, and a university Party chapter wanted to ascertain what in her innermost heart made the student Cresspahl tick—as Faust hankered to learn what holds the world together at its inmost core. Any rancor, perhaps because of her father's deportation to Fünfeichen Concentration Camp, or because of the miscarried house search last summer? The boy played the swain, followed me around, happened upon his 'fellow student' with feigned surprise at eleven at night on Preisnitz Island, between the 'wild' and the 'shipping' Saale; he had inadvertently given himself away, since he was caught waiting on the Bridge of Friendship. He soon betrayed himself, revealing information about Gneez and Jerichow such as hardly comes one's way on a daily basis far from Mecklenburg. His victim appeared guileless, revealing with convincing hesitancy the sort of material likely to be in her file and surely part of his briefing for his mission. He was infected with the kind of dialectic that urges you to view a 'factum,' no matter how arbitrarily established, primarily in the light of cui bono"

"We had that! I know it; 'for whose benefit'!"

". . . the idea being to show that now your 'fact' appeared in a different light, or was canceled out. Necking was another thing the fellow wanted: presumably he had once succeeded in blathering a female into bed. It beats me what makes men so crazy about my bosom; they go on about it as if it were an achievement! As though I could take it off!"

"And the finest legs on bus No. 5 in Manhattan north of 72nd Street."

"Grazie tanto, you American. I prefer having people look me in the face, a problem for the agent provocateur. He thought himself on the way to a sexual adventure free of charge. I kept him on a leash like a Doberman, as an escort. This cost him, or, rather, the reptile budget of the Ministry of the Interior, a hunk of money. For I refused to visit the dance-and-beer mill on Thälmann Square, called Tusculum, entry and pawing free, but let myself be appeased by invitations to the Golden Rose on Rannish Street, or the old Café Zorn on Leipzig Street, lately renamed after Klement Gottwald, the Czech potentate, for reasons of geography. Possibly he thought he saw land ahead when I watched his slim wrist, put into elegant twists when he spoke, clearly well aware of this portion of gracefulness that was his. He also tried to get the future paramour drunk and then nail her with a more com-minative 'factum' than her preference for Romance Philology as a double major. By the time she had admitted, with some reservations, that she thought of the second major field as a 'bourgeois residue,' he was left poorer at Grün's Wine Cellar near city hall by the cost of two bottles of Beaujolais, and the girl emerged sober. She had gone through Cresspahl's school, where a sip of high-proof Richtenberger was pre-scribed as a medicine; she had also celebrated New Year's Eve with Jakob at the Linden Tavern in Gneez, where the basic unit was a quarter pint of vodka. How could she confide to a youthful agent in Saxony that that very night she had swept a Red Army soldier's cap off, ostensibly by mistake, deliberately out of resentment at the settle-ment of his outfit in Gräfin Forest, izvinite, pozhalusta! By the start of my second semester I had become precious to the young man because I had come back from unknown Mecklenburg still dubious about be-coming his, at which point I terminated the game of auscultation under the guise of Eros."

"Pity. I enjoyed that. However, he doesn't deserve a name."

"Satan ride him to hell, or, rather, Tangibly Existing Socialism! He turned up an invitation to a clublike place on Ludwig Wucherer Street where second- and third-year students discussed behind the showy façades of the booming 1870s and '80s whatever they found less than sustaining in Diamat, or Dialectical Materialism: perhaps an essay by Jean-Paul Sartre about 'Being and Nothingness,' Hamburg, 1952. The undergraduate Cresspahl was acquainted with the gentlemen from ta-bles shared at the university library, was greeted by them with ironic acknowledgment; now she was to help deliver them to the noose. For the benefit of the bloodhound she pretended to object to the rule governing these gatherings that a female guest was welcome only when a male member answered for the lady's integrity and discretion. Now he was free to admire her additionally as a champion of feminine independence. Actually she was afraid, and looking for auxiliaries."

"I get it; I know the phrase from you: 'Beware my bigger brother, he has nails under his shoes.' "

"Jakob materialized in the city of Halle-on-the-Saale in a dress uniform of the German Railways, a star or two on his shoulder boards, and accompanied his little sister patiently from one student hangout to another until she could point out her handler to him. While I paraded an untroubled smile for his benefit, Jakob went over to him and spoke a few bars. On Sunday morning, as we strolled to Pottel & Broskowsky on Orphanage Ring, a fine middle-class wine restaurant sporting clean tablecloths and silver cutlery, the stool pigeon looked past us: this would have beggared his expense account. It may well have dawned upon him that his victim wasn't all that vulnerable, that he had sat down to a hotter dish than he would be able to finish. No longer was it his desire to scale in darkened projection rooms the upper slopes of my arms: the smile sat crooked on his face, and stud. phil. Cresspahl was able to behave as if she had forgotten him."

"If I only knew what it was that Jakob told that fellow!"

"Unfortunately, I was curious too at the time."

"It's not curiosity. It's just that I always want to know everything."

"Marie, it was your father's maxim that a man takes forceful action and makes it work; still it is up to him to tell a young woman about it or not."

"Regardless of how many times she may have grown up next to him as if she were his sister?"

"See if you can think up something he might have said."

"My dear sir, I have a long record. Assault and battery."

"So much fuss about a two-bit delinquent? When I asked, Jakob remembered what he had used to shoo him off, and he smiled; but about me, too, with a faint overtone of warning, as though he meant to save me from some unseemly conduct on my own part. For Jakob I was always the younger one. He now wished to have some morning hours at Pottel & Broskowsky's with Cresspahl's Gesine as a celebration; she was to hold a *privatissimum* for him, a one-student seminar about a Professor Ertzenberger and the kindly amusement he derived from the phoneme inventory of a freshman from Mecklenburg. Professor Ertzenberger had departed for a university in the other Germany after the Great Comrade Stalin on January 12 had uncovered, unmasked, and smashed a conspiracy of Jewish physicians in his own city of Moscow, and he, Ertzenberger, had been refused the morning salutation by colleagues in the corridors of Halle University."

"I wouldn't stay in such a country. If only I knew why Jakob stayed!"

"You and I both. Perhaps because he had pledged to do a job for the German Railways. *Some*body has to do the work."

"But *you* got the idea then to leave East German purlieus."

"You are simplifying it because you know of my moving. There

were so many beginnings to this, but I remember only the first: Jakob
nodded at my announcement, although we were sitting under a whole
roof, sedulously looked after by gentlemen in long white aprons under
their tailcoats, with duck on our plates and wine in a bucket of ice.
He pleaded with me not to make up my mind about leaving for three
more months."

"Leave the city of Halle/Saale . . ."

"That was easy; I had known it for six months when I left. I knew
only which of their spires the people there are fondest of; that they
think the world of a little square named Reileck and consider it unique;
I had also learned to understand their language. But I avoided routes
via Robert Franz Ring (they go for 'rings' there in place of streets),
because that's where the administrative offices of the Ministry of State
Security for the state of Saxe/Anhalt were located. At Church Gate 20
you saw the prison facility Halle I, the 'Red Ox' in the vernacular.
Having been to Grün's Wine Cellar, I now knew that around the corner
from there you reached the prison facility Halle II; willy-nilly I had
business on Lesser Stein Street between the polyclinic and the main
post office. And imagine what you must think of yourself, sneaking
along to the Paulus quarter in order to slip through a front door on
Ludwig Wucherer Street an unsigned note warning that someone may
seem eager for confidential discussions of existentialism, and be able
to smile and keep smiling, and may still be a rat!"

"So there you felt they could do without you, and took leave. We
are passing over Omaha, Nebraska."

"That, certainly, but also because since May 1952 there was reason
to fear that Walter Ulbricht, Sachwalter, Caretaker, would close the
borders tighter than a drum. That was the time when the border-guard
troops were subordinated to State Security, whereupon they drew along
the line of demarcation between the two Germanys a patrol strip 10
yards wide, a zone of no man's land 500 yards wide, and beyond *that*
an out-of-bounds territory 3 miles deep, from which they forcibly evacuated the kind of people indicated to them as unreliable—merchants,
innkeepers, artisans, farmers with large holdings. Exactly the types with
whom the Government had made itself unpopular by fiscal harassment
and administrative fines. So the trap was shut right then, you see."

"Such volunteer soldiers, don't they know that they'll have to take
action against the wishes of their neighbors?"

"A lad like that, growing up in the country, he sees bone-breaking
labor all around him, often for strangers; what's more, without a hope
of making a little pile of his own: he is glad to go with the recruiters
for the Armed Police when they promise him a uniform of decent cloth

to wear, better food than farm hands get, lighter duty, and security over a long life. Your average apprentice in the town, he gets sick of filing and grinding, or work as such; he will enter a fixed-term commitment and in this way get higher-denomination food coupons and a claim to housing. (Material incentives—no way for conscience to prevail against them, quoth Anita.) An experienced captain of the ship of state, moreover, will know enough to deploy his Thuringian recruits preferably in Saxony, and the Saxon ones in Mecklenburg. For that matter, the State of Mecklenburg had been abolished."

"Oh, come, Gesine . . . I'm sorry, but tell us another."

"They had a law for this, the 'Statute on Further Democratization of the Structure and Functioning of the State Agencies in the Lands or States of the German Democratic Republic of July 23, 1952. You couldn't speak about 'Mecklenburg!' any longer except in a linguistic or ethnographic sense. For the rest, it now consisted of three regions—Rostock, Schwerin, and New Brandenburg; and the local and central governments were transferred there. In the south, a piece of West Prignitz was added, and the Uckermark territory. Since the statute abolishing the states continued to refer to them by name, the regional diets kept electing delegates to the Länderkammer, their upper house, until 1958; and these had to have sessions over and over again for the purpose of declaring that they had no objection to the law of summer 1952."

"Are you sorry about the passing of the blue-yellow-and-red?"

"About the loss of the blue, because of the golden griffin on blue that was Rostock's. About the scarlet and gold, for Schwerin's sake. About the crimson of the black bison-head's tongue, for the Slavic lands. A piece of regional history has been blotted out."

"And it was also, I suppose, because later the workers and peasants rose up against a government of workers and peasants that you left Mecklenburg."

"What a mouthful, Marie!"

"That's what they teach us at school."

"The American school teaches you this as a primary piece of information about Socialism—so that you might learn to overlook the riots of the Negroes from Watts to Newark!"

"Gesine, you said: only as from October."

"Vesógelieke. Gesine Cresspahl, the way she was made, didn't know any worker intimately."

"One, if you please."

"Two; one by mistake. In May 1953, the Humanities major Cresspahl did find herself out of cash for once, having forgotten to order a free ticket through Jakob. To save some of the railway fare, she went only as far as Schkeuditz and positioned herself at the autobahn cloverleaf there, her book bag under one arm, the other raised and waving. This went on for an hour and a half. Most of the motorists in West German cars saluted with their 'light horns,' fluttering between high and low beam, meaning to say 'sorry,' because picking up riders in the transit zone could mean bad trouble with the People's Police. Rotating flashes, whiter than the morning sun. Who did stop for discouraged female student bound for Berlin were a couple of chunky truck drivers, on their way with household goods from Saxon Vogtland to some People's Own-ery. They seemed pleased with company and kept their guest silent by exchanging multifarious stories, such as the time when some ladies had been waiting at the curb in the night and had expressed readiness to compensate for the free ride in various poses on the seat behind the driver, whereupon he, from the heady foretaste alone, came close to steering the monster truck into the ditch. But then, in Berlin's Frankfurt Street, now reconstructed in honor of Great Comrade Stalin, they advanced on their roadside pickup until she forked over twenty marks, which was more than the railway travel would have cost. Goodnatured threats of readiness to get rough."

"I find that shabby."

"I feel I had it coming to me, by way of a lesson on the community of interests joining transport workers and students between Halle and Leipzig. It's true that this very year the East German state's coat of arms was outfitted with a pair of compasses in addition to the wreath of sheaves and the hammer, to symbolize 'technological intelligence,' which didn't keep two Vogtländers from virtually mugging a student of engineering sciences with impartial enthusiasm. To be sure, we were—"

"We?"

"Anita and her Mecklenburg friend were perpetually amazed by what workers in East Germany were willing to put up with: the abrogation of plantwide wage agreements by an injection of 'socialist content' in January 1953, which, translated, meant a raising of work norms. From a wage earner's viewpoint this implied a gradual erosion of buying power. The Sachwalter wished to take back now what had been decreed to them the summer before in the way of higher wages; he was hard pressed by an excess of purchasing power, caused by his own active hostility, on 'scientific'—that is, ideological—grounds, to the primacy of consumer-goods industries. Now he was able to market too few shoes and cooking pots, but the Party is not human, so it is always right."

"You knew Eckart Pingel's father in Gneez."

"Old Pingel would have given the undergraduate Cresspahl the time of day by a quick wink, which meant the spirited, amused inquiry: 'Well, Gesine, you in this too?' He would have taken his cap off before shaking hands and beginning to talk. Any question about the work quotas in engineering jobs, courtesy of the Soviet Union, he would have side-stepped as though it was a tactless familiarity. For in those days, when Eckart Pingel had nearly been expelled from school ('because he told the truth'), his father took anyone who had a chance to go to a university for a pet of the New State, an ally of the authorities."

"You did know farmers."

"Only a few. After the war, the manorial estates in the Jerichow corner had been divided into small settlements, except for the Plessens' to the south and a much smaller one, formerly the Kleineschultes' manor, on the Baltic. These two were maintained by the Red Army for their own needs of meat, bread flour, and shortening, and a third one, the Oberbülows' estate, was taken over intact as a Peoples Own farm under a contract with the municipal hospitals at Wismar. Among the people who in 1946 had accepted parcels of land measuring between two and four hectares, there were few of the agricultural workers of the past: those knew farming and would not have tried to make a go of it on less than ten hectares. There was one village that had had nothing but peasant farmers since the fourteenth century. Whatever developed there in the way of barter traffic after the black-market era to supply House Cresspahl with potatoes for their cellar was taken care of by Jakob until 1950; by that time Cresspahl had reacquired the art of walking the countryside with a roving eye. Since 1944, the Cresspahl child had been in school in the town of Gneez, even more removed from a rural setting; she knew no farmers. Upon Dr. Kliefoth's request, she did once do a double loop on her bicycle to take in Pötenitz and Old Demwies, and was able to report to him on empty farms abandoned by their settlers when the Sachwalter's men tried to bilk them of their barely six-year-old land allotment by a proposed conversion of farms into agricultural production co-operatives. (We weren't born yesterday!) She had heard unwatered and unmilked cows roar in pain and was cured of the cozy belief that no Mecklenburg farmer would leave a head of cattle without fodder and supervision for even one night. I knew no farmers."

"Georg Utpathel."

"He fared the regular way, but was lucky, since he had been in jail anyway for a long stretch; at least he could take comfort in the illusion that he had lost his farm by the operation of a law. I knew one more farmer!"

"Johnny Schlegel."

"He was one of the exceptions. A man with a higher education and informed views about agricultural communes of the Weimar era. A proletarian in agriculture, he contended, whether or not endowed (bribed) with a cottage, a garden plot, and a grain allowance, would never consider his labor as his very own, since it maintained and increased the property of the landowner or tenant. Under the scourge of Hitler's and his agricultural chieftain Darré's legislation, he had had to work his 120 hectares under the traditional feudal setup. After those two had lost the war beyond the borders and within, he had handed over his inherited acreage in 11 per cent portions to refugees from the lost eastern territories; they just had to be farmers or be willing to learn to be. For each of these donations, normally loans, he had had a fictitious amount entered in the enterprise's statement of assets and into the registry of deeds. Thus under the protection of his friends in the Red Army, he ran an agricultural commune to his own design and taste; even as late as 1951, no inspector of Peoples Own land-purchasing and incorporating outfits could crowd him off the road. Came the scientific recognition by the East German Government that socialist agriculture meant large-scale cultivation; came their astonishment at some people on the Baltic near Jerichow who by 1952 had long worked in a co-operative that had advanced far beyond the socialist 'Type III.' This in the socialist scheme of things was only to introduce joint use of soil, draft animals, implements and tools. At Johnny's, personal householding as well was done in common by all members; the cooking was done in one kitchen, meals taken at one table. The fictitious figures had by now gained substance enough to allow the commune to pay off Mrs. von Alvensleben for her portion when she was asked by her children to join them abroad and assume grandmother's duties. That money was returned instantly, at which point Mrs. Sünderhauf fetched her brother home from the West, where he had had to work as a miner in the Ruhr. Assessed as farmers on middle-size holdings, the members of Johnny's project had to deliver to the state quotas several times higher than were demanded of the colonists and small landholders: 8, not 2, quintals of wheat per hectare; 75, not 25, quintals of potatoes; 59, not 38, quintals of meat. And yet by the end of 1952 they were still in such sound condition that Johnny was able to tell worried visitors: 'There!' "

"Gesine! How can you in an American plane crook your lower arm and make a fist?"

"This is an international flight. Io sono di Ierico."

"How you frightened the old gentleman across the aisle! He knows what it means, you see."

"Vi forstår desværre ikke amerikansk, kære frøken."

"What's next now? Something on the lines of envy being an unpopular quality, even within a socialist administration? That socialist rulers have human feelings, too?"

"How can you even think such a thing? No, they were eager to find out, in the Faustian phrase, what held Johnny's world together in its innermost core; those experts on quotas carried out an investigation in depth at Johnny's farmstead. As it happened, the harvest of 1952 had been pretty measly, causing Schlegel's group to fall into arrears with their milk quota. Generously, and according to regulations, the quota collection offices had given permission to turn over pork instead. If this left a deficit in the pork quota, he was authorized to make it up in beef."

"Which in turn puts even less milk into his bucket!"

"That didn't matter. The mortgaged cow was not impounded; he could keep it in his stable; he had only to pay for it."

"For his own animal?"

"At a quadruple price. If he had offered it as his debit, he would have been credited only with the fixed price of 1941."

"With all these tricks and detours, I'd miscalculate too."

"Johnny's books were accurate and complete. Unfortunately; for now the tax investigators were able to deduce from recurrent drafts that in the autumn of 1947 Johnny had taken off the Von Maltzahns' hands that wedge of land which had been in his way for fifteen years, a couple of hectares; paid off by 1950 via West Berlin to the Maltzahns foreigners' account in Schleswig-Holstein. This was private traffic in foreign exchange."

"An arrest warrant?"

"In February 1953.

"Ah-ah! said the court. Very bad."

" 'Excellent,' thought the judge. And Otto Sünderhauf had exchanged the yield of his share at Frankfurt/Main, where he needed to plunk down only 23 Western marks to get 100 Eastern ones. The criminal exchange rate of the imperialists."

"Supply and demand."

"Thus the defendants were found guilty of being profoundly tainted with capitalist thinking."

"That makes two!"

"No, four. After Sünderhauf they interrogated Mrs. Bliemeister and Mrs. Lakenmacher. For Johnny's group operated on a production plan different from that he had submitted to the authorities in multiple copies. This plan made provision for the death of young animals."

"Gesine!"

"You think it's only small children who die prematurely. A calf, after all, may catch cold and die of pneumonia."

"That's what you have doctors for."

"Of the five veterinary physicians in Gneez, three had meanwhile 'split' for the West, Dr. Hauschildt leading the pack. When Johnny factored in his own knowledge in this field and subtracted the help of trained expertise, losses in the live inventory were to be expected. This was enough for the state, the same state from which the vets ran away, to accuse Johnny of slander. Economic crime. Incitement to boycott. And because Johnny in his final summation asked to know why the court was tearing apart what the Krasnaya Armiya had sewn together for him, they had another crime ready: infraction of the statute for the protection of peace."

"They threw the book at him."

"Fifteen years in the penitentiary. For the rest of the defendants, from eight to twelve. Confiscation of assets. By April, Johnny's co-operative was cleaned out. Its members had skedaddled with all their kids to the refugee camps of West Berlin. Inge Schlegel stayed on for a while; she wanted to try to save the farmhouse at least; somebody had to look after Axel Ohr, send parcels to him in prison. Now it became evident where Johnny had miscalculated in his planning: she needed him there. If one woman all by herself is to keep an extensive farmstead in working order, the place is apt to have sagging doors and holes in the roofs after a month. She had been left with a single horse, Jakob his Foss, the roan. When it was executed, she left. It is a story . . . like those about little kids falling into water butts."

"Tell it, please. I must get over the habit of being afraid of things."

"Marie, let it ride."

"I am eleven years old."

"You'll regret it."

"I accept the responsibility."

"Jakob's roan figured in the books as a medium-rated workhorse. Annual requirements of fodder for one of those are:

    10 quintals of hay
    16 quintals chopped straw
    20 quintals turnips
    18 quintals grain
    30 quintals green fodder,

part of which the animal can forage for in the pasture. If now you set the cost of a half-quintal of oats in 1953 at twenty-five marks—"

"—then such a horse overstrains the student Cresspahl's budget."

"The spring semester of 1953 ended on May 9; the following Monday I was on a visit to Inge Schlegel. She held on to my shoulder when Jakob his Foss was being led by; I followed him to the large feed room. The man who held the lead looked back with a squashed grin, as though inviting me to a spectacle, some surprise. The roan walked briskly, nodding his head good-naturedly to the lout's soothing speeches. A few ribs were showing; he was perfectly sound. His glances said: You starved me for a while, you people; now you are starting to take care of me again. I'll be glad to get along with you. When the gun was applied to his forehead he closed his eyes trustingly: here was something new coming to him from humans. After death had slammed him to one side, his legs jerked violently, every which way, and drummed against the hollow floor it seemed forever. It seemed to express agony and despair; viewed scientifically, nerve impulses were still at work. The warm-hearted beast, Jakob his Foss, was suddenly a revolting slab of meat wrapped in blond pelt, yet recognizable still from his open eyes."

"Oh Gesine! Instead of waiting outside the door!"

"How was I to know that the stranger was a butcher from Gneez? His two assistants with the knife I saw too late."

"Gesine, if you catch me showing off about my age again, will you give me what for? Will you slap my face, but good?"

"Our position is Salt Lake City, Utah."

"Then you had had it."

"Then I still had to watch Elise Bock's bedroom furniture being auctioned off in Gneez. They had become 'people's property' when Elise moved to West Berlin. People pushed and squeezed each other in a narrow dirty courtyard in front of the gaping panes of Elise's windows. Inside, a man in a threadbare suit, the Unity Party's emblem in his lapel, walked on and off, proffering to the assembly pictures, an easy chair, lamps. The bidders, headed by Alfred Fretwust, bawled their facetious remarks as if they were teen-agers or the worse for drink. Then I got ready to leave."

"But you weren't of age then, were you?"

"By East German law, yes. Cresspahl and Jakob's mother—they made me talk all one night till morning. That old woman knew fear on my account, and Cresspahl hoped the child would come to her senses. He talked in terms of a rest. It was to be 'a holiday at Anita's.' "

"And Jakob?"

"Jakob gave the undergraduate Cresspahl a free ticket for her trip to Halle University, made out for the route Gneez-Güstrow-Pritzwalk-Berlin. But think of the child at the border crossing with incomplete papers, under a suspicion that may land her in jail! He forestalled this. And he had taken into account too that in June the mornings are bright; sunlight dances in the forests; the lakes gleam near Wendish Krakow and Plau: she was to see this as she left. Only when a conductor returned to her the ticket with its brown transverse stripe and its German Railway stamp as if she were a colleague—only then did it dawn upon her that Jakob had equipped her with a return ticket."

"Welcome to San Francisco, Gesine!"

And what are the Chinese up to in San Francisco?

Some are standing, flabbergasted, in an alley where you shoot with BB guns at moving targets, and watch a European woman tourist and an American child who exchange words in a foreign language. Now watch this: the woman walks to the stand, takes a gun, and in ten shots has earned an alarm clock, the grand prize. They applaud, free of envy, these spectators. That's what the Chinese are up to in San Francisco.

## August 16, 1968   Friday

To try to find a New York *Times* of current date in New Orleans means *chercher une aiguille dans une botte de foin*, which rougly translated means searching for a needle in a haystack; it may be encountered, like an exotic object, in a corner shop on Canal Street that offers for sale mainly foreign products of the printing press. It is dispensed at a ten-cent premium for the air freight. Its only news item for us: there was a fire in New York yesterday. Yesterday in the early afternoon a middling fire ate the elevated subway platform of Rockaway Park to a bald condition. This was where we had spent Tuesday with Jakob's letter from Olomouc in the C. S. S. R. Marie requested the sheet showing a photograph of the site of the fire (thus swelling our luggage), in order to prepare for a disputation about coincidence with D. E.; for when he would be home again.

Marie has fallen for the Chinese of San Francisco, for the sympathizing way the transient's eye watches the yellow and black and pink people deal with each other on the sidewalks and in the cable cars, where they make room for the stranger by merit of frailty and age, from a feeling of solidarity. A memory of Marie's had something to do with it too, the memory of a Sunday stroll in a New York July with D. E.; there she saw on top of a retaining wall of Riverside Park, next to a sheer drop of fifty feet, a prostrate citizen of dusky hue, with his eyes closed, sleeping in trustful reliance on the sunshine. "That's all we have achieved in this city!" a shamed and disappointed child summed up.

Over her enjoyment of the boats at Fisherman's Wharf it is easy to miss a bus, even a taxi to San Francisco airport; she approved the suggestion to make their route a triangular one. When a young lady escorted by an older one strides past a hotel porter equipped with no luggage except a ticking parcel, the house is honored to accommodate them for the night: if one puts on an air, that is, of doing this every day; "like D. E.!" exclaims the child, looking forward.

This Professor Erichson, who had parted from his existence in a northeast European neighborhood, Marie brings into play once more as she commands her mother for efficient rebooking of flight tickets: "as we learned it from him!" she insists. For his benefit she takes in New Orleans, hoping it might prove a strange place to him, so that she could tell him that you couldn't escape from this airport except in six-seater limousines, whose driver takes them—his last two guests— unasked, to a family boardinghouse between Canal Street and the Mississippi, fetching up against a narrow staircase with the shout: "Folks, I am bringing you somebody!" And again a hotel desk was astonished to see us actually copy our passport numbers into the register!

Provided we are irrevocably booked for a New York flight tomorrow morning, she is willing to tolerate a city on the Mississippi. Not that the river doesn't seem yellowish and dirty, and its harbor ferry a poor thing compared with the one in her city. The balcony verandas in the Vieux Carré, the ornamental wrought-iron grilles guarding the inner courtyards, and in them the magnolia trees with their long shiny leaves, the white and red blossoms—she looked upon all this as a quotation from that Europe which will move in on her with quite sufficient delay on Tuesday. She forbears to complain but does mention the heavy warm moisture, the cooler musty odor—of cemetery, since that's the way she is experiencing it. Mrs. Cresspahl shudders at the prospect of a discussion on coincidence, extended as it will be to intuition or premonition. What met with Marie's approval was a spacious hospital dating to the turn of the century, from which dignified citizens of dusky complexion issued with clouded brows. Newspapers printed on yellow and lavender paper; she likes them for their very novelty. The restaurants she finds grimy in the spots not currently in use; the frying surfaces gleam only at their front halves, don't get polished all over as in New York. Some streets, near Canal Street, are so wretchedly derelict that Mrs. Cresspahl too asked herself how one ever made one's way there—

surely not by plane. In a snack bar, a cat eagerly eyed Marie's double-decker sandwich; the child liked it.

On June 9, 1953, the Sachwalter of the East German Republic made a number of suggestions to its citizen Gesine Cresspahl concerning her possible return under his rod.

His party, the Caretaker explained, intended to renounce henceforward an inhuman one among its virtues: infallibility. It had indeed made mistakes. A consequence had been that numerous citizens had left the Republic. This applies to you, Miss Cresspahl.

Since the Party had gone so far as to set Peter Wulff's scales back to zero, as announced, to "zero gram!" as its zealous exclamation went, it would now overcome its reluctance and permit him to reopen the grocery shop adjacent to his tavern. It also planned to supply him with commodities. Further, he should not worry for the present about the delinquent taxes since 1951 and the Social Security contributions. We are finished with repressive measures, Mr. Wulff!

We now come to your other friends in the Republic, Miss Cresspahl. True to ourselves as we mean to be, we have converted a cooperative farm on the Baltic near Jerichow to the "devastated" category, so that no trustee would want to touch it with a ten-foot pole. If Mrs. Sünderhauf, Mr. Leutnant, Mrs. Schurig, Mrs. Winse with all the English offspring, Epi, Jesus, Huhn, and Häuneken, as well as those under eighteen, would like to reintegrate Johnny's experimental farm, their property would be returned to them and aid extended in the form of credits, equipment, and animals. How would you like that, Gesine Cresspahl?

We seriously intend to send your Georg Utpathel home from where he is serving his sentence, as we will others who were sentenced to only three years under the Law for the Protection of People's Property. We reserve action on those we hold guilty of graver injury, such as Johnny Schlegel, that notorious atheist and antiaristocrat. But perhaps we might be found willing to relent toward Otto Sünderhauf . . . ?

On your last visit to Wendisch Burg you were irate because we kept harassing a girl there, E. Rehfelde, because of her Lutheran faith and her adherence to the Church, until at last Klaus Niebuhr and his Ingrid Babendererde also renounced their graduation certificates, obviously thinking that, for their private consciences at least, this was the way to preserve equality before the constitution. The Rehfelde girl is to be readmitted to classes, Miss Cresspahl. If the students Niebuhr and Babendererde decide upon a return to Wendisch Burg, they shall be permitted to make up the senior examinations they missed. Well—what about it?

Now, turning to your own case, humanities major Cresspahl. We were making an exception when we admitted you to higher education. In the future, though, we plan to proceed this way with gifted young people from the intermediate social strata as a matter of policy. So, far from being handicapped, you may actually end up getting a tuition scholarship, Miss Cresspahl.

Regarding your father too, we would appreciate your acknowledging certain concessions we have in mind. The increment we added in April to food prices will be abolished as of June 15—as early as next Monday, that is. We shall also leave word with the Jerichow town hall that starting immediately Mr. Heinrich Cresspahl, Brickyard Path, is again entitled to coupons for rationed articles.

What do you have to say, young lady? Why not come? We shall consider you as merely returning from a vacation. Should we already have confiscated any of your things, we'll return them, or make restitution. Ration card, German I. D.—all will be yours. Please come accompanied by your friend Anita, Miss Cresspahl.

Thus some suggestions directed to Cresspahl's daughter by the East German Caretaker's Unity Party in case of her return.

Anita addressed envelopes for department stores and ad agencies for the holiday season, at one half pfennig West apiece, until she got in touch with parties who offered her one mark a page for translations from Russian. (Whatever humbug Huguenots they were had better be cloaked in silence; let us merely say that they wanted the work done for the Cultural Co-operation Desk of French Army headquarters in West Berlin. This must suffice.) Whenever Anita had free time, we had a standing appointment at Nicholassee elevated station to go to Wannsee Beach. We had to look sharp "to seek out the cheaper entertainments"; for movie or theater tickets we were too poor. Whether we were swimming up and down the Havel River or I was spending the night at Anita's in Neukölln on Mrs. Machate's ironing board, unfailingly Anita kept wondering that her friend Cresspahl had thought up yet another reason pointing to a rational way back to Jerichow or to Martin Luther University. Once she conjured up the news that in April all the Jewish physicians accused by Stalin of a conspiracy against the Soviet Union had been unconditionally restored to an unblemished professional and civic character. Might one not draw a line from this to the reinstatement of the rule of law in the East German Republic?

"Why don't you tell this to Kogan and Etlinger, the two who died under torture?" said Anita. "And to the Jewish writers he had shot as recently as last summer, the mad killer!" said Anita.

Stalin had died on March 6, the Cresspahl girl interjected mildly.

"And how did you feel when they showed the Moscow funeral rites in the movie theaters of Halle and about the East German mourning extravaganzas—lowered flags and inconsolable music?"

Cresspahl admitted that such sights had indeed caused her a sneaking sense of revulsion.

"So the demise of Stalin, which fills all of progressive humankind with such profound distress, is a particularly grave loss for the German nation? The Socialist Unity Party will always keep the faith with Stalin's victorious doctrine? Always?"

"There is such a promise," confessed Anita's friend.

At this point Anita could have said: You see! What did I tell you? But she abstained from giving advice. Out of solicitude she had the erratic Cresspahl child show her her papers and scrutinized them for gaps, for terms of validity. "Technically you would be safe on a trip to Halle until September 10," she decided, heaving a deep breath, almost a sigh. Anita and Luther's *On Christian Liberty*.

The undergraduate Cresspahl spent June 16 on the Havel River. On the 17th, as she meant to verify by personal inspection the radio news about an uprising in the eastern sector of the city, her streetcar, line 88, was stopped at Lützow Street, where it normally leaves Potsdamer Street to run parallel to the boundary of the eastern sector as far as Kreuzberg; stopped by West Berlin police, vainly trying to clear, one by one, in a southward direction, the streets jammed with sensation-hungry spectators. (She could not summon up the foolhardiness for a transit to East Berlin by the elevated; the station patrols might easily pack her off to Halle/Saale sooner than suited her.) Thus she knows about the uprising only as a news item, verbal and pictorial; by hearsay from Halle students who made it into the refugee camps of West Berlin:

In front of Penal Institution No. 11 on Stein Street, two or three hundred women stood and shouted, "Let our husbands go!" This was seen by a column of striking workers marching up from the synthetic-fuel plants of Buna and Leuna. They took the gate by storm, pulled the prisoners from their cells, many of them women, in deplorable physical condition. The workers proceeded to clear out the court building. A female guard waved her pistol and was beaten up. The Unity Party office on Willi Lohmann Street, the District Office on Stein Gate, the Provincial Office on the market square—all were taken by storm. At the gates of the "Red Ox" by the Church Gate, People's Police were waiting with guns at the ready. The crowd pushes a side door open, is fired on from the roof, disperses. Here, it is said, there were casualties. The Central Post Office has been held by the police since morning. By 6 P.M. 30,000 people have assembled at the Hall Market. The demands voiced by the speakers: general strike to be called against the Government; loyalty vis-à-vis the Red Army. Discipline. Punishment for hoarding, looting, killing. Resignation of the Government. Free elections. Reunification with West Germany. Toward 7 P.M. Russian tanks begin to roll up, cautiously. To join the papers that had sailed out of the windows of the liberated government buildings, there now flutters a leaflet signed by the garrison commander and the military commandant of the city of Halle (Saale), which proclaims a state of emergency, bans demonstrations and assemblies, sets a curfew for the hours between 9 P.M. and 4 A.M., and warns that armed force will be used in case of resistance.

A photograph exists of the march of the strikers, women and men, into Halle. It shows some ninety people completely, the women in summer dresses, the men mostly in working clothes, dark or gray overalls or shirts and pants. They are walking in irregular files, arms swinging, a few waving to each other (unaware of the camera). Two have come with bags. No fewer than eleven bicycles show in the picture. Why on earth would they have brought such costly gear if they had intended violence or expected to suffer it?

On June 21, the Central Committee of the East German Unity Party made an additional suggestion to Citizeness Cresspahl in case of her return: the uprising in her Republic must be taken for no more than a passing event, as the work of the American and (West) German warmongers, who, frustrated by the gains of the peace movement in Korea and in Italy, wanted to throw the torch of war across the Berlin bridgehead . . . unmasked now by the detection of bandits landed with arms and secret transmitters by foreign aircraft . . . by trucks loaded with weapons on the Leipzig-Berlin autobahn . . .

People wrote to her from Gneez that the workers of the Panzenhagen sawmill had opened up the notorious cellar of the District Court building shouting: "We want our bloodsuckers back!" She presumed to claim, in all modesty, that she had better visual knowledge of the workers than the East German Sachwalter could claim for himself; she knew their complaints: the revocation of rebates for railway tickets, bad blood in the family over the reduction of minimum pension rates, deduction of therapeutic-treatment periods from annual vacation time, pollution of working time by police snooping, the *travailler pour le roi de Russie*, illustrated that very morning of June 16 by the Unity Party's insistence on a 10 per cent increase in production norms. She might have gone back if everyone from Gneez to Halle had now been allowed to say: we have seen who rules this country—the Soviet Union. When she decided for departure, it was hardly because in the other Germany the Americans ruled as the occupying power; rather, she was afraid of being called on in a seminar of the university on the Saale to give as her opinion that on a certain date not the workers but . . .

Did she carry her person and case to the refugee camp at Berlin-Lichterfelde? Memory proffers this; insists on it. The writer of these lines is inclined to doubt that this camp was in operation as early as July 1953. Memory asserts that it had been under construction since March 4. Whether at Marienfelde, on Kuno Fischer Street, or on Carolingian Square, it was then that she met for the first time a young man from Wendisch Burg, a gaunt, steep-headed boy with, at that time, fair hair. In an abstracted way he sought acquaintance with her on the strength of social ties with the Babendererdes, both the fishermen and the teacher lines; also with the Niebuhrs of Wendisch Burg. On a stroll around Dahlem and its western university, he watched the local students with some disdain and talked of them as "all these beautiful young people." At first she took him for conceited because of his upperclassman's standing (physics). She described her astonishment at Klaus Niebuhr's giving up his school and his residence in Mecklenburg, impelled solely by his ethical sense to renounce his civil rights to rectify an insult against those of a girl named Rehfelde. Erichson (Dipl. Phys.) was pleased by this; instantly he brought a charge of similar conduct against Miss Cresspahl. "For five years you acquiesced in the distance between what you think and what the teaching institutions had the power up to now to exact from you. Now that the gap has grown a little wider than suits you, you are fed up. Ever heard of the third principle of dialectics, the transmutation of quantity to quality? This has its somatic uses too," he said in answer to her excuse that she was not feeling well. Scarcely a courtship, that. He had had himself flown out of Berlin before she had even reached Prelim Examination I of the Special Admittance process.

The official interviewing process for the recognition of refugee status became more repulsive from one office ("agency") to the next. The medical examiner found her to be the kind of twenty-year-old who caused him no headaches. The responsible authority was Agency 2, in charge of determining competence. After check-up by police and registration came Agency 7, the preliminary examination by the League to Combat Inhumanity. The student under scrutiny did not have the good fortune to please this body, or the next, which was the Investigating Committee of Jurists for Freedom; she considered them aides and abettors in the sentencing of Sieboldt and Gollantz. To make matters worse, she made fun of appeals like the one urging the people of the "Soviet Zone" to demonstrate their resistance by boycotting movie theaters on a certain Wednesday, whereupon, predictably, everyone crowded into the Renaissance Film Theater in Gneez in order to shore up their political reputations. Here, then, she received demerits, poor grades, and this was promptly noticeable at Agency 7c, the Police Commissioner's Office, Department V (Political Section), where their looks classified her as a poor as well as obstinate pupil. For hurdle 7, British Counterespionage, she got Anita to brief her with information about the forced-labor camp at Glowe on the Isle of Rügen, where some 4,000 convict workers, fed on margarine sandwiches and potato soup, slaved at a rail circuit line enclosing four runways for jet fighters and bombers, and a naval base for submarines and light surface craft; this was one of the rumors current in Mecklenburg. (To the detriment of Soviet strategy; Gesine was still upset by the Red propaganda altars at the corners of public squares, known as Stalin's icon corners. She and Anita were in agreement that the Soviet garrison had advanced their tanks on the 17th so cautiously mainly to bring up reserve equipment and troops for a brutal strike, if that were called for.) Alas, the rumor proved well known to the British gentleman in the wooly chin beard; he made a gesture of regret with his pipe. The recording secretary, who wore nine rings too many for her twenty-five years, gazed with prescient gloating, not with fellow feeling, at the child from Mecklenburg who was trying to buy backing toward refugee status with such deflated currency. The next inquiry aimed at those members of Fritz Reuter High School in Gneez who had volunteered for service in the Armed People's Police.

The subject of the interrogation twisted her testimony away to Martin Luther University in Halle, where students of all academic divisions may keep their noses clean by exercising with small-caliber rifles and radio installations in the terrain near the banks of the Saale. She then pleaded indisposition and was sternly admonished to put in an appearance for a resumption of her examination.

Once outside, in a strangely intact neighborhood of private houses and unwalked sidewalks, where only now and then a maid would walk a dog, she was alone with her fear that she might have been of little use to the convict Lockenvitz and be about to do injury to N. C. O. Pagenkopf. If this was the price to be paid for an exit to West Germany, she would rather slip across where no one was looking.

Anita found it, the crooked by-path through the bushes. Did her friend Gesine know of the attorney on Lietzenburger Street who had paid off debts by installments for Johnny Schlegel?

In this way Gesine Cresspahl came by a new-resident's permit for the Land of West Berlin—out of turn, to be sure. Thus she was allowed to register with an ordinary police precinct (instead of the Political Section of Department V) as a permanent resident of the borough of Grunewald. Whoever has a file card there has a right to the I. D. card of West Berlin. With what was left of a loan of 120 marks—the ticket cost over 80—she flew as a private individual to Frankfurt/Main in the third week of July, in a Douglas Clipper, Type 3, at night.

Under the wings of the DC-10 on the way from New Orleans to N. Y. C., one's imagination may now make out the Atlantic and the island barrier far to seaward, the whitish shelf of land where Mrs. Cresspahl attempted to vacation the year before. Marie, looking ahead instead of downward, sees the islands of the Dutch States-General, Manhattan, Long Island.

"Welcome home, Gesine!"

## August 17, 1968  Saturday, South Ferry Day

At Riverside Drive a single cable was waiting in Mr. Robinson Eagle Eye's care. Definitely sent from Helsinki, signature badly garbled: FIT FOR TRANSPORT PRESENTLY STOP ERISINION.

At breakfast a cable from Helsinki. VISIT UNNECESSARY STOP ERISINN. By ordinary mail, a letter with German stamps, official-looking: from the Research Institute for Psychoanalysis at Frankfurt/Main. Deducting the time lost in the mail, this answer arrived within less than four weeks. A professor taking the trouble to write an employee named Cresspahl a three-and-a-half-page letter, on his private stationery!, in his own time.

And has never had the pleasure of making my personal acquaintance (as he wishes to say in all sincerity after reading my letter). He must decline diagnosis at a distance, because of incomplete information, too narrow a base of judgment; nor had she asked for one. But he is ready to offer comments.

If I hear the voices of dead persons, of absent people, and if they answer me, this may be due to "an innate personal predisposition to this kind of experience. (Please extract from my inferences only what may happen to be helpful to you.) A firm bond must exist between this person and her past; that she has put it behind her is out of the question. In assuming that we are dealing with the consequences of hurts, of losses, she is on the right track. But in thinking of Jakob, of Cresspahl, in this connection, she is in error. In actual fact, it started with her mother, who deranged herself out of mind and world. We are talking about you, you Lisbeth née Papenbrock! Alienation, yes; not a figment of delusion. It's just that you have not come to terms with it, the first rejection by your mother (the second, the third). No risk of this being a hereditary trait. One thing, though, is amiss, Mrs. Cresspahl: that you sometimes know your child's answer before Marie has spoken it. This can be an egoistic maneuver, seeking to protect the child, and, in her, yourself. For the child such a symbiosis might be an imminent danger; it hampers her independence. You yourself in your letter used a term for illegal activity which gave you away, Mrs. Cresspahl.

"What you need is the considerable courage to renounce safety devices, even though this might appear as inexcusable negligence, considering what your life has been. You might save time by calling on the services of a—I know you have the word at the tip of your tongue—'head shrinker.' The cutting edge of this headhunter metaphor, however, is directed less at my American colleagues than at yourself; by this allusion you keep yourself from benefiting from a medical service that might lead you to more up-to-date inner security. Such an experiment would be harmless; you would be free to break it off at any point. With kind regards, your A. M."

What he clearly had left out was a reservation concerning inability to work. To judge by my epistolary persona I am still equipped and ready for a foreign assignment, in Prague.

"My dear Professor: It is with some embarrassment that I find myself unable to express my . . ." Serves you right, Gesine Cresspahl. You asked for something difficult, so now rack your brain over the thank-you letter. In three weeks you'll get it done.

At breakfast, the New York *Times*'s news report from Bonn: The West Germans have given another thought to the agreement of September 29, 1938, inherited by them, according to which Messrs. Chamberlain, Daladier, and Mussolini made a present of the Sudetenland to Herr Hitler. Hitherto the formula was to have read "no longer in force." Now perhaps the C. S. S. R. side will get its way, and a signature under the wording "void from its inception."

After Marshal Tito, it is now the President of Romania who is visiting Prague, and Nicolae Ceausescu lets them in on it: a small Communist country, provided it does not loosen its military tie, is absolutely free to seek credits in convertible currency. If, the third day from now, the lady delegated by a New York bank makes an appearance in the capital of a minor Communist country—what of it?

"Now about the undergraduate Cresspahl at a West German university," Marie ordered as soon as she had finished supervising the casting-off of the ferry. "Stud. phil. G. C. at a university . . . what names do they give them in Germany?"

"One was named after Johann Wolfgang von Goethe; it was located in Frankfurt/Main and willing to sign on this rising second-year student from Halle/Saale for the English seminar. (Because I had once been matriculated, you see? Anita's high-school certificate counted for little in the West of Berlin; she had to take a full senior finals 'make-up.') When I saw the schedule of tuition and fees, I gave up."

"You father had Western currency! A few thousand pounds with the Surrey Bank of Richmond, with interest accumulated since 1938!"

"I had left Cresspahl's country, left him, against his will. Think how much more unreasonable I will be when you leave me! Also, he may easily have thought that his balance there had been confiscated as enemy property."

"Your father meant to punish you."

"That would have meant that he hoped to get me back. No, she was to have her way and cut her cloth accordingly. And as for academic work, she had gained insight into herself."

"That was a pity, if you ask me."

"Dr. Gesine Cresspahl—what a joke!"

"Professor Cresspahl—I could live with that."

"Yes—with Marie as first name! Why don't *you* become a professor?"

"Remains to be seen."

"What job can you get with a degree in English?"

"Teaching."

"Any desire for such a profession had been driven out of me in the socialist high school of Gneez. To stand in front of a class with the knowledge one is hiding something, suspected of lying by the students; I meant to spare myself that."

"In a free country you were allowed to teach whatever you wanted."

"Grammar, metrics, the forms, certainly. But no analysis of the content with the kind of dialectic that made sense to me, in 1953! Anyway, all I wanted really was the language."

"Because of your father . . . What did you use for money, Gesine? Here you arrive with 5 marks in your pocket. A dollar and twenty-five cents."

"More like seventy-five cents, probably. The student Cresspahl would have worked in the kitchen of that institution, been glad to. But it would have made the rounds among the 1,500 takers of courses: as a thing that wasn't done. To give you my version of the dishwasher legend: Evenings, in Mannheim, the student Cresspahl manned a checkroom counter and said thank you for every dime put into her plate. Visiting from school came the Rhine maidens, heiresses from the great houses of Düsseldorf or from South America, who even in their third term of English studies considered it a brilliant joke to say 'yes, yes,' or 'I don't have it necessary' for 'I can do without.' They complained to the management: in a night-club, glasses should be washed in public. Her next job was the night shift in a factory that made toys and garden gnomes. And if a faculty member needed something typed, or translated, be sure to apply to Miss Cresspahl. She asks a healthy hourly rate, but what she turns out is ready for the boss. At a later point she was in demand in that northern quarter of Frankfurt where the streets are named for writers, from Franz Kafka by way of Franz Werfel and Stefan Zweig to Platen; that is where the families of the American occupants lived. They went out at night and had their children looked after by a Miss Cresspahl for German currency. She for her part wanted to learn nursery rhymes from the children, and fairy tales, and how you say Auf die Plätze—fertig—los! to start a race. And in her last semester, when she felt assured of her diploma, she was deemed worthy of pay for supervising lab classes."

"You were starving again, Gesine!"

"My own fault! I needed a typewriter, badly. Starved the scientific way, with cottage cheese and rye bread every two hours; with gymnastics you can do it."

"And with two cigarettes a day."

"Smoking was out till 1955."

"And homesickness for Jerichow, for Gneez."

"I had watched the 1953 May Day parade in Gneez, Armed People's Police marching past the reviewing stand on New Market, arms swinging in brownish uniforms, legs in those costly parade boots (and holding fast to their carbine straps, to keep from falling); next the comrade from the District Office screamed, as if he had knife blades on his vocal cords: 'And though today we still talk of the Dü-Dü-Äh'—his D. D. R. the 'German Democratic Republic'—'by next May we shall be able to say Geh-Düdü-Äh!' To me this was a belated decoding of Goethe's words as displayed, centered on a vertical axis, on purely academic occasions on the front wall of our assembly hall:

I HAVE NO FEAR THAT GERMANY MIGHT NOT BECOME ONE; OUR
GOOD HIGHWAYS AND THE RAILWAYS TO COME ARE BOUND TO

CONTRIBUTE WHAT THEY CAN. BUT ABOVE ALL LET HER BE ONE
IN MUTUAL LOVE.

The comrade's acronyms had been notice given of civil war between
the Germanys; should I have felt homesick for that? All-German Democratic Republic, that's what his letters stood for, achievable only by
force of arms. Commenting on this, the student Lockenvitz quoted
what he had found in Voltaire on the Holy Roman Empire."

"That it is not an empire nor Roman nor holy. I did my homework.
And yet you did go to see Jerichow."

I once went on a visit to the north; it was at Whitsun, and among
a slowly crawling procession of urban excursionists my eyes fixed on
the gray sea under an overcast sky, above the radiant yellow of rape
blossom and rain-deep meadow green, on the horizon a strikingly
straight line of land; from the harbor in the evening, the northernmost
stretch of the Mecklenburg coast, blue flecked with white, a hand's
width to look at; next to it, the sea turned inward at Greater and Lesser
Höved bays, behind which, approximately, lay Jerichow. Behind the
sharp angle of the coast at land's end one could look over into the bay,
the west side at right, and across from it, unconnected, the east side
under the inky wind-chased clouds, irregular, with peaks like promon-
tories on a steep shore, coves like harbors, needle-fine points like stee-
ples, cracks like guard boats in ambush. When I close my eyes, the
memory is precise. That similar, that alien drone."

"In 1954 you turned . . . you reached your majority, Gesine."

"Twenty-one years old. And was sent a sealed little package via
Johnny Schlegel's attorney in West Berlin, acting on behalf of Dr.
Werner Jansen, attorney in Gneez, Mecklenburg, in pursuance of a
testamentary disposition by Dr. Avenarius Kollmorgen."

"Don't you dare keep mum about what was in it."

"I'd certainly like to."

"You've got to tell."

"Because it was a pair of gold rings. 'On your majority, my dear
Miss Cresspahl, the undersigned makes bold to lay at your feet . . .
Given the fact that I myself, owing to the intervention of adverse
circumstances . . . any matrimonial attachment whatsoever, if only it
be of your choosing . . . Assuring you of a devotion which . . .' A
whole stratum of language went to the grave with Kollmorgen."

"Wedding rings. From the grave."

"Those are . . . the ones for you. Yours."

"As if I would every marry, Gesine!"

"That's just what the people around me always said about me. Keep that in mind."

"No thought of a return to Jerichow or Halle/Saale."

"No—the radio saw to that. 'The Soviet Union has invented penicillin.' Some disk jockey once announced a certain medley with a sigh: 'One American in Paris—ah, how wonderful it would be!' Over his own brilliance in persiflage he missed the obvious retort; how desirable it would be to have only one Soviet person in the East German Republic, and know him to be on a Baltic vacation near Ahlbeck. As if they had hoped to win on wavelengths! As if they felt strong enough to divide the sky."

"What party were you for in West Germany, Gesine? You had freedom of choice, didn't you?"

"In 1954 the Social Democrats in Berlin declared their resolve, at a Party congress!, under certain conditions to participate in joint efforts to safeguard peace and defend freedom, even by military means."

"Knowing you, I suppose that blew your lid."

"Well, well! You actually know me. The President of the Federal Republic of Germany was a Free Democrat who in 1933 had propped up Hitler by supporting the Enabling Act that strangled the Weimar Republic. Now he advised his fellow citizens to 'deal with,' 'come to terms with,' 'get the better of' their past; and since this was no piece of work or material . . ."

"To accomplish. To master."

". . . only the active verbs 'defeat' and 'subjugate' were left. He abstained from public 'dealing with' where his own person was concerned. The Chancellor was of the Christian Democrats—what an expression—and kept a little dog which was allowed to sing out 'Hear, hear' each time he talked in the Bundestag of a 'restoration of German unity in freedom'; thus he did on June 17. With his other hand, though, he drew his republic into the steely embrace of a supranational mining concern and chained it tightly to a military organization named after the North Atlantic. There was a patriotic song aimed at it; it premiered on May 16, 1950, in Munich."

"Gesine, I wish I weren't quite so inhibited."

"Here we have a child who is embarrassed for her mother on a sparsely occupied ferry where she knows no one among the tourists."

"O.K. If this is part song, I'll take the alto part."

"On your mark—Get set—GO: 'Oh mein Papa / war eine wunderbare Clown / o mein Papa / war eine grosse Kinstler! / Oh mein Papa / Wie war er prächtig anzuschaun . . .'"

"Slandering the state. Punishable."

"In East Germany, definitely. In the West, whoever chanted this with tears of pious devotion was unaware for whom he was praying."

"Gesine, this was to be your homeland!"

The student Cresspahl had tried to think it so, ever since she had been living as an employee in Düsseldorf, in a furnished room near the Flingern-North post office. Her landlady, a widow, functioned as the treasurer of her local Communist group and was grouchy with the renter who had washed her hands of her Party comrades in East Germany; she banned gentleman callers. The disinherited child was not looking for callers; she divided her evenings between the Central Swimming Pool on Grün Street and the State Library on Grabbe Square, where the people were solicitous of a customer who ordered back issues of newspapers by the year, in proper sequence. She read up on the time dodged since 1929; reading, reading, as though after a malignant disease. She regarded Düsseldorf as a terminus, tried to get used to those smoothly integrated house fronts. She held small change in readiness on November 10, when the children went lantern-walking for St. Martin, yet wished she were out of town the next day, when the carnival started. She detoured around the cartwheelers. She dutifully read up on Jan Wellem and Immermann; she started a collection under the heading "Welcome to the New Home: Düsseldorf at the Turn of the Century." She went to Kaiserswerth on foot, found a touch of Jerichow in a shed painted oxblood red, the unharnessing place of an inn in a decayed garden. In a pub she saw a master craftsman's diploma hung on a wall, sporting a swastika in the official seal; in great secrecy she stuck a stamp over it, which at least had the virtue of showing the head of the notorious traitor who was President of this country.

*"Did you see how that man told off the waiter? Has a photo shop now. If we had won the war he would be sitting pretty now. He shot up 64 tanks, that fellow. One day he got ten with fourteen grenades and cracked open a pocket. Has the Knight's Cross, and they gave him a land grant in Bohemia, too. He just let them come eyeball to eyeball, using the earlier wrecks for cover. His turret gunner, he lost his marbles. Rage, that's what it was, not courage. He is a nice guy, not at all conceited. You are so silent, Miss Cresspahl"*

*"With this kind of talk I can't swallow, even if I were hungry. Many thanks for the invitation . . . I must go now."*

Düsseldorf became home as soon as the name Cresspahl was linked with the door of a lockable apartment and a telephone of her own. The associated British and American military, on whose behalf a civilian employee was negotiating in a forest near Mönchen-Gladbach with local German officials over the assessment of maneuver-damage compensation, wanted her in safekeeping and reachable. Nothing but a converted attic, a spacious room with a small bedroom and a kitchen; all windows looking skyward. Düsseldorf-Bilk—that was my neighborhood, sitting between pincers of wheel and rail racket, from streetcars and the railway line to Krefeld and Cologne. Near Old St. Mary's; a daily sight, the plaque commemorating THE OBSERVATORY OF BILK, WHICH PERISHED IN THE NIGHT OF JUNE 11 TO 12, 1942; balanced on the median axis. In a house that had brows over its windows and two balconies; veritable cocked eyebrows. Close by small parks, pump rooms, the South Cemetery for walks; a few streets north, the Municipal Swimming Bath on Konkordia Street. What the apartment still needed when Jakob came to Düsseldorf, that he plastered, screwed in, pasted, and varnished. For Jakob's benefit I splurged on a yellow silk blouse with a loosely hanging collar and long bows—although I knew that this would be wasted on him: he looks me in the face.

"First you surely must go on a visit to Jerichow!"

"Who told you . . . There is only one person who claims that I got off the train on an official trip down the East German rail link to Berlin, breaking the law, and sneaked through the woods to Jerichow. To you, I'll admit it. I had to pay for it. I got myself into the sort of environment that Jakob wanted to shield me from. There was a Mr. Rohlfs, who wanted to talk with me about Jakob; he had me in his files, too, from Gneez to Berlin-Grunewald to the forest near Mönchen-Gladbach. It bothers me to think how completely we all counted on Jakob!"

"How did my father like it in Düsseldorf, in the West?"

"He couldn't care less. What he wanted to know was whether I was making sure of my eight hours of sleep every night; came along on my daily walk to the bus I took to work; asked when I had last had a dental appointment. From Mecklenburg he brought me a scarf, of all things! When I got home near Old St. Mary's at Bilk, Jakob had made me sausage à la Jerichow; think of the man frying and baking away with blood and flour, raisins, marjoram, thyme, and apple slices, so his Gesine might eat one more time as his mother used to make it! Once he knew his way around the delis on Düsseldorf's Count Adolf Street, no sign of envy. To be sure, ten kinds of bread any and every day; he wished his country could have the same—or, rather, the country from which he came. When we passed a construction site and watched bricks being unloaded as gently as if they were china, wrapped in strong paper and tied up six times over, he sighed. And of course he grumbled that the railway in the western republic was running its express trains with just one engineer. Or because the trains eased into motion softly, without warning. He was just visiting, on account of Cresspahl's daughter. There were things that amused him. A cheerful old lady, her rear expanded by the ticket booth, strutting down the aisles before the main feature with an atomizer to give the patrons a last numbing anesthetic. Humphrey Bogart in *The Desperate Hours*, on a day like any other. The words people had fit to the signature tune of North German Radio: 'Are your dues still unpaid?' Two children quarreling: Persian lamb, that's just a sheep; sheep yourself, my mother has one. Depressed he was, though it showed only in a shudder of his shoulders, by the performance of a character actor exiled from the G. D. R., who, in a movie ad, commuted a telephone conversation to a demonstration and eulogy of a shaving machine, all for filthy lucre. When Jakob recognized something familiar in me, smiling wrinkles would creep to the corners of his eyes; as when I asked for the bill without consulting him at the Park Hotel on Düsseldorf's Cornelius Square, same as at Pottel & Broskowsky's on Orphanage Ring in Halle. He was in my town; he was my guest."

"He could have stayed."

"What we discussed for the next year and beyond, up to 1983, projections into the invisible, arrangements for a potential future—all these are now like tales, tales about little children falling into a water butt; whether someone comes and rescues them hangs by the thread of a minute."

"Knowledge is power, Gesine. Tell me about it."

"He takes a train back to the eastern side of the Elbe, in the morning haze crosses a network of tracks he has been in charge of for two years, is caught by a marshaling train, dies under the knife. Cresspahl took care of the funeral and notified Mrs. Abs and his daughter only when Jakob was under the ground. This proved a healthy thing for one, an injury for the other. The one missed the time for killing herself; she wanted to put her house in order, clear the decks first. This is one of the ruses of fate, to make sure someone survives. When suicide was forbidden me, it had almost left my mind."

"Who has any business forbidding you things, Gesine?"

"A strong person. When I poked a finger into her palm, she made a fist. A yard high, with nothing to hold on to, she hung by her firm grasp. A contented person, slept extensively, woke up with soft guttural coos. Four weeks later she looked at me with a look of trust. By the third month she knew my voice—and returned the smile of a Communist widow of Flingern-Nord. By October 1957 she listened to me, signaled agreement with her voice. On St. Martin's Day she turned her head to where my voice came from. By Christmas she turned both eyes, focused, in the same direction. By the New Year she begins to talk, committing herself to the conventional ya, ya, my my; gives a friendly but distant look at her grandmother. In February she laughed at a bottle tipping over, although it was her own. She is proud of her toys, conscious of possessing. In April she hid under my apron when Cresspahl entered the room. In May she tried to stand up. By June she knew the way to South Cemetery, to the Court Park; tossed toys out of her crib to make her mother bring them back to her. In July she knew how to crawl over steps, stood up straight for some moments, knew her name."

"It almost sounds as if you had liked me."

"For you, the difference between good and evil was abolished; which is why in North German mothers call their children 'my heartbeat.' We lived in symbiosis—if you'll kindly look that up; it's something we plan to abolish. You got sick any time I was a little under the weather."

"Knowledge is power, Gesine. Go ahead and tell it if you like."

"When we passed our house, the one with the cocked eyebrows, in September, the instruments were sharpened, the patient prepped. A house trailer stood at the curb, a yellow signboard hung on the front-yard fence. The next day wreckers knocked out the house's teeth, carried windows and doors carefully aside—the reusable items. Then they saw through the house's bones, break its spine, separate it from its neighbor; the neighbor plays deaf. A red-and-white poster appears on every door flanking the victim. At 11 A.M. the house collapses into itself of a blast wound, turning into a pile so little you wouldn't believe it. Splintered beams still stare from it and ruined balcony railings; the dust tastes of air raid. Two Caterpillar power shovels are drawn up to move the rubble, two hauling trucks put in place. Almost to the last, the wrought-iron fence is whole—until it is smashed and swept away in a single bat of a shovel. A young tree gets entangled in this; it is dealt a kick at its root, and is gone. The bared walls of the adjacent house look so unsheltered with their three blocked door breachings, it seems to shiver in the sunlight. Up there in the shimmering air, that's where I lived with Jakob."

"What was my sickness?"

"You caught a fever. 102°; it meant to be stronger than the medicines. Two days you were unconscious. When you woke up, there was Cresspahl at your bedside once more, inspecting his heiress."

"You are first in line, surely."

"Jakob's child—she had priority. For the sake of such a Marie of Jakob's lineage, Cresspahl committed a transgression. By an East German law people were arrested and sentenced if Agency 12 found in their letters abroad any complaints touching on the Sachwalter's wisdom; how much greater threats attended any private foreign-exchange transaction! Instead of registering the account he had at the Surrey Bank of Richmond with the Internal Revenue in Gneez or the East German post office, Cresspahl went to West Berlin to see an attorney on Lietzenburger Street, who also counsels Inge Schlegel, and drafted a letter in English for him. To Jerichow came a postcard with Easter greetings, signed by Anita; its wording is couched for the censorship. Decoded: from Richmond in England a bank reports with some relief (bankers have human feelings too, believe you me!) that a certain Mr. Cresspahl is ready to acknowledge ownership of all those pounds sterling which have waited in its vaults since 1939, with interest and compound interest, unfrozen three years ago and now at the free disposal of former enemy aliens. Cresspahl, at his almost sixty-ninth year, boards an airplane for the first time in order to take a statement of account to Düsseldorf. That was the first half. From Düsseldorf, Cresspahl betook himself to the aforementioned office in the forest near Mönchen-Gladbach, identified himself by means of that halfpenny, mint year 1940, on the obverse a high-spirited caravel, on the reverse GEORGIUS VI DEO GRATIA REX FIDEI DEFENSOR. Honesty and good faith were reinstated: Cresspahl's thirty shillings were paid over to him. That was the other half. Cresspahl, citizen of East Germany, in a will made in Düsseldorf sank two great piles of pounds sterling into a strongbox, made of rods of the Law, which neither I nor you can crack; possibly a guardian invested with testamentary authority could."

"Who is my guardian, besides you?"

"At present you must make do with me."

"I would like your Erichson."

"He . . . has enough on his shoulders. Would you approve Anita?"

"After I have talked it over with D. E., perhaps. Did I show hostility toward my grandfather?"

"At first you were intimidated by such a black overcoat from the year 1932; until you took a liking to the velvet lapels. Soon you found it fun to imitate us and, sitting down opposite him and me, crossed your legs, folded your hands, looked resigned, and let your head drop to express sadness. Cresspahl was embarrassed to have distressed a child by his expression; he held his hands out for you, a spacious tough carpenter's claw, and you whacked it with your cat's-paw fist. You went to sleep without fear when he told you about the days when the devil was still a small boy and had to get kümmel for his grandmother."

"And my own grandmother? For whom I'm named?"

"Mrs. Abs was now afraid of a Jerichow where a Mr. Rohlfs with his State Security badge could take her aside and interrogate her about a Gesine Cresspahl; she remained in Hanover. She had an invitation to come to Düsseldorf to stay, but only paid a visit. So your daytime upbringing came from a kindergarten instead of a grandmother. She looked at you, Jakob's child; her eyes flowed over. She was worried that her grieving might be bad for you. She wanted to live and die alone and lies buried behind the Palace in Hanover."

"Why is this missing from my memory?"

"Because it was kept from you."

"Why did Cresspahl go back to Jerichow? He could have stayed here with us, couldn't he?"

"When it comes to dying, we are all masters and apprentices. He wanted to get through it alone. Not for anything be a burden to anyone, even if it be his own daughter. He kept his promise; he took Joche and Muschi Altmann into the two rooms that had been under German Railways management on Jakob's account. There was no danger

*that I drop dead here and never a one sees me sitting,*
the old folk looking white in the featherbed."

"Am I going to be a woman of property at my majority?"

"Good for five years of university study, anyway."

"And yet, Gesine . . . you were free to use it at a proper time."

"For myself it would have been three times too much. However, he let me share in it: for the child. A child who has been thrown back with her mother into sublet rooms, because business in the inner cities of West Germany is knocking over what the bombs have spared; how can a grandfather allow this to happen? He furnished a garden apartment at Lohaus Dike; for the child's sake. He paid the rent for a year in advance, because her mother was beginning yet another apprenticeship, in a bank; for the child's sake."

"He should have given you a car."

"I bought one for myself when you began to talk; more satisfaction in it that way. From a big dealer, who boosted his chariots with the sign of the (second) hand. A car was a must. Incomprehensible today."

"We were on our way to Denmark."

"You spoke Italian when you were little, and French."

"Never to England. Because of your father."

"If I knew the obstacle, I would show it to you."

"The vacations in London with D. E., they cured you."

"Thanks, Doc."

"Now I want to remonstrate with you, seriously. Düsseldorf has become your city, as Berlin has Anita's."

"Or as the Niebuhrs think about Stuttgart."

"When you feel like a treat, you go and have a meal at the Central Station restaurant. When a new bridge is inaugurated in Düsseldorf and named for a Federal President, you grumble at the old gentleman and go to see it. It is your bridge. What Heinrich Heine wrote about Düsseldorf you approve, with bells on. You are ashamed for this town when it disavows this Heine. All of a sudden you pull up your socks and off you go to America, a helpless infant under your arm! Gesine!"

"The person involved was the employee Cresspahl. This person had to display the proper gratitude for praise and the favor of two years of advanced training offered her at a bank in Brooklyn, N. Y., which was 'on friendly terms' with her employers in Düsseldorf. Docility brings its rewards; this might delay her dismissal. For the sake of etiquette she reacted a little coyly, but privately she was relieved."

"To this day you have let me believe that New York was my decision!"

"It is your blueprint. Crédit Lyonnais or a Milan bank, I didn't care. I wanted to get out of the country for a while. In 1959, on Christmas Eve, in Cologne, that is, next door, a synagogue had been besmirched with swastikas and slogans: 'Germans demand: out with the Jews.' Dora Semig had filed for a judgment to have her husband declared legally dead: he was enjoined to report to Municipal Court in Hamburg by September 2, 1960, failing which the writ would be granted. That was one thing."

"Plenty for me."

"Another thing was the career of a politician in the West German Republic. Now I am going to bore you."

"You say that just so I can never deny that you told me so, and on board a South Ferry in New York Harbor, headed for Manhattan, in the afternoon, to be precise."

"Try to bear it. As a young man he was a member of the Nazi student organization. At twenty-two he applied for admission to their Motorized Corps, fulfilling these conditions: political reliability and willingness to engross himself ever more deeply in the substance of National Socialist ideology. During the war he was 'military morale and leadership officer' with an antiaircraft school in Bavaria; prerequisite: National Socialist activism. After the war he posed as a resistance fighter and played a decisive role in the 'denazification' process in the district of Schongau, where he was district commissioner. In 1947 he exclaimed at a public meeting: 'Anyone willing to take rifle in hand yet again, let his hand wither!' Since 1957 he has been denying that this ever passed his lips. He was then a West German minister of defense. When in April 1957 eighteen scientists from Göttingen University warned against equipping the Federal Army with nuclear weapons, he called one of them 'unworldly'; he himself is a high-school graduate. The professor of physics and Nobel Prize laureate Otto Hahn was described by him at the Press Club of the capital as 'an old duffer who can't restrain his tears and can't sleep at night when he thinks of Hiroshima.' In June 1957 fifteen recruits drowned in the Iller River during an exercise for which they had been inadequately trained. The responsible minister, far from resigning, celebrates his wedding the next day, orders up a platoon of almost wartime strength in steel helmets and white leather trim for an escort—and stays away from the obsequies of the victims. The same year produced this odd dictum from him: While he was not a conscientious objector, he was nevertheless no coward. The following year, on April 29, 1958, he provided a national hero to the West German Republic: the policeman Siegfried Hahlbohm was doing traffic duty at the intersection in front of the Federal chancellery in Bonn when the Minister's driver, ignoring the officer's hand signal, crossed, forcing a streetcar to come to an abrupt halt. Hahlbohm reported the driver (who had five previous citations) for four counts of traffic violation and two infractions of the Criminal Code, item 'Causing Traffic Hazards.' The Minister pledges to remove this man from the intersection; when his efforts become public, he talks of 'treasonable breach of security.' In October 1959 a meeting of 'organized Knight's Cross wearers' is held at Regensburg; the Minister sends them three Bundeswehr officers, along with salutes and music. In 1961 he vilifies a political opponent, an emigrant of the thirties, as follows: 'But one question one may surely ask of you: what were you doing in the twelve years outside; just as we were asked what we had done in the twelve years inside.' By the time I read this I was already in New York, relieved to have moved out of this Minister's reach. The day after, he 'bestows upon' his officers a 'full dress suit' with ornamental braid loops or 'Brandeburgs,' better known in Hitler's armies as 'monkey swings,' and prescribes for the other ranks a belt buckle engraved with the words from the anthem: unity and law and freedom. Next he tries to destroy— by denunciations, by lies—a West German news magazine, whose editors had undertaken a conscientious probe of his financial and official conduct. Before the West German Bundestag he knowingly testifies to untruth: 'This is no act of revenge on my part. I have nothing to do with this affair, literally not a thing.' At this point he has to step out of the Government for a while; but in 1966 a German administration found him good enough again to be appointed minister of finance. That man cannot get a hunting license without dirty work and cheating; and now this same man wants to become chancellor of West Germany and get nuclear arms under his red button. Voices in the Bundestag have warned: anyone who talks like the Federal Minister of Defense would shoot too."

"These are simply bad manners, Gesine."

"If I were ever tempted to feel nostalgic about West German policy, I'd hang up a picture of that one."

"Doesn't he get a name?"

"He deserves the bad name he has acquired."

"Now we are in March 1961, on our way to New York City."

"Since the employee Cresspahl had shown herself complaisant, she was granted four weeks' vacation prior to leaving. So we moved in on Anita in Berlin."

"Where one has to watch what one says. You buy a superlong sausage and promptly they ask you whether you are caring for a family of four. Was I proud of my mother when she shot back: No, I am founding a hermitage! Berlin, city of airplanes."

"Airplanes above the chattering skylights, fitting themselves into ruin gaps between the roofs, shearing ridgepoles, adjoining themselves to spire, high rise, rain. On gardens, stadiums, parks, streets, balconies—everywhere airplanes gazed down, veered off, sent others. Invisibly high but far-seeing, the jet fighters of the Red, the Red-Is-Beautiful, the Krasnaya Armiya squeezed through the sound barrier and flung out that punching, rocking, breath-stopping boom. As we took off for Paris, we saw Anita on her forlorn balcony, waving."

"And now aboard the *France,* off to New York!"

"That's all very well, yet I know of a child who much later could still make a sketch of how the furniture was placed by the garden windows in Düsseldorf. Who was close to tears when she thought back to a child's birthday, when a chorus sang: Now you are three! Now you are three!"

"In New York I turned four. Finally we have arrived where my memory knows its way around. Welcome home!"

Cresspahl's daughter was living in New York when he died in the fall of 1962. America is too far away to me for thought. Four and seventy is enough.

He tried to go to sleep lying on his back. He meant to be found near enough to morning. They were to have no trouble with the rigid body because it was positioned differently from how it would have to fit in the coffin. They used to break bones in such cases in the old days. But going to sleep turned him on the side, even though only his head. In the morning, when the night thinned in his brain, the skull turned the nose upright. Soon he felt himself carried, slightly canted by the narrowness of the inner door on the way to the outer, at length in the cool winter sun that was striped by the bare hedgerows. The jolting on the pavement sent gentle waves of blood behind his forehead, as he heard old Dr. Prüss say: With this kind of illness the prognosis is uncertain.

This morning the sleeping daughter once again watched herself get up, swing hand over hand out of the window onto Riverside Drive, across the green-patinaed bridge parapet to the street below. In obedience to the doctor's instructions she wore only a coat over her shift. She pulled the car door closed as noiselessly as a thief, let the wheels roll eastward to the entrance of the tunnel under Broadway, which in daylight is crossed by the subway. By this time she was being escorted by black-lacquered limousines of state; trapped. The journey slid on as smoothly as on rails; she merely had to press the deadman's button. When she had arrived under the cemeteries, she found a circular cavity hollowed out and lined with concrete, articulated by clinic doors. Behind the first one was the linen room; there she was to change for the operation. Along the inner arc of the corridors the doors reappeared, were called Heart, Lungs, Kidneys. Blood. At the last one they handed her a light package, the remains of the section.

The day to be begun once more.

At 5 A.M., WNBC broadcasts popular works by Mozart and Haydn. At 6, WNYC ripostes with Brahms's Requiem and Schubert.

A day free of work. On which Marie wants to give a party for children; a good-by party.

## August 19, 1968   Monday

Issue No. 40,385 of the New York *Times*.

News from Bogotá, Jerusalem, Iraq, Cairo, La Paz, Peking, Biafra, London. Given this, who would doubt the completeness of its coverage? Early yesterday a passenger train of the Long Island commuter line was shot at; one young man killed, another wounded.

*Pravda* has given us to understand what it wishes to be accepted as valid truth from Moscow: If workers in Prague have petitioned for a longer stay of Soviet troops in the country, they are subjected to "moral terror." At every corner in Prague agitators hold forth, demonstrations form: all these are subversive activities of antisocialist forces. Just to make the point perfectly clear . . .

Concerning the West German Chancellor, the *Times*, that mild-mannered usherette of history, considers it newsworthy today that he went boating on Starnberg Lake and saved a dachschund from drowning.

In South Vietnam, troops of the North and associated guerrilla forces mounted attacks at nineteen places. American troops under machine-gun fire sustained, it is claimed, only 10 fatalities, allotting 500 to the enemy. Such handy round figures.

At 6 P.M. tonight, WNRV has scheduled "Just Jazz" with Ed Beach. Even if we had meant to record it, we are missing it right now.

When we were on our way to the United States of North America, it had been just five years ago in April that a staff sergeant of the Marine Corps, with a beer and three shots of liquor under his belt, led a party of inexperienced recruits into the tidal wetlands of South Carolina, where six were drowned. Military Police mounted guard duty over the victims' flag-draped coffins as though they had died for their country. This was why Marie as recently as last year thought it our duty to buy every record of Pete Seeger's, who had brought out a song on this incident, with some line like "the bulging bastard bawled his 'forward march'!"

When we arrived, the States maintained fewer than 1,000 advisers in South Vietnam. The new President, J. F. Kennedy, increased their number to 3,000 in 1961, 10,000 in 1962. Always those round numbers. In 1964, the C. O.s of the destroyers *Maddox* and *Turner Joy* claimed to have come under fire in the Gulf of Tonkin from the coast of North Vietnam, but could report no damage; in August, the new President, Lyndon B. Johnson, had Congress give him a free hand. Without a declaration of war the Marines landed in 1965, bringing the number of their compatriots in Vietnam to 148,000 men. Local guerrilla forces killed eight Americans on February 7, 1965. Bombing of North Vietnam began, and by April 1966 was carried on with eight-engined B-52 bombers. The Soviets didn't budge. 1967 saw the start of chemical defoliation of the Vietnam forests. Grandmother, why do you make my woods so bare? So that I may bomb you better. High among the American allies is an Air Force general who names Adolf Hitler as his political model. After the Tet Offensive of the Communist forces in March 1968, an American president acknowledged his errors: L. B. J. decided not to renew his candidacy. His successor could be one Nixon, Tricky Dicky, nix on him. He gave out as his slogan for 1968 that instead of an American defeat, the subject of consultations should be: how greater pressure could be exerted toward American victory. The weight of near-culpable involvement that burdened our necks throughout the sordid Algerian war of the French, from 1954 to 1962, has merely changed its label.

What was the first dainty morsel of foreign policy that the U. S. offered its guests the Cresspahls? They had been there barely two weeks when, with President Kennedy's agreement, troops invaded Cuba's Bay of Pigs.

That summer, the Party that is always right immured the city of Berlin and drew a barricade around its nation. The dominant fear: that there might be fatalities. "None on the first day," said Anita on the phone; "many in the years to come."

In December, the employee Cresspahl rushed back and forth two underground half hours each day beneath Manhattan and the East River, lost her job in Brooklyn. By chance she had been passing by the investment information counter and manned it to be of help to an elderly customer who tried to look like an American and spoke with a Saxon-German accent.

*German bonds issued in dollars? We do have those.*

*Could it be something from Saxony?*

*We have municipal bonds of Dresden and Leipzig, both paying 7 per cent, of 1925 and 1926, maturing in 1945 and 1947.*

*I have been tipped off that they can be had for a song.*

*You are accurately informed, ma'am. This is because they are excluded from the London Debt Adjustment Pact of 1952 with Germany. It is anybody's guess when these might be guaranteed.*

*You advise me against it, Miss . . . Crespel?*

*Whoever gave you this tip can hardly be your friend, ma'am.*

Her admonition from management: Miss Cresspahl, you are paid by us for selling securities! Here are your papers. If you are so good at investment counseling, be so kind as to open your own broker's office, rather than deal us out of a commission!

Starting in January, the unemployed Cresspahl, with a four-year-old for adviser, went through her savings traveling from the Atlantic Coast to the brown beaches of Oregon, and had no one to share her worries with save the talking road:

Stay on Pavement
Prepare to Stop
Slow Traffic: Keep Right
Passing Lane Ahead
Middle Lane for Left Turns
No Passing
No Parking
CORVALLIS 38,400 Inhabitants
Please drive carefully. We need everybody
This Lane for Passing Only
Railroad Crossing R X R
NO XING
Loose Rocks
Trucks Entering
Right Lane Must Turn Right
Soft Shoulders
Thank You
Thank You

and often she felt like the half-grown girl in pigtails on the black-and-yellow school signs who leads a smaller child by the hand across a stylized road with zebra stripes. Kids, kids!

After this there was Anita with her illegal propositions. Anita was paying the expenses. A woman tourist with an American passport in Prague who asks the way to Wilson Station, which has long been renamed Střed. A woman tourist with French papers who attempts to exchange Czech crowns at the station Berlin-East.

Since the time when our widely revered Vice-President De Rosny entrusted his subordinate Cresspahl with the transfer of a few millions to the Czechoslovak budget, he has confessed to her why he bestowed the job on her despite her earlier demerit: because she admitted her error. Or because of the nature of the transgression.

A mistaken airplane reservation. No one hears a word more out of this "colleague" than courtesy demands. Employed and watched since 1962. Deemed fit in 1967.

In 1962 a certain Professor Dr. D. Erichson found us and proposed matrimony, after he had come to know Marie; for the time being D. E. was all the name he received, because Marie liked the tiny hiccough she placed between the American sound for D and the E. Later she realized Marie had meant Dear Erichson.

In 1963 I was still not-from-here. Was ready for hilarity when facing an office building composed of steel and glass and concrete, which bore its legend in expensive aluminum, but surprisingly confessed itself to be the U. S. Plywood building. And if I was right in translating a golden legend on a green truck, it said: Theatrical Moves—Our Specialty. While my throat was beginning to tingle from laughing, I joined thirteen men in an elevator and saw them all take off their hats. These were my beginnings, you see—or what I thought of as beginnings.

I felt secure. I had been to the Social Security Administration. Somewhere on Broadway, between restaurants and shops, a startlingly businesslike floor equipped with two brass rails. On the ground floor an area as large as a baseball diamond, no partitions. Nearest the elevators, small groups of chairs to wait on. Next, a desk with a notice that endlessly asks: May I help you? On a pillar, a photograph of the President, framed in black like that of one deceased; on its mat, the signature respected by the Soviet Prime Minister. Along the wall, writing surfaces, as meager as in German post offices. The file card wanted to know the name the employee "was using," also the one acquired at birth. I hereby declare under penalty of perjury that I have never previously applied for a Social Security number. Necessity is the Mother of Prevarication.

In 1963 D. E. for the first time ventured a proposition—to enjoy life for what it offered—and I feigned compliance. Mr. McIntyre's hospitality was hard for me to get away from; these were worthwhile conversations. Mr. McIntyre, of the bar at the Hotel Marseilles, arrogated to himself, with apologies every time, the office of teacher and vocalized the American, as distinct from the British, phonetics of English words; he mentioned that a public holiday was a legal one here, and a "proposition" mainly a suggestion rather than, as among Britons, a suggestion and a proposed deal and a case and a consideration and a way out and a scheme and a sentence and an assertion. This in the midst of taciturn gentlemen who had also found the day unsatisfactory and who expressed their wishes so monosyllabically that Mr. McIntyre pretended to mount a defensive position. One was bothered by the ice cube in his glass; he dropped it like a tip into McIntyre's hand, who said, "Just what I always wanted." And I tried to persuade myself that

I was enjoying life because the kindergarten bus was due in ten minutes and the bellboy would sing out Marie's name and she would walk into the bar, watching us with an earnest and friendly expression like Jakob's but her utterances by now in a shameless American idiom, which people would often beg her to produce for them. Then we went hand in hand down the sloping street toward Riverside Park, and I thought it was enough to be alive.

It started in 1964, this business of being homesick for New York in the middle of New York. The noises alone; they demanded the admission that I felt alive. Although the heavy red firetrucks were off toward some danger, after all, speeding in the midst of the water-treading swarms of lowly cars as if they were already too late; although the helmets and the black, yellow-striped, fire-resistant coats were stained from those earlier times when misfortune was still resistless, fire like plague; although the powerful siren tone, staggering back and forth across a one-note interval, recalled with the brutish roar of a horn the old panic; although the expert at the end of all that capable technology eased the overlong vehicle into place as casually as if he were accepting an accident in sportsmanlike fashion.

In July 1964 a policeman, over six feet tall, weighing 220 pounds shot to death a weedy black boy who, with some others, had molested a pink-skinned creature by throwing bottles and garbage-can lids. Four days and four nights the people of Harlem fought with Molotov cocktails, bricks, looting, arson against the Blue Boys of New York with their riot helmets, nightsticks, revolvers, tear gas. For weeks after this, a German woman carried her passport to prove herself a foreigner.

In March 1965 the American military began dropping incendiary bombs over Vietnam. Napalm.

In a bank in New York City the office of a foreign-language secretary was fitted on the outside left of the door with an exchangeable nameplate saying MRS. CRESSPAHL.

When on November 9 at 1728 hours the lights went out in the northeast of the U. S., this boded ill to dyed-in-the-wool New Yorkers. A stranger, who had tried to insinuate herself into at-homeness by studying up, remembered August 1959, when electric power failed for thirteen hours in the area between the Hudson and East Rivers, from 74th to 110th Streets; for this was part of the history of the Upper West Side of Manhattan, her territory. She remembered June 1961; on the hottest day of the year, subway trains came to a stop, elevators got hung up. As for the power failure of 1965, everybody has his own most personal saga. Since Mrs. Cresspahl found her way by the emergency staircase of the bank to the street and went on foot from Midtown to

Riverside Drive and yet had to offer a story, she tells about the conductor of the diesel-driven Wolverine Express, who in Grand Central talked her into buying a sleeper ticket to Detroit. She nods when someone explains the mishap as due to the breakdown of a computer in the switch aggregate of the linkage system that regulates the Niagara power-plant output; she utters noises of dubious assent when someone persists in the suspicion that the military had been holding an exercise looking to civil war. She stands in no need of omniscience; it is enough for her to have been conscious of living that night. She came back to the candlelight in her windows by the park, to Marie's silhouette, as to a home.

The leave-takings were becoming difficult; although they were the gate to vacations in Denmark, in Italy. In 1966, one evening in the Copter Club near the roof of the high-rise building Pan American had planted on Grand Central's shoulders, I felt numbed by the density of haze through which a whirling machine would carry us off to the port now called J. F. K. The lake in Central Park was a paler rag in a fallow swamp. Arrogantly clear and black and white, two office slabs stood guard before the swathed towerscape of houses. One could make out as far as 96th Street the seam of streetlights along Park Avenue. That is where the trains of the New Haven and the Central emerge from the tunnels. Trains would have been safe on such a fogbound day. The south front of the Newsweek building spoke tenaciously in scarlet: 77°; 7:27. The helicopters by this time were taking off every fifteen minutes; their flight numbers corresponded with the starting times. Out of nothing came the rolling boil of rotor blades, which a while later dwindled into nothing. Marie asked to be shown our tickets and checked them for a reservation back to the place we were about to leave.

In 1966 a certain James Shuldiner, thirty-one, tax expert, first sought a talk with a woman from Germany; in a smoky little deli with red-and-white-checked tablecloths, in a narrow pocket behind the passage between the bar and the food counter. Everybody here lives on the verge of crime. And one crime greets another. For one thing, so he lectured, a society that fosters hostile energy instead of transmuting it (police brutality, glorification of misdeeds, violence against small nations) must expect such murders as the one in Chicago every day of the year. (The next murder of the year was impending in Austin.) On the other hand, such killings set a record that it is a challenge to break! And for a long time his Mrs. Cresspahl had tried to conceal from him that as from 1961 she had counted herself one of the students of New York City. Mr. Shuldiner considered that it was by her counsel that he married a Jewish girl who found the work demanded of nurses in

Switzerland too repulsive. Now she is cooped up with her flawed skin in a flawless apartment on Broadway, with a grand piano and a guitar. Marie in her well-bred way helped herself readily to the sweet graham bread held out to her by the arrogant, skinny Mrs. James Shuldiner, who asked her disparagingly if she were starved at home. James looked embarrassed, ashamed, remorseful. His sidelong glances, which were to call for shared guilt from us, we ignored.

Everybody in New York City has his taxi-driver story; Mrs. Cress-pahl is the possessor of two. The first one confided to her his Jewish parentage, which she had gathered from the card bearing his features, name, and license number; and that he had contracted a form of impotence by sexual concourse with a girl from Germany. An inability to erect, to make myself plain to you, lady. Would you be willing to supply the only treatment on earth that can still help me?

The other driver was taking her and Marie to St. Luke's Hospital; the child had something wrong with her knee, a temperature of 104°, the worst pain in the joint; in her distress she begged for help in German. While the mother was carrying the child to the hospital steps, vainly trying to lift the hanging head so as to keep the braids from trailing over the filthy sidewalk, the driver called after her: "I hope your brat croaks, you German sow!"

In 1967, as in every year, a foreigner has to present her working permit to the office where they list the resident aliens, at the southern root of Broadway. Every year she is asked by the gentlemen what impels her to remain in N. Y. C. when she could live and make money in that wonderful country Germany. They look incredulous, baffled by the applicant's reply that if she had to choose between N. Y. C. and Düsseldorf or Frankfurt/Main, she would prefer New York, but would be undecided between Düsseldorf and Copenhagen. The compliment she meant to pay to the officer's home town remained undecipherd by them. Since then she has vaguely mentioned the rate of exchange between Deutschmarks and dollars; it casts an aura of prosperity about her and accelerates the granting of the permit. How their noses would have been put out of joint if she had quoted a certain poet as her witness, and sand gray, the lion's hue of New York.

In 1968 we chose to be an exception to the law whereby one has to wait for the orderly sequence of events, for history to come, before men of dark skin color shall live with pink ones in mutual neighborliness and friendship. We plucked a Francine out of a confused melée of stabbings, ambulances, and police. The small person with the wide-set eyes sometimes drifts into feathery morning dreams, tilting her head and braiding her stubborn stiff pigtails, and says with mockery and longing: "Yes, ma'am . . . yes, ma'am"; at parting, she spreads a white scarf edged with lace over her dusky gaze and head; the color of mourning, she may have died; is lost.

In 1968 came what may be the last message from D. E., who liked the way we lived. That contract concerning a birthday apartment for Marie on upper Riverside Drive—it will remain unsigned. D. E. sends word that he is gone, made off with by an airplane, with fatal outcome.

The people at the air freight agency are leery. Two capacious suitcases and a cabin trunk equipped like a wardrobe, destination Prague, a Communist country that is—what do you think you are doing, lady? The lists, the licenses! "We are not diplomatic personnel, sir. The invoice goes to a Midtown bank; and do you see the sheet of paper with the green lettering under my hand? Which I will now lift off if you prefer? Is the freight consignment going to be waiting for us tomorrow evening at Ruzyně Airport?" "Absolutely. Since it is for a lady like you. Have a good trip!"

"This is your telephone exchange."

"We haven't asked for any calls."

"You have made calls to transatlantic places, Berlin . . ."

"And once to Helsinki."

"We are afraid there's a pretty steep bill coming to you."

"It'll be paid. This is no reason to disconnect our line."

"We were wondering—would it perhaps be more convenient for you to pay this balance in installments, Mrs. Cresspahl?"

"With a customer service like yours, we're bound to keep our connection."

"The pleasure is ours, Mrs. Cresspahl."

On the subway we arrive beneath Times Square at the wrong time. Out of the shuttle trains from Grand Central, dense human columns come to meet us, apportioned by transit police among the three elevators. "All the way down. All the way down." Superiors who adopt a paternal tone today. As soon as they see us, they clear the middle aisle. "Make room for the lady! Make room for the child!"

Waiting around the corner, the airport buses, elephantine bumblebees. The tinted windows draw a shade across the cityscape. The trip will take us over the route between the cemeteries, to a terrain where shrubbery and lawns seek to make a park out of an industrial zone. We'll wait to the last minute for the intercom message recalling us to New York. Until they announce that this is the last, the definitive call for passengers to board the aircraft. *Passagererne bedes begive sig til udgang.* Please proceed to the gate now. *Begeben Sie sich zum Ausgang.*

## August 20, 1968   Last and Final

In a beach hotel on the Danish coast, opposite Sweden. In a dining room for family parties: wicker furniture, linen tablecloth. In the garden, behind the shrubbery leading to the beach promenade. On the beach. From noon to 4 P.M.

An eleven-year-old child whose voice drops from fatigue, wilted. A woman about thirty-five, descending the steps behind Marie, looking forward because she was being called to the hotel desk. Anita has promised herself to us for Prague; Anita is quite capable of welcoming us as early as Klampenborg.

Porter, chauffeur, waitress; hotel staff.

"We want to thank you for calling us so punctually. De har vist mig en stor teneste."

"You are welcome! A gentleman wishes to see you as soon as convenient."

The gentleman is standing on the terrace, shrunken, willfully erect, dressed in black and white under snow-white hair; with raised arms he relishes the welcome, a raven wanting to hide his emotion.

"No! No! This can't be . . . !" (That's how old people from Mecklenburg carry on.)

"Herr Kliefoth. Marie, greet my teacher of English and manners."

"I am very pleased to meet you, Dr. Kliefoth. My mother has told me some of your stories."

"It would be preferable for us, I think, if we stayed outside German. This country was once under German occupation."

"D'accord, my dear Fru Cresspahl. I am here illegally as it is. Your friend Anita, she up and puts a man of eighty-two on a train to Lübeck; to Lübeck she sends him an I. D. to take him to Copenhagen, and the police at Jerichow know nothing, but nothing. But the name in the passport is Kliefoth; it is my picture; I could keep it as it is."

Seen from the front, Kliefoth's head is narrow; his profile brings out forgotten depth. At the table he leans his head in his hand by the temple; the upper rim of his glasses slides over his eyebrows. Now the dark pupils are exactly centered.

"That you should have taken the trouble, Fru Cresspahl! Change in Copenhagen for the sake of a useless person."

"We have Anita to thank for that. She disliked the idea of our changing planes in Frankfurt. We obey Anita."

"She got me a room here for ten days, if it is all right with *me*."

"She is a good human being; we rarely say that."

"Not even necessary. There are times when all that's lacking is onions. Same goes for what used to be called tropical fruit—citrus and bananas. Only when one comes across the advertisement of a fish-smoking plant in a magazine of 1928 and there is mention of thousands of tons of smoked eel—one starts wondering. There's no smoked eel in Jerichow or Gneez. No, I am looking forward to the meal for company's sake; then we can tell each other stories, no?"

"Hvad ønsker herskabet? What is your pleasure, your honors?"

"Pickled herring. Mackerel in tomato sauce. Smoked eel with scrambled eggs; go on, laugh all you want! And which wine would you recommend to us with that?"

"For us it is now six-thirty in the morning, Herr Kliefoth. In our school we are ranked by numbers, placed on a list. I am No. 4 in my class. How did my mother rank as a schoolgirl?"

"It is due, more than anything, to my being the oldest of survivors. I would have to go to the cemetery if I wanted to talk with someone."

Exhaustion keeps his eyes closed. Reaching under the earpieces of his spectacles, he massages his temples with thumb and forefinger of one hand. The skin around his eyes is gray, pleated wrinkles, motionless. He sits there like a corpse; until he wakes himself with those climbing fingers.

"What was said at my father's grave, Herr Kliefoth?"

"Stuff and nonsense. So I threw a monkey wrench. And if you had disliked the wine, what then?"

"It would have gone back. I learned that from a person who . . ."

"What puts this into your mind, of all things? Jakob visited with me five times in the year after you left his surveillance. He came to read me your letters, wanted to know what goes on at interpreters' schools. Your father was a dependable, a caring man, my dear young Miss Cresspahl."

"Herr Kliefoth, I am only eleven years old. Please call me by my first name."

"Your mother, Marie, she was about five feet six in May 1953 and wore her grayish-black hair in a razor-cut bob. Wide shoulders, narrow hips. In Jerichow she preferred knee pants, to get some tan on her bare legs. With her dark eyebrows, wary eye movements, thin lips, the adult face was scrupulously prepared."

"What do they call such weather in Jerichow?"

" 'Finest ladies' sailing weather? Fru Cresspahl. Near and dear ones excepted."

His voice had a saw-edged hoarseness that in relaxed talking look on organ tones in the bass.

"Herr Kliefoth, I sometimes dream of that. I am on a Polish ship; it puts in at Liverpool, then goes on here to Copenhagen. The entrance to Rostock Harbor next to the Old Channel, views through forest clearings in Doberan Wood, the station of Wismar or Gneez. Or, when Jerichow is barred to me, to Wendisch Burg. At worst, Neustrelitz, Waren, Malchin, where nobody knows us, where I may earn enough to afford an apartment with a lake view, a mooring place for a boat, winter mornings by the ice, shade of cattails, a fire in the stove . . . but Herr Rohlfs, long captain of State Security, is dead or has foundered in his own manner against the cliff of major's rank, like the officers of professional armies in peacetime. We are allowed into Mecklenburg only on transit and must proceed to a hotel under supervision; choosing one's own place to stay is out."

"If only someone like myself could be well-to-do in the future, Fru Cresspahl. Really and truly!"

The waistline of the old man's trousers reaches up to his nipples. His threadbare clothing is shortened every so often. We had thought of cigars, of tobacco, but forgotten about material for a suit.

"I willed my furniture to the Rostock Museum. If you were related to me, Fru Cresspahl, you could have got the table and the wardrobe; they are presents from your father, after all. I have a contract with my landlord. In the event of my death: he retains the remaining furniture, but must see to my removal."

Kliefoth kneads his hands in thought. The pain narrows his pupils.

"I cut myself once and, standing, put my foot into Jakob's hand. He looked at it a while, then let the foot slide down in the same rhythm as my hand came to rest on his shoulder. The movement passed through my body without pain. I think that happens to you a single time in your life."

"Må jeg bede om Deres pas? May I request your passport? All I need is your signature; I'll do the rest."

"De er meget elskværdig; that's very kind of you. Where can one deposit the money? It belongs to that gentleman."

"My wife was handicapped by her . . ."

"I had to tell Marie what she had to know, Herr Kliefoth."

". . . upbringing. Such a woman has the most children flock to her apron; in the kitchen, in the garden. Come right down to it, we know only one thing about life: what is subject to the law of gestation must go down by the same law. Don't worry about me—I will do. My Latin has become skittish; memory conducts itself no better than it should. I must thank my stars for having treated me so mercifully. I thank you, my dear Fru Cresspahl. You have contributed to it."

"Herr Kliefoth, may you live as long as you take pleasure in it."

"Your father did me the honor of his friendship. One of his views may be summarized as: history is a concept or draft."

"How life is treating us we have written down, up to our work in Prague, 1,875 pages; with your permission we shall hand the record over to you. What needs to be supplied later is the two-hour flight south. What could happen to us when we travel with a company called Československé Aerolinie, C. S. A., which in its foreign persona operates under the letters O and K? Where we have a confirmed reservation. Tonight we'll give you a ring from Prague."

"Will you take good care of my friend, who is your mother and Mrs. Cresspahl?"

"I promise, Herr Kliefoth. My mother and I, we are on friendly terms."

As we walked along the beach, we got into water. Shingle rattled about our ankles. We held each other by the hand: a child; a man on his way to the place where the dead are; and she, the child that I was.

[January 29, 1968, New York, N.Y.—April 17, 1983, Sheerness, Kent.]